Gary Brandner's

THE HOWLING
TRILOGY

BOOKS of the DEAD

BOOKS of the DEAD

This book is a work of fiction.
All characters, events, dialog, and situations in this book are fictitious and any resemblance to real people or events is purely coincidental.

Edited by James Roy Daley
Cover Art by Daniele Serra
Book Design by James Roy Daley
Proofread by Carolina Smart

THE HOWLING TRILOGY

Copyright 1977, 1978, 1985 by Gary Brandner

For more information, contact: Besthorror@gmail.com
Visit us at: Booksofthedeadpress.com

THE HOWLING

In the dark Arda Forest on the border between Greece and Bulgaria there is a dead gray patch of land roughly one mile square where no one goes and nothing lives. Today no map marks the location; no road leads there. Four hundred years ago it was a village. It was called Dradja.

Even when the village lived it was a place of darkness. Peasants from the surrounding lands made the sign of the cross when they spoke its name. They entered only when they had to, and left as soon as their business was done. Passing travelers were warned to avoid the place. Some who did not heed the warning would later wish they had.

The stories told about Dradja were unfocused and often conflicting. On one point they all agreed: there was Evil in the village. The Evil took various forms, depending on the storyteller. Travelers listened to the stories and nodded. It was bad, but it was not their concern. They would skirt the village and cross themselves and tell each other that some things were best left alone. In the bleak autumn of 1583 all this changed.

In that season a shepherd named Kyust, with his wife Anya and his little daughter, brought his flock to the rich fields near Dradja. The land to the north, where Kyust had always grazed his sheep, had suffered through a terrible drought, and moving the flock was the only way to keep the animals from starving. Kyust had heard the dark tales of Dradja, but his need was greater than his fear.

At sundown of his first day Kyust settled his sheep and then returned to his cottage. After a family supper he fell into a deep sleep. In the morning he found three of his young lambs savagely killed, and the mother ewe bleating pathetically over the remains. The shepherd brought in a dog to keep watch through the next night. In the morning it, too, was dead.

Kyust knew the family could not survive without his flock. He had to catch the killer of his sheep. Through the next night he stayed with his flock in the fields. So that his wife would not be alone with their daughter, he sent for his sister Rachel.

Kyust spent a quiet, uneventful night and then worked all the following day. That evening, his little daughter, who had been playing in a nearby meadow, did not return home. Anya and Rachel called to her and searched as far from the cottage as they dared. Finally, Rachel ran to the field to get Kyust, and all three began to search. In a grove of alder trees near a stream where the child often played, Anya found what remained of her daughter. The small body was so badly torn it was barely recognizable as human.

When the shepherd saw what had been done to his child he let out one horrible scream. He swore vengeance and set off for the village of Dradja, vowing to destroy the Evil that lived there, whatever form it took.

The shepherd Kyust never returned. The sheep, untended, wandered away. Rachel stayed by the side of her sister, who refused to leave without her husband. Knowing she must have help, Rachel left the cottage one morning and journeyed many hours to a place where Gypsies often made their camp. To one of the Gypsies she gave a message for her brothers in their home village, telling of the tragedies that had befallen Anya, and asking the brothers to come for them.

In her haste to return to the cottage Rachel chose a shortcut that took her close to Dradja. Night had fallen by the time she passed the village, and a flurry of movement caught her attention. What she saw in Dradja was horrible beyond belief. The black secret of the place was the last thing she would ever experience.

When her brothers, having received her message, found her mangled body, they gathered a hundred men from their village and marched on Dradja. Armed with clubs, axes, pikes, and a few matchlock firearms, they swarmed into the accursed village and herded the people into the centre of town. They ordered the guilty to step forward. No one moved.

It was clear then what had to be done. In that bloody day every man, woman, and child caught in Dradja was tortured to death. When the ground of the village was a crimson swamp the bodies were stacked with layers of dry wood, soaked with pitch, and set afire. The animals were slaughtered, the village itself put to the torch. When nothing remained of Dradja but ashes, these were plowed under. The fresh-turned earth was sown and sown again, but not even a weed would grow.

1

The September heat lay heavy on Los Angeles. In the condominium community called Hermosa Terrace all the windows were tightly closed. The only sounds were the hum of exhaust fans and the muted growl of a power mower.

In the living room of Unit Two, Karyn Beatty stood on tiptoe to kiss her husband, Roy. Lady, their miniature collie, wagged her approval from the sofa. It started as a casual husband-and-wife first-anniversary kiss, but it quickly became something more. Karyn drew back her head and looked into Roy's clear brown eyes.

"Are you trying to start something?" she said a little breathlessly.

"Darn right," Roy replied, taking her in his arms.

Roy pulled her close, his big, gentle hands warm through the thin material of her summer dress. He kissed her neck where the blond hair curled forward below her ear.

"Won't Chris be here soon?" she said, her lips close to his ear.

"We won't answer the door."

"You couldn't do that to your best friend. Especially after we asked him to come by for an anniversary drink."

"I suppose you're right," Roy admitted. "Anyway, he won't stay long. He has a date."

"Anybody we know?"

"A new one, I think."

"Doesn't Chris ever get serious about anybody?"

"Who knows? I think he's secretly in love with you."

"You don't mean it?"

"Why not? All my friends have good taste."

* * *

Max Quist shut off the power mower and took out a soiled handkerchief to wipe the sweat from his face. He watched as a young couple in sparkling tennis whites climbed out of a sports car and ran laughing across the lawn. They didn't pay any attention to Max. Nobody living in Hermosa Terrace paid any attention to Max. He was like another piece of shrubbery to them.

No, he thought, not even that much.

Max hated these people. He hated them for having all the things he would never have. He would quit this lousy job in a minute if it weren't for his parole officer. Just once he would like to show the smug sons-of-bitches that Max Quist was *somebody*.

* * *

The telephone rang in Unit Two. Roy Beatty picked it up and frowned as he listened to the voice on the other end. He spoke briefly and hung up.

"Anything wrong?" Karyn asked.

"I've got to go to Anaheim. Deliver some books."

"On Saturday? On our anniversary?"

"Dammit, it's my own fault. I promised to drop off a set of inspection manuals at Aerodyne yesterday. Had them in the trunk of the car and forgot all about it. I don't know how it slipped my mind."

Karyn smiled. It was very unlike Roy to forget anything. He was always thoroughly organized, like one of the technical manuals he edited. When she had first met him she had thought Roy Beatty was as stodgy as a church deacon. However, she had soon discovered his warm sense of humor, an open-minded willingness to listen, and a depth of intellect that was not apparent in his All-American good looks. Karyn had been working as a convention hostess for the New York Hilton at the time. Roy was in the city for a gathering of engineers. For the first time, she had broken the hotel rule against socializing with the guests. Roy had stayed on for a week after the convention, and they had been together constantly. When he had returned to the Coast he had said he would be back for her on his vacation. She had not expected him to come, but he had. That was when she had finally admitted she loved him.

"Don't be long," she said as he stood at the door. She kissed him and watched him walk down the winding path through the neatly trimmed shrubbery. Karyn could not imagine how she could be happier. She had Roy and she had an excellent job with a hotel near the airport where she was in line for convention manager when her current boss retired. Tonight she would give Roy her special anniversary gift—the news that he was going to be a father. Yes, her life was just about perfect.

* * *

Max Quist watched the blond young man come out of Unit Two and stride down the walk past him without a flicker. Max might as well have been invisible. The woman stood in the doorway watching him go. Good-looking cunt. Too good-looking. Both of them. Like people in a magazine ad. Young, beautiful, healthy, rich. Max spat on the cropped grass. How he wanted to show them what it's like to be hurt. Hurt them. Yes... hurt them.

* * *

Karyn was in the kitchen putting the lunch things away when the doorbell chimed. Chris was early, she thought. She dried her hands and walked out through the living room to the door. She did not bother to look through the tiny viewer. She never did. There was no danger here. This was Hermosa Terrace, not East Los Angeles.

Karyn opened the door and the heat pushed against the cool inside air. The man in the doorway was not Chris Halloran. He smiled at her.

"Yes?" Karyn said when the man did hot speak right away.

He had thick black hair that was poorly barbered. His cotton work-shirt was dark with perspiration under the arms. He seemed vaguely familiar.

"I'm supposed to check the pipes in your bathroom," he said.

"There's nothing wrong with our pipes."

"It's in the apartment next door. Their shower don't drain right, and it might be plugged up where your drain pipes come together."

Something in the way the man spoke was wrong. The short speech sounded rehearsed. Something about the man himself was wrong. He continued to smile.

"You'd better come back when my husband is here. He knows about those things."

Without making any sudden moves the man had somehow come through the doorway and was standing in the living room. He was still smiling, but it was a different smile. "That's okay," he said. "We won't need your husband."

Over on the couch Lady raised her neat little head and pricked her ears at the strange male voice. After a moment she put her head back down on her paws, but remained watchful.

"I'm sorry, but I'd rather you didn't come in now." Karyn fought to still the tremor of fear in her voice.

"But I *am* in," the man said. He reached behind him and closed the door. Without taking his eyes off Karyn he turned the small knob, shooting the dead-bolt lock into place.

"What do you think you're doing?" Karyn wanted her voice to be angry and strong, but the fear was in her now. She could not hide it.

"You know what I'm doing," the man said.

"I–I don't keep much money in the house. You can have what there is. And my jewelry."

"I don't want your money or your jewelry. But you know that, don't you? You know what I want, and you're going to give it to me." He reached out suddenly and squeezed her breast.

Karyn jumped back as though from an electric shock. "Please, leave me alone!" The sour smell of his body was sharp in her nostrils. "M–my husband will be home."

"No he won't. He just left. We have all the time we need."

She took a careful step backward. The man's eyes traveled over her body, probing at her. His hands shot out and seized her wrists.

"No!" she cried.

"Relax," he said. "You're going to like it."

"Please... you can't..."

The man pulled Karyn against his body and mashed his mouth down on hers. Karyn clamped her jaws together as his tongue pushed in past her lips. He tasted of stale cigarettes.

"Where's the bedroom?"

Karyn shook her head from side to side, afraid to trust her voice.

With a sudden movement the man twisted one arm up behind her back, forcing her to walk in front of him. He marched Karyn into the hallway that opened between the living room and the room Roy used for a den. She stumbled along in his grasp past the bathroom to the open door, through which they could see the bed.

All the things she had read about rape tumbled through Karyn's mind. All the advice for women. Fight back. Don't fight back. Scream. Stay calm. Blow a whistle. Run. Reason with the man.

Lovely advice, all useless. Fight the man? He was at least seventy pounds heavier than she, and certainly stronger. Scream? Who would hear? Hermosa Terrace Townhomes were proud of their soundproofing. Reason with him? Reason with an animal?

They were in the bedroom now. The man spun Karyn around and pushed her backward onto the bed.

The thinking part of her mind shut off and instinct took over. She crossed her arms protectively over her breasts and drew back her feet to kick out at the man when he came at her.

The man laughed at her efforts and batted the kick aside with an easy swipe of his hand. He grasped her by the ankles and forced her legs apart. Karyn writhed on the bed, helpless against his strength.

The man grinned down at her, showing large, strong teeth. Droplets of sweat stood out on his forehead and upper lip. His eyes moved down to her crotch. Karyn felt open and exposed with the thin velour pants pulled tight between her legs.

"I'm pregnant," she said suddenly.

"Bullshit."

"I *am*," she insisted. "Three months."

"Then you don't have to worry about getting knocked up, do you?"

He released one of Karyn's ankles and took hold of the velour pants at the waist. He yanked them down, exposing the smooth, pale skin of her belly. The snap and zipper held at first, but he tugged again and the material tore away.

Then she screamed. Not with any thought of summoning help or frightening the man off. A visceral scream of outrage and terror.

"Shut up." he ordered. He leaned forward and slapped her hard on the face. She stopped screaming.

A sudden high-pitched barking behind the man spun him around. Lady stood braced on her little legs, yapping angrily. The man swung his foot in a vicious arc; the toe of his heavy shoe caught the little dog just below the ribs and lifted her off the floor.

Lady yelped in surprise and pain. Never before had anyone deliberately hurt her. She crouched on the floor whimpering, her eyes pleading for an apology, a comforting pat.

"Get out of here, mutt," the man snapped.

Still whimpering, Lady moved uncertainly toward the door. She stopped and looked back toward her mistress. The man made a threatening motion with his hand, and the dog retreated into the hall. The man kicked the door shut behind her.

"Hell of a watchdog you've got there." He grinned and came at Karyn again.

"Please don't do this. Please don't hurt me." Even as the words came out, Karyn knew they were useless. This unspeakable thing was actually going to happen to her. *Was* happening to her. What had she ever done that she should be brutalized this way?

The man was upon her again, and Karyn's mind ceased to function logically. He tore away the nylon bikini pants, and his fingers crawled over and into her.

Abruptly he dropped to his knees and thrust his face up between her legs. He clamped his mouth on her, and Karyn could feel his tongue like a thick, wet worm probing, probing at her. She pummeled his head with her fists, but the blows had no effect.

Then he pulled his face back and bit her high on the soft inside of the thigh. He bit down hard, and his teeth sank into the clean white flesh until the blood flowed. Karyn's back arched up off the bed in reaction to the pain.

When the man at last unclenched his jaw and stood over her again his lips were crimson with her blood. Breathing in short, harsh bursts, he reached down and unzipped the front of his pants. Karyn twisted her head away, but could not shut out the sight as he freed himself from the damp jockey shorts and bore down on her.

He forced her legs farther apart and positioned himself between them. Blood from the throbbing bite wound left a red smear on the bedspread. With one cruel thrust he invaded her body.

Karyn cried out in pain and rage. She scrabbled at his face with both hands, clawing for his eyes.

"Bitch!" He hit her in the face with a rock-hard fist.

Karyn tasted blood, and the room swam for a moment, but she continued to use her nails to slash at the face above her.

The man pulled out of her for a moment and drove a fist into her bare belly. Karyn felt something break inside, and there was no fight left in her.

"That's better." He planted his hands on her shoulders and rammed into her again.

Karyn squeezed her eyes shut. When she was a little girl in the dentist chair and the drill hurt her, she would dig her nails into her palms, making a small hurt to ease the larger one. She did it now. The lower part of her body was on fire. The wound on her thigh screamed. The man continued to pump away at her, grunting with every thrust.

Get it over with! she cried inside her head. *Get it over with and go away or kill me or whatever you're going to do. Just finish!*

And at last he did.

After endless minutes he withdrew and wiped himself with the satin bedspread. Karyn rolled her head on the pillow and looked up at him, but now the man would not meet her eye. Hurriedly he zipped up his pants and went out into the hall. Karyn heard him go through the living room.

She sat up on the bed and winced at the tearing pain in her stomach. Her insides felt loose, as though they might slide out between her legs when she stood up. She pulled the remains of the velour pants up over the mess on her lower belly and walked carefully to the door. She made it as far as the bathroom and vomited into the toilet.

She knelt there for several minutes on the cold tile with her hands gripping the sides of the bowl, waiting for the spasms of her stomach to ease. The sudden sound of someone moving around in the living room brought back the fear. When the bedroom door opened and the heavy footsteps came toward her she started to scream.

2

When Chris Halloran found Karyn on her knees in the bathroom she was sobbing incoherently. Finding the front door open, he had sensed something was wrong. He walked in, and that was when Karyn began to scream. Chris held her in his arms for five minutes before she could tell him what had happened. He called the police, then left a message for Roy at the Aerodyne Company in Anaheim.

The two months that followed were a painful time for Karyn. The blow she had taken to the stomach had brought on a miscarriage, but no permanent damage. There was an infection from the bite wound on her thigh that was slow to respond to medication. The doctor advised against plastic surgery until the scar had completely healed.

The police, using their new, more sympathetic procedures for rape victims, made that part of Karyn's ordeal as easy as they could. Her description of the rapist led them at once to Max Quist, the handyman, who had a record of assaults on women. Confronted with Karyn's positive identification, Quist pleaded guilty.

It was psychologically that Karyn suffered most. Twice-weekly sessions with an analyst helped a little, and group sessions brought her together with other women who had been raped. Still, her recovery was painfully slow. She would wake up in the night, eyes wide and staring, and scream that someone was biting her. Of all the violations of her body, it was the horror of the teeth sinking into her flesh that she could not erase. She returned to work, but her life at home with Roy suffered. She could not feel comfortable in their lovemaking.

The analyst suggested to Karyn and Roy that they go away from Los Angeles for a while. Restful, rural surroundings, he said, would be the best thing for Karyn's full recovery. The people at Karyn's hotel were understanding, giving her a six month leave of absence. Roy worked out an arrangement with his firm, and they began taking trips out of the city to look for a place.

A friend in the real-estate business told them about an available house in a town to the north called Drago. They drove up to see it, but Karyn was not enthusiastic. The house was weathered and weed-grown, a mile outside the town, which Karyn thought looked like a cheerless cluster of wooden buildings. Roy, however, took to the place immediately. He assured Karyn that the house could be fixed up so she would love it. With some misgivings, she acquiesced.

For the next couple of weeks Roy made the trip alone to see that work on the house was being done to his specifications. He did not want Karyn to see it, he said. She would be surprised. When it was time to move in, he left a day early to see to last minute details. Chris Halloran volunteered to drive Karyn up to the house.

It was a crisp November day when Chris headed north on Interstate 5 with Karyn beside him in the Camaro. In the back Lady stood with her front paws braced on the seat and her face thrust into the wind from the open window.

They left the freeway for a two-lane blacktop road that snaked up into the Tehachapi Mountains. The outside air grew chill as they climbed.

"Do you want me to roll up the window?" Chris asked.

Karyn moved her head, letting the wind play with her loose blond hair. "No, it feels good. Clean."

As they drove on the evergreen forest pushed in closer on both sides of the road.

"How much farther is the town?" said Chris.

"A few miles. Just over the ridge up ahead and down into the valley. Don't blink or you'll miss it."

"I don't doubt it," Chris said. "I've lived in California all my life, and I never heard of Drago."

"Neither had I," Karyn said. "We were lucky to find the place. The house has been empty since the old owners died four years ago. Roy fell in love with it."

"What about you, Karyn? How do you like the place?"

"It's all right, I suppose."

"You don't sound convinced."

"I haven't seen it since Roy had it fixed up. Anyway, it's quiet and out of the way. That's what we wanted. And yet it's only a two hour drive from Los Angeles, so Roy can commute easily."

"You won't mind being alone when he comes into L.A.?"

"Why should I? I've got to learn to be by myself sometime." The words came out more sharply than Karyn had intended.

"That's right," Chris said. "It's none of my business, anyway."

They reached the crest of the ridge and the road leveled off for a stretch before descending into the valley on the other side. The air was pungent with the scent of balsam. Karyn reached out and touched Chris's hand.

"Pull over for a minute, can you?"

Just before the road started down Chris eased the Camaro onto the shoulder and parked next to the metal guardrail. Below them lay a narrow valley, thick with evergreens. Where the road straightened along the floor of the valley a dozen or so toy-like buildings clustered in a clearing of the forest. Several narrow lanes branched off the main road. They could be seen only faintly through the heavy overgrowth. Here and there along the lanes a tiny house sat on a patch of cleared ground reclaimed from the forest. Although the valley was in shadow, no lights shone in the town of Drago.

"It doesn't look like much from up here, does it?" Karyn said.

Chris did not answer.

"May I have a cigarette?"

He handed her one and lit it for her.

Karyn took several quick puffs before speaking. "I really do want to talk to someone, Chris. Someone who cares about me as a person, not as a case history to read at the next psychiatric convention."

She mashed the cigarette into the ashtray. When she spoke again the words came out in a rush. "Chris, Roy and I haven't had good sex together since that day. There's nothing wrong physically, but it's just not working. Roy and I have talked and talked about it, and God knows we do try. We go to bed and I want it so much... I go through all the motions. That's the trouble, all I'm doing is going through the motions. There's no feeling, and Roy knows it. He can't help but know it... he's not a fool. He's been awfully sweet and patient with me, but I can't expect him to put up with this forever. I just don't seem to be getting any better."

"Did you talk the problem over with your doctor?" Chris asked.

"Oh, hell yes."

"Did he give you any advice?"

"Nothing I couldn't have gotten out of *The Reader's Digest*. Good, sound, logical advice, but I still don't feel anything."

"Give it a while," Chris said. "Two months isn't much time to get over what happened to you."

Karyn nodded distractedly.

"Anyway," Chris went on, "that's what you're moving out here to the woods for, isn't it? Rest and rejuvenation?"

With an encouraging smile, he started the car, pulled back onto the road, and drove down into the valley. As they descended, the mountain loomed up behind and cut off the sun. The air grew cold, and they rolled up the windows. When the road leveled out into the main street of Drago, Chris switched on the headlights against the gathering gloom. They drove slowly along, past the buildings, which had a dusty, unused look. There were a couple of stores, a café, a gas station, a tavern, and a theater with an empty marquee. The only sound they heard was the singing of their tires over the pavement.

Karyn shivered slightly in the cool dusk of the tree-lined street. In the backseat Lady whined softly. Karyn reached back without turning around and rubbed the soft fur at the dog's throat.

"Where is everybody?" Chris asked. His eyes ranged along the blank fronts of the buildings.

"I don't know." Karyn shivered again.

"Is your house on this street?"

"No, it's up one of these little cross streets. They all look alike, though, and I'm not sure which it is. We'll have to ask someone."

Chris eased the Camaro along for a hundred yards, then braked to a stop as a powerful looking man in khakis and a Stetson appeared from the shadows.

Karyn rolled down her window and smiled at the man.

"Hello, there. I wonder if you could tell us how to get to the old Fenno house?"

For a moment she thought the man had not heard. He did not answer her smile, nor did he make any move to respond. His eyes continued to watch from the shadow of the Stetson. Then the man came toward them, moving with a deliberate measured gait. He planted both hands on the windowsill and looked in. Involuntarily, Karyn drew back in the seat.

"You want the Fenno place?" the man said. His voice rumbled up from the deep barrel chest.

"Yes. I'm Karyn Beatty. My husband and I are leasing the house, and I can't remember which of these side roads it's on."

The man thumbed his hat brim up a fraction, and a faint smile twitched on his mouth. "Pleased to meet you. I'm Anton Gadak. I'm sort of the sheriff here in Drago. Fact is, I'm sort of the whole police force. But then, we don't need all that much policing." He looked pointedly past Karyn at Chris.

"This is our friend Chris Halloran. He drove me in from Los Angeles. My husband is waiting at the house."

Anton Gadak nodded, apparently satisfied. "The Fenno place is up the last road that turns off to the left, just before you start up into the hills again."

Karyn thanked him and Chris started away from the curb. He found the last turnoff with some difficulty. It was little more than a wide weed-covered path into the woods.

"As I remember, it's up here about a mile," Karyn said.

They passed two weathered old houses, dark and nearly hidden from the road by the brush. At each Chris looked over at Karyn, who shook her head. They came at last to a small clearing with a white frame cottage trimmed in apple green. A fireplace chimney trailed a ribbon of pale smoke across the slate-gray sky. Lights shone in all the windows, pushing the forest back. Chris pulled onto the clearing and parked behind Roy Beatty's Galaxie.

Karyn clapped her hands delightedly. "What an improvement! You wouldn't believe the dismal brown color the house was when we first came out. And the whole place was strangled with brush and weeds. Roy's done a marvelous job."

Chris got out of the car and walked back to open the trunk. As he brought out Karyn's bags the front door of the little house swung open and Roy Beatty came out. He shielded his eyes against the headlights for a moment, then waved a welcome and hurried toward the car.

Karyn jumped out and ran to his arms. "Roy, it's... it's beautiful."

"Didn't I tell you it had possibilities?" said Roy. "Wait till you see the inside."

With his arm around Karyn, Roy walked back to the car. "Come on in, Chris, and take a look at how us rural folk live."

"Thanks, but I've got to get back to the city."

"Are you sure? There's steaks in the freezer, and the martini makings are already set out."

"It's tempting, but I'll pass this time."

"Got a date with a live one?"

Chris smiled and gave a noncommittal wave of his hand.

"Bring her out some weekend," Roy said. "We've got an extra bed and plenty of blankets."

"Maybe I'll do that."

Roy hefted Karyn's two suitcases, then looked around, puzzled. "Where's Lady?"

"She's been acting funny," Karyn said. "I don't think she knows what to make of the woods."

At that moment the dog put her nose out for a tentative sniff of the surroundings, then bounded out of the car and frolicked happily around Roy's feet. He knelt and scratched her ear.

While Roy and Karyn watched the dog, Chris slid into his car and pulled the door closed. Roy walked over and reached through the window to shake his hand.

"Thanks for bringing the family out, buddy," he said. "Sorry you can't stay."

"Maybe next time. I hope the place works out for you, Roy."

"It will," Roy assured him.

Karyn came over and kissed him lightly on the cheek. Chris backed out onto the narrow lane and drove back the way they had come. Soon the glow of the Camaro's taillights was lost among the trees.

"I wish Chris had stayed for dinner," she said as they started toward the house. "I think he's lonely."

"Are you kidding? A handsome thirty-year-old bachelor with a good paying job and an apartment at the marina? You call that lonely?"

"You sound a little jealous, mister."

Roy set down one of her bags, and gave her a swat on the bottom. "That's right, I can hardly wait to dump you so I can grow a mustache, buy a Porsche, load up on stereo equipment, and be a swinging bachelor."

Laughing together, they continued up to the front stoop. Roy stood aside and gestured her into the living room.

Karyn started in, then hesitated. She ran her fingers down the surface of the heavy wooden door. Under the fresh green paint a series of deep vertical grooves like scars slashed the panel at about shoulder height.

"What do you suppose made these?" she said.

"Who knows?" Roy shrugged and went on inside.

Karyn followed, thinking about the marks. Absurd though it was, the angry furrows in the wood suggested only one thing.

Claws.

3

The small living room and the open dining area were spotlessly clean and lit with colorful new lamps. A blaze crackled over logs in the stone fireplace. The dark old furniture that had come with the house had been cleaned, polished, and recovered in bright hues. The floor was freshly sanded and waxed and covered with new rugs. Vases of fresh-cut flowers were everywhere.

Roy Beatty stood back and let Karyn survey the rooms. "Well, what do you think?"

"Roy, it's lovely. I mean it."

Karyn walked down the short hallway and looked into the bedroom. There was new maple furniture and a bright patchwork quilt on the double bed. Across the hall in the bathroom new wood paneling had replaced the scabrous, peeling wallboard. The fixtures were scoured, the air sweetened. Karyn came back out and walked through the dining area, running her fingers over the satiny finish of the heavy oak table. Out in the kitchen everything fairly sparkled. She came back into the living room where Roy waited, unable to conceal his pride.

"It's not Hermosa Terrace," he said, "but cozy, don't you think?"

"Very cozy," she agreed.

"How about a martini to toast our new home?"

"Lovely idea."

Roy went into the kitchen and brought back a bowl of ice, which he set before her on a low table in front of the fireplace. The green hydrant bottle of Tanqueray and the vermouth were already there. As he stirred the cocktails in a tall pitcher Lady began to whine softly and scratch at the baseboard near the front door.

"I think it's time she took a trip outside," Roy said. He crossed the room and held the door open. "Come on, Lady, out."

The dog looked up at him uncertainly, then at Karyn.

"Do you think she'll be all right?" Karyn said.

"Sure. There's no traffic out here, and she won't go far enough from the house to get lost."

Lady crouched lower to the floor, her eyes on Roy.

"Come on, you, out," he said again, in a more commanding tone.

The little dog obeyed at last, moving in a cautious sidling manner. Roy closed the door after her. He then selected two hefty logs from the pile on the hearth and laid them on the dwindling fire. They caught immediately. The flames snapped at the pockets of pitch and leaped up the chimney.

Roy sat down again and finished stirring the martinis. He brought out two iced glasses and filled them at the low table. They touched glasses, sipped at the cocktails, and smiled at each other.

"Did you get everything worked out at the office?" Karyn asked.

"It's all taken care of. I've got next year's publication list to go over. When I go into town I'll bring back whatever raw copy there is for editing. There's no reason why technical manuals can't be edited up here in the woods as well as on Wilshire Boulevard. I shouldn't have to make the trip into L.A. more than a couple of times a week, if that often."

Karyn leaned back on the sofa. "Are you sure you don't mind being cooped up here away from the city and all our friends?"

"Mind? What's to mind? You think I miss battling through the smog and the freeway traffic twice a day? Listen, this is as much a vacation for me as it is therapy for you."

Karyn squeezed his hand. "You're pretty sweet, you know that?"

"Yeah, I know, but tell me anyway."

"What about some dinner? I'm starved."

"Right. I'll get the steaks going while you build a salad."

"Do we have everything we need?"

"We should have. I stocked up this afternoon at the Safeway over in Pinyon."

"Pinyon?"

"That's the nearest town of any size. It's about twelve miles from here at the tip of Castaic Lake."

"Why didn't you do the shopping in Drago?"

"I guess you didn't get too good a look at the town. There's one general store that's about the size of the cheese section in most supermarkets. They had a few canned goods, a few boxes of cereal, a tiny meat counter, and that was it. Oh, yes, the place doubles as a post office."

"At least we do have a post office."

"Not exactly," Roy said with an apologetic grin. "The nearest post office is in Pinyon, but they do bring the Drago mail over once a day to the store."

"And that's where we go to pick up our mail," Karyn said.

"That's it. There's a funny little old lady running the place. You'll have to meet her."

"I hope she's funnier than the sheriff."

"You met Anton Gadak?"

"On the way in. He didn't exactly welcome us with open arms."

"Yeah, well, it probably takes these people a while to warm up to strangers."

"I suppose so." Karyn leaned over and kissed him lightly on the cheek. "You were saying something about steaks?"

They ate together at the big oak dining table while shadows cast by the fire danced across the walls. After dinner they relaxed on the sofa, drinking rich burgundy out of big tulip glasses.

"It seems like a strange little town," Karyn remarked. "What kind of a name is Drago, anyway?"

"I don't know. It's not Spanish or Indian. Has a European sound. Hungarian or something. Tomorrow we can ask in the village. It will give us a chance to meet some of the local people. And we can get some candles to go with this romantic setting."

After she had rinsed off the dinner dishes and stacked them in the sink, she joined Roy back in the living room.

"I wonder what the last people were like," Karyn said, sitting down and lighting a cigarette.

"Who?"

"The people who lived in this house before us. The Fennos."

"The man who handled the lease didn't know much about them," Roy said. "Apparently they were an older couple. Moved out here from somewhere in the East to retire. Weren't here long when they died in some kind of an accident. I didn't get any details."

They both started at the sound of something scraping at the front door.

"Lady," Roy said, relaxing with a little laugh. "We forgot all about her."

He walked over and opened the door. The little dog dashed into the room and across the rug to the couch. There she jumped up and pressed close to Karyn, peering back toward the door with wide, brown eyes.

"She looks frightened," Karyn said.

Roy stepped outside and looked both ways in the darkness. "Nothing out here."

He came back inside and closed the door. Lady stayed close to Karyn on the sofa.

They talked for a while about nothing important while the logs in the fireplace burned down to a dusky red, finally collapsing in a shower of sparks.

Roy stretched his arms up over his head and yawned generously. "I don't know about you, but I'm beat. Ready to go to bed?"

Karyn felt her muscles tighten. "Maybe. I'll have a nice cup of coffee first. Everything tastes so good up here in the mountains." Even in her own ears the light tone of voice rang false.

Karyn took as long as she could with the coffee. She made herself smile at Roy who sat beside her waiting patiently. "Suddenly I'm tired too. Let's go to bed," she said.

They went into the bedroom and Roy turned back the quilt and the snowy top sheet. Karyn's nerves crawled beneath her skin.

She undressed quickly, feeling sure Roy's eyes were fastened on the bite scar—broken red parentheses on the white skin of her inner thigh. She slipped into bed beside her husband and pulled up the covers. Maybe this time it would be all right.

But it was not all right. As soon as they were together in the big comfortable bed and she felt Roy's hand on her—Roy's gentle, familiar hand—a chill spread from her crotch up and throughout her body. Karyn squeezed her eyes shut and ran through all the mental tricks the doctor had given her to blot out the hateful memory of the rape. She clasped her arms about Roy's well muscled back and pulled him down on top of her. She kissed him passionately and whispered their special love words in his ear.

She felt his body grow tense against hers. Gently he pulled away.

"Oh, Roy, what's the matter with me?"

"Nothing is the matter with you, except that you keep thinking something's the matter with you."

"I'm so sorry."

"Cut it out. Everything will be fine as long as we don't force it."

She trailed her fingers slowly across his flat stomach. "Can I do something, you know, for you?"

He shifted his body a fraction of an inch away from her. "Never mind, honey. Get some sleep. Everything will work out."

After that they lay together, their bodies touching, their minds miles apart.

Many hours later, in the cold, empty darkness before the dawn, Karyn heard the howling.

4

Morning came slowly to the valley. The blackness of the bedroom lightened imperceptibly through the shades of gray, and at last a finger of sunlight jabbed through a gap in the curtains. Karyn lay wakeful for a long time waiting for Roy to stir. At last his eyes opened. He looked over at Karyn and smiled.

"Good morning," she said, rolling on her side to kiss him lightly on the mouth. "Sleep well?"

"Sure, I guess so. You?"

"Fine. Except for…" She hesitated, not wanting to start the day by complaining.

"Except for what?"

"Did you hear anything last night?"

"Hear what?"

"Something… like howling."

"No, I didn't hear a thing."

"Maybe it was the wind," she said.

"That was probably it. Blowing over the chimney."

"Probably."

Roy reached over and patted her hip. "Let's have some breakfast. Afterward we can go in and take a look at the town."

Karyn swung lightly out of bed. "You go ahead and take your shower and I'll start getting things set up in the kitchen."

Together they prepared and ate a breakfast of plump country sausages, eggs over easy, muffins, home-fried potatoes, and coffee. Back in the city they seldom had more than plain toast. The food along with the crisp, piney morning air put them in an excellent mood.

Lady was given a helping of canned dog food with a fresh egg beaten into it. She ate as hungrily as the two people, and afterward dashed eagerly outside.

"I'll get the car," Roy said.

"Couldn't we walk into town?" Karyn said. "It can't be more than two miles, and it's such a beautiful day."

Roy grinned at her, his old warm grin, and Karyn felt a rush of affection for her husband. "I keep forgetting that you lived in Manhattan," he said. "I've never seen people walk as much as New Yorkers."

"You wouldn't, being a Southern California boy," Karyn replied. "People here take the car to go to the mailbox."

"Speaking of cars—" Roy began.

Karyn held up a hand to stop him. "I promise, darling, I'll take driving lessons first thing when we get back."

"I don't mean to nag," Roy said, "but there are times when it could be important."

"Yes, sir," Karyn said with mock servility. Roy could not hold his stern expression.

They both turned as the little dog dashed in through the open door and skidded to a stop, legs braced, ready to play.

"Lady will enjoy the walk too," Karyn said. "Won't you, girl?"

With Lady running ahead, Karyn and Roy started down the narrow lane toward the village of Drago. They continued past the old houses which, Karyn saw, were gray and crumbling, with sagging boards and blind windows. The yards had long since gone to weeds.

"Why do you suppose the people moved out and just left these old houses to rot?" Karyn remarked uneasily.

"Who knows? Drago isn't exactly a boomtown. I guess when people die or move away, nobody comes in to take their place."

When they reached the blacktopped road—the main street of Drago—the dog stopped her forays ahead and stayed close to their feet, her ears up, eyes alert.

Karyn and Roy stopped for a moment. Sunlight filtering through the evergreen boughs gave the town a hazy, unreal appearance. The trees sighed under a gentle breeze. No one moved along the street.

"How many people are supposed to be living here?" Karyn asked. Her voice was hushed, as though she were speaking in a church. Or a cemetery.

"I don't know," Roy answered. "Somewhere between a hundred and two hundred."

"Where do you suppose everybody is?"

"Maybe they sleep late."

"Oh, there's someone now," Karyn said. Across the street Anton Gadak stood leaning in the doorway of a small shop. His blocky form was half-hidden in shadows. Karyn and Roy crossed the street and approached him.

"Good morning," Roy said. "For a while there we thought the town was closed today."

Gadak touched the brim of his Stetson and nodded to Karyn. He spoke to Roy. "You'll find us pretty quiet here in Drago."

"That's fine with us," Roy said. "We're pretty quiet ourselves. Are there stores open?"

"You can buy groceries and most anything else down the street at the Jolivets'." Gadak jerked a thumb toward the narrow shop behind him. "And knickknacks you can get in here." He touched his hat brim again and swung off down the street without waiting for further conversation.

Roy looked after him, shaking his head. "I thought he'd never shut up."

"How do you suppose he got to be sheriff?"

"I think it's an honorary title," Roy said. "The town of Drago is not incorporated."

"Well, shall we check out the knickknacks?" Karyn suggested, pointing to the shop. "They may have candles." There was no sign identifying the shop. A curtain was pulled across the show window, and the glass in the door was too dark to see through, giving the place an abandoned look. Roy thumbed the latch and pushed the door open. The clear tinkle of a tiny bell sounded inside. He let Karyn precede him and told Lady to stay put outside.

The interior of the shop was cluttered and dimly lit, but seemed quite clean. A faint scent of sandalwood hung in the air, mingling with the even fainter hint of herbs. A glass-fronted counter ran along one wall of the shop. All around were shelves and small tables filled with colorful and useless objects of the kind people like to give as presents, but seldom buy for themselves. There were china figurines, embroidered pillows, hurricane lamps, ceramic dishes, ornate vases, lace handkerchiefs, costume jewelry, and a collection of boxes and bottles with contents unknown.

"Wonder where the proprietor is," Roy murmured.

A soft green curtain covering a doorway at the rear of the shop moved, and Karyn and Roy looked that way. The curtain parted in the center, sliding along the rod on silent rings, and a young woman stepped through.

The woman's hair was raven black, and soft with glinting highlights. Her eyes slanted just barely, and were a pale green that seemed lit from within. She wore a loose satiny garment that covered her from throat to ankles. When she moved it touched her in a way that revealed the lithe body underneath.

"Hello," the woman said in a smoky voice. "I wondered when you would be in." Her pale-green eyes were trained full on Roy, ignoring Karyn.

"Well, hello," Roy said in a tone Karyn barely recognized. "Were you expecting us?"

"I saw you in the village yesterday. I knew you would be here soon. How may I serve you?"

An old grandfather's clock behind the counter ticked four times before Roy answered. "Candles," he blurted. Then, more composed, "We wanted to buy some candles. We've moved into what I guess is called the old Fenno house."

"Yes, I know," said the black-haired woman. Noting Karyn's quizzical look she added, "In a small town there are few secrets. My name is Marcia Lura."

"I'm Roy Beatty, and this is my wife, Karyn."

"You do have candles?" Karyn said. It came out more sharply than she intended, but the other woman did not seem to notice.

"Oh, yes, Mrs. Beatty, I have candles of all kinds." Marcia Lura turned to face Karyn. In the way she moved and the sharp contrast of pale-green eyes and midnight hair there could be a powerful attraction for a man. Was there also a challenge? Karyn wondered.

"We don't need anything elaborate," Roy said. "Just something for the dinner table. Something romantic." He gave Karyn a quick grin, but his gaze quickly returned to Marcia Lura.

"I understand," Marcia said with a slow smile. "I'm sure I have something that will please you."

Karyn kept her smile in place, but behind it she ground her teeth. Never had she considered herself a jealous woman, but now it infuriated her the way this woman directed her conversation to Roy, and seemed to put double meanings on everything she said. Maybe, Karyn thought, the double meanings were in her own mind. In any case, she did not intend to be upstaged.

"Do you live here in Drago?" Karyn asked, moving a step closer to her husband and touching his arm possessively.

"Yes, I have rooms right here behind the shop. There's not much space, but being alone, I don't need much," Marcia said with a smile. Her mouth was wide and full, a pale-pink shade that might or might not have been achieved with lipstick. "If you will step over this way I'll show you what I have in candles."

They settled for half a dozen slim green candles with a pair of plain glass holders. Not until Roy was paying the woman did Karyn notice that the candles matched the color of her eyes. When they left the shop Karyn felt a vast relief at being back in the fresh air. She reached down and absently scratched Lady behind the ear.

"Striking woman, wasn't she," Karyn said as casually as possible.

"Who? Oh, yes, I suppose you could say she was."

"You didn't notice, I suppose."

Roy snaked an arm around Karyn's waist and pulled her close to him. "Hell, yes, I noticed. Want to make something of it?"

Karyn smiled, happy to have her husband's full attention once again. "Maybe," she said. "Once we get home and get those romantic candles lit."

"Do we need any groceries?" Roy asked.

"I don't think so. You did a pretty good job of shopping yesterday. We could use bread and some milk."

"We can pick that up down at the Jolivets'. He doesn't say much, but she's a character. Anyway, I want you to know where the telephone is."

Karyn stopped suddenly and looked at him. "What telephone?"

"Our telephone. Didn't you notice that there isn't one in the house?"

"No, as a matter of fact, I didn't."

"There are no wires strung out there. Anytime we have to make a call we use the phone at Jolivets' store."

"When we go rural, we don't mess around," Karyn said.

They walked on up the street to a false-front wooden building with a faded sign reading *Jolivet's General Merchandise*. Inside, the store seemed to be stocked indiscriminately with hardware, clothes, and groceries. It had probably looked the same for the last forty years.

Standing at an ancient cash register was a round-faced little woman with a snub nose, rimless glasses, and a bright smile. "Hi, Roy," she said with easy familiarity. "I see the little woman got in all right."

"That's right," Roy said. "This is my wife, Karyn. Oriole Jolivet."

"My, you're pretty as a picture," said Oriole, coming around the counter and taking Karyn's hands. "I just knew a handsome devil like Roy would have a looker for a wife."

"Well, thank you," Karyn said, a little embarrassed, but flattered as well.

"That's my husband, Etienne, over there by the meat case," Oriole said.

A long-faced man looked up from the tray of chops he was arranging and gave Karyn a sad smile.

"You're the first new folks to move into Drago in quite a spell," Oriole told them. "Hope we'll be seein' you around from time to time."

"I'm sure you will," Karyn said.

"No need to wait till you have to buy something, just come on by anytime you feel like chewin' the fat."

"I'll do that," Karyn said.

"Good, good. Do you like coffee?"

"I love coffee."

Oriole's smile got even brighter. "That's the kind of talk I like to hear. Yes, indeed, you and me are going to get along fine, Karyn. Now you wait right there and I'll go out back and pour us all a cup."

"I don't want you to go to any trouble—"

"No trouble at all, honey. Be back in a jiffy." Oriole bustled out and returned in a moment carrying a tray laden with cups of dark, rich coffee, and thick slices of cinnamon-sprinkled coffeecake. Karyn sipped the coffee and chatted with Oriole while Roy prowled around the store. For the first time since arriving in Drago she felt at ease.

When they had finished the last of the coffee and cake, Roy bought a loaf of bread and two quarts of milk. He put the candles in the bag with the groceries and they left Jolivets' store.

Lady, who seemed to sense that they were going home now, bounded off down the street.

Watching the dog, Karyn touched Roy's arm and pointed toward one of the old houses. There a boy and girl of about twelve stood motionless in the front yard watching them. Their faces were grave, their eyes shadowed. A woman came out onto the porch and said something. The children turned silently and went inside.

"You know," Karyn said, "those are the first children I've seen in this town."

"The rest of them are probably in school."

"Where? I haven't seen anything in Drago that looks like a school."

"Maybe they go over to Pinyon," Roy said. "Does it matter?"

5

That night in bed Karyn gave the finest acting performance of her life. She twisted and moaned under her husband; she dug her nails into his back. She caressed him with her hands and with her mouth. She heaved her body to meet his thrusts and clamped her legs around his waist. She cried out words of passion as she felt his climax burst inside her.

And she felt nothing.

She could not be sure if Roy knew. He gripped her with his strong, square hands and tongued her ear and said all the right things as he approached orgasm, but Karyn was not sure that he believed her response. At least, she told herself, he had climaxed. Her performance was not wasted.

Afterward he rolled over and slept. Karyn lay beside him trying to sleep too. But as the minutes ticked into hours she gave it up and lay waiting, listening. She knew it would come, as surely as death. And it did come. The distant ululation. The mournful sinister night cry. The howling.

After that she slept fitfully, waking up time and again to listen breathlessly to the night. Finally she came awake with a start to find that it was light and Roy was gone from the bed. She could smell coffee perking in the kitchen, and hurried to join her husband.

That day, and the next, and the next, Karyn and Roy did not go into the village of Drago. They stayed close to the little house, walking on the trails in the forest and delighting in the birds and wild flowers. Lady loved these outings. She would rush joyfully ahead barking officiously at anything that moved, as though clearing the path for her people. Although Karyn and Roy kept up the pretense of enjoying each other, each was occupied with thoughts that could not be shared.

In the evenings they played cribbage or backgammon. Having no television set, they rediscovered the radio. Sometimes Karyn would read from the stack of paperbacks she had brought from the city while Roy worked at the kitchen table going over the list of his company's technical publications.

At night Karyn tried to let go during sex, but it became harder all the time to pretend she was enjoying it. Roy's lovemaking became perfunctory, and at last he merely kissed her goodnight and turned away. Then while he slept Karyn would lie on her back, her muscles taut, and stare into the dark.

Every night now, the howling came. Karyn no longer asked Roy if he heard it. He never seemed to. Karyn was afraid that if she talked about it he would say it was all in her head. She knew better. Something was out there. Something.

By the end of the first week Karyn had dug out the bottle containing the remaining Seconals the doctor in Los Angeles had prescribed when she came home from hospital. She had never liked taking pills, but at last she was able to sleep soundly.

Roy began to walk in the forest by himself. His excuse was that he wanted to gather wood for the fireplace but Karyn knew there was all the wood they needed within fifty yards of the house. The real reason had to be that he wanted to get away from her.

She became convinced of it the day of Roy's first trip into Los Angeles. Although he made a show of reluctance to leave their wilderness paradise, his eagerness was not hard to read. She watched the Ford disappear down the narrow lane with an increasing sense of fear and uneasiness.

The day was cool with a high overcast. Karyn vowed to pull herself out of her funk. She put on a heavy sweater and took Lady for a long walk through the woods. For a city girl, she had a remarkable sense of direction, and there was never any problem finding her way back. Returning home around noon, she washed the walls and windows, even though they didn't need it. She fixed herself a sandwich, fed the dog, and shuffled through the books without finding one she wanted to read. She began looking up the road for Roy long before he was due to return.

When at last he drove into the yard, Karyn ran out to meet him and they hugged each other enthusiastically and walked back to the house arm in arm.

Karyn had prepared a small roast for their meal. It came out perfectly—crispy brown on the outside, pink and tender within. The candles provided an intimate glow, and the talk came easy. It was almost the way it had been before their trouble started.

After dinner Karyn fed Lady and let her outside while Roy poured their brandy. They moved into the living room and sat close together by the fireplace. Their legs touched, and for the first time in months Karyn felt a surge of desire for her husband.

"Roy," she said, "let's go to bed."

"Sleepy already?"

She shook her head, holding the warm pressure of her thigh against him. "Nope."

Roy looked at her closely for a moment, then took her into his arms. He kissed her. She returned the kiss with feeling. Everything about him—his hands on her back, the taste of his mouth, even the short stubble of beard—excited her.

"Let's not waste any more time," he said. They stood up together and he led her into the bedroom.

When they were lying together, Karyn rolled onto her side to face him. Roy's hand moved down her ribcage and up over the swell of her hip. She reached down for his sex and found him erect and hard. The touch of him in her hand was good. His fingers trailed down across her flat stomach and into the blond fluff of pubic hair. She felt herself open willingly and go moist under his touch.

Oh, God, said a part of Karyn's mind, let it be good this time. Let it be right, the way it was.

Roy was kissing her breast, teasing the erect nipple with his tongue. His hand was up between her legs, stroking, massaging. Karyn was ready for him. As ready as she would ever be. Then she heard it.

The howling.

Not far off in the woods this time, but close outside. Close, deep-throated, and cold as death.

"Roy." she said, sitting up in bed.

"I heard it," he said. He pulled himself up beside her, but his voice did not reflect the urgency that Karyn felt.

Roy's hand moved between her legs. His head dipped again to her breast.

"What was it?" Karyn said. She was whispering without knowing why.

"I don't know. An owl." His tone took on an edge of impatience.

"Not an owl," she said.

"Who cares? Come on, Karyn, lie down."

Obediently Karyn lay back on the sheet. She tried hard to recover the mood of a few moments before, but the terrible howling still sounded in her brain. How could Roy ignore it?

His head moved lower on her body. She could feel his tongue tracing a moist line across her navel and on down...

Abruptly it was not her husband kissing her down there, it was that horrible other thing. The teeth.

With a startled cry she drew away from him.

He pulled himself up. "What?"

Karyn reached out to him, trying to make her touch affectionate, though she still felt the unreasoning revulsion, "I'm sorry, Roy. I... I don't think I can."

"But just a minute ago—"

"I know," she said quickly. "I know, Roy, but now I can't."

"Jesus," he said through clenched teeth, and turned away from her. His broad naked back was like a wall in the middle of the bed.

"Please, darling," she said, "be patient with me for a little while longer."

He gave her an unconvincing pat on the shoulder. "Sure, Karyn, it's all right. I'm just keyed up after driving out from the city."

But it was not all right, and they both knew it. Karyn's throat filled up with words she wanted to say to her husband but could not: *I'm sorry, dear, I was all ready and in the mood, and then something howled outside. No, it was not an owl. And after that the only picture in my mind was that filthy animal with his hands up in me and his teeth biting me and then... and then...*

Karyn forced her mind back from the brink of hysteria, and at last fell into a shallow sleep.

In the morning she was the first one up. She combed out her hair and went into the kitchen. She would prepare a lovely breakfast for Roy—ham-and-cheese omelet with hot muffins, and rich black coffee. But first she had to feed the dog. She took a can of Alpo from the cupboard, then wondered why Lady did not come trotting in at the sound of the can on the countertop. Then she remembered that no one had let her back in last night. Karyn went to open the front door. The dog was not in sight.

Karyn stepped outside and called the dog's name. The forest was unusually silent on this gray, damp day, the only sound, the dripping of moisture from the tree branches. Karyn called again and walked all around the yard. Nothing answered.

She went back inside and into the bedroom, where Roy sat on the edge of the bed pulling on a pair of denim pants.

"Lady's not here," she said. "We forgot to let her in last night. Now I can't find her. She doesn't answer." Karyn sensed the rising pitch of her voice, but she did not try to control it. Concern for the dog was an acceptable outlet for the other tangled emotions that she was not ready to examine.

"I'll go take a look," Roy replied. He went outside, whistling and calling for the little dog. He made several forays into the woods, calling louder, and came back with his jeans wet from the damp brush.

"She's probably off exploring somewhere," he said without conviction.

"Roy, do you think something's happened to her?"

"What could happen? We've been here over a week. Lady knows her way around by now. She'll come home when she gets hungry."

Karyn caught the irritability just beneath his words. She said, "I guess we might as well eat breakfast."

She had lost all enthusiasm for the omelet. While she cooked it, Karyn left the front door open. From time to time each of them would look over that way.

Afterward Roy went to work editing his manuscripts. Karyn sat in a chair by the window with a book open on her lap. She tried to read, but the printed words would not register on her mind. When it was almost noon she could sit still no longer.

"Roy, I think we should go out and look for her. She may be hurt and can't get back to us."

Roy looked over at her, and Karyn could see that he was not as unconcerned as he acted. "All right," he said.

The sun was out now, high and pale, but warm enough to dry off the forest. Roy and Karyn walked the trails that interlaced the surrounding woods. Some were so dim and overgrown that they were hardly there. Others showed signs of recent use.

Roy went in one direction, Karyn in another. She concentrated on looking down as she walked, scanning the ground along both sides of each trail. She saw nothing.

When Roy came upon her suddenly walking from the opposite direction, she started and gave a little squeal of surprise.

He reached out and grasped her arm gently. "No luck?"

She shook her head.

"Roy, let's try going into town."

"What for?"

"Maybe Lady got confused and went that way. Maybe somebody saw her. It wouldn't hurt to ask. It's better than sitting in that house and waiting to hear her bark, or see her come running home." Karyn turned away so Roy would not see the sudden tears. "Damn, how stupid it is to let a little animal become such a part of your life. *Stupid.*"

Roy put his arms around Karyn and held her for a moment.

They did not talk during the short drive. There was no sign of the dog in the roadway or in the brush alongside.

Once they were in the village Roy pulled over to the side and turned to Karyn while the engine idled. "What now?"

Karyn looked up and down the deserted street, confused. "How... how about that sheriff or whatever he is, Anton Gadak? Maybe he would know if anybody has seen Lady."

The words were barely out of her mouth when the broad figure of Anton Gadak appeared up the street, angling across the blacktop toward their car. Roy shut off the engine and got out on the driver's side. Karyn came around and stood beside him.

Gadak put two fingers to the brim of his Stetson. "Afternoon, folks. Haven't seen you for a few days. Everything all right?"

"Everything's fine," Roy began automatically, then corrected himself. "No, the truth is we've got a problem."

"Problem?" Gadak waited politely.

When Roy hesitated, Karyn spoke up. "It's our little dog. We left her out last night and this morning she's missing." Even as she spoke, Karyn thought how trivial it must sound.

"Sorry to hear that."

"We wondered if she might have found her way to town somehow."

"If she did, I ain't heard about it," Gadak said. "Folks in Drago don't keep pets much, so they'd most likely notice your dog if she came in this way. I'll ask around, and keep an eye out myself."

"Thanks," Roy said. "We'd appreciate it."

"No trouble."

As the big man was about to turn away, Karyn stopped him. "Mr. Gadak, are there any large animals around here that might have... harmed her?"

"Large animals?" Gadak repeated.

"Last night, and on other nights, I've heard something in the woods. A howling."

Gadak pulled at his lower lip and looked down at Karyn. His eyes were shaded by the hat brim. "A howling, you say. Coyote, maybe. Sure, could have been a coyote. Been a few of them seen hereabouts. They'll carry off a small animal now and again. How big was this dog of yours?"

"About so high," Roy said, flattening his hand at about knee level.

"Kinda big for a coyote to take on," Gadak said, "but maybe it was hungry."

"It was not a coyote," Karyn said firmly.

The big man turned his shadowed eyes back to her. "Eh, what's that?"

"The thing I heard howling in the woods. It was no Coyote."

"Come on, Karyn," Roy said. "How can you be sure?"

She turned on her husband. "You heard it. You heard the howling last night. Did that sound like a coyote to you?"

Roy's eyes shifted uneasily. "How would I know? I'm a city boy. The only coyotes I ever hear are on *Wild Kingdom.*"

"All right," Karyn persisted, "but that howling last night, that didn't sound like any coyote on television... or any other place."

"Maybe an owl," Roy offered.

"Could be," Gadak remarked, scratching his chin. "The woods has a lot of peculiar sounds at night. 'Specially for folks from the city. You'll get used to it."

"I doubt it," Karyn said quietly. She walked around the car and got in.

Anton Gadak spoke to Roy in a confidential tone, but the words came clearly to Karyn through the open window. "I'll ask around about your dog, Mr. Beatty, but I want to be honest with you. I think it's gone for good. Take my word for it… that was a coyote your missus heard. They can tear up a small animal in a hurry when they get hold of one."

Roy got in and turned the car back toward their house. Karyn kept her eyes straight ahead, but she could see Roy glancing over at her.

Without looking at him, she said in a firm voice, "It was no coyote."

6

That night Roy did not even try to make love to Karyn. He stayed up long after she went to bed, working, he said. When he finally came silently into the bedroom he was careful not to wake her and immediately went to sleep.

The night after that Karyn wore her nightgown to bed. It broke a year's long habit of sleeping in the nude. Roy came to bed late again and did not even notice.

The next morning Roy acted especially cheerful, but obviously something was on his mind. After more than a year of marriage Karyn knew the man well enough to wait until he was ready to tell her about it. During his second cup of coffee he did.

"Uh, look, honey, something's come up with the manuscripts I brought home."

"Oh?"

"I've run into some problems that just can't be solved without getting together with the writer. So it looks like I'm going to have to take a run into Los Angeles."

"Today?"

"Well, yes, the sooner the better. You'll be all right?"

"Of course."

"Is there anything I can do for you before I go?"

"I'm not an invalid, Roy."

"I hate to go, but it's one of those things."

Roy dabbed at his mouth and stood up, anxious to be on his way, but trying not to show it. He gathered up the manuscripts he said were giving him trouble and took them out to the car. Karyn walked out with him. She kissed him goodbye, then turned away and walked back to the house as he drove away. When she was back inside Karyn sat down and cried for twenty minutes.

Then, as abruptly as she had started, she stopped crying. She went into the bathroom and washed her face. A bleary, red-eyed image looked back at her from the mirror.

"You look like hell," Karyn said. She soaked a cloth with cool water and patted her face with it.

"How do you expect me to look?" her image seemed to answer. "Sitting around the house in the middle of the woods with a husband who has turned into a stranger while trying to pretend there's nothing the matter. How would anybody look?"

She took up a brush and began energetically stroking her hair. When her hair had achieved a shimmery golden glow Karyn went back into the living room and sat down in the chair by the window. She picked up a paperback novel.

After a little while Karyn tossed the book aside. She recognized a new emotion building in her. Anger. She had seethed inside since the other day when Roy and that so-called sheriff Anton Gadak had been so patronizing to her with their smug explanations of the howling. Coyote like hell! Owl my foot! Something else howled in the woods around Drago. Karyn decided suddenly that she was going to find out what.

She went into the bedroom and changed into jeans and a suede jacket. She put on a comfortable pair of moccasins and set off walking toward the village. When she reached Drago's main street she was surprised to see that there were several people out walking. No one she recognized, but at least it was evidence that there were other people living here.

She looked over at the little shop run by Marcia Lura. Door closed and dark, curtain across the window as usual. She wondered how the woman could attract enough customers to keep the place open. Or maybe her real business was in the back room. Karyn grinned wickedly.

For that matter, nothing in Drago seemed to do much business. Karyn walked by the open door of a tavern. Inside a solitary customer sat at the bar with a glass of beer in front of him. He looked out at Karyn, his face expressionless.

She continued past the boarded-up theater with its empty marquee. A faded poster tacked behind a glassless frame advertised a motorcycle movie that must have been ten years old.

She crossed the street to Jolivet's General Merchandise. At least there she could count on finding some life and a friendly face.

Oriole Jolivet bustled around the counter to greet her. The little woman wore a wide smile and her eyes twinkled behind the lenses of her glasses.

"Karyn, for gosh sakes, I about decided you'd up and left us."

"Nothing like that," Karyn said. "We've just been staying close to home."

"You ever find your little dog?"

"No."

"Aw, that's too bad. Something like that can really get a person down. How's Roy? Did he come in with you?"

"He had to go into Los Angeles today."

"Oh. You come in for shoppin' or for a visit?"

"For a visit, really, if I'm not taking you away from business."

"That'll be the day. You and me will have us a nice hen party. You're not in any hurry, are you?"

"No, not really."

"Good. I'll put on a fresh pot of coffee. Do you play cards?"

"Roy and I play cribbage sometimes."

"I don't know that one," Oriole said. "How about gin rummy?"

"I used to know how to play that," Karyn said doubtfully, "but it's been a long time."

"Don't worry, it'll come back to you. Just like riding a bicycle." Oriole started back around the counter and beckoned for Karyn to follow. "Come on out to the back. We'll play for half a cent a point, okay? Cards are no fun unless you play for money."

"Half a cent a point is fine," Karyn said, laughing. "You'd better go easy on me, though. I only have about three dollars with me."

"Shoot, I'll trust you for anything over that." Oriole laughed.

As she followed Oriole to the back room of the store, Karyn saw for the first time that Etienne Jolivet was standing silently off at one side of the counter. He gave her a faint smile and nodded. Karyn nodded back and wondered why the man made her uncomfortable.

In the cozy back room Oriole put a big pot of coffee on the stove and cleared off an old kitchen table for their game. She produced a worn deck of cards, a pad of paper, and a yellow stub of pencil.

"The first hand'll be just for practice," Oriole said, "so you can get the hang of it before we start playing for real."

An hour later Karyn was down $2.80, and Oriole was enjoying herself immensely. Oriole was an aggressive player, if not overly shrewd.

Karyn's mind was not on the game.

"You've lived here a long time, haven't you, Oriole?" she asked as the other woman carefully added up the score of the last hand.

"All my life."

"I was wondering…" Karyn hesitated, unsure how to proceed.

Oriole looked up and her bright little eyes met Karyn's. "Anything at all you want to know about what goes on in Drago, I'm the one that can tell you. Not that all that much goes on here."

Karyn smiled in agreement. "It's not really town gossip I was after. I was just wondering… well, for one thing, why aren't there any pets in Drago? The sheriff said the people here didn't keep many animals, but I haven't seen a single dog or cat on the street."

Oriole scratched thoughtfully at her nose. "Guess I never thought much about it. Let me see, there's some people named Hemphill on the other side of town from you folks. They keep chickens. Used to, anyway."

"That's not quite what I meant," Karyn said.

"Never cared much for dogs and cats myself," Oriole said.

"Maybe when you're out here closer to nature you don't feel the need to have an animal in the house."

"Maybe that's it." Oriole scooped up the cards and began to shuffle.

"Is there much wildlife in the woods around here?" Karyn asked, keeping it casual.

"We see deer sometimes. Raccoons. Chipmunks, squirrels. That's about it."

"Nothing… dangerous?"

"Lordy, no. If you start climbing the mountains you might run into rattlesnakes, but you won't find them in the woods. It's too cool and damp for rattlesnakes."

"What about coyotes?"

"Well, now, I suppose there could be a coyote wander in through the pass once in a while. You get into the high desert just the other side of the mountains, and they got coyotes over there. Why?"

"I've heard something in the woods at night. Howling. You know Lady, our dog, has disappeared. I wondered if something out there could have got her. Maybe even a wolf?"

"Well, I don't know nothing about wolves." Oriole began dealing the cards, snapping each one firmly down on the table.

"I'd like to find out more," Karyn persisted. "Is there a library? Somewhere I could get books?"

"Not in Drago. Nearest library's over in Pinyon. If you want to call them, they'll send your books over with the mail. Tell 'em you know me and it'll be all right."

"Thanks, Oriole. If I can use your phone, I think I'll do that right now."

"In the middle of our game?"

"I'll be right back. This business has been on my mind, and I'll feel a lot better about it when I've at least done something."

"Okay, help yourself. The phone's out on the counter, next to the cash register. I'll heat up the coffee."

Through the operator, Karyn got the number of the library in Pinyon. The librarian there, a Mr. Upshaw, apparently had little to do to keep himself busy, and was eager to help Karyn find the kind of books she was looking for, and he said he'd be glad to send them over. They settled on *The Wolf* by L. David Mech, *Never Cry Wolf* by Farley Mowat, and *World of the Wolf* by Russell J. Rutter. All were of recent publication, and all dealt with the wolf in its natural state. For good measure, Karyn asked for the National Geographic book on North American mammals.

Karyn and Oriole played gin for another hour, during which Karyn lost another two dollars. Oriole cheerfully accepted an I.O.U. and said she hoped they could make their card game a regular thing. Karyn said she hoped so too—if she could afford it—but really was relieved to get away. Oriole Jolivet was cheerful company but she had hardly anything besides gin rummy to talk about.

Karyn took her time walking back to the house. Rationally she had given up hope of ever seeing Lady again. Still, sometimes she would start at a sudden sound from the woods, thinking it was the bark of a small dog. But it was always something else. Or nothing at all.

7

When Karyn came within sight of the house she was surprised to see the Galaxie already parked in front. She had expected Roy to prolong the trip to Los Angeles at least until dark. She was also surprised at her indifference to seeing him. It had never been like that before. Unconsciously she slowed her steps as she neared the house.

In their year of marriage Karyn had known only pleasure in being with Roy. Now after he had made excuses for leaving her, she found herself wishing he had stayed away longer. She walked on slowly toward the house.

Roy was moody and distant in his greeting. Since Karyn was not anxious to talk either, she did not press him. They ate an early dinner, preoccupied with their own thoughts. After dinner they sat apart in the living room and pretended to read.

They both started at the sudden crunch of automobile tires on the gravel outside. Roy shot Karyn a questioning look. She shook her head.

There was a knock at the door, and Roy crossed the room quickly to answer it.

Out on the small porch stood a woman carrying a shopping bag. She was tall and thin, with a bony, big-featured face. Her gray hair was indifferently cut; she wore a shapeless tweed suit and heavy-rimmed glasses. The woman smiled at Roy. She had a good smile that softened the lines of her face.

"Is this where Mrs. Beatty lives?"

Karyn moved in beside Roy. "I'm Karyn Beatty."

The woman's smile took in both of them. "Pleased to meet you. My name is Inez Polk. I live over in Pinyon and I happened to be in the library today while Al Upshaw was getting the books together for you."

Roy turned to Karyn. "What books?"

"I called the library in Pinyon today from the Jolivets'," Karyn explained quickly. She turned back to the thin woman.

"I was intrigued by your selection of books," said Inez Polk, "so I offered to drive over here tonight and drop them off."

"It was kind of you to take the trouble," Karyn said.

"No trouble at all. I'm glad for the excuse to meet you. The fact is I get bored to death sometimes over in Pinyon. I teach English there to junior high school students who consider it just another dead language. I'll grab any chance I get to talk to somebody new and interesting."

Inez Polk looked from Karyn to Roy and back again. "If I'm interrupting something, please say so, I appreciate frankness."

"You're not interrupting a thing," Karyn said. "Please come in. Can I get you a cup of coffee? Or a drink?"

"Have you any wine?"

"Burgundy?"

"A glass of burgundy would be nice." Inez took the four books Karyn had asked for and stacked them on the low table in front of the sofa.

Roy leaned down and fanned the books so he could read the titles. He looked quizzically at Karyn. "Wolves?"

Karyn walked past him into the dining alcove, where she poured two glasses of wine from a decanter. "Yes, wolves," she said shortly. "Would you like some wine, Roy?"

"No, thanks. I think I'll get a little exercise. Take a walk before it gets dark." Roy brushed Karyn's cheek with his lips, said goodbye to Inez, and left the house hastily. Like a man set free, Karyn thought.

She carried the wine back into the living room and sat down on the sofa with Inez. In a very short time the two women were chatting warmly. Inez Polk was intelligent and witty, and shared a surprising number of Karyn's interests and opinions. It had been a long time since Karyn had felt completely relaxed with a stranger. By the time she refilled the wineglasses they were fast friends.

"So what is it with you and the wolves?" Inez said, getting around to her reason for coming.

"You won't laugh?"

"Try me," Inez said. Her expression was dead serious.

Karyn told her about the howling in the woods, how it was far off at first, and quite close the night Lady had disappeared. She told Inez about Roy's skepticism and the sheriff's explanation that it was coyotes.

"And you think there's a wolf out there?" Inez asked. "I don't know. It sounded like a wolf to me. If that's what got my dog, it had to be as big as a wolf. Lady was no fighter, but I don't believe a coyote would attack her."

"And nobody else has mentioned a wolf?"

"No."

"Mm-hmm. Well, maybe there's a clue in those books?" Both Karyn and Inez were quick scan readers. They divided the library books and went through them, and soon they had learned more about wolves than they really wanted to know.

From the several species discussed they chose the gray, or timber wolf, *Canis lupus*, as the most likely. This wolf, they read, was the largest found in America—as big as five feet long, including eighteen inches of tail. Some huge specimens had been found in Canada weighing 175 pounds.

Wolves were fierce fighters and exceptionally intelligent, with a diet consisting primarily of smaller animals, but when hunting in packs they could pull down prey much larger than themselves.

The most significant fact the women found was that, except for a few hundred hanging on in the forests of northern Michigan, Minnesota, and Wisconsin, there were no wild wolves left in the United States.

"What do you think then, Inez? Could it have been a coyote I heard? Or an owl, for God's sake?"

The thin woman was silent for a minute while she appeared to organize her thoughts. Finally she said, "No, it wasn't any coyote. Or an owl, either."

"Was it in my head, then?"

"No, you heard something, all right."

Karyn studied the other woman for a moment. "You never did tell me why my ordering books about wolves brought you out here tonight. You have some idea what this is all about, don't you?"

"Yes," Inez said slowly. "I have an idea."

"Well, come on, let's hear it."

"Let me tell you a little about myself first. I am thirty-nine years old, never been married, and live alone with my potted plants, which I do not talk to, no matter how great the temptation. Every summer I take a trip somewhere alone, meet nobody worth knowing, and come back alone. I read a lot and I have a good collection of classical records."

"Inez, I—" Karyn began.

"No, I am not making a bid for sympathy. I like my life the way it is. Aside from a certain lack of intellectual stimulation, I like living in Pinyon. However, people there think I'm a little odd. Not dangerous odd, but kind of amusing odd."

"What makes you think so?" Karyn said.

"You haven't heard it all yet," Inez interrupted. "For one thing, I used to be a nun."

"A nun?" Karyn repeated.

"Yes, I was a Carmelite. There are quite a few of us failed nuns around today. Unlike most of the others, I didn't leave because of any argument with the Church. In my case it was a personal matter."

Karyn studied the angular woman and tried to visualize her in the traditional nun's habit. Inez simply did not have the round, soft face that one associated with the cloister.

"You're not going to tell me I don't look like a nun?" Inez said, smiling.

Karyn laughed. "As a matter of fact, that's just what I was thinking. Anyway, you were telling me about why you are interested in wolves."

"That's the point I'm leading up to. My interest is not exactly in wolves. You see, I've lived in Pinyon for eleven years, and with a lot of spare time I made a kind of hobby out of local history. Before long I noticed a strange pattern of occurrences in and around Drago. I was intrigued because the pattern seemed to tie in with my other hobby."

"Which is?" Karyn prompted.

Inez drew a deep breath before she answered. *"Diabolus."*

"The devil?"

"You think it's an unusual study for a former nun? Let me tell you, Karyn, that a belief in God requires a counter-belief in Satan. You must know your enemy before you can defeat him."

Karyn stared in amazement. "All right. Inez," she said, hesitantly, making an effort at reason, "but what has Diabolus to do with me and Drago? Are you saying it's the Devil who is howling in the woods?"

"No, not the Devil himself." Inez Polk's eyes fell away for a moment, then returned, bright behind their lenses, to meet Karyn's gaze. "I think," she said, "that Drago has a werewolf."

8

Karyn stared at Inez for a full ten seconds after her shocking suggestion, waiting for some indication that she was joking.

"You're serious, aren't you?" Karyn said finally.

"Deadly serious. Karyn, before you close your mind, please hear me out. Do you know anything about werewolves?"

"Do you mean lycanthropy?"

"No, that's just what I don't mean. Lycanthropy is a disease, a form of mental illness in which the victim imagines himself to be a wolf. He acts like a wolf, losing the power of speech, running around on all fours, growling, and eating raw meat."

"But isn't that what a werewolf is, really?"

"No. A werewolf is a human being who actually, physically, changes into a wolf."

Karyn shook her head. "Inez, I just can't relate to this. We're two grown, reasonably intelligent women. And here we sit discussing werewolves as calmly as though we were talking about fruit-flies." Karyn continued very slowly, reasonably.

"Inez, you were a nun. As far as I know, you're still a Catholic. How can you say these things?"

"Nothing I have said is contrary to the precepts of the Church. If I accept the existence of God as Good, I must also accept the existence of Evil. That's capital 'E' Evil. Call it whatever you want to—Satan, the Devil, the Antichrist."

"Do you mean that werewolves and the Devil are one and the same?"

"No. The werewolf is a servant of the Devil. No one becomes a werewolf by chance. It's like witchcraft. In return you pledge your everlasting soul."

"People willingly become werewolves?"

"Once it was not at all uncommon. In the Middle Ages life could be an ugly, painful existence if you were very poor, and the price of your soul did not seem too much to pay for the powers of the werewolf."

"But today surely there can't be people still making deals with the Devil."

"Not many, I imagine. Not in the old way."

"Then where would a modern werewolf come from?"

"The curse is passed on to succeeding generations. Unless the line is wiped out, there is no end."

"So to be a werewolf, you either have to make a pact with the Devil, or have a werewolf for a parent." Karyn was trying to be sarcastic, but it did not come out that way.

"There is another way," Inez said.

"What is that?" This is going too far, Karyn thought. I must stop humoring her.

"The bite of a werewolf, if it does not kill it can infect the victim with the taint. These cases are rare, because when a werewolf attacks, he usually kills. A blessing, in a way."

"I need a drink," Karyn said. "Do you want some more wine?"

"No, thank you."

Karyn went into the kitchen and made herself a strong Scotch and water. The way Inez was talking worried her, but she did not know how to ease away from the subject. She took a deep swallow of the drink before going back out.

"I can see I'm upsetting you," Inez said when Karyn came into the room.

"I'm sorry, Inez. I'm trying to listen seriously to what you're saying. But *werewolves.*"

"Why is it so hard to accept? Don't we travel to the moon? Destroy cities with the force of the atom? Transplant organs from one human being to another?"

"But those are achievements of science. What you're talking about is superstition."

Inez's expression of utter conviction did not change.

Karyn took another approach. "All right, just for now let's say that these things do exist. Why here? Why in the Tehachapi Mountains of California? Why Drago?"

"The history of the town, for one thing," said Inez. "In the sixty-plus years that Drago has been in existence there have been an unreasonable number of strange deaths and unexplained disappearances in and around the village. I have books at home—documents, records, newspaper clippings. I would have brought them with me tonight, but I didn't know you. I didn't know if I should bring up the subject."

"You still don't know me, Inez. I don't believe in your Werewolves or your Devil or your God, and I don't want to hear any more about them." Karyn stopped abruptly as she heard herself turning shrill.

Inez looked as though she had been slapped. "I'm sorry, Karyn. Please believe that I'm sorry. I had given up talking to people about this because I knew they would think I was crazy. As I told you, they already think I'm odd. I can just imagine their reaction if I told them there is a werewolf at large in Drago. I took a chance on telling you because I sensed a sympathetic feeling between us. The last thing I wanted to do was upset you."

"Shall we drop it?" Karyn said. "I don't want to talk about it any more." She placed her empty glass firmly on the table.

"I understand." Inez looked around uncertainly. "Well... I should be going."

Karyn walked with her to the door. "Inez, I didn't mean to snap at you. My nerves haven't been in the best shape lately. Please don't take it personally."

The taller woman touched her hand. "Really, it's all right. Goodbye, Karyn."

Karyn stood at the door watching Inez Polk walk to her car and drive away. Then she turned back and saw the books Inez had brought her from the library. For some reason she felt like crying.

9

As Roy Beatty approached the village of Drago, he breathed deeply the balsam-scented air. He was relieved to be away from Karyn and her hang-ups, even for a little while. And because he felt relieved, he was twisted by guilt. Karyn was his wife. Now, when she was having problems, was no time for him to be making up excuses to go to Los Angeles, or to be rushing out of the house the minute somebody else showed up to take over the burden of keeping her company.

The fact that he could not get to the pulse of his feelings disturbed him. Roy Beatty had always been in control of his life. He was not a complicated man. He did not like surprises, and he did not like conflicts. For most of his twenty-nine years Roy had managed to keep his life running as smoothly as an engineering project.

And that was the way his life had gone—neatly plotted and well within tolerances—until that terrible afternoon when the shaky voice of his best friend on the telephone had brought him rushing home.

Now, just as he had begun to hope that the peace and quiet of Drago might help restore the Karyn he had loved, this business of the missing dog and the howling in the night had upset her again. When, Roy wondered bitterly, would life return to normal?

He came to the main street of Drago and turned to his right before really thinking about his destination. He had not intended to walk all the way to the village, but he had just kept walking. The logical thing to do now, he told himself, was to turn around and start back. However, a curious sense of excitement compelled him to continue down the street. When at last he came to a stop, Roy had to admit this was where he had been coming all along. It was the little shop run by Marcia Lura.

He hesitated for a moment before opening the door. A kind of unnatural stillness hung over the town. He reminded himself that he was doing nothing wrong.

Why should he not come to this shop? He might just find a nice little gift inside to take home to Karyn.

No, that would not do. The idea of the gift had just popped into his head, and he could not pretend to himself that it was the reason he had come. He was here because he wanted very much to see again the dark haired woman.

He walked inside to the sound of the tinkling bell. Marcia Lura was standing in the center of the shop wearing a peasant blouse and a full, flowered skirt. She was looking at him.

"Hello," she said. "I expected you sooner."

"You knew I would come?"

"Of course. When you were in the other day I felt the attraction between us as strongly as you did. Are you going to tell me I'm wrong?"

Roy caught his breath. In the dim light of the shop Marcia looked criminally beautiful. Her eyes seemed to have a light of their own. An intense pale green.

"No," he said. "You are not wrong."

"Are you uncomfortable with me?"

"A little. Believe it or not, I don't usually do things like this."

"I believe you," she said. Her smile showed strong white teeth. "And besides, you haven't really done anything yet."

Roy forced a laugh. It did not come out as casual as he intended. "What I had in mind was some sort of gift for my... my wife."

"Ah, yes. Do you see anything you like?" Marcia's mouth curled faintly at the corners. Her eyes challenged him. "What I mean, of course, is anything your wife would like."

Roy looked around in confusion. His hand closed mindlessly on the nearest object, a china figurine of a little girl in the costume of a shepherdess. It was overly cute with blue saucer eyes and round cherub cheeks. Karyn would hate it.

"How much is this?" he said.

"Is that what you really want?"

"Why not?"

"It is seven dollars."

"I'll take it."

Marcia moved toward him, stopping just before they touched.

"Do you want to go for a walk with me?" she said.

"Walk?" Roy had to clear his throat against the sudden huskiness of his voice. "Walk where?"

"Out in the back. There's a path through the woods. It's very pretty this time of year."

"All right," he said, nodding.

"Come this way." She held aside the curtain at the rear of the shop. Beyond it were a small living room, kitchenette, bedroom, and bath. The rugs and the furniture were in muted earth colors of brown, green, and burnt orange. There were cushions on the floor and candles everywhere. The air held a hint of sandalwood.

Marcia led him through her small apartment and out the back door. There the forest pushed almost up to the rear wall of the building, as it did to all buildings in Drago. A broad path carpeted with pine needles led off among the trees.

"Come." Marcia held out her hand to him. The fingers were slim and white and well shaped. Roy took the hand. The effect of the touch was like the spreading warmth from the first sip of a good martini.

Hand in hand they walked along the path through the forest. The shadows were deepening, and the afternoon was cool. Occasionally Marcia would call his attention to an unusual flower or a bird watching them from a tree. Roy would respond to whatever she said, but his thoughts were far from his words. He was acutely aware of the waves of sensation that pulsed through his body from the point where their hands touched. The green of her eyes, he saw, was darker here in the forest. Deeper. The loose black hair framed her face like softly folded wings.

"Strangely enough," Marcia was saying, "this path leads through the woods and comes out on the road by the old Fenno house." She turned the green eyes full upon him. "I should really say the Beatty house now, shouldn't I?"

"That has a permanent sound to it," Roy said. "We only leased the place for six months."

"Really?"

"That was the plan. It's always possible we might stay longer." He pulled himself away from the compelling eyes, forced his thoughts down another channel. "Speaking of the Fennos, how well did you know them?"

"I hardly ever saw them," Marcia said. "They were quite old, and seldom left the house."

"What happened to them, anyway?"

"I really couldn't say." Her manner chilled markedly. "I had no interest in them."

Suddenly Roy did not give a damn about the Fennos or their fate or anything at all except the woman before him. He gripped her hand and pulled her close, feeling the surprising strength in her arm as he did so.

"Marcia, I don't want to talk about the Fennos."

She looked into his eyes. She was a tall woman and could meet him almost on a level. "I know what you want, Roy. That's what I want too."

He started to speak, but she placed two fingers on his lips to silence him.

"Not yet," she said.

"Why?" he asked in a hoarse whisper. He felt like preadolescent trying for a first kiss.

"It's not the right time."

"When?"

"You will know." Abruptly her mood changed and the contact was broken. "Come, let's go back."

They walked back along the path toward the village. Marcia danced on ahead, humming a melody Roy did not know. He followed along behind, feeling his desire for her flow powerfully through his veins. Still, he knew somehow that she was right. This was not the time. And he knew sure as death that the time would come.

They reached Marcia's shop at the edge of the forest and went in through the back door. They crossed the living quarters and went past the curtain into the front of the shop.

"It's been awfully nice," Marcia said. "We must do it again." The playful half-smile and the spark in her eyes said the things her words did not.

"Goodbye," said Roy. He started toward the door, his eyes still on Marcia.

"Aren't you forgetting something?"

"Am I?"

"The gift for your wife."

"Yes, I almost did forget. The little shepherdess. How much did you say it was?"

"Seven dollars."

Roy pulled a five and two ones from his wallet and handed the bills to her.

"Would you like a gift box?"

"No, thanks. I'll just take it as is."

Marcia slipped the china figurine into a plain paper sack and handed it to Roy. He took the package from her, turned quickly, and walked out. It was a gift, he realized, he would never deliver.

Back out on the street he thought, *This is crazy. No woman has had an effect like that on me since I was sixteen years old.*

It was the mountain air, he told himself. Plus the undeniable fact that Marcia Lura was a damned sexy woman. Even so, if sex were better for him and Karyn, it would never have happened.

But, damn it, nothing *had* happened. He had held a woman's hand, gone for a walk, and got an erection. Why did he feel as though he had cruelly betrayed his wife? There had not been even a mention of sex. Not aloud. Not in so many words. Nevertheless, as his house came into view, Roy had to admit that the short walk through the woods with Marcia had been an erotic experience he would not soon forget.

10

"I'm sorry, Oriole, I'm just not with it today," Karyn said.

This was the third day in a row she had come into the store and sat playing gin with Oriole. Roy had so immersed himself in his technical reports he was hardly stimulating company. He had urged her to amuse herself.

"You can say that again," Oriole replied. "You want some more coffee? A piece of pie? I made some fresh pumpkin."

Karyn looked at her wristwatch. "Gosh, no, look what time it is. I've got to get home and start dinner. Roy's having problems with his work, and I don't want to add to them by making him eat late."

"I'd give you a ride," Oriole said, "but Etienne took the pickup over to Palmdale for supplies."

Karyn walked to the back window and peered out into the gathering darkness. "I'll make it all right, but I'd better get moving."

"There's a shortcut that will save you ten minutes. It comes out on the road not far from your place, if you don't mind walking through the woods."

"No, why should I? Where is this shortcut?"

"It's a nice wide path, easy to follow, starts right behind Marcia Lura's place. You know where that is?"

"Yes, I know."

"I can walk over there with you."

"Thanks, Oriole, I'll find it."

Karyn left the store and walked up the street to Marcia Lura's shop. As usual, the curtain was drawn over the front window, and there was no sign of life inside. A narrow passageway led back between the shop and the boarded-up building next door. Marcia's living quarters were dark too. What did the woman do in there, Karyn wondered. Probably sat with the lights out burning incense and chanting spells. Now where had that thought come from? Enough.

The path through the woods was, as Oriole had said, wide and easy to follow. However, the overhead branches blocked out much of the sky. The night seemed to follow just a few yards behind Karyn.

Someone called her name. Karyn stopped abruptly. A whisper more than a call, but distinct over the other rustlings of the forest. Karyn peered through the heavy brush that grew along the side of the path. At first she saw nothing, then there was a movement. A person. Man or woman, Karyn could not tell, but somebody was there, just a few yards away.

"Who's there? Who is it?"

No response.

Could it be Roy playing some kind of trick on her? No, he would never do that. Oriole Jolivet come to tell her she had forgotten something? But why would Oriole slip through the brush instead of following on the path? Why would anyone?

For an instant panic seized her, and Karyn's impulse was to run blindly for home. She fought it down. The nonsense talked by Inez Polk the other night must have unsettled her more than she realized. If she started running from shadows now, she would really be in trouble.

It was still not quite dark. Karyn parted the brush and took one cautious step off the trail. Then another. She would go just far enough to see what had attracted her eye. It would be some oddly shaped clump of brush, or a fallen branch that would look, when quickly seen, like somebody out there. The illusion, coupled with the call of an unfamiliar bird, would make it seem someone had called out to her.

Beneath the tang of evergreen there was another smell here. Something unpleasant and vaguely familiar. Something on the ground, partly hidden by the undergrowth, caught her eye. Something red with a bit of metal attached. Karyn reached down and grasped the red thing. Her hand came away holding the red leather collar, still buckled. Still on the ground was the head of the dog.

Karyn stiffened in shock. Her breath seemed suspended. A little way beyond where she stood, at the spot where she had thought she'd seen someone, there was no one now. Still, something was here. Something watching her. Something Evil.

Karyn's breath returned in a great ragged gasp. She staggered back onto the path and began to run. She ran blindly, her feet pounding the carpet of needles that covered the trail. Branches seemed to whip out and clutch at her. Behind her, moving silently through the trees, something followed.

When she reached the house Karyn could not make her fingers work to get the door open. She balled her hands into fists and pounded frantically on the panel. When the door opened suddenly she half fell into the room.

Roy moved quickly to catch her. "Karyn! My God, what's the matter?"

Words would not come right away. "L–let me get my breath." Karyn allowed herself to be led to a chair. She sat down and fought for composure, knowing that in her breathless, disheveled state she must look like a mad woman.

Roy held her hand, rubbing it absently as he looked into her eyes. "Are you hurt?"

She shook her head, then pulled in a deep, slow breath. "Roy, I found Lady. I mean I found all that was left of her."

"You found her?" Roy repeated, his eyes searching her face.

Karyn raised her free hand, the one clutching the red leather collar with the buckle still fastened. "Out in the woods, alongside the path between here and Drago. I saw something in the brush and went over to look. Roy, it was her head. Just her head." Karyn broke off as she heard her voice begin to rise, and tried to will herself to be calm.

Roy took the collar from her and held it gingerly. "Poor Karyn, that must have been awful for you."

Karyn chewed her lip, wanting to tell him the rest, but wanting to sound in control.

"It looks like Anton Gadak was right," Roy said. "Some damned coyote got her. It's a rotten shame."

Karyn shook her head from side to side. "No."

"What do you mean?"

"It was something else. I… I think it followed me."

"Followed you home?"

She nodded.

Roy spun away from her and strode to the door. He pulled it open and stepped outside. After a minute he came back in. "There's no sign of anything out there. What was it you thought you saw?"

"I'm not sure. Somebody… an animal… something." She saw his face change. The look of deep concern faded into one of doubt.

"Why don't you go in and lie down, Karyn? I'll make you a hot toddy."

She leaped to her feet and faced him. "I don't want to lie down. And I don't want a goddamn hot toddy. Something is out there, Roy. It followed me home through the woods."

"We'll go out and have a look in the morning," he said in a voice meant to be soothing. "Things never seem so frightening in the daylight."

"Damn you, Roy, don't patronize me." Unable to stop herself, Karyn flailed at Roy's chest with her fists. "I'm not a child! I'm not hysterical." Even as the words came out Karyn realized how childish and hysterical they sounded. Her body shook uncontrollably and she began to cry.

Roy wrapped his arms around her, and it felt good to be held.

"I'll put you to bed," he said. "Then I'm going for a doctor."

Karyn tried to speak, but great wracking sobs made it impossible. Roy led her into the bedroom and helped remove her clothes. He laid her gently in the big bed and tucked the blankets in around her.

"Will you be all right?" he said. "I'll lock the door."

"Roy, I'm not sick."

"Hush. You stay here and rest."

Before Karyn could protest, he hurried out of the house, started the car, and drove off toward Drago.

* * *

Oriole Jolivet was sitting behind the counter working a jigsaw puzzle when Roy entered the store. Etienne was washing down the meat case.

"Well, Roy," Oriole began, "we haven't seen you in a month of Sundays. Karyn was just—"

Roy cut her off. "I need a doctor, Oriole. Is there one in town?"

The stout woman's face sobered. "What's the matter? Did something happen to Karyn?"

"She found the… the remains of our little dog in the woods. The shock hit her kind of hard."

"I bet it did, the poor kid. I was saying she just left here not an hour ago. Bill Volkmann's probably home now. He's the only doctor we got, but he's a good one."

"Can you tell me where to find him?"

"I can do better than that." Oriole came around to the front of the counter, laying aside her apron. "I'll ride along and show you." She looked over at her husband, who was watching them silently. "I'll be back directly."

Etienne Jolivet nodded gravely. Roy and Oriole hurried out to the car.

The house Oriole directed him to was on one of the short side streets between the Jolivets' store and the road that led to Roy and Karyn's house. It was an old two story frame building painted an uninspired brown. The lawn was well kept and the shrubbery trimmed. There were no flowers.

"Bill Volkmann has lived here alone ever since his wife died in '71," Oriole said. "A couple times a week he'll go over to Pinyon to help out in the hospital there, but mostly he's retired now."

They climbed the steps to the front porch and Oriole twisted the key of an old-fashioned doorbell set into the heavy oak door.

The man who opened it was tall and lean, with a narrow, aristocratic face and steel-gray hair combed back from a high forehead. He wore a suit and vest that was of good quality though at least twenty years behind current styles.

"Bill, this is Roy Beatty," Oriole said. "The one that moved into the old Fenno place. His wife is down sick and he wanted a doctor."

"How do you do," said Dr. Volkmann in a deep, resonant voice. "I'm sorry to hear Mrs. Beatty is ill. What seems to be the trouble?"

"I think it's her nerves mostly," Roy said. "Karyn hasn't been really well for a couple of months, and this evening she had a scare while she was walking in the woods. When she got home she was shaking and not making a lot of sense, so I put her to bed and came looking for a doctor."

"Sounds like you did the right thing, but I'll be glad to come out and see her if you like."

"I'd appreciate it."

The doctor picked up his bag, an old-style black satchel, from a hall table and went out with Roy and Oriole to the car. They had little to say during the short drive to the house.

* * *

Karyn was sitting in the living room when they arrived. She was wearing a robe and had the quilt from the bed wrapped around her. She nodded a hello to Oriole.

"Karyn, this is Dr. Volkmann," Roy said.

She smiled at him briefly. "I hope you didn't leave anything important to come out here, Doctor. I'm really not sick."

"Well, you don't look sick," Volkmann said. "And you're taking me away from nothing but a lonely house and a dull book."

The doctor's deep voice and his dark, sensitive eyes were reassuring. Karyn relaxed a little.

"As long as I'm here, I might as well have a look at you," he said.

"It couldn't hurt, I guess," Karyn said. She led the way into the bedroom and sat on the edge of the bed while Dr. Volkmann took her temperature and blood pressure, counted her pulse, and talked quietly about nothing in particular. Roy remained in the living room with Oriole.

Volkmann smiled at her. "Well, young lady, there doesn't seem to be anything seriously wrong."

"I didn't think there would be," she said, "but it's always reassuring to hear it from a doctor. The whole thing was a case of nerves brought on by something that happened today."

"Your husband told me what happened." Volkmann fished in his bag and brought out two small pill bottles.

"One of these is a mild sedative and the other a tranquilizer. I want you to take one of the little white pills after meals and one of the pink capsules before going to bed at night. Will you do that?"

Karyn repeated the instructions.

"Good." Volkmann went into the bathroom and came back with a glass of water. He shook one of the pink capsules from the bottle into her hand. "Take this now, and you should get a good night's sleep."

Karyn swallowed the capsule with water.

"If you run out of the medication, come and see me," Volkmann said. "However, I think you'll be feeling much better by that time. Much better, more relaxed, no problems."

"Thank you, Doctor," Karyn said. She sighed deeply, then returned his smile.

"My house is the brown one on the first road this side of the Jolivets' store. Drop in any time."

"I may do that," Karyn said.

"Goodnight, Mrs. Beatty." Dr. Volkmann snapped off the light and went back into the living room. He left the door slightly ajar.

Roy broke off his conversation and turned to the doctor. "How is she?"

"A slight nervous condition," Volkmann said, "aggravated by her experience in the forest today. I left her some mild medication. The best thing now is rest and quiet and living a normal life."

"Would it help if I took her away from Drago?" Roy asked.

Volkmann pursed his lips. "I don't think so. It would only make your wife feel she's being treated like an invalid. This is probably as good a place for her as any."

"Then there's nothing... seriously wrong with Karyn?"

"Not that I could determine from a very superficial examination, if there are problems, bring her in to see me. I don't think there will be."

"Thank you, Doctor. It was good of you to come out."

"Not at all. I enjoy meeting any new people in the community. We get so few."

"So I understand."

Volkmann shook his head sadly. "Yes, like so many small towns, I fear Drago is dying."

Oriole spoke up. "Bill Volkmann, if you start talking all gloomy like that you'll talk Roy and Karyn right out of Drago."

The doctor gave a soft laugh. "As long as we have people with your spirit, Oriole, the town will be all right."

"How much do I owe you, Doctor?" Roy said.

"Let me see... twenty-five dollars will cover it, but there's no hurry."

Roy went to the desk and pulled out a checkbook. "I come from a family of compulsive bill payers, so I'd just as soon keep us even from the start." Volkmann smiled. "It would be foolish of me to argue with that."

After Roy had driven the doctor and Oriole back to town he hurried home to find Karyn sleeping peacefully. Her breathing was deep and regular, her color good. Roy leaned down and kissed her cheek softly, relieved.

A few minutes later he was very glad that she was asleep. Because in sleep she could not hear what he heard off somewhere in the night. The howling.

11

The pills that Dr. Volkmann left did wonders for Karyn's nerves over the next two days. The grisly discovery in the woods seemed little more than a bad dream now.

Roy stayed close to her and was very attentive. Karyn kept telling him she was really all right, but she could see in his eyes that he was not convinced.

On the second day Roy drove over to Pinyon and came back with a shotgun.

"What's that for?" Karyn asked.

"It's a confidence builder," Roy said. "So you'll know you have a weapon in the house when I'm not here."

"But I've never fired a gun in my life."

"This one's very simple to operate. I can show you how in a few minutes."

They went out to a clearing in the woods and Roy set up a cardboard box for a target. He paced off twenty feet.

"No point in worrying about hitting anything farther away than this," he said.

The gun was a lightweight, single-barrel, 12-gauge model. Roy showed Karyn how to hold it and load it and finally how to pull back the hammer and fire. The first time it jolted her shoulder and the shot spattered up into the trees. Roy had her change her stance, and after that it was not so bad.

It took several more shots before she learned not to flinch when the gun went off, and even then she was still hitting the dirt a foot or so to the right of the box.

"You're jerking the barrel over when you pull the trigger," Roy said. "Squeeze it gently."

To Karyn the whole business seemed foolish, but if Roy had gone to all the trouble of getting the gun for her the least she could do was go along with him. She followed his directions and soon was hitting the target.

The next day Roy drove into Drago for the mail and came back muttering to himself.

"Something the matter?" Karyn asked.

"They've got trouble at the office. Somebody turned up a bunch of errors in a set of weapons system books we did, and there's a man from the Department of Defense coming in this afternoon for explanations."

"Will you have to be there?"

"I'm afraid so. It will probably be a late session tonight, and I may have to go back in tomorrow."

"It would be silly for you to drive all the way back here," Karyn said. "Why don't you stay overnight in Los Angeles and come home tomorrow when you've finished?"

"You're sure you'll be all right?"

"I'm sure. Anyway, I have your blunderbuss to deal with anything that goes bump in the night."

After several more assurances from Karyn, Roy gathered his things quickly and drove off for the city.

With Roy gone, Karyn suddenly felt the emptiness and the isolation of the house. Although she was already ahead of schedule, she went to the bathroom and took another of Dr. Volkmann's tranquilizers.

About noon there was a knock on the door. Karyn opened it and found a young couple standing outside. They were dressed in hiking clothes. The boy carried a backpack and had one arm around the girl, supporting her.

"I wonder if we could use your phone?" the boy said. "My friend's had a fall and hurt her ankle."

"We left our van parked down in the village," the girl said.

"I'm sorry," Karyn said. "I don't have a phone. My car isn't here either, so I can't offer you a ride in. How bad is the ankle?"

"It's just a slight sprain from the looks of it," the boy said, "but it's too painful to walk on unless it's wrapped up."

"I lost the first-aid kit with my pack when I fell," the girl said. "We probably should have stayed on the easy trail up the mountain, but I wanted to try the hard way."

"Come inside," Karyn said. "I have some bandages and things."

"We'd appreciate it," the boy said. "This one doesn't look very heavy, but I don't think I could carry her much farther."

The girl made a face at him as he lifted her gently and carried her inside to the sofa.

The young couple introduced themselves as Neal Edwards and Pam Sealander. They lived together in Santa Barbara and often went backpacking in these mountains. They were a bright, attractive pair, and Karyn felt refreshed by their company.

Karyn found a package of Epsom salts with the medical supplies, and prepared a solution in a deep basin.

"Soak your foot in this," she told Pam, "and the swelling is supposed to go down. Don't ask me why, but it works."

Meanwhile Neal went outside and came back with a stout forked branch. He used a hatchet to shape it into a serviceable crutch.

"Now we're all set," Neal said. "As soon as the swelling goes down we can tape up the ankle and Pam should be able to walk all right with the crutch."

"There's no hurry, is there?" Karyn said. "I'm glad to have some company. Why don't I make some sandwiches?"

"We sure wouldn't turn them down," Neal said, grinning.

Karyn prepared a tray of sandwiches and a pot of coffee. The three of them sat together at the table eating and enjoying the cool afternoon.

"It's lucky for us somebody was living here," Pam said. "This house has been empty for years."

"Yes, I know," Karyn said. "My husband and I just took a six-month lease on the place."

"I didn't think you looked like regular Drago people," Neal said.

"Oh? Why not?"

"It's hard to say exactly. They're... different. I guess part of it is living in this isolated valley out of the mainstream. And maybe it's a heritage they bring from the old country."

"Old country?"

"I just meant that most of the people in Drago seem to be from the same European background. They're sort of a closed society."

"Some of them seem quite friendly," Karyn said. "I'm sure they are once you get to know them," Pam said. "A lot of people are prejudiced because of the stories."

"What stories?" Karyn had an uncomfortable feeling she had been in this conversation before.

"Just a lot of tall tales," Neal said. "The kind of thing kids make up around a campfire. Nothing you'd take seriously."

"Maybe *you* wouldn't," Pam said, "but I'd give it a lot of thought before I came into this valley alone. They say people disappear here without a trace."

"Sure, it's the Haunted Forest," Neal said, laughing. He put an arm around the girl's shoulder. "Anyway, you've got big strong me along for protection."

Pam laughed with him. "I'm so lucky." Karyn was relieved that the conversation had turned away from things she did not want to hear. She excused herself for a moment and took another tranquilizer. She forgot what it was that had disturbed her. It didn't matter.

The rest of the afternoon passed quickly. The young couple told Karyn about their life in Santa Barbara, and she told them about growing up in New York and how different it was in California. Before anyone realized it the sun was gone and the mountain shadows had reached into the valley.

Neal looked out the window, then checked his watch. "It's getting late. How's the ankle, Pam?"

The girl got to her feet and took a few steps with the makeshift crutch. "It feels a lot better. I can make it all right if we go slowly."

"You're welcome to spend the night here," Karyn said. "There's an extra bedroom."

"Thanks," Neal said, "but we really should be getting back. There's a path through the woods not far from here that will take us into town faster than your road."

"Yes, I know the path," Karyn said. Neal wrapped Pam's foot and ankle tightly with adhesive tape, and they said goodbye to Karyn, telling her to look them up if she came to Santa Barbara. With Neal's powerful flashlight showing the way, they moved off toward the path. Karyn watched until the light disappeared among the trees. Then she bolted the door, took a sleeping pill, and began to prepare for bed.

* * *

Neal and Pam were about halfway to the village when Pam stopped suddenly. Resting on her makeshift crutch, she put a hand on the boy's arm.

"What is it?" he said.

"I thought I heard something. Out there."

"Heard what?"

"Listen."

Silence for a moment, then a sharp rustling of the brush as something moved toward them. Something big. Neal beamed the flashlight into the darkness toward the sound.

It came at them fast, bright-orange eyes reflecting the light.

"Neal, what is it?" Pam cried.

Instinctively, Neal placed himself in front of the girl. "I don't know."

Heedless of the heavy undergrowth, the beast crashed toward them. From ten feet away it sprang, and for an instant seemed to hang in the air—thick fur bristling, muscles tensed, black lips drawn back along the muzzle showing vicious yellow teeth.

"My god." Neal gasped, and the beast was on him. It hit him high on the chest, the forepaws bearing him to the ground. The boy had time for one terrible scream before the teeth tore into his windpipe.

The flashlight rolled crazily along the path, throwing leaping shadows among the trees. Pam, her mouth open and dry with terror, used her crutch to club at the dark snarling form that crouched over Neal's body. The jaws worked and there was a sickening crunch of bone.

Again and again Pam struck at the animal without effect. At last the crutch broke in her hands and the beast raised its head and looked at her. The muzzle was dark and dripping.

"No! Oh, no!" the girl screamed. She turned to run, but the ankle gave way and she stumbled and fell forward. The animal landed on her back, blasting the air from her lungs. Her last sensation was the powerful jaws clamping onto the base of her skull.

12

Karyn awoke slowly, reluctantly from the drugged sleep. Outside the morning was bright and fresh, but to Karyn the world seemed to exist on the far side of a gray scrim curtain. Her mouth was stale. It was an effort to move her limbs.

She put an arm over to touch Roy, but his side of the bed was empty. It was several minutes before her sluggish mind recalled that Roy had spent the night in the city. It would have been sweet just to lie there in bed, thinking about nothing. Pull the comforter up over her head and shut out the morning. Karyn sighed. She really ought to get up, she told herself.

Getting out of bed was so much work that she had to sit on the edge for a minute and rest. At last she stood up and went to the closet. She pulled on an old bathrobe of Roy's. It was too much bother to think about a shower or brushing out her hair.

She went into the kitchen, but fixing breakfast held no appeal. There were dishes unwashed from the day before, but they could wait. She walked into the living room and sat in the chair by the window and looked down at her hands.

She was still sitting in the chair at eleven-thirty when a car pulled up outside. Footsteps crunched across the drying grass in the clearing. Someone knocked at the door. With a heavy sigh Karyn rose from the chair and walked over to see who it was.

Chris Halloran stood in the doorway looking casual and fresh in checkered slacks and a brown pullover sweater. The smile of greeting he had ready stiffened when he took a look at Karyn.

"Why, Chris, what a surprise."

It took him a second to answer. "Hello, Karyn. I had a couple of days off, so I thought I'd drive out and see how you guys are doing."

"That's nice."

He waited for her to say something else. When she didn't, he said, "Is it all right if I come in?"

Karyn put on a smile. It felt lopsided. "Yes, of course, please come in, Chris. I'm a little slow this morning."

Chris came into the room, keeping his eyes on Karyn. "Where's Roy?"

"He went into the city. It seems he has to spend more time in Los Angeles than he thought he would. Isn't that interesting?"

"Karyn, are you all right?"

"Why? Is something the matter?"

"You look a little... tired."

Karyn looked down at the old robe she was wearing and put a hand up to touch her unbrushed hair. "Oh, you mean this. I hadn't gotten around to getting dressed yet. What time is it, anyway?"

"Almost noon."

"Really? I must have dozed off in the chair."

"I should have let you know I was coming, but I didn't decide myself until this morning."

"No, that's all right. I'm always glad to see you. Can I get you anything?"

"I'm fine, Karyn. Sit down, please."

"I think I will, if you don't mind." She returned to the chair by the window and eased into it. It was true that she was glad to see Chris, but keeping the conversation going was an effort.

Chris perched uncomfortably on the edge of the sofa. "So tell me what's been happening."

"Not very much. It's a quiet life up here. We lost Lady."

"Lost her? What happened?"

Karyn looked out the window, her face empty of expression. "Something caught her in the woods and killed her."

Chris leaned forward, staring at her. "What are you talking about? What caught her?"

Karyn shrugged her shoulders. She felt loose and disjointed wearing the oversized robe. "I don't know what it was. The sheriff—but he's not really a sheriff—says it was a coyote. Or maybe it was an owl." She giggled suddenly and put a hand over her mouth like a little girl caught laughing in class.

Chris got up and walked over to her chair. He looked down into her face. "Karyn, what's the matter? I told you that you look tired, but you don't. You look sick."

"I'm all right. I have some pills that I take for my nerves and to help me sleep. I'm all right."

"What kind of pills?"

"Who knows? Dr. Volkmann gave them to me."

"Who is Dr. Volkmann?"

"He's just Dr. Volkmann. He lives in Drago. He came out when I was sick."

"I don't know what he's giving you, but it doesn't look like it's helping a lot."

"Is that a comment on the way I look?"

"Karyn, I'm serious. We've been friends long enough so that I shouldn't have to play games. I think you should have another doctor examine you."

"Dr. Volkmann is a good doctor."

Chris started to say something more, then seemed to think better of it. "I'm sorry I missed Roy. We must have passed each other on the freeway."

"I don't think so. Roy drove in yesterday."

"And left you here alone?"

"It didn't matter. I had a nice young couple for company."

"Overnight?"

"No, they had to leave."

Chris shook his head slowly, but said nothing. He made several more attempts to kindle a conversation, but Karyn found it hard to concentrate on his words. She felt one step removed from everything that was happening. In a way it was a comfortable feeling, but in the depths of her consciousness she knew something was very wrong.

After a while they ran out of words and Chris moved toward the door. "I guess I might as well be heading back to L.A."

Karyn rose to walk out with him. She looked into his eyes and saw herself reflected in the pupils. There was something she would like to tell him, but it seemed too much trouble to put it into words. For some reason a tear formed in the corner of one eye and rolled down her cheek.

Chris took a step toward her. "You're not well. Let me take you to a doctor in Los Angeles."

She shook her head without saying anything. The tears came freely.

"Karyn, please, you've got to let me help you." He reached out to her, grasping her shoulders, and pulled her against him.

Since the day she had been assaulted in the apartment no man but her husband had touched Karyn. Now, through some trick of the mind, she was back there. The gentle face of her friend Chris Halloran twisted and changed like a rubber mask into the foul leering thing that had attacked her. Chris's hands on her shoulders became the rough, grasping hands of the rapist. She pulled her head back to look into his face. He was saying something, but all she could see were his teeth. Teeth like those that had torn the flesh of her thigh and left her scarred town there.

"Get away from me!" she cried. "Get away! Don't touch me, you filthy animal!"

Instantly Chris pulled his hands away and stepped back. "Karyn, what's the matter with you? What are you saying?"

She balled her hand into a fist and swung at him. In his astonishment, Chris made no move to avoid the blow, and her fist smacked into the corner of his mouth, slicking his lip with blood.

He seized her wrists. "Have you gone crazy?"

"You'd better get out of here," she said, her voice rising hysterically. "If my husband finds you here he'll kill you!"

Chris touched the corner of his mouth and looked at he blood on his fingertips. "All right, dammit, enough. I don't know what's happening to you up here, Karyn, but if this is the way you want it, it's your business. Excuse the intrusion."

He sidestepped her and shouldered out through the door. Karyn heard the car door slam. The engine roared to life and the Camaro spun away in an angry burst of gravel.

For several minutes she stood by the door, breathing raggedly, feeling her heart pound. The fog that had clouded her mind throughout the day had been shredded by Chris's sudden anger. She walked into the bathroom and ran the cold water. She caught it in her cupped hands and dashed it into her face. The cold shock helped to clear her head even more. She looked into the mirror and saw the pale, unkempt creature Chris had seen. What had come over her to act the way she had? For a terrible few seconds Chris had seemed to become the rapist. She had screamed at him, hit him, sent him away. What was happening to her?

13

Karyn took a long steaming-hot shower, then forced herself to stand for twenty seconds while the water sprayed icy cold. She rubbed her body dry with a big rough towel and went out to the kitchen to start a pot of coffee. While it percolated she put on a clean pair of jeans and a light sweater. She drank the coffee black and strong, then brushed her teeth until her gums tingled. For the first time in days her body began to feel strong, her mind clear, with only traces of cobwebs. It was two o'clock when she left the house and walked briskly down the lane toward Drago.

By the time she had reached the blacktopped main street Karyn's legs ached from the unaccustomed activity after days of little exercise. Still, she felt refreshed and alert. The scent of the pines washed out her lungs as she swung down the drab street. Some movement down the street on the other side caught her eye, and she slowed her pace.

A tow-truck was pulled up there in front of a metallic blue van. The driver was out of the truck attaching a cable to the front of the van. Something stirred in Karyn's memory. She walked over to where the tow-truck driver stood between the two vehicles.

"Are you towing this van away?"

"That's right. You the owner?"

"No, but I think I know who is. Why are you taking it?"

"The Highway Patrol got an abandoned vehicle report. When that happens we pull 'em in."

"Where did the report come from?"

The driver pulled a sheet of paper from his pocket and unfolded it. "Report phoned in by Anton Gadak. You know him?"

"I know him. Is he around?"

"He was here a few minutes ago to sign the tow-away order. I think he went in the tavern up the street there."

Karyn hesitated for a moment. This was really none of her business. Yet in a way it was. She had liked young Neal Edwards and Pam Sealander. She thanked the tow-truck driver for the information and walked up the street toward the tavern where he had said Anton Gadak could be found.

It was dark inside. Most of the overhead bulbs were burned out, and the flickering beer signs behind the bar only deepened the shadows. The air was stale with old beer, the floor gritty beneath her feet. Karyn stood for a moment inside the door until her eyes adjusted to the gloom.

Anton Gadak sat midway along the bar with a glass of beer in front of him. On the next stool sat a paunchy man in overalls. They were the only customers. The bartender sat dozing in a wooden chair at the far end of the bar.

Karyn walked up behind Gadak and cleared her throat. "Excuse me."

The big man swiveled on his stool and looked at her. He touched the brim of his Stetson. "Afternoon, Mrs. Beatty."

"Can I talk to you for a minute?"

"Go ahead."

The man sitting next to Gadak got up and walked back to the men's room without looking at Karyn.

"What's on your mind?" said Gadak.

"There's a truck out in the street getting ready to tow away a van."

"That so?"

"The driver said you signed the order to have it towed away."

"Said that, did he?"

Sudden anger gave heat to Karyn's words. "Is there some reason you don't want to talk about it?"

Gadak's tolerant smile faded. "Suppose you tell me why you're so interested, Mrs. Beatty."

"I think I know the people who own the van."

"That's interesting. There was no registration slip in the thing. It was breaking the law parked the way it was, so I had it towed away."

"Don't you want to know who the owner is?"

"Makes no difference to me. Somebody comes looking for it, I'll tell 'em where they can pick it up. It ain't my job to go find them."

Karyn held back a sharp retort. If Anton Gadak knew more than he was telling, and she felt sure he did, it would serve no purpose to anger the man.

"Thank you," she said coolly, and turned to walk out of the stale smelling tavern. Outside the tow-truck and the van were gone. Karyn crossed the street and went into the Jolivets' store.

Oriole greeted her enthusiastically. "Hey, Karyn, you're a sight for sore eyes. How you feeling?"

"Much better, Oriole. Thanks."

"Maybe we can get in a few hands of gin today. I tell you it's been mighty dull around here the last three days."

"I don't think I'm quite up to playing cards yet," Karyn said. "What I'd like is to use your phone, if it's all right."

"Help yourself. I'll be back in a minute."

When Oriole had gone out through the rear of the store to give Karyn privacy, Karyn riffled through the thin local phone book, praying that Inez Polk was listed. To her relief, the number was there. She picked up the phone and dialed.

Please be home, Inez. Please answer the phone.

"Hello?"

At the sound of Inez' voice Karyn wanted to cry out with joy. She willed herself to be calm.

"Inez, this is Karyn Beatty."

"Oh, yes, how are you, Karyn?"

Keeping her eye on the door leading to the back room, Karyn went on in a low tone. "Right now I'm not too good. I want to tell you first off that I'm terribly sorry for the way I acted the other night."

"Don't give it a thought. Your reaction was mild compared to some."

"Just the same, I was rude, and now I'm seeing things differently."

"Something has happened?"

"I don't want to go into it over the phone. Can you come to my place?"

"I have a meeting at the school here tonight, but if it's urgent I could miss it."

"It's not really that urgent, I guess."

"How about tomorrow?"

"That will be fine. And, Inez…"

"Yes?"

"Those books and things you told me about… would you bring them?"

"I'll bring them. Karyn, are you in any danger?"

"No. It's… I don't think so. I'll tell you about it tomorrow."

Karyn hung up the phone and started to turn. She jumped as she saw Etienne Jolivet standing a few feet away, watching her.

"Did I frighten you, Mrs. Beatty?" he said.

It was the first time Karyn had heard him speak. His voice was a monotone with a soft, unplaceable accent.

"I didn't see you standing there," she said.

Etienne smiled at her. A shallow smile that did not reach his eyes.

Oriole came back from the rear of the store. "Get your call made?"

"Yes, thanks."

"Sure you won't stay? Even for a cup of coffee?"

"No, I want to be home before dark. To be there when Roy gets back, I mean."

"Well, take it easy," Oriole said.

Karyn bought a pound of coffee just to be buying something, and left the store. She passed up Marcia Lura's shop, wanting nothing to do with the shortcut through the woods, and walked on down to where the narrow road turned off. All the way home she watched the brush on both sides as if expecting something unusual.

Once Karyn was inside the little house, the remainder of the afternoon seemed to drag interminably. She wished Roy would come home. She would tell him about the young hikers' van being towed away, and the strange guarded response of Anton Gadak when she asked about it. Maybe Roy would begin to see the strange things happening in Drago.

She prepared a simple cheese casserole so all she would have to do was pop it in the oven when Roy came home. After that she sat down to read, but found it difficult to concentrate. A very light scotch and water calmed her as the sun slipped behind the western mountains and darkness spilled into the valley.

Then came the howling. Karyn leaped from the chair, dropping the book she was reading on the floor. This time it was right outside.

Karyn crossed the room in quick steps and pressed herself against the opposite wall. She stared at the front door, half expecting it to burst open.

Whatever was outside howled again—a wailing night cry that ended in an ominous growl. Karyn forced herself to walk back across the room to the front window. She parted the curtains and looked out. In the clearing in front of the house, less than twenty feet from the door, hunched a dark, sinister silhouette. Without taking her eyes from the window, Karyn reached over and fumbled along the wall for the switch to the outdoor light. She found it and flipped it on.

It was a wolf, but bigger than any wolf should be. As the animal sat on its haunches, the big head came to nearly four feet above the ground. It did not move when the light came on, but glared defiantly at the window. The reflected light of the bulb out in front made the eyes glow like jewels. The wolf's fur was a dull gray-brown color, shaggier around the neck. The chest was full, the large forepaws planted solidly on the ground. As Karyn watched, the thin black lips of the animal skinned back and she saw the teeth.

She fought down the terror that rose like bile in her throat. She would not live the rest of her life in fear. How dare this beast come to her house to intimidate her? Wolf, ghost, or werewolf—whatever it was, she would not yield to it without a fight. Letting the curtain fall back across the window, she went to the closet and took out the shotgun and the box of shells. She checked to be sure it was loaded.

She carried the gun and the box of shells back into the living room. That other time, back in the apartment in the city, she had been defenseless and overpowered when she was attacked. This time it would be different. She had a weapon.

Moving deliberately, Karyn unbolted the front door. She turned the knob and slowly, carefully pulled the door open.

The wolf rose with a rumbling growl. It began to move toward her.

The shooting lessons Roy had given her came back to Karyn in fragments. There was no time to try to remember everything. She shouldered the gun, aimed at the wolf, and pulled the trigger. The gun boomed and dirt exploded two feet to the right of the wolf. The animal stopped coming for a moment, but showed no fear.

Keeping a grip on her emotions, Karyn reloaded the gun, corrected her aim for the trigger pull, and fired again. The charge of shot hit the wolf full in the face. The animal made no sound, but the impact knocked it over backward. For a moment all four feet thrashed the air.

When the beast regained its footing one side of the massive head was raw and bleeding. However, the damage was far less than it should have been, considering the close-range shotgun blast. Karyn broke the weapon open and prepared to reload and fire again, but the wolf gave her no opportunity. It bounded away to the edge of the forest. There it stopped, looking back at her with raw animal hatred. After a moment it vanished among the trees.

Karyn went back into the house and leaned the shotgun against a wall. Breathing heavily, she sat down at the kitchen table to await Roy's arrival.

14

Roy Beatty stopped in the doorway, a greeting frozen on his lips. In a glance he took in Karyn's controlled expression, her rigid posture in the chair, and the shotgun leaning against the wall.

"What happened?"

"It was here. The wolf. Right out in front of the house. I shot at it and hit it, but it got away."

Roy blinked, struggling to catch up. "A wolf?"

"Right outside. I shot it."

He walked over and looked down into Karyn's eyes. She looked frightened, but under control and rational enough. He went into the kitchen and found a flashlight in the tool drawer, then returned to Karyn.

"Show me where the animal was when you shot it."

Karyn got up and led him out the door and into the clearing in front of the house. Roy played the flashlight over the ground as they walked. Karyn stopped walking and pointed down at her feet.

"The wolf was right here," she said.

Roy knelt at the spot she indicated and slid the circle of light over the crisp dry grass. He reached down to touch a dark patch and held the light on his fingers. They were sticky with blood.

"I guess you really did hit something," he said.

"Not something, Roy. A wolf. The biggest wolf I've ever seen."

"All right, you shot a wolf. What happened next?"

"It ran off into the woods."

Roy swept the light over a larger area of ground. He spotted something a few feet away and went over to pick it up. It was a piece of ragged gray tissue the size of a playing card. He held it gingerly between thumb and forefinger.

Karyn came over to look. "What is it?"

"An ear."

Karyn turned away, shivering.

"You go on back in the house," he said. "I'll take a look around in the woods."

"Roy, don't go out there alone."

"I'll be careful. The shotgun's coming along too."

Karyn chewed her lip a moment before she spoke. "Roy, I don't think the shotgun can stop this wolf. I should have killed it with my shot, but it just came up bleeding a little."

"You probably didn't hit it as good as you think," Roy said. "If it's still around I'll finish it off."

They went inside and Roy took the shotgun from where Karyn had propped it against the wall. He put a fresh shell in the chamber and dropped several more into his jacket pocket.

"Keep the door locked while I'm gone," he said. "Don't worry."

When Karyn had closed and locked the door behind him, Roy walked to the edge of the clearing and swept the brush with the flashlight. He moved along slowly, examining the ground and the bushes. At one of the faint paths that led away from the house the light picked up something. Roy leaned down and saw a dime-sized spot of blood on a flat stone. Whatever it was that Karyn had shot must have come this way. Roy straightened and moved off along the path.

Overhead the high cloud layer began to break up, and a bright moon shone through the openings. Roy walked easily along the path with the shotgun in one hand and the flashlight beaming ahead of him.

A movement up ahead caught his eye and he stopped short.

He snapped off the light and stepped cautiously forward. In a small grassy clearing he saw it again—something pale caught in a flash of moonlight. Roy brought the shotgun to a ready position and waited, holding his breath.

"Are you going to stay there crouching in the bushes, or will you come and join me?" The woman's voice mocked him from the clearing.

Roy stepped toward the voice and snapped on the light. Marcia Lura looked back at him, her eyes glowing.

For a moment Roy could not move. Marcia wore a deeply cut gown in green and black, night colors of the forest. Her dark hair folded softly back over wide shoulders that gleamed palely in the light. There was no surprise in her face, just a faintly amused smile.

"My God, I almost shot you," Roy said.

"It's a strange time to be out hunting."

Roy lowered the flashlight beam from Marcia's face down over the lithe body. Its lines were clearly visible beneath the thin material of the gown. Suddenly uncomfortable, he snapped off the light.

"I was following a wounded animal. My wife shot at a wolf, she thinks, and it came this way."

"I saw no wolf," said Marcia, "or anything else."

"What are you doing out here, anyway?"

"I often walk in the forest at night. It's so very private."

"I suppose it would be."

"Have you ever tried it?"

"Not alone."

Roy found himself standing quite close to the tall, supple woman. He was not sure whether he had walked across the clearing or she had come to him. It didn't matter. The scent of sandalwood clung to her. Sandalwood and something else… something wild.

"Would you like to walk with me?" she said.

The pale green eyes caught the reflected moonlight and seemed to draw Roy down into them.

"Or would you rather do something else with me?"

With a swift, graceful movement Marcia unfastened the gown at her breast and let it slide down her body to make a dark pool at her feet. Beneath it she was naked. She stepped free of the fallen garment and moved back so he could see her.

Her body was lean and smooth, her breasts high. Her stomach was flat. Below the navel a wedge of silky black hair pointed to the joining of her legs.

"Do you like me?" she asked.

Roy could only answer honestly. "Yes." He realized he was still holding the flashlight and the gun. He let them drop.

"Come to me," Marcia said. She stood with apart and held out her bare white arms to him.

Roy peeled off his clothes and tossed them aside. He felt the chill night air on his skin, and stepped forward quickly to take Marcia in his arms. The touch of her bare flesh was like a caress all up and down his body. She pressed herself against him. They kissed. Her mouth had the taste of wild berries. Desire for the woman overpowered his every civilized thought.

With Marcia Lura, Roy discovered a savage, abandoned kind of sex, a kind he had never known. His body writhed and twisted in concert with hers. No inch of flesh, no orifice of the body went unexplored. Her long strong fingers were on him, in him. Her mouth swallowed him; her tongue darted and probed. He tasted her, inhaled her; he groped for the essence of her.

The moon came and went as clouds pushed across the night sky. Time stopped. The climax, when it came, was sweet and wild and more complete than Roy had thought possible. They lay together afterward, their bodies cleaved into one. It was Marcia who made the first move. Gently she disengaged herself and sat up. She looked down at him, the curtain of black hair shading her face. The green eyes shone with a light of their own.

"God, you're beautiful," he said.

She reached down and placed her fingertips on his lips. He touched his tongue to her fingers and tasted the mingled juices of their bodies.

Marcia rose and moved silently to where her gown lay on the forest floor. She raised it over her head and let it slide down over her body. With her eyes on Roy, she fastened the garment over her breast.

"When will I see you?" he said.

"When you want me."

Before he could speak again Marcia stepped lightly out of the clearing and vanished among the dark trees. Roy pulled himself upright and found he was sore and exhausted and utterly drained. He moved awkwardly about, retrieving his scattered clothing.

When he was fully dressed again he let himself think about Karyn. She would be wondering why he was so long. Guilt gnawed like a parasite in his stomach.

Enough, he told himself. Feeling guilty would do no one any good. He had never claimed to be a saint. Marcia Lura had been there when he badly needed someone, and he had taken her. Or had she been the taker? It did not matter. The thing had happened, and he knew it would happen again. He picked up the gun and the flashlight and walked back along the path to the house.

Karyn was waiting for him at the door.

"I was getting worried." She stepped back and looked at him over more carefully. "What happened to you?"

Roy looked down at his clothes, rumpled and speckled with dirt and pine needles.

"I thought I saw something and stumbled going after it. Turned out to be just a shadow."

"Oh?" One small syllable containing a world of female doubt.

"I didn't find a thing. As I said, whatever it was you shot at is long gone by now."

"Did you hurt yourself when you fell?"

"No, I'm just tired. Why don't we go to bed?"

"Do you want something to eat?"

"No, just a shower and bed."

Roy stepped around her and went into the bathroom. He undressed and got into the shower, where he lathered his body over and over to wash away the smell of the other woman. As he massaged his soapy skin the memory of Marcia's hands on him began to arouse him again. He turned the water on full cold and stood under it until his erection went down. He dried himself off, fell into bed, and was asleep in seconds. When Karyn got in beside him he did not stir. He was deep in a dream of the dark woods and the savage love of a green-eyed woman.

15

Karyn stood gazing down at Roy as he slept. He had been so exhausted when he came in last night that she decided not to wake him. His sleep was restless. He wore a troubled frown and his body twitched in rhythm to some vivid dream.

Karyn only left him when Inez Polk arrived. Her arms were laden with books and folders that contained old newspaper clippings. Karyn met her at the door and helped carry the books inside and set them on the table. She turned then and took Inez' hands in her own.

"I'm glad you're here," she said. "So many things have happened."

Inez' long homely face broke into a smile. "I'm glad I'm here too. Now, let's sit down and you can tell me what's been going on."

Karyn poured out what remained of the coffee, and they sat down at the table. Inez listened attentively as Karyn related the events of the past few days. She told of finding Lady's remains in the woods, and about the young backpackers who had spent the day with her, then walked away to an unknown fate. She described Anton Gadak's evasiveness when she asked about the van. Finally she told of the huge wolf that had sat outside the house last night, how she had fired at it and wounded it, and how Roy had gone looking for it afterward but found no trace.

"What's your feeling now?" Inez asked when Karyn had finished her story. "Are you ready to talk about a werewolf?"

Karyn took a moment before she replied. "I'm ready to accept the possibility, yes. Every logical bone in my body rejects the idea, but I can't forget the look of that... that thing in front of my house last night. It was much too big and too, well, malevolent to be a natural wolf. Altogether too many unexplained things have been happening. If you tell me there is a werewolf, I'll listen."

Inez arranged the books and papers neatly in front of her and adjusted her glasses. "The first thing we must be sure of is that we understand what we're dealing with. How much do you know about werewolves, Karyn?"

"Not an awful lot. They're something like vampires, aren't they?"

"Not at all," Inez said briskly. "The vampire is a dead creature that sustains a form of life by subsisting on human blood. A vampire may continue in this undead state for hundreds of years. The werewolf, on the other hand, is as much alive as you or me. Its lifespan is no greater than normal, and when once they die, they are dead forever. There are, of course, certain similarities. When he assumes the wolf form, the werewolf, like the vampire, has a strength far beyond normal, and ordinary weapons cannot destroy him."

"Is there no defense against them?" Karyn asked. "Garlic at the windows? A cross?"

"No, those are weapons against the vampire. Only two things can destroy the werewolf—one, is fire, the other silver."

"Oh, yes, the silver bullet."

Inez permitted herself a thin smile. "I guess that's the one everybody knows."

"One thing here doesn't fit with what I've heard of werewolves. During the past weeks I've either heard or seen something almost every night. Aren't they supposed to come out only during the full moon?"

"Oh, no, they can change any night once the sun has gone down. But let me start at the beginning."

Speaking with quiet intensity, Inez related the history and the nature of werewolves. Frequently she referred to the stack of books she had brought. Among them were *The Book of Were-Wolves* by Sabine Baring-Gould, *Lycanthropy in London* by Dudley Costello, *The Cult of the Werewolf in Europe* by Lewis Spence, and *The Werewolf* by Montague Summers. There were books in French: *Le Loup-Garou de Provence;* German: *Volkssagen aus Pommern und Rugen*; and Latin: *Malleus Maleficarum*. And other books in languages Karyn did not recognize.

Inez showed Karyn passages dealing with cases of werewolfism over the years, some documented, some legendary. There was the notorious Peter Stubbe, tried and executed in 1590 for a series of bloody killings near Cologne while in the form of a wolf. There was the doomed crew of the Spanish vessel *Louisa* that met a ghastly fate on the Aegean island of Skiathos, said to be infested with werewolves. There was the lost Bulgarian village of Dradja where the cruelest torture by an avenging mob could not force the villagers to give up the killer beast that dwelt among them.

Most of the stories dated from the sixteenth and seventeenth centuries, but there were reports of werewolves as early as the writings of Herodotus in 450 B.C., and as recently as the New Orleans *Times-Picayune* in 1959.

"The local newspaper clippings you can go over yourself," Inez said. "The earliest I could find was in 1919. Altogether, there have been sixteen reported deaths or disappearances in this valley with no logical explanation. Your two young friends with the van would make eighteen."

"Still," Karyn said, "that's more than fifty years, and this is a wilderness area where a lot of things can happen lo people."

"Those are only the reported cases. I know of at least two that never made the papers."

"Has anyone told you what happened to the people who lived in this house before you?"

"The Fennos? No."

"It was just over four years ago. The old people hadn't been seen in town for a week or so, and there were inquiries. Your friend Anton Gadak came out to investigate. He found the two of them dead. Supposedly, natural causes."

"That's not so strange. The Fennos were quite old, weren't they?"

"There's more. About a week later one of my pupils, a little boy whom I've never known to lie, told me that he and a friend had sneaked into the house to look around. They found it all torn up, with dried blood everywhere, and bits of flesh and bone scattered about. The boys hadn't said anything at first for fear of getting into trouble."

"Did you report it?"

"I told the boy to tell his parents. He did, and they reported it to the county sheriff. The sheriff sent a couple of men out to look the house over, but they found nothing unusual. They put it down to the child's active imagination."

"But you don't think so," Karyn put in.

"No. I think somebody came in here after the boys saw it and cleaned up."

The women sat without speaking for several minutes. Finally Karyn said, "All right, what do we do now? Try to convince someone in authority that there's a werewolf loose in Drago?"

Inez smiled wryly. "What do you think our chances would be?"

"Pretty slim," Karyn, admitted. "But there must be something we can do."

"Wait a minute, maybe there is." Inez was suddenly sitting on the edge of her chair. "You wounded the wolf last night?"

"That's right. I hit him... it... in the face with the shotgun. It tore off an ear, I think."

"Good. You see, when a werewolf is wounded, it can change back to human form, but it will have an identical injury. Their wounds heal unnaturally fast, but if you can find them soon enough it's a giveaway."

When Karyn looked doubtful, Inez referred again to her books. She quoted the story of a traveler through Wales who was attacked by a wolf, but managed to hack off one of the beast's paws and escape. The next morning he was horrified to see his landlady at the inn with fresh bandages covering the stump of her right hand.

And the notorious Parenette Gandillon, after villagers with clubs had driven off a wolf, was found moaning in her bed covered with bruises.

"Assuming these old reports are accurate," Inez concluded, "what we must do is look for someone in Drago with a missing ear."

"And suppose we find him," Karyn said. "What then?" Inez started to answer, but hesitated at the sound of someone moving around in the bedroom.

"It's Roy," Karyn said. "Do you think we should tell him?"

Inez shrugged noncommittally as Roy came into the room pulling a sweater on over his head "Hello, Inez," he said. Then, to Karyn, "Is there any coffee?"

"I can make a new pot."

"Never mind. Fresh air is what I really need."

"Roy, can we talk to you about something?"

"Will it keep? I'm still groggy from last night. If I jog down the road and back it might wake me up."

Karyn hesitated a moment. "Go ahead. It's not important."

"I'll see you later." He went out the door, and they heard him trot off across the clearing and down the road.

"I just couldn't tell him," Karyn said. "Not yet."

"All right," said Inez.

Karyn clapped her hands together and stood up. "I guess it's you and me, pal. Let's head for town and find the guy with only one ear."

16

The two women left the house and walked across the grass to Inez' little Plymouth Valiant. They got in and Inez fastened her seat belt.

"You'll have to buckle up too," she told Karyn. "This is a '74, the model that doesn't start unless everybody is properly strapped in."

"I feel silly," Karyn said as they drove to Drago. "This whole idea is beginning to seem silly."

"It can't hurt to look. We might get lucky. We could ask around too, if there's somebody you know well enough to talk to."

"The only one I can think of is Oriole Jolivet. She and her husband run the general store."

"Can we trust her?"

"I wouldn't want to come right out and tell her we're looking for a werewolf," Karyn said. "But then I wouldn't want to admit that to anybody."

The store was empty when Karyn and Inez walked in. After a minute Karyn walked to the back and called Oriole's name.

"Be with you in a minute," came Oriole's answer from the back room.

Inez strolled around the cluttered store looking at the merchandise while they waited. In a little while Oriole Jolivet came out and joined them. She wore a cotton dress with a big flower print that made her look even wider than she was. Her hair was pinned back, and Karyn was secretly relieved to see no sign of a head wound.

"Hey, how's Roy doing?" Oriole asked after the introductions had been completed. "I'll tell you, Karyn, if I was twenty years younger I'd give you a little competition for that handsome son-of-a-gun." She laughed heartily to show she was only kidding.

"That's really why I'm here, Oriole," Karyn said, improvising quickly. "Roy cut his hand yesterday chopping firewood, and I need some bandages if you carry them." She was surprised how easily the lie came to her lips.

Oriole's smile switched instantly to a concerned frown. "Gee, I'm sorry to hear that. I hope it's not too serious."

"I don't think so," Karyn said, a little ashamed now of her deceit. "It's a clean cut. No infection. I did want to get some bandages to wrap it, though."

"Sure, we got bandages," Oriole said, moving to the far side of the store. She stooped to one of the lower shelves. "What-all do you need—cotton, gauze, adhesive?"

"You'd better give me the works."

Oriole removed the selected items from the shelf and put them in a paper bag. "A person has to be darned careful using an ax."

"I guess it's lucky you have this stuff." Karyn kept her tone as casual as she could. "I don't suppose there's any place else in town I could get it?"

"Nope. Not in Drago."

"You must sell quite a few medical supplies."

"Not so much. People around here are pretty healthy." Karyn did not know how to go any further without blurting out an obvious question. Oriole saved her the trouble by volunteering the information. "The last time I sold any bandages was last spring when the Eccles boy stuck his arm through a window without opening it first." She tapped her forehead. "The boy's fifteen years old now, but up here he's still about three."

Karyn and Inez laughed uneasily and looked at each other. Their best source for town gossip had come up dry. Karyn paid for the purchases and started out of the store. Passing the glassed meat case she suddenly realized she had not seen Oriole's silent husband today.

"Where's Etienne?" she said, turning back to Oriole. "He didn't come in today. Woke up this morning with a headache."

"A headache?" Karyn repeated, carefully keeping the excitement out of her voice.

"It's no big deal. He gets 'em two, three times a year. They last a day or two, then go away."

"I hope he gets better soon."

"He will."

"Tell him hello for me."

"I'll do that. Come again when you can stay awhile. You too, Inez."

"What do you think?" Karyn said, when they were outside and out of earshot.

"It's a possibility. At least we have a suspect now. Before we had nothing." Inez grew thoughtful. "I have a feeling the two of us shouldn't try to take this any further without help. Is there no one else in town we could go to?"

"No... wait a minute. We forgot the most logical person—the town doctor."

"The one who treated you?"

"Yes. Dr. Volkmann. If someone was seriously injured he wouldn't go to the store for treatment."

"Makes sense. Can we talk to him frankly?"

"As you said, we've got to talk to somebody sometime."

"Then let's go and see him. If we get good vibrations we'll tell him the story. If not, well, we'll try something else."

Dr. Volkmann received the women graciously and showed them into the sitting room of his big old house. The influence of his late wife could still be seen in touches like the lace antimacassars on the backs of chairs, and the little animal figurines carefully arranged, but undusted now, on corner shelves.

"You're looking well, Mrs. Beatty," the doctor said. "Did you use all of the pills I gave you?"

"No, I don't think I need any more of them."

"That's good. Too much reliance on pills can be dangerous." He folded his hands and waited politely.

"What we came for is... well, I'd like to ask you a question, Doctor."

"Certainly."

"Did anyone come to you last night or today for treatment of a head wound?"

"Etienne Jolivet in particular," Inez added.

Volkmann studied the women for several seconds before he spoke. "That's an odd question. Do you mind telling me what's behind it?"

"Believe me," Karyn said, "It's very important."

"I can see that it is. The answer is no, I have not treated anyone for head wounds in the past forty-eight hours. I have not treated Etienne Jolivet for anything in more than three years."

Karyn's face reflected her disappointment.

"Now do you suppose I could have an explanation?"

The women's eyes met, and they made a decision.

"I'll tell you, Doctor," Karyn said, "But you might not believe it."

"Let's hear it, anyway," said Volkmann. His voice was deep and serious and reassuring.

Karyn told him the whole story, beginning with the first time she had heard the howling, and ending with the visit a few minutes before to the Jolivets' store. When Karyn was through, Inez told him about the clippings she had saved detailing strange happenings in and around Drago over the years.

Dr. Volkmann listened intently, and did not interrupt. When the women had finished their story he sat silently, studying them.

"So when you heard of Etienne Jolivet's headache," he said finally, "You felt it might be the result of the gunshot wound inflicted on the wolf last night."

Karyn nodded, not meeting Volkmann's eye. It all seemed so farfetched when put into words by someone else.

"I am afraid you settled your suspicions on the wrong man. Etienne has suffered all his life from migraine headaches, just as Oriole told you."

"And there was nobody else with a head injury of any kind?"

"No one came to me, at any rate."

Karyn's shoulders slumped. "What do you think, Doctor? Am I crazy? Are we a couple of hysterical women? Was it all a dream?"

Again Volkmann took his time in answering. "I have lived here in Drago for ten years. I have lived quietly, and have had ample opportunity to observe the town and its people. During those ten years I have noted a number of strange occurrences. Some of them, Miss Polk, were those that you mentioned. People have died and disappeared in this valley with no reasonable explanation ever given. I must confess that I closed my eyes to a number of irregularities that I might have questioned had I been a more involved man. But I was wrapped up in my own affairs. It is, of course, possible that there is something fearfully wrong here."

Inez spoke up. "And what do you think, Doctor, of the idea that it is a werewolf?"

Volkmann's expression remained grave. "As a man of science I am not willing to admit to the existence of something so far outside the laws of nature. However, as a man who has seen more than the normal share of inexplicable happenings, I cannot deny the possibility. Yes, Miss Polk, there may be a werewolf."

"Thank God you believe us," Karyn said.

Volkmann held up a cautioning hand. "This does not mean I am ready to join you in an all-out hunt for the alleged werewolf. I still have serious reservations. I will do what I can, though, to assist you in gathering information. You may call on me at any time."

"Thank you, Doctor," said Inez. "I can't tell you how much it means to have someone else on our side."

Dr. Volkmann walked them to the door. "Have you spoken to anyone else about this?" he asked.

"No," Karyn said. "Only you."

"I think it would be wise to keep it that way. At least until we have something more to go on."

"That's the way we felt too," Karyn said.

"Let me know if anything else happens. And one other thing, ladies…"

"Yes?"

"Be careful."

Karyn and Inez assured the doctor they would be most careful, and walked back to where they had left the car.

They got in, went through the ritual of buckling the seat belts and started home. As Inez reached Karyn's road, Karyn put a hand on her arm.

"Wait a minute. Can you drive back up the street the way we came?"

"Why?"

"I want you to take a look at the man standing back there under the theater marquee."

"The one with the hat?"

"Yes."

Inez backed around and drove slowly up the street. "Who is it?" she said as they approached the figure standing in the shadow of the marquee.

"Anton Gadak," Karyn said.

As they rolled past they could see a fresh white bandage covering the left side of Gadak's head.

Inez started to wheel the car around.

"Where are you going?" Karyn said.

"Back to the doctor's house. We should tell him about this."

"Let's wait," Karyn said.

"But why?"

"Who do you suppose applied that bandage?"

17

Inez braked the car to a stop in front of Karyn's house. She left the engine idling, and the women sat for a minute without speaking.

"I'm going to tell Roy," Karyn said. "I've got to."

"Yes, I suppose you do."

"It isn't going to be easy. He's always so levelheaded and practical. "I've got to try, though."

"I understand," Inez said.

Karyn smiled and gave the other woman's hand a squeeze. She left Inez waiting in the car and ran across the clearing to the house. She found Roy inside at the table. He was bent over a manuscript, making corrections with a red pencil.

"Roy, can I talk to you?"

"Is it important? I really want to finish these books tonight."

"It's important."

With a sigh Roy laid the pencil aside and shifted the chair around so he was facing her. "All right."

Karyn hesitated. Now that she had Roy's full attention, she felt foolish. She did not know where to start, how to convince him that she was deadly serious. She decided that to plunge right in was as good a way as any.

"Roy, do you know what a werewolf is?"

"Did you say werewolf?"

"Yes."

"A guy who turns into a wolf when the moon is full and runs around growling and eating people. Right?"

"Close."

"So what's the point?"

Karyn drew a deep breath. "I believe there is a werewolf in Drago."

"Oh, uh-huh. And this was important enough to interrupt my work?"

"I'm serious, damn you."

"All right, Karyn, let's hear the rest of it."

"I believe there is a werewolf in Drago. I believe the werewolf killed our dog, killed the two kids who came hiking through here the other day, and killed God knows how many others."

Roy was watching her, his face carefully expressionless.

"I believe the werewolf is Anton Gadak."

"Ah, Jesus, Karyn..."

"Listen to me. Last night I shot that huge wolf out in front of the house. You saw the blood, you found a piece of its ear. Today I saw Anton Gadak in town. He has a fresh bandage covering the left side of his head."

Roy stared incredulously. "And on the basis of that you have decided that Anton Gadak is a... a werewolf?"

"It's not only that, Roy. Through the years there have been lots of strange disappearances and unexplained deaths around Drago. Who would be in a better position to cover up what really happened than Gadak?"

"Wait a minute. What's all this about strange deaths and disappearances? You make this sound like the Bermuda Triangle."

"It's true. Inez Polk has clippings from local newspapers."

"I might have known."

"Roy, don't you hear what I'm telling you? Anton Gadak is a werewolf."

Roy jumped out of the chair and spread his arms. "What the hell do you want me to do? Go into town and drive a stake through his heart?"

"I want you to believe me, that's all."

"Those pills you've been taking..."

"I haven't had a pill in two days."

Roy searched her eyes, as though looking for signs of madness. Finally he said, "All right, Karyn, I'll tell you what we're going to do. We're going to get the hell out of here and go back to Los Angeles. That ought to satisfy you."

"Roy, I didn't mean—"

"You can start packing now. We'll leave tomorrow and move into a motel or something in L.A. until I can make other arrangements." He started out the door.

"Where are you going?"

"Into town to settle our bills. I want to get away as soon as possible."

Karyn stood in the center of the room feeling stunned as Roy slammed out of the house. She had handled it badly, but there was no justification for Roy's sudden anger. She had not expected him to instantly accept the idea, but she had counted on being able to discuss it with him. The thought of running back to Los Angeles now seemed wrong. It left an unpaid debt to Neal Edwards and Pam Sealander. And to nameless others who would follow.

Feeling numb and defeated, Karyn left the house and walked slowly across the small clearing to where Inez waited standing beside the car.

"I guess it didn't go too well," said Inez.

"It went badly," Karyn said.

"He didn't believe you?"

"He wouldn't even listen to me. He thinks I'm hallucinating. Could he be right, Inez? Is it possible there is something wrong with my mind?"

"There's nothing wrong with you, Karyn. If you're crazy, so am I."

"Roy might agree with that too."

"Very possibly. He didn't even look at me when he stormed out of the house. Where was he going, anyway?"

"Into town to pay our bills. We're going back to Los Angeles tomorrow."

"Oh?"

"I feel that I'm running out on you."

"Don't be silly. It might be the best thing for you." For a moment the two women faced each other, then Inez put her arms around Karyn. They clung together like sisters.

"Take care of yourself," Inez said.

"You too."

A little self-consciously they moved apart. Inez put her hand on the car door handle.

"Well… goodbye," said Inez.

"Goodbye. We'll be in touch, won't we?"

"Of course."

Even as they spoke, Karyn could see in the other woman's eyes that neither of them believed it. After Drago they would never again see each other.

Inez got into her car and drove off down the road without looking back. Karyn went into the house and sat down to wait for Roy. Suddenly she was very tired.

18

When he was a hundred yards down the grassy road toward the village, Roy Beatty slowed down. His anger had melted away, and he was ashamed of the way he had spoken to Karyn. He reminded himself what she had been through, and that the only reason they came to this isolated valley was to help her. The last thing in the world he should be doing now was losing his temper and storming out of the house like some sulky adolescent.

But a werewolf! It had to be, Roy decided, Inez Polk who was putting such ideas into Karyn's head. He wished now that he had gone over to the car when he came out of the house and had it out with the woman. But at the time he had been too angry. All he wanted to do was get away.

Well, no, that was not quite right. His real reason for going to the village, he had to admit, was to see Marcia Lura one more time. He would have to tell Marcia he was leaving. It would not be easy, but it was impossible to simply go without seeing her again. His emotional bond to the green-eyed woman was too strong to allow that. Roy could not put a name to the emotion between him and Marcia. Not love, certainly, not in the sense that he loved Karyn. Lust was more accurate. Sheer physical attraction. Chemistry. And yet there was more to it than that. Marcia Lura had introduced him to sensual delights that were beyond anything he had experienced. Beyond anything he had imagined. No, it would not be easy to leave what he had found here.

Roy came to the main road that led into the village. As he turned and walked toward the gift shop he tried and rejected a number of opening remarks for what he must say to Marcia. There was no way to soften it.

In a way, he told himself, it was good that this business with Karyn had come up now. Eventually he would have had to break off with Marcia, and the longer he put it off, the more difficult it would be. Her hold on him would grow with every meeting. It was like a strange sweet sickness.

The village of Drago was bright and empty. Eddies of dust curled along the main street in the light breeze. The shadows of afternoon had barely begun to darken the valley. Roy turned at Marcia Lura's gift shop and pushed in through the door.

The bell over the door tinkled, an incongruously merry sound that did not match his mood. He peered around in the perpetually dim light of the shop.

Marcia came in through the curtains in the rear that separated the shop from her living quarters. She wore tight-fitting pants that hugged her thighs and belled out at the ankles. A striped blouse was open several buttons down, revealing an amulet on a gold chain that hung in the crevice between her breasts.

"Hello, Roy," she said. "I wasn't expecting you until later."

For a moment he stood looking at her without speaking. Her pale-green eyes were softly luminous in the dusk. The black hair had an animal sheen to it that reflected blue highlights. She was so beautiful it brought a lump to his throat.

"I have to talk to you, Marcia," he said finally.

"All right. Come in the back." She reached out a slim arm to part the curtains.

For a moment Roy hesitated. Somewhere deep in his subconscious a warning sounded, but the nearness of the woman, the heat of her body, the scent of her, overpowered his doubts. He walked through the curtain into her rooms.

"I was having some tea," she said. "Let me make you a cup."

Without waiting for him to answer, Marcia went to her small gas range and turned up the flame under a copper teakettle. From a canister she spooned crumbled leaves into a cup, then added a few drops of thick liquid from an opaque bottle. Roy watched, fascinated by the grace of even her smallest movements.

When the water was boiling Marcia poured it into the cup and stirred the mixture. She carried the cup across the room and set it on a low table before the sofa.

"Let the tea steep for a minute before you drink it," she said. She sat down on the sofa, patting the cushion next to her.

Roy sat down beside her, but was careful not to let their bodies touch. To keep from looking into her eyes, he busied himself stirring the tea. Its aroma was a mixture of spices with a hint of something bitter.

"You wanted to talk to me," Marcia said.

"Yes."

"About us?"

"In a way. And about Karyn. She isn't getting any better."

"I'm sorry."

"So am I. I'm going to have to take her away from here.

"You're leaving Drago?"

"I have to."

For the briefest fraction of a second Marcia's body stiffened. The pale-green eyes narrowed, and Roy saw flash there of something dark and dangerous. Then it was gone. Marcia was poised again, cool and lovely, and Roy thought he must have imagined the moment.

"How soon must you go?" Her throaty voice was without emotion.

"Tomorrow."

"I see. Your tea should be ready to drink now." Roy looked down at the cup as though wondering where it had come from. He lifted it to his lips and sipped the dark brew. It had a sweet, wild taste.

"Do you like it?" she asked. "It's a very old recipe."

"It's fine," he said quickly. "Marcia, I don't want to talk about the tea."

"About what, then?"

"I hate to leave you. Do you know that?"

"I know," she said "But we never pretended it was forever, did we?"

"No, but I want you to know that it wasn't just a... a fling for me. You've been something very special in my life. You've given me something I've never known. I'll never forget you, Marcia."

Marcia leaned toward him. Again he had the delicious sensation of being drawn into those deep green eyes. Into them and down to unknown depths.

"No," she said softly "You never will forget me. Drink your tea, darling."

He raised the cup and drank. The pungent steam brought tears to his eyes. When he put the cup back down in the saucer he was surprised to see that his hand was shaking.

Marcia watched him. She reached over and placed her hand on his leg. The fingers seemed to sear his flesh through the cloth. His world shrank to this room and this hour and this woman.

He touched her hair. His hand moved to the back of her neck and pulled her head toward him. They kissed, their mouths open, tongues mating. When at last he pulled back a little way, Roy was breathing heavily.

"I do love you, Marcia," he said.

She shook her head. "No. You admire me. You want me. You may even need me. But you do not love me."

Roy started to say something more, but she stopped him.

"Not yet," she said. "You do not love me yet. But you will, my Roy, you will."

He kissed her again. His hand moved down the long smooth curve of her back to her firm, round hip. Marcia's body moved under his hand, and he felt that she was wearing nothing beneath the blouse and pants.

Marcia drew back her head and looked into his eyes. The corners of her mouth curled upward in the suggestion of a smile.

"Tell me what you want, Roy." She ran her tongue across her teeth. "Tell me what you want to do to me."

"I want to make love to you," he said.

"Not like that. Tell me in the real words. The words you say to me when we are naked together."

"I want to fuck you."

"Yes. Yes. And what else?"

"I want to taste you."

"Where?"

"Your breasts. Your nipples. Your cunt. I want to kiss you and taste you there and everywhere."

"And do you want to be inside me?"

"Yes. Oh, yes."

"Tell me."

"I want to be inside you. Deep inside. All the way."

"And do you want me to take it in my mouth?"

"Yes."

"And roll my tongue around it and kiss it and suck the sweet drops from it?"

"Oh, God, Marcia, yes."

All rational thought was driven from Roy's mind by his pounding desire. With every fiber of his being he wanted to possess this black-haired, smooth-limbed woman. He wanted her sexually, carnally, totally. Nothing else was real. At that moment, had it been necessary, Roy Beatty would have killed to get her.

Marcia slipped out of his grasp and stood up. She undid the remaining buttons of her blouse, stripped it from her shoulders, and tossed it away, paying no attention to where it fell. She moved back in front of Roy and leaned down to put a hand on each of his knees. As he sat looking up at her, she spread his legs and stepped between them. She moved her hands then to the back of his neck. Clasping her fingers there, she pulled his face forward into the soft, warm valley of her breasts.

Roy inhaled the mingled musk and sandalwood. He tasted the salt of her flesh and the metal of the amulet she wore. He bit down on the soft chain and it snapped. The amulet fell softly to the carpet.

Marcia backed away from him again, and Roy stood up, fumbling with his clothes. His erection thrust forward like a lance.

Quickly Marcia unzipped the pants she wore and slipped them down her long legs and off. She stood before him smoothly naked, proud of her body. Roy moved toward her, but she stopped him with a gentle hand on his chest. Watching his face, she let her free hand dip down between them. The fingers curled around his penis.

"You are ready for me, my man," she said. "Aren't you?"

"I'm ready," he whispered.

She released him, turned her back, and dropped suddenly to her hands and knees. "Then ride me, my lover. Ride me."

With the blood roaring in his head, Roy went to his knees behind her. She raised her buttocks to him. He thrust forward and penetrated. At once he started to withdraw.

"No," she commanded. "Leave it there. Give it to me there."

With his hands planted on Marcia's ivory-smooth cheeks, Roy drove into her a centimeter at a time. She let her head sink to the floor, the side of her face pressed against the carpet. To meet each of his thrusts she pushed back with her hips. From deep in her throat came a soft growling moan.

With a final painful shove Roy buried the full length of his organ in her. There he was held fast, as though gripped by burning fingers. He knew that at any second he would climax up there.

"No," she said. The single syllable held him like a physical barrier.

They froze in position. The excruciating sensuality made him want to cry out, but he knew any movement would bring on the explosion. Marcia raised her head and turned to look at him. Her eyes blazed green.

"We aren't through with each other yet, are we, my lover?"

Fraction by slow tight fraction he withdrew. Half a dozen times he was an eye-blink from climax, but each time Marcia's phenomenal control of her muscles stopped him, held him in check, until at last he was out of her.

During the timeless span that followed, Marcia Lura led Roy along paths of physical joy he had never traveled. With unfailing instinct she did exactly the right thing at exactly the right moment. By turns she submitted to him wholly, then took the lead and became the aggressor.

Sexual fantasies locked in Roy's mind since childhood sprang to vivid life. Time and again he would be at the brink of orgasm, and each time Marcia would stop him just short of total release and bring him back.

The shadows of evening moved into the valley and darkened the windows of Marcia's small apartment, but the people within had no sense of time. For Roy

Beatty the universe consisted of the hills and hollows, the knowing hands, and the wet, clinging orifices of the wild black-haired woman.

When at last she brought him to the finish he was in a kneeling position. She lay on her back with her head away from him, her elbows propped on the floor, her legs scissored behind his back. Their movement, in and out, together and apart, was not more than an inch. Marcia's eyes never left his face.

"Now." she said suddenly. And again, *"Nowwwwww!"* drawing it out in a husky growl.

Roy let go, and the explosion pulled him inside out. It was like being born, and it was like dying. Every good sensation of his life was jammed into the heaving, sweating climax. He spurted hot and hard and emptied himself into her. They cried out together, and their cry became a scream, and at last it was finished.

Roy fell back, and for long, long minutes he lay motionless on the soft carpet. It was as though all the nerves of his body had been severed. He had not enough strength to make a fist.

Marcia slid up to lie beside him. He did not open his eyes, but he could smell her, smell the sex of her and their mingled sweat, and still the gentle sandalwood. He wanted to cry. Then he felt the tears slide down his face and he knew he was crying.

"Marcia…"

"Hush." She stopped his lips with her fingers. "But I want to tell you—"

"No, there is nothing more to be said. It is time now for you to go." She moved away from him.

Slowly Roy sat up. He felt drained. Empty. Across the room Marcia lit a candle, and for the first time he realized night had come.

She walked around gathering up his clothes and brought them to him. He dressed silently and methodically while she sat in the shadows watching him. When he was finished dressing he crossed to the back door. There he hesitated and turned, wanting to say something to her. She shook her head no, and he went out and closed the door behind him.

* * *

Walking home along the path through the woods, Roy fought against the still-fresh memory of what had happened to him this night. He knew he must not think about it now. Maybe not ever. Not if he was to live a normal life again.

To keep his mind busy he tried concentrating on the problems of his work. No good. His work was too far away, and the feel of Marcia's body was still on his skin. But he must not think of her. He recited the Greek alphabet aloud. Forward first, then backward.

"Omega, psi, chi, phi, upsilon…" He stopped. He was being followed.

The sound was a soft, rhythmic thud as of something trotting after him on padded paws. Roy peered back along the path where moonlight filtered down through the trees to make bright patches on the trail. As he watched, a lean shadow moved swiftly through one of the pools of moonlight.

As the shadow loped through the next patch of light Roy saw what it was. A wolf. But more than a wolf. A long-bodied black creature moving toward him with power and assurance. Its mouth was drawn back in a grotesque animal grin. And the eyes. The eyes knew him.

Before Roy could react the beast pushed off with powerful hind legs and hit him full in the chest. He staggered back under the blow and instinctively wrapped his arms around the animal. The strength of the beast was unnatural. He could feel the play of its muscles under the thick fur. The wolf's hind feet dug into the dirt and it forced Roy steadily backward.

The face of the wolf was only an inch from his own. Its breath, hot and damp, hissed in his ear. The glistening teeth, as long as two of his finger joints, snapped at the air and moved closer to his throat.

Inexorably, a step at a time, Roy was forced back by the superior strength of the wolf. He clutched at the thick neck fur, but could not pull the thing's face away from his. As he was pushed back off the path, Roy's foot caught in a tangle of fern and he crashed to the ground on his back.

With the beast astride him now, Roy flailed at it with his fists, but his blows had no more effect than those of a baby. The thin black lips of the wolf stretched in a snarl of triumph.

While Roy still struggled to free himself, the wolf's head dipped and the cruel teeth bit effortlessly through his shirt and the flesh of his shoulder. Through the explosion of pain Roy could hear the teeth grating on bone. His right arm went dead, and his will to resist died with it.

In his last moment of consciousness Roy looked into the face of the wolf. The muzzle was smeared now with bright fresh blood. And again the eyes. He knew the eyes. And he knew he was lost. Roy arched his neck, baring his throat to the killer teeth.

19

Roy lay with his eyes closed, waiting for the final burst of agony that would come when the teeth of the wolf ripped away his throat. Incredibly, nothing happened. He forced his eyes open and saw the beast, bloody-mouthed, watching him. The cruel mouth stretched again in a triumphant snarl. Then the beast backed off, turned to the forest, and slipped away into the night.

Minutes went by and there was only the darkness and the sounds of the small forest creatures. Roy tried to rise, but the pain in his shoulder was like a hot iron. His mind would not work. Thoughts crumbled into fragments of visions, making no sense, forming no pattern. With his body operating on instinct alone, he began to crawl through the brush. He crawled until finally he was back on the path. With a wrenching effort he raised himself to his feet. With his right arm dangling he stumbled along the path toward his house. Again and again he fell heavily to the ground, but each time he rose again to stagger on.

* * *

Something jolted Karyn Beatty out of her sleep. She looked around, disoriented for a moment. She was in the living room of the little house. In the rocking chair by the window. She must have dozed off. What was she doing out here? Waiting for Roy, that was it. She remembered then, sitting there through the afternoon, waiting while he did not return. She had opened a can of soup for her dinner, then sat down again. Then she must have fallen asleep.

The gray luminescence of the window through the curtain told her it was dawn. She had slept here though the night, and Roy was still not home.

What had awakened her? A noise outside the house. Something out there. She hurried to the closet where the shotgun was kept and brought it back into the living room. Cautiously she unlocked the front door and opened it just enough to look out. The sky was lightening, but the forest was still dark and secret beyond the clearing. There seemed to be nothing... then she looked down. There at her feet, his body twisted into an awkward position, lay her husband.

Quickly Karyn put the gun down inside the house and knelt beside Roy. His clothes and his hair were covered with pine needles, twigs, and dirt. He was alive, but flushed and feverish. His breathing was shallow, his face damp with perspiration.

"Roy, my God, what's happened to you?" There was no reply.

Karyn cradled Roy's head in her lap. His eyes fluttered open. For an instant they had a look of unspeakable terror and she felt his entire body go rigid. Then his expression clouded and he relaxed. His eyes were still open, but he seemed to see nothing.

"Roy, what is it? What happened to you? Oh, please answer me."

His eyes closed again, then opened with the same blank expression. With her hands under his arms Karyn managed to heave him to his feet and steer him into the house. She got him into the bedroom and eased him into a sitting position on the bed. When she pushed him gently back he lay down without resistance. She took off his shoes and loosened his belt. His shirt was badly torn at the shoulder and stained with what looked like blood, but there was no wound underneath.

Karyn covered him with a blanket, pulling it high around his shoulders.

"Roy... Roy, I'm going for the doctor. Can you hear me?"

He groaned deep in his chest—a sound that might or might not have been an answer.

"You stay here and keep warm. I'll be back as soon as I can."

Karyn ran out of the house. The sun was visible now through a gap in the mountains, slanting down through the trees, warming the shadowed places.

For one of the few times in her life Karyn truly regretted that she had never learned to drive. There in the clearing sat the Ford—so accessible, so ready, so useless to her. She considered for a moment taking it anyway and trying somehow to drive it as far as Drago. She had sat next to Roy often enough to know the procedures. But no, it would be foolish now to risk smashing up the car on top of the other urgent problems. She began to run down the narrow lane toward the village.

She ran until she was out of breath, then walked, then ran again. Soon she reached the blacktopped road and turned toward Drago. No one was out in the early morning. She had the town to herself.

The street where Dr. Volkmann lived was still in shadow. The window blinds in the house were drawn. The doctor's dusty old Buick stood in the driveway.

Karyn ran up the wooden steps to the porch and rang the bell. She waited a minute, then rang again. This time she heard someone moving inside.

Dr. Volkmann opened the door and blinked down at her. He wore a faded blue bathrobe and slippers with no backs. His thin gray hair was in disarray.

"Why, Karyn, what is it?"

"Something's happened to Roy, Doctor. Can you come and see him?"

"Happened? What's happened?"

"I don't know. He went into town yesterday afternoon. I fell asleep in a chair waiting for him. A little while ago a noise woke me up and I went to the door. Roy was just outside lying on the ground."

As she finished speaking Karyn began to sob, the pent-up emotion breaking through.

"I'll be right with you," said the doctor. He reached into his worn bag on the hall table and took out a bottle.

He shook two pills into his hand and gave them to Karyn. "In the meantime you'd better take these. They'll calm your nerves. You can take them with a glass of water from the kitchen while I'm getting dressed."

Karyn walked down the musty hallway to a large, old-fashioned kitchen. She found a drinking glass in one of the cupboards and ran it full of water. She looked down at the pills and hesitated. No more of these, she reminded herself. She dropped the pills down the sink drain and poured the water after them. She walked back into the front hall in time to meet the doctor coming down the stairs. He wore a sweater and pants and shoes hastily pulled on over his bare feet.

"Let's go," he said.

Volkmann snatched up the medical bag and he and Karyn hurried out to the old Buick. It started at once, and Volkmann gunned the engine up the street to the road that turned off toward the Beattys' house.

"What were Roy's symptoms when you found him?" the doctor asked.

"He was only semi-conscious. His face was all red and he felt as though he had a fever. He opened his eyes, but they didn't seem to focus on anything."

"And when you left?"

"I put him in the bed. He seemed to be sleeping, but his breathing was uneven and his body seemed tense."

"Any marks or injuries?"

"That's a curious thing. His shirt looked as though it was stained with blood, but there was no wound that could have bled like that. Only scratches on his hands and face that could have come from the brush. There might be something else. I didn't undress him."

Volkmann pulled the Buick in behind Roy's Ford, and he and Karyn went into the house. Roy was still in the bed where Karyn had left him. His eyes were closed. His head rolled fitfully on the pillow.

"Help me get his clothes off," said Volkmann, "And we'll give him a going over for injuries."

Roy made feeble sounds of protest as Karyn and Dr. Volkmann pulled off his clothes, but he did not wake up. The doctor examined him thoroughly from head to foot, then rolled him onto his stomach and checked his back. He probed delicately through the blond hair on Roy's head, and finally looked up at Karyn.

"No apparent injuries anywhere. His symptoms are similar to those of a concussion, and that might be the case even though there is no sign of a blow on the head."

Together they rolled Roy over on his back again, and Karyn covered him with the blanket. As she did so he opened his eyes and looked at her.

"Karyn," he said thickly. "What time is it?" Then his expression became more alert. He raised his head. "Dr. Volkmann, why are you here? What happened?"

"We were hoping you could tell us," said the doctor.

Karyn took Roy's hand and pressed it against her cheek. "Darling, are you all right?"

"I... I think so. I feel a little shaky. Confused. What's going on?"

"You went into Drago yesterday afternoon and didn't return," Volkmann said. "This morning your wife found you lying outside the door. She came to get me."

Roy frowned with the effort of trying to remember. "Let's see... I was working here in the afternoon... was that yesterday... when Karyn came home? We talked about... Damn, I can't remember what we talked about. An argument, I think. I don't know." He rubbed his eyes with his fingertips before going on. "That's it. After that I fade out. The next thing I remember is looking up and seeing the two of you standing over me just now."

"You don't remember anything about last night?" Karyn prompted.

Roy shook his head. "There was sort of a dream." His eyes looked far away for a moment, then he went on. "I remember something about an animal. And eyes. Eyes that I knew, yet didn't know. Doesn't make much sense, does it?" He turned to Volkmann. "What's the matter with me, Doctor?"

"As far as I can determine you have no serious injuries. Still, I'd like you to come into town for an examination when you're feeling up to it."

"If you think it's necessary. Actually, I feel pretty good now. Just awfully tired and a little fuzzy in the head."

"I think you should sleep now. Perhaps when you awaken your memory will return."

"I hope so," Roy said. His speech was beginning to slur as his eyes lost their focus.

Karyn stayed behind for a moment as the doctor went out to the living room. She drew the curtain across the window, then came back and sat down carefully on the edge of the bed.

"I'll be right in the next room if you need me," she said.

Without warning Roy's eyes snapped wide open. Karyn recoiled as for an instant she looked into the haunted face of a stranger. Then his features went slack and his eyes closed in uneasy sleep. It had happened so fast Karyn could not be sure she hadn't imagined it. She backed away from the bed and went out. Softly she closed the door behind her.

Dr. Volkmann, waiting in the living room, was quick to reassure her. "Your husband will be all right," he said. "What he needs is rest and quiet."

"We were talking about going back to Los Angeles," Karyn said, "But he doesn't seem to remember."

"It's up to you, of course, but I don't think the added pressure of going back to the city right now would help his condition."

"I suppose we'll stay now, at least until he's better. Doctor..." Karyn hesitated, searching for the words. "Do you think it's possible Roy could have been attacked by... by..."

"By the werewolf?"

Karyn nodded.

"You saw his body. There were no wounds."

"Could it have come after him and he escaped?"

"We have no way of knowing what happened. In the morning you might question him some more about that dream he mentioned. But be gentle. He's not in any condition to be quizzed about a werewolf."

"Doctor, I have to ask you something."

"Yes?"

"Have you treated Anton Gadak in the last couple of days?"

"No. Why?"

"Do you remember I told you about wounding the wolf out in front of the house?"

"I remember. You thought at the time it might have been Etienne Jolivet."

"Yes, until you explained about his migraines."

"What has this to do with Anton Gadak?"

"As Inez Polk and I drove away from your house we saw Gadak on the street. He had a bandage covering one side of his head. And the ear."

"Why didn't you come to me at once?"

"To tell the truth, we thought you might be involved."

"Because you thought I'd put the bandage on and not told you about it, is that it?"

"Yes."

"Well, I didn't, but I can understand your caution. Nevertheless, we'd be better off to trust each other. I'll find out what I can about Anton Gadak's injury. Meanwhile, you be very careful."

"You don't have to worry about that."

"You should be in no danger in the daytime, but if you can avoid it, don't go out after dark alone."

Karyn saw Dr. Volkmann to the door and watched him start back toward Drago. Then she returned to the bedroom and looked at Roy. He was sleeping peacefully enough, except for a nerve that twitched at the corner of one eye.

Throughout the day Karyn kept watch while Roy continued to sleep. By nightfall she was exhausted. She undressed and slipped into bed next to him, being careful not to disturb him. She was so tired she dropped off in minutes.

Sometime during the night she was pulled up out of a dreamless sleep. Roy sat stiffly upright beside her, his eyes wide open, staring at emptiness.

"Roy, what is it?"

Then she heard, in the woods not far away, the howling.

20

Karyn did not sleep again until it was almost dawn. When next she awoke, Roy lay quietly beside her. His eyes were closed, but the frown-line between his brows showed he was awake.

"Good morning, darling," she said softly.

He rolled his head on the pillow and looked at her.

"Hello, Karyn."

"How are you feeling?"

"So-so."

"Are you hungry? Would you like me to bring you some breakfast?"

Roy sat up suddenly and pushed the covers away. "No. Stop treating me like an invalid. I've got to get up and do some work."

"Dr. Volkmann said you should rest."

"Doctors always say that. You rest. I've got work to do."

Karyn got out of bed on her own side. "If that's what you want. But try not to tire yourself."

She prepared a big breakfast of buttermilk pancakes with fried eggs and thick country bacon. Roy only toyed with his food. He answered Karyn's attempts at conversation with monosyllables. His thoughts were far away.

"You should eat something," Karyn said. "You didn't have any dinner last night. Did you?"

"I'm just not very hungry," he said, attempting a smile. "It wouldn't hurt me to take off a few pounds anyway."

Karyn looked across the table into the shadowed eyes of her husband and said nothing. This was a mood she had never seen.

Roy got up, leaving most of the food on his plate, and waited impatiently while Karyn cleared the dishes from the table. Then he spread out his papers and sat down to work. Karyn kept out of the way, but watched him. He grew increasingly restless, cursing at the manuscripts in front of him, scribbling angrily on the pages. Before an hour had passed he threw down the pencil and expelled his breath in exasperation.

"Dammit, there are pages missing. You'd think that somebody would check this garbage before they send it to me. I can't edit what's not here."

"Why don't you take a break?" Karyn suggested.

Roy slammed both hands flat on the table and stood up. He paced back and forth across the room with his fists jammed into his pockets.

"Wouldn't you like to lie down for a while?" Karyn said.

"No, I wouldn't like to lie down for a while," he answered, mimicking her voice. "I'm going out."

Without waiting for a response from Karyn he threw open the door and stalked out of the house. She watched him cross the clearing and take one of the forest paths. When Roy was out of sight she walked back to the table and leafed through the pages of the manuscript. They were all there.

She dropped into a chair and stared down at her hands. Things seemed to be closing in, pressing her down, stifling her breath.

The morning dragged into afternoon. Roy came home in the same irritable mood as when he had left. He refused lunch and sat down to try to work again. It was painful for Karyn to watch.

"Roy, do you think we ought to go in and see Dr. Volkmann?"

"What for?"

"He said he'd like to see you again if you were feeling well enough."

"What's the matter, didn't you pay him for yesterday?"

"That's not fair. He's been very good about coming out when we need him."

"Well, we don't need him now." Roy drew a long, heavy sigh, then got up and came over to Karyn. "You're right, I shouldn't take it out on Volkmann." He started to put his arms around her, then backed away. "I'm just jumpy. Worrying about those hours I can't account for, maybe. Put up with me for a little while longer, okay?"

Karyn gazed at him levelly. "Have you remembered anything more about last night?"

"No, I haven't," he said, the sharpness returning to his voice. "If anything comes to me I'll tell you about it. It doesn't help any to have you nagging at me."

"I wasn't nagging, I was asking."

Roy went angrily back to his papers, muttering something too low for Karyn to hear. She went into the kitchen and made a cup of instant coffee, telling herself she must not lose her temper. When she went back into the living room the front door was open and Roy was gone again.

"Oh, damn, damn, damn," Karyn said aloud. "What am I going to do?"

She looked up at the sound of a car stopping outside. Footsteps crossed the clearing, and Inez Polk appeared in the doorway. With a rush of emotion Karyn ran to her friend and embraced her.

"Oh, Inez, I'm so glad you're here. I need somebody so badly."

Inez patted her gently on the shoulder until Karyn regained her composure and stepped back.

"How did you know to come?"

"Dr. Volkmann called and told me about Roy, and I came as soon as I could. How is he?"

Karyn shook her head. "I wish I knew. He's been irritable all day, pacing around the house like a caged animal. He went out this morning, and he's gone again now. I don't know where he goes."

"Exactly what happened to him last night?"

"I don't know. You saw him after our argument when he went into Drago to pay our bills. He didn't come back the rest of the day or all night. Early the next morning I heard something outside the door, and I found him lying there."

"Was he hurt?"

"Just scratches and bruises, but he couldn't remember anything."

"There was no sign that he'd been attacked?"

"No," Karyn said quickly. "I thought of that too."

Inez frowned thoughtfully. "Karyn, we're going to have to act, you and I."

"What do you mean?"

"Talk to the authorities. Will you come with me to the sheriff's office in Pinyon?"

"I thought we'd decided they wouldn't believe us."

"Not if we told them there's a werewolf here, they wouldn't, but we've got to get them interested somehow. What about those two hikers who stopped here? What were their names?"

"Neal Edwards and Pam Sealander. But I don't see what we can do now."

"Maybe we can get somebody interested enough to start asking questions. At least it's a beginning, and better than just waiting for the next thing to happen."

"Yes, of course it is," Karyn agreed. "I'll leave a note for Roy and be right with you."

Karyn inserted a blank sheet of paper into Roy's typewriter and pecked out: *Dear Roy—I've gone into Pinyon with Inez to do some shopping. I won't be late. Love, Karyn.* She left the note in the typewriter and went out with Inez to get into the car.

They drove down the lane and slowly through the main street of Drago. As usual, there was little activity in the village. A few of the silent people were out on the street. None of them looked up as the women drove past.

Three miles out of Drago, where the road started to climb into the Tehachapi Mountains, Inez turned off on a little-used back road. In a few minutes they reached Pinyon. The contrast to the dark village of Drago was startling. Here flowers bloomed, children laughed, and people smiled at you on the street. It made Drago look like a town in perpetual shadow.

Inez drove to a neat cinderblock building that housed the local sheriff's substation. The women went inside and introduced themselves to the uniformed young man at the desk.

"Good afternoon, ladies," he said pleasantly. "I'm Deputy Paul Spears. What can I do for you?"

"We want to inquire about some missing hikers," said Inez.

"I see." The deputy took a pad from his desk and picked up a ballpoint pen. "What are the people's names?"

"Neal Edwards and Pam—I suppose that's Pamela—Sealander. They have been missing for some time."

Karyn proceeded to tell the entire story, as the deputy took rapid notes.

When she had finished, the deputy looked up. "Are you sure the van you saw belonged to this Edwards and Sealander?"

"I'm reasonably sure. As I said, they told me they were driving a van and they had left it in Drago. When I saw it, it was being hooked up to a tow truck. I went over to ask why. The tow-truck driver told me he had instructions from a man named Anton Gadak."

"Yes, I know Mr. Gadak," the deputy put in. "Since the sheriff's department doesn't patrol Drago, he's been our unofficial contact there."

Karyn's hopes sagged, but she went gamely on. "When I asked Anton Gadak about the van he gave very evasive answers. He didn't seem interested in knowing who owned it. He said there was no registration or identification inside."

"Are you saying that Mr. Gadak was not telling the truth?"

"I think he knows more than he told me."

"I see. And have you any evidence to indicate that these people, as you suggest, met with foul play?"

Karyn's throat closed up, and she could not speak. She looked to Inez for help.

"We have no evidence," Inez said. "There is no proof that anything happened to them. But those two people are unaccounted for, and that should be reason enough to investigate."

"It will be looked into," the deputy assured her. "Now suppose you give me the home addresses of the missing people."

"They're from Santa Barbara," Karyn said. "That's as much as I know."

"We'll check out the names through the police there. If your people are in fact missing, we'll be in touch with you."

"Is that all you're going to do?" Karyn asked.

"Ma'am, excuse me, but this doesn't sound like what you'd call an emergency. After all, from your account, you waited five days before reporting that you were worried about these people."

"I know, but... other things have happened since. Couldn't you do something now?"

"What would you suggest?"

Inez took over. "Come with us to Drago and talk to Anton Gadak. He might be more willing to talk to you about the van."

While Deputy Spears considered the request, another young man in a sheriff's department uniform came into the office.

"Take over the desk for me, will you, Jed?" said Spears. "I'm going over to Drago with these ladies. I shouldn't be gone long." He came around the desk and gestured Karyn and Inez out of the building ahead of him.

While the women buckled themselves into Inez' Valiant, Deputy Spears drove a black-and-white sheriff's car out of the parking lot and pulled up behind them. Inez started down the road toward Drago with the deputy following.

"Do you really think this will do any good?" Karyn asked.

"We can hope," said Inez. "At least it can't do any harm."

Karyn gazed out the window at the trees slipping by. "I only wish I could be sure of that."

21

When the two cars turned up the main street of Drago, Anton Gadak was standing beneath the empty theater marquee, almost as though he had been waiting for them. Under the ever-present Stetson the white bandage still covered his ear.

Inez pulled to the side of the street and stopped. The deputy swung in and parked behind her. Gadak nodded to the women, touching his hat brim, and walked back to the sheriff's car.

"Hi, Paul," he said as the deputy climbed out. "Haven't seen you for a spell."

"They've been keeping me pretty busy," the deputy said.

"What can I do for you?"

Deputy Spears waited for Inez and Karyn to get out of the car and come back to join them. "These two ladies have some questions, Mr. Gadak."

"That so?"

"They're concerned about a couple of people who are missing. Backpackers."

"Yes." Karyn did not look at Anton Gadak. "They parked their van here in town."

"Van?" Gadak rubbed his chin in apparent puzzlement. His callused fingers made a raspy sound.

"It was taken away by a tow truck," Karyn said.

"Oh, sure, the van," Gadak said. "The one you was worried about the other day. That was parked out here on the street for a week. Nobody showed up to claim it, so I called the Highway Patrol to come and get it. That's what we always do with an abandoned vehicle. More'n likely it was stolen by kids and dumped here when they were through with it."

"It wasn't stolen," Karyn said heatedly, "And it wasn't abandoned. It belonged to a boy named Neal Edwards who was hiking up here in the mountains with his girlfriend."

"I wouldn't know anything about that," Gadak said.

"Like I told you the other day, there was no registration. The Highway Patrol can check out the owner through the license number. I ain't equipped to do that."

"And it wasn't parked here for any week, either," Karyn persisted.

" 'Scuse me, Mrs. Beatty," Gadak said, "But that vehicle was parked right here in front of this theater for a full seven days. Otherwise, I would've let it be."

Karyn looked at Deputy Spears. She saw he was accepting Gadak's story.

"You can check it out with the Highway Patrol, Paul," Gadak said. "They took the van over to Palmdale. Sergeant Cutter's the man to talk to there."

"I'll give him a call," said the deputy. He turned to Karyn and Inez. "Apparently Mr. Gadak here acted strictly in accordance with our procedures. Did you have any other questions?"

"Is that it?" Karyn said. "Is that all you're going to do?"

"I can check with the Highway Patrol in Palmdale if you want, but it's their job to get in touch with the owner of an impounded vehicle."

"What about Santa Barbara? You said you could do something there."

"All I can do is send a routine request for information to the local police."

"You're brushing us off, aren't you?" Karyn's voice was tight with anger.

Deputy Spears looked down, but failed to hide a patronizing expression.

In frustration, Inez Polk, who had been standing by watching, spoke up. "Mr. Gadak, what happened to your ear?"

Gadak turned on her suddenly, but his expression revealed nothing. He took off the Stetson and touched the bandage.

"You mean this?" he said. "I had a boil back there. It was pretty sore, but I guess it ought to be all right by now. I probably don't even need this bandage any more."

He pulled the strips of adhesive loose and eased the gauze pad away from his head. Underneath was an ear—intact and unmarked.

Gadak's smile was cold. "I appreciate your askin', but as you can see, it's nothing to worry about. Was there anything else I can do for you ladies?"

"No," Karyn said quickly. "Sorry we troubled you."

Deputy Spears politely took his leave, and Karyn and Inez walked back to the Valiant. The women drove away without a glance to the rear, but Karyn knew Anton Gadak's eyes had followed them.

"Why did you do that?" Karyn said. "Come right out and ask him about his ear?"

"I had to do something. It was obvious the deputy wasn't going to help us."

"But what good did it do? All we found out is that Gadak's ear is all right."

"It is now, but remember it's been three days since you shot the wolf. I told you those creatures heal amazingly fast from ordinary wounds."

"But it could have been a boil, as he said."

"Do you believe that?"

"I don't know what to believe."

Inez turned up the narrow road. Suddenly Karyn could hold herself in check no longer. She broke into great wracking sobs that shook her whole body, and couldn't stop. Inez brought the car to a stop and took Karyn in her arms. Karyn responded instantly, pressing herself against her friend.

For the first time in many days Karyn relaxed completely and let the tears come. Her locked-in emotions flooded out as though a gate had been opened. After several minutes the convulsive sobbing eased and she was able to draw a full breath. Still, in her need for another human being, she continued to cling to Inez.

"Is the whole world insane?" she said, her face pressed to Inez' shoulder. "Or are we?"

"Things will work out," Inez said softly. "We mustn't give up."

"You're the only one I have any more," Karyn said. "Roy is so strange lately, I can't even talk to him. Dr. Volkmann seems so removed from things, and Oriole Jolivet, well, she's just Oriole. There's nobody else. I need you, Inez."

Inez stroked Karyn's arm and leaned close. Her lips brushed Karyn's hair. Abruptly, she pulled away.

"I'll take you home now, Karyn."

Karyn straightened in the seat and looked at her friend. "Is something wrong?"

"Nothing is wrong. I have things I must do, that's all."

She put the car in gear and drove on toward the house. Karyn ran a hand over her hair and kept her eyes to the front.

"I'm sorry," Karyn said. "It's thoughtless of me to take up so much of your time."

"No, it's all right," said Inez. "But I really have to go." She pulled up in front of the little house and Karyn got out. Inez did not meet her eye.

"Well… thanks," Karyn said uncertainly. "Will I… see you again?"

"Yes, of course. I'll get in touch with you."

Karyn stood in front of the house and watched as Inez backed the car around and drove away. She waved her hand, but there was no sign that Inez had seen.

* * *

Inez Polk kept her eyes straight ahead as she drove back out the narrow lane, up through the main street of Drago, and onto the back road that led to Pinyon. Then she pulled off to the side of the road and stopped. She gripped the steering wheel until her knuckles turned white. Her head fell forward.

"Oh, my God," she said in a voice twisted with pain. "I thought that was all behind me."

She could still feel the press of Karyn's soft body against her own. How close she had come to making a terrible mistake.

Irresistibly her thoughts were drawn back through time, back to the years in the convent when she was known as Sister Adelaide. For the thousandth time she re-lived the night the young novitiate had come to her room. The girl was in tears, shaking with a fear she could not name. Inez had taken the girl's hand and sat with her on the narrow bed. She had spoken words of comfort and faith while she stroked the girl's smooth white hand. Gradually she became aware of a response in her body. It was a yearning, a need that was utterly foreign to her.

It had seemed the most natural thing in the world to take the girl into her arms. The girl had come willingly. No, eagerly.

Without consciously making it happen, Inez had found herself lying on the bed with the girl. Naked. The girl touched her and caressed her in ways Inez could not have imagined. The caresses aroused sensations indescribable. Inez' body, her very soul, had caught fire that night. Her reason fled. She wanted only to possess. To be possessed.

It was there in Inez' narrow bed that they had been found. Inez had left the convent and the order immediately and in silence. The girl was turned out, of course. Inez never heard from her again. Never tried to contact her. Tried never to think about her. In vain. For often in an empty night when she lay between chaste sheets in her solitary bed, Inez' hand would stray over her own body and she would remember the delicious, forbidden caresses.

Never since then had she been tempted to act against the laws of God and nature. Never until tonight when she had held Karyn Beatty so briefly in her arms. Inez knew there had been no intent on Karyn's part to arouse her. No response at all in that way. If there had been... if Karyn had really wanted her...

Inez forced herself to break off the thought. She pounded the steering wheel with her fists, letting the pain drive the unwanted memories from her mind. She had to think of other things. She would have a busy day tomorrow doing library research. It would fill her mind. Tonight she would read a very dull book until she fell asleep.

"Please, dear God, don't let me dream."

22

Roy Beatty heard Inez' car approaching well before it reached the house. Since the other night when... when whatever it was had happened to him in the woods, Roy's hearing, along with his other senses, had become unnaturally keen. He was aware of the change particularly at night. As he lay sleepless beside Karyn he could hear a whole symphony of night sounds that had been inaudible to him before. Tiny forest creatures chittered and squeaked. Trees groaned, their branches clacked and whispered in the dark. The house itself had a score of voices as boards creaked, a shingle flapped, the stone foundation settled another millimeter.

The nights were restless times for Roy. He had acquired an ache in his joints that came when the sun went down and made it difficult for him to find a comfortable position in bed. Knowing how worried Karyn was, he held himself still and pretended to be asleep whenever she looked over at him. All the time his mind was fully alert and ranging far from the bed where he lay.

In the daylight hours his nerves jumped like worms on a griddle. Although he tried, he could not sit still for more than a few minutes. Karyn's presence in the same room irritated him for no reason. Only when he walked in the forest did Roy find partial peace. Striding along through the brush, inhaling the myriad new smells, listening to the daytime forest music—so different from that of the night—Roy knew a kinship with his surroundings. But even at those times he felt incomplete. When he returned home after hours of walking in the woods he would be jumpier than ever.

Roy had tried very hard to remember what had happened to him the night Karyn found him lying outside the door. All he could bring to mind were vague, shifting images. There was some kind of an animal, of that he was sure. And the eyes, always the eyes. Green as jade. Eyes that knew him too well.

But the picture would never form completely, and as his head began to hurt Roy would give up trying.

He heard Inez Polk's car drive away. A minute went by before Karyn came into the house. She was blurry and red around the eyes.

"Oh, you're home," she said.

"Yes. I found your note. Is anything wrong, Karyn? Have you been crying?"

She started to come to him, then something seemed to stop her, hold her back.

"Roy, are you feeling well enough for us to leave?"

"Leave? What do you mean, leave?"

"I want to go away from this place. It's not healthy for you or for me."

"Leave Drago?" Sudden apprehension sent a chill through him.

"The other day you said we would go back to Los Angeles. I'm ready now."

"I don't remember saying that."

"If we don't get out of here something awful will happen to us. I know it—"

Roy stepped toward Karyn and put his arms around her. She was stiff and unresponsive. He released her.

"All right, if you want to go, that settles it. We'll go."

"When?"

"We can't just walk away. It will take time to make arrangements. We'll have to do something about this house. And we sublet our place in the city for a full six months."

"How soon *can* we go?"

"Dammit, I don't know." Roy felt an anger building that was far out of proportion to the cause. He made an effort to be calm. "If you're in such a hurry, why don't you go back alone? I'll come after I get things straightened out."

"I don't want to do that, Roy. I want us to leave together."

"All right," he said, "We'll leave in a week. That will give me time to tie up loose ends here and find somewhere for us to stay in Los Angeles until we can get our apartment back."

"Thank you, darling," Karyn said, greatly relieved.

"Sure." Roy continued to fight down the irrational anger. "Now that it's settled, why don't we have a drink?"

"Are you sure it will be all right for you?"

"Hell yes. There's nothing wrong with me."

"I'll mix them. Are martinis all right?"

"Sure, fine." Roy had not taken a drink since his experience in the woods. He had no desire for alcohol now. But having a drink had seemed like a good way to get off the subject of leaving Drago. The raw smell of gin burned his nostrils as Karyn stirred the cocktails out in the kitchen.

She brought in two icy glasses and handed one to Roy. He took a sip, swallowed, and the liquor tore at his throat like broken glass. He fell into a coughing spasm.

Karyn, quickly putting down her own glass, came to his side. "Are you all right?"

It took several seconds for Roy to get his breath back to answer. "Some of it went down the wrong way, I guess."

"Maybe you shouldn't drink on an empty stomach." Roy sniffed at the glass in his hand and his stomach turned over. "Maybe you're right." He set the glass down and moved away from it, trying to mask the overpowering revulsion he felt.

"I'll start dinner," Karyn said. "What would you like to eat?"

"It doesn't matter. The truth is I'm not very hungry."

"You really should eat something. You've barely touched your food the last two days."

"Cut it out, will you? You're starting to sound like a Jewish mother."

What Roy could not tell his wife was that he did have a hunger. A bone-deep gnawing need for something, he didn't know what.

"I only asked what you wanted for dinner," she said.

"I don't give a damn," he snapped. "Cook anything you want to."

Karyn looked up at him quickly. The hurt in her eyes made him want to reach out for her, but he could not. She turned away and went into the kitchen.

For their dinner she prepared pork chops with baked potatoes, creamed carrots, and a green salad. Roy barely picked at the vegetables. He knew his stomach would not accept them.

"Is something wrong with the food?" Karyn asked.

"It's fine. Too bad you burned the pork chops, though."

"They aren't burned, Roy. They're done the way I always do them."

"Then you always burn them."

Karyn chose her words carefully. "You have to cook pork well. You know that, Roy."

He slapped his napkin down and left the table. "I don't want to argue about any stupid pork chops."

For the rest of the evening Roy pretended to work while Karyn pretended to read. At last it was time to go to bed. Roy got in next to his wife and lay rigidly stiff, not wanting to touch her, praying that she would not touch him. The aching in his joints was the worst yet. After a very long time Karyn's breathing eased, her features softened. She was asleep.

Roy relaxed. Through a gap in the window curtain he could see the moon. He could not remember ever seeing it so bright. The light of it kept his eyes open and made sleep impossible. He got out of bed and walked over to the window. He meant to close the curtain, but when he looked out he was stunned by the beauty of the scene. The full moon suffused the forest with a pale silver light that made everything magical. Roy could not stay inside on a night like this. He gathered his clothes and carried them silently into the living room. There he dressed rapidly and went out.

He plunged at once into the deep shadows of the forest, but had no trouble seeing the path. The combination of bright moonlight and his improved night vision made the going easy. He inhaled and savored the tangy scent of the evergreens. The air was deliciously cool. Roy felt he was embraced by the night.

The tiny things that lived in the darkness—the rodents and the night birds—froze in the shadows as Roy approached. But he saw them and smiled. He was a part of their world.

The cramps in his joints grew suddenly worse. Roy slowed down and rubbed at his shoulders. There was a twisting ache in both his knees. He stumbled into a clearing, and the pain was too great for him to go on.

He recognized the clearing. It was the place where he had come upon Marcia Lura the night he had gone looking for Karyn's wolf. It seemed so very long ago, yet it was less than a week.

Breathing became difficult. Roy tore at his collar. It was loose at the throat, yet it choked him like a noose.

He pulled the shirt open all the way down the front and peeled it from his back. Better. The cool night kissed his flesh. He eased into a sitting position and pulled off his shoes and socks. The grass was like velvet against his bare feet. The cloth of his pants rasped against his skin, and he pulled them off too. Roy pulled himself erect, naked in the clearing. He bathed in the clean night air.

Then a violent muscular spasm seized him and he lost control of his body. He dropped to the ground, his hands braced out in front of him. As Roy stared at his hands a growth of short yellowish hair spread over the backs. The fingers shortened and grew claws. The palms thickened into pads, and the hands were paws. Simultaneously, thick pale fur covered his body, his arms and legs twisted into new shapes, his ears grew points, his face lengthened into a muzzle. He flicked his tongue over the new cruel fangs in his mouth.

As his body changed, so did the mind of Roy Beatty. The logical, rational, well-ordered human consciousness was crowded into a far corner of the new intelligence. The mind that now controlled the body was wild and cunning. The mind knew—Roy Beatty knew—what had happened to him. He had become a wolf.

Tentatively at first, then with growing confidence, he tested the new body. He marveled at the way the four legs worked in effortless rhythm, bearing him swiftly over the ground. He turned his head to look down along the thickly furred back. He could see the long muscles moving smoothly under his pelt. And there was the fine thick tail that provided balance for this graceful creature he had become.

The delight he felt at his transformation was beyond anything in Roy Beatty's experience. There were no words for it in the human vocabulary. He wheeled once around the perimeter of the clearing, then bounded off into the darkness of the forest.

He disdained the paths, moving easily through narrow openings in the underbrush. The powerful legs carried him swiftly along, the keen eyes and nose following faint animal trails. On he plunged, growing careless of the protruding twigs and branches as he discovered his body was protected by the thick covering of fur.

As he crashed through the undergrowth the big pale wolf became aware of hungers that squeezed his belly like a giant's hand. The craving was for food and drink, and other things. The need was powerful, but the spark of human intelligence that remained still fought it.

The wolf loped on. The satisfying stretch and pull of his muscles filled the consciousness of the beast and, at least for a while, kept out the dreadful hungers.

Then in mid-bound the wolf tensed and jammed to a stop. A sound from far away in the forest stabbed into the animal's brain. He froze, slowly turning the great head this way and that, sampling the air, listening.

The sound came again, a high-pitched wail of unearthly beauty. The howling. It spoke to the pale wolf, called to him. No steel-jawed trap could have kept the pale wolf that night from the one that howled.

The beast raised his muzzle to the night sky and gave his own answering call. Then with an unerring sense of direction he wheeled and ran back through the night.

It was in the same clearing where Roy Beatty had left his clothes that the pale wolf found her. A lithe she-wolf with sleek fur blacker than the shadows of the night. Her eyes reflected the pale moon in twin green sparks. Her lips drew back from the sharp strong teeth and the she-wolf gave a soft, taunting growl.

The nostrils of the pale wolf distended, filled with the wild, musky scent of the female. He stopped in front of her, feet braced wide, neck fur bristling, and gave an answering growl, low and harsh. The she-wolf twitched her tail and moved away from him in slow, sidling steps.

He sprang at her, but the wolf bitch leaped nimbly aside and he came down on empty grass. The green eyes of the female burned into the darker eyes of the male. Roy Beatty the man had never known such overwhelming lust as now consumed the pale wolf. Again he lunged for the bitch, and again she sidestepped just enough to elude him.

The animal mind of the pale wolf understood the game then. He feinted another leap and the she-wolf moved to one side. Instantly he changed direction and sprang upon her. Their legs became entangled and they rolled together on the grassy carpet of the clearing. Their flashing teeth caught each other wherever there was loose flesh. They bit hard enough to hurt, but not to injure.

Abruptly the she-wolf broke off the mock battle and moved a short distance away. She turned and looked over her shoulder, offering herself to him. The pale wolf was on her in an instant, and took her with cruel animal haste. The climax was sudden and explosive. For a moment the two wolves stood locked together. Then the bitch pulled free and sank to her side. The male wolf dropped beside her, his tongue lolling, his ribcage working like a bellows.

At last they both lay quiet. The male told in soft growls and whines of the other hunger that was still unsatisfied. The female answered him in murmurs that said, *Soon.*

As the moon sank behind a ridge of mountains, the black she-wolf rose suddenly and slipped into the forest. Without a sound she was gone. The big pale wolf got unsteadily to his feet. The animal mind was becoming confused. Images faded and broke up, human and bestial thoughts intermingled.

The wolf's muscles twitched and jerked convulsively.

Its eyes rolled wildly. With its graceful movements turned awkward, the wolf staggered toward the untidy pile of Roy Beatty's clothes.

23

The black night sky was smudged with charcoal at the eastern rim of mountains when Roy Beatty came back to the house. He let himself in and walked straight to the bedroom. In the bed Karyn slept uneasily. Or pretended to sleep. To Roy it made no difference now.

He was deadly tired, but he did not want to get into the bed without bathing. He had to get the dirt of the forest off him. And the smell of the she-wolf.

He cleansed himself under the shower and came back into the bedroom, not even bothering to be quiet. Karyn's eyes were open, staring at the ceiling. She did not speak.

Roy crawled in beside her and dropped instantly into a dreamless sleep.

He slept the day through. When he finally awoke in the evening, his mind was clear, but oddly out of synchronization. Karyn was in the living room when he went out. She made no attempt to speak to him, for which he was thankful. He wanted no intimacies now, physical or verbal, with his wife.

As it grew darker outside the night called to him. He fought against the call as best he could. The portion of his mind that was still Roy Beatty cried out its warning, but its voice was small and far away. Still he made an effort. He built the fire high and sat before it shivering as he fought to stay where he was. And what he was.

Perspiration soaked through his clothes. Every bone in his body ached. The night forest called out to him, and finally it would not be denied. He could not even wait until Karyn was in bed. The hunger was in him and there was no resisting.

He sprang to his feet. He looked at Karyn, and for a brief second his face mirrored the agony of his soul. Then he ran out the door and was lost in the night.

Inez Polk sat alone in her tidy little house in Pinyon. She was surrounded by her books of werewolf lore and the yellowed clippings she had saved for years. The glasses kept slipping down her long thin nose as she bent over the maple desk.

In the two days since she had driven away from Karyn Beatty, Inez had kept herself constantly busy. At school she had volunteered to take the classes of a sixth-grade teacher who was ill. At home she had read over and over these volumes that she already knew so well.

At first her purpose had been self-prescribed therapy to keep her from thinking about Karyn, about what almost happened to her. By total concentration on her reading and note taking, she had been able to fall exhausted into bed sometime after midnight the night before.

Tonight, however, as she carefully read and reread the several versions of the legend of Dradja, something began to tug at her mind. Thoughts of sleep were forgotten as the adrenalin of discovery began to flow.

The people of the old village of Dradja, even when subjected to unspeakable tortures, refused to give up one of their number to the mob.

Why?

Again and again Inez read the words before her. Like a cold draft from an open winter window the truth swept upon her. She knew at last the secret of Dradja. And the secret of Drago.

"God forgive me," she said aloud. "We were such fools to ask, 'Who in the village is the werewolf?'"

Without bothering to put her books away, Inez hurried to the closet to get her coat. She rushed out of the house and got into her car, firing the engine with an impatient twist of the key. If she was too late, if anything had happened to Karyn...

Inez did not let herself complete the thought. She gave her full concentration to driving. Soon the lights of Pinyon were behind her and she was on the road leading to Drago.

Overhead, ragged clouds slid across the moon. The night was alive with shadows. Just beyond the swash of light from the headlamps a hundred pairs of eyes seemed to watch. Inez gripped the wheel harder and drove grimly on.

The main street of Drago was empty and dark. Inez slowed the car as she neared Karyn's turnoff. At the entrance to the rutted lane she braked and turned off the blacktop. She had gone only a few yards when the headlights picked out something moving at the side of the road up ahead. Inez tensed as the cold hand of fear came down on her back. The brush parted and a figure stepped out into the road. A man. He raised his hands toward the oncoming car, commanding her to stop.

"No you don't," Inez said through clenched teeth. "You will not stop me."

She drove on. The man in the road did not move.

"I'll run you down," she said aloud. "I know what you are, and I'll run you down before I let you at me."

The muscles of her arms corded with the effort of holding the wheel straight. She steeled herself for the coming impact. At the last moment she recognized the man standing in front of her, and hit the brake pedal.

Roy Beatty.

The car lurched to a stop not an arm's length from Roy, who stood his ground without flinching. Inez let her head sag forward against the steering wheel. For a moment she was faint with relief. Now she was not alone.

Then she realized there must be something wrong at the house for Roy to be standing out here. She reached across to unlock the door on the passenger's side. Not until the door started to swing open did she realize that the face outside in the dark was not Roy Beatty's. It was not the face of any human being.

Inez Polk screamed just once, then the beast ripped out her throat. There was hardly any pain, just a bubbling sensation of drowning in something hot, and then it was over.

The engine of the Valiant continued to idle softly. The only other sound was the crunch of bone as the pale wolf fed its hunger.

24

Karyn lay on her side with her back to Roy. This was the second night he had slipped out of the house late and not returned until sometime before dawn. Unanswered questions tumbled through Karyn's mind, but she could not find the voice to ask them.

Although they were not touching, Karyn felt a strangeness about Roy's body as he lay next to her. A subtle difference that she sensed rather than saw. Ever since the morning she had found him lying outside the door something had been working on him. In these few days a stranger had moved in and taken the place of her husband.

Roy had always been a gentle man, understanding and compassionate. Now, Karyn sensed a roiling violence that might erupt at any time.

He was sleeping now. A heavy, unmoving sleep. Karyn raised up in the bed to look at him It was the same square, innocent face, the same pale-blond hair and light powdery eyelashes. The broad chest and the powerful shoulders, bare now above the sheet, were unchanged. And yet there was something. Even asleep, the man had an aura of danger.

Karyn lay back down on her side of the bed and stared at the window. She had to leave this place without delay. With Roy if he would agree to go, without him otherwise. One way or another she had to get away from here.

If Roy was difficult, she would need help from someone else. A friend. Oriole? Dr. Volkmann? No, they were too much a part of Drago. She could never explain to them why.

Inez Polk. Inez knew what was happening here. She would help. If nothing else, Karyn could stay with her in Pinyon until it could be arranged for someone to come from Los Angeles. With the decision made, Karyn relaxed. She moved well away from the inert form of her husband and, as the dawn broke, lapsed into a shallow sleep.

When they got up later in the morning Roy was full of energy. His face had lost its pale look of recent days and had a ruddy glow. He was in high spirits. Too high. Almost manic.

He threw open the window and stood naked before it, breathing deeply. "Just smell that air. Better than wine."

Karyn watched him carefully. "What shall we have for breakfast?"

"You have whatever you want. I don't need any breakfast. The beautiful day is my breakfast. The trees, the sky, the song of the birds."

Karyn tried to smile. "That's very poetic, but not awfully nourishing. Seriously, what would you like to eat?"

Without warning his mood darkened. "Nothing. Isn't that what I said? I'm not hungry."

"Roy, we've got to talk."

"Go ahead. I'm listening."

"This place is destroying us."

"That's ridiculous. I've never felt better."

"You said we would leave Drago in a week."

"Did I?"

"Yes, you did. But I don't think a week is soon enough."

"What's the matter? There's no great hurry, is there?"

"I think there is. I want us to go now."

He turned to face her squarely. "That sounds like an order."

"I can't help what it sounds like. I will not stay in this valley any longer."

"What if I refuse to go?"

Karyn caught her breath, but answered in a clear, firm voice. "In that case, Roy, I'll go without you."

A shadow of hurt darkened his eyes for just an instant.

"This is not some crazy whim," Karyn went on. "I have good reasons—"

"I don't want to hear your reasons," Roy spat out. "If you're going to come at me with orders and ultimatums, you can forget it." His face hardened into a mask Karyn did not know.

"I'm going to town," she said. She turned and went out the door without waiting for a response.

The trees moved restlessly on both sides of the narrow road. A hot desert wind was blowing, funneled into the valley through a gap in the mountains to the east. The walk to town seemed much shorter than the first time she had tried it. If nothing else, the stay in Drago had made her physically stronger.

Oriole Jolivet hurried out to meet her as she entered the store. "Hey, Karyn, did you hear what happened?"

"Can it keep for a minute, Oriole? I have an important phone call I have to make."

"Well, sure, help yourself."

Oriole's hurt feelings could be soothed later. Karyn picked up the phone and dialed Inez Polk's number in Pinyon. This was Friday, and Inez had classes only in the afternoon.

The receiver buzzed in her ear as the phone rang on the other end. Karyn waited for the five rings she usually allowed, then five more. No answer. Maybe Inez had gone to school early. Karyn hung up.

"Nobody home?" Oriole asked.

"Apparently not."

Karyn leafed through the telephone book, looking for the number of the school.

"You weren't trying to call that friend of yours from over in Pinyon, that Inez, were you?"

Something in Oriole's voice gave Karyn a chill. "Yes."

"Then you haven't heard." Oriole bit her lower lip and shook her head sadly.

"Heard what?"

"She was killed last night."

"Killed?" Karyn felt as though she had been punched in the stomach.

"Ran her car smack into a tree. It happened on the turnoff up by your place. Looks like she might have been on her way to see you."

"A car accident?" Karyn's mind wanted to reject the words. "How did it happen?"

"Hard to say. Anton Gadak thinks she must have dozed off at the wheel. It was him that found her about six o'clock this morning."

It would be Anton Gadak. "Was she dead when he found her?"

"Yep. Looked like she died instantly, Anton says."

"Where did they take her?"

"The hospital over in Pinyon, but I don't think you want to go see her. She was cut up awful bad, Anton says. Must have gone through the windshield."

Not with her seat belt fastened, and Inez' car would not start without it. Karyn closed her eyes for a moment, realizing the full horror of the situation. Inez must have learned something and have been coming to tell her about it.

The only thing that would have brought her over late at night was the identity of the Drago werewolf. Somehow the beast had got her.

Oriole came over and laid a pudgy hand on Karyn's shoulder. "I'm awful sorry, Karyn. It really hits a person when a friend dies. At least it happened fast. I knew a woman once…"

Oriole's voice droned on, but her words faded from Karyn's mind. First Roy, now Inez. One by one she was losing the few people she could call on for help. Who was left? A name jumped into her thoughts. Chris Halloran. She had forced herself not to think about Chris since the day she had so cruelly sent him away. She had thought vaguely that she would make it up to him someday. Now she had no time.

She wondered if Chris would even speak to her after her hysterical performance. But he was all she had left.

"…know how you feel, Karyn, but these things happen. Like they say, life goes on." Oriole's voice came back into her consciousness.

"Is it all right if I make a long-distance call?" Karyn said. "I'll ask the operator how much it is and pay you for it."

"Sure it's all right. Who you calling?"

"A friend. In Los Angeles."

Oriole stood her ground until Karyn made it clear by standing with her hand on the receiver that she was not going to place the call until she was left alone.

"I'll, uh, go attend to some things in the back," Oriole said.

Karyn nodded. It was too late to bother with the niceties of courtesy. When Oriole had gone she asked for the Los Angeles information operator and got from her the number of Chris's company, Western Industrial Design. She dialed the number, and a woman's voice answered with the name of the firm.

"I'd like to speak to Mr. Halloran."

"Mr. Halloran didn't come in today. Can someone else help you?"

"Do you happen to have his home phone number?"

"I'm not sure I should—"

"It's all right, I'm Mrs. Roy Beatty. My husband and I are personal friends of Mr. Halloran."

"Oh, yes, Mrs. Beatty, I've heard him mention your name. Hold on a second, I'll get the number for you."

As Karyn waited, Etienne Jolivet came in the front of the store. He nodded to her solemnly.

"Is that you, Etienne?" Oriole called from the back. "Can you come out here a minute?"

The tall man moved silently past the counter and through the door into the back room.

The girl came back on the line and gave Karyn Chris Halloran's home telephone number. Karyn memorized it, thanked the girl, and hung up. She called the operator back and asked the charges for the call. It came to $1.19. She noted the sum on the back of a brown paper bag and picked up the phone again. She dialed the Los Angeles area code and Chris's home number.

Be there, she thought. Oh, please, God, let him be there. The receiver buzzed in her ear. Halfway through the second buzz there was a click. Karyn went weak with sudden relief. She opened her mouth to say hello, but before she could frame a greeting, Chris's voice came on the line.

"Hi, this is Chris Halloran. Sorry I'm not home at the moment. What you're hearing is my answering machine. If you'll wait for the beep, then leave any message and your number, I'll get back to you as soon as I can."

Karyn wanted to sob in frustration as another hope flickered out. She started to lower the receiver back into the cradle, then the electronic tone beeped faintly. There was still the possibility that Chris was just out of the apartment for a moment. It would be foolish for her to have come this far and not even leave a message.

What could she say? How much time did these things allow for a message? Sixty seconds? Thirty? In as calm a voice as she could manage, Karyn began to speak.

"Chris, this is Karyn Beatty. I'm in trouble, and I need your help. If you hear this, please come to Drago for me. And, Chris... bring a gun."

She hesitated, knowing how crazy the rest of it would sound. She forced herself to go on. "Load the gun with silver bullets if you can. There isn't time to explain anything now, but please, oh please, Chris, believe I need you."

Gently she replaced the instrument and stood for several seconds staring down at it, wondering what effect her words would have on Chris Halloran. Wondering if he would even hear them in time.

"All through with your phone calls?"

Karyn started, then put on a smile as Oriole Jolivet came up beside her.

"Yes, I am. I'll just find out how much it was." She dialed the operator and was told that the charge was another $1.19.

"The total comes to $2.38," she told Oriole. She dipped into her change purse for two dollar bills, a quarter, dime, and nickel.

"I'll owe you the two cents," Oriole said.

"I guess I can trust you for it." Karyn tried to smile, but her face felt all wrong.

Oriole regarded her soberly. "Listen, Karyn, if there's anything I can do, anything at all, just say the word. People sometimes think I'm just a fat, silly woman. I'm more than that."

"I know you are, Oriole," Karyn said softly.

"And maybe I'm not an old friend, but I can be a good one if you'll let me. You know where to find me. You tell Roy hello for me, now, and come on back when you feel like playing some gin."

"I will," Karyn said. "And thank you, Oriole. Goodbye."

She went out of the store, and the hot desert wind pushed against her as she walked up the street. The dry heat sucked away the moisture of her skin, leaving it feeling scaly. In Los Angeles they called it the Santa Ana wind. They said it made people a little bit mad.

In the shadow of a doorway on the far side of the street—*always in the shadow*—stood Anton Gadak. His eyes were invisible under the brim of the Stetson. Karyn looked away quickly and hurried on.

When she reached the turnoff to the road that led to her house, Karyn stopped and looked around. There was no tree anywhere near the road that was big enough to smash a car. Whatever had killed Inez Polk, Karyn was sure it was not an accident.

A short distance up the narrow lane, something glittered on the ground. Karyn bent down to look, and recognized the metal frame, now twisted, and thick lenses of Inez' glasses. She slipped the ruined glasses into her pocket and started home again when something else caught her eye. At the side of the road, partly hidden by the brush, was a tennis shoe. A worn Adidas, white with blue stripes. Roy had a pair like that.

Karyn shuddered, despite the hot wind, and turned away. She walked on rapidly toward the house. In a very few hours it would be dark.

25

Chris Halloran's hopes of getting away early for a weekend of loafing in Ensenada were fading fast. He had planned to hit the border by midmorning, but here it was afternoon and he hadn't left yet. His mistake had been to drop in on one of the clients of his engineering firm to see how a new tool design concept was working out. There were problems. Nothing serious, but as long as Chris was on the scene he could hardly refuse to have a look. By the time he finished it was two o'clock.

On the way home he had made one more stop at a drugstore to pick up a few small items for his traveling bag. He waited impatiently in the checkout line while everyone ahead of him, it seemed, had to cash a check written from a Hong Kong bank.

At last he pulled into the underground parking area of the Surf King Apartments. The image conjured by the name had always amused Chris. Blond young giants in deep tans and cutoffs hanging ten as they hotdogged in with the heavies. Actually, the average age of Surf King tenants was comfortably over thirty, and there weren't half a dozen of them who could stand up on a surfboard. The whole marina scene was beginning to pall on Chris. The same funky-chic people in the same overpriced bars on Friday nights, telling the same lies over the same drinks and looking for... what?

Chris shook the thought away. He was not by nature a moody young man, and he did not much like himself when he became gloomy. That was the main reason for spending a weekend in Baja. He would go down by himself, get a small, comfortable hotel room, drink a little tequila, maybe do a little fishing. Or maybe just loaf. He liked to walk among the local people on streets where the tourists didn't go. He smiled in anticipation of tortillas hot from the fire and beans and Mexican chills washed down with icy Carta Blanca. A weekend in Ensenada had always been effective therapy for Chris. He was in a hurry to be on his way.

Back in his airy two-level apartment Chris quickly packed his one small travel bag. He pulled on a comfortable old suede jacket and headed for the door. He stopped before going out to take a last look around. This was the day the cleaning lady came, so everything was shipshape—the big mirror polished, the ash trays gleaming, magazines fanned on the coffee table, cushions geometrically arranged on the three-piece sectional sofa. Chris walked over and pushed the magazines into an untidy stack. When he came back he did not want to feel he was walking into a setting for *Home* magazine.

He started out the door again, but once more he hesitated. Should he play back the morning telephone calls? What if there was one from his office with some problem or other that would mean further delay? He could ignore the message, of course, but it would bother him all the time he was in Baja. If he never heard the message, he wouldn't feel guilty. And who else but the office would call on a Friday morning?

No, he could not ignore it. Now that the thought had occurred to him, he would have to play the tape. It shouldn't take long, and then he could leave with a clear conscience. He walked back into the apartment, dropped onto one end of the sofa, and switched on the machine to play back the taped telephone calls.

The beep sounded, there was a short silence, then a male voice said, "Oh, the hell with it." A hollow click followed, and the rest of the allotted thirty seconds was dial tone. Many people, Chris had found, refused to talk to a machine. He didn't much blame them.

The machine beeped again. Karyn Beatty's voice came over the tiny speaker, and Chris sat suddenly upright. He was so surprised to hear her voice that the first time through the message did not fully register. Something about being in trouble and a gun and silver bullets. He rewound the tape and played it through a second time, listening carefully.

It was not a joke. There was no mistaking the urgency in Karyn's voice, and she was not the type to play this kind of a joke, anyway. But the message... *Load the gun with silver bullets...* It was crazy.

Chris played back the thirty seconds of Karyn a third time, trying to pick up any kind of clue or hidden meaning. As far as he could tell, there was none. He had to assume that she meant exactly what she said. But, *silver bullets?*

He played out the rest of the tape to see if there was anything more from Karyn, but the only other call was a reminder from his dentist to come in for a checkup.

Chris snapped off the machine and sat for a moment frowning in thought. He would go at once to Drago, of course. It was possible that Karyn was imagining some kind of peril—she had certainly acted irrationally the last time he had seen her—but something in the way she spoke told him the danger was real.

His first impulse was to call the police. But what would he tell them? "My friend's wife is in a little town called Drago and she needs help and says to bring silver bullets." It didn't take much imagination to picture some desk sergeant's response to that. And Karyn must have reasons, or she would have called the authorities herself. He would have to go on his own.

Bring a gun. That would be no problem since he did own one: a .22-caliber Stoeger automatic patterned after the old German Luger. He had bought it a couple of years before for plinking at cans in the desert, and had not fired it since. It was not a weapon that would knock down a moose, but there was no time to get anything bigger. It would have to do.

But silver bullets? Where the hell did you go to get silver bullets?

He had to start somewhere, so he grabbed the fat Los Angeles Yellow Pages and riffled through to *Silversmiths*. He called the firm with the most impressive ad.

A young man's voice answered. "Glendenning Silver, good afternoon."

"Hello," Chris said, feeling foolish, but trying to sound businesslike. "I wonder if you do anything in the way of making bullets?"

"You said bullets?"

"That's what I said. Bullets."

"I think what you want is jewelry. We deal primarily in silverware and plating."

"I don't mean *jewelry* bullets, I mean *real* bullets. Real silver bullets."

"Perhaps you'd like to speak to our manager, Mr. Roth."

"I don't have time to play games with your manager. All I want to know is, can you or can you not make me silver bullets?"

The young man's voice went cold. "We do *not* make bullets, not gold, not silver, not any kind."

Chris slammed down the phone and swore at it. All right, silversmiths do not make bullets. Who does make bullets? Try a gunsmith. Back to the Yellow Pages. Chris picked out the K & K Gun Shop. Their ad featured a businesslike revolver and stated that their services included ammunition and reloading. He dialed the number.

"Yeah?" a gritty voice answered.

"K & K Gun Shop?"

"Yeah."

Might as well get right to it, Chris decided. "Can you make me some silver bullets?"

"You mean bullets made out of silver?"

Stay calm. "That's what I mean."

"Sure."

Chris stared at the phone. As easy as that.

"Bring your own silver. I don't stock that. Naturally."

"I'll bring the silver," Chris said. "Let's see, you're located at…" He read off the Vermont Avenue address from the advertisement.

"Yeah. I close at six, so if you're coming in today you better hurry it up."

"Yes, it has to be today." Chris checked his watch. Jesus, could it be after four already? "I'll try to make it by six, but wait for me if I'm a little late, will you? I'll pay you for any overtime."

"This ain't a joke, is it?"

"It's no joke."

"Okay, but be here as soon as you can."

"I will."

Chris hung up and turned quickly back to the Yellow Pages.

Silver Bullion—See Coin Dlrs. 547

He flipped the pages quickly and found the Excelsior Coin Co., Gold—Silver––Platinum Coins & Bars Bought & Sold. The address was on Venice Boulevard in Culver City. There was no need to bother with another telephone call. He could save the time by heading straight over there.

Chris started out the door on the run, then snapped his fingers and turned back. He went into the bedroom and reached up to the high closet shelf for the Stoeger .22. He checked the magazine and chamber to be sure it was empty, then pulled the trigger to test the action. The pistol gave a sharp, satisfying click. He dropped it into a jacket pocket and hurried out to his car.

It was twenty minutes to five when he pulled into the lot beside the Excelsior Coin Company. The sun was low in the west and turning an angry red. Chris jumped from the car and ran into the building. A clerk looked at him in surprise from behind the counter.

"I want to buy some silver," Chris said.

"Yes, sir. Coins or bars?"

"Bars, I think."

"In what quantity?"

"What sizes do they come in?"

"Most of our bullion transactions are in five-ounce and ten-ounce bars. For anything larger we'd have to—"

"Those should be large enough. Can I see what they look like?"

"Certainly." The clerk stepped to the rear of the store and returned in a minute with two ingots of pure silver in the shape of tiny Hershey bars.

Chris hefted them, one in each hand. How much silver did it take to make a bullet? He said, "How much for the ten-ounce bar?"

"A single bar is sixty dollars, but if you intend to purchase in volume—"

"One will be enough."

Chris walked over to the cash register to discourage further conversation. He paid for the ingot with his Master Charge card and took it back out to the car.

The Santa Monica Freeway was clotted with rush hour traffic. Chris pounded the steering wheel in frustration as all lanes jerked along in an angry dance of flashing taillights.

The sky was dark when Chris finally turned off the freeway at the Vermont Avenue exit. The surface street traffic was lighter, and he reached the K & K Gun Shop in a few minutes.

The inside of the shop smelled of cosmoline, wood polish, and leather. The walls were lined with rifles and shotguns. In a heavy glass case were handguns ranging from tiny Derringers to a cannon-sized .44 magnum. In the back of the shop a chunky man in a t-shirt worked a piece of metal on a lathe.

"Hello," Chris said. "I called you earlier."

The man turned off the lathe and looked up. "Oh, yeah, the silver bullets."

"That's it."

The gunsmith came around the counter and locked the front door. "Might as well close up," he said. "Won't be no more customers tonight." He pulled an expanding steel lattice across the show window and locked it into place. "Hell of a neighborhood for a gun shop. Did you bring the silver?"

Chris fished the ingot out of his pocket.

"Uh-huh. What caliber bullets you want?" Chris showed him the Stoeger. "To fit this."

"Twenty-two Long Rifle," said the gunsmith.

"How many?"

Chris had not thought about it. The magazine of the Stoeger held eleven. And one in the chamber. Surely that would be enough.

"Twelve," he said.

"Jeez, you brought enough metal."

"Well, use whatever you need."

"Come on in the back."

Chris followed the gunsmith into the workroom and watched as he shaved off what looked like very little of the silver bar and put the shavings in a crucible.

"Is that enough?" Chris asked.

"Hell, yes. A .22 Long Rifle slug only weighs forty grams."

The gunsmith placed the crucible over a gas flame and turned to a shelf behind him to select a mold.

"How hot does it have to get to melt the silver?" Chris asked.

"Nine hundred and sixty point five degrees Centigrade," the man said without turning around.

"You know that by heart?"

The man turned to face him. "Look, buddy, I didn't go to no fancy college and I don't read a whole lot of books, but guns and ammunition are my business. I'd be a piss-poor gunsmith if I didn't know the melting point of metals."

"Hey, no offense," Chris said. "I'm impressed, that's all."

The gunsmith relaxed into a grin. "Don't mind me, I've had a long week." He stuck out a big hand. "My name's Buzz Klinger. Call me Buzz."

Chris took the offered hand. "Glad to know you, Buzz. I'm Chris Halloran."

Klinger returned to his work and went about it with the smooth economy of motion that comes with true craftsmanship. Chris stayed out of the way and watched. When the silver shavings had melted, Klinger poured the molten metal into the molds, filling twelve of them exactly.

"You want regular load or high-power in the cartridges?"

"Better make it high-power." It occurred to Chris that Buzz Klinger had not asked what he wanted with silver bullets. His respect for the man increased.

When the silver had cooled in the molds, Klinger mated the twelve slugs to the loaded cartridges and handed them to Chris along with the unused portion of the silver ingot.

"What do I owe you?" Chris said, "Ten bucks will cover it."

"How about your overtime?"

"I figured that in already."

Chris peeled off a bill and handed it to Klinger.

"Thanks, Buzz. It was a pleasure watching you work." Klinger unlocked the front door and Chris started out.

"Hey," the gunsmith called as Chris started down the sidewalk.

Chris turned back.

"Give my regards to Tonto."

26

The little house was empty when Karyn returned after her call to Chris Halloran. In a way, she thought, it was just as well that Roy was not there. He had been so strange lately that it was difficult for her to be around him. The prospect of being alone tonight was not pleasant, but it would be the last night she would spend in Drago.

She locked the front and back doors and all the windows, making sure the heavy screens on the outside were secure. While she was in the bedroom, Karyn went to the closet and looked through the pairs of shoes, hers and Roy's, on the floor. She found one of Roy's white-and-blue Adidas. Just one. No time to dwell on the implications of that now. Roy would have an explanation when he came home.

Moving to the hall closet, she took out the shotgun. She loaded the weapon and propped it up beside the front door. Against the thing she feared was out there, the shotgun was almost useless, but it was better than nothing.

Karyn sat down and directed her thoughts to Chris Halloran. Would he come for her? She tried to remember exactly what she had said into the recorder but the words would not come. She could only hope that it would not sound too crazy when Chris played it back.

If he played it back. Karyn knew she could not count on Chris or anyone else to help her tonight. She had only herself.

With a suddenness that shocked her, the sun dropped behind the mountains and darkness claimed the valley. Karyn turned on every light in the house. She flicked the switch for the outdoor light that illuminated the clearing in front. Nothing happened. A hell of a time, she thought, for the bulb to burn out. She took a good bulb from one of the lamps and opened the door to put it in the outside fixture. Then she saw it was not a burned-out bulb. The old bulb had been smashed, and the metal socket battered out of shape, making it impossible to screw in another bulb. Karyn slammed the door and leaned against it, breathing hard. After a minute she returned the good bulb to the lamp and lit a fire in the fireplace.

The blank windows, with nothing but the night outside, seemed to Karyn like inward-staring opaque eyes. She drew curtains over the glass.

She went into the kitchen and put on a pot of coffee, making it twice as strong as she usually did. There would be no sleep tonight. On the counter she found a carton of Roy's cigarettes. She lit one and pulled in the smoke hungrily.

Soon Karyn found she could not stand it with the curtains closed. Her imagination populated the night with worse horrors than could possibly be there. The moon had come out, so at least she could see a little in the front of the house. The desert wind had not subsided at nightfall, and the boughs of the surrounding trees moved restlessly.

To keep her mind active Karyn thought about what she would do the next day. Whether Roy came back or not, one way or another she would leave this cursed town. Consider the possibilities. Call from Drago for a taxi to come in from Los Angeles and get her, and damn the expense. If an L.A. taxi would not make the trip, try Pinyon.

They must have some sort of taxi service there.

If she couldn't get a taxi, she would go out on the road and hitchhike. Take the first ride offered in either direction just to get away from Drago.

If there were no other way, she would take Roy's car and somehow drive the damn thing. She only had to go far enough to get away from Drago. And what did it matter if she damaged the car? It would be a small price to pay for escape.

Satisfied with this plan, Karyn went into the bedroom and searched through Roy's things until she found the spare set of keys. She tucked them into a pocket and felt better, as though she were already on her way.

Back in the living room the fire had dwindled. Karyn put on another log and jostled the coals with the poker. New flames sprang up and crackled reassuringly.

"Karyn!"

The unexpected sound of her name startled her into dropping the poker. Someone, a man, had called from outside the house. Could it be Chris? But she had heard no car drive up.

She crossed quickly to the window. Roy's Ford was there, gleaming dully in the moonlight. That was all.

"Karyn!"

This time she recognized the voice. Roy. Calling her from somewhere outside. Why not at the door?

"Karyn!"

There was a throb of pain in the voice. Pain and something more.

From the edge of the window, standing close to the wall, she looked out to make sure the doorway was clear. From the bookshelf, where Roy had left it, she took the flashlight. Holding it in one hand, she eased the door open just enough to look out.

"Roy, are you out there?"

"Help me, Karyn."

"Where are you? I can't see you."

"Over here. Come and help me."

Opening the door a little wider, Karyn swept the brush beyond the clearing with the beam from the flashlight. She moved the light along slowly until it picked out a face, pale against the shadows. Roy's face.

He was standing partially hidden by a clump of chaparral, looking at her. His expression was tortured. He seemed to strain toward her against invisible bonds.

Karyn stepped halfway through the doorway. "What is it, Roy? What's wrong?"

"Oh, Karyn." His voice was a strangled whisper.

He needed her, and for a moment everything else was forgotten. Karyn left the safety of the house and ran across the clearing toward her husband.

"No." The single word was ripped from Roy's throat, then he vanished back into the shadows.

Karyn turned to run back to the house, then she froze. Standing between her and the door, its shoulders humped, the cruel mouth stretched into a canine grin, was the wolf. The beast's jaws opened and closed. It growled, a sound of unearthly evil.

Karyn could not get her breath. She stood paralyzed as the wolf came toward her stiff-legged, its eyes never leaving her face.

"Run, Karyn!"

The voice that shouted at her from somewhere back in the trees was like Roy's, and yet it was not like his. The sharp command freed her to move again. With the wolf between her and the house, Karyn turned to run in the other direction. Even as she broke away she felt the futility of trying to outrun the beast.

Abruptly the car was in front of her. Roy's Ford, only a few yards away. Karyn lunged the last few steps, jerked the door open, and fell inside. As she pulled the door closed behind her, the heavy body of the wolf thumped against the outside panel.

Karyn grasped the steering wheel and pulled herself upright. Through the window she saw the wolf up on its hind feet, paws braced against the car, biting at the door handle. Karyn punched the lock button down with her fist, then made sure the other doors were locked too. She slid to the far side of the seat and cowered there. The wolf, with its forepaws against the roof, glared in at her with a deeper hatred than Karyn would have believed possible on the face of a living creature.

A fogged patch grew and contracted on the window as the wolf breathed against the glass. Karyn could not pull her eyes away from its face. She pressed herself back against the far door.

Abruptly the wolf's head dropped out of sight. Karyn heard the rhythmic pad of its feet trotting away. Was it leaving? Karyn held her breath, not daring to hope.

There was silence for a moment, then a soft galloping sound and a jarring thud as the animal hit the side of the car. The Ford rocked with the impact. Karyn pulled herself up in the seat and saw the wolf gather itself and walk back to charge again. It turned ten yards away, crouched, and sprang forward like a greyhound after a rabbit. Six feet from the car the wolf leaped into the air and hit the door again with stunning force.

A spider-web of cracks appeared on the window next to the driver's seat, and flecks of glass sprinkled the seat. In the fragmented view through the cracked window Karyn saw the wolf pick itself up and move away for another run. She knew there was no way to keep it out, and wondered if this was how Inez Polk had met her death.

A third time the wolf smashed into the side of the Ford. The damaged window shattered and big chunks of glass fell away from the plastic core. It could not withstand many more blows.

Karyn jabbed a hand into her pocket and her fingers closed around the leather case that held the car keys. She brushed the glass fragments from the seat and moved over behind the wheel, stabbing the key at the ignition lock on the side of the steering post.

Thump!

More glass sprayed across the inside of the car, and the plastic window core bulged inward. Karyn saw that her arm was bleeding, but paid no attention.

She found the ignition lock and twisted the key. The starter ground, the engine coughed and finally came to life. While she deliberately did not look at the wolf, Karyn struggled to remember the motions Roy went through in driving the car. She pressed down on the accelerator pedal and yanked the shift lever from P to R. The car lurched backward across the roadway and rammed into the brush on the far side. She knocked the shift lever back to P and fought to control her shaking hands.

She groped for the headlight switch, but could not find it. Outside in the moonlight she could see the wolf moving toward her. Forgetting the headlights, she cranked the steering wheel around to head toward town, stamped down on the accelerator, and forced the shift lever through the detents until the car jolted forward. The wolf sprang out of the way and vanished in the shadows as Karyn fought the wheel, fishtailing the car from one side of the narrow road to the other.

With only the moonlight to guide her, Karyn could barely make out the road. Tree branches slashed against the windshield as she veered from left to right and back again. She kept her foot heavy on the accelerator and battled to keep from plowing into the trees.

Without warning she hit the blacktop road that led into Drago. Traveling too fast to make the corner, Karyn stamped on the brake, but too late. With tires screaming, the Ford slid across the road and dived crazily into a drainage ditch on the far side.

The engine died. Karyn started to reach for the ignition key, but she saw by the steep angle of the car that it would be futile to try to drive. She clawed open the door. The rest of the window fell out.

The cold wind whipped her hair into a tangle as she struggled up the side of the ditch onto the road. She looked up the lane toward the house, but saw nothing coming after her. Yet.

She started off at a run toward the village. She did not look back.

No light showed in the dreary buildings of Drago. The streets were deserted. Karyn crossed the short street where Dr. Volkmann lived. His house was dark, like the others. The Buick was not in the driveway. No sanctuary there.

On down the street she ran. The only sounds were the wind and the slap of her shoes on the pavement. Panic controlled her. She had no destination; she only knew that somewhere behind her it was coming.

Then there was a light. A blessed light up ahead in the store building. Safety. When she reached the door Karyn was sobbing with relief. She beat against the panel with the flat of her hand.

Oriole Jolivet opened up and peered through the doorway, her face a round caricature of surprise. "Karyn, what in the world are you doing here?"

"Let me in," Karyn gasped. The breath tore at her lungs. Her side hurt like a knife wound from running.

Oriole put an arm around Karyn and supported her as they walked back to the rear of the store. There was the light Karyn had seen from the street.

"Don't try to talk now, honey," Oriole said. "Just sit yourself down here until you get your wind back." Karyn sank gratefully into the wooden chair and let her head sink forward. Oriole stood by stroking her hair and making little clucking sounds of sympathy.

After many minutes Karyn's breathing slowed, though the pulse still pounded in her ears. "Thank God you were here, Oriole," she said.

"Sure, I'm here, honey." Oriole patted her shoulder awkwardly. "What happened to you?"

"Give me a little time, okay? I'm not quite ready to talk about it."

"Hey, I understand. How about a nice cup of hot coffee to perk you up?"

"I'd like that."

As Oriole went in back, slowly Karyn's nerves began to unknot. Her mind was still not ready to think about what had happened, but her body was beginning to relax.

Oriole returned with a mug of steaming coffee. "There you go. Don't drink it too fast, it's real hot."

As Karyn reached for the cup, Oriole saw the cut on her arm. "Oh, look at that, you hurt yourself."

"It was glass. From the car window."

"You smashed up your car?"

Karyn nodded.

"You poor kid, no wonder you're shook up. Let me get something to put on that arm."

Oriole walked around behind Karyn's chair and rummaged in a cupboard. "There should be iodine in here, and I'll get bandages out of the stock up front."

The muffled sound of Oriole's last words made Karyn turn around in her chair. To her surprise, Oriole was pulling her sweater off over her head. She wore nothing underneath.

"What are you doing?" Karyn said.

Then Oriole pulled the sweater free, and Karyn saw what was happening to the woman's face. Oriole smiled, and the blackened lips pulled back over a double row of sharp yellow teeth.

27

Karyn sat stunned as Oriole Jolivet, or the thing that had been Oriole, continued to peel off clothing. Oriole's mouth and nose had pushed forward into a muzzle, and her skin was now covered with coarse reddish hair. Acting by instinct rather than will, Karyn leaped to her feet and threw the cup of steaming coffee into the creature's face. Hearing a howl of pain, she ran out through the store to the front door.

Once she was outside Karyn stopped. She tuned one way, then the other. Where could she go? Was there safety anywhere in this terrible night? With tears dimming her vision, Karyn began to run up the street. The darkened buildings of Drago seemed to crowd in on her from both sides.

Something was coming.

Karyn stopped and wiped her eyes. Moving silently toward her down the middle of the street, eyes glittering in the moonlight, came a wolf.

"Oh, God, another one," Karyn cried. She turned back in the direction she had come from and was almost run down as a car slammed to a stop inches away from her. Karyn dropped to her knees sobbing. The door of the old Buick opened and Dr. Volkmann jumped out. He ran around to the front of the car.

"Mrs. Beatty, what is it? What's wrong?"

She clutched at the doctor's coat and pulled herself erect. "Dr. Volkmann... help me... the wolves..."

Volkmann put an arm around Karyn and helped her into the car. He got in himself and sat behind the wheel with the engine idling. He watched Karyn carefully as she fought for composure.

"Oriole," she got out at last. "While I was with her just now she... changed."

"Are you saying Oriole Jolivet is a werewolf?" Volkmann's voice was calm and reassuring.

"Yes. And she's not the only one."

Something banged against the car, and for an instant the savage face of a wolf appeared at the window behind Volkmann. Karyn jerked away, but on her own side there was another, and more coming now from the dark buildings. One of them hit her window with its paws. Karyn ducked away and the side of her head cracked into the steering wheel. There was a flash of pain, and everything slipped out of focus.

Karyn's next sensation was one of floating. She was riding along on a gently flowing river. But there was danger. She had to swim to shore. She tried to move, but something held her fast. Suddenly awake, she thrashed wildly to free her arms and legs.

"It's all right." The voice of Dr. Volkmann was deep and commanding. "You're home now."

She was being carried, Karyn now saw, in Volkmann's arms. He was walking toward the little house, where the lights still blazed as she had left them.

"No." she cried. "They're here too. The wolves."

Volkmann stopped and swung her feet down to the ground. He steadied her as she tried to stand. Her head hurt and she staggered against him.

"You say they're here?" Volkmann said.

"Yes. One came at me, but I got away in the car. I went into a ditch, then ran into town looking for some place to be safe. I found Oriole, and she..." Karyn could not complete the sentence. "We've got to get away."

The two of them turned back and started toward the Buick. Before they could get close, a lean black wolf slipped out of the forest and moved between them and the car. The wolf was joined by a second. Then a third.

"We'll never make it," Volkmann said. He spun Karyn back toward the house and they ran across the clearing to the door. Volkmann pushed it open and they stumbled inside. He slammed the door behind them and Karyn shot the bolt into place.

They stood for a moment watching the door as though expecting it to burst open.

"What about the back door and the windows?" Volkmann said.

"I locked everything before."

"Where is your husband?"

There it was, the thing Karyn had refused to think about. Part of her must have known when she found Roy's shoe near the place where Inez had died, but she would not let herself admit it. When he called her out of the house, she had gone, and they were waiting for her. She had lost him.

She said, "I think Roy is one of them."

Volkmann frowned and shook his head.

"I don't know how it could have happened," Karyn said.

"It must have been the night he did not come home," said Volkmann. "If he was attacked by a werewolf and lived…"

"But he had no wounds."

"None that showed, but remember the blood on his shirt."

Karyn turned away. She was not ready to talk about Roy. She went into the kitchen and ran a glass of cold water. Through the small window over the sink she saw more wolves coming out of the shadows.

"They're all around us," she said.

"We'll be safe inside the house."

"They broke the window of the car. They can get in."

Volkmann looked over to where the shotgun was propped against the wall.

Following his eyes, Karyn said, "That can't stop them."

Perhaps it will slow them down."

"Can we make a run for the car?"

Volkmann peered out the front window, then turned back, his face grim. "Take a look."

Karyn moved closer to the window. What she saw froze her blood. The grassy clearing in front of the house was alive with wolves. Different shapes and shades, but all of them large and deadly looking. Occasionally one of them or another would make a menacing move toward the house, but mostly they just shifted restlessly about, watching the house. Waiting.

Karyn backed away from the window, hugging herself for warmth. She spoke in a toneless voice, barely above a whisper. "Oh, the time we wasted wondering who in Drago was the werewolf. It isn't just one of them, it's the whole town. Inez must have realized that somehow. She was coming to warn me when they got her."

Volkmann continued to stare at the animals outside.

"It's the legend of Dradja," Karyn said. "The people would not give up their werewolf even under torture because the werewolf was all of them. When the village was destroyed some of them escaped. These things outside are their children."

"Incredible," Dr. Volkmann muttered.

"You've lived in Drago for years," Karyn said. "Did you never suspect?"

The doctor spoke without turning from the window. "I'm afraid I kept apart from the people of the town. Who could imagine a thing like this?"

Outside, the night sounds changed. Under the sighing of the wind there was a growing rustle of movement. A series of heavy blows thudded against the door, rattling dishes in the kitchen cupboards. A wolf crashed against one of the window screens and rebounded. Another hit a window on the opposite side.

Karyn and Dr. Volkmann looked at each other.

She said quietly, "They're coming for us."

* * *

The red Camaro hit the crest of the hill to the west of Drago and plunged down the winding road into the dark valley. At the wheel a grim Chris Halloran fought to keep the car on the road without slackening his speed. The gun loaded with silver bullets hung heavy but reassuring in his jacket pocket.

At last he reached the valley floor and the road straightened for the short drive to the village. As he entered Drago, Chris wondered why there were no lights. He slowed the car passing the dark buildings, looking for signs of life. He saw no one. Then what appeared to be a large dog showed up in the headlights. Chris hit the brake pedal and the car slowed to a stop. The animal never flinched, just stood there looking at him.

Now he saw it was not a dog. It was too big, and the eyes were not right. A wolf.

He started to ease the car around the animal, and a movement at the side of the street caught his eye. Another wolf was coming toward him. No, there were two of them. With a growing sense of alarm Chris looked along the street and saw half a dozen more of the shadowy forms. These were no common wolves.

He gunned the engine and wheeled the Camaro straight at the wolf that stood ahead of him. He tensed for the coming impact, but at the last instant the wolf sprang aside and the car roared past.

When he reached the turnoff to Karyn's house, Chris saw the rear end of a car jutting up from a drainage ditch across the road. He steered in that direction to let his headlights fall on the ditched car. A Ford. Roy Beatty's Ford.

Chris pulled the Camaro off on the shoulder and started to get out. He had one foot on the ground when a snarling beast charged him from the ditch. He pushed himself back inside and slammed the door just as the wolf hit the car.

His first thought was the gun. He drew the pistol from his pocket, then hesitated. He still had to reach Karyn. He could see there was no one in the Ford, so she must be at the house. He had only the twelve bullets, and from what he had seen so far he might need all of them.

* * *

Inside the house Karyn stood with her back to the inner wall next to the fireplace. She held the shotgun leveled at the door, in which two vertical cracks had opened under the constant battering from outside. She knew the gun was no defense, but it was better than waiting passively for... whatever.

On the other side of the fireplace, Dr. Volkmann stood watching intently as the cracks in the door widened with each blow. He had not spoken for several minutes. Nor had Karyn. There was nothing to be said.

Then, over the banging at the door and the rush of the wind, Karyn heard a new sound. The high-pitched whine of a straining engine. A car was coming. Coming fast. With a cry she dropped the gun and ran to the window. Bright white headlights washed across the clearing and the wolves.

"It's Chris," she cried. "Dr. Volkmann, it's my friend. He'll help us."

Outside the Camaro plowed into the wolves, scattering them for a moment, and jolted to a stop behind the Buick.

"Dr. Volkmann, did you hear me? We're going to be all right."

Karyn turned to where the doctor was standing, but he was no longer there. His clothes lay on the floor. She started for the fallen shotgun, but a lean gray wolf sprang from the side of the room and stood between her and the weapon.

"Oh my God," Karyn gasped. "You too."

The wolf came at her.

28

The pack of ravening wolves around Karyn's house was like a preview of hell. Chris Halloran aimed the Camaro at two of the animals nearest the roadway and drove into them. He felt the sick soft thump as the wolves went down under the wheels. They should have been crushed. Looking back, Chris saw the two animals lie still for a moment, then get back to their feet in jerky movements. Their eyes blazed with wild hatred.

Now he knew for certain what they were. His rational twentieth-century mind had rejected the word, but it had been on the edge of his consciousness from the time he had played the tape and heard Karyn ask for silver bullets.

Werewolves.

He pulled up behind an old Buick that blocked his path to the house. Someone appeared for a moment at one of the windows. It might have been Karyn. Chris calculated his chances of reaching the house on foot. Between him and the door were more wolves than he could count. Right now they seemed indecisive, their attention divided between him and the house.

Chris took the gun from his pocket and stepped out of the car. The wolves watched him intently, but made no move. He started walking carefully toward the house. At the same time from inside came a loud growl. As though it were some kind of signal, the wolves came for him.

Chris took quick aim with the pistol and fired at the nearest animal. The sound was a disappointing little pop, and Chris longed for a heavier-caliber weapon. A puff of dust kicked up a foot in front of the wolf. He had missed. At pointblank range. One precious bullet gone.

For his second shot Chris steadied his right hand with his left, the way pistol shooting was taught. He aimed carefully at a point between the eyes and fired. A round black hole appeared magically in the short fur of the wolf's head. The animal's legs stiffened for a moment, then buckled, and it fell, the eyes open and empty.

The other wolves drew back for a moment, then came together in a mass between Chris and the door. Holding the gun straight out in front of him, he advanced cautiously. Off to one side, a lone pale wolf bounded from the forest and charged the house. Oblivious to both the man and the other animals, it crossed the clearing in powerful leaps and sprang for the window, forepaws outstretched to take the impact. The screen collapsed inward, the window glass shattered, and the pale wolf disappeared into the house. A woman screamed.

* * *

When she realized what had happened to Dr. Volkmann, Karyn edged away from the window, keeping her eyes on the lean gray wolf that now stood in her living room. She wanted to believe that Chris would reach her in time, but she had seen how many wolves blocked his approach to the house.

The muscles of the gray wolf bunched as he crouched to spring. With nowhere to go Karyn backed into a corner, holding her arms crossed in front of her in a feeble attempt to ward off the attack.

But before the blow came there was a splintering crash and fragments of glass peppered the room. A pale-yellow wolf, broad through the chest, landed on all four feet between Karyn and the attacker. She screamed.

To Karyn's astonishment, the pale wolf turned not toward her, but the other way to face the lean Volkmann wolf. The two squared off, growling deep in their throats. The pale wolf made the first move, springing at the other. The gray wolf stepped nimbly aside, and the newcomer overshot and slammed into the sofa before he could turn. The gray wolf moved in fast, his jaws open wide, teeth bared for battle. They collided with a thump and rolled across the floor, the fury of their combat shaking the house. From outside Karyn heard the popping of a small-caliber gun.

She watched the fight with a strange detached fascination. The lean gray wolf was the quicker of the two, but the pale newcomer was the stronger. The gray wolf would back away, inviting an attack, then leap aside like a matador and slash at the other as he went by. Each time the sharp teeth ripped through the yellow fur, leaving a streak of blood, and each charge by the pale wolf was a fraction slower than the last.

The end came with startling suddenness. The gray wolf moved half a second too late, and the other was upon him. Using his superior weight, the pale wolf forced his foe slowly to the floor. Then he struck, powerful teeth clamping on the other's throat. A terrible, bubbling cry came from the downed animal just before his windpipe collapsed.

Still pressed back into the corner, Karyn looked directly into the eyes of the pale wolf as it raised its head, muzzle dripping with the other's blood. A shock of recognition went through her.

"Roy," she said softly.

At that moment the weakened door splintered and Chris Halloran burst into the room. He looked down at the mutilated wolf, then at the other. He pointed the Stoeger pistol at the survivor.

"No." Karyn cried.

With his finger tight on the trigger, Chris looked over at Karyn.

"Don't kill him," she said. "Not this one."

Chris let his gun arm fall, and the pale wolf leaped out through the smashed window.

Karyn staggered for a moment, and Chris moved swiftly to catch her.

"Hang on," he said. "We've still got to get out of here." She nodded and drew a shuddering breath. "How many bullets do you have left?"

"Only four, if I counted right."

Through the open doorway they could see the dark shapes moving cautiously nearer.

"We can't stay here," Karyn said. "We've got to get to the car."

Chris nodded toward the shotgun that lay across the room. "Can we use that?"

"It's no good. Only silver can stop them."

Outside the wolves grew bolder.

"Is there nothing else?" Chris asked.

"One thing," she remembered. "Fire."

Chris looked over at the dwindling flame in the fireplace. "See if you can find something to use for a torch. I'll watch the doorway."

Karyn ran to the bathroom and took Roy's long-handled shower brush from its hook over the tub. She wrapped two heavy towels around the bristle end, fastening them with adhesive tape. From the cupboard under the sink she took a can of lighter fluid and poured it over the towels. From out in the living room came the sound of shots. She ran back and saw two more wolves down on the floor.

Chris took the makeshift torch from her hand and touched the wrapped end to the fire. Flames enveloped the towels immediately.

"Stay close to me," he said, and led her out the front door.

Wolves were everywhere. They backed away when Chris thrust the torch at them, but just far enough to avoid the flame. He fired at one and killed it.

As they inched across the clearing the wolves circled them like a city gang of juveniles waiting for an opening to attack.

Chris handed her the gun. "You take this. I'll try to scatter them with the torch while you make for the car. There's one bullet left. If you have to use it, make it count."

"What about you?"

"Once you're inside the car, be ready to whip the door open for me. When I come, I'll come fast."

Karyn squeezed his arm, then gripped the pistol firmly and started running. She forced herself to look nowhere but straight ahead at the car. With every step she expected to be pulled down from behind by powerful jaws. Behind her she could hear the frenzied growling of the wolves as Chris menaced them with the torch.

The blood pounded in Karyn's temples as she covered the last yards to the car. Just two steps away from safety a lithe black wolf sprang between her and the car. For a frozen moment the woman and the beast were face to face. The green eyes of the wolf blazed with hatred. The timeless hatred of the female.

"I should have known it was you, Marcia," said Karyn.

The she-wolf gathered herself and leaped at her. At the same instant Karyn fired. One of the green eyes burst like a ripened grape as the bullet pierced it and sank into the brain. The black wolf screamed once and tumbled lifeless to the ground at Karyn's feet.

She stepped over the animal's body and snatched open the door on the passenger's side of the Camaro. Without looking back she dived inside and slammed the door behind her.

As Karyn pulled herself upright she saw Chris running toward the car with the torch held out in front of him. He slammed into the fender, did a body roll across the hood, and came down on the driver's side still gripping the torch, Karyn banged the door open for him, and he levered himself inside, hurling the torch back at the raging wolves.

The burning torch traced a fiery spiral arc through the night and landed in the dry grass. The wind caught the flame, and in seconds it had spread across the clearing to the oily chaparral at the edge of the forest.

Chris got the car going, swung around, and sped back toward the road leading out. Behind them they could hear the growing roar of flames and screams that were neither animal nor human.

They did not slow down until they reached the crest of the mountain. There Chris pulled to a stop and they looked back. Below them in the valley the red-orange glow of the fire had spread into the village of Drago, whipped on by the desert wind.

"Some of them will get away," Karyn said.

Chris did not answer.

She looked down at the fire as it ate through the wooden buildings and thought of the long-dead village of Dradja. "Some of them always get away."

A sudden deep chill made her shudder. Chris put an arm around her shoulder and drew her close to him. In a little while the chill subsided.

"Can we go away from here?" she said. "Far away?"

"Yes," he said. He pulled the car back onto the road and drove on over the mountain.

Just as they started down the other side Karyn heard it. She clapped her hands over her ears, but could not shut it out. The howling.

THE HOWLING II

LOS ANGELES (UPI)—A fire of undetermined origin swept through a narrow valley in the Tehachapi Mountains north of Los Angeles yesterday, virtually wiping out the tiny village of Drago. Firefighters from Los Angeles and Ventura Counties brought the blaze under control early this morning, and had it extinguished before it could threaten any of the neighboring communities.

As yet there has been no reported contact with any of the residents of Drago. Authorities refused to make an estimate on the number of casualties as crews were still sifting through the ashes for victims.

The only known survivors at this hour are Mrs. Karyn Beatty and a friend, Christopher Halloran, both of Los Angeles. Mrs. Beatty's husband was missing and believed to have perished in the fire. Halloran and Mrs. Beatty declined to speak with reporters.

According to U.S. Forest Ranger Phil Henry, the final death toll may never be known. Since Drago was not an incorporated town, no accurate records were kept of its population. It is estimated that between one hundred and two hundred people lived there. So intense was the blaze, which destroyed two hundred acres of timber in addition to the village, that searchers are finding it difficult to distinguish human remains from those of animals.

1

Karyn knelt on the moist grass and worked with her fingers in the dirt around the roots of the rosebush. There were no flowers on the bush, and there should have been. Karyn felt she was somehow responsible. Although David had never mentioned it, she was sure his first wife had been a gifted gardener. That was the trouble with marrying a widower—the departed wife was always good at everything.

As for Karyn, except for her houseplants, which enjoyed a special place in her affections, she had little interest in or aptitude for gardening. Outdoor plants, she felt, ought to be able to take care of themselves. However, David and Dr. Goetz thought getting outside and working with her hands was good for her, and she did not want to disappoint them.

While she poked idly at the damp earth, Karyn let her mind wander. There was vacation time to be worked out for Mrs. Jensen, the housekeeper, and a Parents' Day coming up at Joey's summer school. She smiled, pleased at the commonplace concerns that occupied her mind these days. It was a healthy sign, she thought.

Karyn did not hear the soft approach of the padded feet behind her. The first indication she was not alone was the huff of warm breath on the back of her neck. She started to rise, lost her balance, and fell awkwardly to the ground.

She looked up and saw the other face staring down into hers. Its black lips were stretched in a canine grimace, the yellowed teeth bared. She tried to squirm away, but two heavy paws pinned her as the animal dropped its weight on her chest.

In that instant, all the horror of Drago flooded back from the closed-off portion of her mind. The wolfish face with its long, cruel teeth came at her. She screamed. The weight on her chest lessened for a moment, and she rolled away, curling herself protectively into a ball. She felt the animal prod at her, trying to turn her over. She screamed again.

The back door of the house banged open and a solid woman with graying, blond hair rushed out. She ran heavily toward Karyn, still lying on the ground by the rosebushes.

"Bristol, stop that!" the woman called. "Come here, you bad boy."

Cautiously Karyn opened her eyes. A few feet away, Mrs. Jensen stood with her hands planted on her hips. Sidling toward her, a 'don't-hit-me' look in its eyes, was a coltish young German shepherd.

"Shame on you," Mrs. Jensen scolded the dog. "Frightening people like that." She seized him by the collar and tapped him lightly on the nose. "I'm sorry, Mrs. Richter. He's just an overgrown puppy. He wanted to play, that's all."

The back door burst open again and David Richter hurried out. He was a man of forty-eight, with a strong, serious face. He wore a sweater and slacks, this being Sunday, but he never seemed really comfortable without the three-piece suit he wore daily to the brokerage.

Karyn rose unsteadily to her feet. David ran across the lawn to her side and took her arm.

"Are you all right?" he asked.

"I'm fine," Karyn said, still out of breath. "It's nothing."

David turned on Mrs. Jensen, who was still holding the dog by his collar. The dog kept lunging up, trying to lick her face.

"What's that dog doing here?" David demanded.

"It's my sister's puppy." Mrs. Jensen said. "He didn't mean any harm."

"You know we don't allow animals here," David said.

"I was just watchin' the dog for an hour while my sister went to the dentist. She didn't want to leave him alone."

"Well, get him out of here," David ordered. "And don't ever bring a dog to this house again."

"David, it's not that serious," Karyn said. "The dog just caught me by surprise."

"He didn't mean any harm," Mrs. Jensen said again.

"Yes, yes, all right," David said, softening his tone a bit. "But I want him out of here right now."

"Yes, Mr. Richter," she said. And to the dog: "Come along, you bad boy."

As Mrs. Jensen led the dog around the side of the house, a dark-eyed boy of six dashed through the door and across the lawn to where Karyn and David stood.

"What happened," the boy said, looking from one of the adults to the other.

Karyn ruffled his hair. "It's all right, Joey. I was just startled by a dog."

"A dog?" The boy looked around eagerly. "Where is he?"

"Never mind," said David. "Mrs. Jensen took him away. You go inside now and wash up for dinner."

Joey looked wistfully off in the direction the housekeeper had taken the dog. "Can't I just go and see him? Just for a minute?"

"Inside, Joey," said David. The boy trudged back across the grass and into the house.

"I feel so guilty because he can't have a pet," Karyn said.

"It won't hurt him to do without one. Now let me help you inside. You're still shaking."

"Really, David, I'm quite all right," Karyn said, but she allowed herself to be led into the house.

"Sit down there in the big chair," David said when they reached the living room. "Put your feet up."

Karyn did as she was told.

"Now wait right there and I'll get something to calm your nerves." He went off to the kitchen, and returned a minute later carrying a tall glass.

"Here's a nice glass of milk," he said.

A nice shot of Scotch would do her nerves a whole lot more good, Karyn thought, but she smiled her thanks and took the glass from David's hand.

He stood with his arms folded, studying her gravely as she sipped at the milk. "You gave me quite a scare."

"I'm sorry."

"What a shame that this should happen just when you seemed to be getting better."

Karyn set the glass down carefully on the end table next to the chair. "I hate that expression," she said. "Getting better. It's a constant reminder that I'm a convalescent mental case."

"I didn't mean it that way. It's just that I'm a little disappointed that, after a year, Dr. Goetz hasn't done more for you. Do you think we should try someone else?"

"Dr. Goetz is as good as any of them," Karyn said. "Really, David, you're making too much out of this. The dog came up behind me and took me by surprise. I overreacted, that's all."

"The dog," David said, watching her. "It reminded you of that Drago business, didn't it?"

Sure. *That Drago business.* The unpleasantness in the mountains. Nothing remarkable, really—just fighting off a pack of werewolves and seeing your husband change into... Karyn broke off the thought and shuddered.

David moved quickly to her side. "I'm sorry dear, I shouldn't have brought that up."

Karyn squeezed his hand. "No, darling, it should never become a taboo subject, or I *will* be in trouble. And you're right about the dog. Seeing its face suddenly so close to mine took me back for a moment to Drago. It's been only three years, you know, and we've got to expect incidents like that from time to time."

"And you're still having the dreams, aren't you?"

"Yes," Karyn admitted. "But not so often, anymore."

David frowned. "When is your next appointment with Goetz?"

"Tomorrow."

"And you really think he's helping you?"

"As much as anyone could."

David patted her hand awkwardly. "All right, then, we'll go on with him. I just hope he can make you see that this Drago business is all... behind you."

As she lay that night in bed beside her sleeping husband, Karyn recalled his words. She knew that what he had started to say was, "All in your mind." She would be happier than anyone to be convinced of that, but it was not so. Drago was as real as the moon outside their bedroom window, and much closer. The werewolves were real too. And somewhere, Karyn knew, one or more of them survived.

* * *

Nine hundred miles away, in the grape country of California, another woman lay awake beside her man. Her long, supple body gleamed like old ivory in the moonlight. Across the pillow, her hair spread in gentle waves of glossy black, shot through with a startling streak of silver.

The man stirred in his sleep. The woman quieted him with a hand on his broad, bare shoulder.

"Rest easy, my lover," she whispered. "Soon we will have much work to do."

2

From the window of Dr. Arnold Goetz's office in the new Farrell Building, Karyn could see the sailboats skimming across Lake Washington under a stiff westerly breeze. It was one of those brightly washed summer days when the dreary months of rain are forgotten and the people of Seattle go outdoors to celebrate the sun.

Karyn stood at the window talking in a flat, emotionless voice. Finally she said, "So that's all there was to it. Just a silly incident with a dog, and it was all over in a minute."

Dr. Goetz waited a full fifteen seconds. It was a technique of his that Karyn recognized. The purpose was to encourage the patient to elaborate on, or perhaps contradict, the last thought. When Karyn did not offer to continue, the doctor spoke.

"There is no doubt in your mind, then, that it was only a dog yesterday."

Karyn spun around to face him. "Of course it was only a dog." She walked over and sat down in the chair facing the doctor's desk. "I was frightened for a moment because it brought back bad memories. That's all."

Dr. Goetz nodded sagely. "Yes, I see. And tell me about the dreams. You say you still have them?"

Karyn bit her lip and frowned. "Yes. And they worry me more than the business with the dog. Will I ever stop hearing it at night, Doctor? The howling?"

"You *do* understand that it is only in dreams that you hear this... howling?"

Karyn leaned back in the chair. Sunlight from the window caught her pale blond hair and made it a glowing frame for her face. She was twenty-eight now, and there were little lines at the corners of her eyes, but the touch of maturity only emphasized her beauty.

"Yes, Doctor," she said wearily, "I know it only happens in dreams. Now. But three years ago in Drago, the howling was real. As real as death."

Dr. Goetz touched his glasses. Karyn had determined that it was his unconscious gesture of disbelief. He put on an understanding smile.

"Yes, I see," he said.

"Bullshit."

The doctor brightened. Gut reactions always encouraged him.

"You don't see at all," Karyn told him. "You don't believe Drago actually happened any more than my husband does. Any more than all the other people I've told about it."

After his customary wait the doctor said. "Karyn, whether I believe or not isn't important. What happened in the past or didn't happen really doesn't concern us. Our bag is the here and now. All that matters to us is how you feel about it."

Karyn met the doctor's sincere gaze. He was having a difficult time making the transition from the traditional Freudian to the trendy transactional school of analysis. Everybody's got problems, she thought.

"What it makes me feel is scared shitless," she said.

Pause.

"Why?"

"Because I know they aren't all dead."

"When you say 'they' you mean—"

"I mean the wolves," Karyn supplied. "The werewolves."

She watched closely for a reaction—the narrowing of the eyes, or the little quirk, which she had seen so often at the corner of his mouth. Dr. Goetz held his expression of friendly concern. He was good.

"Do you want to tell me about it?" he said.

"Doctor, I *have* told you about it."

"Tell me again, if you think it would help."

Hell, why not, Karyn thought. There was no pain in the telling any more, and that, at least, was an improvement. Maybe if she heard the story often enough herself it would become meaningless, the way a familiar word repeated over and over eventually becomes a nonsense sound.

She stood up again and walked back to the window. There, watching the peaceful scene down on the lake, she repeated the story of the damned village of Drago, and the six months she spent there with Roy Beatty.

She described the way it began, with the howling in the night. Then there had been the cruel killing of her little dog. She told of the strange people who had lived in the village, and the huge, unnatural wolves that had roamed the woods at night. In a quiet, controlled voice she spoke of the black-haired Marcia Lura, who had bewitched Karyn's husband and finally taken him forever with the virulent bite of the werewolf. Finally she told of the escape from Drago as she and Chris Halloran had fled the burning village.

Dr. Goetz waited, then spoke. "You said they aren't all dead. The wolves."

"As we drove out of the valley with everything behind us in flames, I heard it again from off in the forest. The howling."

Abruptly Karyn stopped talking and went back to her chair across from the doctor. "Telling the story doesn't make it any better or any worse," she said. "All it does is keep the memory fresh. What I want to do is put Drago out of my mind, now and forever."

"I can understand that," Dr. Goetz said reasonably. "And that's what we're working toward, isn't it? But, Karyn, before we can finally put this idea out of your mind, we have to find out what put it in."

Karyn stared at him. She spaced out her words carefully. "What put this *idea* into my mind, God-dammit, is that it happened."

"Yes, of course," the doctor went on. "Maybe when you were a little girl there was some experience, something ugly, with wolves or large dogs."

Karyn shook her head wearily. "No, Doctor, not when I was a little girl. My only traumatic experience with wolves came when I was a full-grown woman. Three years ago. In Drago. You're telling me the same old thing, aren't you, that it's a delusion?"

"Delusion is a term we don't use much any more. We understand now that things that happen in the mind are every bit as vivid, and often more damaging than what we call reality. I'm sure your experience in Drago is as real to you today as this room we are sitting in. The important thing, as I said—"

Karyn only half-listened as Dr. Goetz droned on in his silky, reassuring voice. He was saying the thing everyone else did. Namely, that she had imagined the whole Drago episode. Maybe in time he could convince her of that. If he could, he would be well worth whatever David was paying him. In the meantime, it did help a little to be able to talk.

There was a subtle change in the doctor's tone, and Karyn saw his eyes flick over at the discreet little clock on his desk. Her hour was up.

3

Karyn drove slowly north over the Aurora Bridge toward Mountlake Terrace, where she and David had their home. Her thoughts, as usual when she left Dr. Goetz, were on Drago and what happened afterward.

There had been one moment of triumph at the very end when she had fired the deadly silver bullet into the head of the black she-wolf. But that small victory, like the escape with Chris Halloran, had lacked a ring of finality. Even as she and Chris had paused to look back on the valley in flames, neither of them had really believed it was over.

For six tempestuous months they had tried to pretend it was, and that they were just another ordinary couple. After sharing the horror of Drago, it had seemed a natural thing to stay together. How wrong they were.

For a time they had traveled aimlessly from place to place, living on pills and nervous energy. Before long their pent-up emotions were turned against each other. At the end of six months these two people, who had shared more in a day than many couples do in a lifetime, were living on the edge of violence. The most insignificant squabble could erupt in an ugly word battle. They were staying in a Las Vegas hotel when the final blowup came.

Karyn had spent the morning in their room. She had the air conditioner turned up full and wore a sweater buttoned to the throat as protection against the dry cold. Chris had gone down to the swimming pool early, after making only a half-hearted attempt at persuading her to come with him.

At noon Chris returned. He glanced briefly at Karyn and went into the bathroom. Not until he had showered, shaved, and dressed, did he speak to her.

"Do you want to go down and get some lunch?"

"Can't we have something sent up?"

"Why?"

"I'd rather not leave the room, that's all."

"For God's sake, Karyn, you can't just sit up here and hide from the world like a frightened child."

His words cut into her like a dull knife. She fired back, "I can do anything I want. Who are you to tell me what I can't do? Nobody asked you to run my life."

Chris's eyes had turned dark and dangerous for a moment, then he whirled and stormed out the door. Karyn fought down the angry impulse to throw something after him.

The rush of blood through the veins made a roaring in her ears. She walked over to the window, parted the draperies, and blinked at the bright white Las Vegas sunlight. Twelve stories down, she could see people in the pool and on the deck around it. Everyone seemed to be laughing and having a fine time. Was she the only one in the world, Karyn wondered, who was miserable?

She let the draperies fall back across the window, and returned to the chair where she had sat all morning. She was still there, shivering with the cold, an hour later when Chris returned.

He closed the door firmly behind him and stood looking at her. "Why the hell don't you turn the air conditioning down?"

"I like it this way."

She could see him start to get angry, then, with an effort, relax.

"Karyn, we have to talk."

"Why?"

"Because we're destroying each other."

"Is that a fact?"

"Cut it out, damn it. I've had all of this I can take."

"Poor you."

"This continual picking at each other is tearing me apart. It isn't doing you any good, either. Have you looked at yourself closely in the mirror lately?"

"Well, thank you very much."

"Will you please stop playing childish games? I know what you went through at Drago, but—"

Karyn sprang out of the chair and faced him angrily. "You have no idea what I went through. You were there only at the very end. I spent six months in that place. Six months in hell."

Chris spoke in a carefully controlled voice. "I know that, Karyn. I know you suffered a lot. What I want to do now is help you."

"Oh? And just how do you think you can help me?"

"It would be a start if we brought the whole thing out in the open and talked about it."

"I don't want to talk about it," Karyn snapped. "Not to you, not to anybody."

"I'm the only one you *can* talk to about Drago," he said. "I am the only person in the world who would believe it, because I was there. I saw the wolves, and I know what they were."

Karyn clapped her hands over her ears. "I don't want to hear. I don't want to think about it. Why don't you let me forget Drago, so it will go away?"

"It will never go away," Chris said. "It will always be locked in the back of your head. If we could just talk about it—"

"There you go with your 'talk about it' again. You sound like one of those fucking parlor psychologists. Tell me, where did you get your medical degree, *Doctor?*"

"Cut it out. I can't take any more of this."

"Don't then. Don't take a Goddamn thing you don't want to. Nobody's holding you."

"That's right," he said in a voice that had gone suddenly cold. "Nobody is."

In thirty minutes Chris Halloran had packed his clothes and left the hotel. That had been two and a half years ago. Karyn had not seen him since.

* * *

The weeks that followed the Las Vegas breakup with Chris were fragmented in Karyn's memory. She knew that during that time she was very close to losing her hold on sanity. Somehow, she had made her way back to her parents' home in the Los Angeles suburb of Brentwood. For two months she had a full-time nurse, and never left the upstairs bedroom that had been hers when she was a little girl. The days were blanks and the nights were filled with shadows where lurked unspeakable horrors.

Then gradually the world came back into focus. Karyn at last learned to talk about the summer in Drago. Then as now, no one really believed her, but they listened sympathetically. She learned that Chris had been right. Talking about it *did* help.

After six months in the quiet, comfortable house with her family, Karyn began to feel whole again. She tried to contact Chris Halloran, but learned he had taken a traveling assignment with his engineering firm and was seldom in town for long. Maybe, she decided, it was better this way. She would have liked to say she was sorry about the bad days at the end, and keep at least a part of Chris's friendship, but seeing him might just open old wounds.

Instead, she had accepted the invitation of a college classmate and flown to Seattle for a visit. That was when she met David Richter.

David was twenty years older than Karyn, and solid as Mount Rainier. He did not have the dreamy romanticism of Roy Beatty, nor the charm and dash of Chris Halloran, but he was exactly what Karyn needed. She had been a little hesitant about meeting David's son, but she need not have worried. She and Joey hit it off immediately.

The big test, in Karyn's mind, came when she told David the story of Drago. He had listened patiently and seriously, without laughing or patronizing her. He did not, of course, treat it as reality, but accepted it as a minor eccentricity as he might have accepted a slight limp.

David asked her to marry him two months after they met. He offered her security and stability, and a kind of quiet love she had never known. She said yes.

All in all Karyn was content with her life as Mrs. David Richter. Now if she could just stop dreaming of the wolves, and shake the feeling that someday, somewhere, they were going to kill her.

4

In the San Joaquin Valley of California a band of gypsies made their camp in a clearing at the edge of a forest. Their camp was not much like the romantic fiction of operettas and the movies. Instead of colorful horse-drawn wagons their vehicles were vans, pickup trucks, travel trailers and campers. The music in the camp came from transistor radios and tape decks, not from the fabled wild violins and tambourines.

Some things, however, remained little changed over the centuries. Although many of them worked for daily wages in the neighboring fields, the gypsies remained wanderers. An entire camp might pack up and vanish one night, to appear next morning in another place miles away. And the gypsies still had their own methods of communication, which carried news between distant camps more swiftly than the mails.

In yet another way these modern gypsies resembled their forebears. They had a deep respect for the old beliefs. They still held that a man's future could be seen in the lines of his hand. The turn of a card could chill the blood like the whisper of Death. And the gypsies knew there were those who existed outside the laws of nature, creatures to be feared and never, never betrayed.

For this reason the gypsies stayed well away from a battered old trailer that rested on blocks at the periphery of the camp. By their heritage they were bound to protect those who dwelt there, but the wisdom of their ancestors kept them wary.

* * *

Inside the trailer was shadowed, the sun filtered by green cloth curtains across the two small windows. There was a tiny alcove for cooking, with a butane stove and refrigerator. There were a table and benches, which folded up out of the way when they were not being used. At the far end of the trailer, across its entire width, was a bed, covered with a profusion of pillows, silken scarves, soft blankets over a billowy mattress.

Amidst the pillows and scarves on the bed were the wet, naked bodies of a man and a woman. The man was blond, and broad through the chest and shoulders. The woman was dark and long-bodied, with compelling green eyes and hair of midnight black shot through with a streak of silver.

The body of the man strained over the woman. Her long, strong legs locked him between her knees. With a last powerful thrust the man buried himself deep inside the woman. With a sharp intake of breath, she clasped him tight against her. He groaned deep in his chest. Her teeth sank in and marked his shoulder. They cried out together, and it was finished.

Roy Beatty rolled over on his side. The woman rolled with him, still holding him tightly in the circle of her arms. Roy's breath came in ragged gasps. As always with Marcia, their climax had been a devastating experience, leaving him spent and drained as no other woman ever had. Since the first time he saw her in the hamlet of Drago—had it been only three years?—Roy Beatty had belonged to this woman. He had been hers even before she had claimed him in the ancient way. Now they shared the power and the curse, and he was hers forever.

"Are you at ease now, my Roy?" Marcia Lura let her fingers wander through the damp golden hair across his chest. "Did I please you?"

Roy pulled a breath deep into his lungs and exhaled slowly. "You please me like nothing else on earth."

"And you will never leave me?"

He pulled back his head to look at her. "Leave you, Marcia? Impossible."

"That is good." Her fingers massaged the corded muscles where his neck joined his shoulders. "We will leave this place soon."

Roy pulled away from her and sat up. He ran his hand over the smooth length of her body. "Are you sure you're well enough to travel?"

"I am as well now as I will ever be. I know these have been difficult months for you, my Roy, nursing a sick woman, but now it is over."

"All that matters is having you near me," he said.

"I will always be near you," she said. "I will be all the woman you will ever want. But now, you know what we have to do."

Roy's eyes shifted away. He reached down for his clothes where they had fallen beside the bed. "You mean… Karyn."

"Yes!" Green fire flashed in her eyes. "That woman."

He turned back to face her, feeling the impact of her hatred. "Do we have to go through with this?" he said. "So much time has passed."

Marcia ran her eyes over him slowly. When she spoke there was a chill in her voice. "You can't be saying you still have tender feelings for her. Can you?"

"She was my wife," Roy said.

"Your wife!" Marcia spat out the words. "What did that woman know about being a wife? If she had pleased you, you would not have come to me."

"But it all seems so long ago."

"Does it? Does it, Roy? To me, it seems like yesterday." Marcia touched the slash of silver that ran through her dark hair above the left eyebrow. "I think of that woman every time I look into a mirror and see how she marked me when she fired the silver bullet into my head."

"She was defending herself."

"And now *you* are defending her."

"Marcia, no, I am with you always. You know that."

"And yet you take the side of the woman who tried to kill me."

"She couldn't have known it was you. All she saw was a wolf."

"You underestimate her, Roy. She knew. Oh, how well she knew. Yes, she saw the body of a wolf, but what she tried to kill was the spirit of the woman who had taken her man."

He reached out and stroked the satiny black hair. "My poor Marcia. You were so close to dying."

Marcia's mouth tightened. "But now I am well and strong. At least the woman part of me. As for the other—it might be better if the silver bullet had struck a fraction lower and done its work completely."

Roy looked away.

"You know, do you not, what that woman stole from me with her silver bullet? She stole the power of the wolf, the freedom of the night. Do you remember, Roy, those nights when we ran wild and free? Do you remember the times together? The pleasures we gave each other? The pleasures we took?"

"I remember," he said. Still he did not look at her.

"Never again will I know that wild joy," she said. "Now in the night you must walk alone."

Roy faced her. He looked deep into the green eyes. "Is there no way—?"

"None. The thing that happens to me now is my curse for as long as I live. I must bear those nights alone."

"Let me stay with you," Roy said.

"No. The change—I would rather die than have you see the thing I become. Now that my strength has returned, I can control it on most nights, but sometimes, when the moon is low and full, as it is tonight..." Marcia left the sentence unfinished.

Roy stroked the smooth, naked curve of her waist where it flowed into the lean hip. "I love you, Marcia. I would share anything with you."

"Not this," she snapped. Then her tone softened. "But you can share with me the vengeance against the woman who has destroyed half of me."

Roy nodded slowly. He would do whatever he must to keep this green-eyed woman.

Marcia looked over at the darkening curtain across the window. Outside, the daylight was falling. "If it were possible, we would leave tonight," she said, "But I cannot travel when the moon is full."

"Are you—can we be sure Karyn is still in Seattle?"

"She is still there," Marcia said. "The gypsies watch her for us. She can make no move that the gypsies do not see."

"Why do the gypsies do this for us?" Roy asked.

"Because they fear us. They know the power we have, and what we could do to them and their children if we wished. We have their help and their protection only because they fear the werewolf."

"I don't like to talk about it," Roy said.

Marcia's eyes were bright and mocking. "Oh, don't you? Tell me you don't like it when the night comes and you feel your body change. Tell me you don't like the taste of living flesh and raw hot blood."

Roy could not answer. The woman's words brought on an excitement that was almost sexual.

"Of course you like it," Marcia went on. "Out under the moon you glory in the power of the werewolf. You are unstoppable, invincible. No living thing can hurt you. Nothing can kill you. Nothing, save the fire..." In the dim light her teeth gleamed. "And silver."

It grew dark inside the trailer. Roy could barely make out the long, white shape of the woman lying among the cushions. Outside, the night had come. A pale glow beyond the green curtain signaled the rising moon. Roy felt its pull in the quickening of his senses and the uneasiness in his joints. His eyes were drawn toward the curtained window.

On the bed Marcia's body jerked in a sudden spasm. Her mouth twisted in pain.

"Leave me now," she said.

"Marcia, I—"

"Leave me!" The green eyes blazed with pain and pent-up fury.

Roy rose awkwardly to his feet. He stumbled to the door at the rear of the trailer. He pushed it open and stepped out into the cool night. As he closed the door he heard the rusty bolt scrape into place on the inside.

He turned toward the edge of the clearing where the moon was coming into view over the tops of the trees. To his sharpened senses the night held no secrets. He heard the scuttling of small creatures through the brush, and saw them darting among the shadows. The scents of the trees and the grasses and the night flowers were sharp in his nostrils.

The change from man to wolf, Roy had learned, could come on any night. He could will himself to change or, sometimes, prevent it. But on a night like this, with the moon at its full power, the call was impossible to resist.

Roy pulled at the collar of his shirt, letting the cool night air flow in at his throat. He began to walk toward the forest that rimmed the clearing. He tore his shirt open, heedless of the flying buttons, and pulled it free of his belt. The muscles jumped beneath his skin, his limbs twitched against the growing ache in his joints. He stripped the shirt from his back and let it fall to the grass. His breath came in short, hot bursts. He began to run.

5

The upper rim of the full moon edged above the tops of the Douglas firs on the hill to the east of Karyn Richter's home in Mountlake Terrace. Karyn stood at the French windows, watching it, her mind far away.

"How did it go with the doctor today?"

Startled, Karyn turned to see David standing in the room behind her. "I didn't hear you come in," she said.

David Richter had a strong, clean-shaven face. He kept his graying hair short and neatly combed. He was in good physical condition, except for a slight bulge around the middle, and looked younger than his forty-eight years.

"Were you watching something out there?" he asked, nodding toward the window.

"No, just daydreaming." She gave a small, unconvincing laugh. "Can you daydream after dark?"

David smiled briefly, but his eyes remained serious.

Karyn shrugged. "Dr. Goetz said 'Come back next week.' Aside from that he didn't have much to say. No suggestions, no advice, just 'See you next week.'"

"Well, you look good, so he must be helping."

Karyn smiled at her husband. Dear, stolid, loyal David. In his heart he was surely convinced that her fears were the delusions of a borderline hysteric, but he would spring to her defense if any other man suggested as much. It was for David's sake as much as her own that she had to rid her mind of the horrible memories of Drago. For David, she would go on seeing Dr. Goetz or any other doctor he wanted, as long as there was a chance of getting better.

They both turned at a commotion in the next room, and six-year-old Joey Richter dashed in and skidded to a stop in front of them.

"Can I stay up and watch television?" the boy said hopefully, switching his gaze between Karyn and David. "It's Clint Eastwood," he added, as if this would influence the decision in his favor.

David looked to Karyn, signaling with his eyes that this one was up to her.

"What did Mrs. Jensen say?" Karyn asked. The boy looked down at the scuffed toes of his tennis shoes. "She said no," he reported.

"Then it's no," Karyn said. "It's time for bed, and anyway, you've seen Clint Eastwood."

"I saw *Dirty Harry*," he explained patiently. "Tonight it's *Magnum Force.*"

"To bed," Karyn said firmly.

"Oh, okay," Joey said, with all the martyrdom a six-year-old could muster. In another moment, though, the defeat was forgotten as he kissed first his father, then Karyn, goodnight.

"Will you come up and tuck me in?" he asked Karyn with his arms tight around her neck.

"I'll be up just as soon as Mrs. Jensen gets you ready," she promised.

At the sound of her name, Mrs. Jensen appeared in the doorway. To Karyn and David, she said, "He was trying to get you to let him stay up, I suppose."

"There was some mention of a Clint Eastwood movie," Karyn said.

Mrs. Jensen clucked her tongue in disapproval. "Always he wants to watch the shoot-'em-ups. Such trash. You couldn't force him to watch a nice wholesome Walt Disney."

"They're dumb," Joey complained. "Nobody ever shoots anybody."

"That's enough, Joey," David said, not unkindly. "Go along up with Mrs. Jensen now."

From a standing start the boy took off and dashed past the housekeeper and out the doorway. They could hear his small feet pounding up the stairs to his bedroom. Mrs. Jensen sighed and rolled her eyes in a long-suffering expression that did not hide her affection for the boy. She followed him out of the room.

David stretched and yawned. "I think I'll turn in early myself tonight. How about you?"

Karyn felt the tightening of her skin that always came when she thought about sex. The years of therapy had helped her considerably, but she still had problems.

She could never completely forget those last weeks with Roy, when he was going through the terrible change. She had not known at first what was happening to him, but found his touch suddenly repellent. Then after Drago, there was the crazy time with Chris Halloran. They had plunged into wild sex games, hoping to dull the remembered horror. Finally, inevitably, they had failed.

David Richter was a gentle, if unimaginative, lover. Sex with him had been satisfactory most of the time, still, for Karyn, the residue of fear remained. Naturally, she had talked about it with David and with Dr. Goetz. They were both most reassuring and supportive, but there was always the worm of doubt.

She took David's hand and pressed it warmly.

"I'm not really sleepy," she said. "I think I'll stay up and read for a while."

"Do you want me to get you a pill?"

Karyn did not miss the flicker of David's eyes as he glanced through the window at the rising moon. Normally he did not approve of her taking sleeping pills, but he knew how the full moon disturbed her.

"I don't think so," she said. "I haven't used a pill in months, and I'd just as soon stay away from them."

"Would you like to play a little backgammon? Give me a chance to win back some of my losses?"

Karyn smiled at him. She knew he was reluctant to leave her downstairs alone, and she loved him for it, but it was high time she made it clear that she was not an invalid.

"You go on to bed, dear," she said. "I know you have to get up early. I'll be along in a little while."

Mrs. Jensen reappeared in the doorway. "The young man is ready to be tucked in."

Karyn and David went up together to Joey's room at the head of the stairs. The wallpaper featured the exploits of Spiderman. It was chosen personally by Joey to replace what he called "those dumb ducks" that had decorated the walls when the room was a nursery.

Karyn smiled down at the boy and remembered how the idea of being a stepmother had worried her at first. When she was married to Roy, they had talked now and then about having children, but there was always a list of things they wanted to do first.

David Richter had become, unexpectedly, a father at forty-two. He treated the child with a kind of careful affection, as though afraid he might somehow damage the boy. Joey was three when his mother had died of cancer, and David had a couple of rough months trying to be both parents until he found Mrs. Jensen. Karyn was the first woman David had been seriously involved with since his wife's death, and he was delighted when she and Joey had hit it off.

The boy sat up in bed and hugged first his father, then Karyn. He lay down again while Karyn went through the nightly ritual of tucking the blankets close to his firm, wiry little body.

"G'night, Mom," the boy said. "G'night, Dad."

David and Karyn had spent considerable time discussing what Joey should call her after they were married, but the boy solved the problem for them immediately, figuring that if the blond lady was married to Dad, she was Mom, and that was that.

Leaving the door open a couple of inches, the way Joey liked it, Karyn and David stepped back into the hall. Karyn kissed her husband lightly.

"Go on to bed," she said. "I'll be in soon."

She went back downstairs and into the living room. A stack of magazines was spread across the coffee table. Karyn picked out this month's *Redbook* and carried it back into the family room. She could hear Mrs. Jensen's television set playing faintly in the housekeeper's room at the rear of the house. Karyn smiled at the distant popping of gunshots. Mrs. Jensen was watching *Magnum Force*.

For perhaps a quarter of an hour Karyn tried, but failed, to focus her attention on the magazine. What she needed, Karyn decided, was something to really occupy her mind during the day. Something that would take enough effort to leave her honestly tired at bedtime. There was little for her to do around the house. Mrs. Jensen ran it with cool Scandinavian efficiency. Karyn was grateful for the help, but secretly wished that once in a while the housekeeper might leave something for her to do.

To help fill in the days, Karyn spent a few hours a week doing volunteer work at the Indian school. It was useful work, but also very 'in' this season, and they had more volunteers up there now than Indians.

What she really wanted to do was to go back to work. Karyn had experience in working with conventions, and felt she could find some sort of related work with one of the large Seattle hotels. She could handle it now, physically and mentally, Karyn was sure. David might not be enthusiastic, but if she really wanted to do it he would not stand in her way.

Finally she laid the magazine aside and stood up. She was still not sleepy, and did not want to go up and lie awake in bed, disturbing David. She wandered into the kitchen and took down the plastic spray bottle and long-nosed watering can she used for her plants. Karyn had an understanding with Mrs. Jensen that Karyn alone had responsibility for the plants. It pleased her to look after them—tiny living things which were hers alone, and which depended on her for their existence. After the sadistic slaughter of her little dog that summer by the creatures of Drago, Karyn would never again keep a pet. The plants were as close a substitute as she felt she could handle.

They grew in pots in an airy room at the side of the house. David liked to call it the sunroom. It amused Karyn, a Southern Californian, that any room in any house in Seattle should be called the sunroom, but she never told that to David.

Karyn went first to the chlorophytum, the spider plant. The graceful green leaves, with their white stripes, arced like a fountain up and over the edge of their hanging pot. Karyn felt the soil with her finger and found it moist.

No drink for you today, she thought, just a nice little spray to perk you up. She pushed the plunger on the plastic bottle, and a fine mist of water dampened the leaves. Talking to plants, Karyn knew, was foolishness for addled old ladies. But it didn't count, she told herself, if you didn't do it out loud. At any rate, she stopped short of giving them personal names.

Her next stop was the Boston fern. She stood back a little and admired the buoyant arch of the fronds, their fine, lacy detail. She stepped closer and saw that a little spider had moved in and was busily spinning a web among the leaves. Karyn started to pinch the spider off in a piece of Kleenex, but stayed her hand in midair. You have a right to live too, she thought, and balled up the Kleenex and stuffed it into her pocket.

She always went to the philodendron last, because it was her personal favorite. It was a masculine plant, growing strong and glossy, climbing the moss-covered pole like an athlete. We'll soon need a bigger pot for you, my friend, Karyn thought. She gave the healthy leaves a light spray and added a touch of water and plant food to the soil, where the tough, sinewy roots drew their nourishment.

When she was finished Karyn stood back and smiled at her little garden. Then she took the spray bottle and watering can back to the kitchen. She went around the house, checking all the doors and windows, making sure they were all locked. She knew, of course, that Mrs. Jensen did that every night before she retired, but it made Karyn feel better to see to the locks herself. The last thing she did was draw the draperies across the French windows, shutting out the cold light of the full moon.

6

Moving in strong strides across the moon-bright clearing, Roy Beatty reached the edge of the forest. It was like coming home. He stripped off all his clothes and let them fall to the ground. Standing upright made him feel constricted, and he sank gratefully to his knees, leaning forward to dig his fingers into the soft earth. He stretched out full length and lay for a moment with his face pressed to the sweet-smelling carpet of moss and leaves. With a deep sigh he rolled onto his back. Above him, through the cross-hatching of branches, he could see the full moon riding high and cold. The rush of blood through his veins became a roaring in his ears.

A short, sharp pain stabbed into his forehead, and he cried out. His body jerked over onto one side as though controlled by wires. He cramped into a curled, fetus-like position. As he lay there, the man's face stretched and distorted like modeling clay until all resemblance to Roy Beatty was lost. His nose and jaw thrust forward and became a muzzle. His ears grew longer and tapered themselves into blunt points. A series of convulsions seized his body. When the tremors quieted he stretched again, and new, powerful muscles moved under the skin. Where there had been bare flesh, thick fur, golden tan and glossy, now covered his body.

In minutes the change was complete. The creature that had been a man rose to its feet, unsteadily at first, then more confidently as it gathered strength. Braced on four sinewy legs, the beast pointed its muzzle to the night sky.

The wolf opened its throat and howled. A quavering cry that chilled the blood of the gypsies, locked away in their trailers nearby. The wolf exulted in the renewed power of its body. It moved easily through the forest, picking up speed as it went. Finally it charged ahead at its full speed—faster than a man could run, faster than any natural wolf. It crashed heedlessly through the undergrowth, the thick coat of fur protecting its hide from thorns and broken ends of branches. The essence of the man that had been Roy Beatty shrank and retreated to a dark tiny corner of the mind of the beast. All rational thought was wiped out. There was only the raging hunger of the werewolf.

* * *

The inhuman howling carried clearly to the trailer where Marcia Lura was locked away from the night. The thing on the floor scrambled over to the door and pressed its face against the cool metal. From the misshapen mouth came a sound: something between a woman's sob and the growl of a wolf.

* * *

Through the forest the huge pale wolf loped on. Dimly remembered in the animal brain were those other nights when the sleek black she-wolf ran at his side. Then the way she looked, moving powerfully, gracefully, and her sharp female scent on the night air, had driven the pale wolf half-mad with animal lust. Three years before, on a night of terror in the village of Drago, he had lost the female forever.

On that night, as the fire consumed the village and destroyed the others, the huge, pale wolf had broken through the flames to where the female lay wounded and dragged her to safety. The silver bullet missed ending the dual life of the black wolf and Marcia Lura by the breadth of a hair. Over long agonized months, Roy Beatty had nursed the woman back from near death. Now, at least in her human form, the only mark of the wound she bore was the silver-white streak through her midnight hair. As to the other—Roy could only imagine the things that happened to Marcia on the nights she locked herself away from him. He knew only that the lean, beautiful she-wolf would not return. That hunger would never be fed.

But there was the other hunger, the hunger that drove the werewolf endlessly through the night. The killing. The tearing away of living flesh, the crunch of bone between powerful jaws, the sweet-salty taste of warm blood.

As the werewolf reached the far side of the woods, it slowed and moved cautiously through the last of the trees. Roy Beatty had learned much in the three years since he went down under the slashing teeth of the she-wolf and awoke to find himself forever changed. He had learned to move with stealth and to kill with the smallest possible commotion.

The wolf checked abruptly as a change in the night breeze brought the scent of living prey. Moving crouched and silent through the shadows, he inched to the top of a grassy knoll that overlooked the moonlit meadow. The great yellow eyes searched out the quarry.

Along a rutted dirt road that wound through the pasture land walked a boy of about ten. He was headed toward the lights of a farmhouse a mile away where the highway skirted the fields.

The black lips of the werewolf twitched as the boy scuffed along the road, whacking idly at tall weeds with a stick. The boy had short, reddish hair and a spattering of freckles across his face. He wore faded jeans and a light jacket. The scene stood out in sharp relief under the bright moon.

The muscles bunched in the wolf's haunches as the beast gathered itself for the attack. It would be over in seconds. Before the boy could cry out, the wolf would have him by the throat.

At the last possible instant, the wolf held back. The breeze carried a new scent that held him motionless. As he watched the boy, a shaggy white dog bounded up the road from the direction of the farmhouse, flapping its great brush of a tail happily.

The wolf crouched low again, its belly brushing the ground. Although the wind was in his favor, he saw the dog break off its playful romp around the boy, then brace stiffly, testing the air. The fur ruffed up on the back of the dog's neck as it felt the presence of danger. He barked a warning into the darkness.

It would, of course, be no contest. The dog could not last two minutes against a werewolf. Still, there would be a delay in getting at the boy. The clamor might arouse someone in the house. The boy might escape and alarm the people with a story of seeing a huge, pale wolf.

The boy walked on, calling for the white dog to stop fooling around. The werewolf watched from the top of the knoll, its cruel teeth gleaming in the moonlight. With a last half-hearted bark at the night, the dog trotted after the boy.

Slowly the muscles of the wolf relaxed as the boy and the dog rounded a turn in the road and went out of sight. The wolf turned in a slow circle, sampling the air, sorting out the many night smells. Finding what it wanted, the beast loped off over the meadow, away from the lights of the farmhouse.

After a quarter of a mile the werewolf slowed. Straight ahead was its kill for this night. There a black and white Holstein cow stood methodically chewing her cud. Beside the cow, its gangly legs folded under, rested her calf.

Killing this defenseless creature would not bring to the werewolf the fierce, orgasmic joy that came from killing a human, but it would deaden the wolf's awful hunger. The wolf eased closer. The cow raised her head, listening to the rustle of grass behind her. Its reflexes were far too dull for her to sense the danger.

Anger and frustration at losing the boy aroused the killing lust in the heart of the werewolf. He sprang at the calf, hitting the awkward creature as it was trying to rise. The terrified calf was knocked sprawling at the feet of its mother.

The cow mooed in fear and lowered its head in an ineffectual attempt to defend its calf. The wolf merely turned to snarl at the cow, then returned to the business of killing.

While the cow stomped helplessly around, the wolf clamped its fearsome jaws on the neck of the calf. The spine snapped like a dry branch and the struggling young animal went limp.

Under the sorrowful gaze of the mother the wolf fed on the tender flesh of the calf and drank its blood. With an occasional growl he kept the cow from coming too close.

When the wolf had eaten its fill, it used its teeth to crack away the ribcage. Almost gently the bloody muzzle pushed into the chest cavity and tore loose the still-warm heart.

With the bloody organ in its mouth, the wolf rose from its kill and loped away across the meadow toward the forest. The cow lowered its head and nuzzled the mangled carcass.

* * *

The moon was low over the far horizon when the werewolf returned to the gypsy camp. He crossed the clearing between the forest and the little cluster of trailers with the heart of the calf still in his mouth, stopping at the trailer where, hours before, Roy Beatty had left Marcia Lura. The wolf dropped the heart outside the door and stood for a moment, his head cocked, ears pricked, listening. Then he turned and moved back to the edge of the forest.

Minutes later, as the pale wolf lay out of sight in the underbrush, the bolt lock of the trailer door shot back and the door scraped open. The pale wolf heard, but made no move to approach as something snatched the heart of the calf inside and the door slammed shut again. The sounds that came from the trailer then made those gypsies who lay close enough to hear sweat cold in their beds.

* * *

Hours later, with the first light of dawn streaking the sky, Roy Beatty stretched his aching body, pulled on his clothes, and walked toward the trailer.

7

He knocked lightly at the door of the trailer. Inside, the bolt scraped back and in a moment the door opened. Marcia reached out her hands to him and helped him inside. Roy clung to her and felt some of the woman's strength flow into his exhausted body. He stepped back after a minute and looked at her. Somehow, after she had gone through one of the agonizing transformations, Marcia looked her most beautiful. The silver-streaked hair fell loose to her shoulders. Deep fires glowed in the green eyes. Roy's breath caught in his throat.

"Lie down, my lover," she said. "And let me make you comfortable."

He let her lead him to the bed. It was freshly made with crisp linen, the quilted comforter turned back neatly. Roy sank into the bed and closed his eyes. Marcia's hand was cool and soft on his forehead. In a half-dream, he felt her undo the buttons and ease the clothes from his body. He lay naked on the clean sheet as Marcia sponged him with a cool, aromatic liquid. He felt his tensed muscles gradually relax as the vitality flowed back into his body. He opened his eyes and smiled at her.

"You make me feel reborn," he said.

"I'll give you some tea," she said, "And soon you will feel even better."

He reached up and touched the undercurve of her breast. She leaned forward, letting the warm, round weight settle in his palm. Roy shifted his position on the bed as he felt his desire rise for the woman.

"We don't need the tea," he said.

Marcia placed her hand over his and pressed his fingers against her erect nipple. "The tea will be good for you, my darling. It will restore your body and make you strong."

She leaned down and kissed him lightly on the mouth, then walked over to the compact butane stove where a kettle of water boiled. She poured the scalding water over a powdering of herbs in the bottom of a heavy cup. She added a few drops of a thick brown liquid, and a spicy-sweet aroma filled the trailer.

Roy well remembered the first time he had drunk the wild, sweet brew. It was in the small house where Marcia had lived alone in the village of Drago. Afterward there had been sex more intense than anything he had known before. Throughout that afternoon and into the night he had made love to the green-eyed woman in ways he had never imagined. She had taken him with her to the extreme limits of his endurance, then with a final, crashing climax had left him utterly drained.

It was on that same night, as he walked through the forest to the house where Karyn waited, that the black she-wolf with the strange green eyes had run him down. As he lay helpless beneath the beast, the cruel teeth had bitten deep into his shoulder. Roy had been sure then he was going to die. His head was forced back, and he had not the strength to protect his throat. But then, incredibly, the wolf had pulled back and left him. He had staggered home in a daze. Soon he realized why he had been spared, and what it meant to survive the bite of a werewolf.

Marcia handed him the steaming cup. Roy inhaled deeply. The heady aroma made his eyes tear.

"Drink it down," she said softly.

Holding the cup in both hands, he drank the tea and felt the heat of it hit his stomach and radiate throughout his body. There was a soft singing in his ears.

Marcia rested her hand on his bare leg, letting her fingers curl down across his inner thigh. "I have a surprise for you."

"Really?" he said, smiling.

Her lips curved. "In a little while, but first I have something to tell you."

"Yes?"

"We are leaving here."

"I know. As soon as you are ready to travel."

"I am ready now. We are leaving today."

He frowned. "So soon?"

"Soon? I have waited three years. I am as well now as I will ever be."

"But there are arrangements to make... transportation... a place to stay—"

"The arrangements are taken care of," Marcia said. "I have reservations for us on a flight to Seattle out of San Francisco this evening. There will be a room there waiting for us, not far from where your Karyn now lives."

Roy propped himself up on an elbow. "You did all this without talking to me about it?"

Her fingers moved again on his thigh, slid up between his legs. "I know you aren't interested in tiresome details."

"Just the same, you could have told me."

Marcia guided the cup of tea to his lips, and he drank. "You're not having doubts about what we have to do?"

"No. Only—"

The long supple fingers worked on him. "Don't feel sorry for your Karyn. Remember, she was no wife to you, yet she gave herself freely to your supposed friend. Now she shares the bed of this man Richter. She has crippled me and cuckolded you. Now it is our turn."

Roy drank more of the powerful tea. Visions flashed through his mind of Karyn's slim, naked body convulsed with passion as some faceless man pounded into her.

"Yes," he whispered. "Our turn."

Marcia took the empty cup from his hand and placed it on the floor. She stood up and slipped the silky garment she was wearing off over her head. She let it fall to the floor and stood with her strong brown legs slightly apart, letting him eat her with his eyes. She came toward him slowly, her breasts swaying with each step.

Roy started to rise from the bed to meet her. She laid a hand on his shoulder and eased him back down. He lay back obediently, watching her. She moved his legs apart and knelt between them. Her head dipped forward and her hair brushed his thighs as her lips closed around him.

She made it last a full hour. Then, as they lay together and Roy dozed, voices outside the trailer roused them. Loud voices. Marcia pulled gently away from him and stood up, throwing a light robe over her shoulders. Roy, now fully awake, got up too. They went over and stood at the small window. Marcia eased the green curtain aside enough for them to look out.

Outside, Ignacio, the leader of the gypsies, stood talking to a large, red-faced man. Sniffing nervously about their feet was a shaggy white dog.

"None of the people here would do a thing like that," Ignacio was saying. "I know them."

"Don't give me that crap," said the red-faced man. "There was a trail of blood from the spot where the calf was killed, leading right into your camp. People told me I was makin' a mistake letting gypsies stay on my property, but like a damn fool I didn't listen to 'em."

Ignacio's eyes flicked over toward the trailer where Roy and Marcia watched from behind the curtain. They glanced at each other, then returned their attention to the two men outside.

"I will ask among the people," Ignacio said. "If I find anyone here is responsible for this, he will be punished. Be sure of that."

"That calf was worth plenty," the farmer said.

"You can take the money the calf is worth out of the wages you pay us for working in your fields," Ignacio said.

"Well—" The farmer glowered around the motley collection of campers and trailers, as though trying to spot the culprit. "I guess that will be okay. But if this ever happens again—"

"I assure you it won't happen again."

"It sure as hell better not," said the farmer, "Or next time I bring the sheriff with me."

He started to walk away, but turned back as though he were not yet satisfied. "It's bad enough to lose the calf, but the way it was done—Jesus. All ripped apart. What kind of a man would kill an animal that way?"

Ignacio had no answer, and the farmer clumped off, toward the trail that led through the woods. At the edge of the trees he turned and whistled sharply. The dog broke off its investigation of the trailers and followed the man.

Ignacio remained standing where he was. He turned his head and stared long at the trailer where Marcia and Roy stood watching.

"He knows," Roy whispered.

"Of course he knows," said Marcia, "But he would never dare to act against us."

"Maybe not, but we shouldn't push him too far. I'll go out and tell him we're leaving."

"As you wish," Marcia said indifferently. "I'll gather the things we will want to take with us."

When Roy dressed and went out he found Ignacio sitting on the rear step of the camper where he lived with his wife and small daughter. The gypsy's face darkened as Roy approached.

Roy spoke awkwardly. "Ignacio, I–I wanted to tell you we are leaving."

"Leaving?" The gypsy could not keep the eagerness out of his voice. "For good?"

"Yes. You've been very kind letting us stay with you while Marcia was… ill. I'm grateful."

"You owe me nothing."

"She is better now, so we'll be on our way."

Ignacio nodded gravely. He offered no words of regret at their leaving. Roy knew well why they had been allowed to stay, and Ignacio was not man to waste false words of farewell.

"Goodbye," Roy said.

The gypsy studied him, the black eyes nearly hidden beneath the tangled brows.

"God help you," he said.

8

Karyn stepped out of the elevator in the Seattle Sheraton Hotel, feeling highly pleased with herself. She had a job. At least she would have, starting next month—coordinating the new hotel's banquet facilities. It would be good to feel useful again.

Over the past several weeks there had been several discussions with David, who did not fully approve of her going back to work. Finally, though, he said he would not object if that was what she really wanted. Dr. Goetz thought it was a good idea, and he had helped convince David. She had arranged to work only twenty hours a week, and would have afternoons and evenings free for her family.

This morning she had been so excited about the job interview that she skipped breakfast. Now she was hungry. The hotel's coffee shop opened off the lobby, and Karyn went in. It was eleven o'clock, in between coffee-breakers and the lunch crowd, so the room was nearly empty. Karyn took a table near the window and ordered shrimp salad, boysenberry pie, and coffee. As she waited for the waitress to come back with the order, Karyn began to feel uneasy. At first it was nothing she could define, just a prickling of the skin and a sort of chill down her back. Then she knew what it was. Someone was watching her.

Karyn tried to shrug off the feeling. It was nerves, of course. The excitement of getting a job. Just sit still, she thought, and it will go away.

But it did not go away. Instead, the feeling of being watched grew stronger and more oppressive. The waitress brought her food and gave her an odd look.

Even though Karyn knew it was foolishness, the desire to turn around became too strong to resist. As casually as she could manage, Karyn turned in her chair and surveyed one by one the other customers. There was a haggard young mother trying to keep a pair of little boys in their chairs. A young man with an Army haircut, probably from Fort Lewis. An old man in a black mohair suit, reading a Hebrew newspaper. A woman with dark hair streaked with silver, studying the menu through oversized sunglasses. A fat woman cheating on her diet with a double caramel sundae. A young woman in a beautician's smock, with the name of the hotel stitched over the pocket.

That was all. An ordinary lot. And none of them watching her. At least, no one was watching when she turned to look.

Karyn returned to her food, but found she was no longer hungry. She knew she had to stop these imaginings. Be logical about it, she told herself. *Why* would anyone watch her? What reason could they have?

She snapped upright in the chair. Why would anyone wear dark sunglasses on a cloudy day?

Karyn turned again, quickly this time. Everything was as before—all the same customers sitting where they had been. All, except the dark-haired woman in the sunglasses. She was gone.

What had the woman looked like? Karyn bit her lip and tried to remember. The woman's eyes bad been invisible behind the dark lenses, and the lower part of her face was hidden behind the menu. Deliberately? The only feature Karyn could recall was the startling slash of white through the blue-black hair. And yet the woman seemed familiar.

Karyn shook her head, impatient with herself. This was getting her nowhere. There was no earthly reason for anyone to be watching her. She had to stop these fancies. She resolved to tell Dr. Goetz about it. In his gentle, professional way he could settle her down, explain these irrational feelings.

She paid for her uneaten lunch and left the coffee shop. Outside the day had darkened as the heavy clouds pressed down on the city. There was nothing for Karyn to do at home, and she did not want to spend the day alone in the big house with only Mrs. Jensen for company.

She stood indecisively in front of the hotel and looked up and down the street. The marquee of a theater down the block advertised a movie she had been wanting to see. On an impulse she turned and walked to the theater, bought a ticket, and went in.

The audience was small for the early show, and Karyn found a seat by herself halfway down and on the aisle. She settled down to watch the movie, but soon began to shift uncomfortably in her seat. The feeling of being watched came back. It was stronger here in the darkened theater than it had been in the coffee shop.

Making no attempt this time to be casual, Karyn turned to scan the faces in the reflected light from the screen. No one was looking at her. She did not see the woman with the streak in her hair.

After that she found she could not concentrate on the movie, and soon left the theater. Outside, a light, dismal rain had begun. Karyn hurried the two blocks to the parking lot where she had left her car. At once she stopped and turned suddenly. She caught a fleeting impression of a woman half a block behind her, on the same side of the street. Just as Karyn turned the woman slipped into the entrance of a building. In the brief glimpse, all that Karyn could be sure of was that the woman was tall and dark. She walked slowly the rest of the way, turning several times to look behind her, but the woman did not reappear.

* * *

The Evergreen Motel was a neglected, U-shaped stucco complex at the northern city limits of Seattle. The Evergreen had no swimming pool, no television in the rooms, no automobile club recommendations, but it was private and cheap and did good Friday-night business among romantic couples from near by offices. The couple in Room 9, however, had their minds on other things.

"Are you sure she didn't recognize you?" Roy Beatty asked.

"She never got a good look at my face," Marcia said. She smiled, the green eyes glowing with some deep emotion. "But I touched something in her memory. I let her see me twice, and I know she felt the beginnings of fear."

"Do you think that's a good idea?" Roy said. "Dragging it out like this?"

"My love, that *is* the idea. For what that woman did to me, and to you too, we want her to suffer. She must have time to worry about it."

Marcia lay back across the bed, stretching her long body sensuously. Roy did not look at her. He paced the worn carpet nervously.

"What do we do now?" he asked.

"Don't worry, darling. I have it all planned. I will let her see me again—just a glimpse here and there. Maybe we'll give her a quick look at you. That would give her something to think about. I have watched her at home, and I have a little something in mind there too. The important thing is to have patience. I want your Karyn to finally understand what is happening to her, and why, just before—" She left the unfinished sentence hanging.

"Before what?" Roy said.

Marcia sat up suddenly and swung around to face him. "Don't be stupid, Roy. You know what we have to do."

"Kill her, Marcia? Do we have to kill her? What good will that do?"

Marcia swung her long legs from the bed and walked over to stand in front of him. She looked deep into his eyes, holding her body close to his. Her voice was soft and caressing.

"It will give me peace, darling, after months of agony. It is something I must do. If you don't want to be a part of it, I will understand. Leave now if that's the way you feel, and I will go on alone."

Roy held himself away from the green-eyed woman for a moment, then put his hands on her shoulders and pulled her tight against him. He stroked her hair, gently fingering the streak of silver as though it were a wound. The gentle scent of sandalwood brought to his mind the intoxicating days and nights when they had first been together.

"I can't leave you," he said. "Whatever has to be done, we will do together."

"My Roy," she breathed close to his ear. "My lover." Gently she pulled him toward the bed.

* * *

"What did Dr. Goetz say?"

David Richter held his wife's hand and studied her worriedly.

"He said it was all in my head."

David frowned.

"I'm only kidding. He didn't say that in so many words, but that was the gist of his message. What he said was something like, 'Many people go through periods of mild paranoia. Even people with no other neuroses. For someone with your history, it isn't at all unusual. Nothing to worry about.'"

David squeezed Karyn's hand and nodded sagely. "I'm sure Dr. Goetz knows what he's talking about, dear."

"Not in this case, he doesn't," Karyn said. "There *is* someone following me. A woman. Since the other day when I first saw her in the coffee shop, I've seen her again on the street, once at the library, and again just this morning in a taxi driving by right in front of our house."

"You're sure it was the same woman?"

"I'm positive. She was dressed differently, and always had her face covered or turned away, but I couldn't miss that white streak in her black hair."

David listened thoughtfully. When Karyn finished speaking he rubbed his jaw and gazed off at a corner of the ceiling. "Karyn, about your going to work—do you think we might be rushing things a bit?"

"No, I don't! And what the hell does that have to do with anything?"

"I just thought that, well, the added strain of taking on an outside job just now might... might..."

"Might make me start imagining things?" Karyn finished for him. "Like people following me?"

"I didn't mean that, exactly."

"Like hell you didn't." Karyn saw the hurt look come into his eyes, and she reached up to touch his cheek. "I'm sorry, David. I know. You're trying to do what you think is best for me. So is Dr. Goetz. It's just that neither of you wants to consider the possibility that I am seeing exactly what I think I'm seeing."

David smiled at her, but the doubt was still in his eyes. "I'm trying, dear. I'm really trying."

They talked no more about it that evening, and went up to bed early. David fell asleep almost immediately. It was another hour before Karyn began to get drowsy. Then she was jolted back to full wakefulness. Something was moving around downstairs.

It was not any distinct sound that she could identify. Just a sort of soft shuffling. Then nothing. For a long time Karyn lay tense, staring into the darkness. She fought to convince herself that she had heard no sound, and she prayed that it would not come again.

Then she heard it again. Just the suggestion of movement. She wanted it to be Mrs. Jensen, but knew that it was not. The housekeeper moved with a firm, heavy tread, not the furtive shuffling Karyn heard now.

Her mind groped for possible explanations. The wind. The house settling. Mice. The plumbing. But it was no good. She knew it was none of these. She lay utterly still and listened. For many minutes the only sound was David's deep, regular breathing. Her ears ached with the effort of listening. Then it came again. Something sliding, like cloth on cloth. Then a muffled thump, barely audible, but unmistakably real.

"David." Her voice was a rasping whisper.

"Wha—"

She placed her fingers lightly on his lips to silence him as he awoke. When his eyes were fully open and alert, she took her hand away.

"What is it?" he said, whispering in reaction to her tension.

"There's something downstairs."

"What do you mean?"

"Sssh. Listen."

They sat up in bed, their shoulders touching, and listened. The seconds ticked by. Karyn's chest began to ache, and she realized she was holding her breath. She let it out in a long, silent sigh.

"I don't hear anything," David said. A touch of annoyance had crept into his voice.

"No, I heard something. Really."

For another interminable two minutes they sat in the bed, their heads cocked toward the door.

Nothing.

"Karyn—" David began, speaking now in a natural voice.

"I didn't imagine it," she said. "There's something down there. Or at least there was."

"Why do you say 'something' instead of 'someone'?"

"God, I don't know. What difference does it make?"

With a sigh, David threw back the covers. "I'll go down and look around."

Karyn watched as he got out of bed, pulled on a robe over his white pajamas, and went out into the hallway. She felt foolish. Like some giddy wife in an old television sitcom. *"Ricky, get up. I heard a burglar!" "Aw, go back to sleep, Lucy, ees nothing."*

Briskly she threw off the blankets and got up. At least she did not have to stay up here cowering in bed, playing out her role. Pulling on a quilted robe, she went out the door and headed down the hallway toward the stairs. At the head of the stairs she stopped to look into Joey's room. The boy was sleeping peacefully. Karyn went on down to join her husband.

All the lights were blazing now as David flicked them on as he walked from room to room. When Karyn reached the bottom of the stairs he was just coming back from the rear of the house. Behind him was Mrs. Jensen, her face puffy from sleep, her hair twisted around plastic rollers.

"Nothing down here," David said. Karyn knew he was making an effort not to let his irritation show.

"Mrs. Jensen," she said, "Did you hear anything?"

"Not me. Not until Mr. Richter knocked on my door. But then, I sleep like the dead anyway."

Karyn looked around helplessly. "I'm sure I heard a noise down here."

"Well, there's nothing here now," David said. "You can go back to bed, Mrs. Jensen. Sorry to disturb you."

Karyn waited while David went around turning off the lights, then followed him upstairs. They got into bed and he lay rigidly with his back to her. She wanted to reach out and touch him, bring him close, but she could not. She had to listen. But there were no more sounds from downstairs. After a very long time she fell into a troubled sleep.

9

For the next two nights, Karyn slept fitfully.

She was waiting, straining to hear even the smallest sound from downstairs that did not belong. All she heard were the normal creaks and snaps a house makes as it cools off at night, but her imagination gave them strange and sinister implications.

During the daytime she stayed close to the house. When she walked even as far as the mailbox she watched carefully behind her. No one followed.

Finally she began to relax a little. Maybe, just maybe, she had imagined those things—the watcher, the night sounds downstairs. Maybe everything was going to be all right.

Then her plants began to sicken.

The Boston fern was the first to show symptoms of trouble. While making her rounds with the watering can and spray bottle, Karyn noticed several of the little saw-toothed fronds, curled and brown, lying on the floor under the fern. When she examined the plant more closely she found dying fronds, and the remaining, living fronds had lost their resiliency. She moved on to the spider plant and saw that the bladelike leaves no longer held their proud arch. The pointed tips on several were beginning to turn brown. Her pet, the philodendron, seemed robust still, but even its leaves looked duller than they should be.

Karyn heard Mrs. Jensen out in the kitchen. She called to her, and the housekeeper came out wiping her hands on a towel.

"Yes, Mrs. Richter?"

"Have you been watering the plants?"

"I never touch those plants. You asked me not to, as I remember."

"Yes, that's right. Thank you."

"Is that all?"

"Yes, that's all."

Karyn read the woman's resentment in the set of her shoulders as she marched back to the kitchen. She'd make it up to the housekeeper later, by praising the dinner or something.

Karyn walked around and looked at the plants again. There was no doubt that something was wrong with them. Even the strong philodendron. The trouble was that sick plants looked the same whether they were over-watered, under-watered, or suffering from any number of horticultural maladies. Karyn had always been careful about the watering, and she had seen to it that each got its proper amount of light and was kept within the acceptable temperature range. The soil had been specially blended at the store where she bought the plants; the nutrients she added at specified intervals came from there too.

She had heard the theory that plants can pick up the psychological vibrations of their people and react to them, but she considered the idea ridiculous. All the same, something was definitely wrong with her plants, and Karyn resolved to watch them closely.

In the next 24 hours they got much worse. By then there was a generous scattering of dead brown fronds under the fern. The spider plant drooped sadly, its leaves turning yellow and curling in on themselves. The philodendron had completely lost its glossy good health. The leaves had paled and hung limp from the vine. The whole plant sagged against the post as though it were an effort to remain upright.

Karyn decided to wait no longer. She carried the three plants out to her little Datsun and drove off for Plant World on Aurora, where she had bought them. She felt just a little foolish rushing them off like sick children, but they *were* her responsibility.

She pulled into the parking lot at Plant World and carried them in one by one. She was relieved to find an understanding woman at the counter, and not some smartass who would have to make jokes.

"My, they do seem to be feeling poorly, don't they?" the woman said.

"It just happened in the last couple of days," Karyn said. "What do you think is wrong with them?"

"I'd hate to take a guess. Mr. Bjorklund will be back this afternoon. He's awfully good with sick little fellows like these."

"Would it be all right if I left them here? I could come back tomorrow and talk to Mr.—"

"Bjorklund," the woman supplied. "Of course you can leave them, dear. Don't worry about them. I'll see to it they're made comfortable, and I'll watch over them until Mr. Bjorklund comes."

"Thank you," Karyn said. She resisted an impulse to give each of the sick plants a reassuring pat, and left the store.

A sense of depression came over her as she drove back home. The car seemed empty. She reminded herself sternly that it was just three plants she had left behind, not three children. To get out of the mood, she decided to stop in at the new Kenmore Shopping Mall and look around.

It was one of the new breed of two-level shopping centers, roofed over against the elements, and with an adjoining parking structure. Inside, the mall had bubbling fountains, potted shrubbery, and plastic park benches. The air had a scent of aerosol springtime. Soft, soothing music flowed from concealed speakers.

Karyn strolled slowly along, window-shopping the jewelry and clothing stores. She went into a leather goods shop and began to feel better, enjoying the tangy smell and tough-smooth feel of the merchandise.

She picked out a key case she thought David would like, and paid for it with her Master Charge card. While the clerk filled out the receipt she remembered that her parents had a wedding anniversary coming up soon. She left the leather shop with her purchase and stepped on the Down escalator to reach a gift shop on the lower level.

As she rode down the silent moving stairway, Karyn glanced up at the overhead ledge. Just before she was carried underneath, she saw the face of Roy Beatty.

Her knees started to give way, and she clutched the black rubber handrail for support. The woman in front of her turned around and gave Karyn a look of disapproval.

When the escalator reached the bottom Karyn almost fell as her feet slid over the grate where the steps disappeared. The people coming off behind Karyn jostled her as she stood motionless, staring upward toward the ledge that was out of sight now. After a moment, she took hold of herself and hurried across the mall to where the matching escalator carried people up. She got on and climbed the moving steps, ignoring the irritated looks she got from the shoppers she pushed past.

Once back on the upper level she had to look around for a moment to get her bearings. She located the ledge with the railing overlooking the Down escalator, where she had seen Roy. The only people there now were two young boys who leaned over to watch the moving row of people slide down and out of sight. There was no sign of Roy Beatty, or of anyone who looked like him.

Karyn hurried over and spoke to the boys. "What happened to the man who was standing here?"

The boys looked at each other, then back at Karyn. "What man?"

"He was standing right here where you are now. He was looking down."

"There wasn't any man here that we saw." The boys started to edge away from her.

Karyn started to insist that there certainly had been a man standing right here not three minutes ago, then she stopped, realizing how foolish it would be to argue with the children. In frustration she spun around, her eyes ranging over the people who moved among the shops.

She saw him again just as he vanished down one of the broad aisles leading to an exit. He wore a denim jacket and faded jeans. The hair was longer than Roy had worn his, but it was the same shade of pale tan, and the broad shoulders brought Karyn a pang of memory. She left the two boys staring after her and followed the man.

She reached the exit and saw that it opened on a concrete walkway across to the parking structure. No one was on the bridge. Karyn hurried across and peered around among the parked ears. There was no sign of the man in denim. Karyn looked down and saw her hands were shaking. She leaned for a moment against one of the thick pillars for support. Somewhere she had dropped the package with David's key case, but she did not go back to look for it.

* * *

Dr. Goetz sat facing her in one of his chrome and leather chairs. He wore a professional, concerned expression.

"I feel a little silly," Karyn said, "Calling you from the shopping center as though it were some kind of life-or-death emergency. All the same, I'm glad you could see me."

The doctor smiled gently. "I hate to say, 'That's what I'm here for,' because it sounds so Marcus Welby. But that's what I'm here for, Karyn."

"Now that I'm here, I don't know where to start."

"Tell me about the man you saw at the shopping mall. Did you get a good look at him?"

"Yes. It was just for a second or two, but I saw him very clearly. Then the escalator took me down under the ledge where he was standing."

"Did he say anything to you?"

"No."

"Make any gesture? Any sign that he knew you?"

"He just looked at me."

"And you say he resembled your former husband."

"Dr. Goetz, he *was* my former husband. That man was Roy Beatty."

Dr. Goetz squeezed his lower lip thoughtfully between thumb and forefinger. After several seconds he spoke. "As I recall, you told me Roy Beatty died three years ago."

Karyn felt the beginnings of a headache. She said, "I don't *know* that he died in the Drago fire. I assumed that he did. Obviously, I was wrong. If I saw him in the Kenmore Mall this morning, then he's alive."

Dr. Goetz got out of his chair and came over to sit beside her on the sofa. His pale blue eyes searched her face, then became unreadable. "Karyn, I think maybe we were hasty in cutting you down to one visit a week. If it's possible, I'd like to see you more often. Twice. Three times, if you could manage it."

Karyn wanted to cry. Ever since the crack-up in Las Vegas she had made steady progress in her therapy. Until now. What was happening to her? She knew how it must sound—someone following her, noises in the night, and now seeing her supposedly dead husband. The classic symptoms of paranoid schizophrenia.

For the first time in many months Karyn wondered if she might be losing her grip on reality. Maybe she did need more time with the analyst.

"I'll talk to my husband about it," she said. "Goodbye, Doctor."

* * *

The front door of the Richter house flew open and banged shut with an unnecessary slam. Joey Richter raced in, dumped his schoolbooks on the hall table without slowing down, and made a speedy circuit of the downstairs rooms. He came to a stop at the foot of the stairs.

"*Mom!*" he called

Mrs. Jensen came down the stairs carrying a basket of laundry. "Your mother isn't home. And if she was, she'd tell you not to slam the door."

"Where is she?"

"She had an appointment downtown."

"With the doctor?"

"I wouldn't know."

"Why did she have to see the doctor today? This isn't her day."

"I'm sure I couldn't say."

"She's probably having those dreams again. The ones that scare her."

"I don't know anything about any dreams," Mrs. Jensen said. "Now come in and eat your lunch. It's good vegetable soup."

"Campbell's?"

"No, it's homemade."

"I like Campbell's."

"You're going to like this even better. Come on and I'll dish it up for you."

Joey clumped into the kitchen and ate two bowls of the soup, which he admitted was almost as good as Campbell's. He finished up with a peanut butter and jelly sandwich and a glass of milk while Mrs. Jensen loaded clothes into the washer in the adjoining laundry room.

"I wish Mom would get home," Joey said. "I want to tell her about the face last night."

Mrs. Jensen came back into the kitchen. "Did you say a face?"

"Yeah. Last night it looked right in my window. Wow, was it ugly!"

"You had a dream, you mean."

"Nah, it wasn't any dream, it was a face. All kind of scrunched up and hairy and with great big teeth. Really ugly."

The housekeeper studied the boy for a moment.

"Did it scare you?"

Joey met her eye seriously, then broke into mischievous laughter. "No way. I knew who it was all the time."

"Who?"

"That crazy Kelly in a rubber mask. He's always doing crazy things. Probably climbed up on the roof and thought he could scare me. Crazy."

"What would he be doing up so late?" Mrs. Jensen said with stern disapproval.

"He gets to stay up as late as he wants to," Joey said. "I'm as old as he is and don't even get to stay up and watch '*Kojak.*'"

"It does you a lot more good to get your sleep than staying up to watch junk like that. Or playing dumb tricks like your friend Kelly."

"I'll tell Mom," Joey said. "She'll buy me a mask, a horribler one than Kelly's even, then I'll go to his house and *really* scare him."

"I don't think you'd better tell your mother about it," Mrs. Jensen said.

"Why not? She'll buy me a mask. I know she will."

"Maybe so, but your mother's not been feeling too well, and I don't think it would do her any good to hear about faces at the window and such foolishness."

"Awww."

"You want her to get well, don't you?"

"Sure."

"Then don't go bothering her with this kind of stuff."

"Oh, okay."

Joey jumped up from the table and ran outside, slamming the door firmly. Mrs. Jensen looked after him with a worried frown, then shook off the thought and got busy picking up the dishes.

10

Room 9 in the Evergreen Motel was cool and dim in the pale light that filtered in through the curtains. Roy Beatty sat beside the bed, holding the hand of the woman who lay among the twisted sheets.

"I was worried when you didn't come home last night," he said.

Marcia rolled her head on the pillow and looked at him. There were shadows around her deep green eyes, but they shone as brilliantly as ever.

She said, "I'm all right now. It was frightening when it happened. Last night was the first time I wasn't prepared for it. It must have been the excitement of being so close, of seeing at last what we are going to do. I could not control the change.

Roy stroked a strand of black hair from her forehead. "My poor Marcia."

"It doesn't matter," she said. "There is a patch of trees near their house. I was able to reach them and stay there until daylight. No one saw me, except perhaps the boy, and I don't think he knew what he was seeing."

"Maybe we should forget about this. Go away from here. For your sake."

"Forget about it?" Marcia sat straight up in bed, and it seemed to Roy that he could see the strength flow into her body. "Never! I have not waited this long, come this far, only to turn back. As for what happened to me last night, I will take care to see that it does not happen again. I will keep a tighter hold on my emotions."

Roy sighed and nodded his head slowly. He stood up and walked over to the window where he pulled aside the curtain and looked out over the asphalt of the parking lot. The Evergreen was not on one of the main highways which ran through Seattle, and in the middle of the week there was little business. There were only three cars parked outside, the white Ford, which Roy had rented, and two others. They looked cold and abandoned in the misting rain.

"If it's going to rain, I wish to Christ it would really rain," he said irritably. "This everlasting drizzle is driving me up the wall."

"We won't have to be here much longer," Marcia said. "Your Karyn is frightened and worried now. The way we want her."

"Why do you keep calling her *my* Karyn?"

"I'm sorry. It was just an expression. I won't do it any more if it annoys you."

"Well, it does. Anyway, what's the need for all this?" Roy continued to stare out the window. "Why don't we do what we came to do and get it over with?"

Marcia slipped out of bed and came over to stand beside him. She took his broad hand in hers and held it against her smooth, naked hip. "Indulge me in this, my Roy, and I will make it up to you."

He held himself tensely, not looking at her. She moved his hand across the flat of her stomach and down to the crisp bush of pubic hair. He resisted for a moment more, then surrendered and turned to face her. He whispered her name. His fingers probed between her legs and found the dampness there.

Marcia grasped his wrist and held it, keeping his hand pressed against her. "When this business is over I will make you very happy. I know I have not been a complete woman to you these past months, but I will make it right in a hundred ways. You will never regret being with me, darling." She drew back and her eyes searched his face. "You are with me, aren't you, my Roy?"

"You know I am."

"Good." She kissed him lightly on the mouth, then slipped away and began to put on her clothes. Once again she was businesslike.

"Are you sure you were seen at the shopping center?"

"Karyn saw me, all right," he said. "Once when she rode the escalator below where I was standing, and again as I was going out. She followed me to the parking lot, but I lost her there."

"Good. She will have much to think about, many things to remember when we take the next step."

"And that is?"

"We kill the boy."

Roy drew in his breath and let it out slowly. "Is that the only way?"

"It is the best way. It is the way that will hurt her the most before we finally finish with her." Marcia fixed him with her eyes. "Do you have some objection?"

"It's just… killing the boy—"

Marcia's laugh clattered off the walls in the small room. "Come now, Roy. After the things you have done these past three years? The blood you have spilled? Would one more killing bother you?"

He could not meet her eye. "Remember, Marcia, I wasn't born to this life the way you were. What I am, you made me. I am not all wolf. I still have human emotions sometimes."

Marcia stepped close to him and touched his face. "I understand, my darling. The time will come when you will no longer be held back by remorse. Until then you will take strength from me. I know that when the time comes to act, you will not fail."

"When… will it be time?"

"From now on we will watch the house every night. The first time they leave the boy alone, you will kill him."

11

Mr. Bjorklund shrugged and spread his hands in a gesture of helplessness. "I'm sorry," he said.

Karyn waited for a moment for him to say something more. When he didn't she looked down at the long wooden counter between them. There, each in its familiar pot, were her three plants. They were barely recognizable. The fern and the spider plant were yellow-brown, shriveled and ugly, dead, ropy things that had nothing to do with the vibrant living greenery they had been. Only the tough philodendron had not given up. With the tenacity of the dying it clung to the mossy post, but its leaves were pale and sickly, splotched with brown like the hands of old people with liver spots.

"I'm afraid they're goners." Mr. Bjorklund said. "There was nothing I could do."

"Thanks, anyway," Karyn said dully.

"What have you been feeding them?"

Karyn looked up at him curiously. "I didn't feed them anything, except what you gave me. I kept them in the soil you blended for me, and I was very careful about watering them."

"Somebody fed them," The nurseryman said. "They've been poisoned."

Karyn stared at him.

"I ran a test on the soil in all three pots. Each one is saturated with enough herbicide to kill a Douglas fir."

"That isn't possible."

Bjorklund shrugged again. "All I can tell you is what the tests showed."

"Is there some way the herbicide could have got into the soil accidentally?"

"Nope. It was added to the soil deliberately and carefully. The concentration was heaviest right down around the roots. The way I figure it, somebody jammed the nozzle of a plastic squeeze bottle down in there and pumped the stuff in."

"Why would anybody want to do that?"

"You tell me."

Karyn looked down again at the sorry shriveled things that had been her plants. "Then they're all… dead?"

"As last winter's corsage," he said. "The philodendron might hang on for a while if we transplant it into some rich new soil and feed it special nutrients, but if you want my opinion, it's a goner too. I'll try to save it if you want me to."

"No," Karyn said abruptly. "No, never mind." She turned and started for the door.

"How about replacements?" Bjorklund called after her. "I can fix you up with three nice healthy plants."

"No, thank you."

"What about these pots? They're yours."

"You keep them," Karyn said without looking back. "I have no more use for them."

* * *

The house in Mountlake Terrace seemed painfully empty. Karyn wandered around restlessly, then stopped short as she realized she was avoiding the family room. That was where her plants had been.

For God's sake, they were only vegetables! she reminded herself. And yet she had to admit now that they had come to mean much more to her. Far too much.

She saw the absurdity of her feelings, but seeing it did nothing to lessen her sense of loss. The plants had been hers, and hers alone, and now they were dead. Murdered, if it was accurate to say a plant had been murdered. Who would do a thing like that? And why? It had to be someone who was trying to get at her. The someone who was in her house the other night?

She put aside the suspicions forming in her mind when David came home. She told him briefly that her plants had died, without going into details. There was no way to tell him without sounding more paranoid than ever.

David was very kind. Sensing her mood, he put an arm around her and patted her gently. "You know something, we haven't been out together for a long time," he said. "What do you say we have dinner tonight at Teagle's?"

"But you have to work tomorrow."

"So I'll go in a little late. The business will hold together. How about it?"

"I'd like it," Karyn said. "Very much."

David gave her hand a squeeze. "It will be good for you to get out of the house."

Mrs. Jensen came in and cleared her throat to get their attention. "Will you be wanting an early dinner tonight?" she said.

"We're going out," David told her. "Just make something for Joey."

The housekeeper nodded and turned to leave.

"Oh Mrs. Jensen," David called her back. "There was a ladder left leaning up against the back of the house the other day. I had to put it away."

Karyn looked up quickly. "A ladder?"

Mrs. Jensen made a clucking sound with her tongue. "Ah. That would have been one of Joey's little friends. The Kelly boy."

"I wish Joey would tell his friends to leave things in the garage alone. Or at least put them back when they're finished."

"I'll speak to him about it," Mrs. Jensen said.

It was warm in the house, but Karyn caught herself shivering as though she was caught in a cold draft.

12

At first the idea of getting dressed and going out had seemed hardly worth the trouble to Karyn. It could not change anything. Still, it was sweet of David to make the effort to please her, so she went along with it. However, as she sat before her dressing table applying a touch of pale pink lipstick, she found she was truly looking forward to a night out. As David said, it *had* been a long time.

She stood up a looked herself over in the mirror on the closet door. The long dress clung nicely, flattering her trim figure. Not bad, she decided, for a neurotic lady closing in on thirty. She added a final dab of perfume and went downstairs to where David was waiting.

Mrs. Jensen went to the front door with them as they left.

"We may be home late," David said. He turned to smile at Karyn. "We might decide to go out dancing somewhere after dinner."

Karyn returned his smile.

"I won't wait up, then," Mrs. Jensen said.

"You'll see that Joey gets to bed on time?" Karyn said.

Mrs. Jensen gave her a brief smile that said she had been taking care of Joey before Karyn got there, and could handle it very well now, thank you.

David gave Karyn his arm, and they followed the flagstone walk around to the garage. Halfway there, Karyn pulled up. Had she seen something move in that white Ford parked up the block? Whose car was that, anyway? She was sure it did not belong to any of the neighbors.

"Is something wrong?" David said.

"Nooo," she said slowly. Then more emphatically. "No. I just caught my heel on the edge of the stone. Let's go."

There was nothing moving in the white car now. Probably she had imagined it. The Ford most likely belonged to someone visiting the neighbors. No point in mentioning it to David and getting their evening off to an uncomfortable start.

* * *

Mrs. Jensen watched from the doorway as the Richters drove off. It was high time they had an evening out together, she thought. Much of the time she felt Mr. Richter worked too hard. And Mrs. Richter, well, she had her own problems. She closed the door and went inside.

She let Joey stay up to watch Charlie's Angels, which he said he enjoyed because of the pretty girls. Mrs. Jensen left him to enjoy the girls alone while she went to her own room to watch an old Bette Davis movie on another channel. At ten o'clock she sent Joey up to bed, ignoring his pleas to watch Baretta. When the boy was tucked in, Mrs. Jensen resumed watching her movie on the larger set in the Richters' family room.

The movie ended and the eleven o'clock news came on. Mrs. Jensen got up and switched off the set. They never had anything but riots and killings and plane crashes on the news. Mrs. Jensen figured there was enough violence and unhappiness in a person's everyday life without watching film of it every night on the news before you went to bed. She went back to the little bathroom off her room and began brushing out her hair.

At eleven-thirty, wearing a clean flannel nightgown and with her hair in rollers, she climbed into bed. Sometimes she watched Johnny Carson for an hour or so until she got sleepy, but tonight she was too tired.

Mrs. Jensen closed her eyes and lay warm and cozy under the down comforter she'd brought with her when she came to work for Mr. Richter. Finding this job after her husband died had been a blessing. She had no other family, and really needed someone to take care of. The house here and Joey were enough to keep her busy, but not more than she could comfortably handle.

She had assumed a sort of housemother position for the man and the boy, which worked out well for all three. When Mr. Richter married his new wife he hastened to assure Mrs. Jensen that her place in the household was secure. Nevertheless, Mrs. Jensen at first had misgivings about the new Mrs. Richter. The slim, pretty blonde from California had seemed too young and unsettled for Mr. Richter. Also, having no children of her own, how was she going to get along with Joey?

As it happened, everything worked out fine. The new Mrs. Richter had turned out to be a lot more mature and sensible than she looked, and she and the boy had taken to each other instantly. And if Mrs. Richter was a tiny touch nervous sometimes, well, that only made Mrs. Jensen feel more useful.

She rolled over onto her back and cleared her mind of all daytime thoughts in preparation for going to sleep.

A shadow passed her window.

Mrs. Jensen sat up in bed and stared at the drawn blind.

Nothing.

And yet there had been something. Just outside. She held her breath and listened.

Nothing.

But something had been there, all right. Olivia Jensen was not the kind of woman who imagined shadows in the night. She got up and pulled on her robe, tying the belt securely beneath her bosom. She went to the window and pulled aside the blind. An expanse of lawn, revealing rosebushes and the back of the garage, brightened occasionally as the clouds broke up and the moon came through. But nothing moved.

Leaving her room, Mrs. Jensen went out and began testing the door and windows of the house, even though she was sure she had locked them all before going to bed. When she reached the living room she heard something.

A rustling sound in the shrubbery outside the front door. She looked through the peep-viewer, but could see nothing. She started to back away, then stopped as she heard a kind of snuffling outside. Then a soft scraping sound as of some animal pawing at the door.

Animal? A dog, she thought. Could her sister's German shepherd have gotten lost and somehow found its way here? It was a long way to where her sister lived, but you read about those things all the time. Maybe it was hurt.

Mrs. Jensen opened the door.

The wolf sprang into the air and hit her full in the chest, knocking her to the floor as it tumbled past her into the hallway.

There was no time for Mrs. Jensen to think about what was happening. She could only react by instinct.

The wolf, larger and stronger than any she had seen in the zoo, stood in the hallway, its powerful legs braced. The broad tan head swung to and fro, as though it were looking for something.

Mrs. Jensen stumbled to her feet. The front door was still open, letting the cold air in. Outside, the night was peaceful and clear; inside was terror.

"Get out of here!" she said to the animal. Her voice sounded small and ineffectual.

The wolf swung its head to look at her. The lips slid back to uncover long killer teeth in a devil's grin. It growled deep in its chest, a menacing growl that warned her away.

"Is somebody down there?" Joey's excited treble came clearly from the top of the stairs.

The wolf turned from Mrs. Jensen and looked toward the stairs. With a soft growl it started to move that way.

Acting on the unreasoning instinct to protect the boy, Mrs. Jensen seized the nearest thing at hand that could be used as a weapon: an umbrella from the wooden stand near the door. Brandishing the umbrella like a club, she thrust herself between the wolf and the stairway.

"Joey, get back!" she shouted. "Get in your room and lock the door."

Upstairs the door to the boy's room slammed. The wolf threw her a look of pure animal hatred and lunged to one side of her, trying to get to the stairs. As the animal went past, Mrs. Jensen struck at it with the umbrella, hitting it across the back. The wolf hesitated. Mrs. Jensen threw herself upon it, clubbing at its head.

The impact of her body knocked the wolf off balance, and they crashed against the end post of the banister. The wolf was back on its feet immediately, teeth bared, snarling.

Mrs. Jensen scrambled away on the floor, holding the umbrella out toward the wolf like a sword. She heard her own voice screaming incoherent things.

The last thing she saw was the open-mouthed leap of the wolf. She went down helplessly under its weight as the beast brushed aside the puny umbrella. The head turned sideways and the cruel teeth clamped onto her throat. One flex of the powerful jaws crushed the thyroid cartilage and destroyed the larynx and esophagus. The teeth ripped through the platysma muscle and severed the carotid artery. Mrs. Jensen's life ended in a burbling gasp.

The wolf raised its bloody muzzle from the ruined throat and backed away from the body. It turned and started toward the stairs.

13

One powerful bound carried the wolf a quarter of the way up the stairs. There it stopped suddenly and listened. Outside there was a growing clamor of voices, as the neighbors, roused by Mrs. Jensen's screams, ran toward the Richter house to investigate.

Torn by conflicting emotions—part human, mostly animal—the wolf hesitated. The still-bloody muzzle pointed down toward the open front door, then up the stairs. On the landing, the door to the boy's room was closed. Behind it, the child was crying. The thin wood panel would not keep the huge wolf out for long, but out in front of the house, running feet were already pounding across the lawn.

The wolf chose survival. Leaping gracefully from the stairs, the beast landed on the floor of the hallway just as the first of the neighbors reached the front door. Without pausing, the wolf raced through the living room and sprang into the air, crashing out through a large window at the side of the house. As a babble of voices came from the house, the wolf loped across the lawn, through a border of trimmed shrubbery, and into the trees beyond.

Down the block, unnoticed by the people swarming toward the Richter house, a white Ford started its engine and moved slowly away from the curb without lights.

Inside, the house was all blood and confusion. The first people to come through the door stopped short at the sight of Mrs. Jensen's torn body. They were jostled forward by those who rushed in after them, and sent skidding off balance on the slippery floor.

A man turned away to vomit.

A woman screamed.

"He went out the window!" someone shouted.

"Let's go after him!"

"No, wait, maybe he's got a gun."

"Somebody call the police."

A woman standing on the fringe of the milling group turned to the man next to her. "It didn't look like a man to me," she said. "It looked like a big dog."

The man only glanced at her, shook his head irritably, and pushed forward for a closer look.

On the landing above them the door to Joey's room opened. The boy came out slowly and walked stiff-legged to the head of the stairs. His face was white and puffy, his eyes wide. One of the men stepped gingerly around Mrs. Jensen's body and ran up the stairs. He picked the boy up in his arms and carried him back into the bedroom.

* * *

At one o'clock Karyn and David arrived home to find their street clogged with emergency vehicles, and people swarming over the lawn in front of their house.

The mobile news crew from a local television station had parked its van in the driveway and had set up floodlights illuminating the house and yard. Overhead a police helicopter thundered in a tight circle, sweeping the area with a powerful spotlight.

David jammed to a stop at a wooden police barricade and jumped out of the car. He ran toward the house with Karyn following close behind. A rumpled man with weary eyes headed them off before they reached the front door.

"Just a minute, sir."

"This is our house," David said. "We live here. Who are you?"

"I'm Lieutenant MacCready of the Seattle Police. Are you Mr. and Mrs. Richter?"

"Yes. What's happened?"

"I'm afraid there's been an accident. A serious accident."

"Oh, my God, Joey!" Karyn cried. "Something's happened to Joey!"

"If that's the little boy, ma'am, he's all right," said MacCready. "One of the neighbors took him to their house."

"What is it, then?" David demanded.

"There was an older woman living here—"

"Mrs. Jensen," David said. "She's our housekeeper."

"She's dead, sir. She's been killed."

Karyn's knees turned rubbery for a moment.

David put an arm around her shoulder to steady her. "How did it happen?" he asked the policeman.

"If you could come inside and answer a few questions, you can help us find that out," MacCready said.

David looked down at Karyn.

"It's all right," she said in a small voice.

He turned back to MacCready. "We'll help in any way we can, Lieutenant."

Inside, Mrs. Jensen's body had been taken away and a tarpaulin spread on the floor at the foot of the stairs to cover most of the spilled blood. Lieutenant Mac-Cready led the Richters into the family room, out of sight of the bloodstains.

Yes, they told him, everything had seemed quite normal when they left the house this evening. No, they had no knowledge of anyone who might want to kill Mrs. Jensen. Yes, she was a careful person, in the habit of keeping the door locked. No, it was not likely she would have admitted a stranger to the house.

Lieutenant MacCready scribbled notes in a spiral-bound pad as Karyn and David answered his questions.

"Have you noticed anyone suspicious hanging around the neighborhood lately?"

Karyn started to speak, then hesitated.

The detective looked up. "Mrs. Richter?"

Karyn saw David's slight frown, but went ahead anyway. "Well, there has been someone. But I don't know if it's relevant."

"Anything at all you can tell me might help," MacCready said.

"There's a woman," Karyn said, getting the words out in a hurry. "I've seen her several times lately. I had the feeling she was following me."

MacCready's eyes narrowed. "A woman following you, you say."

Karyn chewed her lip. She looked over at David. He took her hand.

"Do we have to go through all of this now?" David said to the policeman. "My wife has been under the care of a doctor. For her nerves."

Karyn stiffened slightly at David's emphasis on nerves.

"I'll make it as brief as I can," MacCready said. "This could be very important if what we have here is an attempted kidnapping."

"Kidnapping?" Karyn said. "Do you mean someone was trying to take Joey?"

"It's a possibility. Now, about this woman?"

Karyn told him about the dark-haired woman, and how she'd seen her in the coffee shop, on the street, and again riding in the taxi. As she spoke, Karyn realized how thin it sounded, how little it really was to base a suspicion on.

"Are you sure it was the same woman each time?" MacCready asked, his tone cool and courteous.

"Yes. I'm almost certain it was the same woman."

"*Almost,*" the lieutenant repeated under his breath. Karyn could see the interest fade in his eyes. "We'll check it out," he said. "I think that's enough for tonight." He took a card from his breast pocket and handed it to David. "If anything comes up, give me a call."

As MacCready closed his notebook and stood up to leave, another uniformed officer came into the room.

"Lieutenant, do you want to talk to that woman now? The one who says she saw an animal?"

Karyn looked up sharply.

"No," MacCready said shortly. "You take her statement, that's all we need."

"What's that about an animal?" Karyn asked.

David gave her a warning look.

"One of your neighbors said she thought it looked like a big dog that jumped through the window and ran away from the house when the people came in." MacCready dismissed the idea with a wave of his hand. "People sometimes see things like that in moments of stress."

"But is it possible," Karyn persisted, "that it was an animal?"

The detective shook his head. "There are no dogs anywhere around here as big as the one she says she saw. And besides…" His eyes flicked toward the archway beyond which lay the blood-spattered tarpaulin. "There's no dog I ever heard of would do that to a human being."

"What about a wolf?" The question was out before she could think about it.

"Karyn, please," David said.

Lieutenant MacCready answered her question seriously. "No way. Wolves need wilderness. The only wilderness around here is that patch of trees over beyond your house, and nothing bigger than a ground squirrel can exist in there. No, what we're looking for here is a man. A big, powerful man. Probably a psychopath."

"I hope you get him. Lieutenant," David said fervently. "Mrs. Jensen was like part of the family."

"Don't you worry, Mr. Richter," said the detective. "We'll get him."

Karyn turned away from the men. Through the window she could see the moon shining intermittently through the broken clouds. *No, you won't, Lieutenant,* she thought. *Not this one.*

14

After the police and the television people and the neighbors and the sightseers left, David picked up his son from the neighbor's house and took Joey and Karyn to spend the night in a hotel. The next day they took Joey to stay with David's sister, who lived across the lake, in Bellevue. Then they went down to the police station and answered more questions for Lieutenant MacCready. Finally, late in the afternoon, they went back to their house.

David strode around briskly, talking in a very businesslike manner. "We'll have to get the window replaced first thing. And new carpeting in the hall. The stairs and the wall will need a thorough cleaning."

"Do we have to settle it all right now?" Karyn said.

"The important thing," said David, "Is to get on with our lives. Get Joey back home and everything back to normal as fast as possible."

"No, David," Karyn said softly. "It won't work. Things will never he back to normal. Whatever that is."

"Please, Karyn, I know this is a terrible blow. I feel it too, believe me. But it won't do any good to dwell on it."

"Don't you understand?" she said. "Don't you know what it was that killed Mrs. Jensen? No, it was not a dog, and it was no psychopathic killer, either."

"You don't seriously believe—"

"I do. The wolves of Drago are here. The werewolves. They've come for me."

"You're upset. I'll call Dr. Goetz. He can prescribe something for your nerves."

"Dr. Goetz can't do me any good now. No one can. They've found me, and there will be no rest row. What happened to Mrs. Jensen is my fault."

"That's crazy talk. It was a prowler, more than likely."

Karyn took both of his hands in hers. "It was no prowler, darling. I know that, and I think in your heart you know it too. As long as I stay here, there is danger. Not only for me, but for you and Joey, too."

"What are you saying?"

"I have to go away, David."

"No!" he cried.

"I have no choice."

"But... where will you go? How long will you stay?"

"I'll stay until this thing is over, one way or another. And I think it's better if I don't say where I'm going right away."

"I can't agree to that."

"Please, David. I promise you I'll let you know as soon as I can. Meanwhile, the fewer people who know where I'm going, the harder it will be for anyone to follow me."

"I'll go with you," he said. "We'll fight this out together."

Karyn shook her head. "No, darling. Joey will need at least one of his parents with him. He'll need your strength."

"Karyn, I can't let you just... walk out this way."

"I have to," she said. "It would be too dangerous for you and for Joey if I stayed here. If you love me, David, don't try to stop me."

He put his arms around her and pulled her tight against him. "If I love you? My God, Karyn, I love you more than anything in the world."

Karyn let her head rest on her husband's chest. She heard a sound she had never heard before. David Richter was crying.

* * *

The next morning Karyn bought a ticket to Los Angeles at the Western Airlines counter in the Seattle-Tacoma Airport. She did not notice the old woman, bundled up in scarves, who sold paper flowers nearby. The old woman, however, paid close attention to Karyn.

15

When her flight was announced, Karyn hurried to the loading gate, trying not to look at all the people saying affectionate goodbyes. She could still see the puzzled and hurt expression in Joey's eyes as she tried to explain that Mom had to go away for a while. She had hugged him very tight and promised to come back soon. It was a promise Karyn hoped she could keep.

She found her seat on the plane and sat looking out at the rain-slick runway as the jet rolled into position for takeoff. She wished she could be sure this was the right thing to do. Running away, she knew, was never a solution, yet if she stayed to fight she would surely lose. If it were only herself she might have tried, but there were Joey and David to think of. Karyn was sure now that the wolf had been after Joey, and that only Mrs. Jensen's courage and the arrival of the neighbors had saved the boy's life. As long as Karyn was there, the people she loved were in danger.

At last the Western Airline jet received clearance from the tower and thundered down the runway and into the air. In a little while the stewardess came down the aisle, passing out plastic sets of earphones. There was no movie on the short flight, but several channels of recorded stereo music were available. Karyn chose a program of light classics and settled back in the seat, hoping the music would push the troubled thoughts out of her mind, at least temporarily.

But it was no use. Every time Karyn closed her eyes she would see the elusive face of the woman with the white-streaked hair. Or Roy Beatty, who was supposed to be dead, watching her from above. Or the impersonal gray tarpaulin spread over the floor where Mrs. Jensen had died.

How had they found her, Karyn wondered, the wolves of Drago? She was certain now that it was vengeance that had brought the horrors from the past so explosively into her present. Vengeance for her part in the destruction of Drago and most of the unnatural creatures that lived there. Most of them. But not all. Roy had survived. Roy and at least one other.

Marcia!

Karyn jerked upright in the seat so suddenly that the earphones were pulled loose from her head. She saw it now—the woman in the coffee shop, and on the street, and in the taxi. Darken that streak in her hair, take away the sunglasses hiding the green eyes, and you have Marcia Lura. But how could that be? Karyn had fired the gun herself, and had seen the impact at close range as the silver bullet penetrated the skull of the black she-wolf. Never mind how. It was Marcia. Marcia and Roy. And they had come for her.

Karyn sat back in the seat once more, her mind racing. It helped, if only a little, to know what she was up against. Maybe now she could make plans. The stay with her parents could be only temporary. If Marcia and Roy had found her in Seattle, they would find her again. She would not risk endangering any more of her loved ones.

On the telephone to her mother and father, she had been evasive about her reasons for wanting to visit them. They had not pressed her for details. Karyn resolved to stay there only until she could decide on a course of action. What it might be, she had no idea now, but she had to come up with something. She could not live the rest of her life in fear.

The plane made a wide turn over the San Bernardino Mountains and began the long descent to Los Angeles International Airport. Karyn smiled, seeing her parents waiting for her at the Western Airlines passenger gate.

Frank Oliver was tall and straight with fine white hair that was always carefully combed. His wife Nancy had a round, pretty face with smile lines etched at the corners of her eyes. She ran forward to hug her daughter as Karyn came through the walkway from the plane. Frank Oliver came behind her, reserved and dignified, but with the love showing in his eyes.

As they walked out to the parking lot where the Olivers had left their Buick, they all acted as though this were just a normal visit of a daughter to her parents. They compared the weather in Seattle and Los Angeles; they discussed the health of David and Joey; they talked about Karyn's flight down.

During the drive to the Olivers' house in Brentwood, all three ran out of small talk at the same time, and an uncomfortable silence enveloped them.

Karyn's mother, sitting in the backseat while her daughter rode up front with Mr. Oliver, leaned forward and placed a hand gently on Karyn's shoulder.

"Are you all right, dear?" she said.

Karyn patted her mother's hand. She tried to keep her voice casual as she answered. "Of course, Mother. I'm fine."

"I mean *really*," Mrs. Oliver persisted.

Karyn started to say something bland and reassuring, but it caught in her throat. She said, "It's nothing too serious. My nerves acting up, the doctor says. I thought it would do me good to get away for a little while."

"Is it the dreams again?" her father asked. He took his eyes off the road briefly to glance over at her.

"Yes," Karyn admitted. "And other things. I'd rather not talk about it, though. Not right now."

"It's all right, dear," her mother said. "We understand. You stay with us as long as you like, and if there's anything at all we can do, you know we're ready to help."

Karyn turned in the seat to smile at her mother. "I know you are." She reached over to touch her father's arm. "You too, Daddy. You've both been wonderful when I needed you. I'm very lucky."

For the rest of the drive, the conversation returned to inconsequential things. They pulled up to the big, comfortable house on Altair Drive, and Karyn was pleased to see it had not changed at all.

She moved into her old room upstairs in the rear of the house. The room brought back mixed memories: There were her carefree high school days with photos of friends tucked into the frame of the mirror, and posters of the Beatles and Joe Namath on the walls; then there was the nightmarish period right after her breakdown. In the shadows of the room lurked reminders of that time when insanity seemed the easy way out.

Karyn set about unpacking the few things she had brought with her, and concentrated on keeping her thoughts positive.

It was three days before Karyn finally began to relax. At the dinner table her father told a small joke, and Karyn found to her surprise that she was honestly laughing. It was the first time she had laughed naturally in weeks. She realized then just how tightly wound she had been. At last she was sure that coming home had been the right thing. That night she learned she was wrong.

It was the howling. At first, only half-awake, Karyn thought it was the dream again. She sat up in bed and stared at the window—a charcoal-gray square in the blackness of the room. She waited, praying that it had been only the dream. Then she heard it again. The deep-throated, tortured howl of the werewolf. It had no direction, but seemed to come from everywhere. And it was near. They had found her once more.

The werewolf howled no more that night, but Karyn lay tensely awake. By dawn she was exhausted, her nerves frayed.

At breakfast her mother studied her from across the table. Karyn was sharply aware of her pallor and the shadows around her eyes.

"Didn't you sleep well last night?" Mrs. Oliver asked.

"Not really," Karyn said. "A touch of indigestion, I think. I shouldn't have gone back for seconds on your roast."

She got no answering smile from her mother. Mrs. Oliver continued to study her daughter's face.

"I thought that dog might have kept you awake," she said.

"Dog?"

"Somebody must have left him locked out or something. He made quite a racket about two o'clock." Then, casually, "Didn't you hear it?"

Oh, I heard it all right, Karyn thought. Only it wasn't any dog. There was no point, though, in getting into that discussion with her mother. She said, "No, I didn't hear anything."

It was clear that Mrs. Oliver was not fully satisfied, but she did not push it. They closed the topic with a couple of remarks about how people should take better care of their pets.

The breakfast was link sausage and moist scrambled eggs. Ordinarily Karyn would have loved it, but this morning she had little appetite. She ate as much as she could, knowing her mother was watching, but finally had to push the plate away. She was spared answering further questions by the ringing of the doorbell.

Mrs. Oliver excused herself to answer it. Karyn followed her out to the living room and was introduced to a neighbor, Mrs. Gipson, a chunky woman whose face was flushed with excitement.

After briefly acknowledging Karyn, the neighbor turned back to Mrs. Oliver. "Did you hear about the awful thing that happened last night? Over at the Stovalls'?"

"No."

"Somebody killed Zora Stovall's horse!"

"I don't believe it! That beautiful palomino?"

"That's not the worst of it. You should see the way it was done. The poor thing's throat and belly was torn right out. There's two policemen over there now. They say they've never seen anything like it. They say it must be some crazy sadist like the one who was cutting up cows out in the valley a few years back."

Mrs. Oliver glanced worriedly at Karyn.

"Have they any idea who did it?" Karyn asked.

"Not really. They say they've got some leads, but the police always say that. It's a terrible mess. They won't let anybody go out near the corral. Poor Zora is all broken up. She loved that horse."

Karyn had heard enough. She left her mother and Mrs. Gipson looking after her, and went up to her room to begin packing. As she had feared, the wolves of Drago had found her again. There was no doubt in her mind who was responsible for the slaughter of the horse. Now she had to run again.

Abruptly, Karyn's icy calm fell to pieces. She sat down heavily on the bed and began to cry. She could not go on running like this every time Marcia Lura and Roy caught up with her. There was no way she could escape them. They seemed to have no trouble finding her, and could probably take her any time they chose.

Karyn got up and looked at herself in the mirror. She dried her eyes and blew her nose lustily into a Kleenex. Stop this, girl, she told herself. It's time to stand and fight. She felt a little better then, but still knew she could not go up against them alone. And it was futile to try to enlist anyone to help her who did not know the horror. In all the world there was just one man who knew, and might help her now. He had once before. Chris Halloran.

16

In the morning Karyn rummaged through her things and found an old address book with Chris Halloran's phone number. At the time, he was living at a singles' complex in Marina Del Ray called the Surf King. She called the three-year-old number from a phone in her parents' kitchen while Mr. and Mrs. Oliver were in another part of the house.

After a series of clicks a recorded female voice came over the wire: *The number you have called is out of service. Please check your directory to be sure you have the correct number, then dial again.*

Karyn followed the recorded instructions and again reached the disembodied voice. She banged down the receiver in frustration. She should have expected it, of course. In Southern California, where businesses, buildings, and people come and go overnight, it was a lot to expect that a telephone number would get the same party after three years.

There was still the possibility that Chris lived at the same place, but had changed his telephone to an unlisted number. It was, Karyn decided, worth checking out. She could not give up now. She borrowed the car keys from her father and left the house. It was shortly before noon.

The Buick seemed like an excess of automobile to Karyn after the little Datsun she had driven in Seattle, but it rode smoothly, and the power equipment made it easy to handle. She drove down the San Diego Freeway past Culver City to the Marina turnoff.

The Surf King Apartments consisted of four interconnected buildings in cream-colored masonry with harmonizing pastel balconies. Karyn parked in an area marked *Visitors*, and entered the complex through a palm-flanked gateway. She crossed the red adobe central court and passed the Olympic-sized swimming pool where an assortment of young men and women presented their bodies to the sun. They eyed her speculatively from behind their Foster Grants as she walked by. Karyn ignored them and followed a series of arrows past the sauna and the Jacuzzi to the manager's apartment.

She touched the buzzer, and the door was swept open by a muscular young man with a full black beard, wearing a t-shirt printed with the Coors logo.

"Hi," he said, "I'm Ron."

"Hello—" Karyn began.

"You're really in luck," he said. "I have a vacancy opening up the first of the week. You'll love it. It's a bachelorette, balcony, built-ins, dishwasher, wet-bar, sofa makes into a queen-sized bed. Want to take a look?"

"No thanks," Karyn told him. "I'm not looking for an apartment."

Ron's smile dimmed.

"I'm looking for someone who lives here. At least he used to. His name is Chris Halloran."

The manager frowned. "Halloran? It doesn't sound familiar, but I've got two hundred units here with people moving in and out all the time. I'll check the list of tenants."

He sat down at a desk and pulled out several sheets of paper with names typed on them. Many were crossed off and inked over. Ron traced a finger down the columns of names.

"Nope, sorry. No Halloran."

"He must have moved," Karyn said. "I know he was living here three years ago."

"A lot of people come and go in three years," the manager said. "I've only been here four months myself."

"Could you look it up for me?" Karyn said. "You must have the records."

"We have 'em, but they're all locked up out in the back."

Karyn switched on one of her best smiles. "I'd really appreciate it if you could check for me. It's awfully important."

Without much enthusiasm the young man left Karyn sitting on the sofa that probably opened into a queen-sized bed, and he disappeared into another room. After several minutes he came back carrying a ledger-sized book.

"You're right," he said, "Christopher Halloran was in 314-C three years ago. Had the place a year, moved out the next April."

Karyn calculated that Chris had given up his apartment here shortly after their split-up in Las Vegas.

"What was the forwarding address?" she said.

Ron scowled down at the ledger. "There isn't any."

"But there has to be." A note of panic crept into Karyn's voice.

"Well, there isn't," Ron insisted. "There's no law that says you have to give one. Listen, if you're so hot to find this guy, why don't you hire a detective?"

Because there's no time, Karyn thought. I need Chris now, today, before something else happens. Before someone else dies.

"Anything wrong?"

Karyn realized she had been staring right through the manager. She shook her head and managed a smile. "No, nothing. Thanks for your trouble." She turned to leave.

"Sure you don't want to just take a look at that bachelorette? We're building tennis courts, and there're parties three nights a week."

Karyn gave him another small shake of her head and walked on out of the Surf King. The dashboard clock in the Buick told her the day was half gone. She felt a terrible urgency to locate Chris before nightfall.

Her next stop was Techtron Engineering, in Inglewood, near the airport. She went inside and spoke to the personnel manager in his small, functional office.

"Chris Halloran left Techtron two years ago," he said.

Karyn felt a sudden emptiness.

"He took a long leave of absence, and when he came back he was never quite the same. Restless, sort of. We were all sorry to see him go. Everyone here liked Chris. In the last few weeks here, though, he couldn't settle down to handle the routine parts of his job. Said he needed more freedom. So he quit."

Afraid of the answer she would get, Karyn asked the question, "Do you know where he went?"

"Oh, yes."

Hope flickered again.

"Chris and another man who worked here at the time, a man named Walter Eckersall, went into partnership and started their own consulting firm. They were a perfect team. Chris supplied the enthusiasm and the creative thinking, and Walt took care of the solid, practical details."

"Are they still in business?"

"Yes, they are. And doing very well, too. We even call them in to do a job for us now and then."

The personnel man wrote down an address in North Hollywood. Karyn thanked him and hurried out to the Buick. It was mid-afternoon. Time was slipping away.

The building on Lankershim Boulevard was a low, cinderblock structure with clean lines and a modest sign on the front identifying it as E & H Engineering Consultants. Karyn scanned the automobiles parked in the diagonal spaces in front of the building, half-hoping to see Chris's bright red Camaro. It was not there. But of course, she told herself, he would have a different car by now.

Inside, the girl at the reception desk, a chesty brunette, smiled up at her.

"I'd like to see Mr. Halloran," Karyn said.

"Mr. Halloran isn't in," the girl said carefully. "Can Mr. Eckersall help you?"

Karyn's spirits sagged again. Finding someone in real life could be so difficult. In the movies all you did was pick up a phone, and there they were. But in the movies there was always a parking place in front of the bank too.

"I'll talk to Mr. Eckersall," she said.

Walter Eckersall was a tall, loose-jointed man with bushy brown hair. He wore black-rimmed plastic glasses and spoke in a voice of surprising gentleness. "You had some business with Chris?" he said.

"Not really," Karyn said. "It's more personal."

Eckersall's eyes shifted their focus to a far corner of the room. "Chris is taking a little vacation just now. If you're a friend of his, you'll know how he appreciates his leisure."

"Yes, I know," Karyn said quickly. "Can you tell me where he's gone?"

Eckersall looked uncomfortable. "Uh, I don't know if I can, really, uh—"

"I should tell you," Karyn said, "that there is no romance involved here. My personal business with Chris has nothing to do with his private life."

Eckersall gave her a relieved smile. "Sorry. When an attractive lady comes in looking for Chris I sort of assume—well, never mind that. He's down in Mexico now. Staying at a hotel just outside Mazatlán. The Palacia del Mar."

"Thank you," Karyn said. "And don't worry, you haven't gotten Chris in any trouble."

"There's one more thing I'd better mention," Eckersall said. "He's not down there alone."

Karyn hesitated only a moment. "Knowing Chris," she said, "I didn't think he would be."

Heading back to Brentwood in the late afternoon, Karyn silently cursed the traffic on Sunset Boulevard that slowed her progress. Soon it would be dark, and the night, she knew, belonged to the werewolf.

By the time she reached her parents' house the sun had slipped down behind the Santa Monica Mountains. Darkness fell like a curtain. Karyn put the car away in the garage, then stood outside and swung down the counterbalanced door. She started for the house. Halfway along the walk to the front door her heart froze.

A sound.

Something moving in the bushes.

Karyn turned for one terrified look. It was just a dark shape. A shadow moving among shadows. But there was no mistaking what it was.

Karyn fought off the paralysis and ran for the house. *Please, God, let the door be unlocked!* She banged into the solid oak panel, fumbled a split second for the knob, turned it in her slippery hand and half-fell into the house.

Mr. and Mrs. Oliver, startled, rose from their chairs in the living room. Karyn slammed the heavy door shut and cranked the deadbolt lock into place. Outside something thudded softly against the door. Then there was silence.

Her mother came quickly toward her. "Karyn, what's the matter?"

"Is someone out there?" her father said. Karyn stood with her back braced against the door and struggled to keep her voice at a normal level. "It's all right. Something startled me for a moment."

Mrs. Oliver put her hands gently on her daughter's shoulders. Frank Oliver reached for the doorknob.

"If somebody's bothering you—" he began.

"No, Daddy, don't go out there!!" Karyn cried. Her father looked at her sharply, and she went on in a quieter tone. "Please, Daddy. For me."

Reluctantly he drew his hand back.

"Is the back door locked?" Karyn asked. "And the windows?"

"Karyn," her father said, "If something's happened, I want to know about it."

"Frank." Mrs. Oliver's tone caught his attention. "It won't do any harm to make sure the place is locked up. And it will make Karyn feel better."

Frank Oliver looked from his wife to his daughter. "Well, sure. All right."

"Could we do it now?" Karyn said. "Right away?"

Mr. and Mrs. Oliver exchanged a look, then began checking the windows. Karyn hurried through the house and tried the back door. She was relieved to find it locked. After making sure the kitchen windows were secure, she relaxed a little. She knew her mother and father thought they were humoring a somewhat neurotic daughter, but that was all right. Better than taking a chance with the thing that was out there somewhere in the night. The beast was taunting her, Karyn felt. Letting her know it could kill her at almost any time it chose. Well, maybe it would pass up one opportunity too many.

She drew a deep breath and walked back into the living room to join her parents.

"Everything's locked up tight," Mrs. Oliver said.

"And double-checked," Frank Oliver added.

Karyn hugged her mother, then went over and took hold of her father's hands. "Thank you both," she said, feeling the depth of her love for these people. "You won't have to worry about this after tonight. I'll be leaving tomorrow."

"Leaving?" said her mother. "I'd hoped you could stay longer. A week or so, at least."

"I wish I could," Karyn said, "But there's something I have to settle once and for all before I can ever stay anywhere comfortably again."

She waited. Both of her parents wanted very badly to ask her questions. It showed plainly in their faces. Where was she going? Why? For how long? But, God bless them, they held their questions inside.

"I promise I'll tell you all about it," she said, "when I come back."

"I'll tell you *something*, anyway, she thought. Something you can believe.

When I come back.

If I come back.

It was a long a sleepless night, but in the morning she was still alive.

17

A fresh breeze flowed in off the coast of California bringing relief to the damp heat of Mazatlán summer. North of the city, where the tropical forest pushed close to the shoreline, the Palacio del Mar Hotel occupied a half-moon of beach.

On the stretch of white sand in front of the hotel Chris Halloran lay on a beach blanket. He was propped on his elbows, eyes shaded by a tattered straw hat, as he watched a pretty auburn-haired girl play in the light surf. The Palacio was generally favored by an older, quieter clientele than that favoring the new high-rise resorts which had gone up in the city. Chris liked the older hotel because it felt like Mexico. The pastel stucco of the main beach area was not much different from Miami Beach or Waikiki. At the Palacio you could hear Spanish spoken by the fishermen who came down from the village of Camarón, and you could smell the heady aroma of chilies from the kitchen where the hotel employees ate.

Two of the employees walked by on the path bordering the stretch of beach where Chris lay. Roberto, a handsome lad of seventeen, carried a tray of iced tea for a couple from Indianapolis who sat up the beach protecting their sunburns under one of the hotel's umbrellas. Dancing along at Roberto's side was Blanca, saucy and pert in her maid's uniform, her arms loaded with fresh towels for the cabanas. The eyes of the boy and girl spoke intimately to each other.

Ah, young love, thought Chris Halloran as he watched them pass. Had he ever been in love like that? And once you lost it, could you ever get it back?

At the edge of the water, Audrey Vance stood barely covered by a pink bikini. Her slim, tanned legs were planted apart in the sand. She beckoned for Chris to come and join her.

Chris smiled at her and waved no thanks. Audrey was an actress who photographed like a dream, but couldn't act her way into a high-school play. Thus, her appearances on various television series were mainly decorative. Chris had enjoyed her enthusiasm during their stay in Mazatlán, but he was beginning to think it was time he went back to work.

Audrey struck a pouting pose and shook her head at him in exasperation. Chris tipped the straw hat down over his eyes and lay back on the beach towel.

A moment later, cool droplets of saltwater splashed on his chest and stomach as Audrey stood over him shaking out her hair.

"Come on." she said, "Swim with me."

"I'm resting."

"Shit, you can rest any time. I want somebody to swim with me." She reached down and lifted the hat from his eyes. "Maybe I'll go and ask that beautiful young stud who works around here. That Roberto. I'll bet he'd come swimming with me."

"He might at that," Chris said, "but you might have a problem with his girl-friend."

"Come on, Chris. Don't be an old fart." She kicked sand across his bare stomach, then ran lightly toward the water, laughing back over her shoulder at him.

With a sigh Chris pushed himself to his feet and logged over the sand after the girl. While he was in Los Angeles Chris kept in shape with twice-weekly workouts at the gym, along with tennis and handball. Swimming, however, had never appealed to him. Even when he lived at the marina, he rarely used the swimming pool, and went to the beach only to play volleyball.

He followed Audrey as she splashed happily, into the surf. The water was bath-tub warm, and the waves were low and gentle. The girl swam easily ahead of him with long graceful strokes while he tried to keep up with his own windmilling version of the crawl.

Fifty yards offshore, Audrey stopped and waited for him, treading water. When he splashed up beside her she wrapped her arms and legs around him and gave him a big open-mouthed kiss. They sank together slowly below the surface.

Chris came up sputtering and blowing as the girl bobbed up like a dolphin beside him.

"What are you trying to do, drown me?" he said between coughs.

Audrey tossed the wet hair out of her eyes and laughed at him. Chris tried and failed to hold a stern expression.

"You're crazy, you know that?" he said.

She swam over close to him and slipped one hand under the waistband of his trunks. "Have you ever screwed underwater?"

"Sure, lots of times."

Abruptly the girl's mood changed. She backed off and looked at him. "You've done just every damn thing, haven't you?" Without waiting for a response, she struck out toward the beach.

No, he thought as he swam slowly after her, not quite everything. Sometimes, though, it seemed he was trying. Until three years ago he had lived a fairly quiet bachelor life. He raised a little hell on weekends, did his share of womanizing, but on the whole he led a life devoid of extreme highs and lows. Then came the urgent call for help from Karyn Beatty. Answering that call had plunged Chris into a night of hell in the mountain village of Drago, and had changed his life forever.

After the horror of Drago and the fire that destroyed it, there had been the nerve-shattering six months he and Karyn had spent trying to run away from it. When he finally returned to reality he had quit his job and gone into partnership with solid Walt Eckersall, who allowed him to take off two or three months a year. He had moved out of the swinging-singles apartment and rented a house in Benedict Canyon, where he could party when he felt like it and be left alone when he wanted to. When he worked he worked hard, and when he played he went to places like the Kona Coast or Curaçao or Mazatlán. Sometimes he went with a woman, sometimes by himself.

Chris knew that his lifestyle was designed to help him forget the past. Most of the time it worked, but for some reason he had lately found himself often thinking of Karyn. He had never shaken the nagging guilt he felt for not going to see her at her parents' home after the Las Vegas crack-up.

What the hell, he told himself for the hundredth time. She got better, didn't she? After the way things ended, seeing him would have done nothing to help her condition. It could easily have made things worse. Chris put his head down in the water and stroked powerfully toward the shore.

Audrey was waiting for him when he waded up onto the beach. Her momentary irritation was all over.

"About Goddamn time, slowpoke. I thought I was going to have to swim out and haul you in."

"Why do you think I was stalling?" he said.

"I thought maybe you were daydreaming about some old girlfriend."

Chris looked at her quickly, but saw she was just kidding. One of those unconscious intuitive flashes women seemed to get. If they ever harnessed that power, he thought, they could rule the world.

He said, "Do you want to go get some lunch?"

Audrey lowered her eyes demurely and peeked up at him through thick, moist lashes. "Do I have another choice?"

"My God, woman, you're insatiable."

"Damn right, big fella, and you love it. Come on, I'll help you shower off the salt."

They walked hand in hand up from the beach and along the wide veranda of the old Spanish style building that was the original hotel. In the early 1960s, six separate cabanas had been built on either side of the main building, following the curve of the beach. Chris and Audrey turned in at Number 7, the nearest to the main building, on the south side.

* * *

An hour and a half later Chris lay face down, naked, on the bed. His face was pressed against the pillow, his body completely relaxed. Audrey moved restlessly around the room, her tanned body glowing in the light from the afternoon sun that filtered between the slats of the bamboo shades.

"Why do men always want to go to sleep afterwards?" she said.

"Mmmpff," Chris muttered into the pillow.

"It always pumps me full of energy. Makes me want to get moving and do things."

Chris rolled over onto his side and looked at her. "We already did things."

She dropped into one of the two rattan chairs and stroked herself between the legs. "Good things." She gave him a mischievous look. "I'll bet I could get you interested again."

He sat up and swung his feet off the bed. "No question about it, but first, let's go get some lunch."

"Okay, spoilsport."

"Got to keep up my strength, honey. A man my age needs a balanced diet."

"A man your age," she mocked. "Jesus, thirty-three is really getting up there, isn't it?"

"Hand me my pants," he said.

Audrey took a pair of white jeans from the back of the chair where she was sitting and carried them to the bed. As she handed them to Chris, something fell out of the pocket and hit the grass carpet with a tiny thump. Audrey dropped to her knees and looked around on the floor for a moment. Then she reached under the bed and came out with a small silver object. She held it out to Chris in the palm of her hand.

"What's this?" she said. "I've never seen it before."

Chris's expression sobered. "It's nothing." He held out his hand. "Here, I'll take it."

"It looks like a bullet."

The tiny lump of metal winked up at Chris. It was a bullet, all right. A twenty-two caliber long rifle bullet of pure silver. There had been twelve of them, made to Chris's order by a bemused Los Angeles gunsmith. On the night of the werewolves in Drago, he had fired eleven of them. Karyn had fired the last. Chris had returned just once to the burned-out village, and the bullet had gleamed up at him like an eye from the blackened earth. He had pocketed the bullet and never gone near the place again.

"It's just a toy," he said to Audrey. "Let's have it."

"Another secret," Audrey said, sulking. "You never tell me anything really important about yourself.

"What do you mean, honey? I'm an open book."

"No, I'm serious. I know that little bullet has some important meaning for you. Why won't you share it with me?"

"Because it's none of your business."

Audrey closed her fist around the bullet and marched across the room to the closet, where she began rattling coat hangers irritably. "I'll bet it was a present from that woman."

"What woman?"

The woman. The one you had the hot rocks for and was married to your best friend."

Chris studied the bare back of the girl as she sorted through the clothes hanging in the closet. Either she was a lot more perceptive than he gave her credit for, or he was talking in his sleep.

"Get dressed," he said. "I'm hungry."

* * *

As they sat in the hotel dining room awaiting their lunch, the conversation was strained and artificial. It was as though a third person sat unseen at their table, listening.

18

The airport at Mazatlán was small by United States standards. Karyn Richter unbuckled her seat belt as the Aeronaves 727 rolled to a stop. From the window by her seat she watched with amazement the number and variety of aircrafts landing, taking off, taxiing, waiting, and just sitting there.

There were sleek new jets, old DC-3s, corporate Lears, private Cessnas and Pipers, and even a battered old open-cockpit biplane. Karyn could see no pattern to their movements, but she assured herself that somewhere a control tower was directing the traffic. Nevertheless, compared to big, orderly LAX, it was like a downtown intersection on Christmas Eve.

When the door was opened she joined the other passengers and filed out and down the stairway that had been rolled up to the plane. She crossed the expanse of black tarmac to the terminal building.

Inside it was hot and crowded. Over the noise of arriving and departing passengers announcements rattled continually over the PA system loudspeakers, first in Spanish, then English. Karyn located the baggage-claim counter and after an hour was finally reunited with her bag. She carried it out of the terminal building and set it down on the sidewalk. The air outside was fresh and cool with a hint of the sea, and she inhaled gratefully.

"Carry your suitcase, lady?"

The voice close behind her startled Karyn. She turned to see a tall, pockmarked youth grinning at her through bad teeth. The end of a wooden match protruded from one corner of his mouth.

"No thank you," she said, and turned away.

"Ah, come on, lady, you don't want to carry that heavy thing all by yourself."

Karyn looked pointedly up the street, trying ignore him.

"I'm real strong. I can carry anything you got. Want to see my muscle?"

"I don't need anything carried." She tried to keep the apprehension from showing in her voice.

The youth picked up her bag and backed off, hefting it. "See? It's not too heavy for me."

"Please," Karyn said, trying to sound authoritative. "Put that down. It belongs to me."

"Ah, lady, you don' wan' to talk like that."

"*Ay, Chico!*" A deep male voice snapped off the words like a whip. The startled boy looked over Karyn's shoulder, and she turned too to see who had spoken.

A square-bodied man with an enormous Zapata moustache glared at the boy. He spoke in hard-edged street Spanish, punctuating his words by jabbing a finger down at the sidewalk.

The boy's insolent grin fell away. He set the bag down at Karyn's feet and started to back off.

The stranger spoke again in Spanish. His voice was soft, but the words were unmistakably a command.

The boy's eyes shifted over to Karyn. "I'm sorry, lady," he muttered, then slipped away into the crowd coming out of the building.

"Permit me to offer apology for my city, Señora," said the man with the moustache. "That boy was a ruffian, a bad one. We are not all like him. There are many good people in Mazatlán."

"I'm sure there are," Karyn said. "Thank you."

The man gestured toward a mud-spattered, ten-year-old Plymouth parked at the curb. The white painted letters TAXI were barely visible on the door under a coating of dirt. "The taxi of Luis Zarate is at your service, Señora. Also guide service, if you desire."

"Well... I could use a taxi," Karyn said. "Can you take me to the Palacio del Mar Hotel?"

"*Con mucho gusto*, Señora," said Luis Zarate. With a flourish he swept open the rear door of the Plymouth and gestured Karyn inside. He carried her bag to the rear and put it in the trunk, which he closed by tying the lid to the bumper with a frayed length of electrical-cord.

"The Palacio is a beautiful hotel," he said when he was in position behind the wheel. "It is old and comfortable, and not so big that they forget about you."

"That's nice," Karyn said, without really listening.

Luis started the car and they pulled away from the curb with a grinding of gears and the roar of an unmuffled engine. As he drove, Luis proudly pointed out the sights of the city—the twin golden spires of the cathedral, the old Farol lighthouse looming off-shore, the busy fishing docks—until he sensed that Karyn was not paying attention.

"The Señora is troubled?" he said.

Karyn looked up sharply. "What's that?"

Luis Zarate's dark, liquid eyes regarded her seriously from the rearview mirror. "Forgive me, Señora, I do not mean to speak out of my place. But I am a gypsy, *comprende,* and through my blood I have a gift for knowing when someone is in trouble."

"Really?" Karyn said. "You're a gypsy?"

Luis' eyes twinkled at her. "Well, a little bit. My great-grandmother on my mother's side was said to be a gypsy. Anyway, it takes only a little such blood to make you a gypsy, no?"

"I suppose so," Karyn said, smiling.

They drove on in silence for a mile before the taxi driver spoke again. "The Señora is visiting Mazatlán all alone?"

Karyn answered carefully. "No... I'm meeting a friend at the hotel."

"It is well. Mazatlán is a beautiful city, and visitors are welcome, but as you have seen, there are bad people here as there are in all cities. It's not wise for a lady to travel too much alone." He was silent for a moment, then added, "You will be here long?"

"I don't know," Karyn said. "Not very."

"Forgive me," said Luis with a little shrug. "I ask too many questions. I just thought maybe the Señora could use a guide. Someone who will charge you a fair price, and who knows Mazatlán and the jungles and hills behind the city like the lines in his own hand."

Karyn could not suppress a smile. "Someone like Luis Zarate?"

"Si, Señora. Forgive my boast, but it is the truth.

"I appreciate the offer," Karyn said, "But I don't think I'll be doing much sight-seeing."

"Eh, *bien,* you will keep Luis Zarate in mind, yes?"

"Yes," Karyn told him, "I will."

Luis drove on out of the city and along a stretch where tree branches with broad green leaves over-hung the road on both sides. They turned back toward the sea then and followed the lip of a bluff for a short distance before starting down to the crescent of beach belonging to the Palacio del Mar. Karyn was pleased by the symmetry of the white main building with its red-tiled roof and the cabanas, like miniature copies, extending in a curved row on either side like arms embracing the beach.

As Luis drove along the roadway skirting the beach Karyn looked for Chris Halloran, but did not see him. The closer she came, the more her nerves jumped. There were so many questions. What would be his reaction to seeing her? Would he reject her? Was it fair for her to come back into his life bringing a horror that was no longer his concern? For a moment Karyn had a wild impulse to order the taxi around and head back to the airport. But then where would she go? There was no place left. There was no one else to go to.

"Señora?"

At the sound of the driver's voice, Karyn realized they had come to a stop before the hotel's wide Spanish-style veranda.

Luis jumped out and opened the door for her with another flourish. He retrieved her bag from the tied-down trunk and followed as Karyn walked up the steps and into the tiled lobby of the old hotel. She crossed to the registration desk, where a light-complexioned man with a high arched nose watched her with a small professional smile. A metal plate on the counter before him spelled out in raised letters:

J. Davila, Manager

"Good afternoon, Señora," he said.

Karyn nodded to acknowledge the greeting. "I'm looking for a gentleman I understand is registered here. Mr. Halloran."

A shadow flickered across the manager's eyes. "Ah, yes, Señor Halloran. You are... a relative?"

"No, I'm a friend. If he's registered here, I'd like to see him, please."

Señor Davila checked his registration cards in a businesslike manner. He pulled one of the cards out of the file and examined it. "Yes, Mr. Halloran is one of our guests."

"May I have his room number?"

"He is registered in Cabana Number 7."

"Thank you. Is there a phone I can use to call him?"

"I am sorry, there are no telephones in the cabanas."

"Then if you'll show me where it is, I'll go and find him myself."

"Ah, but that would be of no use. Señor Halloran is not in his cabana now."

Karyn's temper began to fray. "Well, where is he? I came here to see Mr. Halloran, and I don't have time to waste."

Luis Zarate stepped up to the desk. "Permit me, Señora," he said, then spoke briefly in Spanish to the man at the desk. When he had finished, the hotel manager turned to Karyn with an apologetic smile.

"Señor Halloran is presently at lunch in our dining room," he said.

"Thank you," Karyn said coolly. "Now if you will just tell me where the dining room is?"

Davila looked uncomfortable. "I am obliged to tell the Señora that Señor Halloran is not lunching alone."

"Oh, for heaven's sake. So he has a girl with him. It makes no difference to me. What did you think... that I was his wife?"

"One is never sure," said Davila. The relief was evident in his expression. Permit me to show you to the dining room, Señora."

"Do you wish me to wait?" asked Luis.

"No," Karyn said, "I don't think so." She paid the fare and added a generous tip.

"*Muchas gracias,*" said the taxi driver. "You will not forget, if you need any form of assistance while you are in Mazatlán, no one is better prepared to deliver than Luis Zarate."

"I won't forget," Karyn assured him.

Luis deposited her bag behind the registration desk and walked back out the entrance. Davila came around the desk and Karyn followed him out through the lobby and beneath an archway into the dining room.

It was a big bright room with sunlight streaming in through tall windows along one wall. The tables were widely spaced, covered with clean white linen and set with gleaming silver.

It took Karyn only a moment to find Chris. He hadn't changed much, she thought. Still the same firm features, the unruly brown hair, and as always a deep tan. He was a touch more serious around the eyes, maybe. But who wouldn't be, after two years?

Chris was seated facing Karyn, but not looking in her direction. On the near side of the table sat a girl with long, shiny auburn hair. From the way the girl sat erect and held her head cocked to one side, Karyn could tell she was young and lively. Karyn was surprised at the pang of jealousy.

The hotel manager started to lead the way across the room to Chris's table.

"Never mind," Karyn said. "I see him."

She walked alone toward the table. When she was ten feet away Chris looked up and saw her. Ever since she had left Los Angeles, Karyn had tried to prepare for this moment when she and Chris Halloran faced each other again after two years apart. However, she was not ready for the montage of memories, good and bad, that flashed across her mind. Chris's face reflected many of the same emotions she felt, with the added shock of seeing her so unexpectedly. He sat frozen for a moment, then rose from his chair.

"Karyn. What... what a surprise."

"Hello, Chris."

"It's been a while."

"Yes, it has."

They stood for a moment looking at each other, with a thousand things to say, and nothing that could be said.

The girl sitting at the table set her water glass down with a distinct thump. Chris looked down suddenly, as though surprised at finding her there.

"I'm sorry," he said. "Karyn, this is Audrey Vance. Audrey, an old friend of mine, Karyn Beatty."

"It's Karyn Richter now."

"Oh. I see. Excuse me."

Audrey looked up from her chair with a dazzling smile. She ran her eyes over Karyn appraisingly.

"It's a pleasure to meet you, Mrs. Richter. I haven't met many of Chris's old friends."

Karyn wondered if she detected a faint emphasis on *old*. "Please, call me Karyn," she said.

Chris glanced warily from one woman to the other. "Have you had lunch, Karyn?" he said quickly. "Won't you join us?"

"Yes, please do," said Audrey.

"I ate on the plane," Karyn said. "But I could use a cup of coffee."

Chris pulled out a chair for her and signaled the waiter.

"I don't think you'll like the coffee in Mexico, Karyn," Audrey said. "It always tastes like they left it brewing overnight. Chris and I usually have the tea."

"That's all right," Karyn said, returning the younger woman's smile. "I like my coffee strong."

The waiter brought a muddy black brew in a heavy mug. Karyn sipped at it and made a show of enjoying the taste.

For the next few minutes Chris made an awkward attempt at small talk while Karyn responded politely and noncommittally. Audrey ate in silence, alert for any vibrations between Chris and Karyn.

Finally Chris ran out of inconsequential remarks. He said, "I, uh, don't suppose you're down here by sheer coincidence."

"No," Karyn said. "I came looking for you."

"Well, you found me."

"It couldn't have been easy," Audrey put in.

"It wasn't," Karyn admitted.

An edgy minute of silence dragged by.

"Are you staying here at the hotel?" Audrey asked finally, holding her smile in place.

"I'm not sure yet," Karyn said. Abruptly she turned to Chris. "I have to talk to you."

"I suppose that means alone," Audrey said, her smile gone brittle.

"If you don't mind too much," Karyn said. "I'm sure you can spare him for a few minutes."

"Oh, I suppose can." Audrey stood up and stretched her lithe young body. She walked behind Chris's chair and traced a forefinger along the back of his neck. "I'll be in our room, darling."

Chris's eyes followed her as she walked out.

"Pretty girl," Karyn said when they were alone.

"Yes," Chris said, dismissing the subject. "What's happened?"

Karyn looked around the dining room. The orderliness of the place and the well-dressed, well-mannered guests enjoying lunch seemed inappropriate for what she had to tell.

"Can we go somewhere else?"

"Sure." Chris signed the check and they walked out of the hotel and down across the beach. They passed the somnolent sunbathers and continued to the wet, packed sand at the water's edge. They walked on to where the sandy beach ended and there were rocks in the surf, and the jungle grew right down to the sea. They sat down on a big rock and watched the incoming waves churn into a green and white froth.

"Do you remember the fire at Drago?" Karyn said, looking out to sea.

"Could I ever forget it?"

"And afterward, how we heard the howling and knew that not all the wolves had died?"

"We don't know that for sure, Karyn. What we heard might have been coyotes or something, and not those... creatures from Drago."

Karyn shook her head. "No, it was the werewolves. I know, because they've come for me."

As calmly as she could, Karyn told him about the things that had happened since she first had the feeling of being watched, less than a month ago in Seattle. She told of seeing Roy in the shopping mall, of the death of Mrs. Jensen, of the flight to her parents' home in Los Angeles and the signs that the wolves had followed her there, too,

Chris sat for a long moment when she had finished her story. Finally he said, "And you think one of them who's come for you is Roy?"

"I'm sure of it. I saw him."

"You couldn't be mistaken?"

"No. And that woman, Marcia Lura, is one of them too."

"Are there any more?"

"I don't know. I don't think so. Just the two of them."

There was another heavy pause before Chris spoke again. "All right, what do you want me to do?"

Karyn turned away suddenly, trying not to cry. "I-I don't know, Chris. I came here because I didn't have anyone else. I can't fight them alone."

Her control crumbled then and she began to sob. Tears spilled freely down her cheeks. Chris put an arm around her and eased her head down on his shoulder.

The words came tumbling out between sobs. "This isn't fair to you, Chris. This isn't your fight. You don't owe me anything. I ran away from my husband and our little boy because I was afraid that if I stayed they'd be hurt. Now I've come here and probably put you in danger. I'm so sorry. I just didn't know what else to do." She made an effort to pull free. "I'll leave now, before anyone gets hurt. I'll go back to… I'll go somewhere. I should never have come."

Chris pulled her head back against him. "Cut it out. Of course you had to come to me. There's nobody else who knows these creatures exist, who has seen what they can do. Now settle down, and we'll think of something."

Karyn relaxed and let herself lean against him. Slowly her sobs quieted. She sat up and borrowed his handkerchief to dry her eyes.

"Is there anything we can do, Chris? Can we really fight them?"

"We fought them before," he said. "We just didn't finish the job. Do you think they've followed you here yet?"

"I haven't seen any signs, but they seem to know my movements."

"Well, let's assume we have a little time, anyway. We'll get you checked into the hotel now, and tomorrow we'll start making plans."

They stood up together and for a moment each looked deeply into the other's eyes. Chris's arms went around her, and Karyn without thinking pressed her body against him. He kissed her long and deeply, and she could feel him becoming aroused.

It was Chris who stepped back first. He said, "Let's go see about getting you a room."

They walked back across the beach to the hotel without speaking.

* * *

Señor Davila, the manager, was all gracious attention now. "Ah, Señora, you are in luck. This is our busy time of the year, but we do have one late cancellation. Cabana Number 12, I can put you in there."

"Which one is that?" Karyn asked.

"It is at the far end of the row where Señor Halloran has his."

"You have nothing here in the main building?"

"I am sorry, Señora."

"That's all right. I'll take it."

Chris squeezed her arm. "I'd better go and square things with Audrey. I think she's a little ticked off at being left alone. We'll see you at dinner."

Karyn completed her registration, and a handsome boy of about seventeen, who introduced himself as Roberto, carried her bag along the path to her cabana. Inside it was not lavish, but it was clean. There was a double bed, bureau, night table, two chairs, and a settee of wicker. Roberto showed her the small closet and the bathroom, and demonstrated how to open the window and operate the heater. Karyn tipped the boy and promised to ask for him personally if there was anything she needed.

As Roberto went out, a young maid with sparkling eyes and lush, moist lips came in with fresh towels. A look flashed between the two young people that told Karyn they were much more than friends.

When the girl left, Karyn kicked off her shoes and stretched out on the bed. She closed her eyes and let her mind drift, steering it away, for now, from the dark things she wanted to avoid. An hour later she sat up feeling refreshed and thinking maybe everything would be all right.

She soaked in a hot tub, then took a cool shower and dressed in a light blue knit outfit, which, she knew, showed off her figure. When Chris and Audrey came to take her to dinner, the look in the girl's eyes told Karyn she had chosen well.

During the meal Karyn's feeling of well being slipped away. The conversation was perfunctory and strained. She could tell there had been an argument between Chris and Audrey, and it made her uncomfortable. As soon as she could, Karyn excused herself, saying she was tired and wanted to go to bed early.

Back in her room Karyn checked the locks on the windows and the door. She turned on all the lights, but the bulbs were of low wattage and did not drive the shadows out of the corners. The cabana cooled off quickly once the sun was down, and Karyn turned up the heater while she got ready for bed.

The sheets were clean and starchy, the pillows thinner than she liked. Karyn lay for a long time in the dark, listening to the whisper of the surf and the night cries from the jungle. She drifted at last into an uneasy sleep.

* * *

The late flight south from Los Angeles banked into a gentle turn and began its descent to scattered lights of Mazatlán, nestled between the black jungle and the black ocean. Back in the tourist section, a broad-shouldered man with pale hair dozed fitfully in his too-narrow seat. Beside him at the window a woman gazed down at the expanding lights of the city. Her eyes smoldered with deep green fires. Unconsciously she touched the streak of white that ran through her midnight hair.

19

When the morning came the sun was bright and hot. The ocean was a calm, bottle-glass green, and the fears of the night were not so terrifying. Karyn was hungry when she awoke. Her first thought was to find Chris and have him join her for breakfast. Then she remembered that Chris was not alone. Best she stay out of his way for now. In her brief sizing up of Audrey Vance, Karyn had caught the clear message: *He's mine.* There were surely enough problems without causing any more friction there. Karyn could wait until there was a chance to see Chris alone to talk about their plans.

There was a discreet knock at the door. Karyn pulled a robe on over her pajamas and went to see who it was. Outside the door stood Roberto. He held a tray with a pot of steaming coffee, a cup, and a sweet roll. Behind him, on the walk that led past the cabanas, Karyn saw a metal cart with more trays and coffee pots.

"Buenas días, Señora. Your morning coffee, compliments of the hotel."

"Thank you." Karyn smiled at the boy's obvious pride in his little speech.

"Do you wish sugar? Milk?"

"No, thank you. I drink it black."

"If there is anything more you wish, Señora, please call for me."

"All right, Roberto, I'll remember. *Muchas gracias."*

The boy's smile widened at her use of the Spanish phrase. *"De nada,* Señora."

The boy went away, and Karyn took the coffee inside. She poured herself a cup and sipped at it. The brew was murky and strong, but better than no coffee at all.

She showered and dressed and strolled down the walk past the other cabanas toward the main building. She noticed the blinds were drawn in Number 7. She continued into the main building, through the lobby and into the dining room where several other guests were having breakfast.

Karyn chose a table apart from the others and looked over the menu. She passed up huevos rancheros and anything else that sounded Mexican, and ordered straight-up fried eggs. The eggs were not bad, but the toast was dry and the potatoes were fried to crisp brown cubes. The coffee was no better than usual, but Karyn was determined to drink it every chance she got, just to spite Audrey Vance.

After breakfast she went back to her cabana and put on a pair of shorts and a light blouse. She had not thought to pack a swimming suit, considering the nature of her business here. She walked out onto the beach, and young Roberto came running up to provide her with a folding chair down by the tideline.

Karyn adjusted the chair so she could see the row of cabanas and the front of the hotel. Shortly before noon Chris came out, blinking at the sunlight. He started for the surf, then saw Karyn and veered over toward her. He wore brief white swim trunks, and Karyn could not help noticing the smooth tan on his well-muscled body.

"Good morning," he said.

"Hi. I hope you didn't interrupt anything important just to come out and talk to me."

"Don't you start now. I'm getting enough static from Audrey. She thinks the only reason you came down here was for my body."

"Oh? What did you tell her?"

"Nothing. It's easier to let her believe that than to try to explain the real reason."

"I see what you mean."

Both of them were silent for a moment, looking out to sea.

"Did you come up with any ideas?" Karyn said.

Chris sat down on the sand next to her chair. He continued to look out over the water as he spoke. "The way I see it, there isn't much we can do until they make a move."

Karyn whirled on him. "Make a move? You mean until they attack someone else?"

He faced her soberly. "Have you got a better idea?"

"I... oh, I don't know. I guess I expected you to magically solve all my problems. I'm sorry, Chris. I shouldn't have come here. It's not fair to drag you into this again."

"Cut it out," he said. "You came to me because there is no one else. It was the right thing to do. Now settle down and we'll try to approach this logically." After a moment he added, "If it's possible to be logical about werewolves."

Karyn drew a deep breath and gave him a small smile. "All right, let's be logical. Where do we start?"

"Do you expect them to follow you down here?" Chris said. "Marcia and Roy?"

"I'm positive they will. It took them no time at all to find me in Los Angeles. I don't know how, but they seem to know my movements. I wouldn't be surprised if they were here already."

"Okay, let's assume the worst. They're in Mazatlán, and they know where you are. Our best chance is to find them in the daytime. They have no special powers then. Once the sun goes down and they can take on the wolf shape, no man is a match for them. Nothing can stop them in that form except fire and silver."

"So if we don't want to meet them at night, how do we go about finding them in the daylight?"

"We don't," Chris said. "They find us. Find you, rather. You're the one they're after. Even with all the power the night gives them, they can't move around freely as wolves without attracting a lot of attention. As you saw up in Seattle, they found you in their human shape first, then when they were ready to attack they came as wolves. It's up to us to be alert, always watching, during the day."

"And at night?" Karyn said.

"At night we are careful as hell."

"Do you think they'll be clumsy enough to let us see them in the daytime?"

"I don't think clumsy has anything to do with it," Chris said. "I think letting you see them was all part of their plan. It was meant to frighten you before they attacked."

"Well, they sure succeeded," Karyn said.

A slim shadow fell across the sand at their feet.

"Hey, how cozy."

Karyn looked up and saw Audrey Vance standing behind her chair. The girl smiled tightly and let her eyes flick back and forth between Karyn and Chris. There was no doubt about it, Karyn thought. The girl did have a body. Her pink one-piece swimsuit was thin enough and tight enough to emphasize her nipples and the bush of pubic hair.

"Hi," Chris said. "Ready for lunch?"

"Yes, if you haven't already had yours."

Chris ignored the sarcasm. He stood up and brushed the sand from his trunks. "I'll go get wet and be with you in a minute." To Karyn he said, "Damned if the girl isn't making a swimmer out of me."

He loped down to the water and splashed into the surf while the women watched. He dived into an incoming wave and disappeared from sight momentarily, bobbing up again as the wave rolled over him and broke on the shore.

"Have you known Chris a long time?" Audrey asked.

"Yes. He was a friend of my first husband."

"No kidding."

There could not have been, Karyn figured, more than seven or eight years difference between her own and Audrey's ages, yet Audrey Vance made her feel positively middle-aged. She was acutely aware of her awkward position, sitting in the low folding chair while Audrey stood, straight and slim, a little behind her. Karyn stood up end faced the younger woman and felt better.

"Let's get something straight here," she said. "Whatever you and Chris are to each other makes no difference to me. I wish you both good luck or happiness, or anything else you're after. Chris is a friend of mine, and I'm here to see him as a friend. That's all."

"Sure you are." Audrey made her eyes wide and childlike. "What else could it be?"

Karyn met Audrey's baby stare for a moment, then turned away.

"Shit," she said.

If Audrey heard, she gave no sign.

Chris came jogging back from the surf scrubbing the salt water out of his hair.

"Let's go," he said to Audrey. Then to Karyn "Want to have lunch with us?"

Karyn hesitated for a moment, just to give the girl something to think about. Then she said, "No, thanks. I had a big breakfast."

Chris and Audrey walked off toward their cabana. Audrey tucked her hand possessively under his arm. Karyn turned back to the beach and saw the young Roberto raking the sand smooth. She beckoned to him and he came running to her, his smile dazzling in the sunlight.

"Sí, Señora?"

"Could you get me an umbrella, Roberto? I think I've had enough sun for today."

The boy nodded eagerly and took off at a run toward the rear of the hotel. In a few minutes he came back carrying a huge beach umbrella, which had alternating panels of orange and green. He planted it in the sand next to Karyn's chair and opened it, taking care to adjust it so she was properly shaded.

Karyn reached into her bag, then looked up apologetically. "I'm afraid I left my money in the room."

"Is no problem, Señora," said Roberto. "If you want to give me a tip, is plenty of time when you check out." Still smiling, he trotted off to attend to another guest who was holding up an empty highball glass.

Left alone, Karyn settled back with the umbrella shading her from the glare of the sun. She closed her eyes, lulled by the susurration of the surf, and dozed in the gentle breeze. Some time later she awoke with a start. The sun had moved to the west and the shadow of the umbrella had crept up to expose her feet and ankles. She decided to see if she could get a sandwich in the dining room.

Karyn picked up her bag and walked through the sand, back toward the hotel. As she reached the main building she saw a small crowd at the far side gathered around the badminton court; Karyn strolled over to see what the attraction was.

On the grassy court, under the approving eyes of the mostly middle-aged guests, Chris and Audrey were playing an energetic, laughing game of badminton. Chris wore his white trunks and a striped rugby shirt. Audrey had changed into a pale blue shorts and halter outfit. They were a fine-looking couple, Karyn thought unhappily. Like a travel ad in a magazine.

At that moment Audrey looked over at her. There was an unmistakable glint of triumph in her clear young eyes.

I could really learn to dislike that girl, Karyn thought, giving Audrey a bland smile in return. She left the badminton game and crossed the patch of lawn to the main building of the hotel.

From his position behind the desk in the lobby, Señor Davila, the manager, gave her a welcoming smile.

"Is it too late for me to get some lunch?" Karyn asked.

"Not at all, Señora Richter. Please go right in."

"Thank you." Karyn started for the dining room.

"Did your friend find you on the beach all right?" the manager asked.

"Mr. Halloran? Yes, he did."

Señor Davila looked puzzled. "Oh, no, señora, I mean the lady."

Karyn felt a chill. "Miss Vance?"

"No, it was your other friend. The dark lady. She asked for you and I told her you were on the beach. Is anything wrong?"

Karyn stared at him. "There was a dark woman here? Asking for me?"

The manager began to look worried. "Si, Señora. Dark, with a mark of white in her hair. The lady said she was your friend. I hope I did not speak out of place."

"No... it's all right," Karyn said vaguely. She turned and started out of the building.

"Your lunch, Señora?" Davila called after her.

"I've lost my appetite," Karyn said, without looking back.

Back at the badminton court, she edged past the people who were watching, and stepped out to where Chris was preparing to serve.

"Can I talk to you?" she said.

He caught the note of urgency in her voice, "What's happened?"

"They're here. Marcia was at the desk asking for me."

Chris frowned. "When we went in to lunch there was a woman who came in a cab. She said a few words to the manager then went away."

"What did she look like?"

"Tall. Slender. Wore sunglasses. Long, black hair."

"With a streak of silver?"

Chris nodded.

"That was her. I forgot that you never saw Marcia Lura. At least not as a woman."

"Damn," he said. "I was almost close enough to grab her."

The people alongside the court were watching them curiously. Across the net Audry stood with her fists planted on her hips.

"Can we go somewhere?" Karyn said.

"Yeah." Chris handed his racket to a paunchy man in a flowered shirt. "Here, you take over for me." He called across to Audrey, "I'll be back in a little while."

They walked away from the court together. Before she turned, Karyn caught the flash of pure female hatred in Audrey's eyes.

* * *

In a nameless cantina in the old Mexican section of Mazatlán, Roy Beatty sat listlessly at a table in the rear. It was dark in the cantina. Roy stared down at his hands, spread out flat on the sticky tabletop. He looked up at the sound of Marcia Lura's footsteps.

Marcia pulled out the chair next to him and sat down. She leaned close and spoke in an excited whisper.

"She's here."

Roy looked at her with dulled eyes, but said nothing.

"Did you hear me? I said she's here. I found her."

"I heard you."

"By now she will have been told that I asked for her at the desk. She will realize now that there is no escape for her."

Roy did not answer.

Marcia reached around behind his chair. She slipped her long fingers under the hair at the back of his neck and rubbed him there. "Don't you feel it?" she said. "This is the end of the chase."

He rolled his head around as Marcia's fingers worked on his tense trapezius muscles. "I'm glad it's almost over," he said. "That's all."

She brushed his ear with her lips. "Maybe you will feel something more when I tell you who she is with."

"Karyn is here with someone? I thought you said she came down alone."

"She did. But she met someone here."

Marcia's tongue probed at his ear, sliding in and out sensually.

Roy pushed his chair away and turned to face her. "Who? Who did she meet?"

"Your old friend, Roy, and her old lover."

"Chris Halloran? Chris is in Mazatlán?"

"You didn't think she chose this place by chance?"

"And you say they're together?"

"Oh, very much together. They're staying at the Palacio del Mar Hotel north of the city. It's very quiet there. Isolated. Perfect for lovers. And perfect for us."

Roy Beatty's lips drew back from his teeth, and for a moment the image of the wolf overlaid the man. He seemed to look out through the walls and across the city to the bed where his imagination put the naked bodies of his wife and his friend.

Marcia watched him. The corners of her wide, pale mouth lifted in a smile.

"Tonight, my Roy, we will pay them back for everything."

20

That evening Chris insisted that Karyn share a table with him and Audrey for dinner. Karyn was reluctant, but decided that any company, even Audrey's, was better than being alone. Her nerves had been ragged since she heard about Marcia coming to the hotel earlier in the day.

She dressed in her cabana, watching nervously through the window as the sun dropped toward the horizon. The day was still warm, but Karyn shivered as she hurried down the walk toward the main building.

Chris and Audrey were waiting for her in the dining room. Chris was unconvincingly jovial. Audrey was plainly unhappy with the situation. She wore a tight-fitting jumpsuit of simulated suede. Her hair was brushed to a coppery glow. Her eyes were continually on Karyn.

"It's so nice that you could eat with us," she said, showing her teeth.

"It's my pleasure," Karyn answered.

"No doubt," said the younger woman.

Chris cleared his throat and made a show of studying the menu. "I'm going to try the crabmeat enchiladas. How about you two?"

There was a short, uncomfortable silence. Finally Audrey said, "I want a steak. Medium well. I don't like the way they fix Mexican food down here. It's better in L.A."

"I'll just have a salad," Karyn said. She kept glancing through the archway that opened into the lobby. She could see the main entrance, and through the glass in the doors, the darkening sky outside.

"You shouldn't worry about dieting when you're on vacation," Audrey said. "So what if you do put on a few more pounds? Relax. Live a little."

Another time Karyn might have taken up the girl's challenge, but there were other things to think about. She said, "I just don't have the appetite."

"Mexico does that to some people," Audrey said. "You shouldn't have drunk the water."

Chris signaled to the waiter and ordered dinner. He tried half-heartedly to keep the conversation going, but had little success. Audrey fell into a sulk, returning her steak twice because it was not done properly. Karyn tried to follow Chris's inconsequential remarks, but her thoughts were outside where the night had once again claimed the world.

When they were finished, the waiter came and took away the empty dishes. Chris ordered sweet little Mexican cakes for dessert. Audrey found something else to complain about when she was told the kitchen was out of tea.

They dawdled over dessert until they were the last ones left in the dining room. It became plain that Chris was stalling. Audrey looked pointedly at her watch every two or three minutes.

Karyn badly wanted to leave, but she was terrified at the thought of walking alone through the dark to her cabana. She wondered how she could suggest that Chris walk with her without causing a scene with Audrey.

Before she could think of anything, Audrey spoke up. "If we're going to sit here half the night drinking this crappy coffee, I'm going to the little girl's room and at least get rid of some of it. You two will excuse me, I hope?"

She left the table and walked off toward the lobby, her heels ringing angrily on the tile floor.

"You'd better take me back to my room," Karyn said.

"I can't let you stay there alone," Chris said. "If Marcia was here today asking for you, it's a good bet that they'll be back tonight."

Karyn shuddered. "What can I do? I asked the manager, and there are still no rooms available in the main building. I can't sit in the lobby all night."

Chris rubbed his jaw thoughtfully. "You can come to our room."

"All night?"

"At least until we can think of something better."

"Audrey will love that."

"Audrey will have to learn that things don't always go her way."

"Have you considered telling her?"

"You mean about Drago and the werewolves?"

"Yes."

"No way. She'd laugh in my face. It's better to let her think I've got the hots for you. That's something she can understand."

"It kind of messes up your relationship though, doesn't it?"

"That relationship is on the down-slope anyway," Chris said.

Audrey came back to the table and sat down, her spirits unimproved. Karyn felt oddly guilty, as though she and Chris really did have a secret love affair going.

Audrey lifted the coffee cup to her lips, then set it down in the saucer with a thump. "I've had all this crap I can take," she announced.

Chris spoke up in a tone of artificial gaiety. "I've got an idea. Audrey, we still have that bottle of tequila that we bought at the airport. Why don't the three of us stop by for a nightcap or two?"

"Karyn's probably tired," Audrey said quickly. "Remember, she was up early this morning."

It was time, Karyn decided, to score a few points for the visiting team. "As a matter of fact, I'm not tired at all," she said, turning on a brilliant smile. "It sounds like great fun. Chris and I can talk over old times. And, you and I, Audrey, can get to know each other better."

"Terrific," said Audrey.

"Fine," Chris said. "Then it's all settled."

He called for the check and signed it. They got up from the table and walked out through the archway. Passing the desk. Chris stopped.

"I just happened to think, how many glasses do we have in the room?"

"I'm sure I don't know," Audrey said.

"If I remember right, there were only two. Big water glasses." He stepped over to the desk and spoke to the manager. "Could we have some small glasses sent out to Number 7?"

Señor Davila carefully avoided looking at the two women. "Of course, Señor Halloran," he said with a professional smile. "The girl will bring them out to you."

"And send along some limes and salt," Chris added. To the women he said, "I'll show you how to drink tequila Tijuana style."

"Whoopee," said Audrey flatly.

They left the building together and walked the short distance down the path to the first cabana, the one where Chris and Audrey stayed. Chris unlocked the door and they went in. The room looked the same as Karyn's, and had been neatly tidied up by the maid. Karyn tried not to make a point of looking at the bed, though it dominated the room. Audrey walked by it deliberately and ran her hand across the spread.

Chris waved the two women to the wicker settee and pulled up the chair for himself. He carried a small table over and set it between them. From a drawer he produced a bottle of tequila. He opened the bottle and sniffed at it.

"This will be good for what ails us," he said lamely.

Audrey and Karyn looked at him without expression.

A knock on the door saved him from having to make further small talk. Blanca, the pretty young maid, came in carrying a glass bowl of fresh lime wedges and three double shot glasses along with a saltshaker.

"Now maybe the party will pick up," Chris said, forcing a laugh. He handed a bill to Blanca, who slipped it prettily down the front of her blouse.

"*Gracias,* Señor," she said, with a coquettish lowering of the eyelids. With a bare flicker of a glance at Audrey and Karyn she went out and closed the door.

* * *

Once outside, Blanca stopped and pulled the bill from its warm valley between her breasts. Five dollars, American. This was a night of good omen. And with the blonde Americian lady busy with her friends in Number 7, it could be a beautiful night.

She hurried to a utility shed at the rear of the hotel where Roberto was busy repairing a broken chair. He looked up from his work and smiled at her.

"Can you do that later?" she said, her eyes flashing with mischief.

"Why? Now that I have started, I may as well finish the job."

"Maybe you would change your mind if I told you a secret," she said, moving close to him.

"A secret about me?"

"About us." She sat beside him on the wooden bench and ran a hand along the flank of his tight black trousers.

"Ay, girl, when you do that I have no secrets," he said.

Blanca looked down at the bulge in his pants and smiled. She brushed it with her fingertips. "Are you saving that for someone?"

"What a question, shameless girl. Take care that I do not lay you down right here where Señor Davila would surly find us."

"Would you like to make love to me now?" the girl said.

"Very much. But we have no bed. To go to your room or mine is too dangerous, and on the beach one gets sand in unmentionable places."

"We do not have to go to the beach tonight. One of the cabanas is waiting for us."

"How is that possible? No one checked out of the hotel today."

"The Señora from California who arrived yesterday spends the evening with her friends in Number 7. Her cabana is at the far end, and there is no one there."

"She might return."

"Not for at least an hour. Maybe more. They have a bottle of good tequila and a bowl of limes, and the Lord knows what games in mind to keep them busy."

"Even so, she will know we have been there."

Blanca clucked her tongue impatiently. "She will know nothing. I will put fresh linen on the bed and leave the room spotless. All these objections! I think you do not really want to make love to me."

Roberto's eyes flashed. He jumped to his feet and seized Bianca's wrist, pulling her up after him. "Come along. I'll show you if I want to make love or not."

Pulling the girl behind him, he ran out of the shed, up along the side of the main building, and down the path until they came, laughing and breathing hard, to Cabana Number 12.

Blanca used her passkey to let them in. She peeled the spread, blanket, and top sheet back from the bed and folded them neatly in the chair, bending low as she did so to let the skirt ride up in back over her plump brown thighs.

She turned to face Roberto, but he had her in his arms before she could speak. His mouth found hers, and his hands raced over her body, rubbing, caressing, squeezing. After a minute they pulled apart just long enough to fumble out of their clothes and let them drop to the floor. Together they fell across the bed. Blanca opened her legs to him. With the exuberance and impatience of youth, he entered her.

* * *

At the edge of the clearing, behind the Palacio del Mar, a huge tan wolf arose from the ground where a moment before a man had writhed silently. The wolf stretched and shook, feeling the exhilarating play of its muscles. Then, leaving the pile of clothes where Roy Beatty had dropped them, the wolf moved silently through the heavy tropical growth behind the row of cabanas.

The last one in this row was the one he wanted. The windows showed no light. She would be inside asleep. Or maybe not asleep. Awake, perhaps, and staring into the darkness, fearing what she must know was somewhere outside. Soon there would be no more fear for Karyn. No more anything. The faint spark of humanity still alive in the wolf brain rebelled at the thought of the coming kill, but the dominant animal part burned with excitement.

A few yards from the cabana the wolf stopped. He raised his muzzle and tested the scent that had brought him up short. The scent of sex. Humans in rut. The wolf cocked his great head and heard the rhythmic slap-slap of naked bodies, one against the other. Belly pounding against belly as the man drove his organ into the woman.

Animal rage blazed behind the eyes of the wolf, rage fired by the memory of human jealousy. The long, sinewy legs stretched out into a loping run as the wolf closed on the cabana.

From inside came the muffled squeals and grunts of humans engaged in sex. The wolf's heart pounded in his broad chest. He would catch them together. The one-time wife and one-time friend.

With a full-throated growl, the wolf sprang from the ground and hit the window with outstretched forepaws. He took screen, frame, and glass in with him and hit the floor in a shower of splinters.

Before the two in the bed had time to react, the wolf was upon them.

Not Karyn! Nor Chris either! Strangers. A dreadful mistake, but too late, too late. The taste of blood was in the wolf's throat, and no power on earth could stop him now. In less than a minute the bed was a sopping crimson mess. Bits of flesh and hair and bone littered the floor. The wolf ripped, chewed, and swallowed, gulping the hot raw meat.

The beast growled softly as it fed, looking warily toward the window. Soon there were shouts from the main hotel building and the sound of doors opening in the other cabanas down the line. It was time to be gone.

The wolf thumped from the sodden bed to the floor. In a single graceful bound, he was back out the window and running in long fluid strides toward the forest. He was safely into the thick undergrowth by the time the first people reached the cabana.

21

The atmosphere in Cabana Number 7 was thick with cigarette smoke and hostility. Two of the three tequila glasses sat on the table half full.

Audrey Vance raised the third to her lips and drained it. She set it back down on the table, tipping it over as she did so.

"Lucky it wasn't full," she said. She righted the glass and poured more tequila.

"You ought to try it with lime and salt," Chris said.

"Fuck lime and salt." Audrey sniffed at the liquor, then held her glass out toward Chris. "Here's lookin' up your cucaracha."

Chris sipped at his own glass, this time forgetting the lime himself. Karyn coughed uncomfortably and lit another cigarette.

She could not remember a more unpleasant evening. She appreciated what Chris was doing for her, and she knew she was probably safer here than in her own room, but the strain of the three way relationship was wearing her down. She looked at her watch and saw that it was a little after midnight. A long, long time remained until dawn. The hell with this, she decided abruptly. She would go back to her own room, lock herself in, and at least would not have to put up with Audrey any more tonight.

Then there was a crash of glass, followed by screaming.

Chris stopped talking in the middle of a sentence and sat motionless for a moment. Audrey started violently, spilling tequila down the front of her blouse. Karyn stared at the darkened window. Although the screams were directionless, she was deadly certain that they came from Number 12.

"Jesus!" Audrey said. She stood up, ignoring the spilled drink. "What the hell was that?"

Chris got up and walked to the door. He opened it and stood there listening. The screams had stopped now, and there was the sound of other doors opening and questioning voices. People began running from the main building along the path that led past the cabanas. Chris started out the door.

"Don't go out there," Karyn said.

He looked back at her briefly. "I've got to see what happened."

"Then I'm coming with you," Karyn said.

"You're not going to leave me here alone," Audrey said. She walked unsteadily over and stood next to Chris, clutching his arm possessively.

For a moment Chris hesitated. They could hear voices shouting from down at the end of the row of cabanas. "All right," he said, "We'll all go. But don't get separated."

The three of them stepped out and joined the people running from the main building. There was no outside lighting along the path, and the only illumination came from the open doors of the other cabanas and several flashlights. At Number 12 the running people came to an abrupt stop. The door stood open. A man reached cautiously inside and snapped on the lights.

There was a gasp from the onlookers, and the crowd took an involuntary step backward. Audrey turned away from Chris and began to retch.

Through the open doorway Karyn caught a glimpse of the bed. Her bed. She saw what appeared to be a pile of bare human limbs on top of it. Everything was splashed a bright, wet crimson. She looked away as Chris gripped her shoulder.

Señor Davila, the hotel manager, rushed up with his thin, pale legs bare under a flannel nightshirt. He began trying simultaneously to calm the guests in English and give orders to the staff in Spanish. The only word Karyn picked out was *policía*. Slowly the people began to move back away from the cabana as Davila selected a pair of unhappy kitchen helpers to guard the door.

Half an hour later Karyn, Chris, Audrey, and most of the other guests were gathered in the lobby of the main building. The initial shock had given way to a sort of desperate camaraderie, as with people who have shared, and survived, a disaster. On orders from Señor Davila hot coffee was being dispensed from the kitchen, and the bar, hastily reopened, was doing a booming business.

The clatter of conversation among the guests eased off as two blue and white cars with the markings of the Mazatlán police wheeled up to the front of the hotel with sirens braying.

A short, neat man in a business suit marched in at the head of several uniformed policemen. He directed the officers to their tasks, then talked quietly with Señor Davila while the guests watched with interest. After a minute he stepped to the archway between the lobby and dining room and held up a hand for attention.

"Good evening. I am Sgt. Fulgencio Vasquez of the Mazatlán Police. As you know, there has been a serious tragedy here tonight. Two employees of this hotel have been killed." He paused for a moment while the guests took in this information. "Temporary, I will use the office of Señor Davila, the manager, to do interviews. I will ask that any of you who have knowledge of this crime remain and give your name to my officer. The rest of you may return to your rooms. Please do not leave the hotel before speaking to me. Thank you for the cooperation."

There was a general stirring around among the guests. No one seemed anxious to leave.

Karyn and Chris exchanged a look. Their eyes asked, *Shall we tell?* and immediately answered, *Take care.*

There were few volunteers from among the guests to supply information, but most of them stayed around in the lobby and the bar to see what was going to happen. There was a good deal of drinking and nervous laughter as people found their quiet vacation had become an adventure.

A blue city ambulance pulled up outside, and the guests crowded out on the veranda to watch. The bodies of the two victims, strapped onto litters and covered with plastic sheets, were brought up and loaded into the back. The ambulance drove out with lights flashing and siren wailing unnecessarily.

Karyn, Chris, and Audrey, sat on a wood and leather sofa on one side of the lobby and watched the others jostle for a look at the departing ambulance.

"They act like it's a holiday of some kind," Karyn said.

"It's a touch of hysteria," Chris said. "What they're saying inside is, 'Thank God it happened to somebody else and not me.'"

Karyn shivered. Chris reached over and squeezed her hand.

"I've got a fucking headache that won't quit," Audrey said.

"Do you want to go back to the room?" Chris asked.

"Not by myself, I don't."

"I'll go see if I can get you some aspirin."

Chris started to rise, but sat back down when he saw Sergeant Vasquez coming toward them across the lobby. The policeman stopped before the sofa and nodded politely. He focused his attention on Karyn.

"Mrs. Richter?"

"Yes?"

"I am told it was your cabana that this unfortunate tragedy took place."

"Yes, it was."

"Will you be good enough to come into the I office?"

Karyn looked questioningly at Chris.

He said, "Is it all right if I come along, Sergeant? I'm a friend of Mrs. Richter."

Vasquez's cool brown eyes took in the two of them. "A friend, you say?"

"That's right. We knew each other back in the States."

"Don't mind me," Audrey said. "I'm just passing though."

Vasquez gave her a chilly smile. To Chris he said, "I have no objection if you wish to come."

Chris tuned to Audrey. "This shouldn't take too long."

"What the hell, take all the time you want," Audrey said. "I'll be in the bar."

Chris patted her knee and smiled. She turned away. He shrugged and joined Karyn and Sergeant Vasquez as they crossed the lobby to enter the small office tucked in behind the registration desk.

Vasquez put them into hard-backed chairs facing him as he sat behind a small desk. He offered his pack of Mexican cigarettes and took one for himself when they both declined. He inhaled deeply, then leaned forward across the desk and fixed them with a steady brown gaze.

"The two of you were together this evening?"

"That's right," Chris answered. "Miss Vance was with us."

"Ah, yes, the young lady in the lobby."

Chris nodded.

Vasquez regarded him for a moment without expression, then he turned to Karyn. "Mrs. Richter, do you know of anyone who might want to kill you?"

"Me?"

"The young people were murdered in your room. The lights were out. It is possible that the killer was after you and did not see his mistake until it was too late."

"I just arrived in Mazatlán," Karyn said carefully. "I don't know anyone here, except Mr. Halloran."

"Ah, yes." The policeman switched his attention to Chris. "And you, sir, have you any opinions about this tragedy?"

"I don't know any more than Mrs. Richter," Chris said.

Vasquez held Chris for a long moment with his somber gaze, then turned it on Karyn. When neither of them reacted the sergeant relaxed a little and gave them a cool smile. "It was just a thought. The truth is we are fairly certain who the killer is, but I do not wish to overlook other possibilities."

"You know who did it?" Chris said.

"In a crime of passion such as this, we look first for the husband. In this case we have no husband, but we do have a former lover of the girl. A man given to violent acts, I am told. He worked here at the hotel and was discharged a month ago."

Karyn bit her lip. "Are you certain this was done by a man?"

"It is not a woman's crime, Señora," said Vasquez.

"That's not what I meant."

"Oh?" The policeman assumed an expression of polite attention.

Karyn felt her face growing warm. She looked to Chris for help, but he gave her only a tiny shake of his head. "I just wondered," she said, "Whether it could have been... an animal."

"Impossible," the policeman said at once. "I do not wish to make light of your suggestion, Señora, but there is no animal capable of doing what was done to those two young people."

A uniformed policeman entered the office. He looked quickly at Karyn and Chris, then spoke to Vasquez. *"Con perdon..."*

"Què?"

The policeman spoke rapidly in Spanish as Vasquez listened and nodded. The man placed an envelope on the desk in front of the sergeant as he spoke. Vasquez opened it and peered inside. From a pocket he produced a pair of tweezers, which he used to withdraw the contents of the envelope. He held it up to the light and examined it, then set it down carefully on the desk. A thick tuft of coarse tan fur. He said something to the man in uniform, who saluted and went out.

"It seems the killer left something behind when he went out the window," said Vasquez. He picked up the tuft of fur again in the tweezers and displayed it proudly, like it was a rare butterfly. "One of the men found this caught on the torn window screen."

Karyn and Chris stared at the bit of fur. Neither of them spoke.

Vasquez smiled thinly at Karyn. "I'm sure it is not what you think, Señora. Torn from a fur-lined jacket, I would guess. It will be most helpful when we pick up our man."

Karyn started to speak, but caught a warning glance from Chris, and held back.

"There is something. Señora?" said Vasquez.

Karyn shook her head. "No, nothing. Is it all right if we go now?"

"Yes, of course. Thank you both for your time."

They walked out of the manager's office and across the lobby. Most of the guests by this time had drifted off to their rooms.

"We can't let them arrest an innocent man," Karyn said.

"What do you suggest? Going up to Sergeant Vasquez and saying, 'Hey, I think those people were killed by a werewolf who used to be my husband'?"

"Please don't be sarcastic."

Chris passed a hand over his brow. "I'm sorry. Getting tired, I guess. But I don't think you have to worry about an innocent man being locked up. Despite what you might have read, the Mexican system of criminal justice is reasonably competent."

"I suppose so," Karyn said wearily. "And you're right. There really is nothing we could do." Without warning she yawned.

"We'd all better get some sleep," Chris said.

"Let's find the manager and arrange for a room for you."

Señor Davila, now fully dressed, but still unshaven, said yes, a room in the main building could be made ready at once for Señora Richter, since a number of guests had suddenly checked out.

As Karyn filled out a new registration card, Chris snapped his fingers.

"Damn, I forgot about Audrey. She's still waiting in the bar."

"You'd better go and get her," Karyn said. "I can handle things from here on."

"I'll see you first thing in the morning," Chris said. He hurried away toward the bar.

Karyn finished signing in for the new room while Señora Davila sent a boy out to see about bringing her things in from Cabana 12. She sat down in a chair in the lobby to wait, and massaged her eyes.

"Señora?"

She looked up, and for a moment could not place the stocky man with the luxuriant moustache who had spoken.

"Luis Zarate?" he said with a rising inflection. "The taxi from the airport yesterday?"

"Oh, yes," Karyn said. She waited for the man to speak.

"If the Señora will permit, I think I can be of assistance."

"Thank you, but I won't be needing a taxi tonight."

"No, Señora, not a taxi, but you do need help, maybe, I think."

"What do you mean?"

"The young Blanca, and her *novio*, Roberto, they died tonight, I think, in your place."

"How do you know this?" Karyn asked. She watched the man intently.

"There is much I know. Remember, I told you I have gypsy blood. I know it was no man who killed Roberto and Blanca."

"Who, then?"

"Not *who*, Señora, *what*. These killings carry the mark of *lobombre*. The werewolf."

22

In the part of Mazatlán away from the sparkling beaches and bright new streets was a section of the city called La Ratonera, the rathole. It was a neighborhood where the sightseeing buses never came, and only a foolhardy tourist ventured. The streets were cracked and pitted, the buildings crusted with the filth of decades.

Doors were always closed, windows covered. The air was heavy with the smell of human feces and human despair.

From La Ratonera came the used-up prostitutes, the burned-out thieves, the hopeless drunkards and the dying dopers. At night they moved like shadows along the broken streets, in the light of day they shut themselves inside.

Here, in a musty room behind a nameless *cantina*, Roy Beatty lay face down on the thin mattress of a rusted iron bed. The wallpaper of the room had long ago peeled away to the brown-stained plaster. Vermin scuttled through piles of debris in the corner.

Marcia Lura stood with her arms folded, looking down at Roy. She was oblivious to the squalor around her. The grace of her body and her fierce beauty made her seem an alien being in this lowly place. The green fires in her eyes snapped with suppressed rage.

"You failed again," she said. Her voice was low and vibrant like a taut cello string, "Three times now you have set out to kill, and three times you have blundered. First there was the boy in Seattle. Simple enough, but instead of him, you killed a useless old woman. Then in Los Angeles you had a chance at your Karyn, but you let her get away. And now you have missed her again. After last night she will be more on her guard than ever, and it will be still more difficult for us."

Roy groaned softly where he lay, but did not turn his head to look at her.

"You know that I have to rely on you," Marcia went on. "I would give anything if it were possible for me to make the kill. You know that. And you know why I cannot. I have put all my faith in you, Roy, and you have failed me. Not once, but three times."

"Enough!"

Marcia started, shocked by the unexpected strength in Roy's voice. He sat up in the bed and faced her.

"I don't want to hear any more about failure," he said. "Two young people died last night. Two people who had done you no harm. Nor me. And yet I killed them. With the woman in Seattle, that makes three. Three innocent people I have killed for you."

Marcia's eyes met his, and she slowly recovered her poise. It was Roy who looked away first.

"You killed them for me, did you?" Her voice was dangerously soft. "Just for me. Look at me, Roy. Tell me you did not enjoy the killing. Tell me you did not exult in the power of your muscles as you ripped the throat from the old woman who foolishly stood in your way. Tell me that as you savaged the naked bodies of the couple on the bed that you did not feel a sexual thrill of your own. Can you tell me this?"

Roy's gaze returned to her, but when he spoke much of the power was gone from his voice. "No, I can't deny those things. Because of what I am, the killing excites me. I need it. But because of what I used to be, it disgusts me."

Marcia walked to the bed. She sat next to Roy on the threadbare mattress and eased his head down onto her large, firm breasts.

"I know the pain you feel, my Roy," she said. "I understand. As the time passes, the pain will grow less. One day all memories of the man you were—that weak, shallow, ignorant man—will fade to shadows. You will glory in what you are.

The strength of the wolf will be your joy, and you will know only joy. Then you and I will truly be together. That is what you want, isn't it, my Roy?"

"Yes." His words were muffled against the silk of her blouse. "That's what I want."

Gently Marcia opened the buttons down the front of her blouse, freeing her breasts. They glowed pale and smooth in the faint light that filtered into the room. Roy took her nipple into his mouth. She stroked the shaggy blond hair at the back of his head and spoke in a low, caressing tone.

"Our mission here will soon be ended. Time is short for us now because the woman has an ally. Her lover, your one-time friend. We must separate them. Together they are dangerous because they know what they are fighting. They know our strength, and will not be taken by surprise."

She was silent for a moment and pressed Roy's head tight against her. "And worse, they know our weakness."

Roy brushed his lips over the upper curve of her breast and kissed her ivory-smooth throat. He pulled back from her and reached out to touch the silver streak in her hair.

"My poor Marcia," he murmured. "They hurt you so."

The blazing green eyes stared into the past. "Never will I forget the pain of that silver bullet. There is no pain to compare."

"I promise they will pay for that," Roy said. "I won't fail you again."

Marcia stroked his broad back. Her fingers caressed the smooth, powerful muscles. "I know you won't," she said. "But it will be difficult. They will seek help against us."

"How can we stop them?"

"There are many gypsies in Mazatlán, people who have come down from the mountains. People who remember the old laws. We will spread the word among them. We cannot allow the woman and her lover to arm themselves against us as they did before. We must strike first."

"Will the gypsies help us?"

"We don't need their help. All we will ask of the gypsies is that they give no help to our enemies. They will not deny us that. They will not act against *lobombre.*"

Roy's body tensed, but he began to relax as Marcia used her fingers on him, then her mouth. In a little while there was no more rebellion in him.

23

In the morning after the bloody business in Cabana 12, the sun had barely cleared the mountains behind the Palacio del Mar, but the grounds and the lobby were alive with people. There were members of the Mazatlán police force along with people from the State of Sinaloa and the Mexican government. The sightseers had not started to arrive yet, since the morning papers were not out with the news.

At a table in the dining room, Karyn sat over sweet rolls and coffee with Chris Halloran and a worried-looking Luis Zarate. They looked around furtively, like conspirators, and talked in low, guarded voices.

"I understand you said last night you could help us," Chris said.

Luis' eyes darted around the room. "I did not say that exactly."

"Well, what exactly *did* you say?"

"What I was going to say is that I know somebody who maybe can help you."

"Damn it, man, get on with it. Do we have to drag every word out of you?"

Karyn laid a hand on Chris's arm. "Please, Chris, let Luis tell us in his own way."

"Gracias, Señora," said the taxi driver. "The one I know, the one who may help you, lives in the mountains back of the city of Mazatlán. She is a gypsy. Very old. Her name is Philina."

"What the hell good is an old gypsy lady going to do us?" Chris demanded. "We're talking about werewolves, not tea leaves. I thought you understood that."

Luis pushed his chair back from the table. With as much dignity as he could summon, he started to rise. "If the Señor is not interested, I will take no more of your time."

"Please, Luis, sit down," Karyn said. "We want very much to hear what you have to say." She frowned at Chris.

"I'm sorry, Luis," he said. "I'm just upset. We don't want any more people to die. And we need all the help we can get, from anyone who will give it. I truly appreciate your offer."

Luis eased back into the chair. *"Muy bien.* Philina is, like I told you, a very old gypsy. She is full-blooded gypsy, not just little part like me." He blinked a smile on and off, then continued. "Philina sees things in your hand. She knows things that are going to happen. If there is anyone who can help you fight lobombre, it is Philina the gypsy."

"Can you take us to her?" Karyn asked,

"I can take you some of the way—as far as the road goes. After that there is a mountain trail that leads to her cabin."

"That's no good," Chris said. "We haven't time to go hunting through strange mountain country for some old woman. If we are caught out after dark, we'll be at the mercy of the werewolves."

"The journey can be made in the daylight hours if one starts early," said Luis. "I have a cousin who lives at the end of the road. He keeps burros for mountain travelers. He will let you have two of them for a small price. The burros know the way up the trail. It is the only one leading up the mountain."

"If we started now, could we make it today before dark?" Karyn asked

Luis glanced through the window, checking the angle of the sun. He nodded.

Karyn and Chris looked at each other. "What do you think?" she said.

"To tell you the truth, I think it's a waste of time, I can't see what good an old gypsy fortuneteller can do us."

"Chris, we have nothing else."

"But palm-reading. Do you believe in that?"

"Do you believe in werewolves?" Karyn said quietly.

"Touché," said Chris.

"Even if the old woman can do nothing for us, all we've lost is one day. And it's just possible that she's for real, and can somehow help us. I think it's worth trying."

Chris rubbed his jaw thoughtfully. "Okay," he said. "I'm game if you are." And to Luis: "How soon can you be ready to go?"

"I am ready now, Señor. My taxi is parked just outside."

"Good. Karyn, I think it would be best if you stay here while I go check out the gypsy lady."

"Not a chance," Karyn said. "I'm going with you." When Chris started to protest she held up a hand to stop him. "Please don't go all macho and protective on me. This is more my fight than it is yours, and I'm not going to sit in my room wringing my hands while you're out doing things."

"All right then," Chris said reluctantly. "We'll both go. While you put on something suitable for burro-riding, I'll go try to head off trouble with Audrey."

* * *

Audrey Vance sat up in the bed and held the sheet wrapped tight around her lithe body as she listened to Chris tell her he was going to leave her this morning. Her gray eyes were like chips of granite.

"I know this isn't a lot of fun for you," he said. "But please believe me when I tell you it's super important."

Audrey stared at him coldly before answering. "And you have to be gone all day."

"Most of it, probably."

"With your ex-girlfriend."

"Karyn is not my ex-girlfriend."

"Whatever the hell you want to call her, then."

Chris sighed heavily. "Yes, Karyn will be with me."

"Very cozy."

"I can't help what you think."

Audrey turned away, letting him see her best profile. "Maybe it would be better if I just went back to Los Angeles alone."

After a moment Chris said, "As a matter of fact that might be the best thing to do."

Audrey turned toward him quickly. She reached out her arms, letting the sheet fall away from her high, firm breasts. "I didn't mean it, Chris. I don't want to go back without you. Look at me, I promised you I'd never be jealous, and here I am doing exactly that. Look, if you've got something important you have to do with the woman, go ahead. I'll find something around here to keep me busy today."

Chris relaxed. He placed his hands flat against the girl's sides, feeling the ribs outlined under the firm flesh. "Thanks, honey. I'll tell you all about it sometime when there's no pressure. If I tried to explain it now, take my word for it, you wouldn't believe me."

Audrey locked her hands behind his head and tried to pull him down with her on the bed. "At least you can leave me with a little something to think about."

He held himself back. "Sorry, honey, I just haven't got the time."

She released her hold immediately and looked up into his eyes. Little white tension lines appeared at the corners of her mouth. "Jesus, thanks a lot."

Chris tried a smile. "When I go to bed with you, I want us to have time to do it right. You don't want to start knocking off quickies, do you?"

"Just go on and do whatever you have to do." Audrey gathered the sheet around her again. "I'll see you when you get back."

Chris stood for a moment looking at her. When she would not meet his eye he went out and closed the door firmly behind him.

* * *

Karyn was waiting on the veranda with Luis when Chris returned. She had changed into a pair of jeans and a lightweight jacket over a sweater.

"How did it go?" she said.

"Not too good."

"I'm sorry."

"Don't worry about it. That's my problem."

As they started down the steps Karyn touched Chris's arm. "There's that policeman who talked to us last night. I want to see him for a minute."

She walked up the path to where Sergeant Vasquez stood talking to a young uniformed policeman, who nodded several times, then hurried off.

"Excuse me, Sergeant," Karyn said.

"Señora Richter, good morning."

"I was wondering—you said last night that there was this friend of the girl, the one who was killed, who you thought might have done it—"

Vasquez raised his hands in a helpless gesture. "Unfortunately for us, the young man has the perfect alibi. For the past seven days, including last night, be has been locked in jail in Culiacán."

Karyn fought to suppress a smile of relief. "I see. Well, I was just wondering. Thank you."

She hurried back to rejoin Chris and Luis Zarate. They climbed into the taxi and rolled away from the hotel toward Mazatlán. Before they reached the city, Luis turned off the highway onto a narrow, unpaved road that led off into the foothills of the Occidental Mountains.

Once they were away from the cooling effect of the sea breeze, the air in the car became hot and steamy. Opening the windows did no good. However, it began to cool off again as the road started to climb.

The rutted road finally came to an end at a pile of boulders. Luis eased the car off into the gravel in front of a weathered shack built of lumber scraps and flattened tin cans. He honked the horn steadily until a swarthy man, with a limp and one clouded eye, came out of the shack. Luis got out of the car and spoke to him in Spanish while Karyn and Chris stood by waiting. Finally Luis rejoined them.

"My cousin Guillermo will let you have two burros for the day for ten dollars. It is too much, but he knows you are Americans, and to ignorant peons like Guillermo all Americans are very rich."

"Tell him it's a deal," Chris said.

Luis passed the word to his cousin, and the man limped back behind the shack and returned a minute later leading two sleepy burros that looked as if the moths had been at them.

"Are you sure they'll make it up the mountain?" Chris said.

"Estos es muy buenos burros," said Guillermo, catching the tone of Chris's voice, if not the meaning of his words. *"Muy robustos."*

"Yeah, I'll bet," Chris muttered.

"What about saddles?" Karyn asked.

Guillermo looked blank.

She patted the seat of her jeans, then the bony back of one of the burros. "Saddle," she repeated.

A light came into Guillermo's good eye. *"Oh, si, las mantas!"* He limped into the shack and returned with two thin, tattered blankets. He folded them carefully and lay them over the backs of the burros.

"Swell," Karyn said. She glanced over at Luis.

"Don't worry," he said. "These burros do not move fast enough to throw you off."

"That's not what I'm worried about," Karyn said dryly.

"We'd better get started," Chris said. "Which one do you want?"

Karyn looked the two animals over. They were about the same size, and their gentle, sleepy eyes told her nothing. She rubbed the ruff of hair between the ears of one of them. The burro did not move.

"I like this one," she said. "He's got spirit."

With help from Luis and his cousin they climbed aboard the animals. Guillermo showed them how to hold onto the rope that was attached to a simple bit in each burro's mouth.

"You're sure we'll be able to find the place all right?" Chris said.

"The burros will take you there," Luis assured him. "They will follow the trail, and the trail leads only to the gypsy."

"And you'll meet us here when we come down?" Karyn said.

"*Si*, Señora. I will be waiting a full two hours before sundown. Take care you are not caught in the darkness. Night comes quickly in these mountains."

"Don't worry," Karyn told him, "We won't take any chances."

They clucked to the burros, and with a little urging the animals started off at a slow, patient, pace up the rocky trail that led into the mountains.

Karyn soon found that riding burro-back was every bit as uncomfortable as she had imagined. In less than half an hour the insides of her thighs were chafed raw, and her buttocks ached from the steady jolting gait of the beasts.

Chris, riding ahead on the narrow trail, turned back. "How you doing?"

"Just great, but I may never sit down again."

After riding up the ever-steepening grade for more than another hour, they came to a clear water spring that bubbled out between two rocks. Karyn and Chris dismounted gratefully and drank deeply of the icy water while the burros dipped their muzzles in the pool downstream.

"How about a short rest?" Chris said.

"I'd appreciate it."

Chris sat down on a rock among the scrubby chaparral that grew along the trail. Karyn eased into a semi-reclining position beside him.

"I sure hope this trip is worth the aches and pains," she said.

Chris grinned at her. "I was willing to come up alone, remember?"

"Come on, cowboy, let's ride," she said, pushing painfully to her feet.

Chuckling, Chris remounted his burro and they set of again.

The sun had passed its zenith when they topped the first crest. On the other side, the trail dipped down sharply into a steep valley of tangled green rainforest.

"God, how much farther can it be?" Karyn said.

"I think this is it," Chris said. "Look over there."

Karyn followed his pointing finger and saw, just over the rise of ground, the top of a cabin. The walls were unfinished logs, the roof a heavy thatch of dry grass. From a hole in the roof a trail of gray smoke drifted into the air. The cabin had an unreal, fairytale look.

"The house of the wicked witch," Karyn said, and immediately wished she hadn't.

They got down off the burros and tied them loosely to a clump of chaparral, undoing the rope bits so they could eat. The docile animals lowered their heads and began to chew on the coarse grass.

Karyn and Chris approached the hut together. There was no door. Instead, the heavy tanned hide of some animal hung across the opening. From inside came the smell of something gamy cooking.

"Hello?" Chris called at the door. "Anybody here?"

No answer.

Chris looked at Karyn with a shrug, then drew aside the hide covering the doorway. The smell of cooking, new and old, hit them like a fist. In the center of the single room a low fire burned in a pit lined with rocks. Over the flame, a blackened five-gallon can was suspended on a pole. Something bubbled sluggishly in the can. The room was oppressively hot.

"*Váyase.* Go away."

For a moment Karyn could not locate the source of the voice. Then, as her eyes adjusted to the gloom inside the cabin, she saw a tall woman, thin as a stick, with straight white hair and a black dress that had been patched many times. The woman stood on the other side of the fire pit, looking at them.

"Luis Zarate told us to come to you," Chris said. He squinted into the shadows, trying to get a clear look at the woman.

The gypsy took a step toward them. The glow from the fire accentuated the highlights and shadows of her face. Her nose was thin and highly arched. The cheekbones stood out prominently over the deep hollows of her cheeks. Her skin was leathery and wrinkled, but in the dark fiery eyes was a hint of the wild beauty she once had been. She fixed them with a steady gaze, Chris first, then Karyn.

"You are the ones, then," she said. Her voice was steady and ageless.

"Luis spoke to you about us?" Karyn said.

"I have not seen him."

"You said… we are the ones."

"I knew you were coming."

"Can we speak to you?" Chris said, his tone automatically respectful.

"Ah, well, come inside if you must," the old woman said.

Karyn and Chris entered the dark interior of the cabin. There was no carpet on the hard dirt floor, and little furniture that was recognizable. When Chris let the hide fall back over the doorway, the only light came from the fire.

The gypsy, Philina, motioned Karyn into an old wooden chair that had no back. Chris stood beside her. The old woman sat down on a pile of rags facing them. She drew her legs up and crossed them beneath her.

"Tell me your story," Philina said.

Karyn began to talk, haltingly at first, then more freely. She told the old woman about the things that had happened to her, beginning with her first encounter with the werewolves in the California village of Drago. She talked about the renewal of the horror this summer in Seattle, and how it followed her to her parents' home in Los Angeles, and finally here to the west coast of Mexico.

The old gypsy listened silently. She did not move or change her expression. The only sign that she was not asleep was the glitter of her eyes in the firelight.

When Karyn had finished there was no sound in the cabin for a long time. At last Philina spoke. "So you have come to me."

"Yes," Karyn said. "Can you help us?"

Philina gazed into the fire for such a long time, Karyn began to think she had fallen asleep. Then abruptly she looked up and said, "Let me see your hand."

Karyn glanced at Chris, then rose and walked over to where the gypsy was sitting. She knelt next to the old woman and held out her hand. Philina took it in her own bony fingers. There was surprising strength in her hand. She traced the lines with a cracked fingernail, muttering to herself in a language Karyn did not recognize.

After a few minutes the gypsy released Karyn's hand and turned to Chris. "Now yours."

Chris came over and offered his palm. Philina scanned the lines briefly, then dropped his hand.

"I cannot help you," she said.

"What did you see?" Karyn asked.

Philina looked up. The shadows thrown by the dull red fire made her face skull-like. "Sometimes it is better not to know."

"For God's sake, let's hear it," Chris said. He took out his wallet and began thumbing through the bills. "I'll pay you. How much do you want?"

The old woman made a dry sound in her throat that might have been laughter. "Your money is of no use to me. If you insist on knowing, sit down and I will tell you what I saw in your hands. But do not blame me afterwards."

With a gesture of impatience Chris put away his wallet. He went back and sat on the broken chair. Karyn stayed where she was next to the old woman.

Philina paused, looking again into the fire before she spoke. "I need give only one reading for the two of you, for I see the same thing in the hands. I see pain. And blood. Much blood. And death."

"No!" The word was out before Karyn could think.

The old woman looked at her sharply. "What did you come looking for, some carnival trickster? Did you expect me to tell you of long, happy sea voyages and surprise gifts of money? Of romantic strangers entering your lives? Bah! You asked me what I saw in your hands. I have told you. Now go."

Chris stood up, but said nothing. He helped Karyn to her feet.

"Is there nothing we can do?" Karyn said.

"Arm yourselves as you did once before," the Gypsy answered. "Then you may have a chance."

"Is there no place we can be safe?"

The gypsy shook her head slowly. "There is no place. Your destiny is here, and you cannot run away from it. It is here that your story must end."

"End?" Chris said sharply. "What do you mean end? End how?"

The old woman returned to staring at the fire. She said nothing.

"Chris, what's the time?" Karyn said suddenly.

He glanced at his watch, then strode to the doorway and pulled aside the animal skin. The sun had moved markedly toward the horizon. The valley to the east of the gypsy's cabin was already in shadow.

"It's time to go," he said.

Karyn crossed the room and joined him at the doorway. Philina remained sitting on the pile of rags, not looking at them. Chris pulled two bills from his wallet wad held them out toward the old woman. She made no move to take the money. Chris laid the bills on the broken chair, and with Karyn beside him left the cabin.

The journey down the mountain trail was much swifter than coming up. The burros, knowing they were headed home, jogged along at a spine-jarring rate. Still, the sun seemed to plunge ahead of them. By the time they reached the shack of Guillermo the burro-keeper it was twilight. Behind them the mountain loomed black and forbidding.

Karyn was vastly relieved to see Luis waiting there for them in his battered taxi. She and Chris quickly dismounted and turned the burros over to Guillermo. They hurried to the car and got in, automatically locking the doors and rolling the windows up tight. Luis gunned the Plymouth down the dirt road toward the highway and the city.

"We did cut it a little close," Chris said.

Karyn turned to look out the rear window. "Yes, for a minute there I thought––"

She left the sentence unfinished, for from somewhere back there in the dark, tangled chaparral came the howling.

24

Roy Beatty crouched in the brush alongside the road and watched as his wife and his friend climbed into the battered taxi. They were not thirty yards away from him. How open they would be at this moment, how vulnerable to the attack of the wolf! Roy looked anxiously off to the west. The sun was almost down, but enough glowing red showed at the horizon to prevent him from changing. Enough to save the lives of these two people. This time.

The shadows of the twilight lengthened and joined and spread like ink spilled from a bottle until there was darkness. Roy tore the soft cotton shirt from his back. He pulled off the canvas shoes he wore over bare feet, and stepped out of his pants. He knelt naked in the fast-chilling night and willed his body to change.

His muscles bunched and released convulsively. His joints cracked audibly as the bones shifted in their sockets. He fell forward to his hands and knees. His neck arched. There was an instant of blinding pain as the change wracked his body. Then came the exultation. The wild joy of freedom as the great tan wolf took possession of the man.

The wolf moved silently out from behind the brush. The head turned and the yellow eyes looked off down the rutted dirt road that wound down toward the highway. Far below, the glowing red taillights of the taxi were still visible. The wolf raised his muzzle to the night sky and howled—a cry of hate and defiance.

In the enclosure behind the shack of Guillermo, the burros twitched their ears at the sound. They looked up from their grazing and stirred restlessly. In their soft, drowsy eyes was the shadow of fear.

The door of the cabin opened the width of a hand and Guillermo looked out. He saw nothing in the night, and quickly withdrew. There was the sound of heavy scraping from within as Guillermo moved things against the door to keep out the evil.

Deep in his throat the wolf growled softly. How futile would be the burro-keeper's attempt to bar the door if the wolf really wanted to get in. Against the werewolf the flimsy shack would offer no more protection than a house of paper. But Guillermo was safe this night. He was of no importance; he knew nothing. But there was another in these mountains who would not be so lucky. One who must learn the price of betrayal. The wolf turned and started up the mountain.

* * *

The fire burned low, and then it died to glowing coals in the cabin of Philina the gypsy. She sat still in the cross-legged position she had been in when the man and the woman were here. The money the man had left lay untouched and unseen on the broken chair. Although the night grew cold, the old woman made no move to rebuild the dying fire. She knew she would not need it.

She had lived many years, Philina. How many was it? Eighty? Ninety? She could not remember. She did remember that once in the long dead past she had been a young girl. A beautiful, laughing young girl. The bloodless lips of the old woman moved in a faint, bitter smile. How long had it been since anyone might have believed that once she was beautiful? Or young?

And yet it had been so. In a village near Torrelavega, where the Cantabrian Mountains came down to meet the Bay of Biscay, the young Philina had laughed and danced and sang and flirted with the boys like any Spanish gypsy girl. Then abruptly it had all ended. The gypsies discovered that she had The Gift.

The Gift! The old woman made a rattling sound in her throat. The *Curse* would be closer to the truth. The Curse of Prophecy. When it became known that she could read what was in the hands, girlhood was over for Philina. The people either clamored after her, begging for a reading, or they shunned her to avoid one. She no longer had friends. And the young men who courted her wanted only to use her terrible power.

In the end she had fled from all of them and crossed the ocean to live by herself. She chose the mountains above Mazatlán because it reminded her of her home in Spain, where she had known her only happiness, for such a short time.

But of course she could not forever conceal The Gift. There were gypsies here, too, and they knew at once. Philina never went into the city, and she discouraged all who would come to her cabin, but still they sought her out. There were not so many now as in the early years, but still some came, like the two young Americans today. They would be the last.

The Gift. In how many hands over the years had she read the future? Happiness, grief, riches, pain, births, illness, and death. She had seen it all. To Philina the gypsy, all hands were windows to the future. All hands, save her own. Some merciful power withheld from those cursed with The Gift that one ability that might drive them mad—the ability to read their own futures.

And yet now Philina knew what lay ahead for her. She knew how short was the time she had left. Minutes. She had read it in the hands of the two young strangers. They had brought her death. They had done so innocently, but they had brought death as surely as though they had plunged a knife into her heart.

The old woman sighed. She was ready. She had lived a long time, and there was nothing left undone.

She heard death coming outside. It moved softly through the grass of the clearing before her cabin. Over the years Philina's sight had dimmed, but her ears were as keen as ever. She heard the snuffling sound as death approached. It stopped just outside her doorway, and she could hear the air rush in and out of its powerful lungs. Still the gypsy made no move.

The hide that covered the doorway was torn away as the wolf burst through. It hesitated a moment, snarling, feet braced on the hard dirt floor. Then it sprang.

Philina made no attempt to protect herself from the murderous teeth. It would have been no use anyway. She had lived a long time, and she was ready.

25

By the following morning the news of the double murder had been widely reported, and the Palacio del Mar Hotel had become famous. Sightseers streamed in from Mazatlán, Culiacán, Durango, and even La Paz across the Gulf of California, for a look at the *'cabana de muerte,'* as the newspapers were calling Number 12. Taxis came and left in a steady procession and at least one tour bus had been rerouted to include the Palacio.

There were still police on the scene, and along with the reporters and curiosity seekers, they gave a sense of great excitement to the normally quiet hotel. Señor Davila, the manager, apologized profusely to the regular guests for the inconvenience, but he was enterprising enough to hire extra help for the bar and double the size of the souvenir stand in the lobby.

The dining room that morning was the only part of the hotel that was relatively uncrowded. It was there that Karyn and Chris sat at a small table, talking in low, tense voices.

Chris leaned forward, ignoring the muddy coffee cooling in a cup before him. "If anybody had told me three years ago that one day I would be making plans based on the ravings of a gypsy fortuneteller, I'd have laughed in his face."

"But it's different now," Karyn said.

"A lot of things are different now."

"So what's our next move?"

"The gypsy said we had a chance if we arm ourselves as we did before."

"How can we do that, Chris? You don't have a gun here, do you?"

"No. And for a foreigner, it's just about impossible to get one. Let alone silver bullets. But the only things we have to fight them with is fire and silver. We can't control fire, so it will have to be a silver weapon of some kind. A knife, maybe."

"Can you get a silver knife?"

"I've got to. There's not much time. Did you check the calendar?"

"Yes. Tonight is the full moon."

"If the gypsy woman was right, and we might as well assume she was, then tonight it all comes to an end."

"One way or another," Karyn said.

"Right. One way or another."

There was an awkward pause. Chris looked at his watch. "I'd better get into town and see about the knife. While I'm gone, it might be best if you stayed in your room."

"No," Karyn said.

Chris looked up sharply. "What?"

"I'm not going to lock myself in like some frightened child. Let me go with you."

Chris shook his head. "I can move faster alone."

"All right, but I have to do something besides sit here."

He saw the look in her eye and relented. "At least don't go off anywhere by yourself."

"Maybe I'll take the cruise in the glass-bottomed boat. How would that be?"

"I'd feel a lot easier if you stayed locked in your room."

"There's nothing to worry about. I'll be with twenty other people. The boat leaves before noon and doesn't stay out more than an hour or so. That will get me back well before dark."

"I hope I'm back well before dark too," Chris said. "I'll make it as fast as I can. We'll stay together tonight and hope that the gypsy was right—that this will be the end of it."

"What about Audrey?"

"I don't have time to worry about Audrey's hurt feelings anymore. She'll just have to do the best she can." He pushed away from the table and stood up. "I've got to get started. See you."

"See you, Chris. Take care of yourself."

"You too." He squeezed her shoulder and went out, quickly disappearing in the crowd of people in the lobby.

* * *

Audrey was still in bed when Chris returned to the cabana. She lay on her stomach with her head turned to one side. Her skin was pale, and there was a film of perspiration on her forehead. The flesh under her eyes was faintly purple.

"How do you feel?" Chris asked as he crossed to the closet.

"Like death. What the hell is that Mexican booze made out of, anyway?"

"Cactus."

"I believe it." Groaning, she sat up in bed and watched Chris pull on a jacket. "Where are you going?"

"Into town."

"What do we have to do in town?"

"Not 'we,' *me.*"

"You're going to leave me here alone again?"

"That's right."

Audrey threw back the sheet and got out of bed. She was still wearing the blue bikini panties she hadn't taken off the night before. She stood before Chris swaying slightly. The color surged back into her face.

"What the hell is going on, anyway?" she demanded. "You invite me to spend a couple of weeks in Mexico with you then you let me sit around this fucking room drinking this foul Mexican booze while you cozy it up with your old lady friend and go off on mysterious trips and—" Anger rose in her throat and choked off the words.

"Go back to bed," Chris said without looking at her. "The rest will do you good."

"Like hell it will. I'm not going to take this shit from you anymore."

Chris turned to face her squarely. "Audrey, you don't have to take anything. Our return tickets to Los Angeles are in the top of my suitcase. You can use yours any time you want to."

Audrey caught her breath. She moved in quickly and wrapped her arms around him.

"I'm sorry, Chris. I didn't mean all that. I'm just hung over. I miss you, that's all. I want to be with you."

He held her for a moment. "I'm sorry, too. I didn't intend it to be this way. Things have come up that I don't have any control over."

"Can't you tell me about it?"

"Not now." He pulled away from her gently. "I've got to go."

Audrey released him. He kissed her lightly and went out.

Chris walked along in front of the hotel, where the driveway was crowded with vehicles bringing sightseers from Mazatlán. Halfway down the line he spotted the battered Plymouth of Luis Zarate. He hurried over and leaned down at the open window on the driver's side.

"Luis, can you take me into town?"

The cab driver looked up, startled. "Oh, Señor, *buenas dias*. I was, ah, waiting for a passenger."

"I'm a passenger." Chris opened the back door and got in. "Let's go."

Luis sighed heavily and started the noisy engine. He turned the Plymouth around with some difficulty and headed back toward Mazatlán. Chris noted the stiff set of his shoulders.

"Is anything the matter, Luis?"

"Matter, Señor?"

"You seem, well, uncomfortable."

"I have my worries."

"Yes, well, I guess we all do."

"Where do you want to go, Señor?"

"I want someone who deals in silver?"

Luis swung around in the seat and looked at him. "Silver?"

"Yes. I think you know what I need it for."

"Mazatlán is not a good place for silver. Taxco is much better."

Chris began to lose patience. "Well, I'm not in Taxco, I'm in Mazatlán. I need a knife made of silver, and I need it now. So take me to a silversmith, or let me get out and I'll find somebody who will."

Luis turned back to the road. His heavy shoulders rose and fell with another sigh. "*Sí*, Señor."

They drove on into the city of Mazatlán and along Olas Altas Boulevard, where most of the big hotels and expensive restaurants were built. Luis pulled off on a side street, made another turn, and rolled slowly along a narrow avenue of crowded tourist shops and street vendors. There were art stores with bright bullfight paintings stacked out in front, guitar stores, shops stacked to the roof with wickerware, souvenir stands with red plaster bulls and painted *maracas*. Along the sidewalk, men and women displayed trays of turquoise jewelry and watches, stacks of sombreros and armloads of serapes.

Chris muttered to himself as he searched the storefronts for a likely looking sign.

"You see, Señor," said Luis, "In Mazatlán it is not easy to find somebody to make you something of silver."

"I can't believe that," Chris said. "Keep driving. In the next block he spotted a narrow shop with a neatly lettered sign in the window that read: JEWELRY MADE TO ORDER. "Stop here," he said.

Luis double-parked in front of the shop and Chris got out.

"Wait for me," he said.

On the sidewalk in front of the shop two little boys rushed up to Chris offering to sell him gum or plastic flowers. An old woman huddled under blankets shuffled along the pavement carrying a basket of withered fruit. She held out a blackened banana toward Chris. He brushed past the old woman and the boys and entered the jewelry store.

A salesman dressed in a neat dark suit hurried forward to greet him. "Good morning, sir. May I help you?"

"Possibly." Chris glanced down at the display case. It contained pieces of jewelry that looked to be of good quality. "Do you do work in silver?"

"Yes, sir. We have a fine craftsman here who will make up any piece to your order. Is it for a gentleman or a lady?"

"I'm not looking for jewelry," Chris said.

"Oh?"

"What I want is a knife. A knife with a blade of silver."

The man's eyes clouded. The smile gradually faded away. "A knife," he repeated flatly.

"That's right. I don't care what kind of a handle it has, but I want the blade to be silver, and I want it about six inches long."

"That is impossible."

"Why? If your man is as good as you say working with jewelry, surely he can make a knife blade and fit it to a handle."

"I am sorry, he does not do that kind of work."

"Can I talk to him myself?"

"He is not here. He is sick. He will not be in today. Probably not the rest of the week."

Chris looked into the eyes of the jewelry salesman. The man's gaze slid away and darted around the room.

"I'm sure you can buy a knife in any of the souvenir stores along this street."

"Not the kind I want," Chris said.

The salesman moved back behind the display case. "I'm sorry. There is nothing I can do for you."

Chris hesitated for a moment, then turned on his heel and strode out of the store. He marched across the sidewalk to Luis' taxi, and did not see how closely the old woman fruit-vendor watched him. He started to get into the car, but Luis reached out and placed a hand on his arm.

"I am sorry, Señor, I can no longer drive you."

"What do you mean?"

"I have other business."

Chris started to protest, but Luis started the engine, and the taxi began to edge away. The stocky driver looked back once with a strange sadness in his eyes. "I am sorry, Señor. *Adiós.*"

Luis stepped on the accelerator and the old Plymouth roared up the street. Puzzled, Chris stood looking after the car. Behind him the old lady in the blankets moved with surprising vigor as she entered the jewelry store.

Chris began to walk down the crowded street. He had a feeling that eyes were following him from all sides, but whenever he turned to look no one was watching him. The difference in Luis Zarate today troubled him. He also wondered about the strange actions of the jewelry salesman. A sense of growing urgency prickled the hair at the back of his neck.

He had walked not quite a block when a hand dropped on his shoulder from behind. He spun around and was surprised to see the salesman from the jewelry store. The man pushed a folded piece of paper into Chris's hand.

"Here you will find what you are looking for," he said. "I cannot say more." With a nervous glance at the people passing them on the sidewalk, the man turned and hurried back toward the store.

Chris unfolded the paper and read: *Tulio Santos, 48 Calle Verde.* The man from the store was out of sight when he looked up.

The thought came to him at once that it might be some kind of trap. People were acting much too strangely today. And yet, what else did he have? Time was passing, and tonight was the full moon.

He hailed a passing taxi, this one a red Ford, somewhat newer than Luis Zarate's Plymouth. He showed the handwritten note to the driver.

"Calle Verde? You sure you want to go there, man?"

"Why not?"

"It's a bad street for tourists. It's a bad street for anybody."

"I'll take my chances," Chris said, getting in, "Let's go."

26

The street called Calle Verde was still another side of Mazatlán. It bore no resemblance to the moneyed boulevard that curved along the shore, nor the gaudy tourist streets just inland. Calle Verde was a narrow, grubby passage, between rows of weather stained buildings which gave no evidence of life within. The few people visible on the street moved furtively, as though they expected to be stopped and searched at any moment. A quarter of a mile away was the blighted section called La Ratonera. Some of its human refuse spilled over into Calle Verde.

The cab driver pulled to a stop. "This is it, man, if you still want it."

"Where?" Chris said. "I don't see any numbers."

"There." The driver pointed to a scabrous wooden building with a blind doorway, where a hollow-cheeked little boy sat playing with a piece of string.

Chris got out of the cab and paid the driver. The child watched him, his young eyes already narrow with suspicion. Chris stepped past the silent boy and pushed through the door into a dark, musty room that looked like the overflow from a junkyard. There was a long workbench along one wall. Both the bench and the floor were littered with blackened pots and pans, dented kettles, tarnished, mismatched pieces of silverware, tools, nails, bits of wire, and odd chunks of metal.

"Anybody here?" Chris called.

After a minute a bald, monkey-faced man appeared from somewhere in the rear.

"Tulio Santos?"

"*Sí.*"

"*Habla usted inglès?*"

"No."

Chris switched to his laborious high-school Spanish. "*Quiero comprar un cuchillo. Un cuchillo de plata.*"

The bald-headed man came closer and peered into Chris's face. "A knife of silver," he repeated, speaking Spanish very slowly for the benefit of the gringo.

"Yes."

"For what?"

"That is of no matter. I will pay your price."

Santos pursed his lips, which made him look more than ever like a monkey. "Ah. Well. A knife of silver. A moment." He vanished again into the gloom at the back of the big room. In a little while he came back carrying a tiny, flat butter knife. He displayed it proudly for Chris. "Here. A knife of silver."

"No, no," Chris said impatiently. "A knife." He looked around for something to draw on. He found a crumpled sheet of brown wrapping paper and smoothed it out on the workbench. With his ballpoint pen he sketched the outline of a long, vicious knife with an upturned, Bowie-type blade. Then gripping the end of his pen like the hilt of a dagger, he made stabbing motions in the air. "A knife," he said again. "Like this. You understand?"

Santos watched him slice the air with his pen, then studied the drawing for a long minute. At last he looked up and shook his head. "I have nothing like this. Not of silver."

"Can you make one?"

Another long study of the drawing, with much frowning and many shakes of the bald head. "Perhaps. But it will be very dear."

"I will pay your price," Chris said. He opened his wallet to show the bills inside. "Make the knife."

Santos looked up from the wallet to Chris's face. He nodded slowly, then turned and walked to a pile of debris in one corner of the room. He began digging through the accumulated junk.

Chris watched the second hand sweep around the face of his watch, and willed the man to hurry. After five minutes Santos gave a cry of discovery. With his sleeve he rubbed the dirt off his find and held it up to show Chris. It was an ornate, badly tarnished silver tea tray.

"La plata," said Santos proudly.

"No, no," said Chris, thinking he still had not made himself understood. "I want a knife." Again he went through the stabbing pantomime. "A knife."

Santos bobbed his head up and down. "Yes, I comprehend. A knife." With a blackened forefinger he outlined on the tray the shape of the blade Chris had drawn."

"You will make a knife from the tray?"

"Yes, yes." Santos grinned happily for a moment, then his smile faded. "It will not be a good knife. The sliver is too soft for a blade. It will not cut."

"It is of no matter," said Chris. "Make the knife."

Santos cleared a space on the workbench and set the silver tray on it. He shuffled about the room, gathering up his tools. To Chris's eyes the man moved with agonizing slowness.

* * *

The soft knock on the door of Cabana Number 7 surprised Audrey. She had not expected Chris back until later in the afternoon. She had intended to be freshly bathed and perfumed and dressed in her most flattering clothes. She wanted him to be acutely aware of what a beautiful young woman he was treating so shabbily. But here she was still in her robe, and without her hair fully brushed out. Luckily, she had at least recovered from the hangover. Audrey belted the robe, smoothed it over her breasts and hips, and opened the door.

It was not Chris who stood outside. It was instead a tall, lithe woman with intense green eyes and shoulder-length black hair shot with a streak of silver.

"Hello, Audrey," said Marcia Lura.

Audrey stared. She felt held in place by the woman's gaze. "Do I know you?"

"No, but we have acquaintances in common."

"Who?"

"Chris Halloran, for one. For another, the woman now calling herself Karyn Richter."

Audrey curled her lip. "Oh, that one."

"I do not like her any more than you," Marcia said.

"Uh, come in," Audrey said uncertainly. "I was just about to get dressed."

Marcia stepped into the room and eased the door shut behind her. She glanced around without interest, then turned her luminescent green eyes on Audrey once more. "Would you like to have Karyn Richter out of your life for good? And out of Chris Halloran's life?"

"Well... sure, I guess so."

"I can help you."

"Why? Why would you help me?"

"It is for myself too. I have an old score to settle with that woman."

Audrey felt a strange weakness in her knees. Her mind was sluggish as the woman's smoky voice and unblinking eyes pushed away all outside thoughts.

"What do you want me to do?"

Marcia took the younger woman's hand and drew her down on the wicker settee. As she spoke, Marcia let her hand rest lightly on Audrey's thigh. Audrey was intensely aware of the heat of the hand through the thin material of her robe.

"I have learned that the woman Karyn is out now in the glass-bottomed boat," Marcia said. "When she returns you will give her a message."

"A message," Audrey repeated dully. The strange woman's touch was awakening new, wild sensations in her.

"You will tell her that Chris Halloran returned while she was out, and could not wait for her. You will say that Chris wants her to come at once to the cabin of the gypsy. He will be there waiting for her."

"The cabin of the gypsy? Where's that?"

"She will know," Marcia said. "Tell her it is of life-and-death importance that she go there at once to meet him."

"I don't understand," Audrey said.

Marcia's hand moved along her leg. "When this Karyn arrives at the cabin, there will be a surprise waiting for her. Someone from her past. Someone who will see to it that she breaks up no more happy couples."

The woman's words had little meaning for Audrey. The important thing was the delicious touch of her hand. When Audrey spoke, it was in a throaty whisper. "What if Chris comes back before I can give her the message?"

Marcia turned on the sofa to face her. As though by accident, her hand slipped under the edge of the robe. For a moment it rested there on the smooth, bare flesh of Audrey's inner thigh. Then the hand moved, now with more assurance, sliding up to the moist nest of hair between her legs. Audrey sucked in her breath.

"Chris won't come back early," Marcia said. "I have seen to it that he will be detained."

"All right," Audrey said. Her hips rolled, moving against the light pressure of the woman's hand.

"The boat will return in less than an hour," Marcia said. "You will give Karyn the message as soon as she steps off."

"Yes," Audrey whispered. Her mind swam. Her body was responding to this woman as though with a will of its own. Her own hand moved down and covered Marcia's. Together, their fingers slipped in past the moist vaginal lips.

Breathing rapidly, Audrey said, "Will she believe me?"

Marcia's slender, sensitive fingers found the secret place, and Audrey gasped.

"You can make her believe you." Marcia said. She probed deeply, gently, insistently. "Have you something that belongs to Chris Halloran? Something very private and personal? Something he might send to this Karyn to convince her his message is genuine?"

Audrey tried to think. It was difficult with the waves of sensation that pulsed through her from the other woman's caress. "I-I do have one thing. I can show it to you."

She moved to rise, but found she could not. She looked helplessly into the green eyes.

Marcia smiled at her. "It's all right, dear. We have enough time." Slowly she drew her hand from between Audrey's legs with a soft, sucking sound. With her green eyes never leaving Audrey's face, she raised her fingers to her lips and tasted them.

Feeling unsteady on her feet, Audrey walked carefully across the room to the bureau. She pulled out the top drawer and removed her jewel box. With numb fingers she fumbled through the rings and bracelets, and finally came up with what she wanted—the misshapen silver bullet that had fallen out of Chris's pocket the other day.

Marcia rose from the sofa and walked over to stand beside her. "Did you find it?"

"Yes. I don't know why, but this seemed to have a special meaning for him." Audrey held out the bullet in her open palm to the other woman.

Marcia recoiled as though it were a tarantula. Audrey looked at her in surprise, but she recovered quickly.

"That will serve very well," Marcia said. "Yes, that will be perfect."

She smiled a dark, secret smile that frightened Audrey for a moment, but then it was gone and Marcia was again looking at her in that knowing woman's way.

Audrey set the lump of silver down gently on the bureau and turned so she was facing Marcia. She could not speak, but her body cried out its need.

The tip of Marcia's tongue slipped out and ran around her pale lips. She reached out and undid the belt of Audrey's robe. The robe fell open, and Marcia's eyes moved over her body like a caress.

"Yes, dear Audrey." she said, "We have almost an hour to spend together." She slipped an arm around the girl's naked waist and led her to the bed.

27

On Calle Verde the minutes dragged slowly on into the afternoon. Nervous sweat soaked through Chris Halloran's shirt under both arms and between the shoulder blades. He paced constantly about the big musty room while Tulio Santos worked with saw, hammer, and file, to fashion a knife blade from the silver tea tray.

He came to a stop behind Santos and watched the man slowly, *slowly* shape the cutting edge of the blade. "Can't you speed it up?" he said, then groped for the Spanish words. *"Puede usted trabaja mas rápido?"*

Santos turned and looked at him with an injured expression. "Señor," he said formally, *"estoy un artesano, no mecánico."*

"All right, all right, I'm sorry," Chris said. "Just... continue."

Santos nodded gravely and went back to his work.

* * *

At the small dock below the Palacio del Mar Hotel the glass-bottomed boat eased into its mooring. It stopped with a soft bump as the wooden dock nudged the old automobile tires lashed to the side of the boat. Karyn stood up on the deck and searched the faces of the people waiting on shore, looking for Chris Halloran. He was not there. Karyn was surprised, however, to see Audrey Vance. The girl was standing apart from the people waiting to take the next cruise. She looked directly at Karyn.

The gangplank was lowered and Karyn crossed to the dock. Audrey came toward her at once. There was an odd brightness in the girl's eyes, but Audrey did not seem to have been drinking.

"Hi," Audrey said. She smiled tentatively.

Karyn did not return the smile. She nodded in greeting and waited for the girl to say whatever was on her mind.

"Karyn, I don't blame you for thinking I'm a bitch," Audrey said. "God knows I've acted like one. It was plain, childish jealousy. I'm ashamed of myself, really I am. I didn't understand the way it was between you and Chris."

"Don't worry about it," Karyn said.

"I'm awfully glad you feel that way. I wish you and I could have got off to a better start. I think we might have been friends. I was just telling Chris that."

"Chris is here?"

"No. He came back from town while you were out on the boat, but he had to leave again right away. He asked me to give you a message."

"What message?"

"He said he wants you to come and meet him at the cabin of the gypsy. I don't know what he meant, but he said you would understand."

Karyn stared at the younger woman. Why would Chris trust her with an important message like this? Maybe there was no one else.

"Chris said it was urgent," Audrey went on. "As a matter of fact, he said life and death. He wouldn't tell me any more, but I know he was deadly serious."

"You say he wants me to go to the gypsy's cabin?" Karyn repeated. "Right away?"

"That's what he said. Repeated it several times to make sure I had it right."

Karyn calculated rapidly. It was now early afternoon. If she started immediately she could reach the cabin before dark, but she could never complete the return trip. Chris must have an awfully good reason for subjecting both of them to the danger of night in the mountains.

"He didn't say anything else?" she asked. "Give you a reason?"

Audrey shook her head. "Oh, I almost forgot." She dug into a pocket of her snug white jeans. "Chris said I should give you this. That you would know what it meant."

Karyn took the lump of silver metal from the girl's hand. A bullet. Scarred and misshapen, but unmistakably one of the silver bullets Chris had made to fight the wolves of Drago. What did it mean? That he was successful in getting a new weapon? But what had that to do with the gypsy's cabin? Whatever the meaning, the silver bullet convinced Karyn that the message came from Chris.

"What's it all about, Karyn?" Audrey asked, her eyes wide.

"I'm not sure myself." Karyn said distractedly. She started for the hotel, then turned back. "Thank you, Audrey. Thanks for the message."

"Heck, that's all right. Listen, is there anything I can do to help?"

"No. No, there's nothing. Excuse me now, I have to get going."

Karyn hurried up the slope toward the hotel. She did not see Audrey's small, cold smile as the girl watched her go.

There were no other messages for her at the desk. She went to her room and hurriedly changed to outdoor clothes. She prayed that there would be good news when she met Chris at the cabin. That the long nightmare would be over.

Back out in front of the hotel she looked for the taxi of Luis Zarate, but the old Plymouth was not there. She would like to have had Luis, but there was no time to try to find him. Another cab drove up. A middle-aged couple got out, wearing straw sombreros with MAZATLÁN lettered across the brims. Karyn hurried up to the driver.

"Do you know a man called Guillermo, the one who keeps the burros for riding in the mountains?"

"I know him."

"Will you take me there?"

"The road to Guillermo's place is very bad. I will have to charge extra."

"I don't care. Just take me there."

Karyn did not wait for the driver to open the door for her. She got in and slammed it firmly behind her. The man backed the taxi around and started off toward the highway.

* * *

At last the knife was finished. Chris had been eager to take the weapon the moment Santos finished shaping the cutting edge of the blade. It was seven inches of businesslike metal with a thin, bare, four-inch shank for the handle. However, Santos had heatedly refused to turn it over without a proper handle. Angry at first, Chris had cooled down when he saw the practicality of this. For the purpose he intended the knife, a solid grip would be essential.

So he had sweated out another half-hour while Santos dug up a rusted hunting knife from somewhere among the refuse. The craftsman dismantled the old knife, took the carved wooden handle with finger grips and affixed it solidly to the silver blade.

Santos was still not satisfied with the balance of the weapon, but Chris took it away from him and peeled off several bills in payment. Santos gave him the leather sheath with belt loop that had gone with the hunting knife. Chris slipped the silver blade into the sheath, fastened it in, and hurried out into the street.

He had expected to hail a taxi immediately to take him back to the hotel, but the street was deserted. Not only was there no taxi in sight, there were no moving vehicles of any kind. Chris wheeled and ran back into the shop of Tub Santos.

"Necesitamo un taxi!"

Santos shook his head and smiled sadly. *"No taxi aqui. Nunca taxi en Calle Verde."*

Chris swore under his breath. *"Hay teléfono?"*

Again Santos shook his head.

"Damn," Chris muttered. He went back out to the street. The building fronts were blank, the doors closed, the windows shuttered and forbidding. Shadows were growing longer as night moved in on the city.

Chris slammed a fist into his open palm. By this time Karyn would be wondering what was keeping him. One thing was certain—standing here on this empty, darkening street would gain him nothing.

He started to run. He headed west, because that's where the city was. There were bound to be taxis, policemen, something. The silver knife in its sheath bounced against his hip. As he ran he made sure he did not lose the weapon. He knew that somewhere tonight he was going to have to use it.

28

The taxi carrying Karyn Richter jolted up the rutted road that led into the hills. The driver complained steadily of the damage the trip was inflicting on his automobile. After a drive that seemed like hours to Karyn, they pulled up at the dry arroyo where the road ended and Guillermo had his shack.

"This is where you wanted to go, lady," said the driver.

"Yes, thank you." Karyn started to get out of the car.

"That's ten dollars."

Karyn gave him a look, but there was no time to argue about the fare. She dug a bill out of her pocket and handed it to the man. She left the car and hurried across the expanse of gravel and bare dirt to the door of the shack. She rapped loudly on the patchwork-lumber door, but heard no response from inside.

"Hello!" she called. "Guillermo! Anybody here?"

Still no sounds from inside the shack. Karyn pushed on the door, but it would not budge. She walked around to the back. Half a dozen burros stood placidly in a rude pen. They looked at her without curiosity. Guillermo was nowhere in sight.

From out in front of the shack came the sudden sound of an engine revving up, followed by the spinning of tires in loose gravel. Karyn ran back around the corner of the building in time to see her taxi bouncing away down the road toward the city.

"Thanks a lot," she muttered after the disappearing cab.

She drew a deep breath and told herself to be calm and consider her circumstances. A ride back to the city was now out of the question. In the late afternoon, it was doubtful whether she could make it back to the highway and civilization before nightfall. When night came she did not want to be alone.

Riding a burro, she could reach the gypsy's cabin before dark, barring mishap. Chris would be at the cabin, according to his message, so that seemed the safest way to go.

She walked back around to the rear of the shack where the burros were kept. She found a pile of old blankets, folded one, and placed it over the back of a burro. She opened the gate to the pen, led the animal out, and closed the gate behind her. She climbed on the burro, urged it forward, and with some reluctance the animal started up the trail.

As she rode, the shadow that preceded her up the mountain grew ever longer. It was a constant reminder of the coming night, and of all the horrors that the night could bring.

Karyn pulled her mind away from those thoughts. She thought instead about Chris and herself and what their futures would be. It would not be a future together—they had tried that once and it had been disastrous. Besides, she had a husband and a little boy to go back to when this business was finished. And what about Chris? Would he go back to Audrey? Or a series of Audreys? Somehow Karyn did not think so. She had seen, these past few days, a maturity in Chris which had been lacking in him before. She hoped with all her heart that he would find happiness.

With agonizing slowness the little burro plodded up the trail. They passed the spring where she and Chris had stopped to rest the last time. No time for resting now. She clucked in the burro's ear and urged it onward.

The shadows closed in fast, and the sun was red and angry on the western horizon when they finally reached the crest where the gypsy Philina had her cabin. The crude log building looked like blessed sanctuary to Karyn. There was no sign of life, but as before, smoke trailed out of the hole in the roof.

Why, she wondered, was Chris not outside to greet her? Maybe he was inside talking to Philina and hadn't heard the burro come up.

Karyn dismounted and walked toward the door of the cabin. Her steps slowed as she sensed something different here. The doorway was uncovered, that was it. The animal hide that had hung there before was gone. Cautiously, she approached and peered into the cabin. A flickering red-orange light from the fire-pit danced over the interior walls. She stopped just outside the doorway.

"Chris? Is anybody there?"

All at once she knew it was wrong. It was all wrong. The cabin did not look right. The burro-keeper should have been down below; the message from Chris rang false. Everything was wrong, and she'd realized it too late. She started to back away. One step. Then another.

Before Karyn could take a third step, a slim, strong arm encircled her throat, clamping her windpipe in the crook of the elbow. She fought to scream, but no sound could escape. She clawed at the arm that was cutting off her breath, but she could not move it.

The world began to go dark. Karyn felt the strength ebbing from her like blood from a severed vein. Red flashes of fireworks burst somewhere behind her eyes. A roaring like the wind filled her ears.

Then blackness.

29

For Chris Halloran, the run through the dreary back streets of Mazatlán began to take on the quality of a nightmare. It was as though all other living things had been snatched from the face of the earth. The only sound was the thud and scuff of his feet on the pavement.

After many blocks he spotted a taxi parked at the curb. The cab was empty, but from a nearby doorway came the sound of recorded music. Chris pushed aside a curtain hanging over the doorway and walked in.

It was a dim, musty *cantina*, stale with cigarette smoke and old chilies. A thirty-year-old jukebox played a tragic Mexican ballad. Along the bar sat several men in faded, mismatched clothing. Their eyes slid over Chris without expression. At a table in the rear, two women, heavily made up for the approaching evening, sat nursing glasses of tequila. They turned their professional smiles on him, but their eyes were empty of hope.

Chris paid no attention to the customers. He leaned on the unvarnished bar and spoke to the man in shirtsleeves who stood behind it.

"Hay cochero aquí?"

The proprietor did not speak, but looked down the bar. One of the customers, a thin man with moles on his cheek, spoke up. "I am the owner of the taxi."

"Will you take me to the Palacio del Mar?"

The man turned lazily back to the bar. "Sure. When I finish my drink."

Chris took a step toward him. His eyes glittered dangerously. "Take me now."

The unmistakable menace in Chris's voice got through. *"Sí,* Señor." the driver said automatically. In a gulp he downed what was left in his glass and walked quickly with Chris out to the cab. He drove well and swiftly, and they pulled up in front of the hotel fifteen minutes later.

The crowd at the Palacio del Mar had increased since that morning. Sightseers wandered about snapping pictures and talking in excited voices about *"la cabaña de la muerte."*

Chris paid off the driver and hurried up the steps, across the veranda, and into the lobby. Señor Davila, the manager, was at his post behind the desk. He was relating, with dramatic emphasis, the events of the bloody night to a small, attentive group of tourists.

Chris pushed to the front of the group and got Davila's attention. "Ring Mrs. Richter's room," he said.

Reluctantly the manager turned away from his audience long enough to operate the key that would ring the telephone in Karyn's room. He rang several times, then turned to Chris with an apologetic shrug.

"Señora Richter does not answer."

"She must be there," Chris insisted. "What time did the cruise boat get back?"

"About noon."

"Have you seen Mrs. Richter since then?"

"I-I don't remember."

"Well, *think* about it." Chris leaned on the desk and glared at Davila.

The manager chewed his lip nervously. "Ah, yes, I recall now. She did stop by the desk to ask if there were any messages. I told her there were none, and she went up to her room."

"Did she go out again after that?"

"I could not say. Please understand, Señor. This has been a very busy day. I could not see everyone that comes and goes."

"Yeah, sure," said Chris. He spun away from the desk and stalked back through the lobby.

Where the devil could she be, he wondered. He walked quickly through the busy bar and the dining room, scanning the faces. Karyn was in neither place.

It did not seem likely she would be on the beach. It was too late in the afternoon for sunbathing. Still, it was a possibility. Chris ran out of the building and down across the crescent of sand to the water's edge. He jogged along the tideline, checking the few people who were in the water and on the beach. No Karyn.

Chris did not like it. Karyn knew he would come looking for her. If she was not going to be easy to find, she would have left a message for him at the desk. Something was definitely wrong.

He stood at the edge of the beach and tried to think of possibilities. Maybe Audrey knew something. Chris loped back across the beach to his cabana. The blinds were down; the door was locked. Chris banged his fist against the panel until Audrey opened up. Her eyes were not quite in focus, and she swayed slightly as she opened the door. Chris could smell liquor on her breath.

"Nice of you to drop by," she said with heavy sarcasm.

Chris pushed past her into the room. The air was stale in the gloom. He walked to the window and snapped up the blind, letting in the afternoon sun.

"Have you seen Karyn?" he said.

"Your lady love? Fuck, no. Why would I see her?"

"I don't have time for bullshit, Audrey. Just give me straight answers."

"You don't have time for much of anything these days, do you, lover boy?"

Audrey knew something. Chris could see it in her eyes. "I'm asking you again, have you seen Karyn? Do you know where she is?"

"Find her yourself, lover boy. A bitch in heat like that one, it shouldn't be hard for you to—"

Chris hit her. A hard, open-handed blow across the side of the face. Audrey staggered backward several steps. She put a hand to her reddening cheek. Tears squeezed out of her eyes.

"Now let's talk." Chris said.

Audrey hiccupped and shook her head. Chris moved toward her, and she began to talk.

"I saw her. She… she's gone."

"Gone? Gone where?"

"I don't know. I just gave her a message, then she went out."

"What message?" Chris said. It was an effort to keep from screaming at her.

"There was a woman here. She said to tell Karyn you wanted her to come and meet you. That's all."

"Who was the woman?"

Audrey's eyes fell away from his, and her voice softened. "I don't know her name. Very pretty. Tall, green eyes, black hair with a streak of white."

Chris ground his teeth. With unerring instinct, Marcia Lura had found the weak point in their defenses. Audrey. Speaking very softly, he said, "Where was Karyn supposed to meet me?"

"I don't remember."

"Audrey, you'll remember or I'll kick the shit out of you."

"It was something about a gypsy. The gypsy's cabin."

Chris swore under his breath. If Karyn had been lured up into those mountains, there was no way she could get back before dark. She would be easy prey for the werewolves, and out of reach of help.

"Didn't she question you when you told her that?" he demanded.

"I-I gave her something of yours so she'd believe the message came from you."

"What did you give her?"

"That little lump of silver you always carried around. The one that looked like a bullet."

Chris's hand went to his pocket. Things had happened so fast the last few days, he hadn't even noticed the bullet was missing. He whirled and started toward the door. He yanked it open, then turned back.

"I'm going out now, Audrey. I don't know how long I'll be gone, but when I come back I don't want to see you here." He went out and slammed the door without waiting for a reply.

The taxi he had come in was gone, but there was another just turning around in front of the hotel and heading back toward Mazatlán. Chris ran toward the car.

"Taxi! Hey, taxi!"

The driver, with a full load of passengers, ignored him. Chris stood in the roadway cursing after the departing cab.

"Señor?"

The voice close behind him made Chris stare. He turned to see Luis Zarate nervously fingering the zipper of his jacket.

"Luis!"

"I came looking for you, Señor. I should not have left you today in the city. I am very ashamed."

"Never mind that," Chris said, "I need you now. They've tricked Karyn into going to the gypsy's cabin. I've got to go after her."

A stricken look came over Luis.

"What's the matter?"

"The gypsy, Señor. Philina. *Ella está muerte.*"

"She's dead?"

"*Sí,* Señor." With a shake of his head, Luis returned to English. "The word was spread today among the gypsies and the people of the streets. Philina is dead, and anyone who helps the gringos will follow her. They will know the vengeance of lobombre."

"That's why the salesman in the jewelry store acted so funny this morning."

Luis nodded.

"And that's why you left me there on the street."

"Yes, but now I am ashamed. My poor taxi is at your service."

"Then let's go. Take me to your cousin's place, the one with the burros."

"Mucho gusto, Señor, mucho gusto!"

They roared out of the hotel compound in the old Plymouth and up the highway toward Mazatlán. Luis swerved expertly onto the narrow rutted road leading into the foothills. The car bounced and rattled and seemed at times about to fly to pieces, but Luis never let up on the accelerator. When they reached the shack of Guillermo the burro keeper Chris jumped out and hit the ground running. Luis followed close behind him.

Chris hammered on the door, but received no response from within.

"Where could he be?" Chris demanded.

Luis stepped forward. "Permit me, Señor." He put his mouth close to the door, and in a voice of thunder shouted, *"Guillermo! Nombre de Dios, abre la porta."*

After a moment there was the sound of something heavy scraping across the floor inside. The door opened a crack, and Guillermo's one good eye peered out.

"What do you want?"

"Has the woman been here?" Chris said. "The woman who came with me last time?"

"She was here."

"When?" Chris's question snapped like a whip.

"Two, three hours ago."

"What did she say to you?"

"She said nothing. I did not open the door."

"Why, for God's sake? What's the matter with you?"

The eye squinted out at Chris from the crack in the door. "There is evil and death in the mountains. It is a time for a poor man like me to stay behind doors."

"Well, where did she go?"

"She took one of my burros and started up the trail."

"Give me a burro," Chris said. "Quickly. I have to go after her."

"I do not think you can help her now."

"I don't give a damn what you think. What about that burro?"

"Go to the back and take one yourself, Señor. It will be ten dollars for yours and the lady's."

Chris started to say something, changed his mind. He pulled a bill from his wallet, tossed it at the crack in the door, and started around the shack.

In the pen he found a sturdy-looking burro and led him around to the front. Luis Zarate was standing there by the Plymouth.

"I would go with you, Señor," said Luis. "But I have both a wife and a mother who depend on me. And the truth is that I am not a very brave man."

"That's all right, Luis. From here on it's my fight. What do I owe you for the ride?"

"No charge. Señor."

"Thanks." Chris climbed on the burros back and urged the animal up the trail.

"Buena suerte, Señor," Luis called after him. *"Vaya con Dios."*

He would need more than luck this time, Chris thought as the burro jogged toward the mountains. Maybe even the company of God would not be enough. He rode upward into the gathering darkness.

30

The pain came back first. Pain in her throat. In the instant before she regained consciousness, Karyn was a little girl again. She was lying on a high, white bed in the hospital, and the doctor had just taken her tonsils out. In a moment she would open her eyes and her mother would be there. And Daddy. And they would let her eat all the ice cream she wanted, and before long the pain would go away.

Karyn tried to reach up with a hand and touch her throat where it hurt. But the hand would not move. Her lungs heaved, pulling in air, but it did not have the sharp, clean smell of the hospital. The roughness against her back was no bed.

She forced her eyes open. No loving faces looked down on her. It took only a moment for her to realize where she was. In the gypsy's cabin. The light from the fire pit cast grotesque shadows throughout the room. Karyn was sitting in the chair with no back. Her ankles were tied to the legs of the chair, her wrists tightly bound behind her. The roughness against her back was the log wall of the cabin.

She turned her head. It hurt her throat when she moved. Beside her was the pile of old rags where Philina the gypsy had sat talking to her and Chris such a little while ago. Beyond the rags she could see another torn bundle. Only the clawed hand, lying limp and palm up, told her that it had once been human.

Karyn looked away quickly. Through the open doorway the world outside was in deepening twilight. Someone stepped between her and the doorway. A tall, slim silhouette with flowing black hair that was shot through with silver.

"Marcia!" Karyn's voice was a rasping whisper.

"I see you remember me. I'm glad. You will have much time for remembering in the hours before dawn."

"What do you mean?"

"I'm going to hurt you, Karyn. I'm going to hurt you very badly."

Karyn squinted in the darkness, trying to get a better look at the woman. "Why? Why are you doing this? Why are you persecuting me? You took my husband from me back in Drago. What more do you want?" She broke off as the effort of talking hurt her throat too much.

Marcia took a step toward her. The fire pit lay between them. The tall woman knelt so the light of the fire shone full on her face, "You want to know why, do you? Then look!"

She raised a hand to her forehead and ran long fingers through the white streak in her midnight hair. "This is why. I have this mark to remind me of the night you put the gun inches from my head and fired. I will never forget the agony of that moment and the long months that followed. In those months, Karyn, I thought of you above all else. I have lived for just one thing—to give you some measure of the pain I felt. And finally to see you die."

"I had to shoot that night," Karyn whispered. "I saw only a wolf. I couldn't know it was you."

"You lie!" the other woman spat. "Just before you pulled the trigger I heard you speak my name. Oh, yes, you knew."

It was true, Karyn realized. In that long-ago night when she fired the silver bullet into the head of the sleek black wolf, she had known full well it was the woman Marcia Lura. What a tragic shame that the creature had not died.

"I have had much time to think," Marcia went on. "In that time I have imagined many ways for you to die. In all of them you suffered greatly. And now things have worked out even better than I could imagine. Now I can kill you in a most appropriate way."

Marcia reached down to the edge of the fire pit. There the taped ends of a long-handled pair of pliers protruded from the fire. The other end, with the pincer jaws, was buried deep in the glowing coals.

"In the Middle Ages," Marcia said, "there were many interesting ways of dealing with people suspected of being witches. Or werewolves." She lightly caressed the taped handles of the pliers as she spoke. "One of the ways was to use a red-hot pair of tongs to pull the flesh from the body of the victim. A pinch at a time. It takes a very long time for someone to die that way. Very long, and very painful." She looked up and the fire struck glowing red sparks in the deep green eyes. "That, Karyn, is the way you are going to die tonight."

Karyn pulled her eyes away from the woman, and from the vicious tool jammed deep into the coals. She looked toward the open doorway. Outside the twilight had deepened to the charcoal gray of approaching night.

Marcia saw the direction of her glance. "If you're expecting help from your friend Chris or anyone else tonight, you're going to be disappointed. Even if he does learn where you are and foolishly comes after you, he will never reach us. There is only one trail to this cabin, and someone is waiting for your friend on that trail. Someone you and I both know very well."

"Roy!" The name tore at Karyn's throat as she spoke it.

The other woman smiled. A slow smile of triumph. "Yes, Roy. Your husband once, but not any more. Now he is mine. He belongs to me more completely than ever he did to you. He will be there to meet anyone who comes up the trail, and he will see that you and I are left alone."

Karyn stared at the dark woman. Fear rose like bile in her aching throat. Slowly, slowly Marcia drew the long pliers from the fire. The cruel pinchers glowed a bright red-orange.

Without warning, one side of Marcia's face jerked for an instant in a tic brought on by violent emotion. She threw one quick look over her shoulder, then came around the fire pit toward Karyn. She gripped the handles of the pliers and thrust the glowing-hot jaws before her.

31

The last red slice of the sun slipped below the horizon, and night came all at once on the trail leading up the mountain. Chris swore at his failure to bring a flashlight. He could still make out the trail itself, but the deep shadows at either side could have concealed anything. To the little burro, day or night made no difference. He plodded patiently upward, breaking into a jog occasionally as Chris dug in his heels.

He tried not to think about what he might find when he reached the gypsy's cabin. The old woman was dead, that much Luis had told him. He did not say the werewolves had killed her, but the implication was clear. What would Karyn have found at the cabin? Would she panic? He could only hope that Karyn had locked herself inside when darkness came, and would stay there until he arrived.

With no details visible in the darkness, it was difficult for Chris to calculate how far he had come. Since the afternoon, he had paid no attention to time and distance, except for the position of the sun. He had been on the trail almost two hours before darkness fell. By now, he reckoned, he should be nearing the crest where the cabin was. He prayed he would find Karyn there alive and unhurt. Together they had a chance to survive this night. Separately—

The thought died in Chris's mind. Subtly, a change came over the mountain trail and the brush alongside. Details became visible as the blackness gave way gradually to a cool, pale light. He looked up through a gap in the trees and saw the round, bland face of the moon edging into view above the ridge of mountains.

With more light, the climb became easier, but the coming of the moon reminded Chris of the horror he must yet face this night.

The burro stopped as though someone had jerked him back on a rope. His ears swiveled to catch a sound, his nostrils widened, testing the air. Chris urged him on, but with a frightened bray the burro moved stiffly backward.

"Up, burro, come on," Chris coaxed. "Don't go spooky on me now."

The burro refused to move forward even when Chris slapped his rump. The animal shivered and showed the whites of its eyes.

"What's the matter, burro? What is it?"

Something moved on the trail up ahead. A shadow eased toward them into the moonlight that now illuminated the trail. The shadow stopped and waited. A huge tan wolf.

The burro bucked and shied away. Its hoofs slipped on lose dirt and the animal fell heavily to the ground. Chris pushed himself away in time to avoid falling under the burro. He heard it scramble upright and go thudding back down the mountain. He was alone on the trail with the wolf.

For a long moment the man and the animal looked at each other. As the wolf moved, the muscles rippled under its shaggy tan pelt. It growled softly, and the teeth gleamed in the moonlight.

Chris reached for the knife, but he was too slow. Before his hand closed over the hilt, the wolf crouched and sprang. Shocked by the suddenness of the attack, Chris dived forward and skidded in the dirt on his chest. He felt the night air stir as the long, powerful body of the wolf passed over him. He scrambled into a crouch as the wolf hit the ground and whirled to come at him again.

Chris slipped the knife out of the leather sheath. He held it out between them so the silver blade glinted under the moon. The pale eyes of the wolf followed the arc of the knife as Chris swung it slowly from side to side. The wolf growled again, deeply and menacingly.

"You know what this is, don't you?" Chris said. "You know what it can do. Now, come and get me if you can."

The wolf lunged forward, Chris thrust at the animal with the knife. The wolf stopped inches away from the blade. Chris slashed out, and the wolf backed off just out of reach.

Again the wolf sprang at him without warning. Chris fell to his right just in time to avoid the slashing teeth, but he was unable to bring the knife around. The wolf landed, spun, and leapt at him again without pausing.

As Chris dived frantically out of the path of the hurtling body something tore away the sleeve of his jacket. In a moment of panic Chris felt his shoulder. There was no blood. He knew too well what the bite of a werewolf could do.

Once more the wolf hesitated, watching, waiting for an opening. He circled Chris in stiff, sideways steps, eyes never leaving the silver blade. Chris turned slowly, keeping the knife always between them, the blade pointed at the throat of the wolf.

For timeless minutes the battle continued, with first man, then beast, feinting, lunging, striking. The wolf was wary of a straight-on attack, and time after time Chris slipped away by inches from the murderous teeth. However, he could not get into position to strike a telling blow with the knife.

As the fight wore on, the superior strength and stamina of the wolf began to tell. Chris's breath came in ragged gasps. His body was bruised from hitting the stones on the trail. Every time the wolf attacked he came a fraction closer. Chris could feel the heat of its breath as the teeth slashed at his face.

He would have to finish it soon, Chris knew, while he still had strength to drive the knife home. He could no longer afford to let the wolf set the pace of the battle.

As he and the wolf faced each other, motionless for the moment, he decided upon a plan. He would feint to one side to draw a reaction from the wolf, then leap on the animal's back and pray he could sink the knife into a vital spot. If he failed––well, one way or another, it would all be over in seconds.

Chris began his sideways feint, but that was as far as he got with his plan. His foot came down on a loose rock the size of a tennis ball, and the ankle bent sharply outward. A dull pain gripped the lower part of his leg. He fought for his balance, lost it, and crashed to the ground. His right hand was flung out to the side, and the back of it struck a sharp-edged rock. The fingers loosened their grip for a moment, and the precious knife fell away.

Before Chris could move to retrieve the weapon, the wolf was upon him. The heavy forepaws pinned his shoulders to the ground. The bristling tan muzzle and killer teeth were just above his face. In the eyes of the wolf there was a gleam of triumph, and something else.

Unable to move, Chris waited for the last searing pain and stared up into the eyes of the beast. Deep in the yellow irises was the shadow of some emotion that did not belong. Sadness?

Unaccountably, the wolf hesitated. Instead of tearing out the man's unprotected throat, it stayed poised over him. Then, ever so gradually, Chris felt the weight on his shoulders ease. He was able to move his right hand. His fingers searched around in the dirt. They closed over the carved handle of the knife.

The pressure returned as the wolf brought its weight down once more on the man's shoulders. The jaws gaped, the teeth moved for the man's throat.

Willing every remaining ounce of strength into the muscles of his right arm and shoulder, Chris drove the knife upward. The silver blade buried itself in the broad chest above him. The wolf's great head jerked back, and from the throat came a howl of dreadful pain that was neither animal nor human. The hot blood of the wolf spilled down over Chris's hand and wrist, and splashed his jacket. Chris pulled the knife free, but there was no need to strike again. The animal lurched sideways for several steps, then fell.

With an effort Chris pulled himself into a sitting position. The stricken wolf raised its head and looked at him. Then, inch by agonizing inch, the animal dragged itself toward him. Chris gripped the bloody knife, but then, he saw there was no more fight in the eyes of the wolf, and he relaxed.

Leaving a smeared trail of blood, the wolf pulled its dying body to the side of the man. The big head rose, and their eyes met. Then the light faded from the yellow eyes, the wolf's head sank down on Chris's knee, and it was over.

Chris laid a hand on the short, thick fur that covered the broad head of the wolf. "Goodbye, old friend," he said softly. "You could have won." There was only the night wind to hear his words.

Painfully Chris rose and tested the ankle. It hurt, but he could walk. He pulled off the blood-spattered jacket and wiped the blade of the knife on the remaining sleeve. Then he spread the jacket over the body of the wolf and limped on toward the gypsy's cabin.

32

The glowing jaws of the pliers reached out for Karyn like the pincers of some hellish insect. Marcia advanced slowly, her eyes on Karyn's face. Behind her the black rectangle of the doorway lightened gradually. Marcia's step faltered. She turned and looked back. The pale edge of the full moon inched out from behind the ridge of mountains. When Marcia turned back, there was terror mixed with the hatred in her face.

With the heat of the glowing metal on her cheek, Karyn pulled her head away as far as she could. Her body tensed, waiting for the searing pain, but it did not come. Instead, it was Marcia who cried out. Karyn looked at the other woman in surprise, and saw her body jerk and twist, as though it were controlled by unseen wires. The pliers flew from Marcia's hand, and she doubled over in agony.

As Karyn watched in horrified fascination, Marcia stumbled and fell to the floor of the cabin. She rolled about in the dirt, tearing at her clothes. The garments ripped away under her slashing flingers, and for a moment the lithe, white body was exposed in the moonlight that now flooded through the doorway. Then she began to change. The white skin twitched and crawled and grew coarse black hair in uneven patches. Her limbs writhed into misshapen things that belonged on neither animal nor human. She continued to roll helplessly on the ground. From the tortured throat came a high-pitched whine.

In the light of the fire Karyn saw the face. There was little left of what had been the beautiful Marcia Lura. The nose had shriveled to a blackened shapeless thing with fat, leaking nostrils. The long black hair, still with the deadly streak of silver, was now a scrubby growth on most of the face. The mouth became a crooked slash, half of it the lipless maw of a wolf, the other half grotesquely human. Only the eyes, the eyes of deep green fire, were unaltered.

The smell of smoke pulled Karyn's attention away from the creature writhing on the floor. Beside her, where the red-hot pliers had fallen, the pile of rags smoldered and caught fire. Flames licked up over the pile hungrily, fed by old oils soaked into the rags, and began to race up the dry log walls.

Karyn made a lunge toward the doorway, but only fell heavily to the dirt floor, still bound to the broken chair. Only a few feet away the thing that had been Marcia jerked and screamed on the ground, driven frantic by the flames.

Karyn strained every muscle, but could make no headway toward the door and safety. With the fire quickly eating away at the cabin, she made a decision, then shut off her mind to the pain that would come. She stretched out her bound wrists behind her as far as she could toward the burning pile of rags. Twisting her head around to look, she saw the skin of her arms redden and blister from the heat. With her teeth biting hard against each other, she forced her hands closer to the flames. A spark danced on the threads of the hemp rope, then another. A puff of flame. Karyn strained, forcing her wrists apart, and with a pop the rope burned through.

Karyn snatched her hands away from the flames and worked with singed fingers at the knots that held her ankles. The fire crackled up three of the four walls now, and fiery streamers raced across the ceiling. The thick, acrid smoke tore at her throat.

At last she solved the knots and was free. Unable to see in the smoke, she stumbled in the direction of the doorway and fell through it to the grass outside with a grateful sob.

Drinking in the clean night air, Karyn dragged herself away from the cabin, now blazing like a torch. From inside the awful screaming sounds rose to a crescendo, then stopped as one of the walls fell in with an explosion of sparks.

From somewhere not far down the mountain came a terrible howl of pain, as though in answer to the death cry of Marcia Lura. Then, except for the crackling flames that consumed the cabin, there was silence.

Someone called Karyn's name.

In sudden fear she turned toward the trail that led up the mountain from below.

"Karyn! Is that you?"

The limping figure of a man came toward her. In the combined light of the moon and the fire she saw that it was Chris Halloran.

"Yes," she said in a hoarse whisper.

"Are you all right?"

"I'm all right." She turned back toward the cabin, where the roof was now gone and the flames were beginning to subside. "Marcia's in there. She's finished now."

"Thank God," said Chris. He dropped wearily to the grass beside her and saw her hands. "You're hurt."

"It will be all right." She searched his face. "On the trail tonight... did you... did you..."

Chris nodded. "Roy was there. He's dead now."

"Then they're both finished. It's over."

Chris turned and looked for a moment back toward the mountain trail. "It's over," he said.

They sat together and watched as the cabin crumbled and the fire burned itself out. Nothing moved in the charred ruin. The night was clear and cold. And silent.

Slowly, Karyn let herself relax. In the days to come there would be much to do, but all she wanted right now was sleep. Sleep with the blessed knowledge that never more would she hear the howling.

THE HOWLING III

1

Sheriff Gavin Ramsay stretched out a foot and nudged the switch on the electric heater to OFF with the toe of his boot. The heater coils twanged as the red glow faded. The voters of La Reina County, all 4,012 of them, would be proud of their sheriff's economy moves.

Ramsay hoisted his foot back to the top of the desk and resumed his contemplation of the view from his office window. Out in front ran S31, a two-lane blacktop with a flaking yellow center stripe badly in need of repainting. S31 was also the main street of Pinyon, California, seat of La Reina County, Pop. 2,109, Elev. 3550.

Across the road from the sheriff's office was Art Moore's Exxon station, a Pioneer Chicken franchise, and Hackett's Pharmacy. On his own side of the road, out of Ramsay's line of sight, was Yates Hardware & Plumbing, the Safeway, the boarded-up Rialto Theater, and the Pinyon Inn. That was about it for Pinyon, except for the library and La Reina County Hospital, which were built off the road on the high ground between S31 and the mountains.

The storm that had hammered the town for two days had moved on in the early-morning hours, leaving everything wet and bedraggled. The landscape would need a couple of days of sunshine to dry out.

Gavin Ramsay was more than ready for some dry weather. The rain depressed him. Elise used to get poetic about the rain. Literally. She would go to her typewriter and turn out pages of tortured free verse whenever a few raindrops fell. Then she would show it to Gavin and ask what he thought of it. In the first year of their marriage he used to lie and say it was good, really good. After that first year he started telling her the truth. By that time it didn't matter anymore.

Today was the last day of March, and with luck there would not be another big storm until fall. Summer would bring its own problems—motorcycle gangs, irritable tourists, lost hikers, and campers with poison oak. Nothing that couldn't be handled as long as it was not raining.

Probably there would be fewer problems with hikers and campers this year. Thoughtful people were not eager to go into the woods since the Drago business. You couldn't blame them. It was peaceful now, but sometimes on a quiet night you could still hear it. The howling.

In truth, there wasn't a whole lot for a sheriff and two deputies to do in La Reina County. Well, one deputy and a trainee assigned here by the state, to be accurate. Right now the prospect of a quiet summer suited Gavin Ramsay just fine. After the double trauma of Drago and his divorce from Elise he could use the time to reassemble his life.

The people of La Reina County were happy to see things calm down again. Drago was enough excitement for several lifetimes. It was kind of fun for a while. Now the folks would just as soon not talk about it.

They still got a fair number of sightseers who detoured off Interstate 5 hoping to see something of the infamous village. They might as well have stayed home. There was nothing left to see.

The asphalt road connecting Pinyon to Drago had buckled and cracked with the heat of the fire, and there were wooden barriers put up by Caltrans to block it off. Still, determined curiosity seekers could get through in a tough truck. Those driving something less rugged turned back to Pinyon, where they searched in vain for souvenir shops. Some of the locals used to joke down at the Pinyon Inn about printing up a bunch of Drago T-shirts with bite marks and red splotches, but those jokes got old in a hurry.

Gavin Ramsay had functioned with his usual quiet efficiency during the Drago business. In a way it was a relief for him to get away from home at the time. Now, like the rest of the people in town, he didn't want to talk about it. Not about Drago or Elise. That did not mean he had forgotten. Nobody who lived through Drago would ever forget. Elise, either, for that matter. You just didn't want to talk about it.

He picked up a paperback novel from the other desk in the pine-paneled office, the one shared by his two deputies. Ed McBain. 87th Precinct. It must belong to Milo Fernandez. The trainee. Roy Nevins's taste ran more to *Hustler*.

Milo was an eager kid, still excited by the idea of police work. Roy Nevins wasn't excited by much of anything these days, except finishing up his twenty years of public service and living the rest of his life comfortably off the taxpayers of California.

They should be returning soon. It was after four and getting dark. Ramsay felt a little guilty about sending them out on what he figured to be a wild goose chase, but he could see Milo getting restless with nothing to do, and Roy had been on the verge of falling asleep. They were not likely to find Abe Craddock and Curly Vane in the woods. Those fearless hunters were more likely holed up in some saloon down in Saugus, where everybody had a tattoo and a pickup truck. Still, Abe's wife had called to say she was worried about him, and it had been three days, so Ramsay was more or less obligated to look into it. Anyway, Milo would probably enjoy getting out of the office, and Roy could sure as hell use the exercise.

The gravel crunched outside and Orry Yates's panel truck pulled onto the parking area. YATES PLUMING was painted on the side in no-nonsense black letters. Orry claimed the misspelling was done deliberately to attract attention. Ramsay had his doubts.

Orry got out of the driver's side of the truck, and two teenagers, a boy and a girl wearing backpacks, climbed out of the other. Orry led the way toward the office.

Ramsay swung his feet down to the floor and waited for them to come in. A tightening in his gut warned that this was going to be trouble.

Orry held the door open for the young backpackers, then herded them over to Ramsay's desk. "Got a little problem, Gavin," he said.

"Oh?"

"These kids think they found a dead man in the woods."

"They think?"

"You know how sometimes the light plays tricks coming through the trees. A tree stump or a mossy log can look like something else."

The boy shot Orry a dark look. "If that's a log laying out there, I'm Beaver Cleaver."

Ramsay studied the young couple. The boy was thin and wouldn't be bad looking if he shaved off the apologetic, little mustache. The girl wore a UCLA sweat-shirt and elastic jeans that showed off her firm little ass.

The sheriff cleared his throat and got businesslike. "Tell me about it."

"We were, you know, hiking," the boy said. "On a trail that leads off the old Drago Road, and Debbie goes, 'Hey, you smell that?' And I go, 'Smell what?' And she goes, 'Like spoiled meat.' And I go..."

"Never mind the dialog," Ramsay said. "Tell me about finding the dead man."

"That's what I'm doing, man."

"Could you speed it up?"

The boy looked sullen and Debbie took over. "We found him a little ways off the trail. A big guy, you know. Smelled really bad."

"How big?"

The girl shrugged. "It was hard to tell. He was laying down. Dead, you know." She looked at the boy and giggled.

"What did he look like?"

"Like a dead man," the boy said.

"His face," Ramsay prompted.

"Who knows?" the boy said. "There wasn't much of it left. Like something had chewed on it."

"Gross," the girl confirmed.

Ramsay levered himself out of the chair. "Think you can take me to him?"

They nodded without enthusiasm.

"You gonna need me anymore?" Orry Yates said.

"Not now, Orry. Thanks for bringing them in."

They walked out of the small wooden building that served as La Reina County Sheriff's office. It was built twenty years before as a sales office for an optimistic developer who thought there would be a migration of Los Angeles residents to the mountains. He was wrong.

Orry Yates climbed into the YATES PLUMING truck, waved, and drove off. Ramsay led the teenagers around to the back where the beat-up Dodge wagon was parked. His Camaro had gone to Elise in the settlement. La Reina County could afford only one sheriff's car, and the deputies were using it.

Ramsay wondered if the dead man was Abe Craddock or Curly Vane. If it was, he owed somebody an apology for mentally placing them in a saloon somewhere. However, if it was one of them, where was the other? An argument? Too much booze and a gun goes off? Better stop building a crime until he had a look at the scene. He kicked the engine of the eight-year-old wagon to life and took off for the old Drago Road.

* * *

Deputy Roy Nevins stopped to pull his uniform pants free from the thorns of a wild blackberry bush. He knew this drill was one big waste of time. Craddock and Vane could find their way around these woods as well as anybody in the county. The only trouble they were likely to get into was when they came back to town and started drinking.

He knew Gavin Ramsay had sent him and Milo out here just to keep them busy. If it hadn't been for the gung ho trainee, Deputy Nevins would have sacked out in the back of the car until dusk, then gone back and told Gavin there was no sign of Craddock and Vane. That's what their search would add up to anyway. Zip. Only difference was now he'd get all wet and scratched up from these fucking thorns and his shoes would be ruined.

"*Roy!*" Milo called unseen from off to the left.

"*Yeah?*"

"Just checking our positions."

Yeah, great. Ten-fucking-four. Milo could be a pain in the ass sometimes. But what the hell. He was only twenty. When Roy Nevins was twenty he'd been gung ho, too. The kid might grow up to be a good cop. Not in La Reina County, where a couple of overdue library books was a crime wave. But it was a start. Three months from now the state would put him somewhere else. Nice gentle way to break in as a cop. Not the way Roy Nevins had done it, on the grungiest street in the grungiest section of Oakland.

Roy had been a cowboy back then himself. No more. Now he was sitting on a pension, just putting in his time. Couple more years and he could buy that mobile home down in Baja. Sit around fishing with a cool Carta Blanca in his fist. A man could still live pretty damn good in Mexico for peanuts. Until then he would have to pass the days as comfortably as he could and put up with a certain amount of shit like slogging through these dripping woods.

"*Hey!*" he yelled in the direction of Milo Fernandez.

"*Yo!*"

"Let's take a break."

Roy stuck a Winston in his mouth and lit it. He eased his broad butt down onto a boulder that looked reasonably dry. Milo Fernandez, neat and slim in his uniform, pushed through the wet underbrush and joined him.

The younger man looked up at the patches of sky, they could see through the thick tops of the pine and Douglas fir trees.

"Not more than an hour of daylight left," said Milo.

"Yeah."

"You think we'll find those guys before dark?"

"Craddock and Vane? No way. Not before dark, not before Easter Sunday. They gotta be lost before we can find them. Those two ain't lost. Shit-faced somewhere, maybe, but not lost."

"How do you know?"

" 'Cause I know them two assholes. Why Betty Craddock wants us to find Abe beats the shit out of me. Best thing that could happen to her, he falls down in the middle of S31 and gets run over by an RV."

"Well… we can give it a try, anyway."

"Sure. Old college try. You go to college, tiger?"

"Junior college, actually. I need two more years for a degree."

"Waste of time. You want to be a cop, don't you?"

Milo Fernandez nodded.

"They not gonna teach you that in college. Only way to learn about being a cop is to be one."

Roy was about to launch into a war story from his days as a real cop in Oakland, but the young deputy's attention strayed.

Milo looked around at the dark, dripping trees. "Roy, where's Drago from here?"

Nevins pointed off toward the south. "That way. Four, five miles."

"I'd like to see it sometime."

"Nothing to see. Dozen or so burned out buildings."

"What was it like, Roy? The fire and all. Was it exciting?"

Roy shrugged. He pulled on his Winston, coughed, spat on the ground. "Sure, if you get off on poking through ashes trying to make out which is human and which is… something else."

The young trainee caught the older deputy's hesitation and looked at him quickly. Roy studied the glowing tip of his cigarette and stopped talking.

Milo Fernandez looked off toward the south as though trying to see the burned out village through five miles of forest. "What do you think was going on there, Roy? At Drago? Before the fire?"

"Who knows? Cult of some kind. Los Angeles types. The people living there never went much outside their own village."

"There were stories."

"Yeah, I heard the stories. Bunch of crap."

"Not human, people said."

"Crap."

"There was howling, they say. In the woods. At night."

"So what? There's lots of funny noises in the woods at night."

"People still heard things out here after the fire. After everybody in Drago was burned up."

"Look, amigo, some other time we'll sit around a campfire and scare the shit out of each other with ghost stories. I'm not in the mood now, okay?"

"Sure, Roy. I'm just curious."

Something rustled the bushes up ahead. The two deputies raised their heads, listening. They looked at each other, then back toward the sound.

"Who's there?" Roy Nevins called.

Silence.

Another rustle of brush.

"Craddock…? Vane…?"

No answer. A flash of movement. A head rose above a clump of brush twenty feet ahead of the two deputies. A face looked at them. A pale face streaked with mud. Dark, matted hair. Eyes wild, with lots of white showing.

"Hey!"

The face ducked out of sight. Squishy sound of running feet on the wet ground.

"Son of a bitch." Roy mashed the Winston out under his shoe and took off. Milo was already ahead of him, chasing the fleeing figure, who ducked and weaved among the trees.

The runner left the trail and fought through the undergrowth. The two deputies followed. Roy Nevins swore as the thorns clutched at him and mud seeped over the tops of his shoes.

"Halt!" Milo Fernandez called out. "Sheriff's officers!"

Roy pounded on, the breath wheezing through his open mouth. He fumbled at the leather strap that snapped to the holster over the butt of his .38 police positive. Regulation.

Never could free the damn thing in a hurry. The hell with it. Firing your piece only meant trouble these days. You had to account for every fucking bullet. Nothing in sight to shoot at anyway. He could only catch glimpses of Milo's back as the young deputy charged after the fleeing figure.

There was a thump of colliding bodies up ahead and a damp thud as they hit the ground. Roy floundered through the brush and almost fell over Milo. The young deputy was applying an armlock to the fugitive, who lay prone on the damp pine needles.

"I got him, Roy."

"So I see. Suppose you flip him over so we can see what we got."

Milo warily eased his hold. When the figure on the ground did not move, he grasped a shoulder and turned him over.

"A kid," Roy said disgustedly.

The face that looked up at the deputies was pale and frightened. Oddly, he seemed not to be breathing hard.

"What'd you take off for?" Deputy Nevins said. The large, frightened eyes flicked from one of the deputies to the other. The boy made no attempt to answer.

"Get up."

The boy rose to a crouch.

"And don't think about running anymore. We're taking a ride into town."

Nevins took the boy's arm and raised him to a standing position. The muscles were firm under the smooth flesh. He gestured with his head for Milo to get going. The younger deputy was staring at the boy's face.

"Let's go," Nevins said. "I want to get him back to the car before it gets dark. What's the matter?"

Milo Fernandez hesitated. "Take a look. There's something funny about his teeth."

2

The room on the second floor of La Reina County Hospital was pleasant and bright. Outside the window of the small private room a night bird sang. The boy sat propped in the bed in a half-sitting position. His green eyes skipped around the room as though searching for an escape.

Holly Lang stood at the foot of the bed and smiled down at him. She was tall and supple, with short dark hair and hazel eyes. Her smile was good, and it usually made other people smile in response. But the boy's expression did not change.

"Well, you look a little better now that you're all cleaned up," she said.

The boy's eyes flicked over her and away.

"How are you feeling?" she asked.

No answer.

"A little scared, I guess." Holly kept her tone soft and conversational. "I don't blame you. Hospitals can be scary. My name's Holly. Do you want to tell me yours? It's all right if you don't. There's no hurry."

The boy's fingers moved restlessly on the edge of the sheet.

"I'm a kind of a doctor."

The green eyes met hers for an instant.

"Not the kind that sticks people with needles," she said quickly. "Mostly, I just talk. And I listen, too, if you want to talk to me."

The boy turned away and stared through the window at the dark trees. His expression told Holly nothing.

Holly waited, watching his face. "What happened to you out there?" she said, more to herself than to the boy. "What's haunting you now?"

La Reina County Hospital had more the look of an expensive mountain resort than an institution. It was tucked into the picturesque wooded hillside overlooking the town of Pinyon. Behind it the Tehachapi Mountains rose from gently sloping foothills. The facilities and the equipment at La Reina were excellent, courtesy of the California taxpayers. The same could not be said of the staff.

Somehow La Reina County Hospital had become caught in the backwash of bureaucracy and was known as a haven for medical misfits. Med school graduates from the lower third of their class found a home there. Doctors with a questionable past, nurses with borderline records... these made up the staff at La Reina County.

There were always more beds than patients in residence. The administration lived in fear that during one of the periodic budget battles in Sacramento someone would ask why the hell they needed a hospital down there at all. The funds would be cut off and a lot of people would be out of work. Somehow, the budget checkers in Sacramento kept missing it.

Dr. Hollanda Lang, known to everyone as Holly, did not belong with the staff of misfits. She had passed up a lucrative private practice as a clinical psychologist to work for the state Social Services Department. When people asked her why, she told them she was absolving her liberal guilt. Holly found it embarrassing to admit how deeply she cared about helping people.

And La Reina appealed to her precisely because of its quirky reputation. Her opinion of the medical establishment was not high, and here among the outcasts she found some original thinkers she could relate to. Her one disappointment had been in the lack of challenge in her cases. Until they brought in the boy from the woods.

Holly looked down at the pale boy now, wondering what it would take to communicate with him. In the two hours since he'd been brought in, the boy had not spoken. She had finally gotten the curious onlookers cleared out of the room and felt the boy was at least beginning to relax with her.

There was a sound at the door behind her. She turned, annoyed at the interruption.

Sheriff Gavin Ramsay stuck his head into the room.

"All right if I come in?"

"Could I stop you?"

"Sure. Just say go away."

Holly felt the muscles tighten at the back of her neck. She knew her aversion to police was an unreasonable throwback to her campus protest days, but she couldn't help it. "Come on in," she said.

Ramsay nodded to her. "Thanks, Miss Lang. I'll make this as short as I can."

"It's Doctor."

"Oh, right. Dr. Lang. Sorry."

She made herself relax. "That sounded pompous, didn't it? Shall we try first names? I'm Holly."

"Gavin," he said.

Not a bad looking man, Holly decided, if you liked the macho type. Sort of a younger Marlboro Man. She had seen him around Pinyon and thought it was a pity that he had to be a policeman.

"How's the kid?" he asked.

"Doing well enough."

"Has he said anything yet?"

Holly looked quickly at the young patient. The green eyes regarded the sheriff warily.

"We're just getting acquainted," she said. "So far I've done all the talking."

"I'd like to ask him a few questions."

The boy seemed to shrink a little in the bed.

"Suppose we step out into the hall," Holly said.

"Sure."

She followed Ramsay out through the door and looked up at him when he turned. Holly was five-eight in her stocking feet, and well built. Not many men could make her feel small. Gavin Ramsay could, and she resented it.

"I wish you'd give me some warning before you barge into the room."

"Sorry. The door was ajar."

"Well… no harm done, I suppose."

"I'm relieved to hear that."

"You must understand it's part of my job to keep my patient from being disturbed."

"Fair enough," Ramsay said, "but you've got your job and I've got mine."

"I'm not sure I understand."

"I've got a couple of hunters missing and a dead man downstairs in the pathology lab."

"What has that to do with this boy?"

"I don't know that there's any connection, but I want to find out. From the looks of the kid when they brought him in, he was out in the woods for at least three days. That's about how long our man downstairs has been a corpse."

"You're not suggesting that this boy has anything to do with it?"

Ramsay's eyes flashed blue fire. "Why not, because he's a minor? Last week a twelve-year-old in East Los Angeles set his mother on fire because she found his heroin stash. A seven-year-old girl in Beverly Hills drowned her baby brother in the swimming pool because he got too much attention. Two boys in Glendale hung a baby girl from a swing set. The boys were six. Want to hear more?"

"No, thank you. I'll concede that there is no age limit on criminal behavior, but I won't jump to the conclusion that this boy is guilty of anything."

"Holly… Dr. Lang… all I want to do is talk to him." Gavin raised his arms. "See, I didn't even bring any handcuffs."

"Well, he isn't talking yet. He's had a frightening experience, and it may take a while. Shouldn't you be trying to find out who he is?"

"I should and I am. I've put his description out on the wire. So far he doesn't fit any missing-boy report." Gavin looked back over her shoulder into the room. "You will let me know if he says anything?"

"Certainly, Sheriff."

He started to go, then turned back. "Is there any chance we can get back to using first names?"

She held a stern expression for a moment longer, then relaxed. "What the hell... See you, Gavin."

"See you, Holly."

The boy's eyes followed her as she came back and sat in the chair next to the bed. She smiled at him, studying his face. The two deputies who brought him in had said there was something 'weird' in the way he looked. Probably a trick of twilight and their imaginations. Holly saw only a frightened boy of perhaps fourteen. High forehead, straight nose, firm mouth. The eyes were a deep, lustrous green. Certainly nothing there that could be considered 'weird.'

"Getting sleepy?" she said.

The boy's head rolled from side to side on the pillow.

A response. The first sign he had given that he understood. Holly kept her voice gentle. "I'll just sit here for a while, then. If you feel like talking, fine. If not, that's fine too."

The boy's eyes never left her. Holly thought she could see his body relax, just a little, under the hospital sheet and blanket. She picked up a magazine from the bedside table and pretended to read. She did not leave until she was sure the boy was asleep.

3

During the next three days Holly spent many hours at the boy's bedside. She could not coax him to speak, but his face brightened when she came into the room, and she was cheered by the small sign of recognition. They watched television together and listened to music. Holly talked about whatever came into her mind, and read to the boy from the books and magazines in the hospital's library.

On the morning of the third day the administration chief of staff met her outside the boy's room. Dr. Dennis Qualen was a soft-faced man with steely gray hair. He was always careful about his diction, as though he was being recorded.

"So, Dr. Lang, how is it going?"

"We're making progress."

"Really?"

"That sounds like you have doubts."

"No, no. Perhaps our definitions of progress differ. I've read the reports and can find no indication that there is anything wrong with the boy."

"Nothing physical."

"Exactly. Which leaves us with mental illness."

"Let's say psychological trauma."

"Terminology aside, have you considered turning the boy's case over to someone better equipped than we to handle him?"

"Who did you have in mind?"

"The State Youth Authority, for instance."

"That's for juvenile criminals."

"I understand from Sheriff Ramsay that there is a very good chance this boy might fit into that category."

"There is no evidence of that."

"Perhaps not, but I must consider the best course for the hospital."

"And I have to consider the patient. Listen, Doctor, I've seen cases like this before—loss of the power of speech due to some psychic trauma. If you give me another week, I'm sure I can show you marked improvement."

"A week is out of the question."

"Doctor, believe me, I can help this boy if I'm just given the time."

Dr. Qualen fingered the medical school emblem on his tie clasp. "You may have two days."

"I could do much more in a week."

"Two days. After that the boy will be turned over to the Youth Authority. I cannot take a chance on him becoming violent."

Without waiting for further discussion, Dr. Qualen spun and marched away down the hallway. Holly suppressed an urge to give him the finger. She went into the boy's room.

He was sitting up waiting for her.

"Hi," she said. "Sleep well?" She looked over at the vertical window. It was cranked open three inches to the tough mesh screen outside. "Fresh air always helps me sleep. But then, I guess you've had all the fresh air you want for a while."

Holly pulled her chair over to the bed and sat down. "I want you to do something for me today. I want you to think about the time you spent out there. No, don't turn away from me. It's important now that you think about it. Then maybe we can talk."

Before she could go any further, Dr. Wayne Pastory sailed into the room. He wore his white jacket over a pale yellow Izod Lacoste shirt. He touched the glossy black hair he was so proud of, which he wore combed straight back in a style of the past.

"Well, well, well, so this is the wild boy I've been hearing about. How are we doing, fella?"

Holly glared at him. She did not like anything about Wayne Pastory. With his sharp features and bright little eyes and the quick way he moved, he reminded her of a weasel. She didn't like his reputation either. He had been kicked out of a genetic research project at Stanford for faking the results of an experiment. No charges had been made, but Pastory's name had gone on an informal medical blacklist.

He walked over to the bed and reached down. The boy shied away from his hand.

"What's the matter, son? I just want to check your pulse."

"His pulse is normal, Doctor," Holly said, trying to keep the irritation out of her voice. "So are his temperature and blood pressure. It's all on the chart."

"Good. If you'll stand by, I'd like to look him over."

"I am not a nurse," Holly said, spacing her words carefully.

Pastory studied her, his mouth quirked in a private smile. "Sorry, Doctor. I meant that you and I would make the examination together, of course."

"The examination has been completed."

Pastory stroked the end of the gold cross pen that peeked out of his jacket pocket. "Aren't you being overprotective of this patient, Doctor?"

"I don't think so."

"Have you given any thought to what we have here?"

"What we have is a boy who's been through a terrifying experience. A boy who could use some rest and quiet."

"What we have," Pastory went on, ignoring her, "just might be the first survivor from Drago."

"There's no reason to assume he's from Drago," Holly said. But over Pastory's shoulder she saw the little muscles tighten around the boy's mouth.

"But the possibility does exist," Pastory said. "And think what this could mean to us if he is one of the Drago people. No one really knows what happened there. If we were to produce a flesh-and-blood survivor... the opportunities would be limitless."

"You're thinking of taking him on the Johnny Carson show?"

"Of course not. I'm speaking strictly of the importance to medical research."

"Doctor, this is just a lost, frightened boy."

"Maybe, but I read the report of the deputies who brought him in. They mentioned some facial peculiarities."

"Take a look at him," Holly said. "Do you see anything peculiar?"

They both looked down at the boy in the bed.

Holly felt a sudden chill. Did the hair grow a fraction lower on the boy's forehead than a moment ago? And his eyebrows... she did not remember them being so heavy. And was there a new hardening around his mouth? She looked away for an instant, then back at the boy. The impressions faded. She must not let Pastory plant suggestions in her mind.

Pastory leaned down over the bed. "I don't know," he said slowly. "There's... something."

"He's tired," Holly said. "I think you'd better leave us."

"Are you in charge here, Doctor?"

"Until I'm told differently."

For a moment the two faced each other. Pastory was the first to look away. "I'll be back," he said.

With a last searching look at the boy, he left the room.

Holly turned back to the bed. What was it she had found strange about his face a moment ago? He looked normal enough now. Just a poor confused boy.

* * *

The hopeful mood in which Holly had begun the day was dissipated by the encounters with Qualen and Pastory. The boy had withdrawn once again, and she was sitting at his bedside feeling discouraged when Gavin Ramsay stopped by.

"Got time to talk?"

Holly glanced at the boy, who had fallen into a light sleep. "Aren't you supposed to read me my rights or something?"

"Hey, I'm just trying to be sociable."

"Were you being sociable when you told Dennis Qualen we had a dangerous criminal here?"

"He's the chief of staff; he's entitled to know what I'm doing here. However, that's not quite the way I put it to him."

Holly drew in a breath and let it out slowly. "Sorry. This day hasn't begun well for me. Not your fault." She got out of the chair. "There's a patients' lounge at the end of the hall with a coffee machine. I'll buy."

They walked to the lounge, which was brightly furnished with comfortable chairs, checkerboards, card tables, and a pinball machine. An old man in a wheelchair stared at the television set, where a game show was silently in progress. The old man did not seem to miss the sound.

Holly dropped coins into the machine. It spilled a stream of brackish-looking coffee into two plastic cups. They carried the cups over to a table and sat down.

"Any word yet on who he is?" Holly asked.

"Nope. As far as I know, he might have stepped off a flying saucer."

"That's not very funny."

"You're right, it isn't."

They sat for a minute sipping at the hot brew, not saying anything. Holly watched him over the rim of her plastic cup. Finally she said, "Can I ask you a question?"

"Ask," he said.

"What are you doing here, anyway?"

"Waiting for your kid to snap out of his trauma so I can ask him what he was doing out in the woods."

"No, I mean what are you doing here in Pinyon?"

"Everybody's got to be somewhere."

"Are you happy being sheriff of a county with a population that could fit into a high school gym?"

"Sure. Why not?"

"There was talk a while back about you running for governor."

"Any such talk was strictly the fantasy of my ex-wife and my ex-father-in-law."

"Forrest Ingraham."

Ramsay gave her a long look. "That's the man. What else do you know about me?"

"Oh, a little. You went to Willamette University, enlisted, of all things, in the army, fought in Viet Nam, won some medals, came home, went to law school, married Forrest Ingraham's daughter, were elected sheriff, got a divorce."

"That sure covers the high spots. Don't I have any secrets?"

"Lots, I'll bet. They're none of my business. I just wonder why you stay here."

"I like it. Oh, I've had other offers. From the police departments in Cleveland, Buffalo, and Jersey City. Would you leave La Reina County for any of those?"

"I suppose not," she said, laughing softly.

"Well, then."

"Why do you have to be a policeman? Do you get some kind of kick out of it?"

His expression hardened. "Sure. I get off on clubbing down peace-marching college kids and locking up widows who can't pay their rent."

"Oh-oh, did I touch a nerve?"

"You're damn right. You ACLU types who spit out policeman like something that tastes bad give me a pain in the ass." He paused for a deep breath. "Sorry. We'd better get off this before I go into one of Jack Webb's old Dragnet speeches."

"I guess we aren't ready for a personal conversation."

"I guess not," he said.

They got up and dropped their cups into a trash container near the door.

"Just one thing," she said. "I don't belong to the ACLU."

"Nobody's perfect," he said.

* * *

Holly's breakthrough with the boy came that night while she sat in the chair next to his bed. She snapped off the television set after The Love Boat.

"I don't know about you," she said, "but I'm tired." She tucked the sheets in around the boy and smiled down at him. "See you in the morning." She paused in the doorway and looked back. In a talking-to-herself voice she said, "Damn, I wish I knew what to call you."

"I'm Malcolm." It was a dry croak, barely more than a whisper, but to Holly it was like a shout.

"Malcolm?" she repeated, trying not to sound too excited.

He nodded.

"That's a good name. Do you remember mine?"

The green eyes watched her.

"It's Holly," she said. "Holly Lang."

"Holly," the boy said in the same dry whisper.

"That's right. Do you have a last name, Malcolm?"

The boy looked confused.

"Well, that doesn't matter now. We have one name. That's enough to start with. Do you want to talk some more?"

The boy's eyes drifted off to a corner of the ceiling.

"That's all right," she said. "You get some sleep, and tomorrow we'll start fresh."

Malcolm looked back at her and nodded again. Holly left the room, elated.

She was in early the next day, eager to begin with Malcolm, but as she passed the reception desk the young woman there called her over.

"Dr. Qualen said for you to come to his office as soon as you got in."

Holly frowned. "Did he say what for?"

"Not to me."

Dr. Qualen stood up behind his rich mahogany desk and greeted Holly formally. "Ah, Dr. Lang. Good of you to stop by. I won't take much of your time."

She hid her impatience, waiting for him to get to the point.

"How are things going with the boy?"

"I've learned that his name is Malcolm."

"I see. Not what we'd call a significant breakthrough."

"That depends. I still have today."

"I wonder if perhaps another approach might speed things up."

"Apparently Dr. Pastory has talked to you."

"As a matter of fact, he has. He tells me you were rather abrupt with him yesterday."

"I was ticked off. He was upsetting my patient."

"The very point I wanted to make. The boy is not officially anyone's patient. As I told you, I am not convinced that the case falls under our jurisdiction."

"I remember. You mentioned the Youth Authority."

"That remains an option; however, Dr. Pastory has some thoughts of his own on the boy."

"What does he want to do, dissect him?"

"That's not very professional, Doctor."

"No, I suppose it isn't. I'm sorry. Is the case still mine, at least through today?"

"Yes, of course. I hope there won't be any more friction between you and Dr. Pastory."

"I'll do my best."

"Fine, fine. I'm glad we had this little talk." Holly swallowed her opinion of their little talk and left the office.

* * *

The boy was waiting for her.

"Good morning, Malcolm."

The boy turned away from Aquaman on television and looked at her. "Good morning, Holly."

"You remembered my name."

"I always knew it."

"Well, good." She came over and sat down. "Today let's see what else you can remember."

A tiny frown line creased the boy's brow.

"Don't worry. I'm not going to hook you up to a machine or give you shots or anything like that. We're just going to relax and talk."

Gavin Ramsay stuck his head in the door. "Is it safe to say good morning?"

"Hi, Gavin," Holly said. "Come on in and meet Malcolm."

Ramsay gave her a brief questioning look, then came into the room and walked to the foot of the bed.

"Hi," he said to the boy.

Holly said, "Malcolm, this is Sheriff Ramsay."

The boy looked to Holly for reassurance, then back at Gavin. "Hello, Sheriff."

Ramsay stuck out a hand. The boy took it and they shook hands gravely.

"Glad to see you're talking again, son."

"We were just about to find out what else Malcolm can remember."

"Oh?"

"I thought we might try hypnotism. Do you know what hypnotism is, Malcolm?"

"You put somebody to sleep."

"Not exactly. It's just a way to relax and let things come back that we misplaced somewhere."

"Does it hurt?"

"Not a bit. In fact, a lot of people say that it makes them feel better. Do you want to try it?"

The boy looked at Ramsay. "Is he going to stay?"

"Not if you don't want him to."

Malcolm considered for a moment. "It's all right; he can stay."

Ramsay pulled a chair back against the far wall and sat down out of the way.

"Now Malcolm," Holly began, "I want you to take three deep, deep breaths. All the way in and all the way out. That's good." She breathed in and out with him. So did Ramsay. "I bet you're feeling more relaxed and comfortable already. I know I am." She spoke in a slow, soothing tone.

"We're going to start our relaxing way down there with the tips of your toes. Think about your toes. Do you have a picture of them in your mind? Now if you try, you can feel them start to tingle and relax, one at a time. Little toe first, then the next, and the next, and now the big toe. Doesn't that feel good? Nice and comfortable. Now your feet, Malcolm. Relax your feet and let that nice warm feeling flow slowly up your ankles. It's like easing your legs into a tub of nice warm water. So comfortable... so relaxed..."

Ramsay was leaning back, enjoying the relaxed, comfortable feeling in his legs, when Milo Fernandez stuck his head through the door and hissed at him.

"Sheriff... hey, Sheriff."

Holly looked up and put a finger to her lips. Ramsay got up and stepped out into the hall. In a moment he returned and spoke softly to Holly.

"I've got to go."

"Trouble?"

"It could be. I'll talk to you later."

When he was gone Holly turned back to Malcolm, who sat propped against the pillows, a dreamy expression on his face.

"All right, Malcolm. Let's go back now into the forest. There are trees all around. Tall and cool. A soft wind is blowing, making the branches sway and rustle. Let's go back there and remember, Malcolm. Listen to the sounds. Sniff the air. Remember the forest..."

4

Memories of the forest came back to him in fragments.

The cushiony feel of pine needles under his feet.

A whisper of rain in the high branches of the trees.

Dappled sunlight filtering down on a summer afternoon.

Fresh smells of evergreen and of flowers.

Night-sounds: monotonous song of a tree frog, the hoot of an owl, the cry of some small creature caught in its talons.

A childhood in the forest village of Drago, with carefree days, deep, dark nights, surrounded by people whose faces were blurred now in memory, but who loved him and cared for him.

Then, without any warning, childhood ended. The years that followed were a jumble of strange schools, narrow beds, cold faces of people who were paid to teach him and feed him and give him a place to sleep. The memories were jagged, like pieces of a broken mirror. A face, a schoolbook, a forbidding house in a strange town. Nothing fit together. It was a lost time.

Then the lost time was over and he was back. Back in the forest. Back in Drago. But it was not the same. The days were troubled, and the nights full of danger. Malcolm was apart from the others of the village. They possessed some secret knowledge that had been withheld from him. Knowledge wondrous and terrible, knowledge he must have. This much he learned when he was brought before Derak, the leader of the village.

Malcolm could not even guess at the age of Derak. Not old, certainly. Not in years. Yet it seemed he had always been there. Derak was strong and vigorous, but there was in his eyes something older than time.

The house where Derak lived was small. It was his alone. The other people of Drago lived in groups—four or six or eight of them to a house. Derak lived alone because he was the leader.

Sometimes a woman stayed there with him. Malcolm seemed to remember a woman from before. When he was little. The woman was dark and lithe and smelled of warm wildflowers. Her eyes were the same deep shade of green as Malcolm's. She was gone now. He wondered about her, but he was too timid to ask.

Malcolm felt ill at ease sitting alone with Derak on a sofa in the small house. He perspired, and he did not know what to do with his hands. Derak smiled. When he spoke, his voice was soft, but Malcolm could sense the strength within the man. A strength that could have broken Malcolm like a dry twig, had he wanted to do so.

"Relax, boy," said Derak, as though he had read Malcolm's thoughts. "I'm not going to hurt you. No one here will hurt you. This is your home. Do you understand that?"

"Y-yes."

"Good. I suppose you want to know why you have been brought back."

"I don't even know why I was sent away."

"It is the way of our life. You have seen, I suppose, that there are no children in Drago, except the very young."

"Yes."

"You, too, were here when you were very young."

"I remember. A little bit."

"A child reaches an age where he asks questions. Questions with answers he is not ready for. When that time comes we have to send him away. To the outside, where he can learn about the world out there. When he is ready to know about us and about Drago, we bring him back."

"Am I ready now to know those things?"

Derak smiled at him. A strange, sad smile. "You are more than ready, Malcolm."

"I don't understand."

"Have things been happening to you? To your body? Things you can't explain?"

"Y-yes. Sometimes… in the night."

"It is usually in the night at first. Or when you are afraid. Or hurt. Or very angry. We always try to bring the child back and explain these things to him before the changes occur. Because of troubles here, we could not bring you back at your proper time. So you are late, Malcolm, through no fault of your own. You have already experienced some of the things that will happen to you, things that you cannot understand."

"Will there be more?"

"Oh, yes. Much, much more."

The boy's throat constricted with a rush of emotions. Finally he got out, "Why?"

"It will all be explained to you, Malcolm. Who you are, what you are. What we all are, and what our lives must be."

"When?"

"Tomorrow. There is a ceremony. Nothing big, just our people—your people––gathering around you to show you our secrets and teach you our ways. You will spend tonight alone. After tomorrow, you will know who you are, and you will never be alone again."

"Why do I have to wait? Why can't we do it now?"

Derak looked out the window at the deepening shadows. "Tonight there is something else we have to do. After tomorrow all of our lives will be changed. You will join us then."

There was a finality in Derak's tone that would permit no further discussion. Malcolm was taken to a small cabin at the edge of the village. There was a low cot of wood and canvas with a woolen blanket, a single candle for illumination, and nothing more. The door closed behind Malcolm, and he was alone.

He could hear them outside, the people of Drago, as they walked toward the big building at the center of the village. The big building was sometimes a barn and sometimes a meeting hall. And there were times of celebration when the people danced and the music was something to hear. Tonight there was no music. The voices of the people as they walked were somber and subdued. Malcolm lay awake shivering on the stretched canvas of the cot and waited.

Inside the building Derak stood in the center of the wooden door. The others entered and took their places in a circle around the leader. The quiet talk among them faded and finally died as they waited for Derak to speak.

"My friends... my family. We have lived in Drago without trouble for many years. Longer than our people might have hoped when first they settled here. Our history is not one of places; it is one of movement. From the Carpathians to the Urals to the Andes. From the icy lands of the far north to the steaming jungles of the equator. Always there comes a time when we are forced to move on. Here in Drago we have lived well, but it is over. Now we must move again. There are people, outsiders, who suspect what we are. They fear us, and in their fear they will try to destroy us. As always before, that means we must go."

Derak turned slowly and looked at the people ranged around him in a circle. Shadows from the flickering lanterns danced and skittered over their faces.

"But before we go," Derak said, "we will give them something to remember."

And he began to change.

Derak tore the shirt from his back and flexed the powerful muscles of his shoulders. His chest swelled and cracked as the bony structure within reshaped itself. His lips drew back to show the strong yellow teeth. The killing teeth.

Around him the others followed the lead of Derak. They threw off their clothes while their bodies twisted and stretched in a jerking dance of metamorphosis. The faces, human a moment before, thinned and lengthened. The ears grew, the noses pushed forward into muzzles. Short, coarse hair sprouted on their bodies. The hair spread, thickened into fur. The human voices became low, muttering growls. And there was the howling.

Malcolm sat suddenly upright on his cot in the small cabin. The candle flame guttered and died in a whisper of the night wind that seeped through cracks in the walls. The voices howling in the night were strange and frightening, yet they touched something deep within the boy. They spoke to him in a language he did not know. They called him. He longed to go to them.

Then there were other sounds. The scrape of heavy booted feet, a crunch of brush, muttered curses. Malcolm began to sweat. He stared into the darkness, fearful of something he could not define.

Inside the barn of a building, they heard the other sounds too late. There was a heavy scrape and a thud as the door was barred from the outside. Those within froze for a moment in wild attitudes of change... half-human, half-beast. They sniffed the air and caught the scent of men outside, then the biting odor of raw gasoline. An instant later in a blast of heat and light, the barn was afire.

Panic.

Three ways a werewolf can die. By a weapon of silver. By fire. And a third way that was never spoken of. The fire was all around them, and the fire was death.

Inside the barn was hell. Humans, wolves, creatures in all stages between, stumbled into the beams and crashed the blistering walls, searching for an escape. Their voices mingled in an outcry of agony and rage. Twisted muzzles pushed through the boards of the walls for air but were seared and sizzled by the flames outside. Claws scratched frantically at the wood. The men with the torches had done their work well. The building was surrounded by a wall of flame.

Some of the creatures in the barn broke through to the outside, their misshapen bodies afire, and ran till they dropped in a blazing, screaming heap. The men with the torches watched grimly as they died.

Most stayed inside the building. They huddled together as the flames leaped up the walls and across the roof. Their terrible jaws gaped in helpless rage. The blazing roof fell, and the screaming stopped.

But not all of them died. A few got away. A few always get away.

At the sound of the agonized howling and the furnace blast of the burning barn, Malcolm bolted from his cot and stumbled out into the inferno that had been his village. Men ran from house to house with cans of gasoline and blazing torches. One after another they were set afire.

For long minutes Malcolm stood in frozen horror. The shrieks of the dying were all around him. The smell of the dead made him retch. His body twitched and jumped of its own volition. The smells around him were keener, his night vision sharper than ever in his life. The message was clear in his mind.

Run!

And Malcolm ran. Away from the carnage of Drago. He was faster and stronger than ever he dreamed he could be. The forest was his as he loped through the brush, darting among the trees, leaping easily over any obstruction. Faster and faster he ran, putting the night and the forest between him and the blazing ruin of Drago. He ran in a deep crouch, his hands sometimes clutching at the ground, helping to pull him along. In the midst of his grief at the loss of his village and his people, Malcolm felt something else. Freedom. Freedom and power.

* * *

On the other side of the burned-out village, on the crest of a hill, a huge wolf-like figure looked down on the dying flames. Its fur was singed, and a ragged gash from a splintered board ran the length of the animal's side. The wound would soon heal. The anger would remain.

If he had escaped, there would be others. To help them survive, be must find them and bring them together. He was the leader.

Derak pointed his muzzle to the sky. The cruel teeth gleamed in the moonlight. He tested the air. There was the acrid smell of burning flesh and fur. The bite of gasoline. The sweat stink of the men. And there was the familiar scent of the others, those who had escaped... and somewhere in the night forest... his son.

Miles away, moving swiftly in the other direction, Malcolm paused and raised his head to listen to the howling.

5

The forest took him in. It sheltered him from the night and hid him from the men who shouted and cursed as they crashed through the brush, searching out the few survivors of Drago. In the morning the shouts were farther away. The smell of smoke still hung in the air. The sun was a pale disk behind a curtain of cloud. Malcolm rested and realized he was terribly thirsty. His instinct was to cry, but he did not. Instead he set out to find water, and the forest showed him where to look. There were shallow pools from the last rain, hollowed-out stumps that held enough to drink, and half-hidden streams that a man could miss if he did not stop to look.

Food was easier. Pine nuts were plentiful, and there were wild blackberries and grapes. The leaves and stalks of goosefoot and the fleshy green purslane were tough and chewy, but they gave him nourishment. Sometimes he ate things that cramped his stomach and doubled him up in pain, but soon he learned which foods to avoid and which gave him the strength to go on.

But where to go? Everything that he had known was behind him, burned. Destroyed. Gone. He had no destination. The days passed. And the nights. He stopped counting. Sometimes Malcolm could hear the men in the woods. They were still out there stalking him. And he could smell them. Smell the acrid sweat of the hunter. The men were clumsy in the woods, and slow moving compared to the boy. Still, he could not risk discovery. The men had guns. Malcolm well remembered what the men had done to his village. To his people.

By night he moved, restlessly and without destination, sustained only by the conviction that he must keep moving. During the day, when he would be more easily seen by the searchers, he rested under a simple lean-to constructed of boughs. It was an aimless existence, and a gnawing ache grew in Malcolm's heart. Somewhere, he felt, there was a place for him, could he but find it.

The growing ache was not only in his heart. For the first time in his life Malcolm knew hunger. Real hunger. The edible plants he found in the forest—the berries, the roots, the bark stripped from tender saplings—these were enough to keep him alive, but he was never completely free from hunger. Hunger for meat. It was a pain that never left him. A pain that grew worse every day.

Then one morning in desperation he snatched at a squirrel that sat on a stump regarding him curiously. Malcolm was surprised at the ease with which he had caught the little creature. He killed it quickly, tore away the fur as best he could with his hands, and devoured it. He ripped the raw flesh from the tiny bones with his teeth. The meat was rank and tough, but it was better than bark.

Soon Malcolm discovered he was quick enough to run down and catch other small animals with his hands. Opossums, raccoons, once even a small deer. The streams were not deep enough to provide fish, but there were frogs to be taken. Malcolm's muscles grew lean and hard in his hunting exertions, his teeth white, his jaw strong enough to crack a bone.

There was no question of making a fire to cook the meat once he had caught it. Malcolm carried no matches, and a fire would surely attract the men. At first he had to force himself to gag down the raw meat, still warm from the living blood, but he learned. Before long, to his surprise, he liked it best that way.

The days stretched out, one indistinguishable from the next. During the nights he continued his aimless travels. Once he circled back to where the village of Drago had been. Nothing was left but ashes. Everything gone. Everyone dead. Malcolm never went back again.

And yet Malcolm sensed he was not alone. They were out there somewhere, others of his kind, running and hiding just as he was. He longed to find them, join them, but he did not know how. Sometimes in the night he could hear the howling. And he cried.

The nights grew colder. During the days it rained often. Malcolm learned to make a more sturdy shelter of evergreen boughs, overlapping them so the needles pointed downward and formed a runoff for the rainwater. He sat cramped for long, cold hours in his shelters, hugging his knees and shivering.

There were fewer men in the forest hunting him now. The danger was not as great, but it was still there. As the scent of the men grew fainter, Malcolm grew careless.

His misstep came on a stormy evening as he searched along the trail for the makings of a shelter. He was hurrying, hunched against the rain. Still, had Malcolm been alert as he normally was, it would never have happened. Before him on the trail was a patch of ground covered with leaves. He should have seen that the leaves lay in an unnatural pattern. But this time he did not look before he stepped.

For a moment he did not know what had happened to him. There was a frightful crunching sound and searing pain shot up through his right leg. He fell heavily to the ground. The pain tore at him like fiery claws. On sheer instinct he tried to scramble to his feet, but the leg would not bear his weight. And something was holding it. Something heavy.

When he looked down, there below the tattered end of his pant leg he saw the steel jaws gripping his ankle. The flesh of his lower leg was shredded, and pinkish-white shards of bone jabbed out through skin. Blood seeped into the cracked leather of his shoe. He tried to move his foot. The grinding sound was almost worse than the new flash of pain. He fainted.

The night was an endless agony with long, dark periods of tortured dreams and stretches of consciousness during which he tried to rip his foot free of the steel trap. Clouds rolled down from the mountains and opened in great torrents of icy rain. Thunder boomed and echoed in the hills. Lightning streaked the sky where it was visible through the treetops.

Malcolm thrashed about on the ground in delirium. While his mind whirled, strange things happened to his body. Once he brought his hands to his face and in a blaze of lightning he saw the pads and claws of an animal. Or did he dream that? Reality blurred as the pain took possession of him.

The storm thundered and crashed through the night, then faded. The dawn was bleak and damp. A steady rain continued to fall. Malcolm awoke slowly in a fever, and for an instant he did not know where he was nor how he had come there. He should be in a warm bed, not out freezing in the forest. Then the pain hit him again, clearing his mind, and the memory of the terrible night came back. He shifted his position and the steel jaws ripped his flesh. The trap. He remembered the trap. But he forgot everything else when he looked up and saw the giant.

Well, maybe not a giant, but a big, big man. From Malcolm's point of view, lying there on the trail, the man loomed like a mountain. The wild beard and the hair that hung to his shoulders were a dark, fierce shade of red. One of his hands could have covered both of the boy's. His chest and shoulders were massive as granite. He wore tough, ragged jeans and a buckskin jacket. Even through his pain Malcolm felt fear, sensing the immense power in the big man's body. Then he saw the giant's eyes. They were brown and bright and immeasurably kind.

The giant knelt beside him. Malcolm saw the brown eyes narrow with reflected pain when he looked at the ruined ankle. When Malcolm tried to sit up, the giant pressed a strong, gentle hand on his forehead and eased him back down.

"You sure got yourself into a fix, son." The bass voice rumbled up from the deep caverns of the giant's chest. "You'd best lie still while I have a look."

He moved with uncommon grace for a man of his great size. He was careful to shield the ankle from Malcolm's eyes with his body as he examined it.

"Son of a bitch," the big man rumbled. "Steel teeth, double spring. These mothers are illegal."

Malcolm winced as the big man's hand touched his foot. "Easy, pardner. I know it hurts, but the first thing we've got to do is get this thing off you. It's going to hurt even more in a minute when I pry it loose, but there's no easy way to do it." He turned his head and the kind brown eyes looked down into Malcolm's. "How about it? Can you stand a little more hurt right now?"

Malcolm nodded.

"Good boy. Close your eyes for a minute. Close 'em real tight. Think about the happiest time you ever had."

Malcolm closed his eyes. He tried very hard to think of a happy time, as the big man had told him. But no thoughts would come. Only a blackness with fire and screams of the dying.

There was a loud metallic crack and another fiery shot of pain in his ankle. Malcolm's eyes snapped open. The big man knelt beside him now, holding the cruel steel trap in both hands.

"This is what grabbed you, son," he said. "Damned foul contraption." Then, as the muscles in his arms and shoulders bulged, he twisted the trap like the jaws of a shark until the end of a spring popped loose with a loud twang. He tossed the broken trap into the brush and returned his attention to the boy.

"You okay?"

Malcolm nodded, blinking back the tears. He was afraid to trust his voice, not wanting to show weakness before the big man.

"Ready to take a walk?"

Malcolm looked down helplessly at the mangled ankle. It was free now of the steel jaws, but the torn flesh had turned a puffy blue-black shade. The foot pointed down and back at an impossible angle.

The big man again shifted his body to cut off Malcolm's view of the ruined ankle. "Oh, I'll do the walking," he said. "It's going to jostle you a little bit, but we've got to get you out of here." He slipped his powerful arms beneath the boy and scooped him up as easily as though he'd been stuffed with feathers. The big man rose effortlessly to his feet and started along the trail.

"Feel like talking?" he said.

Malcolm tried, but the best he could do was a small whimpering sound.

"Don't blame you," said the man. "I'll do the talking, then. I'm accustomed to that. And you can listen. That'll be a rare treat for me. Have to talk to myself most of the time."

The big man strode easily through the brush, carrying Malcolm in such a way as to minimize movement of his ruined ankle. The rhythm of the man's pace lulled the boy into a semidoze. When he spoke, the big man's rumbling voice was comforting.

"My name is Jones," he said. "There used to be more to it, but I figure that doesn't matter, seeing as I'm the only one living out here, and not likely to be confused with anybody else. The folks in town know who Jones is. The crazy hermit, some say. The last of the hippies. Nature Boy. I couldn't care less what they call me, just so they leave me alone. And they do. I've been living out here almost twenty years. Never have trouble with people. If you never see them, you can't have trouble with them."

They continued for several minutes in silence before Jones spoke again. "Well, I do see a few people now and again. Hikers. Bird watchers. Lost kids sometimes. Hunters I have nothing to do with. When the animals start shooting back, then maybe I'll talk to hunters. Mostly I meet youngsters out backpacking. They remind me a little of myself back in the sixties. They're not as serious about things as my generation, maybe. More interested in getting a good job than banning the bomb, but I guess you can't blame them. It was a lot easier to get angry about a war if they were liable to draft you to go fight it.

"But there's nothing wrong with today's kids. Different values, that's all. Hell, most of the kids I went on protest marches with are working for IBM now, or somebody like that. Not Jones. I'm forty years old, ought to know better, but I still believe that if the world's going to be made better, it won't be the big corporations that do it. That's why they call me the crazy hermit."

Jones shouldered his way through a dense growth of scrub pine, and suddenly they were in a clearing. There was a neatly tended patch of grass, dotted with wildflowers. A smooth dirt path lead to a solid little cabin of rough logs. A wisp of blue smoke trailed from the chimney. A homey touch was added by soft curtains at the window.

"Be it ever so humble," Jones said, "this is it. There was a girl with me a few years back. Woman, I should say. She's responsible for the curtains. And the flowers. Used to be more of them, but I'm not so great at flower gardening. Veggies yes, flowers no. Her name was Beverly. Blond hair, the longest legs you ever saw.

Dedicated, too. Peace Corps. Save the whales. All that. Beverly thought she wanted to try the natural life. I was glad to oblige."

"What happened to her?" Malcolm's voice was weak and quavery. He had not used it in a long time.

"She moved out." Jones answered casually, as though they had been enjoying a two-way conversation all along.

"Turned out the natural life wasn't quite what she thought it would be. The rain got to her, for one thing. She was a San Diego girl. Never in her life saw it rain more than two days running. Up here sometimes it'll rain for a month, more or less. Doesn't bother me, but Beverly about went crazy. Then there was the baby."

"You had a baby?"

"We did. Little boy. Beverly wanted to name him Star Child, but I wouldn't go for that. I'm not that spacey. Held out for John. Honest name. Solid. Biblical, if you're into that. He'd be a couple years younger than you now. You got a name?"

"I…" Malcolm's mind was suddenly empty, as though sucked clean by a giant vacuum. He was frightened. "I don't know."

"Doesn't matter. With only the two of us, there won't be any confusion about who I'm talking to. Back in town they'll want to know, but maybe you'll remember by then."

Jones carried the boy across the clearing to the door of the cabin. He pushed it open with his foot. Inside there were rough-hewn, comfortable-looking chairs, a table rescued from some thrift shop, sanded down and painted apple green, and a pair of army-style cots with stretched canvas on wooden frames. There was a cast-iron sink with a hand pump for water. On one wall was a stone fireplace with a great iron kettle simmering over the coals of a log fire. Whatever was in the kettle smelled wonderful.

"Beverly hadn't considered that living natural was going to mean no disposable diapers for John. No television to keep him occupied. No baby-sitter. She had to go all the way into Pinyon for the obstetrician. One day she just took him and left. Can't blame her. At least I did the kid one favor. I saved him from a life of being called Star Child."

Jones carried Malcolm into the cabin and kicked the door shut behind him. It was warm inside. The aroma from the simmering kettle wrapped around them.

"Stew," Jones said. "Turnips, zucchini, tomatoes, wild onion, plantain. Care to try some?"

Malcolm bobbed his head, then winced in sudden pain.

"First we'd better see what we can do about that ankle. I'll clean it up for you now. By tomorrow morning this rain will stop and we'll hike into Pinyon and get it fixed up properly."

Jones eased the boy down onto one of the cots. He brought over a basin of water and a soft cloth. Very gently he sponged the wounded ankle, keeping up a running chatter about nothing in particular.

He held the boy's leg in his strong, gentle hands and studied the torn flesh. "Looks like you've got a little infection going there," he said. "I'm going to put some stuff on it now that will sting a little. I boil it dawn from pine bark and a few other things. It'll clean out the infection fast. Better than iodine for sure."

From a shelf over the sink Jones took down a tightly corked bottle. He poured out a thick brown liquid onto a wadded cloth. The concoction smelled of pitch. He sponged it generously on the boy's wounded ankle. And it did sting like fury, but Malcolm never let on that it hurt.

"That ought to get it," Jones said. He wrapped a length of clean white cloth around Malcolm's ankle and foot. He ripped one end to make long strips and tied them in a knot.

"Too tight?"

Malcolm shook his head.

"Okay. Now how about some stew?"

"I am pretty hungry."

"I'll bet you are."

Jones served up the hot stew in wooden bowls along with chunks of coarse bread. To drink there was a steaming, bitter herb tea. Malcolm ate until he could hold no more. The tea, once it was down, warmed him and made him drowsy. The big man helped him ease his shattered ankle up onto the cot and brought a fresh khaki blanket to cover him.

"Get some sleep now, son. We've got to be up early tomorrow."

The pain in Malcolm's foot eased and gradually drained away. He relaxed, enjoying the feeling of a full belly for the first time in many days. The warmth of the cabin and the deep shadows from the dying fire, the soft splash of rain above him on the roof, all combined to lull the boy into a long, deep, untroubled sleep.

6

For long hours after the boy had fallen asleep Jones sat in one of the chairs in the cabin and watched the dying coals. The chair of wood and woven reeds creaked and settled comfortably under his weight. Outside the rainfall softened. It would be clear in the morning. Jones frowned, thinking about the boy he had found in the trap.

In the years he had spent alone in the woods he had brushed the lives of many people with many different backgrounds. This boy was not like the others. Something strange about him. Despite the boy's reticence, Jones could sense a danger that lurked somewhere deep inside him. Something to be feared. Something not quite natural.

The big man dug out an old corncob pipe, stuck it in his mouth unlit, and chewed meditatively on the stem. He had not smoked anything since his teenage years, but it calmed him to chew on the old pipe. It helped him sort out his thoughts.

Tragic fact: the boy's foot was destroyed. No doctor living could save it. When he awoke Jones would give him another draft of the herb tea to keep him drowsy during the long trip they had to make into Pinyon. Jones was not worried about carrying the boy that far. He was confident of his own strength. But a certain amount of jostling would be unavoidable. His strength could not ease the boy's pain.

The kid had been exceedingly brave so far, but he was probably still in partial shock. When he fully realized the damage to his body, he would need a friend close by.

Jones' eyes narrowed and his great shoulders bunched as he thought of the men who had set the deadly trap. He had not struck another human being in anger for more years than he could recall, but at that moment Jones would have happily ripped the trappers' limbs from their bodies.

The boy stirred in his sleep and mumbled something unintelligible. Jones got up and walked over to the cot. He laid his big hand on the boy's forehead. There was a fever, but less than it had been. Jones pulled the blanket up snug around the boy's shoulders and walked back to his chair.

The presence of the boy in his cabin brought back thoughts to Jones of his own son. Sometimes, not often, the big man let himself think about John. What he would look like now. What kind of a young man he would become.

John would now be, let's see, going on fourteen. That would put him in high school. Jesus, it was hard to think of that tiny, helpless human as a gawky teenager. Probably the boy would be living with his mother in some comfortable California suburb, if Jones correctly read the direction Beverly was going. He would have an upwardly mobile stepfather who wore a three-piece suit to work and fired up the backyard barbecue on weekends. Well, what was wrong with that? What if John had stayed here? What kind of a life would he have had with a ragged hermit for a father, living in the woods?

"A damn good life, that's what," Jones muttered aloud. As he had many times in the past, Jones regretted that he had not fought to keep his son. Probably he would have lost, but at least he would have tried. He grunted and bit down hard on the pipestem, consigning the doubts to their place in the closed off attic of his mind.

He got up again and laid a big chunk of fir on the coals. In a moment little flames licked tentatively up the bark. The log was still moist, and it would burn slowly. It would probably last till morning. Jones went back to his chair and sat down, listening to the sizzle and pop as the fire probed at the pitch pockets in the log. He closed his eyes and let himself dream.

As always, his dreams were of Beverly. In his heart he had known from the start that she was not for him. Living off the land had sounded to her like an adventure. Like the six months she spent in the Peace Corps, teaching the Tanzanians things they had no desire to know. She never really saw it as a true lifestyle.

She was happy enough in the commune, where there were other people around to sing folk songs with while they held hands in a big circle around a campfire. Having a shopping center with a big Safeway nearby didn't hurt, either. Jones tried it for a while, but that scene was not for him. Living in one of those hippie communes was like using somebody else's bathwater.

Then as now, Jones was his own man. He did not join movements or march for causes because it was trendy. He did it because he believed. And if he stopped believing, he stopped marching. Why lock yourself into something that no longer made sense?

Beverly, now, she had grabbed on to every hip liberal cause that came around. But if her beliefs did not run as deep as his, Jones didn't give a damn. She was so achingly beautiful it still brought a lump to his throat. He had loved her blindly and uncritically from the moment he had seen her sitting naked under the sun, her shining yellow hair spread like a veil down over those wonderful breasts.

Sexually, she had been everything a man could ask. Something out of an adolescent's erotic dreams. She knew instinctively where he wanted to be touched and how. She could carry him to dizzying heights of desire, then, when he thought he must surely lose his mind, she would bring on his climax, prolonging it to a point where he lay drained, spent, helpless, and happier than a man should be.

Maybe once a month now Jones would go down to the bars around Saugus and Newhall and find a willing woman. There were always a few strays hanging around the bars. He stayed away from Pinyon. Too many people knew him there. He did not want a relationship; he wanted sex. And that was what the women he met in the bars provided. But even in those momentary bursts of passion he could never stop thinking of Beverly. Most of the time he figured it was just too much trouble to hike all the way to Saugus. Then he let his right hand be his woman.

Gradually his massive head fell forward, cushioned by the mat of red beard, and the giant slept.

He awoke at dawn, startled with the sense that something was not as it should be. Instantly he was on his feet. His eyes darted around the gloomy interior of the cabin until he spied the blanket-covered form on one of the cots. Then he remembered. The boy.

While Jones watched, the boy stirred as though he could feel eyes upon him. He came fully awake all at once, like an animal sensing danger. From the boy's expression, Jones thought for a moment he would try to run out the door.

"Hey, easy, son. It's me, Jones, remember? You're safe here."

For the first time since he had found the boy in the trap Jones saw the semblance of a smile on the young face. Thin, and not firmly in place, but undeniably a smile.

"I forgot where I was," the boy said.

"Can't blame you. I wake up the same place damn near every morning, and I still forget sometimes."

The boy started to sit up. Jones said, "You'd better not move around too much with that ankle."

The boy looked down at the hump where the blanket covered his right foot. "Ankle?"

"Don't tell me you forgot about that, too! Maybe it's just as well. At least you got some sleep."

"Was my ankle hurt?"

"I'm afraid it was. Hurt pretty bad. I'd better have a look at it."

While the boy watched curiously, Jones peeled back the blanket, exposing the foot, still tightly wrapped in the bandage he had fashioned. Very gently the big man untied the torn strips and unwound the clean white cloth.

"Holy shit!"

"What's the matter?" The boy struggled to sit up while Jones held his right foot up off the cot, examining it.

"I don't believe what I'm seeing."

He had expected the swollen and discolored skin, torn by the steel teeth, the shattered bits of bone, snapped tendons, ligaments, blood, pus. What he saw was fresh, unbroken skin on a foot that moved this way and that with no apparent discomfort to the boy. The only sign of his terrible wound was a faint patch of shiny pink scar tissue where the trap had bitten through the flesh.

"I flat don't believe it," Jones said again.

The boy sat up, bracing himself with his hands, and looked curiously from his foot to the face of the big man.

"Doesn't it hurt?" Jones said.

The boy shook his head.

"Not at all?"

"Nope."

"Can you stand on it?"

Still handling the foot gingerly, Jones put it back on the canvas of the cot. The boy swung his feet out to the wooden floor and stood up. He took several steps away from Jones, then back. He jumped up and down. He did a little impromptu dance step.

"Well, I'll be damned."

"Feels fine," the boy said.

Jones sat on the edge of the cot, staring down at the boy's feet. "Either you are the fastest-healing son of a gun the world has ever seen, or we've just witnessed a miracle."

"Maybe it wasn't hurt as bad as you thought."

Oh, yes, it was hurt all right, Jones thought. Nothing in the world of medicine was going to save that leg much below the knee. He was not likely to make a mistake like that. He opened his mouth to say as much, then saw the strangely pleading look on the boy's face. The boy did not want to hear just now that there was something very strange about him.

"Maybe you're right," Jones said. "Anyway, you appear to be in fine shape this morning. You ought to be able to walk into Pinyon with me. Save me a load."

The boy looked up. "Do we have to go?"

"Course we do. Somebody's going to be looking for you."

"I doubt it."

"Sure they will. You've got folks, haven't you?"

"I-I don't remember."

"Well, they'll remember. And they'll be damn worried about you."

"I could stay here with you."

"No way. That's all I'd need is to have a big-ass search party come crashing in here and find me with a runaway boy. So far the local people haven't called me a kidnapper or a pervert, but all they'd need is something to put the thought in their heads. I'm taking you back, boy, and that's final."

The boy was silent for a moment. Then he said, "Does it have to be today?"

"Well..." And immediately Jones cursed himself for weakening. The boy's face lit up with a smile, a real one this time.

"I don't eat much, Jones. And I can help around here. I can cut firewood. I can help with your garden. You've got a leak right over the door. I'll bet I could fix that."

"I could fix it myself if it bothered me that much," Jones said grumpily.

The boy looked at him sideways. "My foot's still a little tender."

Jones ran his fingers through his wiry red beard. "Well, I suppose it wouldn't hurt to give it a day's rest."

The boy's happiness was so obvious that Jones was embarrassed and turned away. What kind of life must this kid have been living to want so much to stay in a broken-down forest cabin with a burnt-out hermit?

"But tomorrow, bright and early, rain or shine, we head for Pinyon, hear?"

"Whatever you say, Jones." The boy sat on the bed and began happily lacing the blood-caked shoe onto the foot that by all rights should have been a mangled stump.

"Tomorrow," Jones repeated in his deepest no-nonsense voice. "Tomorrow we hike."

It was four days before they started for Pinyon. During that time the boy had not only repaired the stubborn leak over the door that had plagued Jones for a year; he had cleaned out the weeds from what remained of Beverly's flower gardens and helped Jones straighten up his vegetable plot. He had chopped and stacked a month's worth of firewood and brought back pails of wild blackberries and pine nuts from the nearby woods.

More than all that, he gave Jones somebody to talk to. The big man had forgotten how good was the sound of another human voice. Even better, another ear to listen, for in fact the boy talked very little, while Jones almost never stopped. Jones talked about how it was living off the land. He talked about his own memories as a boy. He talked about the turbulent time of his young manhood. He talked about Beverly. And he talked about John.

The boy listened. He listened, and whether he fully understood or not, he nodded at the right places, asked the right questions, and agreed when it was important to agree. He still claimed to have no memory of his own past, and Jones did not press him. If it was true, there was nothing Jones could do about it, and if the boy was concealing something, that was none of Jones's business.

On the morning of the fifth day, Jones was wearing his heavy boots and buckling up his backpack when the boy awoke. When the boy started to speak the big man held up a massive hand to silence him.

"Before you say a word, forget it. Today's the day."

"Aw, Jones…"

"No. I set out a pair of boots there that might fit you if you put on three or four pairs of socks. Don't worry. I've got plenty. You wash up and I'll get some breakfast going." They ate hot biscuits with butter and blackberry jam and washed them down with some of Jones's powerful coffee. The boy made no more protests, but as they left the cabin and were halfway across the clearing he stopped to look back.

"It was a good time, Jones."

The big man waited until the boy was ready, then they turned and walked together into the heavy forest. "Yes," he said. "It was a good time."

* * *

Abe Craddock and Curly Vane were mad as hell. They had caught something in their trap almost a week ago and some son of a bitch had let it out. No animal would ever get itself out of one of those traps. It could very well have been one of those things from Drago. There were still a few of them in the woods. They had heard the howling.

What made it even worse, whoever had freed the animal had deliberately ruined the trap. Those babies didn't come cheap. You couldn't get them at a regular sporting goods store. So as they tramped through the woods for the fifth straight day of looking for the trap robber, Craddock and Vane were mad as hell.

Moreover, they were drunk. Each of them had put away enough Jim Beam to knock out a normal man. But Craddock and Vane were experienced drinkers. Over the years they had built up a tolerance for the stuff as they tore up their livers.

Abe Craddock was a beefy man with a perpetually red face and an ass that stretched the seat of his jeans. Curly Vane was thinner, less talkative, and if anything, meaner than his companion. The two of them, when they got to drinking, were as welcome around La Reina County as the Mexican fruit fly.

It was Curly who heard the sounds in the woods off to their left. He held up a hand to warn Craddock, and the two of them stood there holding their breath, listening.

Something was definitely moving through the brush. Something big.

"Bear?" Craddock said in a hoarse whisper.

"Maybe." Both men brought their guns up to ready.

Curly Vane carried a heavy old Winchester deer rifle that could put a copper-jacketed slug through a brick wall. Craddock, whose marksmanship was poor, favored a twelve-gauge shotgun that he loaded with 00 buckshot. Anything he came close to with that cannon was as good as dead.

They waited. The sound of their own heavy breathing muffled the noise of whatever was approaching through the brush. They had never encountered anything bigger or more dangerous than a deer in these woods. Whatever was coming toward them now, they convinced themselves, was no deer.

The brush parted twenty yards away with a suddenness that made both men jump. A fierce, hairy head rose above the low chaparral and glared.

"Bear!" shouted Craddock.

Curly Vane squeezed off three shots.

Craddock's shotgun thundered.

The rifle slugs pounded into Jones's chest like three rapid hammer blows. For a second all he felt was the impact, then came the pain as the cold air hit the tunnels the bullets had bored into his lungs. He roared and started for the hunters. His only thought through the pain was to get his hands on the rotten bastards. Then the load of Craddock's buckshot blew away most of his head, and Jones's pain was over.

"Oh, fuck me, it was a man!" Curly moaned.

"What'd you shoot for?" Craddock said. "I wouldn't of shot if you didn't."

"Shut up, you stupid fuck. We got to get out of here." Craddock seized him by the arm. "Hold it! There's another one."

"Oooh, shit!"

They turned back and saw that there was, sure enough, a companion with the man they had killed. More of a boy than a man. He knelt over the bloody remains of the big man, sobbing. Then he raised his head and looked straight at Craddock and Vane. Curly Vane brought up the Winchester.

"What are you doing?" Craddock said.

"We've got to kill him, you dumb fuck. He seen us."

Vane's rifle cracked. A branch snapped off inches from the boy's face. For one frozen instant the boy stared at the hunters. His lips spread in a snarl unlike anything the men had seen on a human face. Then he was up and running.

Curly fired again, but the boy was already lost in the brush. They could hear his feet pounding the carpet of fir needles. He was fast.

"Come on," Curly urged. "We've got to catch him."

The two hunters crashed through the brush, heedless of the branches that whipped their faces and tore at their clothing. Ahead they caught glimpses of the fleeing boy. Their only thought was to kill.

* * *

There was yet another witness to the killing of Jones. After many weeks of searching out the scattered survivors of Drago, Derak, the leader, had finally found Malcolm. He saw him leave the cabin with the big man and start for the town. Derak had paced them silently, awaiting his chance to move in and take the boy. He knew of Jones and had no wish to harm the big man. But Malcolm had to be brought back to his own kind.

Then the other two had approached. The drunken men with their guns. The scent of them alone, their sweat, the whiskey on their breath, had been enough to start the change in Derak. He felt the bones shift and crack and reshape themselves under his skin. He stripped away the restraining clothes and dropped silently to all fours. His jaw worked silently as the teeth grew to their terrible length, strong, yellow, and sharp as knives.

Without warning the men had fired and Jones fell. Malcolm dropped beside him, and for a moment Derak thought the boy was going to go through the full change for the first time in his life. If it happened before he was prepared, it could be devastating. But the boy's body was not quite ready. He rose and fled.

The men fired at him and gave chase.

The ancient rage of his kind welled up in Derak. He flexed the powerful muscles under the thick coat of coarse fur and bounded after them.

The men were far too clumsy to elude him. Derak broke from the bushes with a roar and fell upon the one nearest to him, the one with the thin body and the head of tight black curls. He bore the man screaming to the forest floor and tore out his throat. The other threw down his useless gun and ran.

As his rage ebbed, Derak's hunger grew. He pushed his muzzle into the raw open flesh of the man's chest and fed.

7

Abe Craddock was a mess.

On his best days Abe Craddock did not look like anything a man would want to take home to dinner, but when Gavin Ramsay entered his office with young Milo Fernandez, Craddock was in worse shape than the sheriff had ever seen him.

He was sitting stiffly in one of the office chairs with both hands clamped around a Styrofoam cup of coffee. He tried with little success to hold the cup steady. Much of the coffee had spilled down the front of his denim jacket, adding to other stains that crusted the man's clothing.

Deputy Roy Nevins leaned against the far wall of the office, well away from Craddock, who smelled like a sewer. The fat deputy turned gratefully when the sheriff and Milo entered.

"Hi, Gavin," he said. "One of the lost sheep is found."

"So I see. Is he hurt?"

"Doesn't appear to be."

"Then what's the matter with him?"

"Damned if I know. He stumbled in here half an hour ago babbling about lions and tigers and bears, or some damn thing. I couldn't make heads or tails out of what he was saying, so I sent Milo down to the hospital to get you."

"Has Mrs. Craddock been notified?"

"Yep, I called right away. Betty Craddock says as far as she's concerned we can lock the so—" He glanced over at the shivering hunter. "Lock the guy up and throw away the key."

"Have we got anything to lock him up for?"

"Damned if I know. Defacing the local scenery, maybe."

"I'll talk to him," Gavin said. "You can go get some lunch if you want to."

"Thanks, but the smell of our friend here ruined my appetite. I wouldn't mind some fresh coffee, though." He nodded at the Styrofoam cup gripped by Craddock. "That was the last of the office pot."

"Go ahead," Gavin told him. "I'll give a yell if I need you."

"I'll be at the inn," Nevins said with obvious relief. He shrugged into a jacket and hurried out the door before the sheriff could change his mind.

"Is it all right if I stay?" Milo asked.

"Sure. I need a second officer here for interrogation anyway."

Abe Craddock swiveled his head toward Gavin. Fear glittered in his small, red-rimmed eyes. "Interrogation?" he croaked.

"That means I want to ask you some questions, Abe."

"I t-told the fat guy everything."

"Sometimes Roy doesn't get all the details straight," Gavin said in a soothing tone. "You don't mind telling me again, do you?"

"I-I guess not." Craddock carried the cup to his mouth and sipped noisily. A brown trickle ran down his unshaven chin. He wiped it away negligently with the back of a scabbed hand.

Gavin walked over and perched with one buttock on his desk. The sour smell of Abe Craddock was sharp in his nostrils.

"Okay, Abe, any time you're ready."

"It was a bear," Craddock said. His eyes darted nervously about the room. "We shot a bear."

"You said 'we'?"

"Yeah."

"Is that you and Curly Vane?"

A spasm shook Abe Craddock, spilling most of the coffee left in the cup. "Yeah. Me and Curly. We was out together. Hunting. It was a bear."

"You are telling me that you and Curly Vane saw a bear?"

"Shot it. Shot at it."

"Right up here in our own Tehachapi Mountains?"

"Yeah. Bear." The big man in the chair seemed to try to pull his head down into his shoulders.

Ramsay took a kitchen match from his shirt pocket and stuck the end of it between his teeth. He did that sometimes when he wanted to look rustic and relaxed. He also did it to keep himself from losing his temper and yelling at a citizen.

"Abe," he said very quietly, "there has not been a bear reported in La Reina County or anywhere within a hundred miles of here since the 1930s." Ramsay had no idea if his figures were correct, but they were close enough to make the point of what he thought of Abe Craddock's bear sighting.

"It was a bear," Craddock insisted. "A big one."

"Where's Curly, Abe?"

The sudden question seemed to jolt the big man, as it was supposed to.

"It... it got him."

"The bear got Curly?" Ramsay fought down his rising impatience.

"Not the bear. Worse."

Craddock began to shake. He raised the Styrofoam cup and swallowed the dregs of the coffee, gagging as he did so. Ramsay moved over and took the cup from his hand. He shook the few remaining drops of coffee into the metal trashcan.

To Milo Fernandez he said, "Get me Roy's office bottle."

The young officer looked doubtful. "Gee, Sheriff, I don't—"

"It's in the center drawer of his desk. Behind the Mexican travel brochures."

Milo sat down and pulled open the desk drawer with obvious reluctance.

"Don't worry," Ramsay told him. "I know it's there and Roy knows I know. I don't give a damn if he has an occasional shooter. Right now I'm appropriating the bottle for official use."

Milo pulled out a bottle of Seagram's Seven Crown and handed it to Ramsay. The sheriff poured a generous slug into the coffee cup and gave it back to Abe Craddock.

"Here, Abe, this will do you more good than coffee. Steady you down."

Craddock seized the cup and drank greedily, swallowing the entire contents in two gulps. He held out the cup for more.

"That's enough for now, Abe. We don't want you to get too steady. Now do you want to tell me once more about you and Curly and this... bear?"

Craddock slumped in the chair. The shaking in his hands lessened as the whiskey took hold. He spoke in a hoarse monotone. "It looked like a bear. We thought it was a bear. No shit."

"And you shot at it."

"Curly did."

"He was the only one who fired?"

"Well, I guess I did, too."

"Did you hit it? The... bear?"

Craddock's head dropped. He frowned down at his hands as though they had betrayed him. In a voice barely audible he said, "We hit it."

"It wasn't a bear, was it, Abe?"

"No." The words were wrenched out of him. "It was a man." He looked up beseechingly at Ramsay. "It looked like a bear, though. Anybody would of thought so. All hairy the way he was, and he jumped up so fast. How was we to know?"

Ramsay drew a deep sigh and walked back over to sit on the edge of his desk again. It was Milo Fernandez who finally broke the silence.

"Is it the guy over in the hospital freezer?"

Ramsay nodded. "I picked up the pathologist's report this morning. Three thirty-oh-six slugs in the chest, face blown away by a shotgun blast. Nibbled on by small animals." From the corner of his eye he saw Abe Craddock flinch. "Name's Jones. Kind of a local character. Been living up in the woods since before I got here. Came to town once in a while to do odd jobs. Harmless. Kind of likable, matter of fact."

"We didn't know it was no man." Craddock's voice took on an unpleasant whine.

Ramsay turned back and gave him a hard look. "Tell me about Curly Vane."

Craddock began to tremble again. "Something got him."

"Not another bear?"

"No." Craddock shook his head emphatically. "It was real. Like a wolf, kind of."

"Come off it, Abe," Ramsay said. "I didn't buy your bear, and I sure as hell don't buy your wolf. What happened to Curly? Did you shoot him, too?"

"No, Gavin, I swear to God!" Craddock braced his hands on the arms of the chair and strained forward. "It was like a wolf, but it wasn't a wolf. Bigger. Bigger than a man, even. And it kind of... stood up." His voice faded, as though he knew his words lacked conviction.

"What did you do then? Did you try to help him?"

"There wasn't nobody could help Curly when this thing hit him."

In spite of himself, Ramsay felt a chill between his shoulder blades. "Do you have any idea what it was, Abe?"

Craddock nodded, his eyes shifting toward the door. "It was one of them things from up at Drago. Some of them got away, you know."

"Give it a name, Abe."

"All right, damn it, call me crazy if you want to. It was a werewolf."

For half a dozen ticks there was dead silence. Then Ramsay said, "Keep an eye on the office, Milo. Abe and I are going for a ride."

* * *

There were about two hours of daylight remaining when Gavin Ramsay brought Craddock to the spot where the two young hikers had stumbled across Jones's body. Although he paid little attention to the fantastic stories about Drago, the sheriff had no desire to be caught in these woods after nightfall.

He gestured at the patch of ground where they stood. There were dark stains visible on the carpet of fir needles.

"This is where we found him, Abe," Ramsay said. "Remember the spot?"

Craddock looked at the ground, then quickly away. "Yeah. You can see the bush here where he kind of reared up. We had no way of knowin' if it was a man or what."

"So you blasted away."

"Honest, Gavin, I'm tryin' to tell you how it happened."

"Okay, okay. After you shot and he fell, what did you do?"

"Then we saw the other one and we—"

"The other one?" Ramsay snapped.

"Oh, yeah, didn't I say?"

"No, Abe, you didn't."

"Well, when we came closer we seen there was another guy. Smaller. Like a kid, maybe."

"A kid," Gavin repeated.

"Yeah. Well, he saw us coming and he took off running. We went after him."

"Why, Abe?"

"Well, we, uh, thought he'd be scared and might hurt himself or something."

"You weren't going to shoot him, too, were you, Abe?"

"Jesus, Gavin, shooting the hermit was an accident. What do you think I am?"

I know damn well what you are, Ramsay thought; I know what Curly Vane is, too. Or was, as the case may be. He said, "Which way did you go?"

Craddock looked around, seeming to sniff the air. He was on surer ground now. He pointed off at an angle. "That way. The kid left the trail and took off through the brush. Curly and me went after him."

"Show me."

"I am showin' you." Craddock jabbed with his forefinger. "Off that way."

"Let's go."

"You don't want to go in there, Gavin."

The muscles tightened around Ramsay's jaw. "I said let's go. I'm not playing games with you, Abe."

Craddock met the sheriff's hard gaze for a moment, then turned and led the way through the brush in the direction he had pointed.

"I want you to show me where this 'wolf' or whatever it was jumped Curly," Ramsay said.

Some fifty yards into the brush Craddock stopped. He pointed. "It was up there at the base of that leaning fir tree. I was just about here when it hit him. He never had a chance. Nobody would of had a chance with that thing."

Ramsay walked in careful steps to the tree Craddock had pointed out. He hunkered down at the base of the trunk and examined the ground. The dead needles were stained dark and crusted. He pulled out one of the plastic Ziploc bags he had brought from the office and carefully scraped a few of the needles into it. There was also a whitish powder and bits of what might have been bone. Ramsay took some of that too.

A flash of color beyond the tree caught his eye. He walked over and prodded the brush aside with his foot. A bright red cap with a Budweiser logo on the front lay there upside down. There were shredded bits of a jacket, tough denim pants, a boot, part of another boot. All of it was stiff and black with clotted blood.

Ramsay turned and beckoned. "Come here, Abe."

Craddock approached reluctantly, taking care not to step where the ground was stained dark.

"Recognize these?" Ramsay said.

"Oh, shit." Craddock turned away. He clapped a hand to his mouth too late. The coffee and whiskey he had taken in sputtered out between his fingers. He bent over and retched until nothing more would come.

Ramsay stood quietly and waited for him to finish.

Finally Craddock stood up. His normally ruddy face was pale and bloodless. He nodded. "That's Curly's hat. The other stuff, that's his too, as best as I can tell."

Ramsay scanned the area. "It sort of looks like that's all that's left of him."

From off toward the mountains came a sound that froze the two men where they stood. A long, wild, ululating howl.

In the sudden deeper silence that followed, Abe Craddock turned a stricken face to Ramsay.

"Sheriff, do whatever you got to do to me, but in the name of God, let's get the fuck out of here."

Ramsay hesitated only a moment, then he nodded and they started back toward the trail.

8

"I am going to count up to five, Malcolm," said Holly Lang. "At the count of one you will begin to awaken. When I reach five you will be wide awake, and you will feel rested and refreshed."

The boy sat propped comfortably in the hospital bed. His eyes were closed, the lashes moist and dark against his pale skin. He smiled gently and nodded.

"You will remember everything you have told me," Holly continued, "and you will not be frightened. I am going to begin now. One. You are beginning to wake up."

The boy on the bed stirred. His slim fingers flexed, testing the texture of the hospital blanket.

"Two. You are feeling good, feeling rested, a little more awake now."

The boy sighed. A soft, contented sound from his chest. "Three. Waking up now, feeling refreshed and rested." His eyelids fluttered. His lips parted slightly. "Four. You can open your eyes now, Malcolm, and look around if you want to. You can hear the birds outside in the trees, feel the breeze coming through the window."

The boy opened his eyes. He blinked. His eyes moved comfortably about the room, settling on Holly.

"Five. Wide awake now. Wide awake and feeling fine." Holly smiled at the boy. "Hi, Malcolm."

The boy pulled in a deep breath, stretched his arms, and returned the smile. "Hi, Holly."

"That was pretty easy, wasn't it?" she said.

"I didn't really go to sleep, you know."

"I told you it wasn't like that. None of this trance stuff. That's only in comic books."

"I knew what was happening all the time. I could hear you asking me questions, and I felt myself answer you. It was just that all of a sudden I could… remember." A shadow crossed the boy's face.

"And now you remember everything that you told me, don't you?"

"Yes. I remember the fire. And living in the woods. Running, always running, because men were trying to catch me. I remember the trap. And… oh, I remember

Jones." Malcolm stopped, a look of pain on his face.

"It's all right, Malcolm," Holly said gently.

"He's dead, isn't he?" the boy said.

"I don't know that for sure."

The boy nodded. "He's dead. Jones was the best person I ever knew. And they killed him. Those two men. But I told you all about that, didn't I?"

"Talk about it all you want to," Holly said. "Sometimes talking helps take away the hurt."

"They killed him. With guns."

Holly watched closely as the boy's gaze drifted off somewhere beyond the walls of the hospital room. She leaned forward in the chair where she sat beside the bed. Was there a change in the color of his eyes? Or was it a trick of the late afternoon sun slanting in through the window?

"Something happened after that and I can't remember. Did I tell you what it was?"

Holly shook her head silently. There were still empty patches in his memory that the hypnosis had not penetrated. She did not want to break into the boy's train of thought now. He did look different. She was sure of it. The shadows were deeper under his cheekbones. And there was something strange about his nose and his upper lip.

"I don't know why the men didn't kill me, too," Malcolm went on. His voice had grown deeper and had a rasp to it.

His throat must be dry from all the talking, Holly told herself. But his eyebrows… weren't they heavier now than a moment ago? And she did not remember them growing all the way across the bridge of his nose.

"The next thing I remember I was running again. I didn't know if the men were chasing me or not. I just knew I had to get away. I was afraid again, only this time it was even worse than before. It was worse because Jones was dead. He was my friend, and I lost him."

"It's all right to grieve for a friend," Holly said softly. "It hurts to lose someone, but at one time or another it must happen to all of us. There will be other friends."

Malcolm was silent for a minute. Then he spoke again. "I was so tired of running. When the other two men saw me, the ones who brought me here, I didn't try very hard to get away. I knew they were different from the first two, the ones who killed Jones."

"How did you know that, Malcolm?"

"I could tell by the way they smelled. You know you can smell it when somebody wants to kill you. Or when they're afraid of you."

Holly nodded. She knew the sweat glands emitted a different chemical under the stress of fear, but few humans were equipped with a sense of smell keen enough to recognize it.

"Excuse me, Malcolm," she said, standing up. "We don't need those curtains drawn anymore. Let's catch what we can of the last of the sunlight."

She spread the curtains all the way open, brightening the room with an orange glow from the setting sun. With a reluctance she could not explain, Holly turned to look at the boy in the bed.

He smiled at her. Just a normal, somewhat thin fourteen-year-old boy. His eyes were a warm green. There were no unusual shadows under the cheekbones.

Straight nose, well-formed upper lip. Rather fine, arched eyebrows. Nothing strange here at all. As she had thought, it was a trick of the lighting.

"The funny thing is," Malcolm said, "it seems like only a few minutes ago you were going to hypnotize me. But that was morning, and now the sun's going down."

"Sometimes hypnotism plays tricks with time," Holly said. "A few seconds can stretch into hours. Or the other way around. How do you feel otherwise?"

"Fine. Tired, though. I feel like I did all that running all over again."

"You'll get a good night's sleep tonight," she said. "I'll have your dinner sent up right away."

"Thank you."

Holly gave an unnecessary tuck to the blanket on Malcolm's bed. She smiled at him and started out of the room.

"Holly?"

"Yes?"

"About Jones. You said it hurt to lose a friend, and it does. And you said there'd be other friends. I wonder… will you be my friend?"

"I'd like that," Holly said. "I'd like that a lot. See you." She slipped out of the room into the corridor and stood for a moment with her back against the wall. She swallowed hard to get rid of the lump in her throat. Right now she should be feeling quite pleased with herself. In a remarkably short time she had brought the boy out of an apparent catatonic state and restored at least a portion of his memory. Why, then, did she feel this chill of apprehension? There was more to Malcolm's story. Much more. Holly Lang was not sure she wanted to know it all.

Enough of that kind of thinking. She had work to do. She turned to start down the corridor and gasped as she almost ran into Gavin Ramsay. The tall sheriff caught her to avoid a collision. He held her for a moment with his strong hands on her shoulders, then released her.

"I was just on my way to call you," she said.

"And I was looking for you."

"After you left this morning, Malcolm talked almost nonstop. He told me all about your dead man in the woods."

Ramsay nodded. "Jones."

"You know?"

"Your pathologist caught me on the way out of here this morning with my deputy. He told me who the dead man was and how he died."

"Then Malcolm isn't in trouble anymore?"

"Not with me, he isn't. But we still don't know who he is. Did you find out?"

"Not really." She hesitated. "I think he's from Drago."

"No kidding."

"His memory begins with a fire that destroyed his town."

"If he is from Drago, he'll be the first survivor to turn up," Ramsay said.

"You understand I'm not sure. I'll want to work with him a lot more."

"No problem. The Drago business is none of my affair, anyway."

"One thing will probably interest you… he remembers the two men who shot Jones."

"I know who they are, too, but the boy's testimony will be important."

"Could it wait until tomorrow? He's pretty tired."

"I don't suppose a day will make any difference." Gavin rubbed his jaw, bringing a rasp from the stubble of beard.

"You have any plans for tonight?"

Holly turned brisk. "I always have plans. Tonight I'm going to write up my reports, go home, take a long bath, grill myself a steak, and watch an old Bogart movie on television."

"Let me rephrase the question," he said. "Will you have dinner with me?"

"A date? Why, Sheriff, I had no idea…"

"I hate it when they get cute," he muttered.

Holly laughed. "Dinner sounds like fun. But considering the quality of restaurants hereabouts, why don't you come to my place? I've got two of those steaks."

"That is an offer I can't refuse. What kind of wine do you like?"

"Something dark red and dry. You pick it out. Is eight o'clock all right?"

"Fine. Where do I show up?"

"I have a little house in Darnay. Seventy-one Garden Street. I'll leave the porch light on."

"I'll find you."

He winked at her and swung off down the corridor. Holly looked after him for a moment, feeling foolishly lightheaded about the date. She shook herself back into a serious mood and headed for the tiny office where she could type up her notes on today's session with Malcolm.

* * *

Dr. Wayne Pastory stepped quickly back into an alcove when he saw Holly Lang approaching. He had done a good deal of research during the day and had decided on a course of action. Right now the lady doctor was the last person he wanted to see.

When Holly was safely around a corner in the hallway, Pastory stepped out of the alcove and headed for the stairs. He climbed to the second floor, passed through the glass doors into the administrative wing, and stopped at the reception desk before the office of Dr. Dennis Qualen. After the obligatory banter with Qualen's matronly receptionist, he was allowed to enter.

"Ah, Wayne, you caught me on the way out," said the chief administrator. "I hope this isn't anything that will take a long time."

"No, no, just a few words," Pastory said. "About the boy in one-oh-eight."

Qualen pushed papers around on the polished mahogany desk. "That one. Malcolm Something-or-other, his name seems to be. Our sheriff was just in here talking to me about him."

"Oh?" Pastory tensed, hoping his plan had not been derailed.

"Apparently we are not harboring a juvenile murderer. According to Ramsay, someone else was responsible for the dead man in our basement."

"But no one has claimed the boy?"

"Unfortunately, no. Nor has anyone come forward with an offer to pay his bill. Certain members of our staff seem to be under the impression that we are a charitable institution."

"I think I know who you mean," Pastory said. "My reason for wanting to see you is to suggest a way to get us off the hook."

"Oh?" Qualen was interested but noncommittal.

"As you know, I operate a modest clinic of my own north of here."

"Ah, yes, I believe you have spoken of it. I forget... where, exactly, is it located?"

"My suggestion," Pastory said, passing quickly over the question, "is that the boy be transferred there. I am quite well equipped to take care of him, and I think the boy will be useful in some important research I'm conducting."

"What sort of research?"

"I'm not really prepared to discuss it at this stage. You understand, sir."

Dr. Qualen drew a finger along the aristocratic line of his nose. "What you suggest is not normal procedure."

"I realize that, sir," said Pastory. "But I think in this case it might pay to bend the procedures a bit. For one thing, this will relieve the hospital of additional expense, and I understand the budget is under some scrutiny at Sacramento."

"I don't see how all the necessary arrangements could be made without going through channels."

"These things can be expedited, as we both know. The thing is, time is short. I'd like the boy transferred to my place tomorrow."

"Tomorrow? Nothing can possibly be accomplished that quickly."

Pastory produced a manila folder with a flourish of a magician making a rabbit appear. "To speed things along I went ahead and did the necessary paperwork."

"You are in something of a hurry to get on with this, aren't you?"

Pastory leaned confidentially forward across the desk.

"I'll be frank with you, sir. If my theories about this boy prove out, there will be considerable recognition, acclaim even, that will go beyond the medical community. More than enough recognition for one man."

Qualen stiffened. "That sounds unpleasantly like a bribe, Doctor."

"Nothing of the sort, sir. But it doesn't hurt to remember that quite a few of our friends in high places got where they are by finding a way around the normal procedures."

Qualen glanced over the multicolored forms. "I'm still not at all sure I can go along with this. It's highly irregular."

"You'll notice," Pastory put in, "that I have entered my own name in every case where there is a question of responsibility. Not that I expect any trouble about a routine transfer, but if there should be, it's on my head."

"I see." Dr. Qualen slipped oh a pair of reading glasses. "Give me a few minutes to look these over. If, as you say, everything is in order, I see no reason why I should delay the transfer of this patient into your care."

Pastory smiled. "A good decision, sir. I'm sure it's in the best interests of everyone concerned." He leaned back in the chair and waited with a confident smile.

9

The beast moved silently through the darkening forest. Small creatures of the night skittered from its path or froze into attitudes of self-protection. The beast padded forward in a balloon of silence as the smaller creatures ceased all sound and movement at its approach.

But tonight the smaller animals had nothing to fear from the beast. It was intent on other matters. Every few yards the beast would pause and rise manlike on its hind legs, lifting its muzzle to the sky. It would sniff the air—testing, searching. And then, finding the one scent among many, it would drop again to all fours and move on.

At the crest of the final hill the beast stopped. The coarse fur bristled at the base of its powerful neck. Below lay the sprinkling of lights that were the town of Pinyon. Directly at the bottom of the hill was a large rectangular building with many lights. From the building came a profusion of scents. Some sharp and medicinal, others heavy with death and decay. The scent of humans was powerful. Humans in their sickness. Yet among the confusion of the many odors the beast again picked out the one it sought.

Moving stealthily on great padded paws, the beast crept down the wooded hillside toward the hospital.

* * *

Gavin Ramsay leaned close to the mirror over his bathroom sink and gave his face a critical look. Unsatisfied, he buzzed the electric shaver over his chin for the third time. He had a chin cleft that Elise had always said was cute but that sheltered a tiny ridge of whiskers that were hell to shave off. He tested the area with his fingers and decided it was as smooth as it was ever going to be. He blew out the shaver, splashed on some English Leather, and walked back into his combined living room/bedroom/kitchenette in the Pinyon Inn.

Gavin's was the only room at the inn with cooking facilities. He seldom lit the stove, and he used the half-size refrigerator for little more than keeping beer cold. Most of his meals were eaten downstairs in the coffee shop or brought home from one of the fast-food places down the road in Darnay. Still, having a kitchen, however inadequate, made the room seem a little more like home.

He and Elise had lived in a spacious California ranch house in Darnay until the divorce. The house, like the Camaro, and damn near everything else, had gone to Elise. Gavin had been stunned to find how suddenly cold and calculating his loving bride had turned when she decided the marriage wasn't going where she wanted it to. While he had stumbled through the proceedings with a nice-guy lawyer whose heart was back in Iowa, she had latched on to a high-powered firm from Los Angeles with half a dozen names on the letterhead. It was no contest.

But what the hell, it was over now. The last he heard, Elise was in New York dating some hotshot political columnist for the Times. That would suit her. Her father, too. Gavin had been a great disappointment to both of them.

He pushed open the accordion door on his closet and surveyed the meager wardrobe therein. Two khaki uniforms of the La Reina County Sheriff's Department. One suit, blue. Two sport coats, gray tweed and camel hair. Three pairs of slacks, gray, blue, and brown. Two neckties, one with stripes, one with little fleurs-de-lis. Assorted shoes.

These, except for the uniforms, were the clothes he hardly ever wore. His real clothes were in the dresser drawers. Jeans, corduroys, soft cotton shirts, sweaters.

During the marriage Elise had outfitted him like the rising young politician she hoped he would be. He had had two full closets then of suits, jackets, and pants from the best tailors in Southern California. Gone now, all gone. No, Elise had not taken his clothing, but Gavin had wasted no time giving most of it away when he moved out. It was one thing from his marriage he definitely did not miss.

For tonight, however, jeans and a sweater simply would not do. Holly Lang was not just another date. His dates had been few since the divorce. Generally, they consisted of a few drinks in a quiet bar, dinner maybe, then off to bed. Neither he nor the women involved had any stake in the relationship beyond an evening's entertainment. That was the way he wanted it. For some reason he felt differently about Holly.

He chose the camel hair jacket and gray slacks. Briefly he considered wearing a necktie, but he decided that was too much and settled for a soft blue sport shirt.

"You look terrific," he told his image in the mirror. "All ready for the prom."

Downstairs he climbed into the old Dodge wagon, shoving the accumulated debris off the seats. He frowned at the coating of dust and wished he had washed it more recently. He would have to remember to park in the shadows.

He drove the ten miles along the dark highway to Darnay, listening to a golden-oldies rock station from Los Angeles. He had no idea what songs were played, nor did he care. The music was company, that was all.

Entering Darnay, Gavin stopped at a liquor store and bought a bottle of California cabernet sauvignon. He found Holly Lang's address with no trouble. It was a yellow clapboard bungalow with white shutters, set well back from the quiet street. The lawn was neatly mowed. A row of flowers before the house looked like somebody cared about them. As promised, Holly had left the porch light on.

She met him at the door, wearing a colorful silk blouse with a soft, dark skirt that followed the smooth curve of her hips. Gavin realized it was the first time he had seen her out of the more severe lady-doctor outfits she wore while working. He decided she looked pretty damn good, and told her so.

"Thank you," she said. "I like your jacket."

He held up the bottle of wine for her inspection. "Is this okay?"

"Perfect. If you want to pull the cork we'll let it breathe for a while before dinner."

They entered through a small living room that she had furnished in shades of brown, gold, and rust. In a dining alcove a table was covered with a white linen spread and set for two, complete with candles and long-stemmed wineglasses.

He followed her into a sparkling kitchen and managed the corkscrew while Holly bustled about, straightening things that did not need straightening.

"I don't exactly know what that 'letting it breathe' business is all about," she said, "but it seems to be part of the ritual."

"Like rolling the cork between your fingers and sniffing at it," he added.

"And what's the difference between the aroma and the bouquet?"

"I didn't know there was one."

At the same time they stopped and looked at each other.

"We're babbling, aren't we?" she said.

"Uh-huh."

"We're both adults; we've been in the company of the opposite sex before. There's no excuse for mindless social chatter, is there?"

"None at all."

"Whew. With that out of the way, would you like a drink before I throw on the steaks?"

"I'd love one."

"I have vodka, Scotch, bourbon, and gin. I can make a pretty good martini."

"Scotch will be fine."

"Do you like anything in it?"

"Ice."

She made his drink and a vodka and tonic for herself. They carried them into the living room and sat on the sofa with the drinks before them on a hatch-cover coffee table. Some easy cocktail jazz was playing on the stereo unit. Gavin could not tell if it was a record or the radio.

"Do you ever hear from your wife?" she asked suddenly.

For a moment he was startled into silence, then laughed. "*Ex*-wife," he amended. "You sure know how to break the ice."

"If we're going to start dating, we ought to know about each other, don't you think?"

"Are we going to start dating?"

"I think we have, don't you?"

"Apparently." He sipped at the Scotch. It was good, heavy stuff, not one of the lightweights with pretty labels and no flavor. "No, I never hear from Elise. Ours was not one of those friendly divorces you hear about. Now and then I hear about her from mutual friends. They mean well, but I'd just as soon they wouldn't bother."

"You sound bitter."

He considered for a moment. "If I do, that's something I've got to fix. Bitter people are no fun to have around, and I certainly don't want to be one. They pollute the atmosphere like sour meat. I don't hate Elise. I am not down on humanity or women, or even the institution of marriage. I got gouged in the divorce, but I guess that was mostly to soothe my wife's pride. Elise never lost anything in her life, and if I was going to get away, she was going to be sure I didn't take much with me."

"I saw her several times when you both lived in Darnay. She's a beautiful woman."

"There's no denying that," he said. "She's also intelligent and witty. And ambitious. Who invited her tonight, anyway?"

Holly colored, then smiled at him. "I have been asking a lot of questions, haven't I? It's only fair that you have a turn. Is there anything you want to know about me?"

"Plenty, but I'll let it come out in the normal course of events."

"I've never been married," she volunteered. "That's not the stigma for a woman in her late twenties that it used to be. Still, there were three whole years that it was always on my mind."

"Not anymore?"

"Not the way it was. I had this *relationship*, you see. He was a doctor. Psychoanalyst, actually. Beautifully handsome, clever, and always in command. He was the only man I saw for those three years."

"But no marriage?"

"There was a small hitch. Bob already had a wife. He was going to leave her, though, just as soon as the time was right. Sure he was. I wasn't really so naive that I believed that, but I wanted it to be true so bad that I hung around three years."

"All over now?"

"Yup. It just about killed me the first time I refused to see him. The second time was easier, and the third. After that he didn't try anymore. I understand he now has a lady lawyer from San Francisco waiting for him to leave the missus."

"Bob's loss is the world's gain."

"Thanks. I wasn't fishing, but a compliment is always welcome."

Gavin pulled in a deep breath and let it out. "I hope the therapy session is over now so we can get on with acting silly."

"Right. Do you want another drink, or should I start throwing dinner together?"

Gavin rattled the ice cubes in his glass. "I'm still working on this one. I hope you're not going to ask for help. Pulling corks and opening cans is the extent of my kitchen talent."

"Mister Macho," she said. "I'll bet you're good at moving furniture."

"Want to feel my biceps?"

"Maybe later. You can come out with me and watch if you want to."

"Sure. I might even learn something."

Gavin found a spot to stand where he was out of the way and watched with honest admiration as Holly moved efficiently about the kitchen. She tossed together a salad of fresh greens, checked the broccoli she had steaming, and switched the oven on to BROIL. She sprinkled some kind of seasoning on a pair of thick New York steaks.

"How do you like yours?" she asked.

"Rare."

"Good. Me, too."

Miraculously, she got everything on the table at the same time. Gavin poured the wine and they sat down.

The salad was crisp and not overdressed, the steak was beautifully rare, and even the broccoli, not Gavin's favorite vegetable, was tender and tasty in a light cheese sauce. Conversation ranged over likes and dislikes in food, favorite television shows, the weather, local events, and came to rest finally on the boy who lay in room 108 at La Reina County Hospital.

"He's a strange one," Holly said. "I don't think he even knows everything about himself."

"Are you talking about the Drago business?"

"Partly that." She studied Gavin's face in the candlelight. "You don't believe the stories they tell about Drago, do you?"

"Werewolves? You've got to be kidding."

"You might be a little more open-minded."

"Okay, I'll try. Let's see, when the moon is full they sprout hair and fangs and go around biting people." He pretended to concentrate. "It's no use. I keep seeing Little Red Riding Hood."

Holly sighed. "The all-American skeptic. Where do you think the story of Little Red Riding Hood came from?"

"The Brothers Grimm?"

"It is based on old legends. Lots of fairy tales are. Ever hear of Peter Stumpp? Clauda Jamprost? Jacques Bocquet?"

"No, no, and no."

"They were documented werewolves of the sixteenth century."

"Documented, eh? By who, Walt Disney?" Holly's eyes flashed a danger signal. "If you don't mind, this isn't something I feel like kidding about."

"I'm sorry. You've been doing some homework, haven't you?"

"Yes, I have, and I'd like to be able to talk to somebody about it without a lot of cheap jokes."

Gavin held up his hands. "Okay. No more wisecracks. If this is important to you, I'd like to understand and talk about it with some intelligence. But it will take a little time. Let me do some homework of my own, okay?"

"Okay." After a moment Holly relaxed and sipped at her wine.

"Just one question before we drop it for the night," he said.

"Ask away."

"Do you think our boy Malcolm is a werewolf?"

She frowned. "I'm not ready to go that far. I think he may be afflicted with some form of lycanthropy. I want to know more about him."

"I'll do what I can to help if you want me on the team," Gavin said.

She held up her wineglass in silent assent. They clinked in a toast and drank to the partnership.

* * *

It was past midnight when Gavin set his coffee cup gently down on the table. He cleared his throat and rubbed his hands together.

"I'd better be pushing off," he said. "Work day tomorrow."

"Right," she said. "Me, too."

He stood up.

She stood up.

"Dinner was terrific."

"Glad you liked it."

"Next time my treat."

"You got it."

They stood facing each other for a long moment, their weight shifting from foot to foot as though they were mirror images.

"I'd better tell you this," he said. "I would really like to go to bed with you. I mean it's been on my mind from the minute I walked in. No, from the minute I put on my best sport coat to impress you."

She watched him, her head tilted slightly to one side. "And if we don't mess up somehow, I'm almost sure you and I are going to do it."

She opened her mouth to speak, and he went on quickly. "But I have the feeling neither of us is ready for it right now."

Holly let out a long-held breath. "You know, Sheriff, you're a more perceptive man than you let on sometimes."

"I just didn't want you to think I was gay."

"I detected that," she said. "Those pants of yours fit quite well."

"Why, you saucy little minx."

"That's me."

Their goodnight kiss was long and warm and deep, and filled with promise.

Gavin drove back toward the Pinyon Inn, grinning foolishly in the dim glow of the instrument lights. He had to remind himself that there was still a whole lot he did not know about Dr. Holly Lang. Her preoccupation with the occult was one thing that disturbed him. His grin faded as he thought about the boy who lay in room 108. Gavin thought about him and about the tales of Drago, and he wondered…

* * *

Malcolm's eyes snapped open and he sat suddenly upright in bed. He sniffed the air and turned toward the window to stare at the darkness outside.

Someone was there. Someone or something. Calling to him. The boy's thin body tensed. His nerves tightened with a crazy desire to run out there and join whatever waited for him in the night. Beads of perspiration broke out along his hairline.

It was as though he belonged out there, in the night, not here in a comfortable bed. That was his place. And yet… and yet things were different now. He had a friend. He was no longer alone, running, always running. He thought of Holly. Made a picture of her face in his mind. The picture held him where he was. Still, the silent voice called to him from outside.

Another sound intruded. The barely audible pad of the night nurse's rubber-soled shoes out in the corridor. Malcolm lay back quickly and closed his eyes, feigning sleep. The door opened. The night nurse looked in, listened to his regular breathing, and backed out again.

Malcolm did not rise. The call from the night was still there, but weaker now. He could block it out if he tried. By and by he fell into a shallow sleep that was troubled by strange urges and wild dreams.

* * *

Out on the hillside, yellow-green eyes glaring across at the many windows of the hospital building, the beast growled from deep in its massive chest. The one it sought was inside, that much the beast knew, but there were too many conflicting scents to tell which of the windows was the right one.

The beast made a complete circuit of the building, staying in the deepest shadows, going to a low, loping run when it had to cross the paved parking area. Instinct cried out for it to smash through the glass doors at the entrance and savage any human that crossed its path until the boy was found. Reason told the beast that this was not the way. It was a time for cunning. The killing would come later.

Effortlessly the beast climbed the hill behind the building and slipped down into the shallow valley beyond. There beneath a bush it found a neatly folded pile of clothing. The beast sniffed the air, judged it safe, then lay down next to the clothing and curled its powerful body in on itself as the painful transformation began.

10

Malcolm awoke sweating.

The gray rectangle of the window told him it was early morning. The sensations of last night jolted back into his consciousness. He remembered the terrible certainty that something out there in the woods had called to him. His own wild urge to answer that call. Then the quieting mind picture of Dr. Holly Lang, and the troubled dreams that followed.

He strained his senses now, and he could still feel the presence of something out there. It was much fainter now, but not completely gone. Malcolm was frightened, yet his blood surged with a strange exhilaration. He resolved to tell Holly all about it. She would understand. She would know how to help him.

A few minutes later the door opened and a nurse entered. She had orange hair and a lumpy potato nose. She was not one of the nurses Malcolm had seen before. She carried a small tray that was covered with a white cloth. When she set the tray down on the table across the room from his bed it made a little clinking sound.

"Well, already awake, are we?" the nurse said in that fake-cheerful voice they use. "And my, how chipper we look. Did we have a good sleep?"

Malcolm did not bother to answer. He knew the nurse wouldn't pay any attention to what he said anyway.

"Are we ready for a surprise this morning?"

Malcolm turned his head away.

"Malcolm's going on a little trip."

He turned back to the nurse. She had a mole on the side of her neck with a single orange hair growing out of it.

"I thought that might interest you," she said brightly.

"A trip where?"

"That's going to be the surprise. I don't want to spoil it for you."

An oily-haired man in a white doctor's coat came through the door. Malcolm remembered him. He was the nasty one who had given Holly a hard time when Malcolm was first brought in.

"This is Dr. Pastory," the nurse said as if she were giving him a great big present. "He's going to be your doctor now."

"I don't want a new doctor."

"You don't know how lucky you are," Potato Nose told him. "A lot of people in your position don't have any doctor at all."

"Where's Holly?" Malcolm said.

Pastory spoke for the first time. "Dr. Lang has other patients to attend to." His voice was as oily as his hair.

"I'd rather have her."

"You will find, Malcolm, that in this life we don't always get what we want." He turned to the orange-haired nurse and said in a low voice, as though Malcolm could not hear, "Give him fifty cc's."

The nurse lifted one edge of the white cloth and took something from the tray she had brought in with her. She held it down low, shielded by her body so Malcolm wouldn't see it. He knew what it was, though.

"How about rolling over for me, big fella?" she said, all palsy again.

"What for?"

"We've got to poke a little medicine into you, that's all. A tiny pinprick in the bottom. You've had them before."

"But what is it?"

"It will make you feel better."

"I feel fine."

Dr. Pastory moved over closer to the bed and frowned down at Malcolm. His eyes were small and bright, and there was something in them Malcolm didn't like.

"Do as the nurse says, Malcolm. We have some strong young fellows working here who can come in and flip you over if you won't cooperate. Do you want me to call them?"

Malcolm looked at the nurse and saw he would get no help from her. Feeling trapped, he rolled over on his side, facing away from them. The nurse yanked the blanket and sheet down and pulled the short hospital gown up to expose his buttock. He felt the sharp sting of the needle and a tightening of the flesh down there as something was pumped into him.

He felt the needle slide out and smelled the tang of alcohol as the nurse swabbed him off. She gave him a familiar little pat and pulled the gown back into place. Malcolm rolled onto his back and looked up at the two of them.

"That wasn't so bad now, was it?" the nurse recited.

"I want to see Holly," Malcolm said. "Dr. Lang."

Pastory showed his small, even teeth. "*I'm* your doctor now, Malcolm. You'd better get used to that."

Malcolm felt a tingling sensation spread over his body. He braced his hands and tried to sit up but found he was dizzy and lay back down.

"Just relax," Pastory told him. "Don't try to fight the medicine. You can't win, you know." The words had a funny echoing sound.

"I don't want to relax. I don't want you for my doctor."

That was what Malcolm tried to say, but it came out all mush-mouth. His tongue felt thick and foreign, like a hunk of strange meat.

"The more you fight it, the more trouble it makes for everybody." Pastory's oily little face swam in and out of focus.

With a great effort Malcolm sat up. The doctor reached for him and Malcolm batted his hands away. "You're not my doctor," he mumbled.

Pastory bared his teeth, and for a moment Malcolm thought the doctor was going to strike him. But he got control of himself and turned to the nurse.

"Better give him another fifty cc's."

"But doctor, for a boy his age, that's—"

Pastory's little eyes flashed, though his voice remained calm. "Please do what I ask, Nurse."

With her cheeks reddening, the nurse turned her back and did something with the things on the cloth-covered tray. Pastory stared impassively down at Malcolm.

"Don' wan' any more shots." Malcolm had trouble getting the words out past the tongue that did not belong to him. "Wan' see Holly."

"Will you please hurry?" Pastory snapped at the nurse, who was still fumbling at the tray.

"No more shots," Malcolm said feebly.

The orange-haired nurse turned toward him, making no attempt this time to conceal the hypodermic needle. She reached down with one hand and flipped Malcolm onto his side. His body would not respond to the messages sent by his brain.

He barely felt the second needle prick. The nurse eased him over on his back and he watched as she and Dr. Pastory floated side by side in some murky void. The room grew warm, then hot. Malcolm could feel the sweat rolling off him, but he could not move a hand up to clear his eyes. His power of speech was gone. All he could manage were soft grunting noises. The light grew dim. And dimmer.

"That s done it." Dr. Pastory's voice floated to him through a long tunnel, distorted and barely audible. "I won't be needing you anymore, Nurse."

The shadow shape that was the nurse floated back away from him and disappeared. Dr. Pastory went away, too, but just for a moment. Then he was back with somebody else. Another man. The features were only a blur to Malcolm, but he sensed that the newcomer was not a doctor or a hospital employee. He smelled wrong. There was none of the astringent tang of surgical soap, medicine, and alcohol that clung to the hospital people. This one smelled of tobacco, stale sweat, and urine.

Malcolm felt himself lifted roughly from the bed and placed on another flat, yielding surface. He sensed the door to his room being opened, and he was floating out through it into the corridor. No, not floating, rolling on soft rubber wheels. Rolling, rolling. The fluorescent lights passed overhead in dim, wavery images, as though seen from underwater.

Suddenly the air was cool on his face. There was a breeze with the scent of pine in it. He was outside. A dim recollection of a voice that called him from out here fought for a space in his consciousness, but the drug was too strong.

Malcolm was lifted again, placed inside some sort of metallic box. A van. Dr. Pastory got in beside him. He gave an order. An engine fired and Malcolm sensed movement. Then the fever returned and consciousness slipped away.

* * *

At ten o'clock Dr. Dennis Qualen strolled in through the entrance of La Reina County Hospital. He was, as always, impeccably turned out. Today he had chosen a dark blue worsted with muted pinstripe and a tie of pale yellow. He acknowledged the greetings of staff and employees with a nod and half smile. Dr. Qualen did not believe in becoming too familiar with the people under him. Particularly since he did not intend to spend one day longer than necessary at La Reina. He had feelers out to bigger institutions in San Francisco, Houston, and Miami. Once he had straightened out the budgetary problems here, and had the figures to show it, he would surely be hearing from them.

He rode the elevator to the second floor, passing an encouraging word to a small boy in a wheelchair. The boy stared at him dully. He watched as the nurse wheeled the boy toward the orthopedic ward, then he turned and walked briskly toward the glass doors to Administration. Once beyond them he felt a tangible relief. Those doors represented a barrier to Dr. Qualen that kept the sordidness of disease and death separate from the nice clean business of running a hospital.

He barely noticed a neatly dressed young man with sandy hair who sat in one of the chairs across from the reception desk. A salesman, the doctor surmised. Some new wonder drug, or a piece of expensive equipment that no modern hospital should be without. La Reina was not in a buying cycle at present, but Qualen tolerated salesmen for the gossip they carried of the outside medical community.

The doctor smiled coolly at Mrs. Thayer as he went by. For his own taste he would have preferred a receptionist with a bit more style, and better tits. However, he knew that the matronly Mrs. Thayer gave his office a solid, businesslike appearance. And she was excellent at guarding his door from patients and other unwanted visitors.

As soon as he settled himself in the burgundy leather chair behind the mahogany desk, the intercom buzzed. With a sigh he reached over and flipped the switch.

"Yes, Mrs. Thayer."

"A gentleman out here to see you, Doctor."

"Who is he with?"

"Apparently he is not representing any firm."

"Then what does he want with me?"

"He says it's about the boy they brought in from the woods. The boy in one-oh-eight."

Qualen frowned. He glanced over at the transfer papers for Malcolm, riffled through them, and saw that Dr. Pastory's name had been correctly entered, making him the responsible party.

He said, "Did you tell him I am not concerned with patients' affairs?"

"The gentleman was quite adamant about wanting to see the man in charge. He's been here since I came in, at eight o'clock."

Damn. Qualen hated to start the day with some petty annoyance. "Does he have a name?"

"Yes, Doctor. Mr. Derak."

It meant nothing to Dr. Qualen. Had an unpleasant foreign sound. He sighed. Might as well get it over with.

"Ask Mr. Derak to come in."

The doctor assumed a businesslike pose and watched as his visitor entered. He was not as young as he had appeared at first glance. It was difficult to guess his age. Something about the eyes, an odd shade of green, seemed very, very old. Nevertheless, he was presentable enough. His sandy hair was cut short and neatly brushed. The jacket and slacks were not top quality, but good. He had a nice smile. Strong.

"Good morning, Mr. Derak," said Qualen with just the right mixture of cordiality and restraint. "What can I do for you?"

"You have a boy here. I understand he was found wandering in the forest and was brought in by deputy sheriffs."

"Ah, yes," Qualen said after a pause to indicate he was trying to remember the case.

"I'd like to see him."

"Mr. Derak, visits with patients are handled through the desk in the main lobby. You must have passed it when you came in."

"I talked to the woman there, and I talked to her supervisor. I could not get satisfactory answers from them. They suggested I see you." A rather unpleasant note crept into Derak's voice.

Qualen resolved to have a talk with that woman and her supervisor at the first opportunity. He said. "You are a relative of…" He made a show of looking through the papers on his desk. "…Malcolm."

"In a way."

The doctor looked up, expecting a further explanation. Derak offered none. His green-eyed gaze was uncomfortably direct.

"As it happens," Qualen said, "that patient has been transferred."

"Transferred?" Derak took a step closer to the desk. "He was here last night."

"That's true. The transfer happened early this morning."

The sandy-haired man became agitated. One hand pulled loose the knot of his necktie. "Where was he taken?" His voice sounded different. Coarser.

"I'm really not at liberty to say. If you will leave your name and address with my—"

"You will tell me now," said Derak. The voice had roughened into a growl.

Dr. Qualen stared at the man in astonishment. He had thrown off his jacket and was actually tearing at his shirt. And his face, my God, it was twisting into something quite inhuman.

The doctor reached for the intercom box. Derak's hand clamped onto his wrist with a grip that crackled the bones.

Qualen stared at the hand. Before his bulging eyes it changed. Grew into a terrible mutant paw. Thick, wiry hair sprouted from the back. The nails thickened and pushed out into claws. Qualen looked up at the face.

Even as he began to scream, the doctor knew the acoustic walls would let no more than a murmur escape to Mrs. Thayer outside.

With a strength born of terror, Qualen wrenched his wrist free of the terrible grip. He ran around his desk and tried to make it to the door. Derak, or whatever this thing was that Derak had become, was faster. He threw himself past the doctor and used that misshapen, hairy paw to roll the dead bolt home, locking them in.

The only other way out was the window of reinforced glass, and that gave on a sheer drop of twenty feet to the concrete parking lot. Qualen backed away, watching in horrified fascination the transformation taking place before him.

The man's body twisted and swelled and grew to a height that towered over the six-foot doctor. There was a terrible cracking as the skeleton reshaped itself inside the creature. The face… the face was all muzzle and teeth and burning eyes of green hellfire.

In a movement too swift for him to follow, Qualen felt himself seized under the arms and lifted clear off the floor. His shrieks echoed dully off the sound-proofed walls. He felt the hot breath of the creature as the great jaws opened; he smelled the stench of it. There was a moment of searing agony as the teeth sank into his throat. A hot gush of his life's blood. A last roar in his ears. Then blackness and oblivion.

* * *

It was the faint but unmistakable crash of glass from inside Dr. Qualen's office that roused Mrs. Thayer. The only thing in there that could make a crash like that was the window. She buzzed the intercom, got no answer. With mounting unease,

Mrs. Thayer rose from her chair, walked to the door of Dr. Qualen's office, tried the knob. Locked. She rapped lightly, then again, louder. There was no response. Something was wrong. Dreadfully wrong.

Mrs. Thayer snatched the telephone from her desk and punched out the internal emergency code. In less than a minute two burly orderlies came running in from the corridor outside.

"There's trouble in Dr. Qualen's office," she tried. "The door's locked and he won't answer me."

The orderlies hesitated only a moment, then attacked the door while Mrs. Thayer stood back out of the way. The door soon splintered under their combined assault. The men rushed inside, stopping as though they had hit a wall when they saw the bloody thing sprawled over the desk of the administrative chief. Behind them Mrs. Thayer started into the room, then gave a little cry and backed away, her hand covering her mouth.

At the same moment the men turned toward the broken window. They crossed the room together and looked out, scanning the parking lot below. Nothing.

One of them pointed up at the hillside. "Look!"

The other followed his pointing finger. "What is it? I don't see anything."

"I thought... for a minute it looked like something up there. Running."

"A man? What?"

"I don't know. I can't see it now. It was more like a big dog. Or... Christ, I don't know. Let's get help."

Later, of all the ghastly events of that morning the two men would remember the sound they heard from somewhere up on the wooded hill. They would remember the howling.

11

The people at the hospital provided Ramsay with a small unused office at the rear of the first floor, next to the kitchen, to use for his interviews with the staff and employees. It had only a desk, two chairs, a file cabinet that would not open, and a hastily installed telephone. There was also a pervasive smell of bland hospital cooking coming in through the single window.

One of the chairs was occupied by a stenographer on loan from Ventura County. She took rapid, silent notes as Mrs. Audrey Thayer, secretary and receptionist for the late Dr. Qualen, answered the sheriff's questions.

Through the window Ramsay could see search parties laboring up the thickly wooded hillside, where the suspect might or might not have been seen running by one of the orderlies who found the body. Overhead was the persistent thrum of helicopters. There was one from the Ventura County Sheriff's office and several from television news departments.

The media had appeared miraculously less than two hours after Ramsay had received the report of Dr. Qualen's murder. So far he had been able to avoid them with the help of deputies Nevins and Fernandez, who stood out in the hallway looking as mean as they could manage.

Sooner or later he would have to talk to them, but Ramsay was determined to get as much as he could of his real work done first. Like most lawmen, he had a healthy distrust of reporters, a distrust he knew was mutual.

"Is there anything more you can tell me about this Mr. Derak?" Ramsay asked the woman across from him. "Any little thing, no matter how unimportant it seemed at the time, might be helpful."

Mrs. Thayer frowned thoughtfully and shook her head. Her hands were busy twisting a flowered hankie into a snake. "I'm sorry, Sheriff, but there really isn't anything more than what I've already told you. He was just an ordinary looking man. Rather pleasant, he seemed at the time. Very insistent, though, about seeing Dr. Qualen."

At the mention of her late employer, Mrs. Thayer's ample chest convulsed in a sob. She unwound the hankie and dabbed at her eyes. Ramsay waited for the spasm to pass before he went on.

"And he said nothing to you about what business he had with the doctor?"

"Only that he was sent up there by Eleanor Chung. She supervises the admission desk in the lobby."

Ramsay nodded. He had already talked to Miss Chung and the woman who was on duty when Derak came in. They said he insisted on seeing the patient known as Malcolm in room 108. Since he could show no evidence that he was related, they explained he would have to wait until regular visiting hours, then clear it with the doctor assigned to Malcolm's case. They declined to give him any more information, and when the man refused to leave, referred him to Dr. Qualen.

"How long was he in the office with Dr. Qualen before you heard the crash of the window breaking?"

"Not long. Not more than fifteen minutes. I don't see how he could have... could have..."

Ramsay spoke up quickly to head off another outburst of sobs. "And you heard nothing before that because of the soundproof construction of the walls. Is that correct?"

"Nothing. Once, very faint, I thought I heard a voice, but I couldn't be sure."

Milo Fernandez entered, glanced at Mrs. Thayer, and spoke to Ramsay. "Dr. Underwood is outside with his report."

"Good. Thank you very much, Mrs. Thayer. That'll be all for now."

"You'll catch the... the terrible person who did this, won't you, Sheriff?"

"Yes, we will," Ramsay said with a lot more conviction than he felt. "He won't get away."

Reassured, Mrs. Thayer gave him a teary smile and left the office. Ramsay told the stenographer to take a break, and sat back to wait for the pathologist.

Neal Underwood was a man happy in his work. He was plump and pleasant and had thinning blond hair that still had a curl to it. His biggest satisfaction in recent years had been the cancellation of Quincy, the farfetched television show that had a choleric pathologist rushing around shouting at everyone, solving crimes, making fools out of doctors and police alike. Dr. Underwood did his job in a quiet and efficient manner and had far more friends than enemies. He could make small jokes about how his patients never complained, and he did not even mind being referred to around the hospital as Dr. Underground.

He took the chair across from Ramsay and laid a folder on the desk between them.

"As savage a killing as I've seen in some time," the pathologist said pleasantly.

"What was the cause of death?"

"My preliminary findings show it to be loss of blood from a severed jugular. The lower face, throat, and upper chest were severely lacerated. Many of the wounds, I'm relieved to say, probably occurred after the victim was already dead. He died very quickly."

"Any guess as to the weapon?"

"You're not going to like it."

"Try me."

"Teeth."

Ramsay let several seconds go by while he held the pathologist's mild gaze. "Teeth?"

"I told you that you wouldn't like it."

"Human teeth?"

"Not likely. The human jaw is not constructed for attack. To kill with its teeth, an animal needs a protruding muzzle. That allows the jaws to open like this." Underwood demonstrated with his two hands, touching at the heel, making teeth of his fingers.

"What kind of an animal might that be?"

"Oh, lots of them. Shark, alligator, tiger, hyena…"

Ramsay saw him hesitate. "And?"

"And a wolf."

"Uh-huh. Would you say it's possible to construct a weapon that would make wounds like that, resembling teeth?"

"I suppose it would be possible, but it would make a damned inefficient weapon. It would be an awkward thing to carry around, too. Impossible to conceal."

Ramsay pinched the bridge of his nose. He felt a headache coming on, but the next question had to be asked. "Have you seen a killing like this before, Doctor?"

Underwood nodded slowly. He was no more eager to answer than Ramsay was to ask. "Similar. Several of them."

"Like to tell me where and when?"

"Right here. Last year. During the business at Drago."

Ramsay groaned inwardly. The damned dead village of Drago was destined to haunt him. "What do you think killed those people?"

"Wolves," Dr. Underwood said without hesitation. "Yes, I know there hasn't been a wolf sighted around here since the turn of the century, and I know none was ever found, but that's my story and I'm sticking to it. Wolves. Where they came from, where they went, that's not my problem."

"You heard the stories?"

"Werewolves? Sure, I heard them. Who didn't? But if you think I am going to write werewolves and witches and fairies into my reports… well, forget it."

"It was no wolf that walked into Dr. Qualen's office," Ramsay said quietly. "A man walked in there. One man. He carried no visible weapon."

"Sheriff, I don't envy you your job." Underwood slapped the folder he had laid on the desk. "There's my preliminary' report. Make out of it what you will. Beyond the medical facts and observations contained therein, I have nothing to offer."

"Easy," Ramsay said. "Believe me, Doctor, I don't want werewolves any more than you do. I've just got to come up with some answer as to how a single man could do that kind of damage in a short space of time, then jump through a reinforced plate-glass window to a concrete slab twenty feet down, then run off up into the woods and somehow elude a professional ground and air search party."

Underwood gave him a sympathetic smile. "Sheriff, I'll bet nobody told you it was going to be easy. Are you through with me?"

Ramsay waved him away. "Yeah, thanks, Doctor. I'll be down to talk to you later. Try not to mention you-know-what to our reporter friends, will you?"

"Are you kidding? I walked past a bunch of them in the lobby, and all they're talking about is werewolves. I even saw a couple of them sharpening wooden stakes."

Ramsay could not resist a smile. "That shows how much they know. Stakes are for vampires."

Dr. Underwood nodded sagely and left the office. It was past two o'clock and Ramsay had not eaten since his coffee and donut early that morning. His stomach rumbled, reminding him of the omission. He got up and went to the door where the deputies stood guard. To Fernandez he said, "How about seeing if you can scrounge something to eat? I'm not ready to run the gauntlet in the lobby yet."

Before the young deputy could answer, Holly Lang appeared, wheeling one of the hospital food carts.

"I thought you men might be getting hungry," she said.

"You're magic," Ramsay told her.

She gave a tray to each of the deputies and wheeled the cart into the office. Ramsay closed the door behind her.

On covered plates there was coleslaw, roast beef, hot rolls, mashed potatoes, and peas. There was Jell-O for dessert and a thermal carafe of coffee.

"Not exactly cordon bleu, but nutritious, or so they tell me in the cafeteria."

"It looks great. And I promised the next meal was going to be on me."

"I'll catch up with you," Holly said. "Dig in while it's hot."

Ramsay began to eat. He could feel Holly watching him.

"Go ahead and ask," he said.

"All right. How are you doing?"

"Just swell. It appears that a nice-mannered fellow named Mr. Derak walked into Dr. Qualen's office, bit him to death, jumped out the window, and disappeared. It's a piece of cake."

"You know Malcolm is gone, don't you?"

"Yes, of course."

"The nurse, Rita Keneally, says Dr. Pastory came in early this morning, had Malcolm sedated, and took him away."

"So?"

"Don't you think there's a connection? This man Derak came here wanting to see Malcolm."

"If there is a connection, I'm sure it will come out when we talk to Dr. Pastory."

"But I've asked, and nobody knows where he is."

Ramsay swallowed a mouthful of roast beef. "Holly, I am investigating a murder. I have two capable deputies and more help than I really want from the sheriffs of Ventura and Los Angeles counties. Suppose you stick to curing the sick and leave crime to me."

"God, I hate it when they get condescending."

"If by 'they' you mean me, I'm sorry that's the way it sounded to you, but I do have an awful lot on my mind."

"Isn't kidnapping a big enough crime to get some attention?"

"Kidnapping? You're talking about Malcolm?"

"Who else?"

"As I understand it, that was a fairly routine transfer of a patient from one facility to another."

"Bullshit!"

Ramsay lowered a forkful of mashed potatoes back to the plate. From a desk drawer he drew a clear plastic folder with several sheets of a printed form inside. The sheets were spattered with a brownish stain.

"I have here," Ramsay said, "what they tell me are the official and correct forms for transfer of our patient Malcolm from La Reina County Hospital to some clinic. They are a bit messy, because they were found on the desk of the late Dr. Qualen, who was more or less lying on top of them."

"Have you read them?"

"Well, no, but—"

"I have," Holly snapped. "And there are some glaring irregularities."

"How did you get hold of these reports before I did?" Ramsay asked.

"I have friends here. The point is that although Dr. Wayne Pastory's name is all over those forms transferring Malcolm to his own clinic, nowhere is the location of that clinic spelled out."

"So?"

"So I want to know where Malcolm was taken."

"When Dr. Pastory shows up we'll ask him. How about that?"

"Fine, but what makes you think he's going to show up?"

"What happened here this morning won't exactly be a secret by the time the six o'clock news hits the air," he said. "Unless Pastory is a damn fool, he'll show up here voluntarily and give us his version of what happened."

"Pastory is no fool," Holly said tightly, "but he may be something much worse."

"What does that mean?"

"It means Malcolm could be in real danger. While you sit here waiting for Pastory to stroll in and chat, he could be harming that boy in some dreadful way."

"Now listen to me, Holly. I know you have a special feeling for Malcolm, but it seems to me you're letting it get in the way of your professional judgment. I will want to question Dr. Pastory as a witness, but as far as I know, he has committed no crime. This man called Derak is a bona fide murder suspect. That is my number one priority, and it's going to stay that way until I have reason to change my thinking. Is that understood?"

She glared at him. "Oh, absolutely, Mr. Sheriff, sir. You just go ahead and play Dirty Harry and hunt down your phantom murderer. I trust you won't mind too much if I do what little I can to try to find a boy who may be in trouble like you've never imagined."

"Do whatever you want to, Holly," Gavin said, making an effort to soften his tone "But I'll appreciate it if you'll try not to interfere with the investigation."

She sprang to her feet and glared, fists clenched at her sides "Don't worry, Sheriff. I won't come within shouting distance of your precious investigation."

Without giving him a chance to reply, she spun on her heel and marched out of the office, startling Nevins and Fernandez, who were finishing up their lunches out in the corridor. By the time Ramsay got to the door she was not in sight.

"What did you do to the lady doctor, Sheriff?" Roy Nevins asked. "She came out of there like her tail feathers was on fire."

"I asked her to please stay out of my way."

"Oh. Well." The deputy nodded as though that explained everything.

* * *

When he could postpone it no longer, Ramsay made his way out through the crowded lobby of the hospital. Every third person seemed to be carrying a television mini-cam on his shoulder. Those who didn't have cameras had tape recorders and phallic microphones, which they thrust at anyone who moved within range. When Ramsay appeared they surged toward him like piranha to a goldfish.

"Have you made an arrest, Sheriff?"

"Any suspects?"

"What kind of wounds did the dead man have?"

"Is it true his head was bitten off?"

"Is there a link to the killings last year at Drago?"

"What's your opinion of the werewolf theory?"

Ramsay held up a hand like a traffic cop and waited a full minute until the reporters subsided into near silence. He said, "There have been no arrests. We are following up on several possible suspects. I cannot describe the fatal wounds at this time for fear of jeopardizing the investigation. The victim's head was not bitten off. No connection has been found to any other crimes. In my opinion werewolves exist only in cheap horror movies. Thank you all very much."

As he started toward the door the reporters crowded in around him, thrusting their ball-headed microphones close to his face, gabbling questions all at the same time.

"Excuse me. I'm sorry. I have a very important meeting that could be vital to the investigation. No, I cannot give you any more information. Excuse me."

Ramsay's progress through the crowd slowed to a near standstill as the mass of bodies around him pressed closer. As he was about to be pushed backward, a thick-shouldered man with forearms like Popeye shoved his way through the crowd, ignoring the complaints and curses from the reporters.

"Right this way, Sheriff. The car's outside."

The man was vaguely familiar, but Ramsay could not immediately place him. However, this was no time to ask for ID. He fell in behind the man like a running back behind his pulling guard, and together they plowed a furrow through the gaggle of reporters, out the door, and down the wide walkway to a beat-up Volkswagen Beetle. Ramsay jumped into the passenger's side and the other man wedged himself behind the wheel. He slammed the little car into gear and they took off, barely missing a camera crew from the Los Angeles ABC affiliate.

By the time the reporters had collected themselves and dashed for their own vehicles, the Beetle had roared around the corner and turned off the road onto an all but invisible wagon track that led out of sight behind a row of eucalyptus trees. There the driver stopped and cut the engine.

When the caravan of media cars had roared past on the highway, Ramsay turned for a better look at his driver. "Thanks for the rescue," he said. "You've got a handy way with crowds."

"I played a little football years ago at Stanford."

"Do I know you?" Ramsay asked.

"You might have seen me around. Name's Ken Dowd. I own a little shop in Darnay. Heard about what happened at the hospital this morning and thought maybe I could help you out."

"That so? In what way, Mr. Dowd?"

"Call me Ken. Well, I heard how they're saying this killing was like the ones they had over at Drago before the town burned down. Werewolves, you know."

"I know," Ramsay said wearily.

"Well, back then I had occasion to help a fellow out. Came up from L.A. Had to go into Drago after a woman or something. He came to my shop."

"What do you call your shop, Ken?"

The broad-shouldered man looked embarrassed. "The Spirit World. My wife's idea. I told her it sounded like a liquor store, but that's what she wanted, and half the money to set it up was hers. We sell occult books, Ouija boards, powders, potions, charms, chants. You name it."

"That's interesting, Ken, but I don't see how it's going to help me."

Dowd reached behind the seat and brought up a cardboard box the size of a double deck of playing cards. He handed it to Ramsay. The box was surprisingly heavy for its size.

"What is it?"

"Take a look."

Ramsay raised the flap and looked inside. It took a moment for him to recognize the contents.

"Silver bullets?"

"Caliber thirty-eight. I figured they ought to fit your police revolver."

"You're not joking with me, are you, Ken?"

"I am not. And I won't waste a lot of time arguing with you about whether there's such things as ghosts and vampires and werewolves. I have my own beliefs, but I'm not interested in convincing anybody else. I saw the way some of those people died in Drago, and I don't want to see any more. You can take these bullets or not, whatever you want. I happen to think they might save your life, and maybe some others, too."

Ramsay looked closely at the man and decided he was not drunk or crazy or a fool. He hefted the box of bullets and dropped it into a side pocket of his uniform jacket.

"Thanks, Ken. I'll take them."

Dowd nodded soberly. "I don't think you'll be sorry, Sheriff." He fired the Volkswagen engine and drove back to the road.

12

It was impossible for Malcolm to tell how long he rode inside the van. There were moments when he was almost awake and he could see Dr. Pastory sitting close by, watching him. There were heavy curtains across the rear window, and the only illumination came from up front in the cab, where the other man was driving. Malcolm did not have the strength to turn and look up there, and he soon lapsed back into unconsciousness.

He had only vague sensations of when the ride ended. First the vibration of the engine stopped, then there were the metallic sounds of doors opening and closing and the voices of the two men. The chill of outdoor air was on his face briefly, then it was warm again. He felt the familiar touch of sheets on his body and the slight give of a mattress under him. To his drugged brain that meant he was back in the hospital. Safe. Holly would be here soon. He slept.

When finally his brain cleared and he came fully awake, Malcolm saw at once he was not in the hospital. The bed was similar, and the room had the same kind of medicinal smell, but there was a coldness here. Not in the temperature, for the room was quite warm, but in the atmosphere. Malcolm had no idea where he was; he only knew it was a bad place.

The room was very plain. There was his narrow bed, a four-drawer bureau, a little nightstand, and a straight wooden chair. The room had one door, no window. In a corner was a white enameled sink with a mirrored cabinet above it. On one wall hung a picture of a dog on a hillock overlooking a flock of grazing sheep. The picture showed storm clouds building on the horizon.

Malcolm peeled back the covers and swung his feet out of the bed onto the floor. He was dizzy for a moment and had to shut his eyes. When he opened them he felt a little better. He looked down and saw that he was still wearing the foolish little garment they had given him at the hospital.

He stood up, walked carefully the few steps to the door. He tried the knob. Locked. Malcolm was not surprised. He prowled around the room touching things, feeling their surfaces.

He ran some water over his hands at the sink and splashed it on his face. He looked at himself in the mirror. The young face that looked back at him was very sad. Dark half-moons shadowed the eyes.

The bureau was unfinished wood of some kind. Malcolm pulled out the drawers one by one. Three of them were empty, but the top drawer contained clothes. There was underwear, jeans, t-shirts, sweaters, socks, tennis shoes.

"Well, hello, Malcolm. How are you feeling?"

The voice startled him so that he spun away from the bureau and almost lost his balance. Dr. Pastory stood in the doorway. He had opened it without making a sound.

"I see you found the clothes. It's all right; they're for you. I hope they fit. I'm not used to buying clothes for a boy. Young man, I should say."

Malcolm shrugged.

"I thought you'd be tired of wearing that hospital gown. I don't blame you."

Pastory was trying hard to make his voice friendly, but it was still oily and cold to Malcolm. The doctor came over and took his arm to guide him back to the bed. His touch was as unpleasant as his voice. He had an antiseptic smell to him. Malcolm sat down on the bed. Pastory took the chair and hitched it over close.

"Now then, how do you feel?" he said again.

"Sick to my stomach," Malcolm told him.

"Well, that's not unusual. The drug does that sometimes. It's nothing to worry about. We'll get some food into you and you'll feel tip-top again."

"Where are we?"

"It's a little place of mine where we can get you all well again."

"I'm not sick."

"That's a matter of opinion, Malcolm. Definitely a matter of opinion."

Dr. Pastory was looking at him in a strange, piercing way, but then he put on the fake oily smile again. "Why don't you put on some of your new clothes? Are they what boys are wearing today?"

"They're okay."

"Good. You just get dressed now and I'll show you where we're going to work together."

"Work?"

"In a matter of speaking. You're an unusual young man, Malcolm. I'm going to give you a few tests—oh, nothing that will hurt or anything like that—and see if we can find out what makes you so unusual."

"I don't think I want to take tests."

Pastory's little eyes glittered. "I told you before, Malcolm, in this life it doesn't always matter what we want. Now will you get yourself dressed, or should I bring in somebody to do it for you?"

"I'll do it."

"Good. That's the spirit I like to hear." The doctor went out. The door closed soundlessly behind him. There was a whispered click of the lock. Malcolm turned the knob just to be sure. It was locked, all right.

He tried on some of the clothes from the bureau. Everything was a size or so too big, but not so much that it mattered. And it did feel good to be wearing real clothes again.

When he was dressed Malcolm sat down on the bed and waited. In a few minutes Pastory came back in bringing a mug of some hot brown liquid. There was another man with him. The other man was big, with a barrel chest and thick neck and bristly black hair. His lips were thick and set in a permanent sneer. He smelled bad. Malcolm recognized the smell from the morning he was taken from the hospital. Was it only this morning? Whatever they shot him up with had messed up his sense of time.

Pastory handed him the mug. "Drink this. It's full of vitamins and other good things."

Malcolm drank. It tasted like a heavy beef broth. Not too bad.

"Later on you can have solid food, but I think for now we'd better stick to liquids."

"How long am I going to be here?"

"That depends." He pulled the door all the way open. "Come along now."

"What are you going to do?"

Pastory dropped the fake pleasant expression he'd been wearing. "I haven't time to explain every little thing to you. Kruger, bring him along."

The big man grabbed Malcolm by the shoulder and dug his thumb into a nerve there.

"Hey!" the boy protested.

"The doctor wants you to come along." Kruger had a high singsong voice that did not fit with his size. He pulled Malcolm to his feet and propelled him out the door.

He was taken along a short hallway and into another room, larger than the one where he had awakened. A skylight in the ceiling made it very bright. There were shelves on the walls holding all manner of bottles, vials, beakers, and jars. Some of them contained liquids or powders; others were empty. Along one side of the room was a counter with a stainless steel sink and a little gas burner. All along the counter there was a cluster of instruments and equipment that meant nothing to Malcolm.

In the center of the room was a high, narrow table, padded, with tough leather straps riveted to the sides. Under the table was a complicated system of gears so it could be tilted in any direction.

"This is a laboratory," Malcolm said.

"Very good," Pastory said, as though to an apt pupil. "Would you like to jump up on the table there?"

"No."

"I think, my boy, we had better understand how things are run around here. When I make a suggestion, it is not really a suggestion. It is an order. And when I give an order, you obey. That way we will all get along much better. Now get up on that table."

Malcolm felt his face growing hot. His shoulder still hurt where Kruger had dug into the nerve. He walked to the table, turned around, and gave a little jump so he was sitting on it.

"That's the idea," Pastory said. "Now lie back, please."

"What for?"

Pastory snapped his head at the big man who was standing by eagerly. "Kruger!"

Before Malcolm knew what was happening, Kruger had pushed him down flat on his back and had buckled a strap around one of his wrists. He flailed out with his free hand.

"Cut it out!" he yelled.

Kruger drew back a massive arm and cracked the back of his hand against Malcolm's cheek. Malcolm tasted blood. His eyesight blurred for a moment and there seemed to be an edge of fire around everything. There was a strange growling sound in his ears, and Malcolm was surprised to realize it came from his own throat.

Pastory hurried over to the table. "Did you see that? Wonderful! Get the other hand strapped down, Kruger. And his feet. Quickly!"

As the doctor peered down on him Malcolm's flash of anger drained away, to be replaced by a numb feeling of hopelessness.

"There, he's changing back now," Pastory said. "But did you see it, Kruger? Did you see what happened to his face?"

"It looked funny there for a minute. Like his teeth were too big for his mouth, or something."

"Or something!" Pastory repeated. He leaned very close to Malcolm, took his chin in one hand, and turned his head this way and that. His breath had a minty smell.

"Are you all right now, Malcolm?" he asked.

"I want to get up."

"In time, my boy. In time. Tell me what you felt just then, when you tried to get at Kruger."

"I-I was mad. He shouldn't have hit me."

"No, you're quite right. I'll see that it doesn't happen again."

Pastory walked back to the counter and began to write furiously in a hardbound notebook. He spoke more to himself than to the others in the room. "It appears that anger triggers the change. I wonder if other powerful emotions will have the same effect. We will have to look into that."

He returned to the table. "Open your mouth, please."

Malcolm hesitated.

"It's only a thermometer. See? All I want to do is take your temperature. Now open, please."

Reluctantly Malcolm obeyed, and the doctor slipped the glass tube expertly under his tongue.

"I am going to take a sample of your blood now. A very small bit, Malcolm. You'll never miss it."

The boy watched as Pastory inserted the hollow needle into a vein on the inside of his elbow and drew crimson fluid up into the cylinder.

"There now." The doctor withdrew the needle and taped a wad of cotton over the tiny hole it left. He took the thermometer out of Malcolm's mouth and examined it. "A touch above normal. Nothing to be concerned about."

"Can I get up now?" Malcolm said.

"Very soon, my boy. There is just one more shot now, one that will relax you and make you feel good. Then we'll get you up and get you something to eat."

Pastory gave him the needle in the shoulder, then backed away, looking very pleased with himself. "You just relax for a minute or so, Malcolm. I want to go and check some references. If you need anything, just tell Kruger here. Okay?"

Malcolm rolled his head to look at the doctor, but he did not answer. A heavy feeling was spreading through his body. He did not want to do much of anything.

As soon as Pastory went out and closed the door, Kruger came over and stared down into the boy's face. The man's heavy features were twisted in open hostility.

"You'd better not do anything like that to me again," he said.

"Didn't do anything." It was an effort for Malcolm to get the words out.

"You know what I'm talking about. That thing you did with your face and your teeth. I don't care what the doctor says. You'd better behave or I'll hurt you."

The big man talked to him some more, but Malcolm floated off to a warm, cozy place where the words made no sense.

After that, time had little meaning for Malcolm. He knew he was being measured and weighed, prodded and pricked, tested, retested, fed, and purged. He did not care about any of it. Sometimes he would be left alone and Kruger would be there. The big man glowered at him constantly and made threats, but Malcolm had no energy to respond.

The worst part was when he was strapped to the table. Then Pastory would do things to him that he didn't like to think about. Things with little electric wires and such. Sometimes the doctor made it very cold in the laboratory, sometimes unbearably hot. He was always writing in his book, looking very excited. With the drug in him, Malcolm couldn't care.

Then Dr. Pastory made a mistake with one of the shots he regularly gave Malcolm. The boy moved his arm just as the needle went in, and the drug squirted harmlessly onto his sleeve. So intent was Pastory on watching Malcolm's face that he did not see. When he went away Malcolm could feel himself growing steadily stronger and more alert.

Later that night—or maybe it was day, Malcolm could never be sure—Kruger came into his room. The boy saw him but pretended to be asleep.

"You awake?" Kruger demanded. "Yeah, I can see you are. Come on, it's time to get you up and get you dressed." He started toward the boy.

"Don't touch me," Malcolm said. "Keep away."

"Listen, you don't tell me what to do and what not to do. Maybe you need to be reminded of who's boss around here." Kruger lumbered over to the bed, reached down, and seized Malcolm's wrist.

A dull anger pushed its way into the boy's clearing mind, but he still did not have the strength to pull away.

Gripping Malcolm's wrist with one hand, Kruger pulled a cigarette lighter from his pocket with the other. He snapped on the flame and brought it slowly up under the boy's palm.

The sensation of heat quickly grew into pain. It brought back terrible memories of a night of flames and screaming and the stench of burning flesh. The flesh of his people.

In a sudden convulsive movement, Malcolm snapped his head to one side and clamped his teeth on the hairy wrist of the man who held him. The skin broke easily, and he worked his jaws from side to side, biting through the tougher muscle meat. His tongue felt the slick, ropy tendons through the taste of blood.

Kruger's scream shattered around his head like breaking glass. The cigarette lighter dropped to the floor. Malcolm bit down harder, finding a wild joy in the sensation of sinking his teeth into living flesh.

"Kruger!" The shout came from Dr. Pastory, who had run into the room in response to the big man's cry.

"Get him off me!" Kruger shrieked, trying to pull his arm free.

Malcolm, eyes closed in a kind of ecstasy, bit down all the harder. He felt bones grind against his teeth.

There was a short, sharp stab in the back of his neck, and Malcolm recognized it as the jab of a needle. Instantly he lost feeling in his face. His jaw muscles slackened and Kruger pulled his lacerated arm free.

"Look what that little son of a bitch did to me! Look at my arm! I'll kill the little bastard!"

"Shut up, Kruger."

Malcolm watched dully as Dr. Pastory pulled his assistant away and looked at his arm.

"He took quite a chunk out of you," Pastory said.

"Damn near bit through the bone. Will it get infected or anything?"

"I'll dress it for you in a minute. What I want to know is, what did you do to provoke him?"

"Nothing. I didn't do nothing."

Pastory stooped and picked something off the floor. "What's this?"

"My lighter. I-I must have dropped it."

"Don't lie to me, Kruger. Don't ever lie to me. You know all I have to do is say the word to have you put back in the bad place."

"Please don't, Doctor. I was just fooling around. I didn't mean to do anything to him."

"Get out of here. Go to the laboratory and I'll come in and take a look at that bite. It may even turn out to be helpful to me."

Cradling his injured arm, Kruger left them alone.

Pastory came over and touched Malcolm's face. The anesthetic had left him without any feeling there, but Malcolm could see the doctor poking at the flesh and muttering to himself.

"Incredible. Absolutely incredible. Malcolm, you are going to make me a very rich and famous man. We have a lot of work to do in the next few days, but then we'll start reaping the rewards. And don't you worry, my boy. I'll take very, very good care of you."

Malcolm sank back on the narrow bed. All the anger was gone. All he felt now was an icy despair. He was ready to give up and die, except for one thing. He still held in his mouth the delicious taste of Kruger's blood.

13

Sheriff Gavin Ramsay of La Reina County had moments during the next few days when he seriously questioned his choice of career. The investigation of Dr. Dennis Qualen's murder was not going well. It was, in fact, going very badly.

The search of the surrounding hills turned up nothing. The only flurry of excitement had come when one of the searchers shot another in the foot. After that the fun was out of the whole thing. The volunteers had gone back to their jobs. The helicopters had returned to their home counties or their TV station heliports. Only a few men from the State Forestry Service now combed the woods, doing mostly cleanup and repair of the damage to the environment done by the searchers.

The detailed pathology report had arrived from Dr. Underwood and had done nothing to lift Ramsay's spirits. The wounds that had killed Qualen were definitely identified as having been made by teeth. Unfortunately, they were not the teeth of any animal known to exist on the face of the earth. The traces of saliva were no more helpful, falling somewhere on the spectrograph between human and canine.

While the sheriff suffered, the media had a field day. Every man, woman, and reasonably articulate child in Pinyon had been interviewed at least once. Deputies Nevins and Fernandez became media heroes, the first to his delight, the latter with some embarrassment. All the old horror stories of Drago were dug up and embellished until La Reina County was presented to the rest of the nation as a sort of

Southern California Transylvania, where no one walked out of doors at night.

Most galling to Ramsay was the fact that Abe Craddock had been bailed out by one of the supermarket tabloids and was being kept in seclusion while his personal eyewitness story was being ghostwritten for the paper. Rumor had Craddock collecting a comfortable five-figure price for his lurid recollections of the thing that had eaten his buddy.

And, in fact, a pall of fear had descended over the tiny mountain town. Blinds were drawn, shutters reinforced, doors double-locked at night where before no one had bothered with so much as a hook and eye. Nightly patronage at the Pinyon Inn dwindled to a few hardcore regulars who drank little and talked in guarded tones. They came and left in pairs or groups. No one wanted to be alone.

The tiny library was immediately denuded of all books touching on werewolves, vampires, witches, or anything remotely occult. Then the librarian refused to stay there alone any longer and the doors were locked.

The happiest man in the county was Ken Dowd, whose Darnay occult shop, The Spirit World, emptied its shelves of all manner of charms and talismans that might protect the bearer from whatever evil lurked in the woods.

Nor was the occult dealer the only beneficiary of the werewolf boom. The Light of the World Christian Store, also in Darnay, had a run on crucifixes from customers who did not know Calvary from the Seventh Cavalry. The Light of the World people had to reorder crosses on a rush basis from a religious supply firm in Los Angeles, and still they could barely meet the demand.

Bibles were also a hot item in La Reina County, with King James topping the list, but even the updated versions were outselling the newest Garfield book. Enterprising roadside peddlers appeared with pictures and statuettes representing Jesus, Mary, and a variety of saints, and were doing fine business until local authorities clamped down. From outward appearances, La Reina County was the scene of the greatest Christian revival since Billy Graham filled the L.A. Coliseum.

As if all this were not enough to add gray hairs to the head of Sheriff Ramsay, Holly Lang was after him continually to devote more of his efforts to locating the missing boy, Malcolm. The sheriff was trying to maintain an expression of gentle concern on an early morning several days after the killing as Holly stood across the desk from him, gesticulating angrily.

"Damn it, Gavin, that weasel Pastory is keeping him somewhere," she insisted. For a moment Ramsay thought she was going to pound on the desk, but she brought herself under control. "Why aren't you doing something? Why aren't you looking for him? You're supposed to be the sheriff."

"Comments from the public are always welcome," Ramsay said. "Maybe you will be kind enough to suggest where I might look."

"That's just it. I've talked to everybody at the hospital, and nobody knows where this mysterious clinic of Pastory's is, or if it even exists."

"Ah, then you see part of my problem."

"Problem, hell. I want to hear solutions from you."

"I am doing the best I can, Holly," Gavin said with all the patience he could muster. "I have a want out on Pastory as a material witness. His relatives, of which there seem to be very few, deny all knowledge of his whereabouts." He pulled a sheet of paper from an overflowing basket on his desk. "To quote his brother Kyle in Boise, Idaho, 'I don't know where the S.O.B. is and I don't give a damn.' His clinic is not listed with the California Medical Association or any other group that I've been able to turn up."

"So what are you doing now?"

"Right now I am doing what I can to find the killer of Dr. Dennis Qualen."

"So, are you making any progress?"

"I have before me reports of all killings in the western United States during the past five years that were in any way similar to that of Dr. Qualen."

"And?"

"And you'd be surprised how many people are ripped to pieces. When I eliminate the chain saws and the axes and the certified mad dogs and the circus maulings and one farmer in Oregon who seems to have been eaten by his pigs, do you know what's left?"

"Please tell me," Holly said.

"Drago."

"Oh, Jesus!" she said in exasperation.

"Amen," he added piously.

"I trust, Sheriff, that you won't mind if I do what I can on my own to locate Dr. Pastory and Malcolm."

"Holly, I hope you are not going to get a gun and go rushing off like a crazed vigilante."

"I do not believe in guns," she said.

"I am relieved to hear that. As long as you stay within the law, I can do nothing to stop you. I have to insist, however, that you will in no way interfere with the actions of legitimate police officers."

"That sounds like something you memorized," she said.

"It is," he admitted, "but I mean it."

"Good enough, Sheriff. You go your way and I'll go mine."

She turned smartly and marched out of the office, giving him no chance for a reply.

What reply could he make, anyway? Everything she said was essentially correct. He was the sheriff, and he was doing a lousy job. Moreover, this business had split him and Holly apart just when he was thinking something good might develop there. It was with an honest feeling of loss that Ramsay watched her climb into the little Volkswagen Rabbit with the Greenpeace emblem and drive off, scattering as much gravel as she could manage with the underpowered car.

* * *

Holly was so angry when she left Gavin Ramsay that she had to exert a force of will to pull her foot up off the accelerator. She felt like the fabled knight who leaped on his horse and rode madly off in all directions. This was not like her. She was a calm, reasonable woman, always in control of her emotions. What right did that Gavin Ramsay have, anyway, keeping her awake nights thinking about the way they had kissed at her door?

All right. She would handle it. She got the Rabbit down to an acceptable speed and headed west on Highway 126, which ran along the Santa Clara River. She kept the window on her side rolled down to let the moist morning air flow in and cool her feverish face.

She drove through Fillmore and on toward Santa Paula, taking deep breaths, feeling the muscles at the back of her neck and along her shoulders gradually relax as she ordered her mind, putting everything into its proper compartment.

Number One. She was worried about Malcolm. The boy had special qualities that she had only begun to discover. In time she would have found out who he was and what he was and helped him to live with it. That time had been stolen from her.

It hurt to know that she had been gaining the boy's trust. It was she he had first spoken to. She for whom he had called when he was hurting. What must he think of his new friend now?

Number Two. She was mad as hell at Gavin Ramsay. He brushed off her suggestions and her requests like some hysterical woman. Well, maybe that was overstating the case. Nevertheless, he was a whole lot more interested in catching his Werewolf Killer, as the media were now calling it, than he was in locating a missing boy. But wait, she cautioned herself, isn't Gavin doing his job the very best way he can? Was she being unfair? Maybe so, but what the hell, life was unfair. If he was going to treat her like some addled, helpless female, then to hell with him.

By the time she pulled into Ventura and parked on a bluff overlooking the Pacific Ocean and the Holiday Inn, she was under control and feeling better. She had a plan.

The foremost supplier of medical equipment in the area, Landrud & Co., was located in Ventura. If Wayne Pastory had ordered anything medical for this phantom clinic of his, it would have been from Landrud.

Holly restarted the engine and drove until she found a Texaco station with public telephones. She riffled through the Yellow Pages and located the number for Landrud & Co. She dropped a coin into the slot, punched out the number, and asked the switchboard operator to connect her with the Sales Department.

"Hello," she said, making her voice brusque and businesslike when she was put through. "This is Dr. Hollanda Lang of La Reina County Hospital. I wonder if I might see someone there about an order for new laboratory equipment."

"Of course, Dr. Lang," came the answer. "We'll be glad to talk to you. Would you like to come in this afternoon, or any time tomorrow, at your convenience?"

"As a matter of fact, I'm rather pressed for time, and if possible I'd like to make it sooner. I'm only about ten minutes away from your building right now."

She could almost hear the salesman calculating the probable commission on the other end. "Well, yes, I'm sure that would be possible. I can reschedule one of my own appointments and see you right away."

"Thank you, I appreciate that. Your name is—?"

"Schaeffer. Olan Schaeffer. I'll leave word with the receptionist to expect you."

"Very good. I'll see you in a few minutes, then, Mr. Schaeffer."

Holly replaced the receiver and drew a deep breath. She had managed a couple of white lies there without even flinching. And Gavin Ramsay thought she would get in the way of his police work. Hah!

Damn, why did she keep thinking about the loose-jointed sheriff with those hard blue eyes that could soften like anything? So what if he was one hell of a kisser? Nuts to him.

Landrud & Co. was in a low, unimaginative cinder-block building with lots of glass around the entrance and some fake-looking greenery in front to soften the antiseptic effect. Holly parked brazenly in a slot marked CUSTOMER and entered the chrome-modern reception area.

She handed her business card to a lacquered-haired receptionist and said, "I believe Mr. Schaeffer is expecting me."

"Oh, yes, Dr. Lang. He asked me to tell him at once when you got here." The receptionist smiled with several thousand dollars worth of porcelain and touched a button on her telephone panel. Maintaining the smile for Holly, she said into the mouthpiece, "Dr. Lang is here, Mr. Schaeffer." A moment's pause. "He'll be right out, Doctor."

Olan Schaeffer was a short, ruddy-faced man with thinning hair and cigar breath, which he disguised inadequately with Tic-Tacs. His suit was a muted shark-skin as befitted the serious nature of the product he sold, but he allowed himself a touch of playfulness in the orange and blue figured tie.

"Well, Dr. Lang," he said after seating her in his compact office, "I believe you said you were interested in laboratory equipment. I have our catalog here, and several brochures you might want to glance through."

"Actually, that won't be necessary," Holly said, wishing she had better prepared her story. "I'd like to talk to you about equipment ordered by a colleague of mine, Dr. Wayne Pastory."

Schaeffer's smile slipped a notch, as though he felt his commission shrinking. "Uh, was that order placed for La Reina County?"

"No. Dr. Pastory is associated with us, but the equipment I'm interested in was ordered for his own private clinic."

"I see," Schaeffer said, not seeing at all. "May I ask specifically what it is you want to know?"

"We've had excellent reports at La Reina County," Holly improvised, "about the quality of Dr. Pastory's equipment. And the price offered by you people, of course."

They exchanged little insider smiles.

"Our board of directors is interested in making a similar purchase for a new wing we have under construction."

"Ah, yes, I see. Excellent." The commission light returned to the salesman's eyes. "Well, we'll just punch it up on the old computer here and see what we shall see."

He swiveled his chair around and lifted the dustcover from a computer terminal as though unveiling a prized *objet d'art*. "Everything's done on the computer nowadays. Sometimes I kind of miss poking through the old filing cabinets, but I guess that's progress."

Holly forced herself to sit quietly and smile while Schaeffer flipped on the terminal and waited for the screen to come to life. She crossed her legs to give the man something to look at other than her smile, which was becoming strained.

The computer beeped politely and prompted him in pale green characters to get on with it.

"Would you spell the doctor's name for me?" he asked. Holly wrote it out for him on a desk-pad. Stiff-fingered, he punched the proper command keys, then spelled out WAYNE PASTORY, M.D. The computer beeped and buzzed and Holly began rehearsing her exit in case no information came up on Pastory. She needn't have worried, for after a final buzz and beep the screen was filled with pale green readout that listed dates, medical apparatus, prices, and other coded information.

"Dr. Pastory has been quite a good customer," Schaeffer said. "Especially in the last month.

Ah, yes, that's what I understand," Holly said, leaning forward, trying to decipher the computer language on the screen.

"Can you tell me specifically what pieces of equipment you're interested in? Or I could run a printout of the whole file, if that would help."

"Yes, yes, I'm sure it would, but I want to be certain this is not material the doctor ordered for La Reina. It's his own clinic that I'm interested in."

"Of course. The computer knows all, tells all." Schaeffer tapped several additional keys. "No, all this was shipped to his clinic up near Bear Paw. Is that the place?"

Holly almost laughed with relief. "Yes, Bear Paw. A funny name that I can never remember. That's the place."

"Not much of a town, from what I hear," said the helpful Schaeffer. "Gets a few skiers in the winter is about it. Anyway, they've got a post office and your Dr. Pastory's clinic."

Holly stood up. "Thank you so much, Mr. Schaeffer. I can't tell you how helpful you've been."

The salesman scrambled to his feet. "But the equipment. Didn't you want to go over the list?"

"Why don't you run off that printout and send it to me in care of La Reina County Hospital? I look forward to doing business with you."

Holly made her second hasty exit of the morning, leaving a befuddled Olan Schaeffer wondering whether his commission had just sailed out the door.

14

While Holly Lang took hasty leave of the offices of Landrud & Co. in Ventura, Abe Craddock was draining a can of Coors in the old Whitaker place. It was a falling-down cabin set well back in the trees at the south end of Pinyon, and had not been used since old George Whitaker's Dodge had slipped off a jack while he was under it down at Art Moore's Exxon station.

The cabin had been rented from old George Whitaker's widow by a smart-talking writer fella from Los Angeles who was doing a story for one of the scandal sheets they sold where you paid for your groceries, over at the Safeway. This so-called writer had bailed Abe Craddock out of jail and promised him a cool thousand dollars just for telling him the story of what happened in the woods that day with Curly Vane and the wolf thing. The catch was that Craddock would tell his story to no one else.

Abe figured he flat had it made. Not only was he living fairly comfortable in the cabin with Betty out of his hair; he was taking this smartass L.A. writer for all the booze he could drink, and figured he could probably up the dollar price on him, too. As for the manslaughter charge against him for blowing up Jones, that was no sweat anymore. With the kid gone and Curly nothing but raw meat, there were no witnesses. It was an accident, pure and simple. Yes, things were surely going old Abe Craddock's way for a change.

The L.A. writer, Louis Zeno by name, was hammering away at the old typewriter he'd brought with him like he was trying to set the thing on fire. Abe had never in his life seen a man who could type so fast.

Zeno ripped out the page he was working on and handed it over to Craddock. "All right, Abe, I want you to take a look at this and see if it sounds all right. Remember, this is supposed to be you telling the story, and I want to be sure the facts are reasonably close to what really happened."

Craddock took the page, set aside the Coors can, wiped his mouth, cleared his throat. He began to read in a labored schoolboy manner:

"When Curly Vane and I entered the dense, dripping forest outside Pinyon on that fateful afternoon, perhaps we should have sensed..."

Abe stopped reading and looked up, frowning.

"Something the matter?" Zeno said impatiently.

"It's that dripping forest business. The forest don't drip. Least, I don't remember no dripping that particular day."

"That's alliteration for effect," Zeno told him.

"Huh?"

"Don't worry about it. Read the rest."

Craddock went through his preliminary mouth-wiping and throat-clearing again and continued:

"...should have sensed a certain foreboding, an ominous presence lurking unseen in the shadows. But in our innocent good spirits, neither of us could foresee the unspeakable fate that would befall one of us before we would see the sun again..."

Abe stopped again, shaking his head.

"What now?" the writer said wearily.

"Uh, I ain't sure I get that business about the sun. I mean, it was up there all the time. We weren't in no cave, you know."

"Never mind that," Zeno told him. "That's just for atmosphere. All I want you to do is make sure that what I say you say happened is more or less what happened. So if anybody asks you about it after the story comes out you can tell them, sure, that's the way it was. Okay?"

"Yeah, okay. I get it." Craddock sucked noisily at the empty beer can. "Reading this stuff is mighty thirsty work, and damn if I don't think this is the last of the Coors."

"Jesus, Abe, it isn't even noon yet, and you've put away a whole six-pack and part of another."

"Hell, that's nothin'. You should of seen me and Curly when we really got down to some serious drinking. Hell, we wouldn't leave no bottle untapped in three counties."

"I'll bet," Zeno said unhappily.

"An' you did say you'd provide the drinking stuff as long as I gave my story to you and nobody else. Ain't that right?"

"That's right, Abe," Zeno said. "Let's just finish this part where you walk into the woods and first see the Wolfman."

Craddock coughed loudly. "Damn, Lou, I just don't think I can rightly concentrate anymore without something to cool down my throat."

"All right," the writer snapped. "I'll go get some more beer. Do you think a twelve-pack will hold you till lunchtime?"

"Might be," Craddock said. "If you get the sixteen ounce cans; it'll go farther."

"Yeah, yeah, sixteen-ounce." Louis Zeno lowered the cover onto his precious portable Royal and stood up.

Someday, some blessed day, Louis Zeno would finish the book that was finally going to make him some real money and free him forever from writing trash for the supermarket tabloids and dealing with scum like this foul-smelling Abe Craddock. He had the outline tucked away in his apartment in West Hollywood. All he needed was a free month or so to get it down on paper and off to a publisher.

In the meantime, he would just have to keep turning out stories about mothers who stuffed their babies into microwave ovens and country girls fucked by green men from outer space and assholes like Abe Craddock and his imaginary werewolf. He could look forward to one small victory when Craddock tried to collect the imaginary thousand dollars Zeno had promised him. The writer crossed the cabin's single room to where his jacket hung from a bent nail.

"You might pick up some Fritos while you're at the store," Craddock suggested. "One of the big bags."

"Big bag. Sure."

"When you get back I'll tell you the part where I took on that wolf thing with my bare hands after I seen what he done to Curly. I mean, I was holdin' my own, too, maybe gettin' the best of things. If only I hadn't of caught my boot there in them bushes and tripped myself up it might of been a whole 'nother story."

"Yeah, Abe, swell, but let's just stick to the story we've got. I'll ask the questions and you tell me what happened in your own halting words. I'm the professional. I know how to put these things together."

"I guess that's right," Abe said slyly, "but without me you wouldn't have nothing to put together. Ain't that so?"

Fuck you, you stinking ignorant redneck bastard! is what Louis Zeno thought. What he said was, "Yeah, that's so, Abe. Without you I'd be standing in the unemployment line."

"Well, don't you worry, Lou buddy, you and me are going to make us a whole shitpot full of money with this before we're through."

Zeno shrugged into his jacket and headed for the door.

Neither man looked toward the dusty windowpane at the side of the cabin. If they had, they might have seen the eyes that watched them. Eyes that gradually changed color until they seemed to glow an unearthly green.

* * *

Derak watched the man from the city leave the cabin and stalk down the trail to the clearing where he had parked the little orange car. The engine fired and the city man drove off. Derak looked back through the window at the gross, murdering hunter. The smoldering hatred inside him kindled to a flame. Derak moved a short distance away from the cabin and carefully removed his clothes so they would not be shredded as the transformation began.

* * *

Abe Craddock thumbed a wad of Copenhagen into his cheek and sucked out the good tobacco flavor. He should have told the writer fella to pick up a couple of tins of that, too. The dumb prick would bring anything Abe wanted as long as he got what he called an exclusive on Abe's battle with the werewolf. In Abe's mind the whole thing by now had actually taken place as he told the story and retold it. He came out looking a little more heroic every time.

There was no doubt in Abe's mind that he could milk more than a thousand dollars out of this. Hell, he could probably get double that. Those papers must pay good money for a story like this, and if Zeno was going to use his name he was going to have to pay for it.

Something scratched at the door.

Abe took a look at his waterproof Timex. It was much too soon for Zeno to be back from the liquor store. He didn't want to see any of the reporters who were still hanging around Pinyon, so he'd have to drive clear to Darnay.

Something scratched again.

Could the damn fool writer have forgotten something and come back for it? No, they had a special knock that Zeno would give to show it was him. He didn't want anybody else getting close to Abe before he had the exclusive story all written and handed over to the editor. That was the whole idea of hiding up here in the Whitaker cabin where nobody had come in years.

Scratch. *Scratch*.

You don't suppose the widow Whitaker would of told somebody they were up here? Not likely, since she didn't know what the fool city man wanted with her broken-down cabin and was just glad to get the ten bucks Zeno offered her.

Thump.

There was sure as hell something outside the door. Well, it wouldn't hurt to take a tiny peek. Zeno had bored a hole in the door at eye level and stuck a patch of leather over it so he could look out in case anybody came sniffing around.

Abe went over, lifted the leather patch, and put his eye to the hole. He had a full two seconds for his brain to register the fact that he was looking into another eye of the most terrible fiery green.

Then the door splintered inward like it was dynamited.

Abe staggered backward, knocking over the card table with Zeno's typewriter on it and stumbling among the empty beer cans on the floor. The thing that came at him had to bend down to get its head through the doorway. Even inside the cabin the thing's pointed, hairy ears brushed against the ceiling. The terrible black-lipped muzzle had a wet, just born look. And the teeth. My God, the teeth. Abe Craddock vividly recalled what those teeth had done to Curly Vane, and all his heroic fantasies dissolved before the roaring reality.

"No don't, no don't, no don't!" Abe cried. He might as well have appealed to the wind.

His back thumped against the opposite wall of the cabin and he could retreat no farther. A voice he did not recognize as his own whimpered in his ear.

The beast paused before him, its mighty chest twice the girth of Abe's own. The powerful jaws worked up and down. The beast seemed to savor the helplessness of the man before it.

When the beast struck, it was faster than Abe Craddock's eye could follow. He was intent on those terrible teeth when it struck out at him with a forepaw. The razor talons ripped four parallel gashes down the front of him from sternum to pubic bone.

For an instant Abe felt nothing. He looked down, stunned at the slashes through his t-shirt, his jeans, his jockey shorts, and the fatty flesh beneath. Then the pain came. And the blood.

The blood oozed at first, then bubbled out of him, splashing the bare wooden floor where he stood. Abe clutched at himself, trying to hold his intestines in place. But they bulged and coiled out over his hands like a nest of wet red snakes.

The beast let him scream for a while as his legs gave out and he sank to the floor in a pool of his own blood, guts, and shit. Abe saw the gaping mouth come down toward him. Felt the teeth clamp on his head. Heard the crack of his skull...

* * *

Derak curled himself on the ground near the pile of his clothes and focused his will on the shape change. The transformation from beast back to man held none of the wild joy that was a part of becoming a wolf. Ideally, there should be a full, uninterrupted night to let the tension ease and change back gradually. When it had to be forced and speeded up, the changes to the body were painful in the extreme.

However, there was no help for it now. Derak had a mission, and it was only partly complete. He had set himself the task of returning Malcolm to his own people before the boy could do irreparable harm to himself or others of his kind. If along the way he could destroy some human garbage like Abe Craddock, it would add pleasure to his task.

Derak's body shuddered. He ground his teeth against the pain. The internal organs shifted and jumped under his skin. His skeleton cracked as the bones returned to human form. The body hair vanished as though sucked back into the hide. The ears shrank and rounded off; the muzzle pulled in; the killing teeth receded into the harmless molars and incisors of a man.

Slowly, slowly, the pain eased. Derak moved, straightening his body, testing his limbs and extremities. He shivered with the cold on his naked flesh.

As he pulled his clothes back on, Derak froze at a sound from the road below and ducked behind a bush. The little orange car chugged into the clearing and stopped. The man from the city climbed out, bringing with him a half case of beer and a crinkly bag of chips. Derak watched as the man labored up the path with his burden toward the cabin. The wise thing would be to destroy him, but the blood lust was stilled, and Derak had no wish to kill now without reason.

He waited until the city man had lumbered past the bush where he crouched, then he loped silently down the trail to the car. The door was unlocked. He tore away a fiberboard panel beneath the dash and found the ignition wires.

At the top of the trail the man from the city had seen the shattered remnants of the door. He dropped the beer and the sack of chips and walked stiff-legged toward the cabin.

Derak stripped the wires with a tough thumbnail and twisted them together.

By the time Louis Zeno staggered out of the cabin, white-faced, with his mouth agape in a silent scream, his little orange car was turning onto the road toward the town of Pinyon.

* * *

As he drove, Derak pulled tissues from a carton on the dash panel and wiped away what he could of the blood and mud from his face. He was a fastidious man, and it made him uncomfortable not to bathe after a killing. However, this time the change back had to be done so fast, there was no time.

Derak's mind had not completely reoriented, and as soon as he had a chance, he pulled the car off into a sheltered spot alongside the road next to an Exxon station. He was startled to see only then that the backs of his hands were still thickly overgrown with hair. He tucked the hands away out of sight, leaned back in the seat, closed his eyes, and let himself slip into a light doze.

He awoke sometime later, refreshed and alert. He rubbed his hands front and back to be sure that the change was now truly complete. Only then did he realize he had brought the little car to a stop almost directly across from the office of La Reina County's sheriff.

Derak immediately choked down an impulse to panic. If anyone were still looking for a man of his description after the wild werewolf tales that had clouded the killing of Dr. Qualen, they would hardly expect him to be sitting in a car parked almost in the sheriff's lap.

Using mental techniques learned from those who had traveled his road before, Derak settled into a quiet watchfulness that had protected his kind through the ages.

A small, square car pulled into the parking area before the sheriff's office. A young woman got out. The doctor. Derak had followed closely the events in Pinyon, and he knew that she, of all the people here, was the most anxious to find Malcolm. If anyone could lead him to the boy, it would be she.

Derak slid lower in the driver's seat and watched as the young woman got out and went into the office.

15

Deputy Roy Nevins was alone in the sheriff's office when Holly entered. She barely recognized the man. Deputy Nevins's uniform was spotless and pressed, complete to the military creases in the shirt. His boots, belt, and holster were shined. He was freshly shaved, had obviously just had a haircut. He was even making an effort to hold his stomach in.

"Morning, ma'am," he said, getting to his feet. His speech seemed to have softened into more of a western drawl.

Remarkable, Holly thought, what a touch of fame will do.

"Good morning, Roy. Is Gavin around?"

"The sheriff and Deputy Fernandez are out on a call, ma'am. Left me in charge. Seems there's been some trouble down at the old Whitaker cabin."

"Will you cut out the ma'am stuff, Roy? You make me feel like Dale Evans."

The deputy grinned a little sheepishly. "I just thought we ought to be a little more businesslike around here, what with all the reporters and television people and whatnot."

"Well, I suppose it couldn't hurt. How soon do you expect Gavin back?"

"That's hard to say. Seems whoever it was made the phone call wasn't bein' very clear about what the trouble was at the cabin."

Holly chewed at her lower lip. Why was there never a cop around when you needed one?

"Anything I can help you with?"

"It was just a message I wanted to give the sheriff."

"You're welcome to sit yourself down and wait for him." Roy wheeled one of the unused swivel chairs over for her.

"No thanks, Roy, I'm in kind of a hurry. I'll leave him a note."

She tore a page from Ramsay's calendar pad and wrote:

Gavin:
I managed to find out where Dr. Pastory's clinic is without getting in the way of any of your 'duly authorized police officers.' I'll let you know when I've found Malcolm. Good luck with your big murder investigation.

She read it over, then crumpled the page and threw it into the wastebasket. Cheap sarcasm was not her style. On another calendar sheet she wrote:

Gavin:
Dr. Pastory's clinic is located in Bear Paw. I'm on my way up there. I'll check with you as soon as I find anything.
Take care,
Holly

She placed the note in the center of his desk blotter, anchoring it with a stapler.

"Thanks, Roy," she said. "I'll see you."

"Anytime, ma'am," he said, reaching for the brim of the hat he was not wearing, then, grinning, "Oops. I'm kinda getting into the habit, I guess."

Before leaving the office, Holly checked the big map tacked to one wall. It covered all of La Reina County and included parts of Los Angeles, Ventura, and Kern counties as well. She located the tiny community of Bear Paw just on the other side of the Tehachapi Pass, beyond Clarion. She figured it as a two-to-three-hour drive, depending on road conditions. There certainly wouldn't be much traffic between here and there.

She filled the tank of her little Rabbit across the road at Art Moore's station, then headed north. Holly's mind was filled with thoughts of what she was going to say to Wayne Pastory when she found him, and she did not pay any attention to the little orange car that pulled onto the road behind her and followed her out of town.

The roads were good all the way, although narrowing to a cramped two lanes as she left the state highway. It took her slightly less than two hours to reach the community of Bear Paw. Had she not been actively looking for it, the entire town would have been easy to miss.

There was the Bear Paw Ski Lodge, a faintly alpine A-frame building with the windows shuttered and a chain across the driveway leading to the entrance. A hand-lettered sign hanging from the chain read: CLOSED FOR THE SEASON.

That was it, except for a paint-peeling frame building that was combination post office/grocery store/gas station/tavern. Out in front were parked a grimy Ford pickup and an equally grimy Plymouth some twenty years old.

Holly pulled to a stop at the old-fashioned gas pumps. When no one appeared after a minute, she got out and went into the building. Three men, none of them younger than seventy, sat around—not a potbellied stove—but an electric heater. The temperature inside was a stifling eighty. Behind a scarred wooden counter a grossly overweight woman with a mustache sat on a stool while she read a paperback novel called *Love's Raging Heart*.

The three men looked up when Holly entered. The woman continued to read. No one spoke.

"Hi," Holly said finally. "This is Bear Paw, I hope."

"Sure is, honey," said the woman. She marked her spot in the book with a forefinger and looked up. "What can we do you for?"

"I was wondering if you knew of a clinic around here. Owned by Dr. Wayne Pastory."

One of the men around the heater worked his lips noisily over toothless gums. "You a friend of his?"

"Not exactly. We sometimes work together. The clinic is around here somewhere?"

Another of the men spoke up. His hands were gnarled and knobbed with arthritis. He kept them lying awkwardly in his lap as though they did not really belong to him. "What you want to go up there for, anyhow?"

Holly started to tell the man it was none of his damn business, but brought herself under control. "I have to see Dr. Pastory about something," she said as courteously as she could manage.

"You sick?" said the woman.

"I'm a doctor."

"You don't look like a doctor," said the third man. He had one eye that appeared to be glass. Cheap glass.

"Well, I am." Holly began to feel more than a little irritated with these unpleasant rustics.

"If you're sick, you'd do a lot better to go to Doc Simms down in Clarion," said the man with arthritis. "Good man, Doc Simms. Been around long enough to know what he's doing. Your Doc—what's his name, Pastorini..."

"Pastory."

"Whatever. He don't look like he's dry behind the ears yet. Name sounds like a foreigner, besides."

"Look," Holly said, putting some authority into her voice, "I'm in something of a hurry. Could you please tell me where the clinic is?"

"No need to get snippy about it," said the toothless man. "You want to go to the doggone clinic, that's you're business. We sure ain't stoppin' you."

"Where is it?" Holly was surprised at the whip-crack in her own voice. The four people stared as though really seeing her for the first time.

The woman finally spoke. "Go on up the way you're headed about a mile and a half. There's a logging trail turns off to your right. It ain't easy to see if you're not watchin'. Drive up that two, maybe three miles. And there you are."

They stared at her for another long moment, but no one spoke again.

"Thank you very much," Holly said. She hurried out of the store, into the car, and headed up the road.

* * *

At approximately the time Holly was pulling out of Pinyon on her way to find his clinic, Dr. Wayne Pastory was leading Malcolm from his room to a part of the clinic where he had not been before. It was a high-ceilinged room that was bare of decoration. The furniture consisted of two plain wooden chairs. There was one door and a high-up window that showed nothing but the dark trees outside.

Inside the room was a cage of heavy-gauge steel wire mesh that was backed against one wall. The cage measured about seven feet square and contained a stretched-canvas cot and a bucket for waste.

Pastory unlocked the door to the cage and guided Malcolm inside. "I'm sorry to have to lock you up like this, Malcolm, but I have to drive into Clarion for supplies. I shouldn't be gone more than three hours, and I trust you won't be too uncomfortable in that time."

"Why do I have to be locked in here?" Malcolm said. His mind was still fuzzy from the sleeping drug he'd been given the night before.

"Security, my boy, security," said Pastory, giving him a little pat on the shoulder. "It's as much for your own safety as anything else."

The doctor backed out of the cage, closed the steel-framed door, and snapped a heavy padlock through the hasp. "If there is anything you absolutely need before I get back, Kruger will be here." He turned and called toward the open door of the room. "Kruger!"

The big man entered so quickly that he must have been standing outside listening.

"I want you to stay here with our young friend," Pastory told him. "Get him anything he wants, within reason. That is, anything that will fit through the mesh. I do not want you to unlock the door except in the gravest emergency. Is that understood?"

"Don't worry, Doctor. I'll watch him good. And I won't let him out." Kruger's thick lips twitched. His tongue slid out over them.

Pastory stood for a moment looking from one of them to the other, then nodded to himself and left the room, closing the single door behind him. A minute later the sound of an automobile engine could be heard starting outside. Tires crunched on the dried pine needles that carpeted the roadway. The sound faded as Pastory rolled down the overgrown logging trail toward the county road.

Kruger hitched one of the chairs close to the front of the wire cage and sat down facing Malcolm. He smiled. The fatty tissues around his eyes squeezed them into slits.

"It's just you and me now, freak-boy. All alone. How do you like that?"

Malcolm sat on the cot and did not answer.

"You don't care if I call you freak-boy, do you? 'Cause that's what you are, you know. A freak. A goddamn freak."

When Malcolm still did not respond, the big man's smile faded. He wiped a callused hand across his lips. "The doctor treats you like some kind of a prince, but all you are's a goddamn freak. Oh, I seen what you do when the doctor has you out there on the table. Your face gets all funny and long, kinda. Your fingernails grow. Like a woman's or something. And you get hair on you where hair don't belong. What do you say about that, freak-boy?"

"I don't know what you're talking about."

"Oh, you don't, don't you? I know how to make you do it, too. I watched the doctor. You want me to make you do it, freak-boy? Want me to turn you into a goddamn freak?"

"Just leave me alone."

"Just leeeeave me alone," Kruger whined in a mocking falsetto. "You know, I was number one around here until you showed up, freak-boy. The doctor used to treat me real nice before you came. He took me out of the bad place and he said I'd never have to worry about anything again. He'd take care of me. And he did, too, but then he found you, and we had to bring you here, and now he don't have time for me anymore except to tell me to go fetch this or go empty that. You're the hotshot now, freak-boy. But you know something? It ain't gonna last. One way or another I'm gonna see that it don't last."

Malcolm felt the anger start way down deep somewhere. "Why don't you shut your ugly mouth?"

Kruger hitched his chair closer, pleased that he had gotten a reaction. "Oh-oh, is he going to get mad? Is freak-boy I going to get mad? Go ahead. Let's see you do those things with your face. Then we'll see who's ugly, freak-boy."

Malcolm felt the heat rising within him. His hands began to twitch. He forced himself to breathe slowly and deeply. He closed his eyes and thought of the words Holly Lang had used when they put him into hypnosis. So relaxed. So comfortable. Drifting, drifting. Farther and farther away. Gradually the fire within him cooled. His hands lay quiet in his lap. He felt the waves of relaxation wash over him. Mind and body were once again under control.

"Almost had you goin' there, didn't I, freak-boy?" Kruger said. "Oh, yes, I did, all right."

Malcolm opened his eyes. He looked through and beyond the thick, ugly man. He smiled softly to himself.

"You're not makin' fun of me, are you?" Kruger said. "They used to make fun of me in the bad place. Laughed behind my back when they thought I couldn't see. I knew, though. I knew what they were doing. I took care of them, too. That was before the doctor came and brought me here."

Malcolm breathed in and out slowly. So relaxed. So comfortable.

"I know how I can get that silly smile off your face," said Kruger. "I know. You just wait here." Then, as though realizing he had said something funny, he laughed. "That's right. You just wait here." He laughed again and left the room.

Malcolm tried to hold on to his state of calm relaxation, but the mood was fading. Dr. Pastory was a dangerous man, and he did some unpleasant things to Malcolm, but he was always solicitous about the boy's welfare afterward. At least that was the way he acted. And there was always the hope that when Pastory had finished with his study, whatever it was, he would return Malcolm to the hospital in Pinyon. Holly was there. He could put up with Pastory as long as there was the hope of a reunion with his friend.

But Kruger was another matter. The brute had a damaged brain and was barely kept in check by Pastory's greater strength of will. If he ever went over the edge Kruger could be dangerous. Malcolm began to worry about what the ugly big man might do.

Before he could reorder his thoughts, Kruger returned. He carried with him a wand, shaped like a stubby pool cue. The thicker end was wrapped with leather at the grip. The greater length of the wand was metal. Two wires protruded from the butt end and ran into a flat leather packet that Kruger had attached to his belt.

"Do you know what this is, freak-boy? It's a cattle prod, that's what. The cops use 'em sometimes. Dr. Pastory used it on me when I first come here from the bad place. Then I wised up and he didn't have to use it no more. I found out where he kept it, but I never told him."

Malcolm stared at the metal prod as Kruger waved it back and forth in front of his face.

"Want to see how it works? Watch."

Kruger thrust the metal tip of the prod to within half an inch of the wire mesh of the cage. He touched a switch on the belt pack. A blue-white spark jumped with a loud crack.

Malcolm flinched away from the spark.

"What's the matter, you afraid of it?" Kruger said. "The doctor's been using something like it on you in the laboratory when you're strapped down. Only difference is, the one in there is a lot smaller and it don't hurt as much as this one. Want to see?"

In a movement surprisingly swift for so big a man, Kruger thrust the prod through the cage, jabbing the tip against Malcolm's face.

The pain was like hitting the nerve of a tooth. Malcolm cried out and put a hand to his cheek. He backed against the rear of the cage, but there was no way he could get out of the reach of Kruger with the cruel cattle prod.

The big man laughed, a high-pitched, mindless giggle. "Aha, gotcha now, haven't I? Can't get away, can't get away."

He stabbed Malcolm's wrist with the tip of the wand. The pain of the shock jolted up his arm. Malcolm felt the fires grow inside him.

"See? See? There you go. I knew I could make you do it. Look at your hands, freak-boy."

Malcolm looked down at his hands. Surely, they had grown larger, the palms broadening and the fingers stretching out. Even as he watched, the nails pushed out through the skin, thick and horny, bringing a trickle of blood from the tips of his fingers. The boy clamped the horrid hands out of sight under his arms.

Kruger caught him under the chin with the prod. His facial muscles twisted and jumped in the sudden agony.

"I'll show you what you really are, freak-boy. I'll show you who's ugly." Kruger capered grotesquely around the three exposed walls of the cage, stabbing here, there, anywhere he could find a bit of exposed flesh.

Malcolm's legs bent on him in a strange way and he fell to the floor. The sound that came from his throat was half whine, half growl. Like nothing human. His mind was a jumble of images—the forest at night; flames; burning flesh; a kind, bearded giant; a beautiful woman who was his friend; a doctor who drugged him and took him away; a thick-necked, witless lump of a man who tortured him.

The hands before Malcolm's face no longer bore any resemblance to his own. They had darkened and stretched and grown patches of fine black hair.

The pain continued; the anger grew. And the fire within him burned hotter.

16

Even watching closely, Holly missed the logging trail the first time past, and she had to drive back at ten miles an hour with her head craning out the window to find it. The old trail was no more than two faint paths through the weeds leading up the hill. Years before, logging trucks had hauled the huge Douglas fir logs down from the mountain to sawmills that had long since disappeared.

Minutes after she headed up the grade, the little orange car appeared. It stopped for a moment while the driver peered up the hill, then followed Holly up the trail.

Holly drove carefully up the grade. The second-growth timber had almost reached the density of the virgin stand that attracted the lumber companies in a previous generation. On both sides the thick brush made it difficult to see. Rocks and stumps jutted unexpectedly from the center, where the weeds grew unmashed. The Volkswagen Rabbit was not designed for off-road adventure, and Holly winced with every scrape and bump against the underside of the little car.

As she emerged from one especially thick clump of trees, Holly came suddenly and unexpectedly upon the clinic of Dr. Pastory. It was a dark, two-story house of redwood shingle and heavy oak beams, with an overhanging roof.

The house was built in the 1920s by the owner of a Hollywood studio as a playhouse for his favorite starlet. Sadly, before she could occupy it, the starlet died from drinking bootleg gin and laudanum at a party hosted by a popular slapstick comedian. The house had remained empty since that time until the studio magnate had died, several years before. It had been put up for auction, and because of its remote location, Wayne Pastory was able to buy it cheaply.

There was no other vehicle in sight, and Holly felt a rush of disappointment at the thought that she might have made the trip for nothing. However, fresh tire tracks told her that someone was using the place.

She snugged the Rabbit in under a tree and walked across the cushion of pine needles to the heavy front door. There was no bell, so she reached for the heavy cast-iron knocker.

Before she could lift the knocker, Holly froze at a sound from somewhere inside the house. It was a cry of mingled fear, rage, and pain. The voice was distorted, yet something in the tone made her sure it was Malcolm. Reacting to a sudden blaze of anger, she tried the latch of the heavy door, found it open, and walked in.

The interior of the old house had been redone and modernized, if not improved, with metals and plastics. Wallboard had been added to section the large old rooms into many smaller ones. Holly kept moving, following the sound of the voice, which continued to cry out every few seconds.

She passed along a hallway with doors on both sides. Some of the doors stood open, revealing cell-like rooms with narrow beds and a minimum of simple furnishings. Most looked unoccupied. In one of them, however, the bed was rumpled and recently slept in. Holly paused to look at a crumpled bit of white fabric stuffed into a wire wastebasket. She recognized the stitched blue lettering that would spell out LA REINA COUNTY HOSPITAL. A patient's gown.

She hurried on through what appeared to be a laboratory dominated by an examination table with heavy straps riveted to the corners. Although she did not pause to look around, Holly was impressed by the quantity and variety of equipment in the lab. No wonder Olan Schaeffer at Landrud & Co. had been so eager to do business.

There was a large, well-equipped kitchen, then a short flight of steps leading down to a wing of the house that was on a lower level. It was from a room down there that she heard the agonized cries.

The door to the large room on the lower level was ajar. Holly could see it was brightly lit within. She was close enough now to hear a crackling sound along with the cries of pain. She stepped through the door and stood for a frozen moment, stunned by what she saw.

A thick-shouldered brute of a man with scrubby black hair on a bullet head turned when she entered. He held what appeared to be an electrified metal rod in one hand. He was standing in front of a steel mesh cage. Inside the cage a pitiful figure writhed on the floor. A boy, Holly thought, though she could not be sure. He lay curled on the floor, muscles twitching, his limbs bent into strange, unnatural positions. On the visible areas of skin grew uneven patches of hair.

"Malcolm!" she cried. "My good God, what have they done to you?"

The face that looked up at her from the floor of the cruel cage wrenched Holly's heart. She recognized in it the boy Malcolm, yet it was not Malcolm. The bones seemed to have shifted subtly, elongating the face. The eyes were a strange luminescent green. He said something that might have been her name, then quickly covered his mouth with a darkened, long-nailed hand.

"Who are you, girlie?"

It took a moment for Holly to realize the brutish man was talking to her. She turned toward him and fought down the rage inside her. Her impulse was to strike out blindly at him, but she knew this was a time for control.

"I am Dr. Hollanda Lang. I demand to know what you are doing to this boy."

The *Doctor* seemed to confuse the man, to draw from him a touch of respect. At least temporarily. "How did you get in?" he asked.

"I walked in. The door was open."

"You shouldn't of done that." A sly look crept into his dark little eyes.

"I want you to release this boy at once."

"I can't do that. Dr. Pastory said I was supposed to keep him in there."

"Did Dr. Pastory also give you orders to torture the boy?"

"What are you talkin' about?"

"Answer my question."

"Are you a friend of the doctor's?"

The figure in the cage had pulled itself half erect on the steel mesh. The hands were more human now, the boy more recognizable as Malcolm. He looked so terribly young and vulnerable in the oversized pajamas.

"Holly," he said, his voice hoarse but clearing.

"Malcolm, thank God I've found you. Are you badly hurt?"

The boy looked down at his hands, which still bore patches of dark hair. He let go of the screen and tried to hide the hands behind him.

"I... I..."

Holly moved quickly to the cage. She laid one hand flat against the diamond mesh. He backed away.

"Don't be afraid, Malcolm. And don't worry. I'm going to get you out of here, and I'm going to help you."

She turned at the sound of a movement behind her. The big man had taken a step toward her. He was clenching and unclenching his hands. The metal rod hung forgotten at his side.

"What's your name?" she demanded.

The authority in Holly's voice held him for a moment. "K-Kruger," he stammered. "Dr. Pastory left me in charge while he's gone."

"Well, Kruger, you just get the key to this lock and open the cage right now." She spoke with an assurance she did not feel. This Kruger was obviously unbalanced mentally. God only knew what sadistic tortures he had been subjecting Malcolm to, but Holly knew she was treading a thin line with him.

Kruger shook his bullet head slowly from side to side. "No, I don't think I'm gonna do that."

She tried softening her tone.

"It's all right, Kruger. I'll explain to Dr. Pastory that I told you to let the boy out."

A crafty smile slid over the man's thick features. "Oh, no you don't. I know who you are. You're that Holly woman. The one he" —Kruger nodded toward Malcolm— "keeps calling for. You ain't no friend of the doctor's."

"You just let him out of there. Right now, Kruger, or you're going to be in a whole lot of trouble."

"Not me, girlie. It ain't me who's going to be in trouble." Moving with surprising speed, Kruger crossed the room and placed himself between her and the door.

"Run, Holly," Malcolm said in a strangled voice. "He'll hurt you."

Sensing the menace in the big man's tensed body, Holly tried to step around him to the door. He seized her by the arm above one elbow and squeezed it painfully.

"Let go of me!" she demanded, but her voice betrayed the fear that was building within her.

Kruger felt it, too. "Your little freak friend is right," he said. "I can hurt you if I want to. So you better be nice to me. You understand?"

"Let go!" Holly said again.

Before she could move, she was pulled hard against Kruger's body. His thick, moist lips covered her mouth. His tongue tried to force itself past her clenched teeth.

Acting on instinct, she pumped one knee up between the big man's legs. Her knee slid off the hard muscles of his inner thigh, weakening the blow to his testicles.

Kruger grunted and pulled his head back. "Bitch!"

He balled one huge fist and hit Holly on the point of the jaw.

It seemed her head had been slammed up against the ceiling. The lights went out for Holly Lang and she fell heavily to the floor. Kruger laughed and knelt over her.

* * *

When Gavin Ramsay returned to his office, supporting a hysterical Louis Zeno, two men in neat business suits were waiting for him with Deputy Nevins. They introduced themselves as Hoyden and Placerman from the California Attorney General's office.

"We got your request," said Hoyden, the senior of the two, "to assist with the investigation you're running down here."

"I can sure use you," Ramsay said. He briefly described the scene he had found at the old Whitaker cabin. "I left my man Fernandez in charge there. He'll keep the sightseers away until we can secure the area."

"This a witness?" Hoyden said, nodding toward Zeno.

"He found the body."

The writer took this as a cue to start talking. "It was the worst thing I've ever seen in my life. I'm talking bad, man. Blood everywhere. Pieces of my man all over the cabin. My typewriter was ruined."

"Did you get a look at the guy who did it?" Deputy Nevins asked.

"No man did that," Zeno said.

"What do you mean?"

"No one man could make an unholy-mess like that in the little time I was gone."

"Gang of some kind?" Placerman suggested.

"Shit if I know. That's you guys' job. You figure it out."

"Try to relax, Mr. Zeno," Ramsay said. "Deputy Nevins here will take your statement."

"Stole my car, too," said Zeno.

"What's that? Who stole your car?"

"Whoever... whatever tore up Abe Craddock. Drove off in my car right when I came out of the cabin."

"What kind of a car was it, Mr. Zeno?"

"Datsun. 1972. Orange."

"License number?"

"I... I... oh, shit. I *know* it."

"Hey, I think I saw that car, maybe an hour ago," Nevins interrupted.

"Where, Roy?"

"I was watching Holly, Dr. Lang, drive away, and this orange Datsun pulled out right behind her and went off in the same direction."

"Holly was here? When?"

"Like I said, maybe an hour ago. She left you a note." Nevins pointed at the sheriff's desk.

Ramsay snatched up the sheet from his calendar pad and read it swiftly. As Holly had done, he glanced at the wall map to check the location of Bear Paw.

"I'm going after her," he said. "Will you be all right here, Roy?"

"I can handle it, Gavin," said Deputy Nevins, sucking in his stomach.

"Good. I'm sure Hoyden and Placerman here will give you all the help they can."

The attorney general's men nodded their agreement.

"I'll be back as soon as possible."

Ramsay started out of the office, then hesitated. He looked thoughtfully at Louis Zeno, who was still pale and shaking from what he had found at the cabin. Ramsay himself had been shocked at the inhuman violence done to Abe Craddock. He strode back to his desk and unlocked the bottom drawer. From it he took a heavy, square box and dropped it into a jacket pocket.

"What's that, Sheriff?" Roy asked.

"Bullets," he said. "Just in case." What he did not add was that they were the special bullets given to him by Ken Dowd, the owner of the occult shop. Silver bullets.

* * *

Malcolm watched in tearful, helpless rage as Kruger fumbled with the snap at the waist of Holly Lang's jeans. His fingers clamped over the heavy steel mesh like the jaws of a caged beast.

Kruger paid him no attention. He popped the snap and slid the zipper down, revealing the filmy blue bikini pants Holly wore underneath. The man's breathing grew louder. His eyes glistened.

"Leave her alone," Malcolm cried. In his voice was a strange new quality. A growl. Even Kruger, in his lust, stopped and turned toward the cage.

"Hey, look at freak-boy! Look at that face! Too bad the doctor ain't here to see this. Maybe you get off on watching, huh, freak-boy? Well, you pay attention, then, 'cause I'm gonna give you plenty to watch."

He returned his concentration to pulling the tight jeans down Holly's legs. She moaned softly but did not regain consciousness. The bluish bruise from Kruger's fist was already beginning to show on her jaw.

With some difficulty, Kruger pulled the jeans completely off, taking Holly's boots with them and exposing her long, slim legs. He reached up and touched her pubic mound through the blue nylon.

Malcolm snarled. The fires inside burned hotter than ever before. The sinewy, hairy hands that now grew at the ends of his arms gripped the steel mesh and pulled. With a loud rip the material of his pajamas tore at the shoulders, where new muscles bulged and humped. The mesh of the cage bent and started to pull apart where he gripped it.

Kruger, his fingers now hooked under the elastic of Holly's bikini, looked over. His wet, red mouth opened in surprise.

The window high on the wall above them burst inward. A beast, lithe and muscular, dived headfirst through the shattering glass. The beast landed gracefully on all fours, his great shaggy head swiveling to take in the situation. The black lips peeled back in a snarl.

Malcolm froze where he stood. The mesh of the cage before him was ripped wide enough for him to slip through, but he could not move.

Holly moaned again. Her eyelids fluttered. She tried to raise her head.

Kruger let go of her and scrambled to his feet. He stared at the creature now advancing on him.

"Get back! Get back!"

Malcolm, from inside the torn cage, stared at the beast. It rose on hind legs to a full seven feet. The talons, the gleaming teeth, the powerful jaws, all were capable of killing a man in seconds. The eyes glowed an unholy green.

But Malcolm felt no fear. There was recognition. A kinship. As the eyes of the creature held his own, the boy sensed the message in his mind: *Flee!*

When he looked down at his hands there were again smooth, smallish, normal boy's hands. He touched his face. It was his own unmarked, beardless face.

Flee! The message sounded again in his mind. A command. Malcolm squeezed his slim body through the split he had torn in the steel mesh.

"Hey! Where d'you think you're goin'?" Kruger, remembering his orders, turned his attention for a moment from the towering beast to the boy.

The beast opened its great jaws and roared. Kruger whirled to face the menace. Malcolm, compelled by the telepathic command, slipped past Kruger and the beast to the open door. There he stopped and looked down at Holly.

Conscious now, she raised herself on an elbow. She shuddered at the sight of the beast but saw that its full attention was given to Kruger. She looked to Malcolm, who hesitated in the doorway. Unable to find her voice, she motioned with a hand for him to run. Malcolm opened his mouth as though he would speak, then turned and vanished through the doorway.

The beast roared again and advanced on Kruger.

The big man, his mouth loose and drooling with fear, backed away. He stumbled, and remembered suddenly the cattle prod hanging by the wires from his belt pack. He seized the leather-wrapped grip and switched the current to its highest level. He thrust the rod out before him like a rapier.

"Awright," he babbled, "you want some of this? Come on, I'll give you some. I'll give you all you want."

He stabbed the metallic tip of the prod at the advancing creature.

The beast swatted at the measly weapon the man brandished and felt the electric shock that coursed all the way up to the hump of shoulder muscle. The shock was no more than a tickle to the beast, but it knew now what had been done to the boy Malcolm. It understood what had driven Malcolm to change as much as he had. The tiny shock was exactly what the beast needed to rekindle the bloodlust that had been so recently satisfied in the cabin outside Pinyon.

Kruger literally did not know what hit him. One moment he was holding the cattle prod, jabbing it at the huge, hairy thing that had burst through the window. The next moment his arm, fingers still twitching on the leather grip, was lying on the floor at his feet. He stared dumbly at the empty shoulder socket, where arterial blood pumped out in rhythm with his heartbeat.

Sitting now on the floor, Holly sucked in her breath as the beast cleaved Kruger's arm from his shoulder with one swift blow. She squeezed her eyes shut and turned away, unable to watch any more. She heard, however, Kruger's mewling little cries, and the crackle of teeth on bone.

* * *

Gavin Ramsay kept the accelerator to the floor all the way from Pinyon to Bear Paw. He did not bother with red lights and siren. There was not enough traffic along the way to make any difference. By the time he hit the brakes at the faint logging trail that led up to Pastory's clinic, the three-year-old Plymouth Fury bought by the taxpayers of La Reina County was sweating and snorting like a used-up racehorse.

He jounced up the grade, swerving against the brush on both sides, finally jamming to a stop when he came suddenly upon the old high-roofed house among the pines. Louis Zeno's orange Datsun was parked at an angle out in front, one door hanging open as though the driver had abandoned it hastily. Tucked neatly under a tree-was Holly's little Volkswagen.

A sound came from inside the house that raised the short hairs at the back of Ramsay' s neck. A snarling growl that reminded him of nothing so much as the feeding of big, dangerous animals at the zoo.

A door banged at the rear of the house. Ramsay galloped around the side of the building in time to see a figure running swiftly away, darting between the trees.

"Halt!" he called, unhoistering his revolver.

The running figure never slowed down, vanishing as Ramsay watched. A shot would be fruitless at that range and with all the trees between him and the target. Anyway, Ramsay never fired his piece without knowing what he was shooting at. Another growl came from inside the house, and he abandoned any thought of giving chase.

He started in through the open back door, then came to a stop. He thumbed the catch and rolled out the cylinder of his revolver, ejecting the copper-jacketed .38 cartridges onto the ground. Sweating with concentration, he jammed a hand into his jacket pocket and dug out six of the silver bullets. He slipped them into the cylinder, locked it in place, and ran into the house.

Ramsay almost fell down several steps into a semi-sunken room but caught his balance in time to stumble upright through the door. He took in the scene with a fast, sweeping glance. Against one wall stood a ruined cage. Rising shakily from the floor, clad in a sweater and bikini underpants, was Holly Lang. But dominating the room was a huge, wolf-like beast that stood upright holding the armless, headless body of a man.

"Holly!" he called.

She looked up at him, dazed and unbelieving for a moment, then scrambled toward him.

The beast, still holding the dismembered body, glared at him with bright green eyes. Ramsay raised the pistol.

At the moment he fired, Holly Lang stumbled into him, throwing off his aim. The soft silver bullet smacked into the far wall. Where an ordinary slug would have bitten out a chunk of concrete, the silver bullet flattened on impact and bounced to the floor.

The beast looked down at the bright blob of metal, then back at Gavin. A flash of understanding passed between them. The beast let the mangled body fall, dropped to all fours, and bounded past Ramsay and out the door before he could bring the revolver back into play.

Ramsay did not try to go after the thing. He stood where he was and wrapped both arms around Holly. He held her close to him until she finally stopped shivering. Then, supporting her with one arm, he picked up her jeans and her boots and led her gently out into the clean air.

Several minutes later they sat together in the front seat of the sheriff's car, which was still parked before the peaceful-looking house that Dr. Pastory's clinic. As Holly calmed down she told him all that had happened to her since she had left his office early that morning.

"Then that was Malcolm I saw running into the woods," he said.

"Yes. We've got to find him, Gavin, and help him."

"I'm not sure we can."

"We've got to try. If you won't help me, I'll go after him alone."

"No you won't," Ramsey said quietly. "We're together in this thing now. Wherever it leads."

"You know what we're up against?"

"I know," he said. "I saw it in there. But I'm not going to try and convince anybody else. I would suggest that you don't either, unless you want to locked in a rubber room."

"No," she said. "I don't imagine we could get anybody to believe us. Not anybody who could help."

"I'm afraid that's it," he said gently. "It will have to be you and me, Holly, and that's it."

She laid her head against his shoulder for a moment, then looked up at him. "I think I'd like to be kissed now," she said.

He complied.

17

He was alone again.

Alone and running.

Malcolm stumbled blindly through the forest, tears blurring his vision. Only an ancient instinct saved him from repeated collisions with the trees. He ran on tirelessly with no thought of direction or destination. He knew only that he could get away, far away from the terrible house where the men had done hurtful things to him. He blanked all thoughts from his mind except escape.

And he ran.

Alone and crying through the forest.

The daylight waned and the light crept in and Malcolm ran on. The sky was tinted gray with the coming dawn when he finally dropped to the ground, sobbing. He had used up his youthful body, and in seconds he fell exhausted into a dreamless sleep.

When he awoke, it was night again. He was hungry. And he was cold. He still wore only the oversized pajamas provided for him by Dr. Pastory. Both top and bottom had been ripped by thorns. The legs were soaked through by the dew. His feet were bare, though remarkably uninjured after his wild run through the forest. Malcolm sat hugging his knees and shivering. He pushed away the panic that nipped at him and willed himself to relax.

The smell of wood-smoke was in the air. Not the greasy smoke of the raging fire he remembered from the night of terror in Drago. This was small. Almost friendly. A campfire. There was the aroma of boiling coffee. Malcolm rose and tested the air. Where there was a campfire there were people. People meant food and clothing.

Malcolm followed the smell of the campfire, moving without sound through the trees. He heard the lapping of small waves as he approached a mountain lake. At a safe distance he stopped and hid himself among a cluster of fallen fir boughs. From there he silently watched the camp at the lake's edge.

There was a tent and two men. The men sat across the fire from each other and talked with the familiarity of old friends. Their backpacks leaned neatly against the trunk of a fir. The play of the flickering flames across their faces stirred in Malcolm memories of the drunken hunters who had killed his friend Jones. As the remembered rage returned, a growl built in his throat.

But watching these men, Malcolm sensed that they were not like those others. These were fishermen, not killers. They laughed easily together and talked with rough affection of the wives they had left behind for this weekend excursion. Malcolm's anger subsided. The growl never left his throat.

It grew late and the fire crumbled into glowing coals. The men banked the dying fire carefully and laid out their sleeping bags.

"Funny, isn't it?" said one. "Here we can stay up as late as we want, and I'm dead tired at nine o'clock."

"It's the mountain air," said the other. "Anyway, we can get an early start in the morning. Get at the fish before they've had their coffee."

"You going to sleep in the tent?"

"Nah, it's too pretty out here. Nothing in these woods to worry about."

"Except the Drago werewolves."

Both men laughed. They crawled into their sleeping bags and soon fell silent.

Malcolm waited patiently until the snoring of the men assured him they were asleep. Then he stole down to their camp, placing his feet with care so there would not be the smallest sound.

His vision at night had always been nearly as sharp as in full daylight, and he quickly found the men's supplies. Their backpacks still leaned against the fir. Malcolm opened the packs carefully and took only the clothing he needed—underwear, a woolen shirt, tough denim pants and warm jacket, heavy socks, a pair of boots. Then, selecting food he could carry easily, he slipped away.

He moved softly until he was far enough from the camp so the men would not be awakened, then broke into a loping run. After a mile he stopped and rested and examined the things he had taken.

He ate a portion of the food and dressed himself in the men's clothes, carefully burying the torn pajamas. The clothes were too large for him, but he cinched up the pants and rolled up the cuffs of the shirt and jacket and the pant-legs. He put on both pairs of thick socks under the boots. Then he moved on again. More slowly this time; he had to think, to plan.

The days passed. Malcolm knew he would have to leave the area. The town of Pinyon, the county of La Reina, would never be safe for him again. Yet he had to return one more time. There was something he had to know.

He waited for a cloudy night when the moon and stars were hidden, then crept down from the hill behind the hospital. There were still searchers in the hills, but they were amateur woodsmen and easy to elude. There were no helicopters or organized parties as there had been when the doctor was killed. Several times Malcolm passed within yards of the searchers without being seen.

He found a vantage point from which he could see everyone who entered and left the building. Then he waited. In the afternoon of the following day he saw the one he waited for. His friend. Holly Lang.

She walked up to the entrance of the building with the tall sheriff. They stopped to speak, then kissed briefly, and Holly went inside. Malcolm watched with a mixture of unfamiliar emotions as the door closed behind Holly and the tall sheriff walked away. There was the joy of seeing Holly and knowing she was safe. But there was also the pain of knowing he could never go to her again. Because of what he was. Holly's place was with people who were normal. People like the tall sheriff. Malcolm's place was... where?

* * *

When night came again Malcolm left La Reina County for the last time and made his way to the coast above Ventura. There he left the forest and took to the highway. Hitching rides, he headed north.

In San Francisco he stopped for a time. In that city he found acceptance among the street people. Many of them were outcasts like him. They asked no questions of him, and he offered no explanations.

There were times when powerful emotions and strange hungers took over his body, and he felt the changes coming upon him. At those times Malcolm would find a hidden spot in some alley or a field and there struggle against the strange transformation that he was just beginning to understand.

In that terrible sunken room of Dr. Pastory's clinic, when the beast had crashed through the window, Malcolm knew, really knew for the first time, what he was. The beast was Derak, and Derak was Malcolm. Or what Malcolm would become.

The knowledge filled him with horror. Malcolm wanted to live among people and not be a thing of loathing to them. He despised the thought that he might lose control and attack someone who meant him no harm. During the times of changing, he fought against what he was, and while his body cried out for release, he was able to slow and finally halt the transformation, and eventually he would come back. But the effort cost him dearly.

In the city he could not live off the land, so he learned stealing and all the tricks and skills of the street boys.

It was an ugly existence, but he survived. Moving on, always moving so he would not become well known in any one place. He moved from the cities to the smaller towns and through the countryside, taking a bus when he had money, hitching rides when he didn't. Surviving. Searching. He knew somewhere his destiny waited. He would find it, or it would find him. There was no escape.

* * *

In La Reina County the sensation faded slowly into yesterday's news. For a few weeks there were reports of 'werewolf' sightings, but they turned out to be somebody's dog or a tree or an unfortunate bearded hiker. The hunt continued for the sadistic killer, but official opinion was that he had left the area. The search spread beyond county and state boundaries. The hunt for the killer was based on the description of the mild-looking man who had been seen entering Dr. Qualen's office. It was the best lead they had. As for Malcolm, a runaway boy held a low priority.

For a time writer Louis Zeno was held as a possible suspect in the Pinyon killings, but he was never considered seriously. When he was released, Zeno hurried back to Los Angeles and went to bed for a week. When he emerged, Zeno avoided all discussion of Pinyon, Abe Craddock, and what he had found in the isolated cabin. He still planned one day to write that book, but for the present he was content to crank out articles about two-headed calves and movie stars' romantic problems.

Dr. Wayne Pastory was questioned at length when he returned to his isolated clinic to find a dead assistant, a missing patient, and a sheriff and lady doctor waiting for him outside. However, his transfer of Malcolm from the hospital in Pinyon to his clinic had been handled according to the rules, and there was no crime he could be charged with. Nevertheless, the new administrative chief at the hospital, replacing the late Dr. Qualen, made it clear that Pastory was no longer welcome there in any capacity.

There were changes, too, in the office of the La Reina County Sheriff. Milo Fernandez finished up his training tour and returned to school to study police science. His next assignment would be at some larger jurisdiction than La Reina County, but it could hardly be as exciting. Milo left with regret, and with good wishes from all.

Roy Nevins, having had a taste of real excitement for the first time since his early days in Oakland, had second thoughts about retiring. The law would allow him to stay an additional five years. He sold the idea to his wife by pointing out that the pension would be bigger. The real reason was that Roy Nevins, past fifty, had found a pride in his profession. He had started watching his diet and running and had lost so much weight that he had to buy a whole new set of uniforms. It was money he was glad to spend.

Gavin Ramsay watched the departure of one deputy and the transformation of the other with, respectively, regret and pride. The investigation of the local killings had largely been taken over by other agencies as the search for the killer widened, and it was the old routine again in the sheriff's office. Given Roy's new dedication to the job, one deputy was enough to handle the workload.

The sheriff found himself for the first time in months with spare time. Fortunately, he had a place to spend it—with Dr. Holly Lang. It was natural that they should be together because of the terrible secret they shared. As they had promised each other, neither had spoken of the nature of the beast that destroyed the brutish Kruger in Pastory's clinic.

There were people around who would be only too ready to embrace the idea of werewolves in their midst. But they were the same people who believed in little men from outer space and went to flying saucer conventions. Their support could only hinder the very personal search of the sheriff and the doctor.

They did make one attempt. On a morning about a month after their return, Gavin had said, "I know one man who would believe us."

"I thought we agreed that kooks were out," Holly said. "This guy is no kook.

He knows about these things, and he might be able to help us."

"Then by all means, let's give him a try."

They went together to Ken Dowd's shop, The Spirit World, in Darnay. Ramsay was disappointed to see the shades drawn and a CLOSED sign taped to the glass on the inside of the door. He and Holly went into the neighboring leather goods store to inquire about the owner.

"Ken Dowd?" the young clerk repeated. "He closed up about three weeks ago. He made a bundle during the werewolf boom, then locked the store and split. Wish I could have had a piece of his business at the time."

"Do you know where he went?" Ramsay asked.

"Back east somewhere is all I know. Cape Cod or something like that. Him and his wife. Told me he was going into the antique business. Something that couldn't possibly scare anybody, he said. Maybe he hasn't checked the price of antiques."

"You have no address for him?"

"No. You might try the real estate company that's selling the store for him."

Ramsay thanked the young man and he and Holly left the shop.

Back out on the street, he turned to her with a shrug. "I don't think it's worth chasing him to Cape Cod. You got any suggestions?"

"Afraid not. But we've got to keep looking, Gavin. I'd feel we were abandoning Malcolm if we gave up."

"Hey, nobody said anything about giving up. I thought Ken Dowd might help us from the, well, occult end. We missed him, but we can sure as hell keep looking. I told you we were in this together, didn't I?"

"Yes, you did. All the way, you said."

"And all the way I meant. Let's go."

* * *

Ramsay received hundreds of pictures from police agencies all over the country. Pictures of boys—delinquents, runaways, pickups, strays. He and Holly spent hours going over them. Many resembled Malcolm in one small way or another, but Malcolm himself was not among them.

One evening at Holly's little house, after a session with a new batch of photos from the police chief of Seattle, Ramsay shoved the pile of glossy prints aside irritably.

"What's the matter?" she asked.

"I'm sick and tired of looking at pictures of young boys," he said.

Holly laid a hand on his knee. "I know it's boring, but it's one thing we can do."

"Well, I'm beginning to feel like a damned pedophile."

"Are you going to sulk now?"

"Sulk, hell. It's been half a year."

"You said—"

"I know, I know, and I'm not backing out on you. I understand how important Malcolm is to you, and I'm willing to make every reasonable effort to find him. But do you realize how much time we're spending looking for a boy who could be anywhere in the Western Hemisphere by now? Or dead?"

"Malcolm is alive," Holly said stubbornly. "I know he is. I can feel it."

"Okay, so he's alive. He's becoming an obsession with you. We can't even go to the movies without Malcolm sitting there between us."

Holly's cheeks showed pink spots of anger. She took her hand away from Gavin's knee. "Oh, is that so? I don't remember a lot of complaining from you last night about the bed being too crowded."

"Last night was fine," Gavin admitted. "But those times are getting to be mighty rare. We started out with what I thought was a pretty good sex life. Lately it's Malcolm this and Malcolm that, and we're lucky to have an uninterrupted twenty minutes for fooling around."

Holly stood up abruptly from the couch. Gavin scrambled to his feet to face her.

She said, "If you want out, Sheriff, you've got it. Thank you very much for sticking it out this long. I'll handle it myself from here on. Goodnight."

"If that's the way you want it, goodnight!" he said, and stomped out the door.

Ramsay had stomped all the way down the walk to his car and had his hand on the door handle when he stopped. Asshole, he told himself. He squared his shoulders, turned, and walked back up the path to Holly's little house. As he reached for the bell the door opened in his face.

"They always come back," she said.

"You're too smart for your own good, lady. Want to look at the pictures some more?"

"Not tonight," she said.

"Want to go to bed?"

"Try me."

He gently closed the door behind them.

18

The weeks passed.

And the months.

Malcolm wandered up and down the long, diverse state of California. He had been in and out of cities, towns, villages; crossed mountains and desert. Several times he had ventured near the state line. He had looked across into Oregon, Nevada, and Arizona, but he had not crossed the line. Although he was a young man without roots, he still felt that it was in California that he would find what was waiting for him. It had all begun for him in this state, and he sensed that this was where it would end.

Once, during the winter when he was seeking warmth where he could find it, Malcolm did travel a short distance into Mexico. He had looked hard at the verdant hills below Tijuana and felt the presence there of others like himself. Yet they were not his own people, the survivors of Drago. He had no doubt now that there were survivors. Many times he had heard the howling in the night—calling him. Though his body yearned to answer their call, he fought against it. He was not ready.

Despite the vagabond life, Malcolm's body filled out over the year. He grew stronger. His shoulders broadened out and his shoulders expanded. Such work as he was able to find helped harden him. His muscles were supple, his hands rough and callused. Although he took a boyish pride in his more manly appearance, there were new problems.

In the dim outlaw world he was forced to live in, physical conflict was common. Malcolm had seen men fight to the death over a bottle of wine. In the early days he had often been challenged by the boys and men he met in his travels. Every time, although his body ached to respond, he had backed away from a fight. He would suffer any humiliation to avoid combat.

They laughed at him and called him a coward. The taunts did not bother him, nor the name. He sensed how swiftly and terribly he might destroy these people if he yielded to violent emotions. Their name for him then would be far worse than coward.

More frequently as the weeks passed Malcolm felt his body strain to change its shape when some passion gripped him. The urge to let go was powerful, but Malcolm continued to fight it. By intense effort of will he had so far resisted the full change, but he knew the day would come when he could resist no longer. He could only hope by then he would know what to do.

While his body grew strong, the unsettled life took its toll on the young man's emotions. On a cloudless afternoon in late spring he felt he had hit bottom. He rested that day in the Inyo hills and thought about bringing his painful life to an end. But he did not even know how to do that. With his education cut off by the fire at Drago he understood very little of his kind. There were three ways, it was said, that they could be destroyed—silver, fire, and a third, which was never mentioned. Had one of their people ever killed himself? Was such an act possible? Malcolm had no way of knowing.

Suddenly he tensed, cocked his head, and listened. Faint, but unmistakable, there came a cry of mingled pain and fear. Malcolm tested the air, determined the direction from which the cry came, and climbed swiftly up the grassy slope.

The cries ceased as he drew near. Malcolm knew that the creature in pain sensed his approach and feared him. He moved on cautiously, guided by his sense of smell.

Behind a patch of scrub oak he found it—a young coyote, hardly more than a pup. Its forepaw was caught in a trap.

Memories flooded back to Malcolm of his own anguish on that night more than a year ago when his ankle had been crushed by the trap. He knelt beside the coyote pup, his eyes filling with tears. He reached his hand out tentatively, palm up, to show the creature he meant no harm.

The trapped coyote sniffed at his fingers. Its lip drew back in an instinctive snarl, but it made no attempt to bite him. Very gently Malcolm touched its muzzle. His fingers stroked the gray-brown fur of the head between the velvety, pointed ears. The young coyote shivered under his touch.

"Easy, little guy," the boy said. "I'm not going to hurt you."

The pup whined softly.

"I know how you feel. Believe me, I do."

The coyote looked up at him with cautious eyes. Its shivering quieted.

"That's the boy," Malcolm said, speaking in a slow, soothing tone. "Now let's see how bad you're hurt."

He moved the pup gently to get a better look at the damage done by the trap.

With relief he saw it was not the bone-crushing kind that had caught him in the woods outside Pinyon. This was the legal, non-maiming trap designed to catch and hold, but not to do serious injury.

"You're a lucky fella," Malcolm said. "I know you probably don't think so, and it's no fun to be caught in any kind of a trap, but believe me, you could have it a lot worse."

He slipped his fingers between the smooth jaws of the trap and pulled against the spring. Was there no place, he wondered, where a wild creature could be left alone?

Down in the valley he had seen a flock of sheep. He supposed the rancher had set out the traps to protect his flock. Malcolm could not fault the man for that. At least the man had used this less destructive trap, and he had not resorted to poison. Still, a lamb was natural prey for the coyote. Where was the right or wrong of it all?

Slowly Malcolm forced the jaws open. The young coyote drew back the injured paw but did not try to get away. Malcolm ran gentle fingers along the leg that had been caught.

"Nothing's broken. Your foot will be sore for a while, but like I told you, it could be a lot worse."

The coyote tested its weight on the paw, raised it quickly, then tried again.

"See, it works all right," Malcolm said. "You can get along back to your family now."

The pup looked up at the boy, then lowered its head and butted gently against his leg. Malcolm scratched the coyote behind one ear.

"I wish I could keep you with me, little fella," he said. "It would be nice to have somebody to talk to. And we've got something in common, haven't we?"

The little coyote licked his hand. Malcolm drew it away. "But it can't work that way, so don't get all friendly with me. First thing you know I'll be giving you a name."

From behind him, Malcolm heard a soft growl. He turned and saw a female coyote standing with her legs braced, the fur bristling on the back of her neck.

He looked back at the pup. "I think your mama's here." The young coyote's eyes flicked from Malcolm to the female, then back to Malcolm.

"Go on," Malcolm said. "You know where you belong."

The pup hesitated a moment longer, then trotted, limping slightly, to join the female. The two of them were quickly lost from view in the scrub oak.

"I wish," said Malcolm to the empty hillside, "that I knew where *I* belonged."

He sank down on a mossy spot sheltered by a boulder and began to weep. Malcolm was not much given to crying, but there, alone and isolated, he gave himself up to the feeling of despair.

And as he wept his body began the spasms of the shape change. He could feel his downy beard growing thicker and coarser. He tasted blood as the long teeth pushed out through his gums. Because no one was around to see, this time Malcolm did not try to fight it. He was weary, and it had been a long, very long day.

* * *

It had been a long day, too, for Bateman Styles. It had, for that matter, been a long several years for Bateman Styles. A carnival showman, he was an outdated man scraping out a living in an outdated profession.

Until this year, however, he had managed somehow to find a spot every summer, even though it was with progressively smaller carnivals. In recent years he had fronted for a kootch show, an all-takers wrestler, a shooting gallery, funhouse, ring-toss, wheel of fortune, and finally a freak-tent. This year he had barely made it with the broken-down Samson Supershow. Or so he thought until early that afternoon when he was summoned to the Airstream Trailer of Samson himself, otherwise known as Jackie Moskowitz, former midget.

Styles had a premonition when the kid who ran the Ferris wheel told him the boss wanted to see him. It was the day before they were to open in Silverdale, and Bateman knew his freaks were at best a borderline attraction. But what the hell, he reminded himself, the Samson Supershow was not Barnum & Bailey, and Silverdale, California, was not San Francisco. Or even Eureka.

Even in its boom days Silverdale had never been much more than a last watering hole for travelers coming down through the Inyo pass and heading for some insane reason into Death Valley. Today it did not even show on many maps. When pressed for a location, residents would say it was five miles from Wheeler. If that reference drew a blank look they would admit the town was fifteen miles out of Lone Pine. Anybody who did not know Lone Pine deserved no further explanation.

A far cry from the old days, Bateman Styles reflected as he tramped across the dusty field to Moskowitz's trailer.

When he was a boy—Lord, that was fifty years ago—carnivals had played towns throughout the South, the West, and the Midwest without slowing down for nine months of the year. In those days the carnival was a big attraction in the towns, and even in cities of fifty thousand or so population. Even with the Depression, people found dimes to spend riding the Octopus or trying to win a Kewpie doll.

It was a lot different now. But hell, what wasn't? Bateman himself had been slowing down steadily for several years. He didn't have a lot of time left, but he always said he wanted to go out running a pitch somewhere. Only suckers die broke in bed.

He reached Jackie's trailer and banged on the aluminum door.

"It's open," piped a squeaky voice from inside.

Bateman entered. Jackie Moskowitz sat on a bench at a fold-down table playing solitaire. He brought himself up to table level by sitting on two copies of the Los Angeles Yellow Pages. He did not look up immediately.

Bateman remembered Jackie from the days when he was Major Tiny, an ill-tempered midget with Gallagher's Greater Shows. That was in the fifties. It was a phase out time for carnivals, and just as well for Major Tiny, whose faulty pituitary gland unexpectedly betrayed him. In a period of less than a year he grew to four feet eleven. Not a big man in the outside world, but laughably tall for a midget.

Luckily for him, Jackie had saved his money and was able to buy a piece of the Gallagher's show when he got too big to work. It had since declined steadily until the ragtag collection of grifters, kids, and burnouts that made up Samson was all he had left.

"What's up, Jackie?" Bateman said, squeezing his paunch into the narrow space behind the table across from Jackie.

"I gotta cut back," said the little man.

"Oh?" Styles braced himself for the bad news.

"Your show's gotta go."

"Why mine?"

"Because it's the weakest in the whole shebang. I carried you last year for old times' sake. I was ready to do it again, but I got to lookin' at the bills, and I can't hack it."

"My tent's better than the kootch show," Bateman protested. "Those bimbos couldn't give a hard-on to a Mexican sailor. Or what about the Wheel of Fortune? Umbach's got his foot on the pedal so heavy it raises smoke when he stops the thing. Even the yokels aren't going for that."

"Forget it, Bateman," squeaked the little owner. "You're gone."

"Why me? Just give me a reason."

"Okay. That bunch of so-called freaks you carry around wouldn't get a second look at a Kiwanis convention. Your giant, what is he, six-seven?"

"Six-eight-and-a-half," Styles protested.

"Some giant. The yokels can see kids bigger than that at any high school basketball game. And your bearded lady—you call that a beard?"

"You would if you kissed her."

"God forbid. That five o'clock shadow don't impress anybody, not even when she darkens it up with pencil shavings."

"She's got three kids."

"That don't make her no freak."

"I mean, how's she going to take care of them?"

"That ain't my problem. Let her do shave cream commercials. And your sorry fire-eater—what's he call himself, Torcho?"

"Flamo."

"It's always one or the other. Do you know how old his shtick is? I mean, blowing lighter fluid out of your mouth went out with handlebar mustaches."

"Handlebars are back."

"Don't confuse the issue."

"So my people aren't exactly New Wave. What of it? Most of the carnival is things that's been around for years. Nostalgia, that's what brings the folks in."

"Well, in your case it ain't bringing enough of 'em in. You and your freaks are out, Bateman. Sorry, but that's the way it is. In another year I'll most likely be out, too. You and me, we're the tail end of this business."

Styles seemed to crumble where he was wedged into the small seating space. He stared blankly down at the worn cards laid out before Moskowitz.

"Can't you give me a week?"

"No way. Everything's too tight. Hell, Bateman, you can probably collect more on Social Security than you make traveling with a tin can outfit like this. You're sure as hell old enough for it."

"They tell me to collect any of that you have to show you put some in over the years."

"No bull? How chicken shit."

"What if I come up with another gimmick?"

"I don't want your freaks, period."

"Okay, if they got to go, that's it. Maybe I can come up with something else."

"Come up with what? We open tomorrow."

"Lemme think about it, okay?"

"Sure, you think about it, Bateman, but I don't want to see those freaks in the morning."

"I'll give them the word."

"Good."

Moskowitz returned his full attention to the solitaire game. Styles levered himself out from the confining seat and left the trailer.

Breaking the news to his people—like most old-time carnies, Styles would never call them freaks—did not go too badly, all things considered. Colossus shook his hand, thanked him for a year of work, and said he'd have no problem getting a dishwasher job in some joint. They liked to have a big guy who could come out from the back if the bouncer got into it with somebody tougher than he could handle. Colossus was no fighter, but he was big and looked mean, and that was enough to discourage a lot of mouthy punks.

Flamo said little when Bateman gave him the bad news. He merely belched and chewed his Maalox tablets. He guessed maybe he could go back to his wife in Bakersfield if she had kicked out the twelve-string guitar player she'd been shacking with.

With Rosa it had been tougher. Tears had welled in her great brown eyes and rolled clown into her inadequate mustache. Bateman took her aside and slipped her enough for bus fare back to Flagstaff, where she had parked the kids with a sister. It was the best he could do.

Now, walking in the late afternoon on the hill above Silverdale, Styles missed all of them. In his years as a showman he had seen a couple thousand people come and go. He could never get used to it. They were his family. And in his heart he knew, once somebody left the carnival, you never saw them again. It was like they died.

Speaking of which, unless he could come up with some fast spiel for Moskowitz by tomorrow morning, Bateman Styles would himself be leaving the carnival. When he'd made the pitch in Moskowitz's trailer he had some half-ass idea about setting the midget on a flashy new idea. The trouble was, he didn't have one. All the ideas were used up.

Bateman stopped frequently to rest as he walked. The hills were steeper than they used to be. And it was hard for a man to catch his breath at this altitude.

He sat on a rock and looked at the view. Silverdale might not be much shakes as a town, but you couldn't buy the view for a million dollars. To the east, flat and parched, stretched Death Valley. It shaded delicately from gold to chocolate brown. To the west, just beyond the Inyo foothills, stood big-shouldered Mount Whitney.

His contemplation of the scenery was interrupted by a sound very close to him. Not quite a sob and not quite a growl, but a little of each Bateman stood up and looked behind the rock he had been sitting on.

There on the ground lay a boy, or young man, his body twisted into an unnatural position. He was huddled there, his face away from Styles, his limbs twisting and jerking as though yanked by invisible wires. It was the boy who was making the sob-growl sounds.

Styles' first thought was that the kid was having an epileptic seizure. He had once worked with a high-diver who was an epileptic. They all figured someday

Carlo would throw a fit while he was up on the tower, looking down at the tub. Sure enough, one day he did. Carlo's last dive was by far his most spectacular.

Bateman knew you were supposed to keep an epileptic from swallowing his tongue. He leaned down and tried to roll the young man over onto his back. Then he saw the face, and forgot all about epileptic seizures.

Ten minutes later the young man was looking reasonably normal. All muddy and soaked with sweat, but not a bad looking kid. Styles leaned against the rock, smoking an unfiltered Camel.

"Hi," said the showman.

The boy said nothing.

"You got a name?"

"M-Malcolm."

"Mind telling me how you do that, Malcolm?"

"Do what?"

"Make yourself go all hairy and fierce looking like you just did."

Malcolm stared at Bateman Styles. He was silent for a minute as he seemed to make up his mind about something. Finally he said, "I don't do it on purpose. It just... happens. Sometimes I can control it."

"Anything special that makes it happen?"

"When something makes me feel really sad. Or really mad. Then... things happen to me."

"No kidding. What makes you mad, Malcolm?"

"I don't know. Lots of things."

"How about being in a cage with people standing around looking at you, pointing, saying things about you?"

The moment he said 'cage' Styles knew he'd hit it. The boy's eyes deepened to a dangerous shade of green, and his lips pulled away from his teeth like an animal. Then he got hold of himself.

"Yeah," Malcolm said. "That would make me mad."

Bateman Styles drew in deeply on his cigarette, coughed, and said, "You want a job?"

19

Bateman Styles leaned back from the fold-down table and lit up a Camel. He coughed. He watched as the boy Malcolm shoveled in the beans and sausage he had heated on the small butane stove. It looked like his grocery bill was going to go up fast, but if the kid could manage that trick he saw today, he'd soon pay for it.

"That was good, Mr. Styles," Malcolm said when at last his plate was empty. "Thanks."

"Sure it was enough?"

"Well..."

"It'll have to be," Styles said quickly, "until I can get to the store."

"I wish I could help pay," Malcolm said.

"You will, my boy, you will," Styles said. "However, before we start making permanent arrangements, we'd better go see the boss about taking you on."

"You're not going to ask me to, you know, do it for him, are you?"

"Not if you don't want to, my boy. That act's our bread and butter, and there's no use giving it away, not even to the boss."

"It isn't that I don't want to, Mr. Styles; it's just that I can't, like, make it happen just any time."

"I get the picture, lad. You need the stimulus. Anger, despair, some powerful emotion. We'll work that out. By the way, 'Mr. Styles' makes me nervous. Call me Bate."

Malcolm grinned shyly and nodded.

"What we need now is a name for you."

"I have a name."

"No, no, no. Malcolm definitely does not fill the bill. We need something to draw in the marks. Something to whet the people's appetites for what they are about to see. Like Flamo the Fire-Eater."

"I don't eat fire."

"I know that, boy. I was merely using it as an example. As a matter of fact, it didn't do much for Flamo either." Styles was silent for a long minute. He closed his eyes, laid his head back, pursed his lips, and passed a hand over the wisps of gray hair that remained on his scalp. Suddenly his eyes popped open. He smiled broadly, showing brown-stained teeth.

"I've got it. Wolf Boy. Grolo the Wolf Boy." He waited for a reaction.

Malcolm frowned.

"Something wrong?"

After a moment's hesitation Malcolm shook his head. "I don't want to be called that."

"What's the matter with Grolo?"

"That's okay. It's the other part."

"Wolf Boy?"

Malcolm nodded.

"Judas Priest, why not? It's short, descriptive, and has a nice scary ring to it."

"I don't like it." There was a new, cold note in the boy's voice.

"Then we shall discard it," Styles said decisively. He again went into his thinking posture—eyes closed, head back, lips pursed. This time he was out of it in thirty seconds.

"Animal Boy." He studied Malcolm through narrowed eyes. "Can you live with that?"

"I guess so."

"Then it's Grolo the Animal Boy. I don't think it has the same appeal as Wolf Boy—"

Malcolm's eyes darkened.

"But, after all, you are the attraction here, and we'll call you anything you like."

They left Styles' antiquated trailer together and tramped across the dark field toward Jackie Moskowitz's Airstream. The concession stands were up, the tents in place, the small Ferris wheel erected, all ready to go at ten the next morning. Some of the attractions, like the kootch show and Bateman's tent, would not open until evening.

In the back of the food tent the perpetual poker game was in progress. The laughter and good-natured cursing of the carnival hands floated through the clear night. Elsewhere it was quiet. The town of Silverdale, immediately to the north, showed only a sprinkling of lights.

The showman and the boy came to a stop at the owner's blimp-shaped trailer. Styles gave Malcolm a reassuring wink and banged on the aluminum door.

The little owner was wearing yellow pajamas and a cutoff robe when he opened the door. He looked at Styles and the boy with distaste.

"Jesus, Bateman, is this important? I just took a sleeping pill."

"I told you I'd get a new show."

"Well?"

Styles swept his hand in a grand gesture toward Malcolm. "I give you Grolo the Animal Boy."

Moskowitz squinted up at them. "Come in here in the light."

Styles urged Malcolm into the trailer, then followed. The showman stood back while Malcolm shifted nervously from foot to foot. Moskowitz walked slowly around the boy, examining him from all angles.

"Animal Boy? What the hell does that mean? He's not a geek, is he?"

Styles was offended. "Jackie, you've known me long enough to know I wouldn't bring you a geek. Grolo here will turn into a raging, roaring, frothing animal before the eager eyes of the paying customers. He will be a sensation."

"Yeah? What's the trick?"

"Jackie, please. Would you ask Houdini how he did his Water Torture escape?"

"I would if he was looking for work."

"This is by way of a trade secret. Even *I* do not know how he does it."

"Okay, okay, so don't tell me." Jackie picked up one of Malcolm's hands and examined it. "He don't look much like an animal."

"Not now, he doesn't. Just wait until tomorrow night when there's a tent full of marks waiting to see him."

"I don't know, Bateman. I was thinking of using your space for a baseball pitch. I haven't had one for two years."

"A baseball pitch? Can you imagine people paying more to knock over weighted metal milk bottles than to see a genuine, bona fide Animal Boy?"

"People like to throw baseballs."

"They like to be scared, too. Why do you think horror movies clean up?"

"Well…"

"Jackie, let me try it for this one week in Silverdale. I'll guarantee you a minimum."

"Guarantee?"

"More than that. If we don't outdraw the kootch show and the ring-toss, I'll make up the difference out of my own pocket. And if we bomb, you can leave us here and you're out nothing."

"Are you sober, Bateman?"

Styles held up a right hand. "Not a drop since early this afternoon."

The little man cracked off a huge yawn. "Okay, you got a deal. I want to see this act myself. But remember, if your animal boy is a dog, it's adiós."

"Fair enough, Jackie, fair enough."

"Now get out of here and let me get some sleep." He looked up doubtfully at Malcolm. "Uh, so long, Grolo."

"Good night, Mr. Samson," Malcolm said.

As they walked back across the field together Styles clapped Malcolm on the back. "Congratulations, my boy, you're in show business. This calls for a toast to our future success. Or do you indulge?"

"I don't drink, but you go ahead, Bate."

"Thank you, my boy, thank you. I believe I will. Then perhaps I'll take a stroll over to the kootch girls' trailer. Care to join me in that?"

Malcolm flushed. "Well, I, uh, don't know if I, uh…"

"That's all right. Plenty of time for sport. Probably better for you to get a good night's sleep. I'll fix you up with a blanket roll in the trailer and try not to wake you when I come in."

* * *

Malcolm jolted out of a light sleep when Bateman Styles returned to the trailer sometime after midnight. It took him a moment to realize where he was, then he closed his eyes and feigned sleep as the showman bumbled about the trailer, trying clumsily to be quiet. Soon Styles was in his bed, snoring. Malcolm dozed off again with a tiny, contented smile on his lips.

Bateman was up at dawn, apparently none the worse for his night's carouse. He scrambled some eggs and made hash browns for the two of them, then left Malcolm alone.

The sounds and smells of the carnival as the people started coming in were enticing, but Malcolm stayed in the trailer. He was not yet ready to move among people again. In mid afternoon Styles returned, looking pleased with himself.

"Good news, boy. At virtually no expense, I have procured a cage," he said. "We can't convince the good people you're dangerous without a cage, now can we?"

He saw Malcolm's expression darken and went on quickly. "It isn't much of a cage, really. It would barely hold a determined pussycat. However, it will do until we can find something more impressive. It was lucky that Clete Matthews still had it from the time he was carrying a chimp act. The thing still smells faintly of chimpanzee, but I daresay we can get used to that, right?"

"Sure, I guess so."

Bateman studied the boy for a moment, then sat down on the rumpled bed. "Kid," he said, "I want you to understand what's going to happen tonight. You'll be in the cage inside the tent with a curtain pulled to hide you till we're ready. I'm out front talking, turning the tip, as we say, to get the marks to part with their coin and come inside. Then I come in and say a lot of things to you and about you that won't sound nice. Don't you pay any attention. It's show business. I want to get the marks riled at you so you can work up enough passion to… do the thing you do. You just… let yourself go, or whatever it takes, okay?"

"Okay, Bate."

"Fine. We're going to make us a few bucks, my boy. And maybe have some chuckles along the way." He pulled out an old-fashioned turnip watch. "Are you ready to go at it?"

"I'm ready if you are."

"Then let us proceed."

* * *

Styles put up the same garish canvas paintings that he had used for his dismantled freak show. There had been no time to prepare a new one, and Bateman reasoned that any pictures were better than no pictures. He climbed up on the platform and observed for several minutes the trickle of locals who passed on the sawdust walkway below him. Then he blew into his hand mike, heard the resultant blast from the speaker, and began to improvise a spiel.

"Inside, ladies and gentlemen, inside, inside, inside. Inside this tent you will positively *not* see"—he pointed to the garish pictures in turn—"Colossus the Giant. You will *not* see Rosa the Bearded Lady. You will *not* see Flamo the Fire-Eater. All this I promise you. What, then, you ask, *will* I see on the inside for the price of one lonely dollar? A fair question. I would tell you, my friends. I would describe in detail the wonder inside, but frankly, you would not believe me. You would not believe me, and I would not blame you. For inside, inside, inside, for the price of one dollar, I have for you the most inconceivable, incredible, impossible, astounding, amazing, astonishing sight on the face of the earth."

A few strollers stopped to listen to the spiel, grinning at the cascade of superlatives. Styles noted that nobody was reaching for his wallet yet.

"At monumental expense and superhuman effort the Samson Supershow has brought from faraway shores the most bizarre attraction ever presented in the Western world. Yes, in this very tent, my friends, blessedly caged to keep us from being attacked, is Grolo... the Animal Boy!"

The tip was building, but not fast. The Wheel of Fortune across the way had twice as many waiting to dump their coins on Umbach's crooked wheel. Styles forged on.

"Before your very eyes—no mirrors, no tricks with the lights—before your very eyes Grolo will become the fearsome, the terrible, the fantastic... Animal Boy!"

The showman continued to improvise in this vein while a few people paid their dollars and straggled into the tent. For the first time since he had watched Malcolm's remarkable transformation this afternoon, Bateman began to have doubts. What if the kid couldn't do it? What if he hadn't really done it in the first place? Styles had put down a few belts of Old Overholt earlier to brace himself for delivering the bad news to his people, and it would not be the first time he had seen things that did not happen.

He pulled aside a flap and peeked into the tent. One good thing—if the kid did funk out on him, he wouldn't have a lot of money to refund. Not more than a dozen people stood on the dirt floor waiting for the show. Might as well get on with it, he decided.

Styles broke off the spiel and entered the tent. He stepped up onto the low platform at the far end and paused dramatically with a hand on the worn velvet curtain.

"My friends, in the next few moments you are going to see something no other human eyes have—"

"Get on with it, old man," said a teenager who had come in with two friends. "We already heard the bullshit."

"Yeah," said a man with the weather-beaten face of a farmer. "Let's see what you got back there."

"Very well, my friends," said Styles without breaking stride. "Your impatience is understandable. Without further ado I give you… Grolo the Animal Boy!"

He snatched aside the curtain to reveal the chimp cage. Seated inside, for the top of the cage was too low to allow him to stand, was Malcolm. He looked around at the small crowd, his eyes large and apprehensive.

After the first intake of breath, a muttering rose in the crowd.

"That's an animal boy?" somebody said.

"What else does he do?"

"It's just another phony!"

"Fake!"

"I want my money back!"

The last comment triggered Bateman Styles to action. He glared into the cage, giving Malcolm a wink that the marks could not see.

"I don't blame you one bit, my friends, and believe me, every penny will be refunded to you. You see, it is not only you but myself as well that has been flim-flammed here. I was given the most solemn assurances that this was, indeed, the authentic Animal Boy you may have read about or seen on television. I am embarrassed to admit to you that this young imposter hoodwinked me."

Speaking directly to Malcolm, he said, "Young man, you are a liar. A cheat. You misrepresented yourself to me and you have tried to steal the money from these good folks out in front. You are nothing more than a contemptible juvenile hoodlum. You should be caged in prison."

To the people out front, who were enjoying his tirade, Styles added, "Go on friends, tell this young imposter what you think of him and his type." Searching for a reference they could relate to, he added, "This is the same kind of punk who tears in here on a motorcycle, freaked out on drugs and who knows what all, and rips up the landscape, then goes roaring back to the city, leaving you to clean up his mess. Go ahead, tell him what you think of him and his kind."

The people watching understood that this was somehow part of the show, yet they were carried along by Styles' florid speech.

"Boo!" came the first tentative yell.

"Get out of here!"

"Dirty biker!"

"Go home, faggot!"

Someone picked up a small stone from the ground and threw it. The stone clanked off the bars of the chimp cage.

Malcolm listened to the shouts and jeers and tried to concentrate on what Bateman Styles had told him to do. Styles had been kind to him and asked no questions, and he did not want to let the showman down. He concentrated. Nothing happened.

The boos got louder. Styles began to sweat as he anxiously watched Malcolm through the bars. The marks were getting carried away by their own voices. One of them heated a penny with a cigarette lighter and tossed it into the cage.

Malcolm blanked Bateman Styles out of his mind. He got off the stool and walked forward in a half crouch to seize the bars. He looked down into the taunting faces and summoned back a series of images. The fire. The trap. The hunters. Dr. Pastory and the table. Kruger and the cattle prod. Kruger hurting Holly.

He felt it begin.

The jeers of the crowd died in their throats. For a moment there was silence in the tent. Bateman Styles, along with the paying customers, stared in awe at the boy in the cage.

"What's happening to his eyes?" a plump girl asked her boyfriend.

"Look at his face," somebody else said in a strangled tone.

"And his hands! My God, they're growing!"

"The teeth! Holy shit, the teeth!"

Styles watched the contortions of the boy in the cage. Even though he had seen the process before in reverse, he was stunned by what was happening in there. The growls that came from the boy could surely not be human.

He let the transformation continue until blackened hairy hands started to bend the inadequate cage bars. Then he caught the message flashed from the dangerous green eyes. This must go no further. Without ceremony the showman snatched the curtain back in front of the cage.

"That's it, my friends. I think each and every one of us can agree that we got our dollar's worth here today. Grolo the Animal Boy. There will be another show in one hour by the clock. Tell your friends. I thank you."

The dozen people who had witnessed the performance filed out silently. Once outside, they all began to talk at once, the general topic being speculation on how it was done. They scattered excitedly over the small carnival grounds to spread the word.

When he had seen the last of the customers leave, Bateman Styles hurried back through the curtain and helped Malcolm out of the cage. He was relieved to see that the boy looked normal again, if somewhat sweaty. Malcolm gave him a tired smile.

"How did I do, Bate?"

"Lad, you were sensational. We will never again have a crowd that small, or I do not know this business. How do you feel?"

"Okay. A little tired."

"Think you can do it again in an hour?"

"Yeah. I found out there's a kind of a trick I can use to make it easier."

"Whatever the trick is," said the showman, "don't tell me. There are some things a man should not know. Go catch a nap in the trailer if you want. I'll call you in time for the next show."

"I think I'll just walk around, if that's all right."

"Sure. If you want to see any of the shows, take a ride, tell 'em you're working with me. You're one of us now."

One of us. Beautiful words. He really wasn't, of course, but it was as close as Malcolm had come to belonging anywhere in a long time. He strolled around the small carnival, savoring the tinny music from the merry-go-round, the thumping drum from the kootch show. He inhaled with pleasure the raw smell of sawdust mingled with cooking grease and cotton candy. He gazed happily at the colored lights strung above the walkways. When he told the other carnival people he was working with Bateman, they accepted him without question. Nobody asked what he did or where he came from. He was almost one of them.

As Styles had predicted, the crowd was much larger for the second show. Many who had been at the opener came back to see it again. Jackie Moskowitz himself came in, positioning himself in the front row, where he would not have to look through people's armpits. Styles shortened his spiel this time and let the act speak for itself. Again the Animal Boy was a sensation.

When they closed out the week in Silverdale, there was no more talk of leaving Bateman Styles behind. The Animal Boy *did* bring in more than the kootch show and the ring-toss combined.

The sponsoring civic organization was so pleased with their share of the carnival's take that they invited the Samson Supershow back to Silverdale for another stand late in the summer. Jackie Moskowitz, with holes to fill on his schedule, was only too happy to oblige.

As they traveled north with stops at Manzanar, Crestview, Mono Lake, Markleeville, Sattley, Ravendale, and a dozen other California towns nobody ever heard of, the fame of Grolo the Animal Boy spread. People were driving fifty or a hundred miles to see the amazing change of boy into beast. Bateman Styles was supremely happy. He had a real attraction again. Jackie Moskowitz was talking long-term contract.

As for Malcolm, he was as close to being content as he could remember since childhood. Sometimes he would awaken in the night from a terrifying dream, then relax as he recognized the tacky trailer of Bateman Styles. There was still the nagging worry that someone would find him and take him back to answer for the business at Pastory's clinic, but over the weeks that faded, too.

It happened in mid-July. The Samson Supershow was playing a small town outside Red Bluff. Two men from Los Angeles paid their dollars and walked into the show, and Malcolm's life was about to be changed forever. By mid-July, with the Samson show playing a town called Castle Rock, Malcolm had relaxed enough to laugh out loud, something he had not done since his days with Jones. He felt sometimes that his life here was too good to last.

He was right.

20

"What am I doing here?" Louis Zeno complained.

"What's the name of this town again?"

"Castle Rock," said Ted Vector. He was a bony, loose-jointed man with quick eyes. He wore a bag of camera equipment slung over a shoulder.

"Castle Rock," Zeno repeated. "That's not a town; that's a dance craze from the thirties."

"Don't be so negative. Once you see what I've got for us here, you will forever remember Castle Rock as our El Dorado."

Zeno came to a stop on the sawdust midway and stared at his companion. "Tell me something. What made you think of me, anyway?"

"Actually, it was Ed Endicott who suggested you."

"The editor of *National Expo?*"

"Do you know another Ed Endicott? He said he liked the way you were handling that werewolf business down in Pinyon until you got yourself in trouble."

"Yeah, trouble. I could have got myself eaten," Louis Zeno muttered.

"So when I told him what I had here, he said you'd be the perfect one to write it."

"Wonderful. Now I'm the *National Expo's* werewolf man."

"You would rather be the two-headed-calf man?"

"Okay, okay." They walked on a short distance in silence. Then Zeno said, "You really think this Animal Boy is legitimate?"

"What the hell, he's close enough. They're talking about him all over the state. Ed Endicott was convinced enough to give me an advance, and you know the Expo don't throw money around."

Zeno sighed. "Let's get on with it, then. This'd better not turn out to be some turkey in a rubber mask."

Grolo the Animal Boy had his own sign outside the tent now. Two garish paintings flanked the platform where Bateman Styles was delivering the pitch. One showed a figure with the body of a boy and the head of some nightmare animal with huge tusks leering out from between two trees. The other had the Animal Boy carrying off a terrified, near-naked woman in the tradition of 1940s horror movies.

Zeno stared up at the pictures. "For this you had me drive up from L.A.?"

"Lighten up, pal. You can't spend your life writing about Burt Reynolds and Bianca Jagger." Vector told him. "Anyway, it's what's inside that counts."

The photographer stopped to click off several pictures of the front of the tent, then they joined the large crowd listening to Bateman Styles.

"...It is my duty to warn you, friends," Styles was saying, "to stay well away from the front of the stage. Grolo is inside a sturdy cage of tempered steel, but his full strength when the rage is upon him has yet to be tested. Therefore, for your own safety, please stand clear. Everyone will be able to see everything that happens."

He paused and made a mental count of the spectators. "Now let us go in for the first show of the evening. For those of you who cannot fit inside the tent this time, your tickets will entitle you to first admittance at the next show one hour from now by the clock."

The showman stood next to the girl selling tickets and smiled contentedly. When he spotted Ted Vector's camera bag he leaned down from the platform.

"Sorry, sir, no pictures."

Vector looked up in innocent surprise. "What'?" Then he smiled and tapped the camera bag as though he had just remembered he was wearing it. "Oh, this? I don't plan to take any pictures inside. I'm a tourist, you know. Never go anywhere without my camera."

"Well, as long as you leave it in the bag..." Styles said doubtfully.

"Absolutely," said the photographer. He and Louis Zeno paid their money and filed into the tent with the rest of the crowd.

The people were packed shoulder to shoulder in the tent. There was no air circulating except that flowing in through the entrance. The combined body heat was oppressive.

Zeno tucked himself in behind Vector and followed the photographer as he pushed his way to a position near the front. He mopped perspiration from his neck with a handkerchief and stared gloomily at the moth-eaten velvet curtain.

"This'd better be good, Ted. Remember, I could be home among the Beautiful People covering some swinging Hollywood party."

"Sure, sure, I know how you cover those parties—you open a can of beer, sit in your bathtub, and fantasize. Watch now, here comes the man."

Bateman Styles made his appearance at one end of the curtain. It was a refinement he had added since the crowds became too big for him to walk easily through from the entrance to the stage.

"Ladies and gentlemen, welcome to the most astounding, the most amazing, the most incredible phenomenon on view in America today. In a very few minutes I am going to pull this curtain aside and reveal to you the Ninth Wonder of the World!"

"What happened to the eighth?" Zeno whispered to the photographer.

"Wasn't that King Kong?"

"Of course. How could I forget?"

Styles gave the two men a stem glance and they fell silent. Then the showman went on with his pitch, the grandiloquent speech rolling smoothly off his tongue in effortless flowery sentences. After many years in the business, Bateman Styles no longer had to think about what he was saying. The sentences, each with a verbal exclamation point, formed themselves and marched out of his mouth while he thought of other things.

He wound it up. "And now, ladies and gentlemen, the moment for which we have waited in an agony of growing suspense! I give you... Grolo the Animal Boy!"

He swept aside the curtain to reveal Malcolm seated on the stool in the confining chimpanzee cage. The boy gazed shyly out at the crowd.

By this time people knew the routine of the act from the reports of others who had seen it. They launched into the derisive hoots at Malcolm without prompting from Styles.

"That's no animal."

"Get off the stage, you fake."

"He doesn't even shave yet."

"Course not, it's a girl!"

"Refund... refund!"

"Booo!"

Louis Zeno took no part in the harassment of the boy in the cage. Nor did he pay any attention to Ted Vector, who was fumbling in his camera bag. Something about the boy's luminous green eyes as they locked on his for a brief moment made the writer acutely uncomfortable.

"Let's get out of here," he whispered to the photographer.

"Are you crazy? The show hasn't even started. Take notes or something."

As always, when the boy began to change, the jeers of the crowd died abruptly. No matter how prepared they were for what was about to happen, the actual transformation on the small stage never failed to shock.

"Jesus," Zeno muttered through clenched teeth.

"See? See? What did I tell you?" Ted Vector had his camera out of the bag now and was holding it down low where it would be concealed from Bateman Styles.

The writer was not listening. He was back in the cabin at the moment he entered and saw torn bits of Abe Craddock everywhere. His stomach lurched, and for a moment he thought he was going to vomit.

"I've seen enough," he said. "Let's go."

"What do you mean? Aren't you going to interview the pitch man or anybody?"

"Who needs interviews? I can make up the quotes, like I always do. Let's go."

"At least let me get some shots of Grolo. Your story is worth shit without pics."

"Well, hurry it up."

Zeno tried not to watch what was happening in the small cage, but a terrible fascination kept pulling his eyes back.

The boy's face had sprouted a coarse black hair. His body had broadened and stretched and changed its shape with a crackling of bones. He had to bend far over as he clutched the bars to keep from banging his head on the low ceiling.

The eyes glowed with deep green fire. The teeth... visions of Craddock's savaged remains swam back up in Zeno's mind.

Vector brought the camera up with no further attempt at concealment and began clicking pictures. The creature in the cage caught the tiny sound. The ears pricked and the great head swiveled toward the source. It gave an inhuman growl; the taloned hands gripped the bars and began to bend them apart.

"You!" Bateman Styles jumped to the center of the stage and stabbed an accusing finger at Ted Vector. "Out! I told you no pictures!"

"Come on," Zeno said, tugging at his friend's arm.

"Just one more."

Click.

The bars separated. A powerful black-haired arm reached through.

"Shit, he's coming out!" someone yelled.

Styles' voice rose above the others. "Get that camera out of here before you get somebody killed!"

Zeno took a firm grip on the photographer's arm and tugged him back through the tense crowd and out of the tent.

"I got some great stuff," he said when they were back out on the midway.

"Yeah, you almost got us ripped apart, too."

"You convinced now?"

Zeno modulated his voice. "It's a good trick. Looked real in the dim lights in there."

"Bet your ass it looked real. How soon can you have the story written?"

"Tomorrow morning."

"Good. I'll develop this stuff tonight and we can hand the whole package to Endicott and collect the rest of the bread." The photographer gazed around the carnival. "You feel like seeing anything else? A couple of the girls in the kootch show aren't too bad, and they go all the way."

"What I feel like," Zeno told him, "is getting the hell out of here. Now."

* * *

CAGED ANIMAL BOY TERRORIZES CARNIVAL

The headline sprang out of the copy of National Expo being browsed by the shopper ahead of Holly Lang in the Safeway checkout line. And the picture—a horribly distorted mingling of human and animal features. But the eyes... she knew the eyes. Beyond any doubt, it was Malcolm. Holly snatched her own copy of Expo from the rack and paid for it along with her groceries. She got into her car and drove directly to the sheriff's office.

Gavin Ramsay frowned at the half-tone photo in the tabloid. He said, "Are you sure this is Malcolm?"

"Of course it is. Don't you see it?"

"Frankly, no. They do some wild things with makeup these days."

"Damn it, Gavin, you're just being obstinate. You know it's Malcolm."

"Well, there's a chance."

"So let's go. We'll find that carnival and get him out of there."

"Right now? Just like that?"

"Why not?"

"For one thing, we don't know how old this photo is or where this"—he scanned Louis Zeno's story—"Samson Supershow is playing. It doesn't sound like a very big outfit."

"You can find out, can't you? You're a cop."

"I suppose I can," Ramsay admitted, "which brings me to my second point. I have a job here, and the taxpayers would probably not approve of me rushing off to do some private business on their time."

"I can go," Holly said. "You don't have to come along."

"Uh-huh. I remember the last time you rushed off to handle things on your own. As I remember, you were in kind of a fix when I got there."

"This is different," she said. "I won't have a Wayne Pastory to contend with. Chances are these carnival people don't know what they've got. All I'll do is go to the carnival, find Malcolm, and bring him back."

"Assuming that this *is* Malcolm," Ramsay said. "What if he doesn't want to come back?"

Holly was flustered for a moment. It was a possibility she had not considered.

"In that case I'll... I'll let him decide for himself. The least I can do is tell him he's not in any trouble over what happened at Pastory's."

"I don't want you to get in any trouble either." She softened her tone. "I promise, Sheriff, if there is the least hint of any rough stuff I'll come running back for reinforcements. Okay?"

He could not hold the stern expression, and relaxed into a smile. "Okay, Doctor. Let me see if I can locate this Samson Supershow for you."

He made a call to the sheriff's office in Los Angeles County. A deputy he knew there said he would check with the theatrical booking agencies. Half an hour later the L.A. deputy called back with the information.

"He says Samson is booked this week in some place called Silverdale over in Inyo County," Gavin told Holly. "If you want to wait a couple of days, maybe I can arrange to go with you."

"Thanks, Gavin, but I don't want to let any more time go by. It's been over a year since we last saw Malcolm at the clinic."

"Then what difference would a couple more days make?"

"I just don't want to wait, that's all."

"You will call to let me know what's happening."

"That's a promise. I'll call as soon as I know anything." She came around the desk and gave him a warm, affectionate kiss. "Thanks, Gavin."

"Don't mention it."

She skipped out of the office to her waiting Volkswagen. Ramsay sat watching her, a worried frown on his face.

* * *

It had not been a good year for Dr. Wayne Pastory. After the unpleasantness at the clinic and his dismissal from La Reina County Hospital, he had been unable to get a practice started anywhere else. His reputation in the medical community, never the best, had fallen to a new low.

He was living in Stockton, eking out a living providing uppers and downers to minor league ballplayers. As he pondered his reduced circumstances, Pastory nourished an ever-building rage. His chance for a real breakthrough—a study on an advanced case of genuine lycanthropy—had literally been stolen from him. Those people had had no right to break into his clinic and make it possible for Malcolm to escape. Yet it was he, not they, who suffered the ostracism. The injustice of it ate away at his mind like a steady drip of acid. Someday... someday he would make them all pay. When he saw the picture and story of the "Animal Boy" in the supermarket tabloid, Pastory could have cried out for joy. It was Malcolm. Malcolm as Pastory had seen him when he applied the electrical charges, only further along in the transformation. What must be happening to him now in the hands of some unschooled carnival showman?

It was an easy matter to learn where the carnival was playing. Wayne Pastory locked up the small apartment that was serving also as his office and headed for the town of Silverdale.

21

An authentic carnival, even a rinky-dink outfit like the Samson Supershow, was a new experience for Holly Lang. She had grown up a city girl, and the closest she had come to the carnivals of small towns were theme parks like Disneyland and Magic Mountain. Those had been exciting at the time, but there was always a sense of antiseptic unreality. People dressed in oversized animal costumes. Here in the carnival the sights and smells were real. The people were real. And always just beneath the surface of cotton candy and jangly music there was a sense of danger. Things could happen in a carnival that would never be allowed at Disneyland.

These thoughts danced in and out of Holly's mind as she made her way along the sawdust midway. The carnival was an experience she would like to take the time to savor one day, but tonight her entire attention was given to finding Malcolm.

She had no trouble locating the tent. It was the largest on the grounds, and the crowd outside it was bigger than any of the others. Jungle sounds blared from a loudspeaker that Bateman Styles had recently added.

As Holly approached, the entrance flap was pulled back and a crowd of people spilled out. Apparently the show had just ended. From their expressions, it appeared the audience had enjoyed themselves.

Holly frowned up at the huge paintings flanking the entrance. She listened to the comments of a couple who were just coming out.

"I wonder how they do it," the woman said. "Search me," the man answered. "I was watching him like a hawk the whole time and I didn't see anything funny."

"You don't think it could be real?"

"Are you kidding? People don't turn into animals except in the movies."

"Yes, but in the movies they can use camera tricks. This wasn't any picture."

"Well, it looked real. I'll say that."

"I know. I thought for a minute he was coming right through the bars."

"It's all part of the act."

"Well, I hope so."

The couple drifted off toward the food tent. Holly waited until the last of the crowd had come out, then she started toward the entrance.

She pulled aside the tent flap and was met by a fat man with a red nose. He wore a bright checkered vest and straw hat.

"Sorry, Miss, the show has just ended. There will be another in one hour. You may buy your ticket now, if you wish, and be guaranteed of getting in."

"Are you Mr. Styles?" Holly asked.

The man's expression turned guarded. "Do I know you from somewhere?"

"We've never met. I read the story about you in the National Expo."

"Ah, yes, that piece of drivel. Since that was published I don't even allow a camera into the tent. I would ban writers, too, if there was a way to tell them from other layabouts. How may I be of service to you?"

"I, er, think I know your... Animal Boy."

"Grolo? I hardly think that's likely, Miss..."

"Dr. Lang."

"Doctor," Styles amended. "What makes you think you are acquainted with my protégé?"

"In the first place, his name is Malcolm."

"I'm afraid you've made a mistake, Doctor. I don't know any Malcolm."

"Holly!" The joyful cry came from the rear of the tent. "I thought I recognized your voice."

Holly and Bateman Styles turned: Malcolm jumped down from the stage and ran toward them, smiling broadly.

"You know this lady?" said Styles.

"It's all right, Bate," the boy said. "She's a friend of mine."

As he reached them Malcolm stopped, suddenly shy. Holly opened her arms and he responded with an enthusiastic hug.

"Malcolm, Malcolm, where have you been? I've been looking for you for more than a year."

"I've been a lot of places. Since May I've been traveling with Mr. Styles. How did you find me?"

"A story in the paper."

Malcolm frowned. "That one with the awful picture?"

"Yes."

"It was just a lot of made-up stuff."

"I was sure of that," Holly said, "but I thought it might be you."

Styles cleared his throat. "If you will be good enough to excuse me, I have a number of errands to run, and I'm sure you have things to talk about. Malcolm, why don't we skip the next show and close out with the ten o'clock."

"Can we afford it?"

"Don't worry about that, my boy; we're well ahead of the game. A reunion with your friend certainly takes precedence."

"Well, thanks, Bate," Malcolm said.

"Think nothing of it. I will see you at ten." He touched the brim of his straw hat. "Good evening, Doctor."

Holly nodded to him, and she and Malcolm walked off up the midway arm-in-arm.

"I can't tell you how happy I am to have found you at last," Holly said.

"So am I," said the boy.

"You've grown."

"I guess so."

Holly squeezed his arm. "If you can get your things together, we can leave right away and be back in Pinyon in the morning."

Malcolm's happy expression faded. "Are they looking for me back there because of, you know, what happened at that clinic?"

"Nobody is looking for you, except to help you, Malcolm. What happened up there at Bear Paw was not your fault. Everybody knows that."

"They do?"

"You have my word for that. You trust me, don't you, Malcolm?"

"Yes."

"Good, then shall we get started?"

The boy looked doubtful. "I don't like to leave Bate just like that."

"Why on earth not? The man has been exhibiting you like some kind of a freak."

"It's not that way, Holly. Mr. Styles has been good to me. I was feeling really bad when I met him, and he gave me something to do with my life. Besides..." He hesitated.

"What is it?" Holly prompted.

"I am some kind of a freak."

Holly came to a stop and turned to face him. She spoke sharply. "Don't you ever talk that way again, Malcolm. You are... different, through no fault of your own. Some people are born with terrible deformities. They can't help it either. But you are not a freak. Not something to be put in a cage and shown to a lot of curiosity seekers."

"It really isn't that bad," Malcolm said. "I don't even think about the people who come to see me. When I'm up there on the stage I think about... other things."

"You don't want to go on doing it, though, do you?"

"No, I... I guess not. I'm always afraid that someday I'll lose control for real."

"Then come back with me, Malcolm. Let me try to help you."

"Do you think I could ever be... cured, Holly?" His eyes searched her face.

Holly hesitated before she answered. "I don't know, Malcolm. I want to be honest with you, and not give you any false hopes. Your case is so different from anything doctors have dealt with that no one can say if there is a cure. One thing I will promise you: I will do everything I can, and so will a lot of other concerned people, to help you in any possible way. Okay?"

"Okay," he said. They smiled at each other.

"One thing, though," the boy added. "We're still booked here for tonight and tomorrow. I'd like to stay and do those shows for Mr. Styles."

"He is important to you, isn't he?" she said.

"I never knew my real father. I would have liked him to be like Bate."

"All right," Holly said. "I'll take a motel room in town. Maybe I'll come down and watch your act."

"No," he said quickly. "Don't do that."

"Not if you don't want me to," she said.

"I'd rather you wouldn't. This is a different part of my life. It doesn't have anything to do with you, and I want to keep it that way."

"Then I'll just stay in my motel room until you're ready to go."

"Thanks, Holly," he said, relieved.

"Well," she said brightly, "we have a couple of hours to kill. What would you like to do?"

"Let me show you around the carnival. We can go on the rides free, since I work here."

"That sounds like fun," she said "Shall we try the Octopus?"

* * *

When Malcolm came back to the tent for the ten o'clock show he found Bateman Styles sitting on the front of the stage with his legs dangling. Beside him was a bottle of Old Overholt and a plastic cup from the food tent. The showman seemed to be studying the shine on his shoes.

"Hi, Bate," Malcolm said cheerily.

"Hello." He did not look up.

"Something wrong?"

"Wrong? What could possibly be wrong?"

"You're mad, aren't you?"

Styles poured rye whiskey into the cup and swallowed it. "No, Malcolm, I'm not mad. I always knew you had a life of some kind before I found you, and I'm not surprised that it would catch up with you someday and pull you back. You are leaving, aren't you?"

"Yes."

Styles hopped down from the stage and came over to stand beside him. He clapped a hand on the boy's shoulder. During the summer Malcolm had grown an inch taller than the showman.

"I want to wish you the best of luck, my boy. If you have something to go back to out there, I don't blame you. The carnival is no place for anybody who has roots. We did have a good season together, didn't we?"

"A good season," Malcolm agreed. "Bate, I want to finish out the date here. I'll do tonight's show and tomorrow's."

"You don't have to do that. I imagine you're anxious to get going with your friend, the doctor."

"I want to do it," Malcolm said. "You can pitch it as a farewell appearance and jack up the admission price."

A smile spread slowly over Styles' ruddy face. He began to laugh, then subsided in a coughing fit. When he recovered his breath he said, "Malcolm, my lad, you are beginning to sound like a real carnie. Go and get yourself ready while I step out front and turn the tip." He laughed again. "Farewell appearance. I'm proud of you."

Malcolm stepped behind the curtain and changed into one of the sets of cheap shirts and pants Bateman had bought for the act. There was no sense wearing anything good, since when his body changed it pushed right out through the clothes.

Lately the change had seemed to go further each time before he could reverse it. It had begun to worry Malcolm, and he was glad to be going with Holly. If there really was help for him, he knew Holly would find it.

As he buttoned up the shirt and tucked it down into the pants, he heard Styles warming up to his spiel out in front.

"Yes, ladies and gentlemen, tonight and tomorrow are absolutely the last and final opportunity you will have to see the Ninth Wonder of the World! The sensational what-is-it that people all over the country are talking about! The inimitable, the incomprehensible, the indescribable... Grolo the Animal Boy!"

Malcolm smiled. Over the weeks he had built a real affection for the showman, and he sensed that Styles liked him, too. In other circumstances he would be glad to stay with the carnival as long as Bate wanted him, but his future was too uncertain. What they were doing might be just a fun-scary show to the marks, but Malcolm knew. They were playing a deadly, dangerous game.

"Yes, my friends," Styles continued out in front, "tonight and tomorrow are absolutely and irrevocably the farewell appearances of the Animal Boy! Never again on this continent or any other will you have the opportunity to see this amazing metamorphosis! Therefore, my friends, since you will be witnessing something no one will ever see again, the admission for tonight and tomorrow's shows will of necessity be slightly higher, a still very reasonable five dollars! And if any of you think you can get a better buy today for five dollars, please tell me and I'll go with you!"

Malcolm heard the crowd laugh with Styles and he knew the showman had them in his pocket. He was glad that Bateman would make a few extra dollars these last two days. It would be partial repayment for the happy time this summer that Styles had given him.

He finished dressing and entered the old chimpanzee cage. Styles had talked about getting a more elaborate cage but had not got around to it. Malcolm had developed a feeling almost of affection for the cage. The door in the back was never locked, of course, and when the power of the beast flowed through his body he could have easily ripped it apart. The marks did not know this, of course.

He sat on the stool and listened to the babble of voices beyond the curtain as the crowd streamed in.

When the tent was full, Bateman slipped in through the rear and winked at Malcolm. "Everything all right, lad?"

"Everything's fine, Bate."

"Good. Let's give 'em their five dollars' worth."

Styles stepped through the curtain for his introduction speech. He was in masterful form, and he had the marks howling for action even before the curtain was pulled aside. Malcolm smiled happily.

"And now the moment for which we have all waited..." Styles intoned. "And paid our five dollars for," somebody in the crowd added.

"I give you, for the very last time, in his farewell appearance… Grolo the Animal Boy!"

He pulled back the curtain and Malcolm assumed the puzzled and rather embarrassed look they had perfected over the summer. He sat on the stool, hands folded in his lap, and tried not to smile as he thought about rejoining Holly Lang.

"Well, what's the matter, Grolo, off your feed tonight?" Batmen said in his tone of mock anger. "Surely this is not what the good people paid to see."

The crowd joined in enthusiastically.

"Yeah, what a phony!"

"Do something, stupid!"

"What is it, a wax dummy?"

"Give us our money back!"

"Look, he's even smiling!"

Malcolm left the stool and walked in a crouch to the front of the cage. There he clutched the bars as he always did and stared out at the people hurling insults at him. He tried, as he had taught himself, to summon up the hateful, painful things that had been done to him in the past. But tonight, try as he might, all he could think about was going back with Holly and maybe… just maybe finding a cure that would make him normal, like other boys.

After several minutes of no action the tone of the crowd changed. Where the insults and jeers had been good-natured, a part of the act, they began to turn ugly as Malcolm stood gazing out over their heads with a half smile on his face.

"Come on, we haven't got all night!"

"What's the matter with him? I thought he was supposed to change into an animal."

"Hell, he's not doing anything!"

"We've been robbed!"

"Come on," a burly tattooed man yelled, "let's pull him out of there and make him do something!"

Bateman Styles, who had been watching Malcolm anxiously, turned quickly to the crowd when he heard the last comment.

"Ladies and gentlemen, I'm very sorry, but the Animal Boy is not feeling well tonight. He will be unable to perform."

"Bull! It's part of the act."

"I assure you, young man, this is an unscheduled interruption. If you will kindly file out, I will personally hand each and every one of you a pass to tomorrow's show."

"Pass, hell, what if there ain't no show tomorrow?"

The crowd shifted, looking as though it might advance on the stage.

Styles said quickly, "You're absolutely right. Your money will be refunded out in front; each and every dollar will be returned with my sincerest regrets."

"You can stuff your regrets," somebody said. "Just give us our money."

The crowd laughed, and the ugly moment had passed. They trooped out of the tent and Styles followed with the cash box. As he passed through the entrance flap he turned for a long, sad look at Malcolm, then continued outside to return the money.

When the showman returned Malcolm had left the cage and was sitting slumped in a wooden chair behind the curtain.

"I let you down, Bate," he said. "I'm sorry."

"Nonsense, my boy, nonsense," boomed Styles. "You could no more help yourself than I could jump over the Ferris wheel."

"I tried. Really I did."

Bateman pulled the stool out of the cage and sat next to him "I know that, Malcolm, and I think I know why it didn't work. You're happy, aren't you?"

"Well, yeah, I guess so."

"Of course you are. I could see it in your eyes when you came out and saw that Dr. Lang tonight. You like her a lot, don't you?"

Malcolm nodded. "Holly was a friend when I needed one. Like you, Bate."

"Thank you, my boy. I appreciate being included in that company. However, as they say, sometimes friends must part, and I guess this is the time for you and me, right?"

Malcolm swallowed hard. "I guess it is. Holly's a doctor, and she's going to try to cure me. Make me normal."

"Unquestionably a worthwhile endeavor."

"If it works out, and I'm just like everybody else, I'd be no good to you, would I?"

"Utter nonsense, my boy. You are a natural for the carnival life. Anytime you want to come back, just look up Bateman Styles and we'll work something out."

"Sure, Bate. Thanks."

Styles lit a Camel and coughed into a handkerchief. "I'd better go clean up out front. Will you be staying in the trailer tonight?"

"If it's all right. Then I'll leave tomorrow with Holly."

"Of course it's all right. I may be in a bit late myself. I'll try not to wake you."

Styles pushed through the curtain and eased himself down off the stage. He started for the front of the tent, slowing down when he saw a man standing in the entrance flap.

"Sorry, bud, the show's over. No more shows tonight."

"I know," the man said. "I saw the last one."

"What's the problem? Didn't you get your money back?"

"I don't want my money back. I have a proposition for you."

Styles looked more closely at the man. He was not big, but he was wiry and seemed charged with nervous energy. His hair was slicked back, his eyes bright and a little too close together.

"What kind of a proposition?"

"First let me introduce myself. I am Dr. Wayne Pastory."

22

It seemed to be his day for meeting doctors, Bateman Styles decided. The first had taken away his livelihood; now this one was offering him a proposition. Holly Lang appeared to be authentic, but Bateman was inclined to be skeptical about Wayne Pastory. He had known too many self-proclaimed 'doctors' who used the title as part of a scam. And this wiry man had the over intense look of somebody not playing with a full deck.

"You say you have a proposition, Dr. Pastory," Styles said carefully.

"Yes, I think it might be of some interest to you. Is there somewhere we can talk?"

"Right here is as good a place as any."

Pastory looked back doubtfully at the entrance. "We won't be disturbed?"

"There won't be anybody coming in," Styles told him. "The rest of the shows have been canceled."

"Ah, yes, so I understand. That rather undercuts your income, I would guess."

"You could say that."

"Perhaps I can make that a little easier for you." He looked quickly at Styles. "I don't know what your relationship has been with this, er, Animal Boy, but I assume he is of no further use to you."

"The relationship has been a professional one," Styles said slowly. "And no, it doesn't look like we'll be performing again."

"All right, here's my proposition—I'll take him off your hands."

"Off my hands," Styles repeated.

"Exactly. We both understand he has no future with you. Oh, I expect to compensate you, of course, but in as much as he is worth nothing to you now, I wouldn't think we'll have to do a lot of haggling over the price."

"No, I wouldn't think so," Styles agreed. He tilted his head to one side and stared down into Pastory's bright little eyes. "May I ask, Doctor, precisely what your interest is in the Animal Boy?"

"I don't see as that is of any importance to our transaction."

"Call it curiosity."

Pastory sighed and spoke rapidly, like a man who knows he is talking over his listener's head. "I am a researcher in psychobiology. The, er, phenomenon of the boy's physical change is of great interest in my field. I want to complete a series of experiments that will shed greater light on his condition."

"And maybe make you a few dollars?"

"I am a researcher, Mr. Styles. Monetary gain is not important to me."

"Ah, yes, of course. Forgive me."

Pastory nodded brusquely. His eyes flicked hungrily up to the curtained stage.

"But as you saw tonight," Styles continued, "this phenomenon, as you call it, is not so reliable."

"There are laboratory methods of triggering the process," Pastory said. "Shall we get down to business?"

"I'd like to hear more about these laboratory methods," said Styles.

"I don't think they would be of much interest to you. Highly technical, you understand."

"That so? What makes you think these methods of yours will work?"

"Because they have before." Pastory was losing patience. "I assure you it is nothing you could duplicate here. The boy was in my care for a short period about a year ago and I was making significant progress until an interruption by outsiders brought my experiment to an end."

"What a shame," Styles commented.

"Yes, yes, but that's not important now. I can pick up where I left off. How does a hundred dollars sound for transferring the boy to me?"

"A hundred dollars. My, my." Styles rubbed his nose thoughtfully.

"I'll make it two hundred just because I am eager to resume my work with the boy."

"You must be."

"That's cash, of course."

Pastory reached for his wallet. He opened it and slipped out four fifty-dollar bills. He was careful not to let Styles see how much more he was carrying.

Bateman took the money. "Ah, yes, two hundred United States dollars." He held the bills up one at a time to the light bulb that was suspended from the top of the tent. He grasped them by the edges and snapped them out. "Crisp new currency; yes, indeed."

"The money is quite genuine," Pastory said. "Can I see the boy now?"

Even from behind the curtain Malcolm recognized the voice of Wayne Pastory immediately. He felt that his past was catching up with him from all directions.

He parted the curtain just a crack and peered out into the tent. The sight of the doctor made him shiver with remembered terrors.

As the conversation continued between Pastory and Bateman Styles, Malcolm's high spirits of a short time ago plummeted. The showman, his friend, was actually dickering to sell him out. Malcolm felt a sob rise in his chest. He forced it back. His vision blurred as tears squeezed into his eyes.

He let the curtain close and sank slowly to his knees. His face was feverish, yet his body shook with a chill. He felt the muscular spasms that preceded the change. He ground his teeth and fought for control.

Be reasonable, he told himself. He couldn't blame Bateman for taking a few dollars from Pastory. Malcolm knew he would never go back to that hateful clinic anyway. Holly was waiting for him. Why did it matter to him what kind of a deal Bateman made with Pastory? His body jerked convulsively.

"Do we have a deal?" Pastory said.

Styles continued to hold the bills in both hands. "Let me be sure I understand," said Styles. "You are offering me two hundred dollars for the boy. I take the money and you take Malcolm."

"Yes, yes, can we get on with it?" The doctor looked at his watch. "My time is limited."

"Yes, well, so is mine. So let me tell you without further palaver what you can do with your two hundred dollars. You can take these bills, roll them up, and stuff them one at a time up your ass."

Pastory blinked. He stared at the showman. "I don't think I understand what you're saying."

"I don't know how I can make it any plainer."

"Is it a matter of more money?"

"It is a matter of you getting the hell out of my sight. So you're a doctor. Good for you. I'm a carnie. Been one all my life. I'll tell you something about carnival people, Doctor: we have a code of our own, and we try to live by it. Sure, we may work a scam here and there, put pictures out front of attractions we don't have inside, weight the milk bottles so they won't tip over. But there are some things we do not do. We don't sell human beings. Not for two hundred lousy dollars. Not for any price. Now get the hell out of my tent."

Styles let the four fifty-dollar bills flutter to the dirt floor. Pastory stared at him for a moment, then bent to pick them up. When he straightened again his face was mottled with anger.

"You don't know what you're doing. Malcolm is not just another boy. He is a unique specimen of active lycanthropy. I want him."

"Get out of here," Styles said. "I can't stand to look at you."

Pastory reached out and seized the lapels of Styles' brightly checked coat. "Damn you, old man, you can't do this to me. I want that boy. I will have him!"

Styles opened his mouth to shout, and Pastory's fingers moved up to clamp around his throat, shutting off his air. The smaller man squeezed. The tendons stood out like cables in his forearms.

Styles' eyes bulged. His face turned an unhealthy bluish color. He scrabbled ineffectually, trying to pry loose Pastory's fingers. He staggered backward, Pastory following, until the smaller man's grip was broken.

Styles pulled in a wheezing breath. He gave a strangled cough, clutched at his chest, and staggered into one of the tent supports, making the canvas shiver. His eyes rolled up into his head and he fell heavily to the dirt floor, his chest heaving. Pastory came over and stared down at him. Styles body bucked once, twice, then lay still.

Pastory looked quickly toward the entrance to the tent. Assured that no one had heard the short scuffle, he ran to the stage at the far end, mounted it, and pulled aside the curtain.

The hate-filled face that glared up at him from the crouching figure only faintly resembled the boy Malcolm. The muzzle was pushed well forward, the eyes slanted deep green, the ears pointed and cocked. The black upper lip curled back to show the outsized killing teeth. It growled.

Pastory spread his hands as one does with a strange dog to show he carried no weapon. He advanced slowly.

"It's all right, Malcolm. No one is going to hurt you. You remember me, don't you? I'm your friend. You know that. I'm going to take you back with me to where no one hurt you again."

Another growl. The creature drew back slightly. The shoulders and deep chest were covered with coarse hair. The clothing he had been wearing hung in tatters.

Pastory could barely contain his excitement. This was furthest along in the change he had yet seen the boy. He ached to get Malcolm back to the laboratory. This time there would be no bungling Kruger to mess things up.

"Come along now," he said, putting just the right note authority into his voice. "There is nothing more for you here. Your place is with me."

The answering growl this time was deeper. The teeth seemed to have grown.

For the first time, Pastory felt a small doubt about his ability to control the boy. He took a step back. "I'm here to help you, Malcolm. Now stop this foolishness and come along."

The attack was so swift that Pastory had no time to cry out. From the crouching position on the floor Malcolm sprang at him. The flashing teeth seized him by the throat; the powerful jaws clamped together. Pastory felt the hot splash of blood down the front of himself. He screamed, but all that came from his gaping mouth was a soft bubbling sound. He had a last impression of the hot, snorting breath of the beast on his face, then the life drained out of him.

The beast, with its jaws still clamped on the man's throat, carried him the way a dog does a rabbit. Blood splattered the wooden floor of the stage, the velvet curtain, the canvas of the tent, the cage. Finally he dropped Pastory's pale and broken body with a thump.

He came through the curtain and in two long bounds was at the side of the still figure of Bateman Styles. The muzzle poked down close to the showman's livid face and snuffled questioningly. There was no answer from Styles. No movement, no breath, no heartbeat.

The beast whirled from the body of the showman and ran out through the opening in the rear of the tent. Outside he lifted his bloody muzzle to the night sky and he howled.

It was a sound Malcolm had heard many times from others in the night. He howled again—a long, ululating cry of loneliness and rage and despair. From up in the distant hills, faint but unmistakable, came an answer.

Along the carnival midway people stopped and turned to stare toward the unearthly howling. Small children began to cry. Women pressed closer to their men. The men glanced at one another, each waiting for someone else to make the first move. Then several of the carnival people started toward Bateman Styles' tent.

Malcolm heard them coming. He swung his great beast's head to and fro, searching for a way out. Seeing a path that led off toward the town between the parked trailers and trucks, he ran. Ran with ground-devouring strides. If any of the carnival men saw the powerful figure loping across the field they did not try to give chase.

23

Gradually Malcolm's pace slackened. His breathing grew labored. He became aware of an ache in his muscles and the slap of his bare feet on the pavement. He slowed to a walk, watching behind to be sure there were no pursuers.

The shadows seemed to deepen. He listened to the tiny chirps and rustlings of the night creatures. The air was cold on his skin where the clothing was torn, and he realized that the transformation had reversed itself. Once again his appearance was that of a normal human.

He gathered the torn remains of his clothing about him and looked around to get his bearings. He saw he was on the state highway that formed the main street of Silverdale. A mile ahead he could see the scattered lights of the town. A couple of hundred yards before him was the neon sign for the motel where Holly Lang was staying. He hurried on.

There were only four cars pulled into the spaces to accommodate the twelve rooms of the motel. Curtains were pulled across the windows in the occupied rooms. In the office Malcolm could see a young Oriental woman working on a crossword puzzle.

He crept along the wall to the motel room with Holly's Volkswagen parked before it. Softly he knocked.

When Holly opened the door her shocked expression reflected the boy's disheveled appearance.

"Malcolm, what happened to you? Are you all right?"

"Can I come in?"

"Of course." She stood aside while Malcolm entered the room. She led him to a chair, then snapped off the old movie that was playing on television.

Malcolm sat stiffly in the chair for a moment, breathing hard. Then he started to cry. At first he made an effort to hold back the tears, then gave in to them. All the pent-up sorrows, frustrations, and pains of his young life burst forth in uncontrolled sobs. Holly took a chair across the room and sat quietly, letting him cry it out.

After a while he subsided. He used the tattered sleeve of his shirt to wipe his eyes, and looked shyly over at Holly.

"I've never done that before," he said.

"Then it was about time you did. Everybody has to let the hurt come out once in a while."

"It does feel better."

"Of course it does. People shouldn't hold those things inside."

The boy's faint smile faded. "Oh, Holly, it's all over now. I've ruined everything."

"Why don't you tell me about it."

The boy spoke haltingly, glancing at Holly's face from time to time for a reaction. Mostly he kept his eyes downcast.

"Dr. Pastory came to the tent tonight."

"How did he..." Holly interrupted, then caught herself. "No, never mind. Go on."

"He... he wanted to take me back. He offered to buy me from Mr. Styles. For a minute I thought Bate was going to do it, but he never would have. He told Dr. Pastory to get out. Pastory grabbed him and there was a scuffle. Mr. Styles choked and fell down. I was behind the curtain and heard the whole thing."

The boy paused. His gaze drifted off to a corner of the ceiling, as though seeing there again the events of the night.

"I didn't want it to happen to me then, Holly. I didn't want to change. I tried to fight, but I couldn't help it. When Dr. Pastory came to get me, I couldn't help myself."

"There's blood on your shirt," Holly said. "Did he hurt you?"

Malcolm shook his head. "It isn't my blood. It's his. Pastory's."

"You... attacked him?"

"I killed him, Holly."

"Oh, Malcolm, are you sure?"

"I killed him, all right. And do you want to know what else?"

"What?" Holly said quietly.

"I liked it. I hated him so much, both for what he did to me and for hurting Mr. Styles, that all I wanted was for him to die. And when he did I was happy."

Holly stretched out a hand and touched him on the shoulders. "Oh, my poor, poor Malcolm."

"Then I went to Mr. Styles and I saw he was dead. If I could have killed Pastory again right then, I would have. I ran out. People started coming toward the tent. I just kept running until I got here."

"I'm glad you came to me," Holly said.

"I shouldn't have. They'll be looking for me soon. I'll just get you in trouble, too."

"You mustn't think that way, Malcolm. What happened was not your fault. Wayne Pastory was an evil man. Whatever happened to him I'm sure he provoked."

"But I killed him, Holly. I turned into an animal and I killed him. If they catch me, they'll lock me up."

"Not if I can do something about it," she said. "Come with me, Malcolm. Now, tonight. We'll go where there is help for you."

"Why should anyone want to help me?" he said.

"You are not to blame for what happened. You have to remember that. What you have is like a sickness. And sickness can be cured."

"But this is... I'm... different," the boy said.

"Yes, Malcolm. And it is because you're different that you can't be held responsible."

"It could happen again," he said.

"We must see that it doesn't. You were put under unbearable stress tonight. The man you most hated attacked and killed a good friend. A lot of so-called normal people would have lost control, too."

Malcolm was silent for a long minute. Then he said, "What can we do, Holly?"

"The first thing is to get out of here. I can pack in ten minutes, then we'll start back to Pinyon. There are people there we can trust."

Malcolm looked at his torn, blood-spattered clothes. "I can't go like this."

"I doesn't matter, Malcolm," Holly said. "No one but me will see you."

"I don't want to," he said, trying to cover himself. Holly sighed. He was, after all, an adolescent boy with the normal adolescent's dread of being embarrassed.

She said, "I might have something you can wrap yourself in, at least until we get to Pinyon."

"I have some things in the trailer," Malcolm said. "Mr. Styles' trailer. I can go and get them."

"Do you think that would be safe?"

"I'll be careful. If there are people around, I won't go near it."

"I think you're taking a big risk just to pick up some clothes."

"They're kind of special," the boy said. "Mr. Styles bought them for me. I don't have anything else to remember him by."

"All right, Malcolm, if you feel you have to. Promise me you'll be very, very careful."

"I promise," he said.

They walked together to the door. Holly looked out to be sure no one was around. Then she gave the boy a hug, and he slipped away into the night.

He stayed in the shadows of the brush at the side of the road as he made his way back toward the carnival grounds. Circling the perimeter, he saw that all normal activity had come to a stop. The lights still blazed, but the sounds of the carnival—the jangly music, the rumble of the rides, the talkers, the laughter of the people along the midway—were missing. A car from the Inyo County Sheriff's Department was parked near the entrance gate.

Malcolm slipped onto the grounds between the food tent and the shooting gallery. He could see a crowd milling around in front of the Animal Boy tent. A man in a sheriff's uniform stood guard out in front to keep back the curious. So far there seemed to be no one back where the trailers were parked.

As he made his way toward Bateman Styles' battered old trailer, Malcolm stopped suddenly. The breath caught in his throat. Ahead of him a man-size shadow detached itself from the others and moved into his path.

"Hello, Malcolm."

It took a moment for him to make out the sandy-haired, mild-looking man who stood regarding him calmly. Then recognition came with a jolt.

"Derak! How did you find me?"

"We've known where you were for months," he said. "One or more of us was always nearby, waiting for you to call and tell us you were ready. Tonight you did."

"I called you?"

"We heard it from the hills. The howling."

"I didn't mean to do that," Malcolm said. "I couldn't I help myself."

"I understand," Derak said. "The fact remains that you called to us. By now you have learned that you cannot live among the others as one of them. It is time for you to join us."

"H-how many of you are there?"

"More than you might think. There is a band of us now in the hills above this town. Some of them you will recognize from Drago. We're all waiting for you, Malcolm."

The boy peered into the darkness. He thought he saw movement among the shadows. "Are there others here now with you?"

"Yes. You will meet them all when you join us. Come, let's waste no more time."

Malcolm hung back. "Derak, I-I'm not sure this is what I want to do."

The eyes of the sandy-haired man lost their mild look. They glittered, reflecting the lights of the carnival. "My son, you have no choice."

"But I do. I have a friend who says there may be a cure for me."

"*Cure!*" Derak snapped the word off like the crack of a whip. "Cures are for sick humans. You are not sick. And Malcolm, you are not human. You belong with us. It is your only hope for survival."

Malcolm pulled in a deep breath. Although Derak seemed to draw him like a powerful magnet, he was determined to assert his own will.

"Dr. Lang has promised to help me."

Derak snorted in contempt. "Dr. Lang? That woman in the motel room? What do you think she can do for you?"

"I don't know," Malcolm admitted. "But she promised to try, and I believe her."

"You're a fool. She will only exploit you like that other doctor."

"No," Malcolm said stubbornly. "Holly is different. I trust her."

"You have much to learn," Derak said. "Not only about humans but about yourself."

"I'm going with her," Malcolm said. "You can't stop me."

"Can't I?" Derak said darkly. "You don't know how easily I could take you right now."

"Then you'll have to do it that way." The boy braced his feet wide apart and faced the man.

Derak made a sound deep in his chest. He took a step toward Malcolm. For a moment the light gleamed off his teeth, suddenly grown longer. Then he stepped back into the shadows.

"No, Malcolm, I will not take you by force. I want you to join us of your own choosing. I ask you once more... come with me."

Malcolm shook his head. "No. If there is a chance I might be helped, that I might live as a normal human being, I have to take it. I'm going with Dr. Lang."

Derak's eyes glowed dangerously. "Very well. It is a foolish choice, one you are going to regret. However, the choice is yours to make. When you are ready to come to us, you know we will be near."

As Malcolm watched, Derak seemed to vanish into the darkness. A second shadow shape moved, too, and the boy was left alone.

He continued to Styles' trailer, relieved to see there was still no one around. He slipped inside, leaving the door ajar. For a moment he was overwhelmed by the familiar surroundings that had been his home during the happy summer months. He moved about, running his fingers lightly over the cupboard where they kept their supply of food for the butane stove, the board where the old man had been teaching him chess, the perpetually rumpled bed where Bateman slept, his own bedroll neatly tucked away under the fold-down table. Even the stale smell of Bate's Camels brought back happy memories.

Malcolm shook himself out of the mood and quickly selected a few articles of clothing. He slipped them on, taking the tattered old ones with him to dispose of along the way.

He made his way back to the highway, buoyed by the thought that in an hour he would be back with Holly. Then they could be on their way to a new life for him.

* * *

At that moment, however, someone else knocked at the door of Holly's room. Expecting Malcolm, she opened it to a surprise.

24

Malcolm quickened his steps as he approached the motel. The same cars that had been there before still stood in the parking spaces. The Oriental woman dozed in the office. Holly Lang's Volkswagen waited outside her room.

He stopped. There was a prickling of his skin as when someone draws a fingernail down a blackboard. Everything looked the same, yet something was different. He could sense it. Something unknown was waiting for him behind the drawn curtains of the motel room.

He approached slowly, looking in all directions, listening, sniffing the air. Nothing moved in the night. There was no sound. He could detect no foreign scent. And yet, he had this feeling...

He knocked lightly at the door, his muscles tense, nerves jumping.

The door opened.

The woman who stood in the doorway was not Holly Lang. She was two or three inches shorter than Holly. Her compact body was beautifully rounded and displayed to good advantage in a tight skirt and top of black leather. The woman's hair was black as midnight, her mouth wide and inviting. She smiled. Her eyes were wide-set and playful. They were green. Deep, deep green.

"Hello, Malcolm," she said.

The impact of the woman in the doorway kept him from speaking for a moment. He felt very young and clumsy.

"Are you going to stand out there staring all night?"

"Who are you?" he managed finally.

"I am Lupe. I've been waiting for you. Come in." She stepped aside and watched him with amusement.

Malcolm entered the room hesitantly. No one else was there. He saw Holly's suitcase lying open on the floor, her things packed neatly inside.

"Where is Holly?"

"We have her now."

"We?"

"Oh, come, Malcolm, you know me. We can always recognize each other."

"What do you mean you have Holly?" A blade of fear stabbed into him.

"Oh, not *that* way," Lupe said. "She's still all right, as far as I know."

"You're one of Derak's people?"

"Yes, of course. Derak has your friend."

"Where has he taken her?"

"To the hills. I can show you."

"Well, come on!" He started toward the door.

"What's your hurry?" The dark woman's voice was husky and insinuating. "He won't do anything to her. Not until you get there, anyway."

"What do you mean?"

"I think you'd better hear the rest from Derak. We'll go after them in a little while."

"Why not now?"

"There are other things we can do now." She reached up and undid the top button of the leather blouse. "How old are you, Malcolm?"

"Almost sixteen."

Another button.

"Have you been with a woman?"

"Yes."

The third button.

"Many?"

"No."

"I'll bet you have never been with a woman like me."

She undid the last button and dropped her arms. A shrug and the leather top was on the floor. She wore nothing underneath. Her breasts were large and firm and proud. Malcolm could not pull his eyes away.

Lupe reached for the fastening at the side of her skirt. "Have you?"

"What?" Malcolm's mouth was dry.

"Have you been with a woman like me?"

"No."

"I didn't think so."

A soft snap, a zip, and the leather skirt joined the top on the floor. Lupe stood straight before him. She touched the dark triangle of pubic hair, slid her hand up over the rounded belly, and cupped one heavy breast. Her finger played with the nipple until it stood erect.

"Do you like me?" she said.

"I-I have to find Holly."

"I told you I'll help you. But first, wouldn't you like to get to know me better?"

She came toward him, stopping inches away. He could feel the heat of her naked body. There was an ache between his legs.

"I can make you feel really good," Lupe said. "Would you like that?"

She reached down and touched him. His erection grew under her fingers.

"Well, what do we have here?" she teased. "And only sixteen years old. You are going to be quite a man, Malcolm."

He began to perspire. He could feel his shirt going damp at the armpits. Conflicting emotions ripped him. He wanted to take the hand of the taunting woman away, and he never wanted her to move it.

She opened his pants and slipped her hand inside. The sensation was unbearable pleasure.

He tried to speak, but all that came out was a long "Aaahhh!"

"Take those things off," Lupe told him. "Come into bed with me."

She peeled back the spread, blanket, and top sheet, then lay down, spreading her midnight hair over a pillow. She cocked one knee and massaged the velvety inside of her thigh with gentle strokes of her fingertips.

"Hurry," she said in a husky whisper.

With his eyes never leaving the woman in the bed, Malcolm stripped off his shirt and pushed the pants and shorts down his legs. He pulled off shoes and socks and lay down on the bed beside her.

Instantly Lupe was on him. She kissed his mouth, her tongue probing deep. Her hungry lips nibbled at his chin, his throat, and down across his chest to his belly. The green eyes looked up at him teasingly.

"Feel good?"

"Y-yes."

"Want me to stop?"

"No."

"I told you so."

She took him into her mouth then. Her tongue and lips worked on him, her white little teeth giving him gentle love bites. Her cheeks hollowed as she sucked. Malcolm felt as though he were being pulled inside out.

Just when he thought he could not last a second longer, she drew her head back, her mouth making a little popping sound as he slid out. She rubbed the length of her body up along his, the flesh lubricated by their mingled sweat. She raised her head and looked down on him. Her hair was a shiny black curtain framing her face. She smiled. Her teeth were very white and very sharp. And not so little anymore.

Slowly, tantalizingly, she lowered herself down on him and took his length inside her. He felt the heat radiate through his body.

"Good?" she said, her breath moist on his face.

He could not answer.

She began to ride slowly up and down on him, pausing at the top just before he would have slipped out, then sinking gradually to swallow him up again.

Malcolm closed his eyes, giving himself to the sensations of his body. Sitting on him, riding him, Lupe stepped up the rhythm and the vigor of their joining until her buttocks smacked his upper thighs with a report like a pistol shot.

His climax came a second before hers. She dropped down on him, her arms wrapped about his neck, nails digging furrows in his back. They cried out together and rolled back and forth over the king-size bed until his seed was spent. Then they continued to cling to each other like drowning children as their breathing slowly returned to normal.

Lupe was the first to speak. "I told you you'd never had a woman like me."

"Mmmm," was all Malcolm could manage.

"It gets better."

"I don't believe it."

"Oh, yes. When you really know about yourself and about what we are, there are ways to make it much better."

Malcolm opened his eyes. He rolled to one side and pushed the woman away. "You said you'd take me where Derak went with Holly."

"Did I say that?" Lupe's eyes danced with mischief. "I don't know why you're so anxious to see Derak."

"We have to settle something."

"You're not thinking of challenging him?"

"Why not?"

"Because you are just a pup. Derak has been a leader of his people for a long time. You're lucky he has let you come this far on your own."

"Let me?"

"Of course he has. He could have taken you many times over the past year."

"Then why didn't he?"

"You don't know?"

"I'm asking."

"Because he is your father."

Malcolm sat up and stared at her. Derak, his father? The knowledge hit him like a fist. Malcolm knew him as a leader, a teacher, one to be respected. And perhaps feared. But a father? How was it possible? He felt closer to Holly, to Jones, to Bateman Styles, than to the quiet-spoken man with the deep green eyes.

"Don't start thinking that makes you too special," Lupe went on. "Derak was father to half the children in the village of Drago. Of course, many of them did not survive the fire. Maybe that is why he is so patient with you."

"And my mother?" he said.

"She died in the fire. You must not think of her. It is not important, as you will learn."

He swung his feet off the bed and began pulling on his clothes. "Take me to Derak now," he said.

Lupe reached over and slid a hand between his bare buttocks. "So soon? We've just gotten started."

He stood up, moving back out of her reach. "You're wrong. We're finished.

Let's go."

"You mean you had your fun and now you're through?" she said petulantly. "What about me?"

He glared at her. "You promised."

She patted the damp sheet beside her. "Come back. Once more, then I will take you to Derak and your lady friend."

He cinched the belt buckle tight and crossed to the door.

"If you won't help me, I'll find them myself."

"Go ahead, if you think you can," Lupe taunted him from the bed. "But it will be much nicer in here with me."

"The hell with you."

He went out and slammed the door. The night surrounded him. He looked at the lonely cars crouching like abandoned beasts in the painted spaces. The lights were out now in all the rooms, except the one where Lupe waited. Malcolm felt terribly alone.

He walked back past the motel units to where the land sloped up into the foothills. Up there somewhere was Derak. And he had Holly with him. But where? How to find them in all that expanse of dark, rolling country? The boy's doubts made the night even colder.

Then he heard it. The howling.

Unmistakably, it was a call to him. Malcolm closed his eyes. He sniffed the air. Small, invisible changes happened inside his body. And the night was not so cold anymore.

When he opened his eyes, their green color had deepened. He started confidently up into the hills.

25

Gavin Ramsay sat staring at the little digital clock on his desk in the La Reina County Sheriff's office. He caught himself counting the seconds as they ticked off, and angrily turned the face of the clock away from him.

All right, so Holly Lang had not called last night. That didn't mean anything. There were a hundred reasons she might not have telephoned him. Yeah, he told himself grimly, and about fifty of them were bad news.

The new, slimmed-down version of Deputy Roy Nevins came into the office. His leather gleamed; his uniform was freshly pressed. He was shaved, trimmed, and looked maybe ten years younger than he had a year ago. Gavin marveled at the varying effect exposure to violence had on different people.

"Any action, Roy?" he asked.

"Not to speak of. Somebody used the deer-crossing sign for target practice again. I collared a speeder from L.A. trying out his new Porsche. Had to break up a couple of guys who had pulled off the road to do some smooching."

"Couple of guys?"

"I should have mentioned that they were from San Francisco."

"Oh. Well."

Nevins sat down to type out his report in two-finger machine-gun style. Ramsay sighed and turned the clock back around to face him. The hell with this. He was worried, and there was no use pretending he wasn't. He picked up the phone and direct-dialed the number of the Silverdale Motel.

The female voice that answered had a pleasant, foreign-sounding lilt.

"Is there a Dr. Hollanda Lang registered there?" he asked.

"Yes, sir. She in room twelve. I ring for you."

He listened while the line buzzed five times in his ear.

"Sorry, sir, she not answer."

"This is Sheriff Gavin Ramsay of La Reina County. I'd like you to take a look in Dr. Lang's room to see if she's all right."

"Is something wrong with lady?" The woman's voice rose several tones.

"There's no reason to think so," he said soothingly, "but I'd appreciate it if you would take a look."

Yes, yes, I look. You want I call you back?"

"I'll hold on," Ramsay said.

There was a clunk as the receiver was set down on the other end. Ramsay counted seconds on the clock for five minutes. Roy Nevins had stopped hammering the typewriter and was watching him.

"Hello, Sheriff?" The sudden return of the voice in his ear startled him for a moment.

"Yes."

"I look in room. Nobody there. Lady's clothes put away all neat. Car outside. Maybe she walk down the road for breakfast."

"Yeah, maybe," Ramsay said. "Thank you."

"Trouble?" Roy Nevins said when he had hung up.

"I don't know. Holly was going to call me from Silverdale. She didn't. Now she's not in her room. It's probably nothing."

"Sure." Nevins went back to his report, but he continued to glance over toward Ramsay.

Gavin made a try at studying his calendar for the coming week. Talk to the Darnay Boys' Club, lunch with local Kiwanis, oversee motorcycle hill climb east of Pinyon, entertain police science class from La Reina College. It was no use; he could not concentrate.

He picked up the phone again and called Inyo County. The sheriff there was a man named Fielding whom Ramsay had met once or twice. A stolid lawman with good instincts but little imagination.

Ramsay identified himself to the switchboard and was put through to the sheriff, who sounded harried.

"Good to hear from you, Ramsay. What can I do for you?"

"A woman from Darnay, a Dr. Hollanda Lang, checked into the Silverdale Motel yesterday. She's still registered there, but the woman in the office couldn't find her. I'm a little worried."

"Any reason to think something might have happened to her?"

"Nothing concrete, except the business she was doing there."

"What business?"

"It had to do with the carnival."

Fielding exhaled a blast of air into the mouthpiece. "I don't know anything about your doctor, but I've got plenty of troubles of my own with that carnival."

"Oh?" Ramsay leaned forward.

"Couple of men died there last night under suspicious circumstances."

"Two men?" Ramsay said. "What happened?"

He could hear other voices talking excitedly in the background at Inyo County.

"I've got to go now, Ramsay," said Sheriff Fielding. "Give me a call back this evening and maybe I'll have something for you."

The phone went dead in Ramsay's hand. He hung up the instrument, then dug into the bottom desk drawer for the silver bullets that had rested there since he had last used them at Pastory's Bear Paw clinic.

He said. "Think you can manage things here for a day or so, Roy?"

"No problem," said Nevins. "Is Holly in some kind of trouble?"

"I hope not," Ramsay said, "but I think I'll take a run over to Silverdale to check on her. If you need me, call Sheriff Fielding, Inyo County."

"Will do," Nevins said.

As he drove through the Inyo Pass and started the descent through the hills to Silverdale, Ramsay began to wonder what he would say to Holly if he found her safe and sound in the Silverdale Motel. How would he explain galloping over here like John Wayne on the chance she might be in trouble?

Hell with that. There *was* trouble here. Two men were dead on the grounds of the Samson Supershow, and Ramsay would be damned surprised if Holly and the boy Malcolm were not somehow involved.

He had to pass the carnival grounds on his way to the motel, so Ramsay pulled off there first. He identified himself to the Inyo County deputy who was posted at the entrance. In the tent that displayed pictures of 'Grolo the Animal Boy' he found Sheriff Fielding and an agitated little man named Moskowitz, who seemed to be the owner of the carnival.

Fielding gave him a rundown of the previous night's fatalities. "One of the dead men was Bateman Styles. He ran this Animal Boy thing. Cause of death seems to be a heart attack, but there were suspicious bruises. The other one was definitely not a natural death. Had his throat ripped out."

"Got a suspect?"

"A pretty good one," Fielding said. "It seems this so-called Animal Boy hasn't been seen since the killings. Nobody knows where he went. Not that they're telling, anyway."

"You're on the wrong track there, Sheriff," piped Moskowitz.

The lawmen looked down, surprised. They had forgotten for a moment that the little man was there.

"What makes you think so, Mr. Moskowitz?" said Fielding.

"The kid did a kind of wildman act, but that's all it was—an act. When he wasn't working he was just a shy, sweet-natured kid. No way he could kill anybody. Besides, he thought Bateman Styles was Jesus Christ."

Ramsay had a sudden thought. "What was the name of the second victim?"

Fielding consulted a notebook. "The name in his wallet was Wayne Pastory. A doctor, apparently."

The muscles tensed in Ramsay's upper back. "I know that one," he said. Briefly, he filled the Inyo sheriff in on Pastory's background in Pinyon.

"Could you take a look at the body and give us a positive ID?" Fielding said.

"Sure. But there's something I have to do first."

"Check on your Dr. Lang?"

"I'll get back to you."

* * *

Holly Lang's little Volkswagen Rabbit looked so natural and peaceful parked outside unit twelve that for a moment Ramsay felt his fears might be foolish after all. However, the apprehension returned as he knocked and waited for a response.

A woman with glossy black hair and mischievous eyes opened the door. She wore a motel bath towel wrapped around a sensual olive-skinned body.

"Sorry to keep you waiting," she said. "As you can see. I was in the shower."

Ramsay pulled his head back and checked the room number again. "I'm looking for Dr. Hollanda Lang. Maybe I have the wrong room."

"You have the right room," the dark woman said. "She's not here."

Ramsay fumbled out his identification. "My name's Ramsay," he said. "Sheriff, La Reina County."

"I am Lupe," said the woman. "I was told you might be along."

"Told? Told by whom?"

The woman shivered. "Do you mind if we go inside? I'm getting a chill standing here."

Ramsay stepped into the room. Lupe closed the door behind them. He looked over the impersonal motel furnishings, searching for some sign of Holly Lang. Aside from a blue overnight case beside the bureau that might have been hers, he could find nothing.

"Where is Dr. Lang?" he said.

"Why is everyone so interested in finding that woman?" Lupe said. "Won't I do?"

"I don't want to play games. If you know where she is, please tell me."

Lupe pointed up into the foothills that rose immediately behind the motel. "She's up there."

"Up there, where?"

"She's with a friend of mine."

Ramsay took a step toward her. "Let's stop wasting time. I want to know where Holly is, and I want to know now."

Lupe clutched the towel to her breast in mock fright. "And what will you do to me, Sheriff, if I don't want to tell you? Give me the third degree?"

With an effort Ramsay brought himself under control. "I think we'd better talk to the local authorities. They're investigating a couple of deaths at the carnival, and they might want to ask you some questions."

The woman's green eyes lost their playfulness. "I don't think you want to have me arrested. Not if you want to see your Holly again."

Ramsay ground his teeth. "Where *is* she?"

"I told you—with a friend of mine. His name is Derak."

"Should the name mean something to me?"

"He is from Drago."

Ramsay stiffened. "And you?"

"Yes."

"Jesus." Unconsciously his hand brushed the jacket pocket that was heavy with the silver bullets.

"I see you are beginning to understand. She will not have been harmed yet, but if you want her to stay that way, you had better be nice to me."

"What about the boy, Malcolm? Is he with them?"

"If he is not, he soon will be," Lupe said. Ramsay moved toward the door. "Where are you going?"

"To organize a search of these hills."

"A search?"

"Men, helicopters, whatever it takes."

"That would be a mistake. Your men and helicopters did not capture Derak the last time. They are no match for him. All they can do is make him angry. And then what do you suppose he might do to your Holly?"

Gavin stood indecisively halfway between the woman and the door.

"There is another way," Lupe said in a throaty voice.

"Well?"

In a sinuous movement she pulled away the towel and let it fall to the floor. Gavin stared at the smooth naked body.

"Come make love to me and I'll tell you about it." she said.

"Are you crazy?"

The green eyes flashed. "No. I'm hungry. Last night I had a boy. He just gave me a sharper appetite for a man." She opened her arms. "Come. Let me show you what a woman like me can do for a real man."

For a moment Gavin was actually close to accepting the challenge. The woman's body was wonderfully inviting, and the faint musky smell of her made him feel a little drunk.

He shook off the impulse. "I'll bet you're something." he said, "but strange as it may seem to you, I'm not in the mood. See you."

He turned and walked to the door. As he gripped the knob she called to him. "Wait."

He turned back. She reached down and picked up the towel but made no effort to cover herself. "I'll take you to them."

He eyed her suspiciously. "Why would you do that?"

"Because I don't want her to be one of us. That's what happens, you know, when someone is bitten and doesn't die. They become… what we are."

"So I've heard," Gavin said.

"Lately I have been Derak's woman. I don't want to share him."

"All right," Gavin said. "Get dressed and let's get started."

* * *

The first half hour was rough going as the slope grew steeper and there was no usable trail through the heavy brush. Lupe, in spite of her soft shoes and leather outfit, moved easily up the hill while Ramsay struggled. He was breathing hard by the time they reached a trail that angled up the hillside at a more gentle grade.

Lupe was waiting for him as he topped the rise onto the trail. She contrived to brush her breasts against him. "Want to rest? Or something?"

"No, I'm fine. Let's go."

She made a face at him, but they continued up the trail. After another hour they were making good time. The trail forked, each leg angling up the hill in a different direction. Ramsay turned to Lupe for a decision. She suddenly cried out and fell to her knees. She rolled to a sitting position, clutching her right leg.

"What's the matter?" Gavin said.

"It's my ankle. I stepped on a rock and I heard something pop in there. It hurts."

Gavin knelt beside her and took the leg gently in his hand. He eased the soft leather shoe off her foot. Lupe grimaced.

"Do you think you can walk on it?" he said.

"I don't know. It hurts really bad."

He ran his fingers gently along the skin of her leg from knee to instep. There was no irregularity that might indicate a broken bone. In spite of the urgency of the situation, he was aware of the smooth feel of her flesh.

"Maybe it's higher up," she said. "Above the knee. Why don't you feel there?"

He turned and saw she was grinning at him.

"Go ahead," she said. "Feel my leg. It's already getting better."

"Damn you," he began, but before he could say more, Lupe grasped him behind the neck and pulled his head down into a steamy kiss.

He pulled away, a little bit surprised at her strength. "Will you for Christ's sake cut it out?" he said.

She leaned back on her elbows, looking at him. "What's the matter? You do like women, don't you?"

"I like women just fine," he said slowly. "And I like sex with women. But I like it with the woman I choose and at the time I choose. Now quit crapping around and let's go."

Lupe did not move. Her eyes flashed angrily. "I'm not good enough? You've got to have a lady doctor, is that it?"

He opened his mouth to answer, but the words died when he saw what was happening to Lupe. Her mouth opened in snarl to show strong canine teeth. Hair sprouted from her face. Her body jerked in a convulsion as she tore away her leather clothes. Claws pushed out of the ends of her fingers as the hands stretched and blackened. She rose, standing on the powerful hind legs of a wolf.

Ramsay looked up at the creature that now stood a good head taller than he. All resemblance to the beautiful seductive woman was gone. What remained was a deadly, ravenous creature covered with glossy black fur. He pulled the revolver from his holster.

"Get back!" he said. "Silver bullets."

Lupe, or what had been Lupe, gave a deep-throated bellow that echoed faintly of the woman's derisive laugh. She came at him.

Ramsay hesitated for a near-fatal moment. He could not erase the image of the vibrant, sexy woman who had been there a moment ago. The oversized hands caught him, the claws digging through his jacket into the flesh of his back. The creature's jaws creaked open. The teeth came down toward his throat. Her breath stank of carrion.

Ramsay pulled the trigger. The sound of the gunshot was muffled against the huge body of the werewolf. She gave a shriek of mingled pain and shock. The grip of the claws relaxed and she staggered backward.

Blood pumped in a steady stream from a hole in the belly of the wolf. The green eyes fogged over and the creature fell, raising a puff of dust from the trail. The jaws opened a last time in a long, wailing howl, then the head dropped back lifelessly.

Ramsay stood for a long minute looking down at the dead thing that had been a woman. The revolver was still in his hand. He was surprised to see it shaking.

He put the gun away and turned his gaze up the trail into the hills. Finding Holly would be a tough job now without Lupe to guide him. But he knew she was up there, and he was not going to turn back. As he concentrated on choosing one of the two trail forks before him he heard a voice high in the hills and off to the left. Howling.

He knew now which direction to take.

26

Holly Lang leaned her back against the rocky face of a cliff. The ledge where she sat was some thirty feet wide. Beyond it the trail sloped sharply down the hill through heavy brush. The silence was broken only by the chirping of birds off in the forest. Holly shivered with the chill of the morning. She hugged her knees and waited.

They were all waiting. Derak with his arms folded, his eyes on the spot where the trail came out of the brush, the rest of them sitting, standing, crouching. There was little conversation. They were waiting. Waiting for Malcolm.

Holly looked around, studying the people gathered on this rocky ledge in the Inyo Hills. There were men and women ranging in age from young to very old. Some were thin, others fat. To all appearances it was a group of normal people spending a day in the mountains. Their faces betrayed nothing beyond a mild anxiety. Nothing at all was remarkable about them. Nothing, except that they were all werewolves.

When Derak had taken her from the motel last night, Holly fully expected to die. Instead she had been brought here, given coffee and a candy bar for breakfast, and told to be still and she would not be hurt. She understood now that she was the bait that would lure Malcolm back to these people. Whatever happened, they still might kill her. She simply could not let herself think about the possibility.

She had considered running and had actually made an attempt shortly after Derak brought her there and left her alone. When no one seemed to be watching, she had plunged down the steep grade toward the trees. They let her flounder thirty yards or so into the forest, then two of the women had simply come and gotten her and brought her back. These people moved in the wilderness with a natural ease that she could never hope to match. After the aborted escape attempt she had sat quietly like the rest of them. Waiting.

At noon he came. Malcolm walked straight up the trail with no attempt at stealth. His eyes flicked over the assembled people and came to rest on Holly. She thought he looked a little tired. And somehow older.

The boy started toward her, but Derak stepped into his path.

"The woman has not been harmed," he said.

Malcolm faced him coolly. "Why did you bring her here?"

"So you would come. I tried to make you understand that this is where you belong, but you were stubborn. Taking the woman was the only way."

"And now you expect to keep me here?"

"I expect you to stay."

"What if I don't?"

Derak's mouth compressed into a tight line. He looked over to where Holly now stood against the face of the cliff. "You are fond of the woman, I think."

"Are you saying you would hurt her?"

"What happens to her depends on your decision."

Holly spoke up then. "Don't let him destroy you, Malcolm. You can be helped. I'm sure you can."

Derak looked over at her with a bored expression and turned back to Malcolm. "You see, she doesn't understand the realities of our life. She doesn't know that there is no turning from the course that is set for us from birth. And she also doesn't know what we can do to her."

A muscle twitched in Malcolm's cheek.

"But you know, don't you, boy?" Derak continued. "You know, but you have been unwilling to face the truth."

"I was told you are my father," Malcolm said.

For the first time Derak's poise slipped a little. "Yes, but that makes no difference here. Don't expect any special treatment."

The slim young man and the stocky older man faced each other. Malcolm said, "If I stay with you, will you set Holly free?"

"I'm glad you've decided to be sensible."

"I want your word first."

Derak's face clouded. The green eyes glowed from some inner fire. "I don't make bargains with pups."

Malcolm pulled at his shirt collar as though it had suddenly grown too tight. "I want you to let her go."

"You *want*? You... *want*? Do you think it matters to me what the devil you want? You like this woman, do you? Maybe you would like her even better if she were one of us. Have you thought about that?"

"*No!*" Malcolm cried. He took a step forward and flexed his shoulders. The muscles bulged and pulsed until the shirt stretched tight across his upper arms. He spoke to Derak through bared teeth. "It's your fault that I've never known who I am... what I am. You're my father. You should have told me things. You withheld the truth from me."

"I was waiting until you were ready. That's the way it is always done."

"I *was* ready! You should have told me." The seams of his shirt split with a loud tearing sound. "There are things I should know. What am I? Why am I this way? How do I control it? What can hurt me? You never told me the third way a werewolf can die. Fire, a silver bullet, and what else, father?"

Holly and the others stood in a semicircle, mutely staring at the confrontation Malcolm's teeth began to grow, pushing out through the gums. His nose and mouth stretched into a muzzle. The dark fur sprouted as he ripped away his clothing.

"You fool!" Derak growled. He pulled off his own clothes and laid them aside as his body began the shape change with a popping of bone and tendon. The fur that grew over the older man's flesh was sand-colored. His face twisted into that of a wolf. It bore the scars of old battles.

When he spoke his voice had deepened into a hoarse rumble. "The third way we can die is never spoken of because it is unthinkable. It is the one unforgivable crime for our kind. We can die by fire, as you remember from Drago. We can be destroyed by a weapon of silver, as mankind learned long ago. And the third, most terrible way... one werewolf can kill another."

There was a soft moaning sound from the others. They shrank back a step from the father and son. Holly's throat was dry as she watched the two figures evolve from men into huge and terrible beasts.

It was the first time Malcolm had completed the metamorphosis. As a wolf he was taller by a head than his father, but Derak was more muscular, more sure of his body. They circled each other warily.

The dark wolf attacked first. He lunged wildly at Derak and was batted aside by a clawed hand. He lunged again, and again Derak evaded him, dealing a painful blow as he did so. The son bellowed in anger and frustration. The father was watchful, conserving his strength.

For an hour the battle continued much in the way it had begun. Malcolm, younger and quicker, struck time after time, but Derak's experience and cunning made him miss repeatedly. Before long the blows struck by the older wolf were taking their toll. Malcolm's lunges became more clumsy, his own wounds deeper.

Holly bit into her knuckle as she watched. She had once seen two chimpanzees fight to the death during an experiment on the animals with PCP. It had been agony to watch, but this was more terrible by far. Not only was it beast against beast; it was father against son. And the son was losing.

As Malcolm slowed perceptibly, Derak began to go to the attack. He moved in with teeth and claws and drew howls of pain as he slashed through fur and flesh. Once Malcolm fell and Derak stood over him, teeth bared for the kill, but he backed off and gestured Malcolm toward him like a taunting prizefighter.

As Malcolm pulled himself erect, blood trickling from a dozen wounds, Holly had to look away. As she did so, she saw a man emerge from the brush along the trail. Gavin Ramsay. She ran toward the tall sheriff, ignored by the others, who were intent on the battle.

Ramsay stared at the two beasts. He opened his arms and gathered Holly in as she came to him.

"Are you all right?"

"Yes." Her voice was no more than a whisper.

Ramsay could not take his eyes off the wolves. He drew the revolver and leveled it at them.

Holly seized his wrist, forcing the arm down. "Don't," she said. "One of them is Malcolm."

"Jesus." Ramsay looked around at the others, who had now taken note of him. Normal-looking people, but in their eyes lay a threat. "Are they all...?"

"Yes," Holly said. "You might be able to kill some of them, but the rest would get us."

"Jesus," Ramsay said again. He put the gun away, and the others returned their attention to their leader and the young challenger.

The battle continued. Big patches of dark fur had been ripped from Malcolm's body. A tooth was gone, leaving a bloody socket. One of his ears was nearly torn away. It seemed only a matter of time before the more experienced of the two would finish the fight.

Then with shocking suddenness, Derak sprang at him. The killer teeth of the older wolf tore through his chest. Malcolm fell, blood streaming from this last and deepest wound. Derak poised for a moment over his fallen son, then cracked his jaws wide and bent down for the kill.

But Malcolm was not quite through. With an effort that brought blood pumping from his chest, he twisted where he lay so that when Derak came at him, his own throat was seized in Malcolm's jaws.

The muffled crunch of bone drew gasps from those who watched. The powerful wolf body of Derak thrashed and bucked, but the teeth of the younger beast were sunk deep. With a last strangled cry from Derak, it was over. Slowly the jaws of the son opened. The father lay limp and silent. The fur of both creatures was matted with blood. Malcolm turned his battered head to look over at Holly. She reached out to him.

Dragging himself painfully a few inches at a time, Malcolm came to her. Ramsay started again to reach for the pistol but held back, Holly dropped to her knees as the beast that had been a boy reached her. He rested his great torn muzzle against her for a moment, then he died.

Holly stroked the tangled fur of his head, smoothing it down. After a minute she stood up. "It's over, Gavin," she said.

He looked back along the ledge and frowned. "Where are the rest of them?"

Holly followed his gaze. The two of them were alone. They and the dead beasts. "They must have slipped away into the trees."

"Should we report this back in town?"

She looked deep into his eyes. "What do you think?"

"No," he said after a moment. "They'd put us away."

She nodded and squeezed his hand.

He said, "We'd better try and make it back before dark. Are you ready to walk down?"

"I'm ready," she said.

Gavin circled her waist with an arm and they started down the trail. From somewhere in the hills behind them they heard it one last time. The howling. They did not look back.

Available from
Books of the Dead Press

J.C. Michael - Discoredia
As the year draws to a close a mysterious stranger makes a proposition to club owner, Warren Charlton. It's a deal involving a brand new drug called Pandemonium. The good news: the drug is free. The bad news: it comes at a heavy price, promising much but delivering far more. Euphoria and ecstasy. Death and depravity. All come together, at Discoredia.

Weston Kincade - A Life of Death
Homicide detective Alex Drummond is confronted with the past through his son's innocent question. Alex's tale of his troubled senior year unfolds revealing loss, drunken abuse, and mysterious visions of murder and demonic children. Is he going insane? With the help of his friend, Alex must find the source of his misfortune and ensure his sanity.

Julie Hutchings - Running Home
Death hovers around Ellie Morgan like the friend nobody wants. She doesn't belong in snow-swept Ossipee, New Hampshire, at a black tie party—but that is where she is, and where he is: Nicholas French, the man who mystifies her with a feeling of home she's been missing, and the impossible knowledge of her troubled soul.

John F.D. Taff – The Bell Witch
A historical horror novel/ghost story based on what is perhaps the most well documented poltergeist case to occur in the United States. The Bell Witch is, at once, a historical novel, a ghost story, a horror story and a love story all rolled into one.

Justin Robinson - Everyman
Ian Covey is a doppelganger. A mimic. A shapeshifter. He can replace anyone he wants by becoming a perfect copy; taking the victim's face, his home, his family. His life. No longer a man, but a hungry void, Ian Covey is a monster. Virtue has a veil, a mask, and evil has a thousand faces.

Mark Matthews - On the Lips of Children
Meet Macon. Tattoo artist. Athlete. Family man. He's planning to run a marathon, but the event becomes something terrible. Macon falls prey to a bizarre man and his wife who dwell in an underground drug-smuggling tunnel. They raise their twin children in a way Macon couldn't imagine: skinning victims for food and money. And Macon, and his family, are next.

Bracken MacLeod - Mountain Home
Lyn works at an isolated roadside diner. When a retired combat veteran stages an assault there her world is turned upside down. Surviving the sniper's bullets is only the beginning of Lyn's nightmare. Navigating hostilities, she establishes herself as the disputed leader of a diverse group that are at odds with the situation. Will she - or anyone else - survive the attack?

Gary Brandner - The Howling
Karyn and her husband Roy had come to the peaceful California village of Drago to escape the savagery of the city. On the surface Drago appeared to be like most small rural towns. But it was not. The village had a most unsavory history. Unexplained disappearances, sudden deaths. People just vanished, never to be found...

Gary Brandner - The Howling II
For Karyn it was the howling. The howling that had heralded the nightmare in Drago... the nightmare that had joined her husband Roy to the she-wolf Marcia and should have ended forever with the fire. But it hadn't. Roy and Marcia were still alive, and deadly... and thirsty for the most horrifying vengeance imaginable...

Gary Brandner - The Howling III
They are man. And they are beast. Once again they stalk the night, eyes aflame, teeth flashing in vengeance. Malcolm is the young one. He must choose between the familiar way of the human and the seductive howling of the wolf. Those who share his blood want to make him one of them. Those who fear him want him dead.

James Roy Daley - Into Hell
Stephenie Page and her daughter Carrie are driving down an empty highway. They pull off the road at a gas station that has a restaurant attached to it. Carrie enters the restaurant in need of a bathroom. When Stephenie steps inside the building she discovers that the restaurant has become a slaughterhouse. There are dead bodies everywhere, The worse part is: Carrie is suddenly missing.

James Roy Daley - Terror Town
Hardcore horror at its best: Killer on the warpath. Monsters on the street. Vampires in the night. Zombies on the hunt. Welcome to Terror Town. The place where no one is safe. Nothing is sacred. All will die. All will suffer.

James Roy Daley - The Dead Parade
Within the hour James will witness the suicide of his closest friend, be responsible for countless murders, and become a fugitive from the police. In the shadow of his mind, a demon lurks. Bloodlust is a virus-it's infecting his logic. James has become a pawn in a game he does not understand, and only one thing is clear: Survival is not an option.

Tonia Brown - Badass Zombie Road Trip

Jonah has seven days to find his best friend's soul, or lose his own, dragging a zombie across the country with a stripper who has an agenda of her own, while being pursued for a crime he didn't commit... and dealing with Satan. 2,000 miles. Seven days. Two souls. One zombie. Satan.

Matt Hults - Husk

Mallory Wiess is a typical teenage girl... or so it seems. When she moves to rural Minnesota she discovers her new home won't be as boring as she'd feared. Who is the dark figure watching her from across the street? What is the shape hanging in the shadows of the old barn? And why has someone begun digging up graves at the ancient cemetery? In the end, one night will decide if the dead will rise.

Tim Lebbon - Berserk

The army had said it was a training accident. But why had the coffin they sent home been sealed? On a dark night, in a deserted field, Tom begins to unearth the mass grave where he hopes - and fears - that he will find his son's remains. Instead, he finds madness: corpses in chains and dead bodies that still move. And one little girl, dead and rotting, who promises to help Tom find what he's looking for...

Best New Zombie Tales - Volume One

Includes Amazing Fiction by: WHC Grand Master Award Winner, Ray Garton / New York Times Best Seller, Jonathan Maberry / Bram Stoker Award Winner, Kealan Patrick Burke / Bram Stoker Award Nominee, Jeff Strand / Micro Award Finalist, Robert Swartwood / British Fantasy Awards Nominee, Gary McMahon / Bram Stoker Award Winner, Kim Paffenroth... and so much more.

Best New Zombie Tales - Volume Two

Includes Amazing Fiction by: Bram Stoker Award Winner, David Niall Wilson / British Fantasy Award Nominee, Rio Youers / Bram Stoker Award Nominee, Nate Kenyon / Authorlink New Author Award Winner, Tim Waggoner / George Turner Prize Nominee, Narrelle M. Harris / Bram Stoker Award Winner, John Everson / Pulitzer Prize, Bram Stoker Nominee, Mort Castle... and so much more.

Best New Zombie Tales - Volume Three

Includes Amazing Fiction by: Anthony Award Winner, Simon Wood / Bram Stoker Award Nominee, Joe McKinney / New York Times Bestselling Author, Tim Lebbon / Arthur Ellis Award Winner, Nancy Kilpatrick / British Fantasy Award Nominee, Paul Kane / Bram Stoker Award Nominee, Jeremy C. Shipp... and so much more.

Best New Werewolf Tales - Volume One

Includes Amazing Fiction by: New York Times Bestseller, Jonathan Maberry / Bram Stoker Award Winner, John Everson / Bram Stoker Award Nominee, Michael Laimo / Aurora Award Nominee, Douglas Smith / Bram Stoker Award Winner, David Niall Wilson / Bram Stoker Award Winner, Nina Kiriki Hoffman / Golden Bridge Award Winner, David Wesley Hill... and so much more.

Best New Vampire Tales - Volume One
Includes amazing fiction by: Bram Stoker Award Nominee, Michael Laimo / Bram Stoker Award Winner, David Niall Wilson / Authorlink New Author Award Winner, Tim Waggoner / Bram Stoker Award Winner, John Everson / International Horror Guild Nominee, Don Webb / British Fantasy Award, Science Fiction Award Nominee, Jay Caselberg / Arthur Ellis Award Winner, Nancy Kilpatrick

John F.D. Taff - Little Deaths
Named the #1 Horror Collection of 2012 by Horror Talk
Named top 5 books of 2012 by AndyErupts

You think you've got bad dreams? Consider author John F.D. Taff's nightmares. Taff has the kind of nightmares no one really wants. But it's nightmares like these that give him plenty of ideas to explore; ideas that he's turned into the short stories he shares in his new collection.

James Roy Daley - Zombie Kong
Big. Bad. Heavy. Hungry. While a 50-foot tall zombie gorilla smashes the hell out of a small town, Candice Wanglund drags her son Jake through the hazardous streets in an attempt to get away from the man that is determined to kill them. She wishes her husband Dale was by her side; he would know what to do. The good news: Dale's alive. Problem is, he was eaten by the gorilla.

James Roy Daley - 13 Drops Of Blood
13 tales of horror, suspense, and imagination. Enter the gore-soaked exhibit, the train of terror, the graveyard of the haunted. Meet the scientist of the monsters, the woman with the thing living inside her, the living dead... James Roy Daley unleashes quality horror stories with a flair for the hardcore. Not for the squeamish.

John L. French - Paradise Denied
This is one of the best collections you will ever read. There isn't a single story in this collection that feels like filler. Vampires, zombies, tough cops, faeries, heroes, or super-scientists, John French has got a tale for you and it's amazing. Again and again, readers agree: this is the book you won't be able to put down. A must read.

Zombie Kong - Anthology
Zombies are bad, but ZOMBIE KONG is worse. Way worse. Big. Bad. Heavy. Hungry. This is the most original zombie anthology of all time. In the jungles, in the arctic, in the cities, in the towns -- Zombie Kong rules them all. All other zombies must bow to their god... ZOMBIE KONG!

Paul Kane - Pain Cages
Reminiscent of Stephen King's classic, bestselling book Different Seasons, Paul Kane gives us an unforgettable collection of four novella-size stories. Each story is refreshingly original and delivers an emotional impact that is rarely seen in today's literature. Dark and moody, clever and well-written... Pain Cages speculative fiction at its best.

Matt Hults - Anything Can Be Dangerous
Anything Can be Dangerous contains four amazing stories:
Anything can be Dangerous ~ the simple things in life can kill.
Through the Valley of Death ~ a dark vampire story that will make you remember fear.
The Finger ~ zombie literature has never been so extraordinary.
Feeding Frenzy ~ lunchtime in a place called Hell.

Bill Howard - 10 Minutes From Home: Episodes 1 - 4
When a viral outbreak hits Toronto, Denny Collins and his best friend Thom Washington find themselves trapped over 100 km from Denny's home in a town called Pontypool, where his wife and daughter remain. As the streets begin to teem with violence, they must first find safety, then find a way out of the now deadly metropolis.

Bill Howard - 10 Minutes From Home: Episodes 5 - 8
The journey gets bloodier as the group runs into hordes of the infected in a suburban neighborhood. Thom must make some drastic decisions when the survivors encounter a military camp. But does the camp provide safety, or just another hurdle delaying Denny's expedition home?

Classic - Vampire Tales
Includes: J. Sheridan Lefanu / Bram Stoker / M. R. James / F. Benson / Algernon Blackwood / F. Marion Crawford / Mary E. Wilkins Freeman / James Robinson Planche / Johann Ludwig Tieck

Thank you for reading this book!